ELEVENTH CYCLE

MISTLAND

BOOK ONE

ELEVENTH CYCLE

KIAN N. ARDALAN

Line Editor: Aubrey Spivey
Cover Illustration: NinoIs
Cover Design and Interior Layout: STK•Kreations
Map: Justin Cullen
Symbols: Hafizhtedho

Trade paperback ISBN: 978-3-200-08673-9

Worldwide Rights
1st Edition

Kian N. Ardalan
Wohlmutstrasse 15-17, top 24
Vienna, Austria, 1020
www.KianNArdalan.com

To my father.
Thank you for giving me the life
you never got to have.

FOREWORD

If you've gotten this far, it means that you are either reading a sample or have the book in your hands. I'd like to give you a message before you enter this world. Eleventh Cycle is a story about many things, and tackles subjects which many may feel uncomfortable with. It deals with disability, with mental illness, with abuse, and even descriptive sexual content. I included these matters not for the sake of it. Not to simply shock with a blunt weapon, but rather to deliver the image of a raw world. The material this book is based on is dark; it doesn't shy away from unsettling matters. However, it is about perseverance in the face of absolute hopelessness. It is about tearing down the veil and facing whatever face evil wears.

It is about people living in an indifferent world which will pull no punches, and finding your own path. However, I need to also take a moment and mention the late Kentaro Miura, author of Berserk. Without him, the Souls franchise may not be where it is today and this book may never have reached your hands.

I won't tell you how to enjoy this piece, but I will give you one piece of advice for the journey. Too often are books about clarity, about being as succinct as possible. This isn't true to life very often. As you read this book, you may find yourself confused, or unsure of how it all fits together. Only once one reaches the end will the pieces align themselves.

CHARACTERS &
GLOSSARY

Aeolus: A tall spawn of a Yungblood with an equine and salmon coloured body, and ever shifting horns. Seen as a companion for the Seed.

akar: A race born from the end of the 6th cycle with large, charcoal-hue bodies and monstrous strength. The receding mists have turned them into feral opponents of the Elders.

Beck: A friend of Dalila's.

Ben: Dalila's younger brother.

Blacksmith: The Elder Blacksmith charged with forging weapons for Elders. His lower half is missing and he is bound to his eternal forge as punishment.

Bolton: The third major city of Bravnicka and seen as an industrial city where Haar is primarily bottled after being collected.

Bradley: Nora's closest friend.

Brother Clemence: A blind member of the Brotherhood of the Faithful.

Candice: Another member of the Sisterhood of the Faithful.

Cassidy Femur: Son of Jason Femur, and a nobleman delegated to Erefiel's company under his father's wishes.

Chitons: The behemoth insects slumbering in Mount Duran.

Chroma: Born to an akar refugee camp beside Crowtown. Chroma longs to live up to his father's legacy and be a warrior worthy of his akar heritage.

Cleria: The capital of Bravnicka and also known as the golden city. The centre for scholarly pursuits of magic and where the main military is housed.

Dale: Son to Gallivax. Is a musician with dreams of becoming an Inspired.

Dalila: A farmer girl and the only daughter of the Reed family.

Duncan: Nora's uncle and discharged soldier. Now works in Bracken.

Elder King: The highest being of all the lands and known to be the most ancient. The Seed is always born from his blood and he holds the most power.

Elders: The strangest and most powerful beings akin to gods.

Erefiel: Born as a Nephilim and son of White-Hawk and Lady Imrie. Erefiel is half Zerub and half-human. He leads as a high ranking captain in the Clerian army.

Father Maurice: The bridge which connects the Elders to Mount Morniar through delivered letters. He is also the head of the Brotherhood of the Faithful.

forgotten: Those who are forgotten are stricken from mind and memory.

Frank: Nora's father.

Fredrick: Dalila's older brother. Lanky and tall.

General Commander Orson: Highest ranking general of the Clerian Militia.

Gron: Akar and member of the Demon Hunters.

Haar/Nif: The two terms to describe the mist at the edges of the world. Nif is the term used by higher beings.

Hachen: A seer Zerub from Mount Morniar.

Howard: Nora's Lieutenant. Strong and reliable and with a calm disposition.

Ida: A blind mystic who joined a band of Demon Hunters.

Ievarus: The eventually bestowed name of the Eleventh Seed.

Jasper: A guard of the akar settlement.

Jeremiah: A plump and full-cheeked boy. Nora's brother and raised as a Witness.

Judge Felicie Auburn: A judicator who brings judgement in Cleria.

Juta: A large akar fighter and a mentor to Chroma.

King Aston: King of Cleria.

Kolotha: The most prominent akar among Chroma's circle of friends with a deep voice and sprawling tattoos.

Lady Imrie: Also known as the White Lady who was once a noble human. Her marriage with White-Hawk resulted in her taking from the fruit of Ascension and transforming into a lady of ice. Mother of Erefiel.

Martha: Nora's mother.

Master: A mysterious, hooded being with just a woven web and a crawling spider for a face.

Maxin: An Inspired bard who plays a lute. Can conjure magic through instruments.

Mother Lucia: An old witch who joined the Sisterhood when very young.

Mother Maiden: The guide of Mount Morniar's halls.

Mother Margret: Carer for the ill at the akar camp but also a teacher at the sisterhood.

Mother Vinrie: The head of the Sisterhood of the Faithful

Muk'tow: Chroma's father.

Munasen: Real name is James; is a brawler at the Toothfairy.

Museya: A city built entirely around the concept of Inspired and artistry.

Nedalya: Chroma's love interest and another akar.

Nora: Born as the daughter to emotionally abusive parents, Nora runs away from Basksin in order to pursue a career as a soldier in Cleria.

Perry: A friend and Dalila's love interest.

Plithy: A viscount who is an adviser to the king.

Preceptor: An Elder with a tentacle face and is able to communicate telepathically. The Eleventh Seed's teacher.

Richard Ericson: A lieutenant with a penchant for gambling.

Rot: A sickness where a black substance eats away at a person's life.

Saru: A shavinu and willing employee of Erefiel. Lost his third eye of prophesied death due to a dishonourable vision.

Seamus: Leader of a Demon Hunter band.

Seed: A child of the Elder King spawned through a surrogate to end a cycle. Sexless and without an idea yet instilled.

Sielie: An Elder with bound leather garments and wielding two sickle blades.

Sirmy: An Elder who observes the Eleventh Seed.

Stamence: Nora's Lieutenant. Reliable but known for his levity.

Stoya: Member of the Demon Hunters.

Tom: The youngest of the Reed family and Dalila's youngest brother.

Trem: A lithe akar befriended to Chroma.

Victor: Nora's Lieutenant. Analytical and precise.

Vol'tar: The last dragon chained in the belly of Mount Morniar.

White-Hawk: One of the first Zerubs to be born with the body of man and head of an albino hawk.

Yungblood: Spawn of an Elder born through a surrogate. They reside in Chainhearth and are second only to Elders.

Zarien: Chroma's mother.

zerubs: The first race born from when Xelxidon concluded the first cycle. They all don the features or head of an animal and embody that animal's traits.

Prologue

Minethria was born from mist, shaped and moulded by the Elder King himself. Many cultures have different names for it. The Bayrish language calls it the Haar, yet the higher beings name it Nif. Though its shaping comes naturally to the higher beings, talented mortals have also shown a proclivity for being able to mould it into equipment or magical objects.

—Guide into understanding Haar manipulation.
An introduction for mages in Cleria

The mist trailed an unmade land, a land so white it was like a virgin canvas waiting to be painted. There was no floor to tread, nor way to discern between up or down. This was a place of things that could be, but weren't. But it wasn't entirely without form.

Here, a great egg stood. Perhaps an egg which was yet to be, or one that already was. Not big. Not small. For there was nothing to compare it to.

It cracked, a fractured line running through it. Next it echoed, a brittle thing which filled the void. And when the egg split, it bore no chick or babe, but rather a single scion. The scion grew into a powerful sage tree, its roots dug deep into the lapping mists as the branches spread themselves into a great, protective canopy.

It stood there with its still leaves and wrinkled bark, as from the rooted base a river of colour flowed.

The sage tree waited. It waited endlessly in resigned acquiescence and such stoic silence that it pierced the quiet in a way a scream never could.

The tree would wait until the end of the world.

≪ ≫

Within the bowels of Mount Morniar, through its many disorienting tunnels which wormed and shifted, there was a room. The armchairs looked as if they had serpents writhing beneath the surface, coiling in wait for someone to sit. Forked sconces of gold filigree were latched onto the mortar walls.

Mounted paintings watched the surrogate whose wiry form was like a charred willow tree; burnt and with wrinkled bark. But her bloated belly roiled with green. There was something inside; its time nigh.

A hand burst through the embryonic shell which held the Eleventh Seed.

The surrogate shrieked. A deep bone-chilling wail filled the coven of stone-black mortar. Yet the boundless tunnels of Mount Morniar buried the cries within its abyssal depths.

"*Cometh, brethren and sistren of mine and witnesseth! The new Seed hath been b'rn,*" spoke a slithering and enigmatic voice, tones of different metres were stitched together to give the impression of words.

The Seed's arm stretched through the surrogate's belly. The green liquid clouded the visage within.

The surrogate writhed, her marred and coarse skin rippling as her digitigrade feet buckled. Her lithe, black fingers clasped the wound. The arm which pierced through curled its fingers and stretched its limbs. The surrogate fell to her knees.

The green slime covered the birthed arm of the Seed, sliding from it and plopping to the floor where it sizzled. The arm returned inside

2

its shell and spread open the tear; without so-much as a sound. The surrogate screamed till her vocal cords tore. It came through the black spiral which was her face until she fell into silence. What was left of the green belly was flat and smoking. It gave a sweet and nauseating smell like sulphur. The surrogate went rigid, her body sputtering in twitches till her joints groaned like and she appeared truly carved from a tree.

A curious body lay there from the birth. They were naked from head to toe save the green substance from inside the surrogate. The new-born shivered. Lanky arms tried desperately to hold onto warmth. Vapour trailed all about the curled up body.

Arrhythmic steps filled the chamber.

"Rise, O' King's Seed." A booming, other-worldly voice gave out the instruction with divine decree. The Seed obliged. Slime stretched from their body and obscured much of their features.

The being had some semblance to a humanoid child except for their stretched limbs on a emaciated skeleton, their willowy strands of silver hair, and their androgynous body.

Gaunt limbs hung long and awkward from shoulders and hips. Corded muscle stretched along its entire body like a mass forgotten to be filled. Where one might have expected some sex between the legs, there was just a smooth and hairless bump.

Great and long strands of white hair, like woven spider silk, hung from their scalp down to the lower back. Their cheeks were sallow and stretched over a thin and long face. Great, milky eyes peered out inquisitively at the amassed and oddly shaped figures.

"Wh—"The Seed hesitated, words coming to lips which must have been so alien and unfamiliar. "What is this?"

"Thou art the Eleventh Seed, born of King's blood. Thou art the saviour of man, saviour of Elders. Thou art the eleventh child of promise." The voice was impermanent, strange and drawn-out, syllables clinging to twisted tongues.

They were creatures of cloaked black, with many limbs and contorting faces. An ever-moving mass of bodies with unfathomable definition, faces hidden under masks and indiscernible protrusions.

The Seed blinked dully at the gathered crowd.

"Thou art b'rn, Seed of King, Blood of King, to delivereth Minethria from festering Evil like Seeds before thee; all so that land be birth'd from mist and the Eleventh Cycle may finally end."

Chapter One

DALILA

What has happened to the lands since the enclosing Haar? Thick-
wood burgeoned like a welt upon the world and the beasts turned mad.
Cultures and cities such as Heimur or the Eternal Library of Deglut
are presumed lost to mankind. The Asamanian kingdom and its desert
has been equally swallowed up. How long before the rest of it goes?

—JOURNAL ENTRY OF A CLERIAN

Nothing made me feel as small and insignificant as staring
at the sheer cliff wall known as Mount Morniar. Its umbral
body was a distant tidal wave coming to drown all of the
lands. Its size was so unfathomable, I thought it held up the sky itself.

A knell came from it, a reverberating sound that reached every
corner of Minethria. It was otherworldly, filling me like a sonorous
chord stretched thin, working its way into my bones and making sure
I felt it deep to my core.

It was the break of dawn when rigid clouds lined the sky and the
peaking sun pushed back the autumn grey. It was the kind of morning
where even the world was drowsy and reluctant to wake. Father had
dragged me out and put me in line with my siblings and Mother. Our

field lay bare and looked as frigid as I felt cold. That scent of autumn dew clung heavy about us.

Fredrick rubbed the sleep from his eyes and tried to hide a yawn behind long fingers. I could tell his overall was put on hastily, as one strap lay limp and the other was twisted before being latched on. He didn't complain though—Fredrick never did.

Benjamin, on the other hand, was too tired to complain. His eyes blinked in and out of wakefulness as he swayed like a supple reed.

I knew better than to complain—Father had been waiting for this moment his entire life.

Only Tom didn't follow suit as he cried his lungs out. Granted, the child was only a few months of age.

"Quiet that child, Miriam!" my father groused.

My mother cradled Tom and gave a stern frown of her own. She tried to comfort my baby brother, his cries pierced the fragile half-light of morning which was like thin frosted rime reaching over a winter lake. If Tom's cries were an ice-pick chiselling at the lake, then the booming knell from Mount Morniar was an elder-damn monstrosity: I could still feel my body quake with every ring—I could only imagine how large the bell needed to be.

Neighbouring farms emitted a halo of bleeding light. A sombre and soft fog made the entire scene even more depressing. It gave the luminous halo of buildings a certain frosted look.

"Robert! Tom hasn't even lived through his first summer! Let him be." Mother lulled Tom with a placating back-and-forth, while her lips offered soothing shushes.

"It's okay, Dad. This is a big moment," Fredrick said, brown-nosing as usual. It earned him a proud grin as the wrinkles under Father's eyes bundled up.

"Yes son, indeed it is." Father ruffled Fredrick's maple curls even though my brother was almost a head taller than him. It didn't help that Fredrick resembled a malnourished scarecrow with stretched out limbs and height. I trembled at the thought—his fingers were incredibly creepy.

"Dalila!" I snapped out of my reverie. "Pay attention to this moment. For we are blessed to bear witness to the birth of a new Seed!" His momentary temper faded as quickly as it came. His expression took on a more sombre shade. "If only your grandfather was here to witness it," he said wistfully. "The man would never shut up, telling me every day that 'today may be the day when the new Seed is born.'"

I stared past the thin veil of fog and the stretch of open land which went for miles. Mount Morniar was like an obsidian sentinel placed at the border of the land, the realms of the higher beings were built black and dark against the face of the mountain. I only ever saw the faint impression of some great fortress, yawning and wild in its dimensions as if built from a dream. Often I would stare and the longer I did, the more skewed it all seemed as if I was looking at the roiling edges of reality.

Some days, I could make out rising spires like stalagmites pointed at the heavens, other times it was only domed buildings with flashes of colour-magic blossoming from them. Only once did I have a chance to hear the guttural and most terrifying rumble which came from Vol'tar: the last dragon. The other kids said Vol'tar was the size of a mountain; I didn't believe them till I heard its roar. Father had said the Elders chained him like a guard-dog.

I could make out the great wall which even Vol'tar could not surmount without taking flight. The vertical face of it scaled ever upward to peer down at us. I imagined how at the very peak, the Elder King stared out at all his subjects.

Ben shook the sleep from himself and listened to the deep knell ring out. It was the sound of a dormant titan's heartbeat. "Dad, why is the bell so important?" he asked.

I tensed for a second, expecting Father to lash out. Instead, Father relished in telling us all about the Elder King and his Seed. "Long ago when the king first came to be, there was nothing, only mist from the Haar."

I noticed more and more faint lights from neighbouring farms and distant Crowtown. Silhouettes braved the sapping, autumn cold to acknowledge the new Seed's birth.

"He made worlds, cities, created life from the Haar and stretched out the borders to where the Haar now resides."

"What is the Haar, again?" Ben asked.

"Robert, he's just a child," Mother interjected before Father could scold Ben.

Father exhaled, letting another intermittent ring of the bell cleanse him of his wrath. "The Haar is the mist, it is the mist that encircles *all* of Minethria." Father swung his arms wide to make his point. "It is endless potential but not everyone can control it. The Elder beings have their own word for it."

Father's patchy brown beard would suddenly fill with such life. His deep brown eyes widening and becoming so expressive as his crooked teeth regaled Ben with wonder. His calloused hands gesticulated wildly to breathe as much joy and hope into the tale as they could.

"The Elder King created more Elders along the way; great, immortal beings of such awesome power that they could sunder mountains and drain seas! Even the Elder King's eyes became our moon and sun!"

Ben lit up and gasped—perhaps it was the knell of Mount Morniar, or the gathering of people early in the morning, but Ben was a lot more interested in the tale than ever before.

"But along with it came the rising evil in man's heart. We brought about decay and tyranny despite the King's generous gift and thus he created time."

Father pointed along to a floating island far in the distance. It held a wandering minaret of sparkling gold as it continued on its route, glistening with what bare light grazed its unblemished spire. "The King created the Grand Archon, the first of the angels who governs time. But it didn't stop the Great Evil from taking root."

"Where did the evil come from?" Ben asked, as the great King's eye drifted over the horizon and climbed upwards.

Tom had stopped his crying and suckled on Mother's tit. A tender smile spread across her lips—I had to admit, watching Ben be filled with such liveliness was contagious.

"From us!" Father answered. "Every thousand years, the evil would take root somewhere in the world beyond the cradle of humanity, growing as it bides its time, turning turgid from our sins. So the King gave birth to the first Seed, his first child. First born as they, but then they became a she with the name of Xelxidon: the first of the Cycle born of King's blood. She ventured forth with her allies and slayed the Evil, bringing back its heart so it may be sacrificed. In turn, the Great Creator would spread out the Haar and provide more land for our people to live in, to farm in, and to work in. But our sins would also be absolved, removed like an abnormal growth from Minethria."

Father pointed to Mount Morniar, across the long and stretching land towards its foreboding presence.

"That, my son, is the sound of the Morning Bell. It tells of a new coming age with a new Seed, a Seed born every thousand years, the eleventh of their name so that another month will be added to the Archon's schedule. This will grant us eleven months to our year in their limitless wisdom."

I was absent-minded as I shifted my feet along my bare toes in our yard. "King Aemir already had an Eleventh Seed." The words had wormed their way from my subconscious and took advantage of my drowsiness. I regretted the words as soon as they slipped out.

Mother gasped, upsetting Tom once more. Fredrick stepped away with arms behind his back as his lower lip went cold-white. Only Ben was confused.

Father's cheeks went a burning fury-red as frenzy claimed his wide eyes. "How dare you use the Elder King's name!"

The knell of the bell now sounded like that of my funeral. It threatened to shatter the silence.

"Father, I'm sor—"

"There is no Eleventh Seed!" Father grabbed me by the arm and dragged me back into the house.

"Father, I'm sorry!"

"The Eleventh Seed is forgotten!" Father roared, more so to himself than just to me. Each time he repeated himself, more desperation filled his tenor.

"Father! Let me go!" I cried, as tears streaked my flushed cheeks and I became fully awake. "I'm sorry! I'm sorry!" My words bordered on shrill screams.

"I will make sure you forget, too!"

As the bell continued to ring and the light of day filled the world, Father brought me into the house and over his lap, his strapped belt buckle already prepared.

I doubt anyone could hear the sound of the belt over the knell of Mount Morniar.

Chapter Two

DALILA

Two ailments in particular threaten our world. The first being the rot. It is indiscriminate who it affects and eats way with its touch. It is an ailment so black as if it had dripped from the night-sky itself. The second is that of the forgotten. Those who disappear from sight and from memory without any trace. How do we know, then, that the forgotten are even a thing? Because the hole they leave behind is unmistakable.

—HIGHER TEACHING AT THE SCHOOL FOR THE FAITHFUL

I didn't notice when the bell ceased its tolling. I sat on the wooden steps of our home and wiped away my tears. My rear was sensitive to the touch. The rest of my family had returned inside while I submitted myself to autumn's chill. I couldn't stand the tension.

The Elder King's watchful eye rose as an imposing sun far in the distance, past the valleys, hills and towns which obscured the sea itself. The world transitioned from dull grey to tawny shades.

I sniffled and hugged myself tight, trying to withhold shivering limbs from the cold. I heard footsteps behind me, followed by the door creaking on its hinges. I hadn't said a word to anyone since Father's punishment. Fredrick came to find a seat beside me; his long spindly legs propped awkwardly.

"What do you want?" I asked.

Fredrick shrugged. "Mom told me to check on you. She would do it herself, but Tom's in a bit of a mood after everything."

Fredrick had fixed his overalls, his faded white shirt was tucked in and straps secured. "It was stupid, what you said."

"Thanks," I said.

Fredrick smiled. He was bad at this, always was.

"Do you believe any of it?" I asked.

"Believe what?"

I pointed out into the distance towards the great peering sun. "Do you believe that's truly the Elder King's eye?"

"Shhhh!" I heard the fear in his shushing.

"What? The Elder King can't *hear* us."

"It's not the bloody Elder King I am worried about!" Fredrick turned to stare at the door he'd left ajar and counted the seconds, expecting Father to leap out like some sort of demon.

I thought it silly, but seeing Fredrick tense like that made his worry infectious. Only when he felt the danger had passed did he speak in whispers.

"It doesn't matter if I believe in the stories, little sister, what matters is I believe in Father's wrath."

"So, you don't believe in the Eye?"

"Maybe I do, maybe I don't. I'm telling you: what's important is that Father believes in it, and that's enough for me. You better learn this lesson very quickly." Fredrick tapped my knee and stood to leave.

He was right, of course. I thought back to the incident and Father's frenzied look. It wasn't just rage in his eyes; he was scared. There had been only one other time I'd seen him frightened. The time when I caught my father alone in the barn. He was encircled by goats as he flagellated himself. I had caught the words '*Forget the Seed*' between lashings, it came out as a pained groan. The leather tails snapping onto his scratched back, digging bit by painful bit till the flayed ends were coloured crimson. I couldn't help but feel he was cutting the name into his flesh.

Part of me felt guilty as I'd indirectly made him remember the forgotten Seed. The nameless one. It was a crime to even think of it, but it was impossible not to.

The door behind me creaked open for a second time. I turned and found Ben standing there. I wiped the rest of my tears and sniffed the last of my runny nose.

"Did I get you in trouble?" Ben asked sweetly.

"No, Ben, no. Not at all. I said something I shouldn't have. It had nothing to do with you."

Ben nodded, leaning against the door's weight to hold him upright.

"Dad asked you to go get some water from the well." Ben's voice became even softer.

I gathered my strength and nodded. "Thank you," I said with my most reassuring smile.

⋄ ⋄

The sun returned colour to the world. Birds chirped as they burst forth from canopies, and a pair of dragonflies dashed in tandem before me and then left.

The trek to the well went down a slope where few outside our family tread. The farm where we lived was out of the way of any major road. The scent of rain still lingered from two nights earlier and the path was wet with mud. The best I could do was raise my stained, brown dress and sidestep.

I looked to the sun and wondered if Father allow me to see my friends. Should I ask him for forgiveness, or sneak out and hope for the best?

I certainly wouldn't be missed as it was mostly Fredrick who took over the hard work and though Ben had begun to get a feel for the labour, majority of the attention went to Father's favourite. I vented my frustration on an unfortunate stone and kicking it.

I longed for the days when Father would spoil me with tales from the Kaseluda instead of taking me over the knee or sending me to fetch water from the well. Xelxidon was always my favourite Seed, even when I was younger, and there was nothing I wanted more than to be like her. Lady of Light, the first Seed born from king's blood. A warrior who braved great trials with burnished armour and a blade of pure sunlight. She had paved the way to the first parting of the Haar.

Father thought it was cute at first, me wearing a cape and waving around some stick like a sword, but the older I became, the more grating he found it. Told me to know my place, that it was our duty to venerate and serve best we could.

When I reached the well, I readied my bucket and swatted away a few flies.

"Fredrick..." I voiced in irritation. The well's rope wasn't resting on the edge of the wall, but instead dangled inside the shaft.

With a defeated sigh, I leaned over the edge of the well and reached out.

"'Look at me, I'm Fredrick, my daddy loves me so much,'" I burlesqued as my fingers reached further and further. "Come on!" I said through gritted teeth, fingertips grazing the rope.

My foot slipped.

The mud gave way. I flipped over the well's lip and was greeted by the depths. My heart stopped.

At the last second, I grabbed one of the wooden beams which supported the rope and stared deep into the pitted darkness. My heart beat against my ribcage and thrummed in my ears.

I heard my breath echo down the well's stony throat. Yet what I didn't expect was something staring back at me.

Was I just imagining it? I squinted, looking deep into the pool below, and could have sworn I'd seen green emerald eyes, three on either side of some V-like constellation.

"Dalila!" I heard my name as I grabbed the rope and turned around to see Fredrick working his way down the path. When I turned back to the well, the strange vision was gone.

◃ ▹

Convincing Father to let me see my friends was an uncomfortable trial. I had to seem contrite and as vulnerable as possible without appearing too desperate. But I also needed to convey a believable amount of regret.

"Fine. Just remember to be back by supper."

It was practically a herculean task, trying to hide my grin and relief.

"Dalila," father said before I could run out of the barn where he was feeding the goats. I turned and bowed my head, feigning demureness, and straightened my dress.

I heard a sigh, the kind of sigh which reminded me that my father was a good man with plenty of love in his heart—I just felt sometimes it was too much. He moved closer to me as my body tensed. The beating from the morning worked its way through me.

"I am not going to hurt you," father reassured, hovering his calloused hand over my shoulder before reconsidering. It fell onto my arm instead with a loose grip.

He held pain in his eyes. "I am sorry I had to punish you. But I did it because I love, because what you spoke was blasphemy." Father let the last word fall from his lips like it were an unfortunate truth.

He bit his lip. We were thinking of it, of the event. And indirectly, thinking of the forgotten Seed. I didn't envy my father at that moment. How do you reassure someone when you weren't allowed to talk about the very matter?

In the end, father simply settled on words which came from the heart. "I love you, my sweet, sweet Dalila. Though you will see your fourteenth winter soon, you are my child, and I only want you to live a good life. Do not speak the Elder King's name, ever. It isn't our name to be spoken."

I nodded meekly, though truly glad father granted me his forgiveness. I wanted nothing more than to move on, for everyone's sake.

15

"Good." Father smiled, tenderly caressing my cheek with his thumb before returning to work.

"Be back before the King's eye sets."

I nodded and went on my way.

❧ ❧

I worked my way down to the riverbed where Perry, Beck and Jeremiah squatted over the water and dropped stones. Only Dale was missing.

"Sorry I'm late!" I said.

"What took you so long?" asked Beck.

My cheeks warmed. "Dad got angry with me today."

The other boys raised their eyebrows. "What did you do?" Jeremiah asked. He was rather chubby-faced but as sweet as they came. He had two years on the rest of us with deep blue eyes and a heart of gold.

I considered my words wisely, catching my tongue as I recalled that which shouldn't be recalled, and then tried desperately to drown the thought. "I said the Elder King's name," I offered as a compromise.

The boys gasped.

"Father would have torn out my tongue for that!" Perry claimed.

Only Jeremiah shrugged indifferently. "Not my parents."

"Did you watch the Knell?" I asked excitedly, trying to change the subject.

Jeremiah shook his head. "I wanted to, but dad and mom were really against it. Told me we were Witnesses, not followers of the Elders. Said to go back to bed or go pray."

Jeremiah and his parent's faith always fascinated me. Mother told me the Witnesses came from a group of people who took note of those who were forgotten. 'Those who are witnessed are those who are acknowledged and cannot fade.' There was a reason why Jeremiah's parents were so fond of the angels and their many-eyed wings.

When I had asked father who the Witnesses were, he said, "They are a cult."

Beck raised his chin. "Yeah, but that's because your parents don't

16

know up from down." Jeremiah hung his head.

I advanced on Beck, and slapped him about the head. He touched the point of impact and turned to me in surprise.

"What was that for?" he asked.

"What Jeremiah's parents believe in is none of your business. He's our friend, so stop bullying him."

"Ow." Was the only bit of an answer Beck provided.

Perry chuckled. Our eyes met, and I turned away before he could.

"You know, the sound, the knell. It was like... a vibration. A thrum deep in the ground which shook me to my core—shook my soul. I felt as if—"

"Reality was breaking." Perry offered.

Beck nodded, awe still lingering in his gaze. A sort of sublime wonder captivated him.

"M... my sister is coming back!" Jeremiah said. I had a feeling he was feeling left out and wanted to also have something to discuss.

"How's she?" I asked.

Jeremiah nodded, his gleaming smile returning. "They beat the akar back to their borders."

"I'm so jealous!" Perry groused. "What I would do to be on the front lines with her, just hacking away at the invaders!" Perry swung his arm as if wielding a sword and grinned. I felt a wave of jealousy.

Beck frowned. "Is she not returning to the garrison?" he asked.

Jeremiah shook his head. "She promised to visit once she was done."

"And your parents are okay with that?" I asked.

Jeremiah rocked back and forth on crossed feet and with his chubby, big goofy smile. "Oh no. Mom and dad are still mighty upset with her for joining the Clerian army instead of settling down with some follower of the Witness. But it ain't like my parents can stop her."

When Jeremiah spoke of Nora, it was with such beatific, brotherly love that it was the one time the unsure lines of his brow would break and his smile would shine.

"What about us? What are we doing today?" Perry asked.

"The forest?" Beck suggested.

Perry shook his head. "How about Crowtown? Gallivax is back today! We can also see Dale!" The others lit up.

"As long as we don't pass by the akar camp," Jeremiah said with worry lining his words.

Beck agreed. "Can you believe they are conscripting akar refugees into the army? How can they trust that lot?" He spat.

"They aren't really akar, they are defectors," Perry rebutted.

"Doesn't change who they are. Living among us for sixteen years! Can't believe the other lords are okay with it."

"Stop." I could sense where the conversation was heading and didn't see it ending well. "Let's just go to Crowtown. We will avoid the settlement. Happy?"

Chapter Three

NORA

An average, fully grown akar has a greyish-to-black charcoal hued skin. They range between seven to eight feet in height and are double the width of your typical Clerian soldier. Generally speaking, they are far more formidable in comparison to humans. However, their propensity for charging without any forethought, and their typically small companies due to lacking leadership make it easy to lure them into our formations and take them out one by one with minimal losses.

—OFFICIAL REPORT ON DEALING WITH THE AKAR — 7C653

The trek from Fort Treb to Greyhill was not an easy one, and even less so as we made our way back from the defensive line where we broke down the akar.

I faintly recalled our original march was filled with the dour grumbles of tired soldiers dragging their feet, complaining about how sweat clung to their padded armour despite the morning cold. I certainly sympathised with the lot but there was no way I would have voiced any of it. Instead, I looked forward, following whichever way Erefiel's path led me.

In contrast, the way back from the front lines was no longer filled with the sound of grousing men, but rather a suffocating silence as damp boots trudged over mud. The occasional groan of the injured could be heard, but our numbers held strong and losses were at a minimum; the same could not be said for the akar.

For many men it was the first time they faced this foe; big hulking forces of destruction with skins of perpetual charcoal. Their eyes were dark beads like pearls stolen from the abyss, small tusks barely poking out from their lower lips, sprawling tattoos scrawled their entire body. It was the fourth time I had the misfortune to face them, and it never got easier. I held back a smile, imagining how Jeremiah would crawl into a ball if he ever met one. It was the self-indulgent fantasy of the older sister.

As the sun lazily rose in the distance, I took a moment to recall my first battle. How I broke formation and dove into the front lines, a childish sense of heroism moving limbs. I would have died if the enemy hadn't failed to see the spear locked in my grip. He fell atop of me, his heart impaling itself, while slick blood ran down the wooden shaft.

Lightning struck and seared the moment into my mind. Charcoal skin, diminutive tusks bleached by the blitz above; great, brutish muscles belonging to a being three heads taller than me and twice my width.

Its body buried me, and I was both relieved and petrified that nobody could hear my screams over the sound of the ensuing battle. Only the shadow of war danced across my vision.

I did better this time around. My bones were locked and heavy, but at least I stood my ground and helped my formation take down three of the great beasts.

Our company's slow march came to a stop. Erefiel reached the crest of our winding road and removed the helmet made in the image of his father, White-Hawk, to reveal slicked back white hair with a handful of equally blanched feathers mixed in.

"Almost home, men." Erefiel turned to us with a morale-boosting smile. It infected us at the front and worked its way back to the rear of our returning hundred and fifty men. We thrust our weapons high and saluted our captain. Despite the toil of battle, Erefiel remained flawless.

His armour grasped the light of a rising sun to magnify his beauty. Even his dried sweat made his half-zerubic skin glisten.

Suddenly, our chanting was crushed under the weight of the Morning Bell. The tolling knell from Mount Morniar was far in the distance and past the impressive architecture of Cleria. From where we stood, Mount Morniar looked like a long ranging black wall from the shore in the west and ran endlessly to the east. Our company went incredibly quiet. A gust of cold air threaded through our formation and moaned, as if it were nature's serenade for the event.

⊲ ⊳

Fort Treb greeted us. It was an unsightly hunk of mortar stone just off the road into Cleria. It was made for efficiency, not extravagance. The parapets had men faced towards the distance, on the lookout for anything which warranted attention, while ballistas on the wall hung forgotten.

We ambled through the raised portcullis. The inside of the keep was divided into a stable, a sleeping quarter for two hundred soldiers, and a training area comprised of a shooting range and a sandpit.

I made my bed upon a haystack piled to the side of the stable much to a horse's annoyance. The brown stallion flapped his lips at me as I pressed a gloved hand to his face and brushed him away.

I took note of the last men coming through the doors and tsked at the sight of our own akar conscripts which trailed at the back. Only three remained from the original seven. Naturally, their strength was put to good use, carrying the heavier items as if it were nothing. I doubted any of us trusted the brutes conscripted into our ranks.

Averse to the sight, I allowed my eyes their rest and let myself sink into the hay.

"Never a good idea to give a horse a reason to dislike you."

A misty breath escaped me as I opened an eye. Bradley stood before me with that stupid grin of his.

"Maybe it left because it saw your ugly mug," I suggested.

21

Bradley gave a bemused chuckle and shook his head. I knew he had no comeback to think of, so he joined me on the pile instead.

"Continue on like that, and the only men who will offer themselves to you will be one of the akar."

I chuckled. "Don't start, I would rather fuck the horse than an akar."

Bradley shrugged and then pondered for a second.

"What?" I asked.

Bradley turned to the stallion which trudged off; the horse had found another haystack to devour. The other men of the garrison were unloading the equipment in the meantime.

"Do you think?" Bradley prodded cautiously, his eyes conveying his lewd meaning.

"Oh…" I shared his sudden curiosity and turned to the horse as well. "For the akar?" Bradley nodded.

Clapping my hands in front of me, I began moving them apart. "Say stop." I grinned.

"Hmmm."

My hands had reached shoulder length apart, and I gasped in-between my immature grin.

"I hope it is kill count you are measuring."

Both Bradley and I jumped to attention; the hay was equally startled and drifting about. Standing with a knowing smirk was Erefiel, who we rigidly saluted.

"At ease," Erefiel said.

Up close, he looked even princelier. Not the snobby entitled brats you would find at Museya but rather the made-up kind in fairy-tales. His celestial nose was like a fragile piece of art, his jawbone so defined, one could sharpen steel upon its edge, his deep white eyes like halos of snow. Even his skin was free of any blemish. His albino hair was short and slicked back along with the few feathers spread atop his scalp. Though nowhere near as overwhelmingly giant as your average akar, Erefiel still was tall enough that I could only reach his collarbone.

Bradley and I relaxed.

"Get back to work." Erefiel pointed to Bradley, who nodded and went to help with the unloading.

"You did well out there," Erefiel said as he took a step closer to me.

"Thank you, sir."

"Yes, you maintained a strong front and followed the orders from training. Surely better than the first time with your one 'kill'."

A great, raging flush worked its way to my cheeks as I stuttered. He didn't say it outright, but his implication was clear. Erefiel waved a placating hand and chuckled to himself. "Don't worry. You did well. And I most certainly admire your drive." His smile was affirming.

"What can I do for you, Captain?" I asked, and straightened my posture.

Erefiel walked away. "Come to my office after you help unload the carts. I have something to discuss with you." His expression returned to that of a fair but stern leader as he moved along to the inner-keep's entrance and gave a few commanding shouts to the workingmen.

⊰ ⊱

"What do you think he wants?" Bradley asked as we helped unload the last of the boxed food from the wagon.

I shrugged.

"Maybe he wants to give you a promotion?" he suggested.

"For lying around and talking about akar dick-size? Highly doubt it."

"I know what he wants." An all too familiar voice had me withhold my urge to vomit.

I turned to see Cassidy's back turned to me, his own manicured hands gripping his shoulders to give the impression he was kissing someone with that venomous tongue of his. He was a worm, a pest upon this world I wish I could weed out. His dirty-blonde locks framed a pampered visage with a stuck up nose and sunken, snakish eyes—it was no secret the only reason he got a spot in the company was because of his father's noble reach inside Cleria.

"Oh! Nora! Oh! Let's have bird-sex!" There were a few dispassionate

23

chuckles from the other men, but none more so from Cassidy's own suck-ups.

"Oh yes, general Erefiel! Please pump me with your bird seed!" Cassidy imitated with an unflattering high-pitched voice.

"Please, go ahead. I bet that is the most action you've ever gotten, and you are not even *in* the fantasy."

He spun to face me. If the chuckles of the other men were indifferent before, they were mirthful this time around. Even Cassidy's own crew had to bite their lips to withhold a chortle. I took pride in the soft blush on the vermin's cheeks.

"What do you know, anyway?" Cassidy pointed a livid finger. "You are the only damsel in this place, fighting under the son of White-Hawk. I wonder who you had to suck off to get here."

The other men made their voices heard with a resounding 'Ooooooh', as they all turned for what was sure to prove entertaining. The only exception were the akar, who knew better than to involve themselves in such troubles.

I held my tongue—I went through such training till the skin upon my palm tore and I bled sweat and sweated blood. I wasn't about to be taunted by a child.

"Let's go," I said to Bradley and turned to leave.

But Cassidy didn't relent. "Maybe you can come here and serve us all. I mean, after massacring those disgusting akar, I feel like we have earned ourselves a bit of reprieve. I downed ten of the beasts all by my lonesome. Did you stay nice and cosy behind our defences? Quivering in your boots while we did all the work?"

I saw red.

Perhaps it was because of Cassidy's advancements or because I saw him curled up into a ball somewhere while the rest of us put our lives on the line. Images of fallen comrades flashed in my mind juxtaposed by Cassidy's cowering form. Or perhaps I was just tired of his stupid-fucking-face. Whatever the reason, I turned and strode to him.

"Woah, woah, woah. No need to be so eager, I am not going anywhere." Like the vermin he was, Cassidy lowered his pants and flaunted his limp, cold cock which shrivelled into its turtle-neck.

The weight of my shin struck between his legs with such force that Cassidy's eyes rolled back. The audience shared sympathy pains and winced and gasped or gave more 'Ohs.'

Cassidy groaned and fell to his knees. His four men stepped away when they met my gaze, more out of stunned surprise rather than fear. I moved in. Cassidy's head hanged limp as I grabbed his locks and pulled so that his eyes met mine. "Listen here." I hissed through gritted teeth. Though I was certain our audience could hear me on account of the silence sweeping through the keep.

"If I ever see your cock again, I will cut it from your pathetic, pampered body and feed it to Vol'tar."

Cassidy's lips trembled and showed me the white of his eyes. I shook him. "Do you hear me?"

No response.

"Nod if you understand."

I shook him hard by his hair, but still no response.

"I said nod!" I roared, my voice echoing through the autumn stillness.

I let go of his hair and grabbed his arm, pulling it taut in a way not intended for limbs, and pressed my knee onto his back so that his face met the dirt. His men and the others noticed too late what I had planned.

"Nora!" was all Bradley managed to say.

"Do you understand!?" The question was stressed by a deafening crack which reverberated from the keep walls. His arm bent at an awkward angle. Cassidy cried in such palpable agony that spittle drooled from curled lips and his red eyes told of coming tears.

"I understand!" The words barely intelligible between the pained groans and pitiful whines.

As my anger ebbed and my breathing stilled, realisation came as a trickle and then all at once. What had I done? I felt a horror like a great stone sinking in the pit of my stomach. Fear filled me.

I had just injured and assaulted not just any fellow soldier, but Cassidy Femur, son of Jason Femur.

"Nora!" My name was called from above. Our collective heads shot up to see the image of Erefiel looming through his window and waving for me to come up with great haste.

Chapter Four

EREFIEL

The first race born from Xelxidon's passing were the zerub; human-oid beings with the head of animals. As such, they have been blessed with living close to the gods atop their mountain. Few zerub descend to the mortal plane for that very reason, but it isn't unheard of. Those who are the offspring of these blessed folk and mortals are the Nephilim. Half animal, half mortal.

—To Understanding Minethria, a never ending endeavour, by Calhaze Lenchin

I thought you said she'd behave!" I leaned against the windowsill and pinching the bridge of my nose. I considered all the ways I needed to kiss Jason Femur's ass to make this go away. Mother would have another go at me, pontificating about how it is to be expected when I keep collecting "strays".

My office was packed with documents and unsigned diplomatic papers which covered the trading of resources and negotiations for troops. Underneath the unfurled scrolls lay maps of Greyhill where I had spent nights poring over. The room itself was not large by any means, but it served its purpose for the shelved storage of documents to my left and right, as well as a simple desk.

Lieutenant Hendrix furrowed his brows together with a sadness to his eyes. "She is a good girl! Steadfast, loyal, strong and driven most of all; you've seen her in action! She's got a fire, Erefiel," Hendrix said, his thick caterpillar moustache just as expressive as the rest of his aged face. He was nearing his forties, but nobody could find someone more sharp-of-mind and wisdom than he, even if his paunch may not have made him as quick or ferocious as other men.

"Her fire is exactly the problem. Jason Femur couldn't give two licks about her record as a soldier! Not only did Nora attack one of my men, but it had to be the son of *that* man. He will want her punished severely."

Hendrix considered his options. "It is only his fourth—"

"Fifth," I corrected.

Hendrix nodded affirmingly before continuing. "Fifth son. Maybe he will be more lenient?"

I shook my head and chuckled with jaded amusement. The idea that Jason Femur would be lenient was laughable. To him, letting go of such an affront was an invitation to challenge his own standing. "You don't get it, he couldn't care less about his son; the issue is the family name. Nora besmirched it by laying a hand on his blood. To Jason Femur, it might as well have been he who was attacked."

A knock on the door stilled us both.

"Come in," I said, leaning against the table, my fingers tightening about the wooden frame.

The door opened to reveal a guarded woman, her brunette hair in a bun and her modestly handsome features knotted in indignation. Nora avoided our gaze and hung her head, she looked like a child who came to be scolded.

"Leave us." I motioned to Lieutenant Hendrix.

As he made his way out, his gloved hand lay gently on Nora's shoulder and he quickly whispered something.

"Now, lieutenant," I said authoritatively. Another supportive pat on the shoulder as Hendrix closed the door behind him.

For long, stretching, seconds I just stared at her. I could tell how guilt and pride warred within her and I assumed there was no winning side yet.

Silence worked its way between us, while the rest of my men could be heard from the courtyard. Surely, the subject of their banter wasn't hard to deduce. Nora shifted nervously, refusing to speak the first word.

I prompted her. "What do you have to say for yourself?"

"He told me to whore myself out for them all!" The words burst from Nora's tongue as if previously nocked and ready to fire. No sooner did she speak, did she shut her lips at the raise of my hand.

"You injured and humiliated the son of one of the most powerful men in Cleria, a man who has King Aston's ear; I don't care if he groped you, you cannot take matters into your own hands."

Nora's expression hardened as she stood strong and lifted her chin. Whatever telling lines of remorse there were, they were pressed completely smooth. "And if he had attempted to rape me, sir?"

I sighed. "Then you come to me." These words were not my own. I hated the implication, but the alternative was worse.

"The last time I made you aware of his behaviour you tried to reprimand him. But it didn't stop the harassment."

She was right. If I were to have my way, Cassidy wouldn't even be part of my regiment. I privately loathed watching him cower as his fellow men laid down their lives—the thought sickened me.

"If this were some regular soldier, then believe me, my actions would have been harsher. But my hands are bound, too. His involvement comes from higher up."

"So I should allow him to keep harassing me? To wave his worm at me? Do nothing if he were to have his way with me?" Her questions were spoken without a hint of emotion; cool and impassive.

I let out a heavy, rueful sigh. She was a good soldier, and I wanted nothing more than to have her in my regiment. Nora always dove headfirst into battle as if possessed, it galvanised the rest of the troops. But there was nothing I could do with politics playing its hand.

"Nora Demiel Rawsom, I will be moving you into another regiment. Until then, I ask that you return home until we send someone for you."

That was all it took to break Nora's composure. Her eyes widened and she allowed the fear in her voice to be heard. "No!" Something in my heated stare made Nora recognize the breach in her emotions. She took a moment to control herself. "Please. I am sorry. There must be something else."

I shook my head. "I am sorry, Nora. This is the best option we have. The Femurs will want you severely punished for what you did. If I act decisively, I may still manage to move you to another regiment and it will be punishment enough. Not to mention, you won't have to worry about Cassidy's behaviour any longer."

"To do what?" Nora's query was unbidden now that she had nothing to lose. "Bring resources? Be a glorified transport unit? Maybe I will stand guard for the akar settlement." She spat on the floor; I could taste the venom in her voice at the mention of akar.

My gaze took in the spit that tarnished my floor, before I coolly craned to stare at Nora. "There are plenty of other regiments which handle akar attacks."

"None of them are under your leadership," she countered, stoically this time. She saw the change in regiment as a demotion; I supposed it was.

"If you were to stay here, do you think Cassidy's harassment will stop?" I asked and looked back at her.

Nora considered it for a moment. "After what I did to him today? I think so."

I chuckled, slightly bemused by Nora's fire, even if it was exhausting. "Maybe so, but his father won't."

Nora hesitated, I could hear her voice break as she spoke. "What about White-Hawk? Your father is renowned and powerful, maybe he will—"

"Let me make sure I understand." I cut her off and fixed her with a seething glare. I strode towards her, each step I took was heavy with intent. "You, a nobody from a small town, were harassed by the son of a nobleman and decided to break his arm. Now you want me, Erefiel Numyana, son of White-Hawk and Lady Imrie, to go running to my father at Mount Morniar so he can wave around a magic-fucking-wand and make it so you can play soldier!?" I found myself staring Nora down as my chest heaved. The treble in my voice grew the longer I had spoken, swelling until my typical brevity was distorted with rage.

I noticed the slight flutter of fear in her eyes. I was close enough for my warm breath to reach her cheeks.

A wave of regret came over me as I realized I had lost my cool. With some composure, I distanced myself and walked over to my table.

"You... you wanted to talk to me earlier," Nora stated softly. I turned back to her. She was bowing her head now.

"Doesn't matter. I just wanted to let you know akar were supposedly sighted at Dreamwood. I wanted you to take a look since you were headed in that direction."

"I can still—"

"I will send some troops to patrol the area. You best be on your way." My words were cold; I had no more rage to give. I turned to the window again and leaned on my table, only hearing the defeated steps of Nora as she closed the door behind her.

I had to stop collecting strays.

Chapter Five

CHROMA

*When the akar refugees came with hands raised, Cleria denied them
any refuge. It was the eccentric and entirely persistent leadership of Crowtown's mayor who permitted them stay. Sadly, Lord Ollicier passed away just
a year after due to the rot. His son didn't share his father's opinion on
the refugees but decided to tolerate their presence. Population control is handled
through denial of rations for families with too many children alongside forced
conscriptions into the defensive force of Cleria. The yearly onset of
Burr deals with the rest.*

—MILITARY REPORT ON AKAR SETTLEMENT AFTER FIVE YEARS 11C1954

Today was the first time I stood at the head of the breakfast line, all thanks to the Morning Bell. I felt it deep in my slumber before I heard it, a resonance which reverberated through my entire body and bones, making my heart palpitate and my mind shudder. It made sure all beings across Minethria heard of the Eleventh Seed's birth, of the coming end to the Eleventh Cycle. But most of all, it made certain that the great Evil, no matter where it was, knew its end was nigh.

I couldn't have cared less. I used the opportunity to grab my bowl and Mother's. She was sound asleep, turning over in her thin blanket of hay. Not really a surprise; she had come home late the previous night after spending it with friends. A smile split my lips at the thought of how she'd react, waking up to the smell of warm breakfast rather than cold sludge.

I ran through the akar settlement, a camp which stood for sixteen years despite its rushed construction of sticks and straw and mud. It was barely enough space for us, even for me, though I was only just graced by my sixteenth autumn.

The refugee camp had swelled to make space for more births, and repairs came often; the good thing was that sticks, hay and mud were in abundance. Some of the more fortunate lived in yurts. More and more homes huddled together. Crowtown always stayed in our sight, but never could we peer past the town walls. The closest we got to experiencing human life was being exposed to the carefree laughter of Crowtown beyond our cage. Our own perimeter was closed by erected palisades made tall enough for our ilk.

The storm from two days ago still showed its passing as I ran across the mud. Mother and I couldn't get a lick of sleep that night. Thunder trickled like the sound of fading cracks in the sky.

Standing before the breakfast table, I waited for the guards and akar to snap out of their reverie. They all stared out towards the sinister outline of Mount Morniar; an endless black wall which held up the sky. I suppose I would have shared their fascination, if not for intentionally trying to resist. There was something magical about the sound, not just the power with which it reached the furthest borders of the Haar. It was like trying to ignore the need to breathe or eat—its very presence demanded notice.

I tried to distract myself by focusing on what was for breakfast. A large pot waited for us. A slight opening gave me a whiff of its contents. A stew of potatoes, a few herbs, perhaps rosemary? There was the earthy hint of mushrooms thrown in there, carrots, a note of pig-meat and parsnips. But I stayed my expectations. Most of it must have been whittled down with water. Feeding the enemy, even if we were refugees, meant that they would take the cheapest route possible.

Another knell came from the Morning Bell. My attention was torn to Mount Morniar; to the mountain and to where the realm of the Elders remained. The bell reminded me of thunder, and called upon my conversation with Mother two nights ago.

"Are they fighting, Mother?" I had asked as I was denied my sleep.

Mother's name was Zarien. Mother and I had laid recumbent on the floor of our small hut. Drops of water came through our straw roof, but never enough to prove distracting. Mother's features depicted a strong sort of beauty with defined facial structures. There was a primal warmth to her beady eyes. She had one arm tucked underneath her dreaded locks which bulged her bicep.

"Yes, Chroma. Our people fight the humans on the border of Muuch'kan, what the people here call Greyhill," she said.

"Why aren't we with them?"

"You know this. Our people fight a meaningless war."

"Look at how they treat us. We are nothing more than dogs here." We had this conversation a thousand times, and neither of us could think of new things to say, just different ways to say them.

"It is not the human's fault."

"I am not talking about the humans." Another lightning strike punctuated my meaning. "I mean *them*, the zerubs, the angels, the damned Elders and their Elder-King. They are the ones who took away our land. Our war is with them, not the humans. The humans just stand in our way."

"We *have* no land, Chroma. We are nomads."

"We are *nothing*. Have nothing," I countered.

Mother and I faced each other in our small excuse for a home; it was nothing more than a cramped tent with a bedding of hay.

After silence threaded between us, I had decided to ask about Father. It always managed to quell the air of any tension.

"Again?" Mother asked. A flash lightning had revealed her momentary smile to me and the small glint of a tusk.

"Not like we will find sleep soon anyway," I joked.

Mother sighed and relented.

"Muktow, your father, the strongest and bravest of all akar.

I smiled, looking down and finding my fingers were fiddling with a piece of hay. I loved the stories of my father: a strong man, a fierce man. But he didn't fight for the sake of fighting, he fought for his people, to protect."

The longer Mother went on, the further she seemed to sink into the memories of the past, far before she came with the other refugees to Bravnicka. She shared of Father, of how smitten and shy he was. Of how he had begun to unite the other tribes and brought hope to us. He is still out there, somewhere, fighting despite the rebellion. I'm sure of it.

Mother had fallen asleep right after her retelling. I remained awake for a while, hoping I will meet my Father one day.

The absence of the knell was even more present than its ringing. Even now when Mount Morniar had gone silent, I could still feel the surrounding air vibrate and the tips of my fingers tingle.

Jasper was the first of the guards to come forward after the bell faded. As always, there were sleepless rings about his eyes.

"Okay! Stand in line! Show is over! Hurry or we can't promise there is enough to feed you all." He called out. Weary eyed and waking akar trotted and groused as they formed a line.

A guard stood on a crate in order to more easily serve with his ladle, but he still struggled to match most akar in size. Except for me, who he had the gratifying pleasure of looking down on from his nose.

I eagerly accepted the ladle of warm grub, and checked to ensure it really did float with its promised contents. It was accompanied by a loaf of bread.

"Sorry. One more. Please." Contorting my tongue to speak the human's Bayrish stunned the guard.

"O-one per person." The guard took a moment to collect himself.

"It is for my mother."

"She can come get her own." The moment wore off, and the guard looked at me with irritation. "Next!" He called out.

⊰ ⊱

I returned to Mother and offered her my bowl. She appeared to have just woken up based on the wide yawn and the stretching she committed to.

"What about yours?" she asked, and took the food. She paused for a moment, allowing the bowl's warmth to spread through her fingers.

"I already had mine," I lied. Mother took a big slurp. I hid my hunger and smiled instead. "Long night?" I asked as a follow up.

"Yes." Her voice hadn't fully awoken yet.

"Oh. I have something for you," she said and turned away. She pulled out a misshapen bar of something dark. That's when I recognized it as chocolate and gasped.

"Chocolate?" I asked and grinned freely.

"Shhh. Not so loud. I don't have enough for the entire camp."

I greedily took a piece and split it with Mother, and then practically devoured my piece.

"Slow down, Chroma! I was going to tell you to share some with Nedalya!"

I felt my cheeks warm. Thankfully, akar didn't really show the red in their skin. "I thought you said not to tell everyone?" I countered.

"Well. Your love interest is an exception." Mom winked at me and I had to roll my eyes.

"But interesting. For someone who already ate, you seem incredibly hungry still," Mother noted with a playful scrutiny.

"I have to go. The human healer will be waiting for me."

"Hey!" Mother managed only the one protesting cry before I was out. She didn't pursue. The settlement began filling with life when I heard a familiar voice speak from my side.

"You're a poor liar, you know?"

I turned to find Mother Margaret flashing her knowing smile. She was a human Sister from the church of the Faithful and the healer I was looking for. She stood in her white robes and appeared almost inexplicably spotless except for the mud which stained the very fringes of her clothing.

"Here," she said, handing me a fresh bowl of grub and two extra loaves of bread.

My mouth instantly watered. "But, I can't. What about you?"

She smiled tenderly—of all the humans I met, I liked her the most. "I already ate," she said with an affable chuckle.

"And you are too good of a liar," I joked, unable to tell if she was telling the truth or not. I considered for a moment, and my stomach took it upon itself to cast in its vote as a great big audible rumble churned inside me.

Mother Margaret laughed heartily. "Just take it. You need it far more than I do apparently."

I did not object and said my thanks.

⊰ ⊱

Mother Margaret and I found a decrepit bench to sit on while I ate. The ascetic presence of the woman was like a sun-dried plumb. Her figure was round and her cheeks full. Her facial muscles had grown weary over the years and let her skin sag until her brows almost threatened to blind her.

"I still can't believe you are already sixteen," she said as I devoured the food.

"Thamph."

Mother Margaret frowned disapprovingly. She leaned away from the bench in an attempt to avoid the spittle. "Remember what I told you, akar! Don't speak with a full mouth," she chided, wiping away the chunks of food from her robe. She wet her thumb to aid her attempts. The woman had taken a shine to me ever since mid-wifing my birth. If my notable education and manners seemed all too human, it was because of her teachings.

I swallowed the contents forcibly. "I'm sorry."

She turned her stern frown to me and gave a pointed finger. "I told you to chew your food."

"Yes, Mother Margaret." I tried to hide my annoyance and let only my embarrassment show. I wasn't the size of a fully grown akar yet but I could have still crushed her. Several factors stopped me from doing so, including the fact that I actually liked her.

"For shame. You certainly refuse to learn some manners." She pointed a wrinkled finger. Mother Margaret was truly fearless when it came to scolding me.

If I lived among the invading trips in Thickwood, I would have been preparing for my first taste of battle. Yet here I was, in a camp being scolded by a human. Why Mother was so trusting of her I will never know.

"I'm sorry," I repeated, more ruefully this time.

"At least you've got the sense to apologize!" Her smile was true and her words loving. "I see you've really taken on the Bayrish language. If it weren't for your appearance or the depth of your voice, I might have even thought you human!"

I chuckled. My gaze caught two glowering akar facing my way. They turned the moment I caught them.

"Don't mind them," Mother Margaret said. She couldn't have known what swiped my smile away, but perhaps she read enough from my expression. Some akar weren't fond of my friendship with Mother Margaret. I despise the humans for many reasons, but not Mother Maragret.

"How do you find time for all this?" I asked in order to change the subject.

"Time for what?" She frowned, seemingly unprepared for the change in topic.

"Helping me? Tending to our ill?"

Mother Margaret shrugged. "Some time ago, it was all a bit too much, but after living through such a life day in and day out, it seems wrong not to do it all." She arched her posture as her angled arms pressed into the small of her back and a pained grimace spread on her face. "Although it seems my body is struggling to keep up, nowadays."

"Are you here because of the akar Burr?" I asked. It was the time of year, after all.

She nodded. "We are to meet Juta first. Sukin tried desperately to communicate that he needs attention."

Juta was the fighting trainer for myself and all the other growing akar. So it wasn't a surprise that his home was a yurt made from stitched leather. I watched as Mother Margaret tended to the brutish giant. Even amongst the akar he was truly huge. Outside, I heard akar getting about their day. Inside, I heard only Juta's strained breaths and his mate's soothing words. Sukin leaned in to plant a kiss on Juta's forehead.

The Burr worked its way through the camp with the coming autumn; it was a yearly thing believed to only affect us. Bed ridden men and women lay in their tents where Mother Margaret would tend to them. I admired her dedication.

Juta was covered in sweat. His tusks glistened from it. His large brows furrowed from fighting a fever. The beast of a man squirmed at Mother Margaret's care.

I focused with split attention; one eye on the treatment delivered by Mother Margaret, while the other rested on the akar. Juta was an honourable fighter, and would never harm someone he didn't deem a warrior. But he was delirious. I looked at his frighteningly large hands and imagined with what ease he could crush Mother Margaret's skull.

"Pay attention, Chroma. Along with the shrinkweed, a drop of clamdew in the tea will deal with muscle cramps." Mother Margaret handed the medicinal concoction to Sukin, who pressed it to Juta's cracked lips. With one hand under her lover's head, she raised his lips to the bitter mix. Juta fell into a mild coughing fit.

"What is that awfulness?" Juta asked with a strained voice in deep akar. He was stuck somewhere between a dream and the present.

"Medicine, my dear," Sukin supplied.

"Are you trying to poison me?" Juta's chest heaved, a sickly cough rasping at his throat. His eyes were shut, but there was no mistaking that the question was directed at Mother Margaret.

"Juta, my love, let her treat you." Sukin leaned in, her hand wrapped around her lover's; if his fingers were the thick branches of a tree then her long, strong fingers were that of embracing vines. The two continued to converse in akar.

"Chroma." Mother Margaret called for me.

I leaned in.

"What are they saying?" she asked quietly.

I strained my ears and tried to grasp as much as I could.

"Nothing, Sukin is just comforting him."

Mother Margaret nodded and continued to work, putting together a damp cloth mixed with more herbs. "Here you use dampweed and yimroot, I added a bit of deer velvet—"

It all happened so fast. Mother Margaret attempted to press the cloth on Juta's forehead and the fragile tightrope snapped. Juta roared and sat up, his giant hand swatting at Mother Margaret.

I only barely dove between them in time. The force knocked me back and into Mother Margaret, bringing us to the ground. Her scream was short and sharp.

Chapter Six

CHROMA

The akar are a proud folk with a culture as colourful and violent as their capricious emotions. One such tale I was able to gather from an akar was about the Scarred Soil tribe. During the age of the Asamanian Kingdom, a tribe of akar committed to a pilgrimage of blood. They walked endlessly till their feet bled and their path was stained scarlet. They only stopped when reaching the oasis which became their home.

—A LOOK INTO AKAR CULTURE, BY SHAUNA LAWLESS

A re you okay?" I asked Mother Margaret.

"I will be fine." She sat on a stool and had a warming blanket over her shoulders. Jasper had brought her a cup of warm tea which she held in her good hand. The other hand was bruised purple so that one couldn't even notice the trail of prominent veins in them. She hadn't broken anything, which was good, but I knew she must have been in some pain after the impact.

Juta and Sukin were moved to a different tent. All they could do now was wait for him to recover.

"You don't need to look at me like that," she grumbled.

"Like what?"

"As if I am some wounded puppy. I know what I am getting myself into," she answered, and took a sip from her tea. I looked nervously

KIAN N. ARDALAN

at the surrounding guards. We sat near the settlement entrance. The guards eyed me, their strafing glances boring in my back. I couldn't hear what they were muttering about and wasn't sure if I wanted to. Jasper suddenly came from the side and slapped them about the head, telling the men to get back to work.

I returned my focus to Mother Margaret and allowed myself the faintest of smiles for the moment. Our roles seemed suddenly reversed where I was the one who was worrying.

"You could have died," I said, only then noticing how Mother Margaret's robes were stained and dirty all over.

"But I didn't. I have you to thank for that." Her tone was warm.

I had nothing to say in turn.

"Now go along, I am done for the day. One near death experience is enough, and I am not much good with my injury." She waved me away with her bruised hand and played at being irritated.

I nodded. It was time to find my friends. I felt excited at the thought of seeing Nedalya.

⋯

There weren't many akar my age, but I had found a bond with the few who were. With Mother Margaret's visit over and nothing else to do, I sought out my friends.

I paced through the settlement and through small gaps in the tents. In a more recluse corner, I found the tree stump which marked our place of congregation.

My heart leapt the moment I set eyes on Nedalya. She sat with the others as they were casting carved bones.

She was a true akar, gifted with greatly defined muscles which formed her shoulders and gave her the disposition of a panther. Her face was more angular and squared with a strong jawline and hollow cheeks. Long lashes framed her dark and beady eyes.

It all came together when she saw me walk up to them and smiled. By Googan; I felt weak in the knees.

42

"Chroma," Trem whispered my name loudly, "You're staring again." Siemeny and he howled their laughter. Only Nedalya and Kolotha remained quiet. I was thankful that our akar complexion hid the colour of my cheeks.

"Stop it." Nedalya fixed me with her stare; I almost buckled under its weight. My knees felt weak—I couldn't help but desire her, even though I knew the likes of Kolotha were more desirable mates given his greater size and strength.

"Join us, lover-boy," Trem teased as I sat with them.

Although we grew up together and were of similar age, I had grown more self-conscious around them over the years. My own body took on the form of a lithe, muscled thief rather than an akar warrior.

Siemeny frowned and cocked her head. The ornaments knotted into her dreadlocks clunked together like bones. "Lover boy?" she pressed.

Trem appeared flustered. "I overheard a guard. Said it to Jasper," he said, almost flustered.

I laughed with the others, thankful to Siemeny for taking the attention off me. We conversed mostly in Bayrish, the human tongue. It was difficult to maintain pride for your own people when all the humans about us saw us as lesser; but regardless, we made the best of what we had.

"'Oh, lover boy,'" Siemeny teased, parodying Trem's voice.

"Shut up," he said mirthfully, tossing dirt at her face.

Kolotha gave a bemused grunt. "You sound like one of them." Kolotha's tone was slightly chiding; out of all of us, he was the closest link to our past we still had.

He was a warrior, his skin marked by our culture. A bar of obsidian stone punctured Kolotha's nose, horizontally. More piercings jutted like thorns from his upper-cheekbone and the rear of his lower jaw on both ends, including a final pair above his eyebrows. White curves were tattooed to form winding rivers along his face and down his collarbone. The only thing about him which wasn't embellished was his voice, like a deep guttural sound coming from the depths of an endless chasm. The only thrum greater came from the Morning Bell.

"And you sound like your throat was fucked by Googan himself."

We all laughed. Even Kolotha gave a hearty chortle.

Trem was only slightly bigger than me with his own wiry and more acrobatic definition. His face was long and his eyes were bunched up and pressed deep into his skull. His lanky build and long features gave him a ratty face.

"Hey, I got something here." Trem reached behind the log he sat on and withdrew a bundle of cloth. He held it close and looked to see if there were any unwelcome eyes. Satisfied, he revealed its contents. "Look what I found." He smiled devilishly.

"Are you crazy?" Nedalya pressed. "If they find out, you will get punished!"

"They won't find out," he said.

I moved away from the tree stump to get a clearer view and re-pressed a gasp at the steaming pig leg. My mouth watered instantly.

"How can you be so sure?" Siemeny joined in.

"By our ancestors, can you all stop being so scared and just enjoy the moment?" Trem insisted. "Plus, if you keep gawking like that, they will get suspicious."

I turned to the gates and was relieved to see a string of tents obscure us from the guards.

"That's not all." Trem raised his eyebrows suggestively and gave a toothy grin as he produced a leather water skin. Nedalya took it from him, but Trem seemed untroubled.

Removing the stopper, Nedalya took a sniff and her eyes widened. "Wine!" she proclaimed in surprise.

"Relax, they were going to throw out the meat and they have so much wine in there they don't even know what to do with it all."

"How did you even get this?" Siemeny asked.

Trem grinned as he was about to share his secret. Being cautious, Trem leaned forward, and the rest of us followed suit. "One of the wooden planks at the fence behind my tent is rotten and the earth has come loose. You can easily remove it, squeeze through and return it again and no one would know."

Trem took back the wineskin and downed a satisfying gulp. "Anyone want to join me? Drinking with company is so much better, especially with stolen food and drink."

We found our way into one of the open yurts made for small gatherings and tried our best to stay quiet. The bones we had brought were used to play Janaham. They were carved with runes to be thrown the way humans throw dice. Usually, the bones would belong to that of our slain foes from battle, but the lack of such resources made us use the bones of animals like cattle and pig. The humans saw it in their good graces to pass us the bones of animals when they were done with the flesh.

The principle of Janaham was simple: akar life was about chance, about believing in the weaving thread of life as you ran headfirst into conflict. Thus the bones were also a game of chance, to bet on a rune, to bet on a combination, to bet on a constellation which included all runes.

The pig leg served as a delicacy and the wineskin didn't last long, but we had a reserve of our own vile creation among the akar called pirine. Better known as 'demon piss'. As the Elder's eye started its descent to bring in the light of dusk, we found our throats burning.

Bones were thrown, bets were made, and laughs were had.

One could take four or five bones and toss them, but one had to also make a claim and a bet. The claim could be that the great eye of Googan will show itself, or perhaps the skull of Ankou awaits. The weave of Nekfet, The Great Loomweaver, So'Ra, the champion's blessing and Kho'Shah's blood. If the symbol showed itself, all those who agreed to the bet had to hand over their losses, while if the thrower lost, they had to offer in turn based on the counsel of the others. Yet the offered bet could be anything and everything.

There were also combinations with higher stakes and higher rewards, where a combination of two or three brought greater bets, especially if this was achieved with just four bones. But if one were to make a claim for the constellation, one could ask for anything in the world, especially with all five symbols.

As we dove into the night's revelries, I once again noted that the name 'demon piss' was a deserved title: it certainly tasted like it. Vile like vomit let out to sit in the summer sun, ground up with crab shells meant to scratch against your throat and just a light hint of something close to rotten eggs. But it got the job done. Our vision blurred and our wits strained. Our laughs boisterous, and our shushing just as loud.

Our ancestors used it to drown away their fears and give them courage in times of battle; we used it for similar reasons, but not for battle.

❧ ❧

"Okay, okay," Trem tried to collect himself.

He had gone back and forth with Kolotha and bet on a combination of three symbols, the eye, the blood, and the spider. In return, Kolotha was supposed to tear out one of his thorn-like implants in his cheek. Trem lost, and in turn, had to tear out a tooth at the back of his mouth. It was covered in blood and more red flowed down Trem's chin. The rest of us cried triumphantly.

As things escalated into the night, more carnal bets were made beside the newly ignited fire of our lodging.

"I make a claim to the champion… and if I get my claim, I want Trem to undress," Siemeny said. It was undeniable what kind of sexual tension simmered in our tent. I was certain this wasn't the first time Siemeny and Trem engaged as they were doing.

The entire tent wooed at the claim and a hunger was ablaze in her stare. The lit fire at the centre of the yurt reflected off her eyes. The rest of us remained seated and just watched.

I gulped. My breath stiffened. Was I excited or terrified? I couldn't tell.

Siemeny got her claim as Trem pulled down his pants. Curiosity made me stare. His phallus was curiously big. I'd never seen another except for my own.

Siemeny got onto all fours and bit her lower lip. There was a hunger to how she prowled. The campfire made her eyes glisten, the golden light grasping tightly to her charcoal skin as the fire was spurred on by the display.

No one spoke a word, and Trem didn't even try to repress his wanton grin.

The fireplace crackled and the shadows danced with heightened zeal. Suddenly, Siemeny inched herself between Trem's loins and seized something the shadows insisted to conceal. She stroked softly, tenderly, until Trem moaned.

The ever-shifting light of the fire was like ethereal hands which cast themselves upon Siemeny's and Trem's form, exploring along their bodies.

My own breath quickened, the space between my legs growing tight. I was captivated by the display, a stray thought wondering how my cock would be compared to Trem's. I thought they were evenly sized. But was Trem's average? Kolotha stared on stoically: he was unimpressed. Alongside my lust I felt insecurity spread.

No, no. That was how Kolotha always looked.

I caught Nedalya staring and we both tore our gazes away from each other. My heart pounded.

Trem spoke the names of our gods.

Kolotha casually reached for his own groin, massaging the telling outline, yet his eyes seemed as unfazed as ever at the sight. I felt our company's heartbeat fall into tandem; the sound filled my eardrums. The heat expelled from our bodies rose in unison and came to fill the space.

I dared another glance at Nedalya and found her also mesmerized by the site. Akar embraced their passion; this was a celebration of body and emotion. Blood pumped through me with the promise of flesh. What I would do to take her. The pirine in my system, the enticing performance before me, the devouring sight of my longing having every important feature revealed by the dancing fire-light. It was like sinking into a warm and venereal embrace. The light bathed against the leather tan of the tent.

Warmth radiated from between my legs. My focus ensnared by the gentle beads of sweat, like dew, which trailed Nedalya's skin.

She looked at me, and now my gaze stayed strong. She too, warred with some inkling of doubt. My sense of self melted underneath her sharp gaze. An invisible force pulled me towards Nedalya.

"Oh, by the words of Googan, I will make sure to steal food every week." Trem muttered half-consciously.

Siemeny chuckled heartily. "You promise?" I heard and then turned to see her commit even more firmly to the act. Pirine had given us courage; made buoyant our desire so that doubt could never threa-ten it.

Kolotha stood and held his own instrument in hand. I shrunk at the sight of the monstrosity; it was akin to a battering ram. Casually, he traipsed over to Siemeny who reached for Kolotha's member. Siemeny stared lustfully up at him and began to pleasure both. This was normal among akar. It was. So why did I feel so uncomfortable?

Nedalya rose and came next to me, the room in my pants tightened. My heart blazed in my chest, and my breathing hastened.

"Relax," Nedalya said, perhaps partially to herself. "I have been wanting to do this with you for a long time."

Her breath caressed my chin as she neared me, causing a shiver to crawl up my spine. The hairs on my arm stood at attention. She smelt of sweat and rosy earth. Her hands were strong and calloused. One carefully worked its way up my thigh.

I could see the worry in her expression. She was nervous. I was lost in her eyes; how small they seemed, how lovingly they stared. It was a gaze of passion waiting to take me, but there was a sense of love mixed in with it.

She shuddered with her own breath as her eyes slowly closed, my hand wrapping itself around her nape, the sweat which sheened her conspiring to make our bodies cling to one another. Her breathing strengthened, I savoured its caress upon my cheek as I drew her closer.

The world melted away.

My lips finally met Nedalya's. I felt cautious fingers explore the shape above my trousers. The meeting did away with any pretence of restraint, our tongues were locked in dance, twirling within the walls of our mouths. The light of the fire danced and flickered, wood cracked and ember sparks shot up like burning petals to celebrate this long awaited kiss. But I went too deep, my heart beating faster and faster as the riptide of my desire proved too much. Fear struck me, a primal fear which defined my existence even if I didn't want it to.

I pushed her away. There was hurt in Nedalya's eyes, confusion even.

"I'm sorry," was all I could manage. I got up to leave.

The first sign of coming night showed itself. The world was painted tawny as the sun set. I worked my way back home crest-fallen and ashamed.

Embarrassment flushed my cheeks and made its way through me. What would Nedalya think?

"I am so pathetic," I claimed under my breath. My fists tightened. The flaring sense of shame battered against the helm of my being.

Why couldn't I have been more like Kolotha? Even Trem got his act together and just did it. Would Nedalya think me a coward now? She gave herself wholly to me and I ran. Perhaps she would want someone with more confidence as an akar.

My cock certainly held no candle to Kolotha's. Was I overthinking it? My body was nowhere near as tall or wide as his or Trem's.

Maybe I should have waited till I had grown a little older? But what if that was it?

I looked up to see Mother outside our tent. The surrounding homes were pitched and still in their rows.

I was about to call out to her but something gave me pause. Perhaps it was the morose ache of my heart or this lone image of mother standing amidst tents. Or maybe it was the clandestine look about her as she headed towards the settlement entrance. Only a handful of other souls roamed about, preparing for night.

Cautiously, mother paced through the empty road and out through the entrance. None stopped her. No alarmed voices cried out into the curdling dusk.

My mind was a quagmire. Too muddled with thoughts of Nedalya and my cowardice to think of much else. I wandered through the rows of tents with only my poisoned thoughts to keep me company.

⋦ ⋗

My heart ached as I thought of Nedalya. I hung my head in my hands, remembering the pain in her eyes. She opened herself to me and I just rejected her.

I owed her an apology, at least.

I visited Nedaya's tent and expected to find her there. It was empty.

"Chroma?" Trem and Siemeny stumbled about drunk and jovial when I turned to them, their expressions turning sour when they found me at Nedalya's tent.

"Hi," I offered sullenly, unsure of what to say.

"Chroma…" Siemeny started, her drunken smile faltering with the last glimmer of day and turning into a sympathetic expression.

"Where is Nedalya?" I asked, fearing the answer.

Their heads hung low and apologetic.

"She went with Kolotha."

⋦ ⋗

I moved to Kolotha's tent and heard the two of them shake the very ground on which they fucked.

The raging, guttural grunts like boars in heat, the sound of shifting hay punctuating the pounding sounds of skin on skin as Kolotha growled like flame in a furnace.

But most painful of all was hearing Nedalya moan. I could hear her tender voice, a voice I had fallen in love with, soft yet strong and robust. A voice which as sturdy as a planted tree and as true as the image of the sea. A voice I always knew would be there without a single glimmer of doubt. It was once a loving sound, now perverted by their cries. I felt an illusion shatter, its shards imbedding themselves in my chest and causing an invisible ache.

My mind's turbulence took form like shifting colours. All I could do was wish her moans were for me and not for Kolotha. It was selfish, I knew I wasn't owed anything, but it didn't make their heated grunts hurt any less.

The thought of Kolotha's entering Nedalya made my cheeks flush with warmth, my heart ache and my cock harden all at once. My own rising lust felt sickening as I listened. I couldn't stay any longer.

I didn't know how long I was a voyeur to their primitive passion, but I retreated to Trem's tent and tried to block out the sound of his own groans with Siemeny. Was it just my imagination that they didn't sound quite as wild as Nedalya and Kolotha?

Careful not to alert the two to my presence, I found the rotten plank of wood Trem had mentioned and removed it, slipping through, and gingerly returning it to its spot.

I stood there. Simply stood with a heaving chest and looked out towards the tranquil scene of an open field. In the distance, I could see forest trees clinging stubbornly to their green despite coming autumn. With the view of an open field, I felt as if I could breathe again, felt as if the grunts and groans of Nedalya and Kolotha previously trapped in my skull had dissipated. A soft and gentle breeze rustled the long field of grass as if grooming it with an invisible tongue. The orange glow of an egg yolk covered it all and the soft touch of grey began to grow like mould over its tapestry.

Then I ran, ran as far as my legs could carry me into the open field under the cover of growing night. Never before had I seen a world outside of the settlement, yet I felt welcomed by this embracing dark which covered all of Minethria, and I sprinted through the field. I could see the outline of a slumbering forest, its silhouette looking much like the curled body of a dreaming giant.

Chapter Seven

DALILA

Time is our mortal leash and divides the gods from us mortals. The golden spire circling about Minethria is a constant reminder of this. The Grand Archon, first of the angels, rules over this heavenly domain and guards the Contract of Time, notching another month to our year after a cycle's end.

—PASSAGE FROM THE KASELUDA

T he path to Crowtown was a leisurely stroll up a road. The road started off patchy with green until we walked past the outline of Basksin and met the beaten path.

Jeremiah was sharing his packed food.

Beck was whining about his sore arms from all the milking his father made him do.

"Must be fun! My dad just does boring paperwork," Perry complained.

Jeremiah interjected. "You think that's bad? There is nothing to do at Basksin! Everything is a sin to the Witness." He gobbled down a loaf of bread as if to stop himself from further blaspheming.

I've heard Witnesses sneer and judge everyone who didn't believe in Oxular, saying they will be one of the forgotten. Father equally stated that when the end of time came, Jeremiah's folk wouldn't be saved by the Elders. I wondered who was in the right.

I looked over to Perry, who mirrored my tender smile. My heart couldn't handle more than a second of connection—that alone was euphoric.

He had wide blue eyes filled with wonder and life; they were always so expressive, even with the tiniest of things. His cheeks were full and his chin small and tucked in. He was fast, faster than the others, still a child, but everything about Perry made him the life of the room without even trying. He even had a few freckles I would mentally connect when I lost myself in his features.

"Do you smell that?" Jeremiah asked excitedly. Repressing my embarrassment at having so blatantly stared at Perry, I looked out at the fringes of humble Crowtown. It was true: there was a buttery scent which often accompanied baked goods and I could tell that the town's commotion had more to do with the impromptu celebration at the sudden ring of the Morning Bell.

It turned out that the birth of a seed was never set for a specific day, but instead lurked around a thousand years. But without fail, all events were dropped when it rang and a holiday was created without prior warning.

The akar settlement which hugged the bricked walls of Crowtown was obscured from our view as we neared the festivities. I looked on towards the extending road, imagining myself following its path till I reached Cleria. Only the grand stories I had been told served to embellish my fantasies.

At arrival in Crowtown, we entered through open gates and took in the sounds of enterprise as people walked to and fro between market stands.

Food stalls and bakeries were energized with the promise of customers, for who wouldn't wish to make an excuse and enjoy some well-earned commodities on such a day?

I could smell the wafting allure of butter-bread, the soft burning of coals in a hearth. The autumn air was dour, but it didn't stop the people from celebrating. Even with the sun's dulled glow, the world had a jolly and spirited buzz which was infectious. We were greeted with welcoming smiles and wished a merry day.

"May the Eleventh Seed protect you," they would say.

Jeremiah was the most wide-eyed out of us all. "Guys, could you tell me about the Haar?" Jeremiah asked.

"What about it?" Perry replied.

We had just squeezed through a moving gap of adults before Jeremiah responded timidly. "Nothing. Nevermind." His plump cheeks decided to ripen a spotted red like ready apples.

Despite being spoiled for choice when it came to the dozens of stands, we already had set our sights on the Merry-Inn; a pun based on the owner's name being Merry-Anne.

Once a week, she opened her doors freely to youngsters and hired a musician to come and play, regaling us with tales of old from the birth of Minethria and the spreading of the Haar. It just so happened that this week, it fell upon the day when the Morning Bell had rung.

We leapt up the three steps and slowed to a brisk pace with little pats of our feet against the wooden floorboards and into Merry-Inn. It hadn't started yet!

Inn tables and chairs were used to form a theatre. The children were huddled together on the floor, cross-legged. The place smelt of spilt ale and wine which worked its way into the floorboards. Burnt pig's fat from candlelight gave the place a greasy aroma. It was a nice smell all things told; it became an inseparable part of the experience.

Once inside, we saw the waving, frantic hand of Dale as he motioned for us to join him with a goofy grin on his face. He had been expecting us. We shuffled over to his corner and took a seat to the sound of creaking wood. The bard was still tuning his lute.

This time around, the bard was Gallivax. Golden curly locks like springs hung long and unbound. His figure was willowy, much like Fredrick, with wiry fingers and a thin form, though at least with Gallivax there was a certain grace. His posture rather relaxed, his long face and thin smile comforting. And even his garishly pointed chin goatee appeared appropriate. His attire spoke of a modest income, enough to afford a brown vest and a clear white tunic which must have cost a hefty penny, but nothing that would have set him apart from the more affluent of Crowtown.

He smiled, holding us in his trance as we waited in anticipation for his first words. His eyes drifted among our little puddle of children and took in every expression.

"What would you like to hear first?"

Many hands shot up from the audience.

"White-Hawk and Erefiel!" Perry requested next to me, unable to decide between the two figures.

"Colour magic!" Cried Jeremiah.

"The akar war!"

"The Asamanian conflict!"

"The third Seed!"

"The hundred year dragon war!"

Many requests were made, and some were lost underneath all the demands. In the end, Gallivax pointed to the one which won out.

"The birth of the moon and the sun!" he declared, apparently only his ears having caught the request.

I wasn't sure who he was pointing at, but perhaps it was Gallivax's plan to point between children and make everyone think it was their neighbour who made the request. He slung one dainty ankle over the other knee and shuffled in his seat, his lute propped upon his hip as he strummed the first chord.

"*The womb of void did teem with mist,*" sung Gallivax, his brows knitting together as he sunk deep into the pool of his creativity and was lost in his own voice.

"It roiled, it coiled, it writhed.
"It waits alone, and with no season,
"Until the Gods arrive.

"Yet none could see, with eyes born blind
"For first we needed light,
"In this umbral black we weep
"Till Elders gifted sight,

"Two eyes of gold the Elder King bore.
"Two nests of bleeding flame,
"To burn to ash the veil of nought,
"And bathe the world in paint and stain.

"And thus his charge as King commenced,
"Grey mould, his light did rend,
"The boon of bliss, did sun's eye show.
"But blight did not yet end.

"A darkness roots inside man's heart,
"It's watered with sermons of greed and blood
"They wear their gilded crowns of thorns
"And reap till naught but mud.

"So weep, did King, on soil scarred deep.
"And birth'd the Archon's wings.
"In spokes of light they bind their wheels,
"And man's age with the rings.

"But King be kind, in their decree
"To cherish months 'fore year's end,
"Is thanks to Seeds who came and bled,
"But some rejected this advent.

"Do woe the men who stole god's eye,
"So they may break their bind,
"For yoke of time is chafing, grating,

"They watch its weave unwind.

"Too late they notice scattered dust
"Becoming stars of night
"Now know in day that all is well
"But fear the fleeting light."

Gallivax strummed the final chord and bowed with a minstrel's flourish.

"So who stole the King's eye?" Perry asked after a round of excited applause.

Gallivax nodded. "The Kingdom of Estria, now a forbidden place of death and decay."

"And they only rise when the moon rises?" Jeremiah asked.

Gallivax nodded again. "Bound to the moon as they are, they can only exist with its presence."

One child looked perplexed as he asked the next question. "So we didn't originally have ten months in a year?" His brows knitted together at the concept.

Gallivax smiled. "The first angel, the Grand Archon, drifts along their golden spire in the sky and denotes the month based on their position. With each cycle ended and each Seed ascending to live with the creator, the contract of time adds a month to the cycle. Ten cycles have been fulfilled: thus we have ten months to a year. The more months there are, the longer we live."

No sooner was one question answered did the next already start. "Did the Elder King's power dwindle after his eye was stolen?"

Gallivax shook his head. "The Elder King is powerful beyond measure. He may have lost the shine of one eye, but none can match his power."

"Not even his Seed?" I asked.

The swelling silence thickened all about us. Wide-eyes jerked and lingered on me, surprise painted across all their expressions. Even Gallivax's smile faded, though he didn't appear annoyed at the question.

"Not even his Seed; traitor Elders and the Bugs of Duran have tried, but none have managed, not even the dragons of Krem."

All I felt at that moment was a shudder as I considered the unimaginable power of the Elder King.

⋞ ⋟

Gallivax spoilt us with a few more stories. Some about the Bugs of Duran, ancient creatures made by the Elder King at about the same time the rest of the Elders were created. Stories told of creatures shaped like beetles, flies, ants, and more, said to be the size of boulders and towers. Father once said if I pressed my ear to Duran Mountain, I could hear a soft vibration believed to be the buzzing of distant wings and chittering mandibles.

Gallivax also told of the sea monsters born from the third cycle, great indescribable beings. Leviathans roaming below the depths of the sea awaiting a daring voyager. Or perhaps a foolish one: some said the Elder King created the beasts to dissuade us from sailing forth to such unforgiving ventures.

The last story Gallivax shared came from a persistent young boy who wanted to hear of Ashen Forest.

It was a place far past Greyhill within Thickwood forest, guarded by the mage's institution of the Faithful. A sect of Mystic derived from the Faithful church supposedly sealed it off.

Gallivax told us of the great Ring of Fire, which one could see up above the forest like an infernal halo. It was supposedly a place of unsettling quiet where ash snowed perpetually to blanket the forest's stillness. Some hired hunters were occasionally tasked with going in and capturing a demon for experiments.

"That will be all for today," Gallivax admitted regretfully to the disappointed groans of us children. He chuckled. "I'm sorry, that's all the time we have."

Merry-Anne stepped forward. "Come on, kids, I have a business to run, out with you all." A demure and reticent girl sprung from the crowd and went to embrace Merry-Anne. All I ever managed to learn was that her name was Georgia. I tried to talk to her in the past, but she never seemed very keen on the idea. Merry-Anne embraced her daughter and patted her on the back. The girl ran past and into the kitchen without once turning back to show her face.

Merry-Anne was a rather bubbly and kind looking woman with fine wrinkles betraying her age but she was just as exuberant as if she were in her twentieth year. It truly felt as if her personality had infused with the building itself. Having been enraptured by all the stories, I almost forgot she was there.

It was a strange thought to me that if we lived during the time of any earlier cycle where the months were fewer, Merry-Anne would have already been dead and I would have looked just as old as she did now.

⊲ ⊳

When the children worked their way out of the Merry-Inn to be greeted by waiting parents, Merry-Anne, Gallivax and a few other workers moved the tables back to their usual positions.

Dale ran up to me. "What did you think?" he queried, all excited and starry-eyed.

I found myself rather taken off-guard as I blinked. "Your father was great."

"I know, right?" Dale was the prime epitome of expression, be it to portray sadness or excitement. It was usually the latter.

"I hope to play like Father does one day," he proclaimed.

Beck chuckled sardonically and sneered. "Your father isn't even in the college of Museya, his music can't even make a plant grow, let alone perform miracles; that's not a hard bar to set."

This time, I swung a full kick into Beck's shin and took pleasure from his cries.

"Why do you have to be such a bully?" I shouted.

My cheeks were warm with bristling fury as Beck limped back with one hand to his injured shin and the other palm raised in submission.

"Dalila," Perry neared me and held me back. "Don't. It's not worth it."

Dale still smiled, but the downward knitting of his frown and faltering lips told of how much wind was robbed from his sails. "It's okay," he said. "He's right."

I walked over to Dale. "No, he's not. Your father may not be able to heal wounds or lend strength to troops like an Inspired of Museya, but what he does do is bring people from all over to listen to his stories and makes children wish it never ended: that is true magic."

Life returned to Dale as he suddenly noticed how close I stood. His light-brown eyes suddenly averted themselves as he gave feeble thanks. "Thank you, Dalila."

I nodded and pretended not to notice the flushing of his cheeks.

"Indeed, thank you."

I turned to see Gallivax stand behind us. Beck had gone a ghostly white.

"It is true," he said to Beck. "It was my dream as a child to follow troops into battle and support them with my music, but I was never one of the gifted." He turned to his son. "Perhaps one day Dale might be. He has a gift I never had, I just wish he would put in the work." Gallivax turned to Beck. "If I can watch your youthful faces light up with such wonder once a week, that is magic enough for me."

I admired Gallivax's composure, though I wondered if he still harboured hurt, and was just too proud to show it. Or perhaps too skilled as an entertainer.

"Father, can I join my friends for a bit?" Dale requested.

Gallivax frowned. "But you have practice today. How can you ever hope to be a bard if you never practice?"

"I am already good enough." Dale rebutted.

"No, son, you are *talented*. There is a difference. You still can't even manage Micrion's Ballad."

Dale looked at us desperately.

"Mr. Tanley. I know his playing is important, but it is the birth of the Eleventh Seed today. It doesn't happen very often," I offered, knowing full well that the softness of my remark would win him over.

"Please, Father," Dale pleaded.

With a defeated sigh, Gallivax finally nodded begrudgingly as Dale gave a loving embrace.

"Thank you, Dad!" He cried.

"Just stay safe! And make sure you take care of your hands," Gallivax said.

"Yes, yes, Father." Dale rolled his eyes.

"Oh, and on one condition." Gallivax went back inside the Inn and returned with Dale's lute.

"You practice on your way!"

"But dad—"

"No 'buts'!"

I jumped in before Dale could dig himself an even bigger hole.

"I will make sure he plays the lute, sir."

Gallivax nodded and left.

Dale strapped the lute to his back begrudgingly. "Where will we go?" he asked.

I smiled. "How about Dreamwood? They say it is the place to go to have wild dreams and awaken your gift!"

We all looked to the sky and noted the setting sun above dancing between motes of dull orange and grey.

"But I can't stay past nightfall," I added.

"That's a great idea! And we'll be fine! We still have plenty of time and your home is right next to the woods, anyway." Perry turned to Dale. "Plus, this way, nobody has to listen to your terrible playing," he teased.

"Hey!" Dale cried.

"Actually, that's why I suggested Dreamwood," I said.

Dale lit up at the prospect.

Beck nursed his shin and stood with us with a rueful expression. "Sorry about what I said earlier," he said.

Dale nodded, and Jeremiah allowed himself a wide smile before slapping Beck across the back in approval. Beck fell flat on the floor.

We laughed until the moment was violently shattered by a blood-curdling scream.

Behind me was a nightmarish woman sprawled on her knees and wailing like a banshee in the night.

"What happened?" I murmured in stock-horror.

Another wail escaped her, so true and pure from whatever core inside her that I fully expected her vocal chords to snap like an overly taut string.

"My son!" The woman wailed. Her hair was frazzled and matted, as if she had lived in the woods for months. Her eyes were weighed down by heavy bags. Cracked lips trembled as she tried to grab at passing folk.

"My son! Who is my son?" she called out, repeating the question and switching between who and where.

"That is Mrs Johnson." We turned to find the tavern owner, Merry-Anne, standing over us with a saddened expression. "She ended up like this over the past few days, screaming to us about her son. She claims he is forgotten. Accuses all of us for not paying enough attention."

Jeremiah's right hand made a circular symbol made of his thumb and forefinger, and pressed it to his forehead with closed eyes. "May he be Witnessed," he said piously.

"Mrs Johnson?" Perry began. "But she never had a son."

Merry-Anne's gaze narrowed with inexplicable sorrow. Something about the scene was terrifying, something I couldn't quite place until I saw how taciturn Merry-Anne was about Perry's query. Realization came to me as a lazy trickle and then all at once.

A deep, existential fear gripped me. I looked at the wailing woman, her arms thin and her nails cracked, her skin a ghostly grey, her wild nest of hair like unravelled strands of her sanity.

Her son was forgotten? What was his name? Did I know him? Was he a friend of mine? Questions by nature of being unanswerable filled me with terror; I wondered if I had known the boy. Did he just fade into nothingness?

The lingering fear was ineffable. Would I one day also be forgotten?

Merry-Anne looked at us and said the only thing she could and in the most reassuring tone she could muster. "You best be on your way, children."

Chapter Eight

DALILA

Dreamwood is known to be a catalyst of inspiration. Though unlikely, some say that making your bed within its domain will grant you with transcendent understanding.

—Myths and Legends of Minethria

T he fading sun peered at us through brief gaps in buildings and sky. Some of the rays were absorbed through spongy clouds as we made our way back up Newmon Road.

Our mood had been dampened by Mrs Johnson's plight. None of us could quite explain the nagging sensation. It was like a sixth sense young children naturally had for noticing bleak atmospheres and things which warranted respect or sorrow. The idea of simply no longer existing came to us like a shapeless fear, a blotch of smeared black in our vision which could not be filled.

Yet the further we distanced ourselves from Crowtown and were distracted by Dale's absent strumming, the less bleak and sullen our moods became.

Pacing at the rear, I pretended not to notice Perry had been drawing ever closer to me. I let my hand dangle, fingers relaxed as I could feel my palm become damp with nervous sweat. There was barely a swing to my arm as Beck, Jeremiah and Dale joked among themselves.

Only a mouse's squeak escaped my lips before I shut them tight as I felt Perry's fingers curl around my own. He must have noticed me tense, for his grip relaxed and he silently fell away. I did my part and held his hand tight before he slipped away and turned to look at him with flustered eyes.

Perry was surprised. He looked away to hide blushing. His own grip strengthened around my hand. Strong. Firm. Gentle.

I looked ahead and saw Dale turn away from us. He strummed his lute and sung even louder.

"O' fair Minethria of our past,
Blistered and scarred, thy gentle land,
Won't ye protect us from akar scorn?
For one day, there will be noone to mourn."

Dale played from Veruk's Hymn, a song I had heard on one or two occasions before. Ever since the threat of the invading akar had grown, more and more of such songs were being written.

"Do you guys feel anything?" Dale asked.

All of us shrugged our lack of change. Suddenly Beck stopped in his tracks.

"Wait," he professed, hand to his stomach as he leaned over.

"I feel something." His voice was a strained groan. "I... I... I feel."

We all froze with anticipation.

Beck suddenly rose up high with burlesque grandeur and sang. *"That you suuuuuuck!"*

We burst into laughter, even Dale who made as if he were about to break the lute over Beck's head. The two were running circles around giggling Jeremiah.

When Dale stopped his chase, he simply spoke aloud his thoughts through a humoured but disappointed smile. "Guys, I am serious! I have been trying over and over again to work some magic through my music but it never works." Dale let his lute hang from its strap.

I glared daggers at Beck, fully expecting him to say something demeaning and inappropriate again, but he seemed to have learnt his lesson.

"I want to be like Veruk, Jasine, or Loran. I want to join their ranks and breathe life into troops as they charge into the fray against the akar."

"It's not easy, Dale. Give it time," Perry said. I imagined he was sympathetic as he too wanted to be on the front lines.

"Veruk could control entire forests with his music when he was my age, I can't even make a potted plant grow faster. It's just so frustrating, no matter what I try, I show no sign of being one of the Inspired."

"Well, maybe you will get inspired at Dreamwood," I provided.

"Y-yeah, I mean. Some of the greatest musicians have gone there to discover their talent." Even Beck tried to be supportive.

Out of everyone, it was just Jeremiah who shied away from the topic and blended in with the scenery. I felt something nagging him.

"You think so?" Dale asked, just the bare hint of hope to his query.

Beck nodded. "Just take a nap there and you will have one of those wild, inspired, dreams and just like that—" Beck snapped his fingers. "You will have what it takes to be a great bard."

"And then you can support me when I am there on the front lines with you!" Perry exclaimed excitedly.

Dale's smile beamed. "Then what are we waiting for? On the double!"

❧ ❧

As we neared the forest and brushed aside the resistance of branches, Jeremiah finally said what was bothering him. He looked like he was going to burst with his puffed up cheeks and tightly shut lips. "Guys, I have a question. But please don't laugh." His cheeks already flushed without even having asked anything, yet.

Beck spun at the call. "I am making no such promises! In fact, it is kind of rude of you to expect that from me."

Perry, being as diplomatic as he was, stepped in front of Beck and lingering Jeremiah.

Jeremiah twiddled his thumbs, as his gaze fell to the forest floor. "I don't know…" the rest was inaudible as he mumbled it.

"What was that?" Dale asked.

"I don't know how magic works!" He practically shouted it this time, his embarrassment painting his cheeks.

"What?" Beck spelled out his incredulity, his grin from ear to ear as his eyes dazzled with the promise of something new to torture Jeremiah with. "Is that why you kept asking about colour magic from Gallivax?"

A quick raise of my leg made his sneering grin fall away.

"What do you mean? You don't know?" Perry asked. There was no judgement in his tone.

Still flustered, Jeremiah answered with his eyes to the ground. "Father and Mother don't want me to learn about it. They say it is not part of our religion. I keep trying to ask Gallivax or someone, but I was just too embarrassed to ask directly."

I could tell there was a silent conflict taking place within the boy with a golden heart, his faith in his own religion battling against a child's natural curiosity.

"Why wait till now?" I asked.

Jeremiah shrugged and looked rather ashamed. His eyes remained down and he was footing some dried leaves as he spoke. "Was just embarrassed… and then I waited and waited, until it became harder to ask. But I feel left out now."

I couldn't pretend like I understood Jeremiah, but I did sympathise.

"Well, what do you know?" Perry asked.

Jeremiah looked up. "That Dale wants to be an Inspired, like those who get accepted into the colleges in Museya. I know only a few gifted who can perform miracles with their instruments."

Perry nodded and stepped towards Jeremiah, placing a hand on his shoulder. "See? You know more than you think." Halfway through his sentence, Perry turned to stare at Beck. Not with any glower, but still it was a silent warning to think twice before saying anything.

"Well, where to begin? You know of the Haar?" Perry asked; Jeremiah's chin lifted itself.

Perry continued. "The Haar is the mist, it is what encircles the lands. The Elder King could fashion more space out of it. So it goes that some of us can do the same. From Bolton you have carriers who gather and transport the mists in special containers for mistmages to control."

"What about colour?" Jeremiah's question was meek but not as frazzled.

Perry nodded. "Colour-magic is drawn from special flowers, each colour having a certain strength to it. Red can instil rage or love or passion but it can also invoke flame. They all have properties here and there. As for the Inspired, I suppose Dale would explain it best."

Jeremiah looked up at Dale. Dale was taken aback at the suggestion, but cleared his throat to explain. It felt as if he had not just borrowed his father's words verbatim, but even his cadence. "Father said art is magic. There are those naturally melded with the spiritual thread of the world and, if fully in tune with their art, they can perform incredible miracles. But an Inspired can come through in any art; scribes in Museya write magic scrolls with poems to instil bravery or strength and there are sculptors or dancers."

Jeremiah nodded, his brows knitting together as he processed it all. "Is it really so hard to get into a college in Museya?" he asked Perry, who in turn looked at Dale.

The minstrel's son had a sombre smile, his hand clutching the strap of his lute till I heard the leather crease and saw his knuckles turn white. "It is damn-near impossible. There is a reason an entire city was built around this gift."

"That's why we are here, Jeremiah," Perry said, picking up the pace again. "Dreamwood is supposed to be a mystical place, some say falling asleep here grants a connection to the truth of their craft beyond mortal understanding."

"Is it true?" Jeremiah asked.

Beck scoffed. "Load of bull, if you ask me. You know Grace? She's the girl living in Jones' farm?"

"You mean the one you fancy?" I teased. There was only a slight flush on Beck's cheek.

"Shu''t," he said with a slur. "Anyway, her brother also wanted to be a musician. Came to the woods and slept there for a whole week! His parents thought him dead and sent a scouting party. When he finally returned, he got such a whooping." Beck laughed in that abhorrent way he did when he was overly excited. His laugh always had a rise but never a fall, and remained stuck on repeat.

Dale was now the hesitant one. "Well, did it work for him?" he asked.

Beck's laugh died down as he looked at Dale with a cocked eyebrow. "He's still here, ain't he? His dreams must have been as inspiring as a skunk's fart," Beck said churlishly.

⊲ ⊳

We continued through the forest, taking advantage of whatever fleeting time was left after the advent of the Morning Bell.

The forest had an unbridled beauty to it. There were great winding trees stacked close, their bodies thick and powerful on uneven footing. Something about the way they stood with interlocked branches and leaning trunks made them appear in mid-dance. Bluffs and steep climbs made for an adventurous experience. The first crickets worked their way out of their burrows to serenade the coming night.

"So, should I bring a pillow or something the next time I am here? Perhaps a blanket?" Dale asked as we climbed.

"Why not a bed while you are at it?" Perry joked, leading the way.

He turned and climbed to the top of the bluff, before lowering a hand down to me. I took it, if for nothing else other than to have an excuse to hold him close.

Perry pulled me up, our chests colliding. I stumbled with my apology.

"Sorry, foot snagged my dress," I explained.

We shared smitten smiles with one another, our lips a short distance from leaning in for a kiss.

"A little help?" Our moment ruined as we turned to see Jeremiah failing to purchase grip or foothold.

Perry and I smiled at our shared moment before reaching down and heaving Jeremiah up.

❧ ❧

Though it was early autumn, the leaves themselves were a dark, heavy, green which showed no sign of its more appropriate rust or mustard shade. Branches and twigs and foliage crunched beneath our wandering feet.

There were light motes of dust which travelled through the air and a distant hoot. I wasn't quite sure how it came to be so, but I never quite noticed how magical the forest could be at twilight.

"Any inspiration yet, Dale?" Beck asked irritably, as he had to unsnag a bramble.

"Not so much as a hymn," Dale admitted.

"A hum?" Perry asked.

"A *hymn*." Dale corrected with great emphasis.

"Hmm?"

Dale was not amused.

"Just pulling your leg," Perry teased with a smile.

As if to punctuate the joke with some irony, Dale's trousers were caught on a thorny bramble. As he pulled hard on his leg, we heard the loud sound of tearing fabric.

"Great!" Dale threw his arms up. "Now I have to walk around with torn pants as well."

"Maybe you can write a song about it?" Perry said half-jokingly.

"Ha-ha!" Dale retorted. He clearly didn't share Perry's affable mood.

"Can we just leave?" I asked, wholly aware of the fading light and coming dark.

"Ah-ha!" Perry pronounced as he worked his way to the root of a thick and wrinkled tree. At the base was a single lone flower with hanging blue buds of such a radiant shade one would think the colour sprouted from a fevered dream or was painted on just moments before we'd arrived.

Perry strutted over to pluck one. The hanging heads could be seen as depressed and sullen, but I preferred to see it as veneration—to me, the flower heads were bowing to us passing visitors.

When Perry returned, he brushed my dirty-blonde hair behind my ear and fitted the flower. Perry was usually too reserved to approach me in such a way, but I could tell from his focused gaze, he was simply lost in the romantic gesture.

"It is a blue-cap flower. It will keep you safe," he promised.

I blushed and felt a warmth spread and relishing the moment—I didn't even bother correcting the fact that it was a bluebell and not blue-cap.

I heard Beck make a retching sound behind me and turned to give him a scolding. The sound of rustling foliage made me start. There was an akar in the woods.

Chapter Nine

CHROMA

*Upon the ruin of the Elder King's left eye, night was born. What
remained of its glow turned into the moon, and the scattered remains
of its broken surface became the stars high above. Yet the question is if
anything lingers between these points in the truest abyss.*

—SCHOLARLY MUSINGS OF A CLERIAN MAGE

I wandered aimlessly through the woods. The crunching of the
leaves sounded like my humourless thoughts. I felt numb. I
could still hear the passionate sounds of Nedalya and Kolotha.
It came like an echo.

The one I loved gave her flesh away to another. Was Kolotha more
akar than me? Perhaps it was his sprawling tattoos? The body I bore
seemed more suited to heal and tend through the teachings of Mother
Margaret than reap scores of men in battlefields. Did Kolotha know
how much he would hurt me by his act?

The truth was that all the listed reasons were bad, but not as bad
as the reality. I didn't want to face that Nedalya embraced me, but I
spurned her.

"Stupid… so stupid." I muttered to myself.

I snapped out of my reverie. My wandering mind had me stumble absently through the dimming forest. It was there my heart stopped when I saw the human children stare back at me.

"Run!" One boy yelled. He grabbed the hand of a girl behind him and sprinted through the covering of trees, running at an angle down the forest incline.

"Wait!" I shouted. It was unlikely that they'd be persuaded.

The one girl among them screamed loud and fierce. It shattered the fragile quiet of the forest.

Googan be damned. I cursed and chased after the children.

This was the worst possible outcome. Akar were not allowed to leave the settlement unsupervised, but crossing paths with human children was far more damning! I couldn't allow them to report me.

"Wait!" I called out a second time as I vaulted over a fallen log that one rather heavy child worked his way under.

"I am not dangerous!" I wasn't sure if they could hear me, but even if they did, they showed no sign of slowing down or stopping their screams.

While I could bound and leap over great distances, the steep incline of the forest provided uneven footing as I slid and crashed into a nearby tree.

"Please! Stop!" I would be heavily punished, perhaps taken away and forced into an army regimen, or worse: executed. What would Father do?

I tried desperately to rise to my feet, but the blanketed leaves robbed me of any clear footing until I finally stumbled forward and resumed chase.

The children split and diverged from each other's trajectory as they ran.

I leapt over two, three, four fallen trees which bridged across a gully and leaned over the last log to grab the boy and girl running below.

The girl screamed, and was pulled low to evade my grip. The boy pulling her promptly returned with a branch, swatting it swiftly against me. The stick broke and grazed my eye. I let go of the log and was in freefall. Vertigo took over. The world spun for a moment before I landed painfully on my back. The impact sent air fleeing from my lungs.

Frightened screams swirled in every direction.

My breaths turned painful as I rose to my feet. It took me several painful blinks before I could see clearly again.

"Please! I can explain!" I gasped for air as my vision refocused. Trying to stand, a charging weight suddenly slammed into my side and sent me right back to the ground.

I gathered what wits I could and quickly distanced myself from where I was. Just narrowly I avoided the sword plunged into the dirt. I grunted, shaking my head and composing myself.

Within the narrow gully stood a human woman at the ready. She wore a thin white tunic, brown pants and fastened marching boots. With laboured breathing, she shook away the hair from her face. Unsteady fingers fiddled with her blade. She went into a wide stance.

"Akar blood. Perfect. Just what I need to relieve some frustration." The woman swung with an eagerness to draw my blood. I jumped to the side and created more distance.

"Please, this is all wrong, I am not the enemy." My heel tripped over a branch and sent me sprawling to the floor—I instinctively rolled to my side without looking, the blade inevitably plunged at the dirt where my heart had been mere moments ago.

With a quick and half-hearted kick in the woman's stomach, I sent her stumbling back. Quickly I jumped to my feet.

"I am from the akar settlement; I mean no harm."

Again, the sword sliced through the air as I hopped out of its reach. My heart pumped harder, my anger slowly bobbing in response. The attacks kept coming till I stepped to the side and the steel clapped against a tree trunk.

"Oh, I know," the woman said with malice. Her stance moved to something more casual, but the ire in her gaze attempted to burn me.

"I know where you are from, but more importantly, I know *what* you are. A disgusting creature, showing your true colours. What were you planning with the children? Kill them? Eat them? Sacrifice them to your vile gods?" She spat the questions with caustic venom.

I could feel my ire bubble, course through my blood; it was a natural response to any goaded akar. It urged me on, tempted me with promises of being unchained and free if my anger could spring to the surface.

I avoided another attack and then another. Juta's voice spoke over my anger, telling me to observe my surroundings. I dodged up another incline to my left and around a tree.

"Fight me!" she demanded.

The woman turned again, her vision seemingly narrowing on the point between my head and shoulder. Her sword slashed, its teeth biting down on tree bark. She noticed too late the kick which exploded from my thighs and into her midsection.

Fingers relinquished her hilt as she was sent hurtling into the dirt, staining her tunic; she was mere inches from the gully's edge.

We locked eyes. Her rotten hatred infected me. More and more I leaned into the offered comfort of blind rage. The way her kind treated us, arming themselves with choice words meant to hurt, the way her kind worshipped the Elders living atop their mountain. All of it and more stoked my flames until I met her challenge with earnest. A single passionate moan of Nedalya rung through my consciousness.

"I am not your enemy," I stated through gritted teeth. "But if it is a fight you want, I will oblige." Juta's teachings coursed through me and wrapped their memory about my form.

I stepped down the slope and saw the woman rise to her feet; her fists ready to box and not an ounce of doubt present on her features. Her brown eyes jumped to the imbedded sword behind me as I stepped down.

"Try it," I dared. I had no way of knowing if I'd win, but anger had a way of snuffing out reason.

Her feet shuffled forward, never leaving the ground. She was patient, knowing full well a single mistake could mean her death. The forest grew unnaturally quiet, as if it became a spectator to our bout. Then we heard it. An ear-piercing scream through the canopies.

The girl from before? But it was unnatural. The way it vibrated was as if it turned sound into tiny needles. The trees finally seemed to acknowledge something as they slightly swayed at the sound. I looked at the woman in front of me, my sudden rage forgotten. She stared back, her fists lowering; concern took the place of hate.

Our chests heaved for one second, then two. It was one second too long. Our conversation wordless and our understanding succinct.

I turned and released the sword from its spot, tossing it to the warrior. In tandem, we sprinted towards the sound.

Chapter Ten

DALILA

—during the rise of the Rashi at the end of tenth cycle, entire towns were swallowed by their bloodthirst. In response, an unlikely hero arose in the form of a small village boy. He chartered a course for his destiny. The farm boy died soon after.

—UNFORTUNATE REALITIES OF MINETHRIA AND ITS HISTORY,
BY ZON MOXIN

The akar was like a great panther, leaping and bounding from tree to tree in search of its prey. He cried something, his sound like shifting earth, but the frantic beating of my heart and rushing wind made it hard to understand.

Perry pulled me through a narrow gully, the akar soared across fallen logs above as his shadow cast over us. The akar's grip barely missed me as Perry pulled me to the floor and then swiftly struck our pursuer.

It was only then when I noticed Nora break free from the cover of vegetation with sword in hand. She jumped with all the force she could summon into the akar who toppled to the floor. Nora's blade just barely missing flesh.

"It's Nora!" I shouted to Perry.

He didn't seem to notice as he ducked under a branch and urged me forward.

"Perry!"

"I know! We have to keep moving!" Perry pressed, his speech laboured and frantic.

We eventually came across Jeremiah, panting and heaving so hard till his throat gave hoarse croaks and he leaned his weight against his knees. Beck fared no better and clasped a stitch at his rib.

"Where is Dale?" I asked.

Almost as if a summon, Dale appeared traipsing through a brush and holding the neck of his lute like a weapon. His torn trouser was split up to his knee.

"We can't stay here," Perry insisted.

"Where is the monster?" Dale asked.

"He is back there. Nora came out of nowhere and started fighting him," I said.

"Nora is here?" Jeremiah phrased it as a question through ostensibly pained lungs. Was it fear or incredulity? Perhaps both? He stood on trembling knees before stumbling forward.

"Where are you going?" Perry asked, and grabbed Jeremiah by the collar.

"I need to save my sister!" Jeremiah said.

"You aren't doing anything of the sort." Perry pulled Jeremiah away. "She is a soldier, she will fare better than we will against an akar."

"That wasn't an akar; not the deadly kind," Dale provided.

"What do you mean?" Jeremiah asked.

"The way he was clothed, his size. I think he was from the settlement."

"Are you sure? I just saw a giant charcoal skinned man," I said. All I had seen was a shadow pouncing from tree to tree as if it was his playground.

"He's right," Perry agreed.

"So why did you run?" Beck asked, one hand grabbing the stitch at his rib.

"Because you all started running and Dalila screamed! What was I to do?"

"It's still an akar! They aren't allowed to leave camp," Beck argued.

"We have to keep going," Perry said. "We need to get back to Crow-town and let the guards know. Nora may need help!" I was surprised to find a slight hint of remorse in Perry's statement.

It was then that we laid eyes on the biggest creature I had ever seen.

I understood what Dale meant when he said the previous akar was not the deadly kind—for the one before us looked like a demon emerging from a volcano.

Its size was of a behemoth. Father wouldn't even have reached his chest and his shoulders strained with great worming veins protruding from swelling masses of muscles. The akar was heavily injured, a wound at his ribs bleeding a shade which was surprisingly human, as his breath misted with hampered breaths.

The akar's face alone was brutish and unwelcoming with a great bone piercing his nose shaft and white tattoos forming crescents. I looked down to his hand, noticing the great club he dragged behind him like a troll from the stories mother used to tell. The akar stared down at us as if we were ants in its path and simply breathed. The lines across his exhausted face hardened. He grunted.

Setting his great bear-sized paw upon a tree, the akar leaned and the tree groaned, its foundations torn from dirt as roots exposed themselves and a spatter of dirt showered us.

"Run…" Perry croaked; he was barely audible.

With another deep exhale from the towering, bare-chested akar, the tree continued to be ripped from its roots and plummeted with a great fall, breaking us from our trance.

"Run!" There was nothing ambiguous or soft about his cry.

This time, the danger was undeniably real. This time, we knew we had crossed paths with a real akar.

We ran down the decline. My heart was beating out of my chest. We reached a narrow brook. The giant roared and pushed over another tree behind us. I didn't dare turn to see, but I felt his pursuit. His feet met the earth and reminded me of rolling thunder.

"Run down stream!" Perry said, leading our group down the babbling water. Gravity aided our escape.

I turned just in time to see the akar crash against the low bluff behind us. Loose dirt showered him. I looked ahead. The monster's roar made my spine vibrate. I barely even noticed the warm which ran down my leg.

The akar was closing in when Perry veered me and the others down another path. We jumped and ran through thorny brambles, and ignored the forest's clawing.

Something caught my eye, a glint between the trees in the distance like light off glass. I remembered it as the glistening emerald shine at the bottom of the well. I could not say what manner of feeling took over me but my body moved before I could change my mind.

"This way!" I pulled back on Perry's tug and with the beast chasing after us, none of us felt it was the time to argue.

Perry chased after me and started to follow my lead. I looked out for the glint of emerald shining through the gaps of trees which seemed to instruct me. I trusted in its shine and the others trusted in me.

I wondered if the light was just my imagination, yet the further we ran the more deliberate its glint was. The akar slid upon wet soil on one turn and crashed into walls. Other paths were narrow enough for us children but denied the akar.

And yet we continued; criss-crossing winding trees and weaving into terrain difficult for our pursuer. The sun's light had completely receded at this point.

"I can't." Jeremiah groaned, his voice barely discernible as we worked our way around the top of a bluff.

All it took was a stumble for his footing to slip, sending Jeremiah's lopsided weight over the edge of our precipice. The tense quiet was broken. We heard the crunch of bone followed by Jeremiah's crying. A cold fear filled me.

Frantically, the rest of us scurried over the ledge in time to see his bent leg and the protruding bone. I gasped.

"Jeremiah!" I called out in hushed tones. If he could hear my voice he was in too much pain to respond. His hands trembled over his shin as if stuck in a limbo of decision.

We climbed down carefully and began to drag Jeremiah's heavy body under the umbrella of a jutting overhang of dirt. Beck had to stuff a cloth into Jeremiah's mouth to muffle the sound of cries and prevent him from betraying our location.

The shadows concealed us. It was dark. I could not see my friends but I could hear their hampered breaths. Our bodies fluxed between cold and sweaty warmth. Crickets all around played their music. Their bowed legs orchestrated a coming crescendo which whipped at our racing hearts.

Barely did I think we eluded the great akar, when heavy steps sounded from above. We all held our breaths. I could feel the monstrous weight of our pursuer press down and shower us in loosened dirt.

Dale caught some on his nose and recoiled, taking in great drags of air to warn of a coming sneeze. Perry jumped forward and placed a hand over Dale's mouth. Dale's sneeze was muffled, and yet still was the loudest sound I'd ever heard.

I held my breath. Time froze.

The akar shuffled back and forth. The seconds dragged on endlessly. Finally, we heard the distancing of feet. The seconds felt like minutes, and it was only after it turned into an eternity of such maddening silence that any of us dared to speak.

"We have to move," Perry said as quietly as he could.

"But how?" Beck whispered back.

I placed a hand on Jeremiah's forehead and stiffened. "He is really cold," I said worriedly.

"We can't move him like this," Beck added.

"Isn't there anything we can do?" asked Dale.

Jeremiah faded in and out of consciousness.

"Hold the cloth in his mouth," I ordered meekly. The others looked just as unsure as I was, but they nodded and held Jeremiah down. Beck tore a bit of his shirt to stuff between Jeremiah's shaking lips.

"Jeremiah," I whispered. "This is going to hurt."

I had no idea what I was doing as I pressed my hands against the wound and felt my blood run cold. I touched the protruding bone. I gagged. Jeremiah's suffocated scream was absolute agony. So much blood. It coated my hands, and ran into the soil beneath us.

"What are you doing?" Beck pressed.

"I don't know," I admitted, tears running down my eyes as I just tried to do something, anything. Somewhere in my broken mind, it seemed logical that I could simply push the bone back in and make it work.

It felt like a dream; some distant, unreal reality as I tried to put Jeremiah back together.

Jeremiah struggled for a time with his hampered cries, his body thrashing from the pain until finally, he fell unconscious.

Seconds passed.

I closed my eyes and felt my trembling hands. A gasp, then two, then three.

"Dalila." My name was spoken with disbelief; I wasn't certain by whom. There was a radiating warmth, probably from the pooling blood.

I opened my eyes and saw a soft, tender light spread from my hands onto Jeremiah's mangled leg.

"What are you doing?" Dale asked in astonishment.

"I... I don't know." But I did know. I was healing him. I could not explain how. Little motes of light like dandelions shone and dimmed in and out of existence. The edges of the shine bristled like light seen through a thin fog. The light created a private bubble for only us to see. The others had a look of fear about them, revealed by this strange power of mine. When it came to Jeremiah's leg, we saw the blood and skin and bone writhe underneath the flesh, spasming to pull the bone back into its housing and heal the wound.

Perry turned to us and smiled.

"Stay here. You have to keep her safe." Perry instructed Dale and Beck.

"Where are you going?" I asked, my worry obvious.

Perry looked scared, terrified even. When his hand reached for my shoulder, I could feel the tremble of trepidation work its way through me. But still he pressed, feigning courage to comfort us all.

"I need to go get help, and if I find the monster, one of us needs to lure it away."

"Why you?" Beck asked.

"I am the fastest. If anything happens, he will come for me, not any of you. I have a chance to survive and buy you some time."

He looked at Jeremiah's leg putting itself back together.

"We will make it," he said, conveying as much conviction as he could. We believed him, I believed him.

Perry nodded.

He worked his way out of our respite and let out a terrified cry. A club fell from above and reduced Perry to a smear of viscera. His warm touch was replaced by splattered blood. My mind failed to understand.

We all just stared on, speechless, our mouths left open. Again and again, my mind replayed the scene at lightning speed, refusing to process the event.

The light from my hands dwindled, and what was being mended together was left as jutting bone from Jeremiah's skin. The process was only half complete.

He groaned, coming to himself with cold sweat running down his cheeks.

"Where am I?" Jeremiah asked absently. "Do I smell blood?" his query disoriented and weak.

The great club dragged what remained of Perry across the floor like some vile paint brush. It scraped sinew, bone, and flesh off its end. The giant's calves came into view. His toenails were cracked and grimy.

The akar knelt down to one knee and peered into the cave with dispassionate eyes.

"Kula, sik tu jar fal Ikh meh Googan." The akar's words reverberated like the strings of a lyre deep within the tunnels of a volcano.

The surrounding crickets picked up the pace of their song as the akar reached out. All I could do was tremble from the coming shadow of death.

First, it came as a whisper. A soft sound, barely discernible.

Then it came as a word, a word spoken by my trembling lips.

Then it came as a scream, a scream which worked its way through my belly and burst from my lips like a shredding storm evoked by the caustic mists.

Reality trembled under the weight of my voice. Beck and Dale covered their ears, and Jeremiah seemed almost lulled to sleep from the melody.

The akar stopped in his tracks, bracing against the force of my cry. Suddenly, his footing was robbed from beneath him. The great giant was torn from his feet and dragged through the air. He broke through one tree, then another, and then another, and then another. The wood shattered like an accompanying choir of thunder to my banshee's scream.

My throat blazed in agony. My curled fists drawing blood from my palms. Muscles burning with a cold warmth as my neck felt like it was about to snap and disconnect from my shoulders.

When the explosive air finally dissipated, as loosened leaves from the canopies drifted like ceremony petals, when only a ringing was left deep in my ears, did I finally feel exhaustion come over me and my eyes blink in and out of wakefulness.

The beast rose to his feet, disorientated. The akar appeared as just a greyish smear in my ever-fading vision.

"Dalila…" Dale said somewhere off to the distance.

I felt Dale shuffle over to me, his hands grasping my arms and trying to shake me awake. "Don't fall asleep on us now."

Beck came to his side and slapped me. But even that transient wakefulness was no more than a blip. My head felt so heavy and lumbering, my neck incapable of carrying its weight.

"Dalila!" The two boys turned frantically back to the akar, who stumbled forward to his feet.

The beast started jogging, then running, the club dragging behind it like some gruesome appendage of war.

"Dalila! Scream! Do something! Dalila!" My vision danced between blurred and clear. I noticed a single drop of blood from Beck's ear.

I stared into Dale's frightened eyes and heard the sprinting akar. He was coming.

"Dalila!"

A second, smaller rumble of thunder met the first. I was still lucid enough to recognize it as the younger akar from before. I wondered how he could have ever frightened me now that I knew of true terror.

I looked past Dale and at the distant figures. The smaller akar came from the side and knocked the other out of his stride. The smaller one was far lither and reached his bigger adversary to the chest, but it didn't stop him from raging against the giant.

Nora suddenly stood over me. "Are you all alright?" she asked with noticeable concern.

She only then noticed Jeremiah. She made as if to go to him. "Oh god. What happened to his leg?" The others were speechless.

Nothing.

"Where is Perry?" Nora asked.

The quiet now turned telling.

Nora turned towards what remained of Perry. I didn't have the strength to crane my neck anymore and see. Or maybe I just couldn't bear the sight.

"By Oxular's grace!" Nora gasped in horror. Her voice was so far away. So it wasn't just some dream. She could see Perry's remains too.

Nora's face twisted with rage. She unsheathed her blade and charged to where the battle was being fought.

That was when my consciousness faded and I sunk into nothingness.

Chapter Eleven

CHROMA

—but be aware she who casts without medium, for such
unkempt chaos is the power of a witch.

—MUSEYA TEXT ON TYPES OF MAGIC

The scream was as if reality itself was shattering, cracks and fissures forming upon its faultless contours. It sent the forest trees swaying back and forth and made my ears ring in a way the Morning Bell could not. Even the scream became distorted the longer it went, coming undone like yarn, distended and stretched till it became unrecognisable.

The soldier and I did not share a single word as we bounded in the scream's direction. She did not object to my coming and perhaps there was something she knew I didn't, something which made her have no choice but rely on me. I hoped that at least my cooperation made my punishment lighter.

Or perhaps the truth was much simpler. The desperate cries for help were what tore me towards the scream. They were just children, after all. It was what Father would have done.

I jumped down a bluff and ducked into a roll to carry my momentum forward. I left the warrior behind in my tracks.

I thought I imagined at first but then knew after several blinks that what I saw was real. An akar; one of my own. The way he dressed with the fur kilt and dangling bones. He must have come from Thickwood! I could talk to him. We could defeat the woman soldier and I could ask him to take me home, back to Father, back to my people where I belonged.

He charged forward, his feet pounding against the soil, a wild bloodlust in his gaze, yet his charge wasn't directed at me. I followed it to an overhanging plateau where vines hung over a shaded part underneath—my akar eyes adjusted to notice the telling outline of young children.

My body moved faster than I could think. I left off the ground and hammered into the akar. He was larger than me, but the weight of my sprint sent him toppling.

The giant stumbled on his feet. His breathing laboured. There was a deep gash on his ribs which ran down silver tattoos.

He peered lazily at me, and the gasping mist of his breath looked fleeting. I could tell he was exhausted. I noticed then blood had been trickling down his ears. More than that. There was a line of broken trees and ploughed soil. What did this?

I didn't have time to think. I bound forward and challenged the akar. He was a giant built for war, but I was uninjured and had a lot more energy to spare than he did.

Leaping into the sky, I aimed a piercing elbow at his scalp. He grunted and barely moved to the side in time. My elbow crashed down onto his shoulder.

I leapt down before his ham-fisted strikes swung forward. With another opening I struck again, landing a perfect kick into trunk-sized thighs. The akar trembled on his knees, but he did not fall.

The mast of his club came swinging by as I ducked just in time to the sound of rushing wind being dragged overhead. The club crashed against a nearby tree, giving me the opening to leap up again and send a fist against his chest; it felt like punching a boulder.

He seized my wrist and pulled me in for a headbutt—stars danced across my vision before I was swung into a neighbouring tree. The titan didn't let go.

Quickly, I regathered my bearings and coiled around the limb. But the akar's arm-span and bulging muscles made it impossible to seize a proper hold; the brute slammed me against the tree again, knocking the air from my lungs this time.

His knee buckled, the akar stumbled back and accidentally loosened his grip.

I collapsed to the ground and blood filled my mouth. Only with pure zeal did I force myself to stand, feeling my natural akar body numbing the pain. As I charged, I spat out a clump of blood.

I landed hits upon joints and openings I could exploit. I had to keep the pressure before my body had a chance to realize how exhausted it was.

My vision tunnelled. The great mast of the akar's club slammed its weight into me—it felt like I was struck by an auroch.

The warrior woman charged behind the akar with her blade unsheathed. He clumsily swung behind him as the woman went low. Her blade found an opening between the back of the giant's knee.

The akar barely winced and swung with a closed fist. The warrior's sword caught the attack, sending her sliding across the forest floor. I was amazed. A single strike of his fist made my bones bend till they felt like breaking, but the fact alone that the woman's steel did not shatter told me volumes about her capabilities.

The woman was again on the attack without a moment's hesitation. The sight ignited a flame in me which said only one thing: I couldn't let a human outshine me.

Rising to shaken legs, I collected my wits before running into the fray with a roar of my own.

The woman was quick and precise.

I forced myself to watch her every move, to see how she possibly held her own.

She wasn't fighting the akar, not really, she was playing something more akin to Janaham, placing bets and playing chances with carved bones, offering false confidence and reaping the rewards when her opponent proved too eager.

She tried to find an opening.

I kicked a knee. The akar roared and turned to me, providing enough time for the precise slash of the woman's weapon to draw more blood. I danced to the other side and took with me the akar's focus. With a leap up into the air, I swung a half-hearted but quick fist into the akar's swelling left eye.

The akar's head whipped back—I struck too hard. The woman was underneath, caught below the stumbling goliath and unable to distance herself in time.

She screamed. The akar found a nearby tree by chance to regain his footing and swung his wayward fist behind him.

It landed.

The blade shattered, sending the woman tumbling through the soil and onto her stomach.

The akar ran forward and raised his foot, bringing it down with formidable power onto the woman-warrior.

I flew through the air, knee raised and knocking against the akar's cheek. The giant's head snapped to the side, a broken tusk falling to the floor as the club was torn from his grip. Yet the akar didn't relent. He struggled to stand to his full height, cuts bleeding from numerous openings and one barely open eye staring me down.

Again, I took to the skies. My roar paled in comparison. He punched me and my own momentum lent his strike power. I flew backwards through the air and landed on my front.

The akar trudged over and stomped down on my back—my roar was closer to his own now.

Blood trickled all around me from the akar's wounds and ran down my cheeks—the scent was overpowering.

He leaned in, pressing more of his bestial weight atop of my back—I could feel my spine bend and knew if I were human, it would already have been crushed to dust. Anger was taking hold, stretching its tendrils through the corners of my vision to guide me.

He spoke in perfect, brutish akar, *"You disgrace your kind."* His voice was like stone grinding against stone. *"You help this human whore. You run to live as pets rather than fighting against those they protect: the Elders who exiled us."*

I screamed, the agony of his weight unbearable.

"Now you get to die like them."

My cheeks expanded, blowing panicked air. I clenched my fists tight and tried desperately to withstand the pain.

I heard the woman's cry. Something about the raw and emotional cry ran into me and took over. It seemed to also halt the akar's stomps. I spun onto my back and caught his leg. With all the strength I could summon, I held on and wouldn't let go.

The woman ran up a boulder and leapt. A shard of her broken sword at the ready as she plunged into the giant's neck.

It was enough. The akar stumbled and howled. His weight no longer on me. I coughed and still felt my body scream, but I had no time to rest as I pushed myself to my feet.

The woman panted, a hand to her ribs. I hoped they were just bruised and not broken.

The akar stood on uneven feet, his hand clasping at the last of his fleeing life. Even the rise and fall of his chest weakened.

I couldn't rest. Not yet. I needed answers. With great pain, I worked myself towards him. The akar stumbled on failing feet before keeling over, as a stone boulder caught him. Dust rose from the weight of his fall.

The giant was much like the boulder that braced him. He wheezed. The flowing trails of his blood was like cracked stone giving way to scarlet veins. Bringing forth my best akar, I spoke. "Tell me about Muktow," I demanded with pained groans.

The akar chuckled and spat dark blood at my feet.

"Tell me about my father," I repeated.

The akar's laugh grew even more humoured despite his fleeting life. His one giant and gnarled hand wrapped about his ribs as he licked the blood from lips.

He raised the good hand from his side and with a grunt pulled free the imbedded blade from his neck so that death may come sooner.

"I hope it was worth it, siding with the humans. I will now go and live with the great Kho'Sha and our ancestors. My name is Ji'sura of the Stone and they will remember me as a warrior; but you will be remembered as a pig—an akar without honour."

I dashed to Ji'sura and pressed my hand to his neck, trying in vain to stave the shadow of death a while longer.

"Tell me about Muktow!" I demanded, the akar's eyes opened and closed with less and less virility.

"Lo'Sai will one day have your head too as he does Sun'Ra's."

The akar who named himself as Ji'sura took the blade and imbedded its end in his neck again, deeper this time. His one good eye was wider and more alive than it ever was during our bout. It went ablaze with the last vestige of his ignited soul.

What fanaticism, what veneration stared back at me in his moment of truth. There was no hesitation in his final moment.

Ji'sura's fist bled across the blade as his quivering hand pulled the steel across his throat and opened an even greater gash. I gasped and shuddered as if his soul had left through my lips.

That one eye; it was a deep, large black which shone with faith, with belief, and with honour. It glistened with such shine that I felt almost overpowered and wanted to look away, but I couldn't. I felt captivated by this warrior's final moments.

Finally, the split was done, and the blood ran free. The hand fell forgotten by his side as Ji'sura was no more.

"You fought valiantly," I said in akar. "Our ancestors will accept your blood." I spoke the words emptily, they felt awkward on my tongue, as if not my words to speak.

Ji'sura's words remained. I was not like my folk. I was locked behind human walls and penned up out of human sight; a target for hatred rather than one of pride.

I rose to my feet, deep in thought, and never expected the weight of the log which struck me unconscious from behind.

Chapter Twelve

DALILA

Among the remnants of human civilization to the north, there is evidence of enigmatic tribes. Some are said to control beasts with the help of their bangles, others are said to have become worshippers to pretend gods.

—A REPORT GIVEN TO KING BALSEM DURING THE RISE
OF THICKWOOD. 11C1460

I saw a blur of intersecting lights; green, and blue, and lilac, and red, and yellow. They shifted like great discs within my unfettered consciousness. I saw a sublime constellation: a connection of six emerald jewels upon the noble head of a stag. I saw an interwoven thread of a spider's web.

I saw antlers.

I then saw amorphous blobs which rippled and shifted in shape like a body of scintillating mass as they crawled lazily across the forest floor.

I saw birds comprised of multiple wings and several heads. The wings retreated into their bodies as more feet grew to scale the floor. Incredibly long toes, disproportionate to the bird's own size, disappearing in the rippling water.

The waters distorted a splotch of motley colours which turned into ferrets with columns of eyes where there would be teats; upon those eyes, there reflected the spider's web. I saw a coloured wheel bound towards an endless kaleidoscope of possibilities.

What I witnessed was bound and limited by mortal words used to describe them, and never anything more. To even get a glimpse of what I saw in that realm of unfettered wilderness would be to inscribe these words to cloth and dip it into a bucket of water and watch as the ink bled. But one thing I confidently ascribed, somewhere in that fever-dream, was the soft but present scent of Perry, and I imagined him smiling at me.

⊰ ⊱

I awoke to find Nora leaning over me, her expression twisted into one of deep worry. Sweat and grime matted her. Her fringed hair clung to her skin as if by virtue of its own fright.

"Oh thank Oxular! You're alive." The relief was palpable as she embraced me. My thoughts were still trying to mend themselves when I noticed the caked blood on my hands. Clarity returned; stalking and cruel.

The scent of blood clung to the air in a way it had no right to. I let go and saw a wounded Jeremiah breathing steadily. His leg had been partially healed, but the white of bone still jutted from ruptured skin. It wouldn't heal properly.

"Perry," I spoke aloud.

Dale and Nora went quiet, their gaze avoiding mine.

"Beck went to get help," Nora said meekly; perhaps to detract from the reality of what had happened.

I brushed her aside and my heart sunk and tore itself apart at the sight of my love, laid so undone to my tear-stricken eyes. I couldn't help but shudder. It felt like my own body was unravelling.

There were bits and pieces of him splattered all over the place like some horrifying art display. I recalled a faint memory of screaming; my throat was still hoarse and sore.

I reached out. My hands trembled. Almost as if by its own volition, my hands gave a soft glow, returning to the same sensation from when I was healing Jeremiah. I hovered over Perry's remains.

"Dalila... what are you doing?" I heard Nora ask me. I didn't respond.

The magic light returned fully now. Whatever will I imposed onto the mound of flesh worked in such a cruel and macabre fashion that it was tantalising. The flesh bubbled as skin and sinew crawled together, trying to stitch back the impossible.

I shuddered a second time. My mind felt like it was about to break. I breathed too quickly. My sight shortened. I took in air that my lungs wouldn't accept. My mind was breaking. The tears flowed.

Nora's hand grasped mine.

"Stop it." Her word was authoritative through the silence. "Stop it." It was comforting this time, pleading even. Her effort sounded just as desperate as mine.

She wrapped her arms around me and stilled my shudders; in its stead, I let loose a great mournful cry. Tears flooded as an inexplicable sorrow claimed me. My sadness burst from its swollen cloud, unbound from wounded heart and into sombre night. Even when Beck returned with the guards, my crying didn't stop.

That was how the first day of the Eleventh Cycle came to an end.

Chapter Thirteen

The number of Elders are unknown and many of their definitions unimaginable, but that isn't the case for all of them. Some are representations of ideas. The Soprano is known from her constant lament, turning her voice into an instrument of death. The Inspired of Museya look to her for inspiration. Yet there are others, such as Aneiso, who sports three heads and three pairs of hands. They cover the eyes of one head, the mouth of another, and the ears of the last. For if these senses are unleashed, their nightmare can be seen.

—Speculative tales of the Elders and the works, by Thiago Ganme

Three days had passed by mortal standards since the ringing of the Morning Bell. The Seed spent most of that time suckling upon the sap of a tree, which offered its leaking branch as a teat. The sap filled the Seed, nourishing them, expanding their body into a lean and muscle-bound form.

Born empty to such an enigmatic realm, the Seed was ushered through Mount Morniar's elusive belly. The winding paths and tunnels were alive with madness as the skittering passed by without being seen, like heavy log-legs thumping louder and then fading past the Seed's presence.

The Seed's guide was Mother Maiden, a lithe and tall being cloaked in ephemeral shadows with the shine of stars to it. Upon her cowled head were features indicative of a face, with slitted slots for eyes and the imprint of lips but no nose. It looked porcelain. But if it was truly her face or a mask, none could tell. Three arms were on either side of Maiden that seemed to be made from enamel, as they lacked flesh or muscle. The bone-thin hands were all steepled and pointing downwards. From within the encompassing cloak there opened a seam, and from there came a mummified hand carrying a lantern. The light which shone from the lantern was strange as it pushed back the stagnant shadows, which themselves seemed to writhe abnormally at the edges as if alive.

The long corridors of this place lent themselves to sudden drops which disorientated and robbed one's sense of up or down. It was maddening trying to discern the paths taken, yet the Seed followed the Maiden who roamed with ease.

Zerubs walked as if trapped in a dream. Beings called Shades moved without direction, like wayward shadows that escaped the walls they were cast against.

The sound of wet flesh moved through this realm, howls and wails so sonorous as if from a maudlin giant. Even Silence had a voice here, whispering from within the left behind blackness.

Time and time again, the Seed was tested and prodded by enigmatic beings. One room led to the next, where creatures opened their maws and cast a beam of light from their gullets.

One such raven-headed creature ran fingers through the Seed's willowy strands of silver hair. Suddenly, the Seed's hair went coarse and rigid, turning into streaking white lightning which shred through the zerub's fingers. Blood dribbled from the wounds, but the zerub watched with disinterest as small drops of blood ignored gravity to drift upwards.

The other beings noted down this interesting ability. The hair could also lax so that it was like sawing wires. Their body also shared this curious ability and shifted between being hard like steel or pliable like rubber.

The impish ravens noted their conclusion. "Healthy and strong, a good body unlike the birth of Kaelu. But no will in this one; listless and empty, eyes carrying the unformed mists of Nif. Plenty of potential.

Body is nourished from the feeding. Strong and reliable."

They squawked their unanimous approval.

◁ ▷

The Seed was again taken through the distended hallways; the dimensions distorted the height of Mother Maiden. They came across seemingly unremarkable double doors which opened to reveal an open circular arena with a sandpit.

Strolling inside, the Seed could see that the top of the ever-rising balconies was truly endless. At the balustrades of these vaulted balconies were further enigmatic beings called Elders. Simply trying to glean shapes or forms from their queer dimensions was a toilsome task.

The Seed stood naked as they peered up to the curious entities, and then a voice spoke.

"Lo, fellow Elders, set thine eyes upon the Eleventh Seed and rejoice," a headless being said, dressed in a robe with fractal patterns that writhed.

Then, from within the opening of the speaker's collar, several serpentine, boneless arms sprouted like the dividing head of a hydra. The words were spoken through a mouth placed within the palm of one such hand while another held up a great ocular eye which stared down to the Seed with undeniable intensity. The rest of the limbs slithered in the air like snakes.

"Rejoiceth, f'r thy King's blood hast birth'd a new Seed! Rejoiceth, mine liege, for thou'st hath come to bear witness of thine own fruit."

The Seed stared up to who was supposedly their father and saw only the mere tatters of an entity. Shadows wreathed the Elder King as casually as a scarf about one's neck. They could only make out the curling ram horns and outlines of a crooked crown; the silhouette of a hunched back betraying the wizened impression of the Elder King. A withered hand with long fingers was curled about the haft of a twisted staff. Blotches of shifting ink clung to the fabric of the Elder King's attire without any purchase, instead sliding across the deep sea-blue surface.

Finally, the only other thing which peered through that veil of darkness was a single emblazoned eye like a distant sun, the golden ribbons flickering about the edges of it.

"*The Morning Bell hath tolled for thee, mine child. Borneth anew, without sin, without desire, without greed. Thou shalt become a vessel for tom'rrow.*" The Elder King sounded like a groaning tree, patient with the drawn out syllables. There was a weight to his ancient words.

"*A hollow'd vessel to slayeth the most wondrous evil and eschew the Twelfth Cycle.*"

The Seed craned their neck to the very top. The balconies were filled with countless beings of frayed conceptuality that stretched and peered and loomed with ancient eyes.

"*Alas, mine blood, mine Seed: prithee. Thou must proveth thy skill and strength for the task at hand.*" The Elder King waved to a figure that stepped into the sourceless light. "*White-Hawk, first of the guard, descendeth into combat and bringeth mine child's head.*" Boomed the Elder King without inflection.

White-Hawk did not delay, and vaulted over the balustrade. His landing was full of grace and befitting his form and avian name. With his gauntleted hands, the zerub removed his helmet to reveal a pristine albino Hawk-head with predatory eyes trained ahead.

He bowed curtly. "It is an honour to meet you, Eleventh Seed," the White-Hawk stated, his expression and tone dream-like.

The Seed gave no response and blinked instead. They appeared indifferent to White-Hawk's existence.

White-Hawk returned his helmet and drew his singing blade, a piece of straight metal, long and gleaming much like his own armour emblazoned with epic reliefs.

"Please take this seriously," he said. "I wouldn't want to summon an-other millennia of suffering." In one swift move, White-Hawk pounced. The blade sung like a bird-of-prey in flight, its screech echoing in search of food, its talons ready to rend flesh. The Seed barely managed to dodge the glint of steel with every strike, despite contorting their form and bending as if their bones were made of rubber. They continued to bob and weave, never striking back. Their motions were reactionary more than anything else, like a swaying blade of silver grass.

White-Hawk's silver cape rippled like wings taking to the sky. Sand trailed by the direction of steel, each strike precise and controlled with unparalleled focus. Cuts did streak the Seed's body; the newborn experienced pain for the first time as they were striped in scarlet. A pained, siren-like howl exploded from the Seed as they distanced themselves.

White-Hawk lowered his centre of gravity, sword in front and resplendent cape dragging across the floor.

The Seed stood casually and licked their wounds. White-Hawk advanced, yet this time, the Seed was learning.

Dancing back and forth, the Seed flicked their neck, their hair lashing out like the end of a frayed whip. White-Hawk's sword met deadly silver hair and birthed sparks from their marriage.

White-Hawk's prowess pushed the Seed till they were backed into a wall. Just in time, the Seed took off into the air with such explosive power and speed, avoiding the clear cleave that would have divided their midsection. Seed's body softened to rubber as they planted their feet on the wall and pushed off over White-Hawk and into the open clearing.

White-Hawk did not relent, the beaked and albino visage not just for show as the speed with which the zerub ferociously pursued his target was truly reminiscent of a hawk.

The skin of the Seed hardened and with propped shoulder and strengthened stance, the brunt of the blade was arrested. The Seed blinked; there appeared to be a slight intelligence to their casualness. The Seed twirled their head in a circle, silver strands gyrating swiftly as the hair hardened mid-spin into sickle blades.

Sparks flew, and the screeching sounded like nails on stone. The Seed's hair recoiled from White-Hawk's armour, who stumbled back.

The Seed bound with growing confidence, rubber kicks turning into crystallised steel upon impact, whip-like motions giving momentum for the bludgeoning force at the last moment. White-Hawk was driven back.

But White-Hawk had experience on his side. In mere moments, he showed his warranted station and leaned into the trade. White-Hawk took on a defensive stance to repel the coming attack.

Strands of serrated hair and steel chipped away, when suddenly, the hair softened and coiled around White-Hawk's blade. With one sudden tug, the blade was torn from the zerub's hand and sent the beautiful hawk stumbling forward.

The Seed leapt up and landed upon White-Hawk's back. They took strands of loose hair in both hands and wrapped it around White-Hawk's feathered neck. The zerub's nimble fingers managed barely to fit between neck and steel threads. The wire-like strands cut through the metal gauntlets as blood seeped through the shredded opening.

"Enough!" The Elder King bellowed, his voice carrying throughout the vast rising fighting pit and balconies.

Yet the Seed did not relent, if anything, their grip tightened. Emotionless and turbid eyes blinked their disinterest. There was a haunting silence except for the choked gasps of a breathless bird. Scarlet dripped to the sand dispassionately. White-Hawk croaked in pain.

"Sielie," the Elder King spoke dispassionately.

In what was just the blink of an eye, there stood a new presence in the pit. Sielie was like a dying tree in a fog-infested grove. The Elder's entire body was lanky and crude, their bent knees shortened the stature of the masked figure who still stood impossibly tall.

Leather clasps ran across Sielie's entire body to seal the dark garments tight against its form, the mask the Elder wore was of glossy metal in contrast and showed only slitted eyes for sight and a single black teardrop painted to the corner of the left eye.

The Seed and Sielie exchanged unimpressed glances—White-Hawk choked as blood stained his previously flawless armour.

The kick which came was as thin and quick as a flash of umbral lightning. It weaved between White-Hawk and the Seed, sending the king's spawn catapulting into a nearby wall and forming a crater.

However Sielie had done it, it ensured that White-Hawk fell to his knees with bloody, gnarled fingers, but with his head still intact. Only his coughs echoed through the silent pit.

Chapter Fourteen

Kaelu the Silent's word changes reality. Once, Kaelu whispered of death. Immediately, the ushered word began eating away at everything. The Puzzler created a container for this word. It is said that the container is hidden in one of the deepest and most unreachable dreams of Mount Morniar.

—A COLLECTION OF ELDER TALES, BY DRUMY. CIRCA 6C154

T he mountain let out a deep exhale, a breath which howled through its halls whilst Silence also roamed, not far from sight.

The Seed was cleaned and dressed again, a great ceremonial garment fashioned from moonlight with shimmering hems to accompany the silver of hair and the unnervingly milky eyes.

Guided through the long halls, there was again the pristine figure known as Mother Maiden with one shrivelled hand carrying her lantern. She led a path through the body of Mount Morniar. When Mother Maiden finally came to a stop, it was in front of double-doors with an arched frame and studded metal running across its midsection. The lantern rescinded back into the robe as darkness stitched itself back together. Silence roamed this place again and spoke without words. The lantern bearing hand returned, accompanied by another, which carried an old bronze key with intricate knots on its haft. Mother Maiden languorously slotted it into the keyhole.

The doors swung open, and Mother Maiden drifted away with indiscernible purpose, and left the Seed without a guide.

Inside the great open chamber there was a rolled out carpet of alive colours, leading to a marble dais, upon which sat the Elder King upon his throne.

"Cometh, blood of mine," the Elder King instructed, and the Seed followed.

The chamber was vast in every sense of the word, but seemed rather empty on account of the scarce furniture. Its very lacking décor gave the place an austere aura that was filled with a powerful presence. There were braziers pressed against adjacent porticoes and great stone statues of Elder Guards; three handed figures with tapering masks. Framed in between the regimented pillars on each side there were tapestries in shaded alcoves that gave glimpses of writhing images. The depictions were made of thread and the Seed lazily observed the impression of dragon's flame slowly shifting and billowing upon hapless mortals. Another tapestry showed a rendition of mortals bowing with offerings to the Elder King or more obscure details of Seeds from previous cycles. Another showed the Flame Knight and Frost Knight breaking the tapestry into halves of ice and fire.

Sielie, the Elder that had interfered with the Seed's bout, stood there at the king's side like the looming gnarled tree that they were. On the opposite side of the Elder King there stood the raven-headed zerubs who had been inspecting the Seed. Further to the right was another towering being with a close-fitted robe buttoned all the way to the top and a plague doctor's mask peering out to give the impression of a wandering tower.

Further down the dais lurked another creature; bloated and with sickly grey skin reminiscent of a pallid swamp. There was no mouth, instead replaced by writhing tentacles with a life of their own and large black beads for eyes.

Finally, the last creature stood naked and matched the Seed in height if one didn't count the ever shifting antlers atop his equine skull; they shifted and turned like a branching road trying to meet its siblings. His skin was a soft salmon-pink and his body stood on two hooved feet. Even when hairless, his snout was unquestionably like that of a horse. His tail began thick and ended at a docile point, coiled about his hooves.

The Seed walked up to the dais and stared upon the king, upon their father.

The Elder King appeared different. Where before the right eye burnt with a great golden blaze, it now was empty and sagging. Instead, the previously empty left socket harboured a grey eye with a sombre glow to it, like a luminescent rock robbed of its light.

The Seed blinked, barely able to discern the fact that the King's gaze never once settled on them.

"Seed born'th of mine own blood, doth thee comprehend mine words?"

"Yes," the Seed said without inflection.

"Seed of mine, doth thee comprehend thy task?" the Elder King asked.

The Seed nodded.

"Fool! Doth thee not notice the King's vision did impair? Speaketh with thy lips!" Sielie demanded.

"Prithee, mine child yet hath been b'rn but yesterday, doth not pressure mine own, lest we chase them away." The Elder King placated with his calm aura alone. It was as large as the sea itself.

"Steppeth, child of mine. Alas, mine good eye raiseth across the h'rizon and bareth me from giving my fullest attention." The Elder King sounded almost remorseful.

The Seed stepped forward. What was this life to the Seed? These strange beings who introduced themselves as such?

From behind the King's monstrous throne, a sudden light bled and filled the chamber in its grace. The Seed was struck by the display; what kind of warm and blessed thing entered their life?

"Ah, yes. Seed of mine own, cometh, permit me to showeth mine realm." The Elder King rose shakily from his throne to reveal his entirety.

From his left eye there shone a great, glowing silver sphere of sombre woe, yet his smile was that of a caring and benevolent god. His brows were thick and of bushy white with interwoven threads; a great white beard hung long from his chin. There was a single wizened hand with thin skin wrapped around old bones brandishing long nails—his other hand was hidden underneath his robes.

A seemingly endless and decrepit tongue did wet his ancient lips, and the size of the king was more than twice that of the Seed who stood taller than any man, but shorter than the tallest akar.

Upon the head of the Elder King, there was adorned a great crown of ash wood. One may have suspected the crown to be an item of its own, but closer inspection revealed it to actually have grown from the king's scalp along with the curlicue horns.

None helped the king as he lumbered his way around the throne, as his staff of oak lent him balance.

Doth not fear thy father, Eleventh Seed. The thought invaded the Seed's mind. They turned to see the tentacle-faced being who drifted with a knowing glint in their beady eyes.

And so the Seed did follow, working their way around the throne. That was when the king's eye, rising as the sun, flooded into the room and caused the Seed to shield their eyes.

"*Worry not, Seed of mine, no creation of my making will bring harm to thee,*" the Elder King reassured.

The Seed peered out a vast balcony to a most beautiful vista, and the first sight which went beyond the cage of Mount Morniar. It was the first time the Seed had shed tears. Each bead glistened and sparkled like reflections of the night sky bottled in glass.

"My chest," the Seed began, putting a hand to their heart. "It pains... it bleeds."

The Elder King nodded. "*That be wonder, Seed of mine own. Lay thine eyes upon my most sacred works and revere! All that my rising eye shineth upon be my dutiful charge given by the Creator; all of it be my issue.*"

The Elder King waved to all of Minethria: great spanning planes of verdant green, ranging forests, never ending mountain ranges to the west and glistening cities out in the distance.

Far beyond, there floated a great golden minaret like a spire in the sky drifting onwards. Further off, there was a large burning ring of flame barely visible but as a candlelight far away. There were folded valleys and winding rivers like veins of the earth.

"Tis be my work, my creation. I careth for my realm and thus I made thee," the Elder King explained. *"Thou shalt slay the prominent evil, bringeth forth the heart so that I may eschew more land from Nif; whenst done, thou shalt rise and joineth thy siblings in our creator's bosom."*

The Elder King turned to the Seed. *"Thus thy quest shall be, child born of Silver Willow. Tis' shall be thy reason, Ievarus, the Eleventh Seed."*

And so, the Eleventh Seed was bestowed upon a name.

Chapter Fifteen

EREFIEL

*My son. I won't forget your name,   . You are my love, my
sunshine. No matter what happens, I won't forget your eyes, or your
face. No. No.   , come back to me. Your face is a blur. I am forgetting. Who am I writing about? Who am I writing about?
Who am I writing about?*

—JOURNAL ENTRY BY MRS. JOHNSON

T hree days had passed since the incident at Dreamwood.
I knew there were reports that of an akar sighting, but I
didn't pay them as much mind as I should have. Now there
was a dead child and an injured one on my conscience, all because I
didn't act decisively.

There was one good thing which came out of it all. I now had a
way to save Nora from Jason Femur's scorn, but there was no way that
I could justify the cost.

On the third day, I rode out personally to the woods upon my
horse, Zephyr. Perhaps not the most original of names but nonetheless
appropriate, for the way he moved was like riding the wind.

But first, I had to make a stop at Crowtown.

I dismounted Zephyr and was greeted by a curt and trained salute
by Nora. Just as I had expected, she had been waiting a great deal of

KIAN N. ARDALAN

time before our appointed hour. The sun barely even rose. Her brown hair was done in a ponytail and she fixed me with a levelled stare.

"You are early," I said.

"Been waiting an hour, Captain," she stated matter-of-factly, as I dismounted.

"Didn't expect any less of you." My remark wasn't exactly praise, though I felt it was all the same to Nora.

Nora was quite possibly the best recruit I had ever seen. Her drive and willpower put many veterans to shame. It made it all the more of a loss that I had to defect her from my regiment. But I was certain she would find a suitable position elsewhere. Still I heard familiar voices chiding me, Mother telling me to stop investing so much attention in others.

On our way through a rousing town, Nora efficiently and succinctly gave her report. The day it happened, she had been on her way back to Crowtown with a wagon and was dropped off just before eve's light. She had gone to the forest to clear her mind and because of the akar sighting, which had made her uneasy, she decided to investigate.

In her original report, Nora had sent two letters. The first an official occurrence of events, while the second was privately addressed to me, relaying the actual events. She had omitted the more tentative parts in the former. I would have preferred such delicate matters to be handled using an enchanted seal-scroll, but they were costly and rare.

Blessed be Nora Rawsom who trusted her intuition. If not for her and the akar boy who aided her, there may have been more bodies to count.

"I put the akar in detention."

My eyes widened. "You did *what?*" I asked, already bristling at the idea.

Nora blinked, taken out of her stride as she gathered her thoughts.

"Where is the akar now?" I asked.

"In the detention centre," she said, with obvious confusion in her tone.

108

I strode towards the other side of town as the first of the sun's light came over the horizon.

I broke through the exit and worked my way around the akar settlement. Guards half asleep roused from their slumped positions at my passing.

"Erefiel."

"It's Erefiel."

"Look."

One guard with a nest of ginger hair and freckled skin walked out of his tent with a wide yawn and buckled his pants. The moment his dreary eyes met mine, a great fright sprung him awake and into a stiff salute.

I paid their gossip no mind nor their clumsy salutes and instead worked my way around to a large shed that one might have mistaken for a stable at first glance.

I walked to the entrance and saw two guards sitting on either side of the door, one squealed at the sight of me.

"Open it." I forced through gritted teeth.

"Yes, sir. I mean Captain. Erefiel." The blabbering idiot awkwardly bowed before swinging open the door. I stepped into the dark stable, but there was very little hay to be had. The barn was abandoned. I paced forward four steps and footed away the straw at my feet.

One of the guards ran up behind me with a lantern chasing away what sluggish shadows still remained. Nora was right behind.

"Open it," I repeated flatly.

The guard rushed to pull the latch and revealed the steps leading down. I turned to Nora. "You, take the lantern and come with me." Nora didn't dare test my mood any further and did as she was told.

I turned to the other guard who opened the latch. "Stay here." He nodded.

The steps led down to a moist chamber that stunk of mildew. Drops of water echoed within and there was the occasional rattle of linked chains within.

The lanterns forced the shadows to reveal its secrets. The metal cages. They were made of iron, each crossed intersection linked with a studded nail. Inside, there was hay, an empty bowl of food, and a bucket of refuse wreathed by flies. The stench was pungent within the enclosure.

Leaning against the bars was a curled up akar child with a guarded expression. His wrists and ankles were bound in chains.

"Free him," I told Nora.

"But sir, he is—"

"I SAID FREE HIM!" I bellowed within the cramped space. Whatever ire I had held back blew the lid from its container.

Nora begrudgingly took the key hanging from a hammered nail and unlocked the door; the hinges screamed. She stepped inside. Nothing but the sound of dripping water, her shuffling footsteps, and clinking chains could be heard.

She did not fear the akar despite her contempt for their kind. Reluctantly, Nora unlatched the cuffs that bound Chroma's ankles and wrists before pacing back out.

Nora returned to me, a fury of her own apparent in her eyes. "May I be dismissed, sir?" The unevenness in her voice told me she was close to losing her own temper.

I nodded at Nora who proceeded to slap the keys against my chest and stride out with heavy steps. A deep sigh escaped me.

"Come. I apologise for how you ended up here."

⊰ ⊱

The akar's name was Chroma, and there was a wild but approachable energy to the way he looked. His smile was joyous and his tusks and teeth gleamed whenever he had reason to smile, despite being locked away in a cell for two whole days.

We sat upon two mounds of bundled hay outside of the basement. I had asked the officers to bring him warm food, a drink, and a blanket. I made sure that what they brought was the good stuff, not the grub which was rationed and peddled to the akar.

"This is really good." Chroma claimed as he took another deep sip of the soup and took a bite out of a chicken leg. He had the kind of excitement I would expect from a human teen, except it was bound into the lean and powerful muscle of an akar. This one seemed less primal and wild than his counterparts, and by extension, more approachable.

"Do you think I could take some for my mother?" he asked.

I smiled; his Bayrish was surprisingly fluent. Again that voice spoke in the back of my mind. *'Stop collecting strays.'*

I shook the thought before it could fully form.

"Absolutely, I will make sure that you can pack a portion for her," I offered solemnly.

Chroma paused, his predatory akar eyes meeting the white of mine. I felt a question coming.

"You are nice to me," he said as if having just noticed.

I chuckled. "Why wouldn't I be?"

"Because I'm an akar."

"And I'm a Nephilim."

Chroma shook his head. "It's not the same, you know it. I see your armour, your hair, the way the other guards look to you. To them, you are half god; but I am a full-blooded savage to them." His tone was guarded.

Chroma tilted his head to the stable entrance. I turned just in time to see the guards look away.

"You are loved, we are hated." Chroma's previous cheerfulness washed away like sleet from stone and there was just a quiet and sullen resignation to be seen.

I leaned in and considered my next words. I licked my lips.

"They may see you that way, but that's not who you are. You saved those children's lives, you know?"

"Not all," Chroma said, slightly rueful.

"If it weren't for your valiance, it may have been worse."

Chroma hung his head but seemed to accept my words based on the bobbing nod he gave.

"Your warrior doesn't seem to think so," he said.

I frowned. "Warrior?"

Chroma nodded at the entrance where Nora stood, her arms folded and her gaze unfaltering.

I turned back to Chroma. "Ah yes." I scoffed bemusedly. "My 'warrior.'"

"Is she not one of yours?"

"I don't know what she is. Her name is Nora. And she is brave. Steadfast. Dedicated."

"A good warrior," Chroma provided, and I gave an affirming nod. Chroma looked agitated by the thought of her.

"Yet her hate for your kind is misplaced, and I worry it will blind her to what can be achieved."

Chroma's features bunched together in confusion. "Did my kind do something to her?"

I smiled and shook my head. "I wish it were so easy, some just hate because it can be rousing to do so."

Chroma tilted his head, and I had almost forgotten how young the boy was. Even his vernacular seemed above most adult humans. He was only slightly shorter than me, but the way he spoke leant itself a certain level of maturity and growth.

"One final thing, Chroma."

He raised his head.

"The events of that night, do not tell anyone about what you saw." I didn't mention Dalila, I didn't have to. Chroma already discerned my meaning with a quick nod. I could only hope that he would keep it to himself.

⤙ ⤚

As I departed, Nora attached herself to me, keeping up with quick strides.

"Captain Erefiel, permission to speak," Nora requested with obvious annoyance.

"Granted," I said just as sourly.

"That akar broke the law, he fled the settlement."

"He also saved those children."

"Doesn't change the fact—"

I veered on my heels and stared Nora down.

"*He* saved those children's lives, and *he* is nothing more than a child himself."

"Did you see the size of him?" Nora proclaimed incredulously. "How is that a child? Granted, he looks younger, but that is no child."

I would have laughed away my scorn if I weren't so livid. "The boy is no older than sixteen!"

Nora was taken aback, a flush working its way to her cheeks. She probably had never known about their physiology given that her interest in them stopped at finding new ways to kill.

"We—well, it doesn't change the fact that he broke the law!" She pushed through.

Exhausted, I drew a hand across my face. "Look, Nora. This has nothing to do with an akar breaking the law. This has to do with your own hatred towards them."

"They're animals! Why are you defending them?"

A voice cut through the conversation in my mind. '*Stop collecting strays*'.

"So when one of them does something right, we do what? Punish him? Nay. This has to do with your own desire to see them suffer. Now, look me in the eyes and tell me you didn't feel frustrated and angry, tell me you didn't just see an excuse to unload that frustration onto an akar? If you hadn't let your emotions take over, Perry might have still been alive."

Nora stood aghast and unable to find her next words. There was a sudden guilt underneath her expression. I had gone too far. The presence of those words lingered, bleeding their emotions into our conversation.

"Forget about the akar. He did well. I saw the size of the beast in question. If you were alone, I wouldn't be having this conversation with you." I knew Nora was tired, and for whatever it was worth, she accepted my olive branch with a short and affirming nod.

"Plus, I have good news."

Nora's gaze refocused, beaming at me. "I will be able to return to the regiment?"

I furrowed my brows, as Nora seemed to catch my meaning.

"Oh," she said, the wind taken from her sails.

"But I assure you, after this, I will be able to move you to a different garrison and perhaps even throw in a good word, you may be able to move up the ranks. I promise, you will most definitely be able to join in on the front lines against the akar."

Nora saluted at that. "Thank you, sir." Her militant demeanour returned. Nora seemed grateful, all things considered.

⊰ ⊱

Nora's brother, Jeremiah, was not so easy to get hold of, and not just because he was still combating a heavy fever, and spoke in tongues. The parents' rather fanatical inclination towards the Church of Witness put my allegiance to the Elder King's throne and my service to the kingdom of Cleria in a rather poor light. I resigned myself to the fact that it was one conversation I wouldn't be having.

By the time I was done speaking with the two young boys, Dale and Beck, the Elder King's golden eye had reached its zenith and I was on the road again, heading towards the most important child that warranted my attention.

I thought back to the spoken report and private letter. Dalila, a young girl of thirteen who mended the leg of Nora's brother when he collapsed, partially refitting broken bone and healing it. Though as I understood things, Jeremiah's leg healed awkwardly for the rest of the way. I was relieved that the remaining boys made no mention to me about the 'incident.'

Nora reassured me that she made it very clear that nothing was to be said—for Dalila's sake.

I bit my lip and allowed my thoughts to wander as Zephyr sauntered the empty road towards Reed farm.

This had to be handled with the utmost prudence, lest there be talk of witches among the suspicious folk of Crowtown and especially Basksin. I thought back to Father's lessons of past incidents, of the last congregation of witches that rose together and began to sow strife and unrest into the lands. How long ago was that? The third cycle? Nine thousand years ago?

The head of their covenant was Nayrien, a most powerful witch, one of the Inspired who was to be offered to the Elders to serve them. She revolted, and in the way of her wrath stood her own kind. Thus began the prejudice against witches. It was never about who could use magic and who couldn't, it was about stomping any symbol of Elder opposition. Dalila's only crime would be being born a woman and casting magic without a medium.

Stories had a bad habit of taking on a life of their own, spreading like a disease, growing until it could no longer be contained. The people, thus, had a rather distrusting inclination towards anyone who could perform magic without the help of an instrument or colours.

I dismissed my thoughts upon reaching the farm and turned right, past the empty harvest. Along the ploughed field laboured a willowy man with a stubbly beard. He was laden in cold sweat and a younger, weedy gentleman with overalls and shirt suddenly also sprouted from the crops.

They stopped their work and observed Zephyr's canter up their road. The ostensible patriarch clapped the dirt from his hands and wiped his sleeve against his face. They seemed to have been expecting me and looked rather unwelcoming.

Thanks to Nora, I knew the father as Robert Reed and I watched him wave his son away.

The younger boy obliged and jogged to their house, shouting something to a woman who came through the door.

When I approached the farmhouse, I had an entire family waiting in a row for me. I dismounted Zephyr who tugged on the reins, seemingly dissatisfied with the scent of manure.

"I will take him," An even younger boy said, motivated by the sight of Zephyr more than any sense of hospitality. I pulled the reins away from the curly-haired child, presumably no older than ten.

"Ah, I am afraid that wouldn't be wise." I ran a hand across Zephyr's neck to placate him. Zephyr bobbed his head as if restless. "Zephyr can be quite… temperamental."

The older son seemed to catch my meaning as he stepped forward. "I will take him," he said. I handed him the reins as the long, dainty boy clicked his tongue and led Zephyr to a brackish trough beside their stable.

The father stepped forward, wiping his hands and face clean with a cloth, but it only managed to smear the dirt. I didn't mind, seeing someone work in their element was always the best way to judge their character.

There was a disinclined hook in the man's brow. He stood guarded. I faced the terrible force of akar tribes in the dozens; the imposing stare of a humble farmer was hardly unnerving.

Truth be told, I was a little surprised. Nora had told me how the Reed family was incredibly supportive and even dogmatic when it came to Mount Morniar. My distinctive appearance must have told them who I was.

My questions were answered when the man looked at the floor, fidgeting with a loose thread on his overall.

"Are you here to take my daughter away?" the man finally asked. Robert looked up at me and stood his ground, his eyes red and with welling tears. He spoke his query without inflection; I could tell that the man did his best not to falter.

I was so foolish! But of course. My sudden appearance must have implied a horrible idea. To these people I must have appeared to be the hand of Cleria, coming to take away their flesh and blood. I placed a gloved hand to the man's shoulder and gave a reassuring smile.

"I am not here to take anyone away, just wanted to ask some questions."

The father looked up at me in disbelief. There was a light shudder of relief from him. And then, the man almost fell.

"There is no reason to take your daughter away," I reassured and I meant it. Witches were to be reported and sent away in the best of circumstances, the less fortunate would meet their end at a stake. All because of what they represent.

"Thank you." The words were almost unintelligible as they fell from his lips. "Thank you," Robert repeated, his voice on the verge of breaking.

He fell to his knees. "Praise be to the Elders, praise be to the First Defenders of Cleria," the man preached as if nothing else would come to his thoughts.

I turned and noticed that there now stood a mother with a young babe in her arms suckling upon her teat, relief and gratitude also apparent in her eyes as she gave a small bow—the most she could manage given the weight of her child in hand.

I entered the farmhouse and had to apologise several times for the wooden step that snapped under my weight upon entry.

Robert's mood improved tremendously, and it truly seemed as if not even burning down his entire home would ruin his day. The man apologised a great deal more than I did for the squalid state of their home or being able to provide appropriate amenities.

Having had to duck under the humble door frame, I found Dalila sitting inside on their dining table facing the door, or she would have been if her head wasn't hanging sullen and low. She stared hollowly towards the shadow of her twirling thumbs as her dangling feet swung in opposing directions.

I looked doubtfully towards the simple chair and table and worried I would break one more thing within the house.

"If you wouldn't mind, I would like to talk with Dalila outside."

⊰ ⊱

Her father was hesitant at first to let me talk to Dalila in private, but what could he have said?

Dalila and I walked for a while. The girl trailed just behind as we went around the perimeter of their farm.

It wasn't large by any means, but it was enough for the size of their family.

A crop field where they could grow corn during the seasons. A few goats in the back for milk and a coop for chickens to lay eggs. I didn't speak much; I wanted Dalila to manage our exchange at her own pace.

I asked her questions about the farm, her siblings, and her duties. I tried my best to steer clear from the topic of friends. She barely answered, all responses were short. The most I could get from Dalila were the names of her siblings.

We paused before Zephyr so I could introduce to her a friend of my own. I could tell that Dalila was timid and shied away from Zephyr's size, but I could also tell she wanted to get closer.

I went to Zephyr's back and unbuckled the strap to my bag, where I retrieved a carrot.

"Here." I offered it to Dalila; she took it sheepishly.

With a bit more encouragement, the young girl neared Zephyr and raised the perishable to the warhorse's lips.

Zephyr was boundless and unrelenting in the midst of battle, an untrained soldier would find themselves on the ground if unable to seize the wind. But Zephyr had come across enough young children during the years and was smart enough to recognize a threat from a treat.

He humoured me and the girl, eating the carrot. I used the chance to hold Dalila's hand.

"Don't be scared; he won't bite," I promised, as Zephyr neared the end of the stick and ate it all without so much as a scratch on Dalila. Finally, he licked her hand and surprised even me.

"That means he likes you. Zephyr isn't so trusting with everyone."

Dalila was pleased and even laughed. The girl had eased up and unfolded her smile.

We sat together behind the stable, away from the house itself, and it proved even more beneficial to earning Dalila's trust.

"What happened that night?" I finally asked.

Dalila was a brave girl. She nodded, pushing down any reluctance, and shared of the events.

She told me that they went to Dreamwood in hopes of sparking some inspiration into Dale. I would have found the tale amusing under normal circumstances.

"It was my idea... I'm the reason Perry..." Dalila said sullenly, her words cut off by a lump in her throat. It was something about the way she said it, the way her tone softened like an incredibly frail piece of glass.

The girl combed her hair behind her ears and revealed a bluebell flower that had been hiding. The flower had begun to wilt.

My heart sank to the low pits of my chest and I felt an unbearable ache.

"Was he your..." I didn't know how to end the sentence. Was 'beloved' the right term? They were both so young. Though younger engagements did happen.

Silence filled the space between us. If only I had taken the sighting more seriously and sent troops in advance.

Dalila remembered something.

"Is the akar okay?"

I blinked. First wondering if the young girl made a mistake. Why would she worry about their attacker? I then understood she meant Chroma and was even more surprised.

I smiled, happy to deliver the news. "He is fine. His name is Chroma."

Dalila twiddled her thumbs. "I was worried. Just saw him and... screamed. I was so scared. But then he came and saved us."

"He is just glad you are safe."

Dalila nodded at that. "Are the others okay?"

"Everyone else is fine, minor bruises and scratches. Your friend, Jeremiah, is recovering and will live." I chose to omit the fact that he would never walk like he used to.

"But I probably won't be allowed to see him again," Dalila stated dourly.

"He will live, that's all that matters. And that's thanks to you."

Dalila sniffled, her fidgeting hands told of festering remorse. I patted her back, acutely aware of how little I knew about dealing with children.

"Perry died because of me." Dalila's voice broke and her tears flowed readily. Her sobs started soft but gained more and more weight.

"But you also saved someone." I turned her to face me. "Jeremiah lives because of you, in fact, all of them live because of you."

I felt my expression change. It turned serious. "There is another reason that I am here, Dalila. Nora mentioned what she saw in the woods, what you did with your hands." I dared not give away any more than I already had. "Dalila, nobody can know of your abilities."

Again I heard that voice. *"Why do you care?"*

Dalila wiped away her tears and nodded understandingly. "Father already caught me healing Fredrick's cut the other day. He hit me for it."

I repressed a disapproving comment.

"Your father has good reason to be worried. If anyone finds out, you will be taken away. Or worse: killed."

"Am I a witch?" Dalila asked.

I smiled. "You are a young, brave, and loving girl. You are Dalila. That is all I see." I was glad to see her still smile.

"May I offer you some advice?" I asked Dalila.

She nodded hesitantly. I took the flower from her ear.

"Perhaps you can press this between the pages of a book? Perry might be gone, but that doesn't mean that his memory needs to disappear too."

⊰ ⊱

When Dalila had finally calmed, we returned to her family.

"I thank you. Your visit here today means the world to me and my family," Robert said. He must have wept privately from relief, and though his smile never faltered, the man looked exhausted.

I felt a tug to my side and turned to see the young boy named Ben look up and point at me.

"Are those real feathers in your hair?"

"Ben!" Miriam, the mother, reprimanded. Her expression along with Robert's was one of shock.

I laughed. "It's quite alright, really."

Leaning down, I pursed my lips and plucked a feather from my scalp, feeling a momentary sharp sting. The spot would itch and feel uncomfortable for a day and strange for one more, but the feather would grow back along with more.

"Here." I offered it to Ben.

The boy lit up as if he was given the rarest artefact of all of Minethria.

"It is a good luck charm, keep it safe."

Ben nodded, but I wasn't so sure he heard me, as his eyes were only for the feather. Ben ran to show his mother and father, who scolded him lovingly in hushed tones.

"I best be on my way," I stated. Mounting Zephyr, who seemed more than keen to leave the ill-scented farm behind.

My final destination proved to be the most difficult. Part of me was relieved that Perry's parents were so understanding, yet still their sorrow hung like a cloud to them that held no foreseeable parting.

Chapter Sixteen

DALILA

Art impacts different people in different ways. The more sensitive an individual is, the more they may be affected. One way to overcome the resistance of such a troglodyte is to gather crowds to perform for. To see one's neighbour be imbibed by emotion makes even the most uncultured person impressionable.

—HIGHER TEACHINGS OF THE MUSES, BY GOLANAD RICKS

T he day after General Erefiel's visit, there was a wake for Perry.

I wore a sombre-blue dress to match my mood. It had shrunk. The last time I wore it was when granddad passed away.

Some scenes I barely even registered anymore. Like when Mother chased after Ben. He was carrying his newly gifted feather wherever he went, even in the comforts of his bed. I stayed awake the previous night until the wicker burnt out, just looking at Ben drift to sleep with Erefiel's feather gripped tightly.

Erefiel's visit had done much good to instil some semblance of calm. Erefiel didn't patronise me like Mother had, nor seemed as emotionally inept as Father. He was honest and open, spoke to me as someone who was grieving and not someone to belittle. There were just some things that could never be said to parents.

Ben and Mother ran past me and noticed Mother's forehead-vein ready to pop. I rose and helped capture Ben to ready him for the wake. He moaned and complained but ultimately resigned himself.

I had nightmares the past few nights, not like the dreams that entranced me in the forest, but rather ones of Perry. His love haunted me as a perverse spectre. I saw the well again with the six emerald eyes at the bottom. Perry climbed out of it as a corpse. What used to be full of life before was now infested with writhing maggots.

He stood there: loving, smiling, confident, but his visage was one of death, with pallid skin and listless eyes. His flesh was exposed, as the boy I loved suddenly collapsed into a heap of viscera and bone. I could hear the akar's deep laugh but could not see him.

One may have thought it morbid and cliche to say, but a part of me truly did die that day along with Perry; a part of me was left behind in that forest of dreams.

I lacked the energy to respond to Fredrick's jabs and missed the irritation that would boil within me. The past two days alone were spent in bed. I was grateful that my parents were too avoidant to say anything to me—the only time they became insistent was when I refused to eat.

The hunger within was numb and paled in comparison to my grief. Even Erefiel's visit, which greatly improved my mood, was but a momentary respite before the roiling clouds.

⋖ ⋗

We arrived at the wake when I realised I hadn't seen the other boys since the incident. Only Fredrick stayed behind with Tom as to not disturb the event. It was the perfect day to mourn. The clouds were a grey that promised rain. The wake was held outdoors.

Beck stood aside with Dale. The young musician lit up at the sight of me. He waved me over and made as if he had been reserving a spot beside himself. Mother and Father did nothing to stop me as I sauntered to my two friends. Jeremiah was nowhere to be seen. I knew he wouldn't be present, but still it hurt.

I saw Nora standing by herself at the edge of the gathering, her attire seemingly a mishmash of anything dark and mourning. The concert of colours was discordant. Her skirt even bordered on a very dark red rather than the appropriate faded blue. Did she not have mourning clothes? I assumed she had to improvise on the spot. The rest of the gathered people were friends and family. The faces alternated between stony remorse or trickling tears.

I looked to the front, and despite the usual tradition of the casket being open, there instead was a closed one. Realising why set off another wave of distinct sorrow. It took all my strength to not cry.

Perry's father was a long-faced man with a stubbled brown beard, a receding hairline causing what little short and curly hair about his scalp to look like an arrow. The mother stood strong and proud, even though the tears still flowed down flushed cheeks.

Dale tapped on my shoulder. I turned and followed the direction of his pointed finger to someone I did not recognize. Then I saw his case, and the filigree patterned waistcoat of deep-sea blue worn over a shirt. The attire was as gorgeous as it was respectful.

"That's Maxin," Dale said excitedly. His smile would have you think that Dale was enjoying himself at a festival rather than a wake. Though I didn't fault him for it. Dale's simple appreciation for all things concerning music and the Inspired College always excited him. I envied that.

"He is a lute player of high renown! Last I heard, he already earned four of his seven Strings and is well on his way to becoming a muse!" Dale harped. "He must have cost a fortune for Perry's parents." He seemed to consider it for a moment, his brows furrowing deeply as he put the numbers together.

A swift hand smacked Dale around the head.

I turned to see Gallivax, his father, standing. "Show some respect." He snapped sharply.

"Yes, Father," Dale replied, bowing his head in admonishment.

When the wake began, a priest with a dark, encompassing robe stepped forward and looked exactly how one might imagine such a priest to look. Bald. He sported about a pronounced and hooked nose at the centre of pocked skin. His full robes were draped over a paunch. It rounded out the features of a man in his fifties. When he spoke, it only added to the image. He held in his hands a dark-leather bound Kaseluda as a symbol of divine authority.

"I thank all of you for coming to pay your respects to this young child so soon robbed of his life."

I turned to Beck and saw him sniffle. At first, I thought it was the cold, but he was truly shedding a tear for Perry. I hadn't stopped to think how the others must have felt. I wasn't sure if Dale's hanging head was due to his earlier admonishment, or because of a deep sadness that I only just noticed.

"… Before even the first cycle began, man lived longer and prospered due to the Elder King's generosity. We flourished far and wide and enjoyed our endless lives. But then, folly took root in our hearts that gave life to the evil, a folly that formed tyrants and sadists that tortured those less fortunate. So the King created the first angel, the Grand Archon and Warden of Time, and with it came the Contract of Time. We, who are not of Elder's blood, are bound to its machinations and forlorn'd, for our days were numbered. Even after the robbing of the Elder's eye and the Kingdom of Estria's betrayal, the Elder King decided to be merciful."

The priest spoke with such piety that it humbled all present at the notion of the Elder's power. He raised a single finger and paused for dramatic effect.

"One. One month is added to each year when a cycle ends. One month more for us mortals to regain the Elder King's favour, the Creator's favour, and return to a time where we, too, can live eternally."

The priest addressed the casket. "Perry Nemias is no longer with us, his death a reminder of our sin; our sin the reason for his short life. It is up to all of us to help the Elders, to live in service of them, so that one day, such a young life would no longer be robbed from this world."

I turned to Father and saw him neither nod nor show any other sign of subscription. Instead, he simply stood with his head bowed and hands in front of him. Mother tried her best to act in kind, but Ben's restlessness as he tugged upon her dress made it a difficult task.

When the priest was done and stepped away from the casket, the man that Dale had earlier recognised as Maxin stepped forward and unclasped his case, putting together his fine and pristine lute in a matter of seconds.

The priest didn't look pleased.

Mother had told me that the tradition of having someone play at your burial and wake was in part linked with the church of Witness. It was a song written and made for the deceased, a song so pronounced, so potent, so vigorous that it burnt the impression of that person indelibly into those present. A truly masterful rendition intertwined the memory of those who passed with the music until the two became interchangeable. The more powerful the Inspired, the greater the lasting impression.

I looked up at the sky. It looked back at me. Their grey dulled the colour of the world and made everything seem like faded ink on canvas. The clouds were ripe with rain,

When Maxin began playing his lute, it was as if that very ink was being restored to its natural colour with loving brush strokes. It did not try to break the sombreness, nor did it try to persuade any present that this was a joyous occasion.

The notes, the tune given from the lute, painted the picture of sorrow whole. The plucked chords reverberated in such a way that it sounded like even the lute was mourning.

It added notes of drab blue to the potted flowers, denoting the sadness of autumn; it splattered great streaks of black to pronounce the bottomless pit of our sorrow; it added detail to the shed tears so that their cries would be noticed. I could feel the sapping wind howl. It mourned alongside us. I could feel the sweeping blades of grass dance. I could feel the beating hearts of our pain linked in ceremony.

So this was an Inspired.

I was overcome with grief and mourning, but I embraced it, relished in it. I took every note, every consequent tone, and threw myself into its arms. It felt as if I were rolling down a flowered hill, trampling petals on the way, before plummeting off the edge and into the depths of grasping waves.

My tears flowed. My heart ached. The hurt, the suffering—I wanted it, I deserved it. *Make me suffer*, I thought. Only then did I realise how numb I had become. I hungered for unbearable pain as it lashed within my chest and broke its chafing chains.

I was a slave to the music, a slave to its sound. It linked me to all others, amplifying my sorrow until my heart beat louder and louder in concert with the melody, until the white stillness of its hurt became desirable.

I felt everyone's sadness. I felt my own. But I felt release most of all; I was not the only one who let loose a deep cry. When it was done, I felt freed.

There was a stillness, an intense stillness amongst our audience, whose speechless response said so much more than any applause ever could.

It was only then, right after that moment of inexplicable silence, that the clouds burst and rain poured, almost as if in response to Maxin's performance. The static downpour silenced my spent thoughts.

Only then was Perry's casket lowered. Six men took the ropes and lowered the casket in tandem. I watched the boy I loved disappear beneath the ground. The laboured hands offered more rope to the darkness. I bit my lip, and hoped truly that I would never forget who he was, never have him become a forgotten after death. The thought of not being able to remember Perry scared me even more than fading away into nothingness myself.

Chapter Seventeen

CHROMA

The first dragon was a force to be reckoned with. Zolas, known to be as large as a black mountain, was once a landmark of Minethria after his death. Scales and bones and teeth were removed to be forged into anger manifest by the Blacksmith. No new weapons can be made since the Haar swallowed Zolas whole.

—Summary on the thousand years of the fourth Cycle by Ennay the Scholar

I returned to my people at dawn. A soft cold worked its way through me. I carried with me nothing, and was told that food would be delivered to my mother.

I reflected on my imprisonment. There was the cold and damp embrace of absolute darkness. Its heartbeat was the slow drip of water on stone. I went through a sort of quiescence typical with my folk. And then came the Nephilim to free me.

My thoughts were scrambled. What would I say to Nedalya? To Kolotha? Did Siemeny and Trem tell them what I saw? Was mother worried? Did they know what happened? I paced outside the entrance when a frazzled Jasper made his way to me.

He looked as if he wore his uniform in a hurry. Was he here to scold me? No. He looked too awkward and nervous. "Chroma," he said to me.

"Jasper."

There was a pause. The guard was unsure of himself.

"I heard what you did out there." The man tapped me on the shoulder, his eyes avoiding my gaze.

"Thank you?" I wasn't sure how to respond.

"Look. I know I am not the friendliest of the guards here, and that is saying something. But one of the kids you saved was my nephew and… obviously you shouldn't have run away in the first place, but if you hadn't been there, who knows what might have happened?"

I blinked. I felt incredibly awkward. Jasper was a rough, stubbly bearded man who seemed like he always woke up an hour too early. He was handsome enough despite his stretched features.

He slapped me on the shoulder a second time, trying to seem laid-back, but it just made things worse.

The pounding in my head only grew.

"It's okay, Jasper. I did what anyone would have done." I meant the words, but struggled to deliver any kind of sincerity.

Jasper almost scoffed. "No. No Chroma. That's the thing, an *akar* would never have done what you did."

I scowled.

Jasper seemed to have noticed his mistake as he stumbled backwards and almost tripped over his own feet. "Wait—sorry, I didn't mean it like—"

"Are there new conscriptions?" I asked. Mother left the encampment just as late as I had, yet I heard no commotion regarding her. Was she being conscripted?

Jasper's fear vanished and was replaced by confusion. "What do you mean?" he asked.

"Never mind." I shook my head and walked away.

I expected a quiet settlement of waking akar, not the crowd which waited for me with tusked grins. They howled when I wandered in.

They approached as a welcoming flood. Juta was there and clapped me on the back in approval. I didn't even notice Mother until she was right on top of me. I flinched, expecting her to hit me, and was left stunned when I realised she held me in a tight hug. The ornaments in her hair clattered. I was glad to see her.

"I was worried," she said.

"I'm sorry. I'm okay." My own arms returned the hug, though not as tightly.

"What were you thinking?" Mother pushed to hold me at arm's length so that I could see her chiding expression.

"I wasn't," I admitted.

Suddenly, her face softened. She stepped aside and threw my hand up to the sky. "My son is a warrior!" She roared. Our people joined in. They cheered and threw their fists into the air.

A smile I had no control over sprouted on my lips. I found Nedalya amongst the mingled crowd. There was an awkwardness to our exchanged glance which only slightly weakened my smile.

My chest tightened and my heart sang. I looked back into the crowd.

"Baatar! Baatar! Baatar!" The people chanted, their stomping feet reminded me of thunder. I was a warrior. The thought hadn't even crossed me until now! It was believed that the akar born within the settlement would never have the honour of bearing that title, and yet, there I was. All for slaying one of our own.

I caught another set of eyes, this one belonging to Kolotha. He didn't appear to share the excitement.

Out of nowhere, the chants died down as my people were distracted by something behind me. I spun to see. Men strolled in with carts chock-full of food; a feast worthy of a war tribe. Jasper stepped forward.

"In the name of Captain Erefiel, son of White-Hawk, a feast is to be put on for the akar camp this coming night," declared Jasper with a booming voice.

I had never seen such a festive gathering before as my folk came together. They drank fine barrels of ale rather than pirine for once. I watched mothers put together bowls of ointment to paint the face of their children. Did my people beyond the forest have gatherings like this often?

Several hours had passed since my arrival. The remaining day was spent setting up the feast. Long wooden tables were burdened with food our folk had only ever heard of. Anything the guards casually had called 'cake' was the first to go. Sugar was the main culprit in all of these things and we unanimously found each bite to be electrifying.

All the expenses were covered by Erefiel himself. I felt uneasy. I asked for food for my mother, not the whole tribe!

I smiled privately and remembered Nora. She would hate seeing such an amount of food given to my people. It made me happy.

Generous cuts of meat were passed around and was just as abundant as the mud beneath our feet.

I felt like an observer; happy for my people and that they got to celebrate, but unable to get in a festive mood.

I stayed on the fringes of the campfire as the shadows of my folk laughed and danced in the night—their stretched, umbral forms were alive. The embers of the fire sent sparks that looked as if they had tried to become stars and then faded.

The guards still stood at the very borders of the camp, but they oddly seemed protective now rather than hostile. It was as if they were unsure how to feel themselves; glad that most of the children were saved, but unsure how they felt about our celebrations.

I caught Kolotha leering. He turned away, as brooding as a boulder.

Juta approached and took a seat. The man truly was giant, his chest heaving as he considered his first words. I flinched as the memory of Ji'sura flashed through my mind.

"You look better," I said.

"I feel better," he replied. "I heard from Sukin what you and the shaman did for me."

I chuckled. "She isn't a shaman." I corrected, in that snarky way adolescents usually felt the need to. I picked at a blade of grass in my hand, tearing the strands into equal, thin lengths.

"Healer. Whatever," Juta groused, his gruff voice sounding slightly irritated.

The large akar cleared his throat as if uncomfortable. "Is the human alright?" he asked, slightly hesitant.

I nodded. "She is fine, a few bruises, but nothing worth worrying about."

"Good," the large man said. I sensed relief. It was the closest he would allow to vulnerability.

I stared at him. My trainer. His jaw drew circles as his teeth grinded. An akar habit when deep in thought.

We were far enough from the others. Whereas they basked in the campfire's glow, Juta and I were graced with its scraps.

"You did a good thing, out there, saving those children." A relaxed hand waved in the direction of the forest, now hidden behind tents and palisades. "I guess my teachings weren't for nothing," he joked. His playful, giant elbow nudged me slightly and earned a smile from my otherwise reticent lips.

"Did you catch the akar's name?" Juta asked more seriously.

"Ji'sura," I supplied.

Juta nodded. "Good. Always know the name of the one you kill."

I still held my tongue.

"You regret it, don't you?" He finally asked the question.

"I don't know what I feel." There were so many thoughts that filled me. "Is it really okay? That I saved humans and stood against my own kind?"

Juta shook his head. "He wasn't your kind." He waved towards the surrounding folk, a deliberate gesture to express the magnitude of his claim. "*We* are your kind, Chroma. The people who have been beside you since you were born."

I thought again to the distant mountains, to a home I would never know. I felt robbed of my heritage. "You never miss home? Wish you could return there?"

"Of course I do! Everyday—it was my home. But not anymore; I am not welcome there. I can't afford to think of the past, there is no going back."

"What was it like?"

Juta chuckled at the query. "Free." That one word, that one single statement, was like a liberating exhale. "Open fields, abundant food. Our problems were our own and simple lives didn't always mean simpler problems." He shrugged. "But it was a good life." His brow furrowed like the surface of weathered stone. "Though things got worse. With the Haar constantly closing in, we lost more and more territory. The forest was cramped and overgrown, but not enough wildlife to feed us all. It was as if the forest was starved. Left it no choice but to cannibalise itself." He nodded. "Things were tough."

"That's why Father brought the tribes together," I said absentmindedly. Perhaps Juta took it as a question. He hesitated for a moment and then nodded with a grunt.

"Muktow started all this. He brought the tribes together to fight back against the Elders; they made their peace, we made ours."

"But Juta, you are a warrior. Is this really the life you imagined for yourself?"

Juta's scoff sounded like a growl, challenging my statement, but not me. "What is a warrior, Chroma?" he asked.

I pondered the question; it seemed rather obvious. "Someone who fights."

"Yes, but you have only just scratched the surface. Someone who fights *what*? Am I a warrior if I were to cut down those guards?" He pointed cautiously towards our human wards. "Would I be a warrior if I went to Crowtown and cut down each and every person? Killed helpless mothers and murdered their children?"

I did not understand what he was getting at, but the query was an obvious one. "No," I surmised.

Juta nodded, satisfied with my answer. His dreadlocks clacked together as he licked his lips in preparation for what came next.

"A warrior is not a killer, is not someone who only fights with axe and shield: it is someone who fights for a reason. I still maintain my warrior spirit by choosing to protect my tribe, to protect my family. Ji'sura sounded like a valiant akar for many reasons. But I do not believe the death of innocent children was one of them."

I was about to ask what it would mean if I wanted to return to my people, return and join their war. I never got a chance.

Juta rose to stand, his great paw clapping down on my shoulder as he pointed into the crowd.

"You did the right thing; know that I am proud of you." What strange words. I found that I appreciated what Juta just said. "Now move along. There is someone else that needs your time." I followed Juta's finger to find a waiting Nedalya. She turned and headed behind tents away from the campfire's reach.

✧ ✥

I walked to where Nedalya had lingered. My heart beat faster and faster the further I distanced myself from the celebration.

My eyes adjusted to the dark. There, I found the familiar and soothing contours of my heart waiting for me.

"Nedalya, I—" My heart strode to me and took my lips into her own. When we parted, I wanted nothing more than to lean back and feel her touch.

There was hurt in her eyes.

"Nedalya—" I tried again, but she interjected.

"I know. Siemeny and Trem told me." Nedalya avoided looking at me.

"That night, when we were in the tent. I know you wanted it." Her words caught me off guard. Was it a statement?

Nedalya forced her eyes to meet mine. "You want me. I've known since we were children and I want you, too." The hold was momentary, her gaze dropping. The powerful hands she had placed on my chest slid down to her side.

"But when you pushed me away that night..." Nedalya grew terribly quiet. Her voice drifted into the night and died.

"I need you to understand. When I was hurt, drunk, and you were nowhere to be found, Kolotha was there." She was looking for forgiveness just like I was.

My words lumped in my throat.

"Please. Say something," she pleaded.

What was I to say? There were a million thoughts, a million things I wanted to tell her ever since I pushed her away. But now that I stood before her, it was like ink washed from paper and my mind turned blank. I choked, my throat tightening. I was scared, not just of rejection, but of what would happen if I got exactly what I wanted—I wasn't ready.

Nedalya's expression began to transform. Her upturned brows twisted into an expression of hate.

She grunted a guttural sound and shoved me.

"Nevermind; this was a mistake."

Don't go. I love you. It's not your fault.

The words refused to come as I watched Nedalya storm away. Confusion whirled into panic.

"Kolotha is twice the man you will ever be." What terrible words said with such tangible spite that it tore a wound in my soul deeper than anything I could think of.

She said it. She confirmed it: I was not worthy of her.

Her words were meant to hurt, they were meant to rend and tear, and I could tell that the hooked edge of her claim would infect my desire and fester what could have been.

Chapter Eighteen

DALILA

"Lo! It is a blessed day, for the ------- has been born! The Evil will be slain once more and the Eleventh Cycle will come to an end! Blessed and hallowed be the name ------- and blessed be the Elders in their boundless wisdom!"

—ARCHIVED PROPAGANDA POSTER CELEBRATING THE BIRTH OF ------

Six months had passed since Perry's burial, six months where I went through the motions and my heart wilted with the coming spring.

Perry visited my dreams often, sometimes as a corpse, sometimes as I remembered him. Often, he would be accompanied by the well and the six eyed shadow at its bottom.

Perry and I would talk about things, things that I never remembered upon waking. I chased after those moments, mere opportunities to escape the reality of it all and join him in hopeful realms of my construction. Upon my waking moment I felt like I was a lost soul, my mind half asleep and simply strolling aimlessly, completing mindless tasks without thought or reason.

"Dalila." Father came into the shed where I was milking one of the goats. I noticed then that my inattention resulted in the chafing of the goat's udders, turning them red.

"Have you seen my shears? I can't find them," he asked, scratching his scalp and surveying the shed filled with the animals.

I smiled half-heartedly. "You lost it several months ago, remember?"

"Yes, but I am still searching for them. How can something just disappear?" he asked.

I shrugged and returned to my task, consciously trying to be delicate with the milking.

When Father left, I waved a healing hand over the goat's udders and a brief flaring light shone, doing away with the chafed skin. I coveted that light, hiding it from prying eyes and especially from my parents.

There were two things that I kept to myself during these days: the first being the magic of my healing light, the second being the queer animals that visited me when I was dreaming, the same ones from the forest. I originally described them as fairies to my family; Father had no hesitation about beating such nonsense from my already muddled and gloomy mind.

✕ ✦

Food that day was soup with chunks of flotsam potato, a side of eggs, and a good loaf of bread with butter.

Father was rambling on about how good the harvest had been, even working our way into spring.

It was true, we had enough to last us until autumn, and Father even sold some for a little extra, using the money to gift mother with a pristine silver necklace. He insisted it was crafted by an Inspired, but I was certain that he was scammed.

Mother didn't seem to care either way and gratefully paraded her present publicly.

Ben still carried Erefiel's feather wherever he went. Even as he took his bowl to his lips and the brown liquid dribbled down his chin, the feather sat snuggly behind his ear. These days, his imagination had taken on a life of its own, outgrowing his own maturity. He would pretend to be a mage and wave around the feather as if it were a wand, donning the rather fashionable name of White Wizard.

The only sense of rather spiteful comfort I achieved was seeing that Fredrick looked as sullen and reserved as I did for once. Maria, a rather rat-faced girl from the farm over, was to be betrothed to my brother. Fred made no attempt to hide his displeasure.

Fredrick didn't dare engage the topic right there at the table, but I had heard his hushed arguments with Father when they thought themselves safe from curious ears. When that didn't work, I heard Fredrick go to Mother instead but had little to show for it.

Father liked the Horsestead family, their devotion to the Elders and their affable relationship made it a certain plus. Although, I was sure that their rather profitable business of raising prize-worthy horses also did not harm the arrangement.

I joked to myself that the Horsestead family opted for Fred because no one else was interested in marrying someone as unattractive as Maria.

❧ ☙

Nothing, and I mean absolutely nothing, that I deigned to do on the farm was more exhausting or loathsome than pretending I was okay.

I had to smile, smile between moments of sheer, empty sorrow because it was easier than the truth. Father wanted to help. I knew he did. He would suggest thinking of positive things, looking to the future, moving on, to lose myself in labour so that I may be free from my thoughts. I didn't fault him for it; he was a problem solver, but trying to solve my woe was like trying to catch smoke.

Mother was no different, but she wished for me to talk, to tell her how I felt, but I couldn't bear to see the hurt in her eyes as she watched her daughter display such numb indifference.

So I lied, I lied because it was easier than telling the truth.

I couldn't smile the entire day. I looked no different than someone losing their mind from the rot or Mrs. Johnson's own erratic outburst. But I had to seem like I was improving, as if each day my smile returned to that same shine it had before everything happened.

I despised the lie.

Having to pretend like I was doing better, smiling in spite of the fact that it felt like my heart was tearing itself apart.

That evening, I finally excused myself after dinner and went out into the shed for some privacy.

Night had not settled yet as I walked out of our home. The bare fringes of the sun's glow still marked the horizon in a soothing lavender which bled red into the sky.

The goats bleated as I entered. I turned to seal the door behind me.

With the help of a lantern to light my way, I worked towards a mound of hay piled in the corner. The goats simply stared like they always did with their blocky pupils and twitching ears.

I rifled through the hay. One of the goats munched at some while watching me with disinterest. I felt the metal grip and pulled out the shears hidden inside; the same ones Father was looking for.

The instrument was fashioned like tongs, a bendable strength to its haft which allowed one to squeeze the blades together only for it to return to its previous shape. My lantern's flame flickered against the metal surface. Rust had corroded its previous shine, eating away like a disease.

One of the goats bleated.

I rolled up my sleeves to reveal the face of my sorrow: it was a temple to my loss. Horizontal tracks worked their way across my arm, healing scars which told despairing tales of my pain. Healing these was not an option.

I stared at the edge of the shears and pressed their blade to my skin. My hand quivered as the first drop of blood beaded and then quickly ran as a thin seam. I moaned in repressed pain and sorrowful release.

The droplets shone, their surface reflecting with the light of my lantern, and I continued to spread a gash across.

The blood dribbled and ran down my elbow, dripping into the hay below my feet. I could feel my brows knitting together, I could feel the pain taking shape into a virulent bloom.

This was my repentance. The price I had to pay to feel anything at all upon my waking hour. The blades made two cuts across, which ran unabated, my blood carrying with it the harbouring guilt I felt within me. My cutting hand shook from the effort, but also from the ecstasy of release.

I knew that whatever weed took root inside would just regrow again, no matter how many times I plucked its body from the soil of my heart; its roots ran too deep.

Yet still, for that one moment, the pain I felt, the waxing numbness within me was gone. I could feel pain, I could feel remorse, I could feel sorrow. It felt like a perverse parody to Maxin's performance, an attempt to recapture that sense of freeing grief, but my display was garish in comparison.

I hated myself then and there; I pitied what had become of the sweet Dalila, what had become of her love.

A tear ran down my cheek, and its salt was as precious as all the ones I had freed before. A single tear fell upon the pooling blood of my arm and made a momentary blot of red in water before being swallowed by the rest.

"Dalila!" I heard from outside.

Panic seized me. My private, intimate retreat meant only for me, the bastardized ritual of my mourning with only the stupid gazes of goats was disturbed.

Frantically, I hid the blood stained shears and rolled down my sleeve to cover the wounds.

"Dalila?" Fredrick broke into the shed.

"Dalila. What are you doing here? Father is calling you."

Fredrick stepped into the light and then paused, taking in the stale and heavy air that surrounded me and the goats.

Blood dripped from my concealed arm and ran down my fingers.

"Dalila! You're bleeding!"

Fredrick ran to me when he noticed my wound, any thoughts of the strangeness of my circumstance gone.

I pulled my arm away from him. I couldn't look him in the eyes.

"I'm fine," I reassured. I was angry that he disturbed my moment.

"Let me see." He pulled my arm against my will. I braced myself.

Fredrick's eyes widened as he pulled up my sleeve, the truth of it all scarred indelibly into my arm.

"What is this?" he asked, terror in his voice.

"It's nothing." My statement had a pleading undertone. I begged him to believe me.

"Did you do this?" he asked.

I didn't answer. He looked at the scars as if he were trying to read the story it told. I pulled my arm away before he could. The move freed Fredrick from the spell. He just stared at me with horror and shock in his agape expression.

He grabbed my wrist. "We are telling Father."

"No!" I kicked and screamed, my free hand trying its best to pry open Fredrick's long fingers coiled about my slender wrist. My blood left a trail in the ground and formed a bridle of blood between his wrist and mine.

I planted my feet, tried to hold on to a post, but nothing stopped me from being dragged along into judgement.

⊰ ⊱

I didn't hear most of what happened. My mind receded into its corner again and I faded into a trance. I looked at Father as he scolded me, tears in his eyes, asking why I would do such a thing. Mother sat in a corner of the room, unable to stop her crying.

Father asked how I could do this to him, to the family. What would our neighbours think?

When he calmed down, Father turned pleading, begging me to return his sweet and innocent Dalila. I wished I could give them what they wanted. I wished I could return to who I used to be before all this madness.

Fredrick stood in a corner of the room, one hand holding his other shoulder in regret as it was now his gaze that avoided mine.

⪻ ⪼

I was forced into my room that night, left to lick my wounds as my blood clotted and the scars began to form. Ben and Fredrick had made their bed outside. I was to be left alone and think about what I'd done.

Father had given me the Kaseluda, which contained the teachings of the Elders.

But that night I couldn't bring myself to open a single one of its pages and instead leaned into my tiredness.

So I shut my eyes and willed myself to my succour of dreams, for where Perry would visit and I could pretend all was well if just for a few hours.

Tears ran down my cheek, and my chin quivered. I sobbed softly.

I wished for escape from this cruel life. I wanted to return to a time before this perpetual autumn which numbed my world.

I wished for death.

Perry never came that night. Yet what I wholly did not expect, were the guards who came to take me away the next morning.

Chapter Nineteen

DALILA

On a lone branch where death's seed sprouts,
Pluck the berry, and state your vows.
Speak the name, of hated foe,
And share with them, your destined woe.

—POEM OF DESTINED WOE

That day, just like any other, getting out of bed seemed like a mountainous task. My bones were lead, the sheets beneath me like muck pulling my limbs under. A weight pressed itself against my chest and I cursed the bubbling sorrow inside me; it wanted to cry yet never found its way through my lumped throat.

I stared at our roof of thatch and mud through pupils which were like filthy windows far above my soul.

Nobody really talked to me. Ben appeared unsure what was happening but avoided me all the same.

I assumed Father and Mother were still trying to teach me a lesson, either that or they still weren't ready to confront me. It was probably both.

Commotion stirred outside our home. It pulled me away from the wall. Something was very wrong. A part of me tried to stand and see what was happening.

Perhaps it was something bad? Maybe mother was injured?

A twitch of my forefinger was the greatest test to my will. My eyes could only blink. I felt like a spectator in my own body. As if a part of me, the true me, screamed and battered and cried within my chest. But her voice was too quiet, too distant to rouse my skeleton.

The voices came closer. It was a dispute; Father was shouting something. I heard Mother plead. My body gave a stiff shudder at the sound of flesh being struck.

Mother shrieked. My heart beat faster, energy flooded my limbs slowly but surely. And still my body felt too numb to rise or do anything.

"Robert!" I heard Mother call, the word muffled through the walls.

The voices came closer.

"Please, no!" Mother wept.

The door to the house burst open.

Finally, the spell broke as I sat up. But I knew there was nowhere to run. I heard heavy boots take exactly three steps.

A door opened. It was not mine; probably my parents'.

"Please! No!" My mom begged. She was crying.

"Quiet, peasant!" someone commanded; a man.

I heard a slap. It brought me to my cold, small feet and had me running to the door.

"Mom!" I cried, flinging the door open.

"Dalila! Run!" Mother cried from the floor she lied on; she had one hand clasped to her reddening cheek.

There was a man. A Clerian guard. He bore the tabard of a golden city holding up the sun.

"I found her!" The guard shouted out through the open door.

"No!" Mother's wail was barely intelligible as she descended into whimpers. She grabbed onto the man's greaves to little effect. "Run!"

I bolted for the open door, stopping short as the shadow of a lax man blocked my escape.

He wore a sneering grin. His stubble beard was rugged and belonged to sagging skin like that of a turkey's neck. A diagonal scar ran from the bottom right of his chin to the upper left of his lips. The wound had never properly healed and thus exposed his gums; giving the impression of a perennial snarl. The man went down on a knee. His cold set eyes were framed by greasy locks. They bore into me.

"You must be the witch," the man said, entirely composed.

Mother stopped screaming. She sobbed in the corner, hands still ringed about the guard's leg. Nobody spoke. The man before me commanded everyone's attention.

"My name is Dalila," I said.

The man seemed somewhat taken aback by that.

"Ah yes, my apologies," he said. "I am Sergeant Richardson, but you may call me Eric." His voice carried a slow drawl, absolutely devoid of any urgency. Part of me half-expected a serpent to slither from his lips.

Patiently, the man tugged upon his right glove, loosening its digits to reveal the hand beneath.

He pressed it to my cheek, and I trembled, almost recoiling from his touch. Eric meant me no harm, though. Instead, he took my hair and tucked it behind my ear. I felt sick.

I fell to my knees and vomited colourless bile.

"I am sorry, Dalila," the man said, sounding truly remorseful.

He leaned into my ear and whispered. "I mean you no harm, Dalila. I am here just for you. If you come with me without any fuss, then no one else needs to get hurt." His words smelled rotten. Not due to any food that he had eaten, but rather how he said those words.

I nodded feebly.

"Good girl," he lauded with a pat on my back.

I rose, numb, but some instinct called upon whatever ounce of control I possessed. I had to protect my family above all else.

"Well, let us be off," Eric said, any friendly pretence gone.

"Please, sir, don't take away my Dalila, she is just a child," mother begged, as if fully waiting until this seditious leader had his say.

The man did not respond. Instead, Eric communicated his wishes with a glance. I shuffled my way to Mother.

"Mom," I said, "It's alright." I tried to offer my strongest smile. I doubted it had any actual strength, but Mother understood. Her grip loosened and fell defeated to the floor. A helpless sob escaped her.

The guard Mother had been holding promptly kicked his feet away from Mother's grip, as if somehow insulted about being touched by a farmer.

"Best be on our way then, sorry for all the trouble," Eric said with a cheerful smile.

I walked over to him.

"Sergeant," I addressed him meekly.

"Please." He smiled affably. "Call me Eric."

I nodded. "May I go and grab something for my travels?"

Eric frowned. "What, exactly?"

"The holy book of the Elders: the Kaseluda."

"There are more than enough of those where you are going."

I nodded. "But this belongs to my family. It will be something to remember them by."

I tried to look as docile and non-combative as possible; given my mood, it wasn't very hard to achieve. Eric pondered for a moment and finally nodded. "If that will keep you quiet," he said.

I ran to my room and grabbed the discarded Kaseluda.

Walking out of the farm, I found Father being held down by two more soldiers. His left cheek had already been swelling and his eye was closing shut from a gnarly bruise. He struggled against their hold, and when the guards finally released him, he dropped to his hands. Tom was quiet in Fredrick's pacifying arms, and Ben was nowhere to be seen.

I allowed myself a final glance back at my home. I wanted to remember it exactly as it was. Decrepit. Old. Flimsy. But it was home nonetheless.

The sun was up and the warmth of spring on my skin seemed like it wasn't my own. I could hear children playing in the distance, oblivious to the cruelty that awaited them.

I stumbled at one point, looking down to see my small, bare feet dwarfed by the guard's footprint. My family all stood there wordlessly, watching me leave. Mother couldn't stop crying. Did she really love me that much?

From the others, there were no waves, no shouts; perhaps giving it voice would have made it too real. I had no idea what to say. I looked to the field where hanging crop heads were already harvested.

We passed by the well. I tried my best to burn its contours into my mind, taking note of the uneven blocks of stone, the obtuse shapes sticking out too far or some slotted too deep. I heard the sound of sloshing water. Was the light still inside? Was it still in the forest? Perhaps it would guide me as it did back then?

It all went by too fast.

I wanted to remember the earthy scent of piled and damp leaves. I wanted to remember the rustling sound of oblivious trees as wind blew through their fingered branches. I wanted to get annoyed with Fredrick again, cover my ears when Tom cried and smile when he cooed. I wanted to smile irritably at Ben when he pretended to be a wizard. Confide in my mother. Please, Father.

It all went by too quickly.

I was brought to sit upon the pulled wagon. The other guards took their seats at the front of the cart as three, while Eric mounted a steed of mud brown and we all set off. I looked out towards the place I had known as home for the past fourteen years and watched it fade from view. My heart had once leapt at the promise of leaving its safety; I just never had imagined it would be in this way.

In my moment of privacy, shaded by the arched covering above me, I took the Kaseluda in hand and opened its page.

There it was, not a word or a page of my particular interest, but rather an item, the only thing that belonged to me and tied me to the boy I loved.

It wasn't perfect, its colour already faded, but the bluebell that Perry had gifted me laid there patiently for me.

I closed the book, wondering what new life awaited a witch like myself.

Chapter Twenty

EREFIEL

Out of the many beings which inhabit Minethria, one sees the least evidence for the Chitons of Duran. Only once did their kind ride upon an umbral host across the buzzing sky, when the Elder King called for help against the dragons.

—HISTORY OF MINETHRIA FROM THE FOURTH CYCLE.
APPROXIMATELY 4C430

My station as Lieutenant General for the defences of Cleria came with perks. Enviable wage or connections with beings of a higher plane among them. But one luxury which had proved itself frustratingly scarce was sleep.

I stared out my window towards the expanse of my garden and those who maintained its appearance. Spring air still lingered. I took in a breath.

Out beyond my gates was the bustle of Cleria's pristine streets.

I looked back to the men and women who worked on tending my home. Things were uneventful.

"Here you go, Erefiel." Saru had entered my study and put down a tray with biscuits and steaming tea onto the edge of my maple desk.

"Thank you." I turned to him, trying to be as sincere as possible as I pulled the blanket draped about my shoulders closer. I had no doubt it was Saru who had covered me while I slept.

There were two things that betrayed the fact that Saru was not human. The first being his lavender skin reminiscent of shavinu people. The second being the vertical slit on his forehead. Except it didn't sport an opened eye typically expected of his ilk. Instead, an ugly scar ran through the shut slit and marked him as an exile.

If it weren't for his coat-tailed outfit or groomed appearance, one would have thought him a vagrant.

"Erefiel, I can't keep finding you like this. You need a proper night's sleep," Saru said.

"Noted," I replied glibly. We both knew we would be having the same conversation again very soon. His sigh of defeat confirmed it.

"I'm serious. Have you been helping people again?"

I dodged the question. "You didn't complain when I saved you."

Saru slightly bristled at the implication. "You can't keep using that excuse to neglect your own well-being."

Ignoring him, I worked my way around the table and drank the tea.

I braced through the tea as it seared my tongue. Black tea wasn't necessarily my favourite, but it did rouse me awake in more ways than one.

I noticed Saru was still standing there.

I lowered the cup. "What is it?"

Saru hesitated to tell me. "A woman by the name of Nora is here to see you."

This was the extra punch my spiced tea needed.

"And? Did she explain why?"

Saru shook his head. "Only that it is important."

"How long has she been waiting?"

"An hour."

I repressed a grumble but Saru still seemed to notice.

"You can be as grumpy as you want. You need to rest." Saru stated without hesitation. Though shorter than me and comically stern, Saru had no qualms in my stare with his amaranthine eyes.

"Bring her in," I said.

Saru nodded and left.

I took another, deeper sip of the black tea and let it scorch my tongue into wakefulness. With a roll of my shoulders, the blanket puddled into the embrace of the seat.

When Nora arrived, I was still wearing the same clothes from the day before. Loose fitting pants and a bland white tunic though my feet were bare. It didn't put into question rank or authority.

She entered and saluted.

I knew that the last time we had seen each other was six months prior, and since then, I had helped her get a new position where she quickly proved herself in the ranks.

"If it isn't Simurgh, the Twilight Bird. Or Undying Flame? I have lost track of the names people give you."

Nora tried to hide her flushing cheeks. "It is good to see you, Captain Erefiel." She gave a respectful but short nod. Her brown hair was done into a ponytail, but she permitted herself the slight act of embellishment by sporting fringes that were cut just above her brow.

"If you are here to tell me about the rot, then I am already fully aware." I frowned. "Don't you have more important things to do?"

Nora shook her head. "I'm on leave, but this is important." I dropped my arms; there was something she was reluctant to say.

"What is it?"

She finally looked me in the eye. There were no tears but there was guilt.

"They know Dalila is a witch. I didn't know who else to come to."

My composure shed itself, just like the blanket did from my shoulders.

"What?" I asked in disbelief. "But how?"

Nora hesitated.

"What are you not telling me?" I asked and stepped up to her.

"My parents. They pried it from Jeremiah. I know that this is above your station, and who you are the child of. But she is just a child. My brother would have been dead if—"

"Demon-shit." I cut her off. It seemed as if Nora had come here prepared to convince me of something, but there was no need for any of it.

I strode quickly out of the study.

"Wait! Erefiel!"

I ignored Nora and turned down the hall to my room. She ran after. "There is more!"

I turned on my heel. "What? What more could there be?"

Nora hesitated as I stared her down. I caught myself in the reflection of her fear and let out a stilling breath.

"I'm sorry. This is not your fault." I laid a hand on Nora's shoulder. "You're just trying to help." I gave a reassuring smile and reigned in my anger.

That sing-song voice returned to taunt me, louder than ever. *Another stray for your collection?"*

"Eric Richardson is the one tasked with retrieving her."

All thoughts abandoned me as I sprinted to my room, promptly removing my shirt and trousers.

Nora squealed. In any other situation, I would have found it amusing that the unfaltering 'Simurgh' was so easily flustered. But at that moment, my mind only raced with thoughts of Dalila and what would become of her.

"When did they find out?" I asked while Nora stood out of sight by the door.

"Four days ago, I only found out due to a letter sent by Jeremiah," she explained. "I followed through and discovered that someone was sent yesterday."

"Good thing you did," I offered, putting on and buckling my new and clean greaves. I dreaded the idea of Dalila having to travel with that serpent.

I turned my sight to the armour stand, realising I could use the extra air of authority granted by it.

"Is there a trial?" I asked.

"Yes, today at noon."

"Saru!" I roared, poking my head out the door and startling Nora. "Saru!" No response. "Where is he?" I murmured to myself.

My eyes lowered themselves to Nora.

"I need your help." I ducked back into my room and began strapping the polished steel plates around my feet.

"What?" Nora asked incredulously. "I can't do that," she admitted.

"Just come here; we are running out of time."

"Let me go get the shavinu."

As she turned to leave, I groused and reached out to grab her and pulled her into the room. "We have no time!"

Nora nodded and caged her insecurities. I instructed her as duly as I could, telling her how to strap the plate, the greaves, and having her help carry the gauntlets so that I could wear them when appropriate.

We ran out of my home. Along the way I caught Saru distracted and looking out of an open window in our kitchen where birds flocked together and chirped lifting songs. I didn't have time to explain myself as I ran to the stable.

Harry, my stable hand, was in the midst of feeding Zephyr and brushing him down.

"Saddling him will take too long," I said.

Nora took my gloved hand and led me out the gate.

"Then we need to find another way," she said and waved down one of the passing coaches.

The paunch gentleman riding it eyed me down. He suddenly seemed to realise who I was. With absolute professionalism, the driver simply tipped his hat and asked where we might wish to go.

"Outer ring," Nora said. "Strait District."

The driver confirmed he could take us and had us board.

⋖ ⋗

As the wagon trundled on, I noticed Nora shifting. She wanted to ask something.

"Something's bothering you. Just speak your mind." If I sounded irritated, it wasn't my intention. My own thoughts were far away with Dalila, thinking what I could do to save her from death.

Nora summoned whatever courage she needed to loosen her lips. "When I came to you, I was fully expecting you to put up a fight." It was unusual to see Nora be so unsure and vulnerable. "Yet, you jumped at the news and were already running to get dressed."

Nora's brow furrowed even further. "Like you said, you are the son of White-Hawk and Lady Imrie. A blessed union that gave us a Nephilim, a union designed to be a protector of Cleria. Why do you care so much about a young farmer girl like Dalila?"

I looked pointedly at her for a moment. "Would you rather I did nothing?" I asked.

Nora got slightly flustered. "N-no! That's not at all what I meant—"

I cut Nora off with a raised hand. Her final words escaped her as a soundless sigh. "It's alright," I reassured, forcing a smile of my own and putting my own haste on hold.

"Did you see Saru? The shavinu who serves me?"

Nora nodded.

"I found him when he was just a child. His eye was mutilated, cast out by his father. It was during an expedition out in Thickwood, during the aftermath of the Assamanian conflict."

"How horrid." There was a suppressed tone of sympathy in Nora's comment.

I nodded before continuing. "I saved him, took him in as my own. It's a bad habit of mine, you see. An incessant need to help others."

Nora nodded, considering what I said. "But why?"

I allowed the most spectral of smiles on my lips. "Because I can, because I am in a position to help." I felt immediate guilt for not speaking the entire truth, yet it was enough to placate Nora.

⤝　⤞

When we arrived, I noticed that I had forgotten my coin purse. Nora wordlessly paid for the fare.

"Are we early?" she asked.

I pondered, dreading the worst. "Maybe we are late."

Cleria was a place of riches and a booming economy. Unless one were inclined to the almost fanatical design of Museya in terms of artistry, anyone who dreamt of avarice would also dream of Cleria. It was all made of winding cobblestone, two-storey homes, and the sound of ringing chimes like a choir whenever someone entered a store. The entire place stunk of money and flowers.

But not Strait district; it was the closest thing to an underbelly. The place was entirely Spartan in its design. Beauty and bliss was made to run off its grey walls. The buildings themselves leered with an oppressive austerity which offered no quarter to the unfortunate.

Other than a few urchins sprawling the city streets and gutters, Cleria really did not have many criminals, but that seemed like low praise when considering a young child was on trial for being a witch.

"There!" Nora pointed, and I turned to follow her finger.

At the building opposite of the prison was the courthouse, a more intricate building with militant geometry.

It was wider than the prison and three storeys tall. There was a cloister inside the decorated courtyard where pillars worked their way around the bottom floor, upholding the colonnade veranda of the second floor.

Walking through the cloister was Eric accompanied by a crestfallen Dalila. Her chained and cuffed hands clanked with every step.

"Eric!" I called.

"Ah, Lieutenant General Erefiel, what an auspicious coincidence." Eric turned, his smile wide and welcoming, but his eyes were anything but.

"Stop it. Where are you taking the girl?"

Eric turned to Dalila. He looked confused.

"You mean the witch? Well, to the judicator, of course. Where else?" he offered placidly.

I nodded, at least grateful that the sorry excuse for a trial hadn't begun. I met Dalila's eyes, and for a moment, I was ready to give her my word that she would be fine. Except that I froze when her soulless eyes peered back at me, vapid and empty; I wasn't even sure if she recognised me.

Eric's look went from indifference to curiosity.

"Do you have some form of interest in the girl?" he asked.

"And what if I do?" I had to repress my anger. I rose to my full height and loomed over the jackal, but all I saw from his own cold eyes was amusement.

His stare held mine. Not once did they falter as finally, he simply shrugged his shoulders. "Whatever, my task is done, I am just to bring Dalila to the judicator." Eric sniffed the air. "Aureate air of this city doesn't agree with me, anyway."

He strode on. I noticed then the extra length of chain attached to Dalila's binds as Eric tugged her into motion.

My blood went raging hot. I tore the chain from Eric's grip and shoved him against one of the pillars.

"I'm sorry General, is something wrong?" he asked glibly.

I dangled the end of the chain before him as if to point out the obvious. "Do you enjoy degrading and ushering an innocent girl to her death?" I pressed through tight teeth, almost hissing. I stood close enough to notice his pocked skin.

He shrugged. "Do I enjoy it? Does it matter? I was tasked with it. If you have any complaints, you can take it up with my captain," he said matter-of-factly. He appeared jaded by my theatrics.

"Oh I will," I promised, more so to myself.

I unclasped the key from Eric's grip and took some satisfaction in tearing down his smile.

Nora stood stoically. She waited firm and patient for when she was needed.

I knelt down to Dalila. Her stare glazed over into the distance and was so listless I felt as if she didn't notice me.

"Dalila, it's me." A hand to her shoulder, I shook her slightly to get her attention. "It's Erefiel, do you remember me?" I asked, my smile weak and uncertain.

Her eyes finally rose to meet mine and they roamed back and forth, as if trying to ascertain who I was.

"Erefiel?" she asked uncertainly.

I turned with accusation towards Eric. "What did you do to her?" I asked.

Eric threw his arms in the air, seemingly as exacerbated as I was. "Nothing!" he said. "She was a bore the entire ride, never wanted to talk. Just kept staring out into the distance in that way." Any pretence of affability was now gone.

I turned to Dalila. "Listen to me, Dalila. You are going to be okay. Do you understand? I promise."

Dalila blinked. "Erefiel," she said, as if noticing my presence all over again.

"Yes?" I leaned in closer, my smile reassuring. I wanted to give her my ear and make sure I heard every last word she spoke.

"My family."

"What about them?"

"Can you make sure they are okay?" she asked, as if not hearing a single thing that I said before.

I nodded. "Of course," I promised.

Nora suddenly came and knelt beside me. "I will make sure they are safe," she said reassuringly.

"Ah, Nora." Dalila sounded so meek, so lost within an empty mind. "Is Jeremiah okay?"

Nora nodded. It was the first time that I truly saw the steadfast woman show vulnerability. Her voice noticeably cracked.

From the opposite end of the courtyard where the double rosewood doors swung open, there now stood a fair-skinned man of notable age and crowned hairline, his burgundy robe and scholarly spectacles noted his position within the courthouse.

"Eric Richardson? The Judicator will now see you." The man's lips curled into a sneer. Even his eyes openly held contempt for the man he addressed.

"Yes." Eric turned to us. "I seem to have been caught up in conversation," he said blithely.

I looked back to Dalila's shackles and quickly unlocked them. It took a lot to not let my displeasure show at her red and chafed wrists flaking with bits of skin.

"Erefiel," Dalila called, an ounce of lucidity to her. "What will happen to me?"

I bit my lip. I wanted to explain, but I couldn't afford to keep the judicator waiting any longer. "You will live." Was all I could promise.

Chapter Twenty-One

DALILA

What happens to those who venture beyond the Haar? Some stories say that you become unravelled. The very fibre of one's being is unmade and returns to its lapping mists. What will happen once the Haar returns to devour us all?

—A SCHOLAR'S MUSINGS BEFORE THE BIRTH OF
THE ELEVENTH SEED

Everything went by like a jaunting river, slow and smooth in its gait, yet blink an eye and one wonders how much time had passed. That was what the past two days were like. More and more my life felt like a living dream as I was torn from my home and hurled into an abrupt and unexpected series of events.

The journey with Eric had been the furthest I ever ventured from home, past Crowtown, past even the crossroads. We had arrived that very same day, and I was greeted by a most bewildering sight. The roads were filled with the cacophony of exchange and my feet felt the touch of cold stone rather than warm dirt.

I felt out of place, an unwelcome and ragged stain still dressed in my nightgown and bare feet. I hugged my book tightly and imagined the pressed bluebell in my mind's eye for comfort and courage. I struggled to gather my thoughts, as it seemed that every little bit of chatter bartered for my attention. My head spun left and right, trying to catch the endless stream of noise. The motley clothing of the citizens bled into each other to form one giant ink blot. A cloud of perfume wafted over me. It was almost as if it demanded to be smelt.

Someone was talking about an affair regarding a nobleman's son and herself with giddy excitement. Another person chatted about a new deal struck at the tailor's store. One raved about the statue of them sculpted by an Inspired and insisted that everyone should come and see. All too quickly, the sound congested into unbearable white noise.

If I had to comment on the second thing that struck me about the city, it would have to be the beautiful roads and homes. The roads were wide, and I wondered why no one walked through the centre. Then I saw the first carriage trudge on by with its gilded frame and beautifully lacquered wood.

The scent of tulips hung from above. I looked up at hanging pots mounted to balconies. Framed windows were opened for the taste of fresh air and washed bedsheets were hung to dry.

On the opposite window was a rather young gentleman who pressed an equally attractive woman against the windowsill. She giggled and playfully seemed to rebuke his advances, though she was laughing so I guessed she was enjoying the attention. The woman swivelled on her heel and shut the curtains.

The homes were somewhat similar to those of Crowtown, made of thatched frames, wooden upper stories, and its foundation was of solid stone. Yet those at Cleria were pristine and masterful by comparison. The doors to each home were preceded by railed steps; the doorframes themselves painted with turquoise blue, calming dark-brown, or other soothing tinges.

I shrunk into Eric's side and held on to the man; he didn't complain. He may have been a snake in human form, but at least he looked just as out of place as I did along those streets. Eric led me through the channel of souls and into a district with muted architecture. Militant shadows towered over me like the presence of Mount Morniar.

They kept me in a small, empty room to pass the time until my trial the next day. My Kaseluda had been confiscated. Eric reassured me he would return it after the trial with an insincere smile. I was too tired to argue. Sleep became my refuge. I found Perry waiting for me. He had been partially absorbed by the bark of a tree to show his grey and decomposing expression.

My heart remained back at the farm, back at the woods. I felt like a hollow and distant shell. My lips were too enervated to ever make a sound. My listless eyes were glued against wooden walls.

The very next morning I was escorted out of my room in a daze and became entirely aware of the strangeness of this place of marbled floor and grand halls. The vastness of this world made me think I entered the home of giants.

Some part of my consciousness remained with Perry, watching his shut eyes and pallid expression upheld by the frame of the tree which absorbed him. He seemed so peaceful, almost as if he was sleeping. I awoke from a daze and saw Erefiel and Nora before me.

I tried to smile and failed.

Chapter Twenty-Two

EREFIEL

While witches who are taken into the Faithful church are forbidden
from practising their magic, other sisters who require a medium face no
such prejudice. They are yet free to use any Haar magic or colour magic
at their disposal.

—Laws of the Abbey by Greshell Fayma

The courthouse's inner lobby proved spacious and decadent in a militaristic sort of way. A wide set of stairs led up and then to the right. The courtroom we eventually arrived at was mostly barren of life except for a few souls. A single judicator waited. She sat behind a high table at the very back of the room.

I recognized her as Judge Felicie Auburn. Everything about her was comparable to an old crone: withered and wizened with skin pulled over slender bones. Her hair was coarse and pitch-black. Intelligent, owl-like eyes peered through beady glasses and her thin lips were perfect for pursing. The woman was built like a switch in her litheness but also in personality. She had a reputation for being quick of mind, efficient, unmovable in her judgement, and ambitious beyond compare on top of that.

I was relieved that it wasn't the likes of Branson preceding over the case. Paunch bellied and unmoving in their ignorance rather than in their opinion. A single word like "witch" would have been enough to condemn Dalila to death at worst, or imprisonment at best.

I knew the law, and Felicie was the best chance at getting Dalila into the church of the Faithful.

There was also a Mother from the Faithful Church, clad in her white robes to portray purity. The other attendees were a bailiff, and one single notary hidden away in her corner with pen, ink, and paper.

"Good day, Judge Auburn," Eric said, tipping an imaginary hat.

Auburn's groan sounded almost like a snarl.

"Go on," I urged and encouraged Dalila with a soft touch to her back. The girl turned to me for just a moment before approaching the podium just in front of the judge's eyeline.

Nora and I took our seats at the very back, while Eric seemed to have wanted a closer view of the proceedings. He propped his muddied shoes on the backrest of a bench in the front. Judge Auburn cleared her throat to dissuade Eric of such behaviour.

Dalila reached the podium but proved too short to make herself seen.

"Bailiff," Judge Auburn's intention noted with a nod. The stout and trusted man needed no further instructions as he grabbed a chair from the corner and placed it to provide Dalila the extra height she needed to look over the lip of the stand.

"Name?" Auburn asked curtly.

Dalila said something entirely inaudible.

"Louder," Auburn commanded, meanwhile scribbling away at her pages.

I heard the brief sound of a name spoken; meek and frigid. Auburn didn't say anything, almost as if waiting for Dalila to still try again. Several still and awkward moments passed and I entirely feared and respected Auburn's command over her realm.

"A little louder, child," said the Mother from the Faithful church with a straight but not unkind tenor. She was a willowy woman of considerable age, her posture straight and confident. I was glad that the emissary sent to observe the proceedings was not a venomous toad.

"Dalila!" Dalila almost had to shout, yet her name barely passed for being audible.

"Last name?" Auburn sounded more and more impatient with every passing moment.

I rose to my feet. "Her name is Dalila Reed. Could we please get on with the proceedings? The girl is innocent."

A tense silence filled the courtroom. Eric gave a bemused chuckle, but not even that cut through the tension. I recognized my mistake the moment I spoke. The regret I felt was not for my sake, but for Dalila. I needed to be patient.

My fingers clenched about the backrest of the bench before me; the wood felt ready to splinter. Nora placed a reassuring hand on mine to instil some calm in me.

"Erefiel Numyana." Judge Felicie Auburn removed her glasses and met my gaze.

"I know not why you are here, and frankly, I do not care. There are proper channels, papers, cases to be made. There are laws here to be followed. This woman has come here to be tried as a witch."

"Yet she is only just a young girl, not a woman—she means no harm."

"That isn't for you to decide," she retorted. "The law states that when such an individual is discovered to be a witch, she is to come forth and reveal herself post-haste. If the individual does not comply, they are to be prosecuted with extreme prejudice."

"At risk of being torn away from the life they knew? To never see her family again? The law is archaic." I thought it wise to not mention the penalty for a witch with intent to practice.

Auburn placed down her pen, and her smile was anything but friendly. Her stern fingers folded over the knuckles of her hands as if in prayer.

"Erefiel Numyana. Do I show up to your garrison and shit on your porch? Do I tell you how to lead your men? Do *I* accost you with things outside my jurisdiction?"

I said nothing.

"I thought so. If you have a vested interest in this girl, you may make your claim in time, but until then, this is my throne room, and I expect you to respect that." Completely unperturbed, her spectacles slotted themselves back onto the bridge of her thorny nose.

Eric did a laughable job at trying to hide his chuckle. I snarled under my breath and returned to my seat.

"She will be alright," Nora whispered.

Dalila understood the issue, and now more clearly introduced herself as Dalila Reed, daughter to Robert Reed and Miriam Reed.

"Good," Auburn said, seemingly mollified.

"Now, Miss Reed, as it were: you stand trial within the holy city of Cleria, and are prosecuted on the grounds of being a witch." A moment of dramatic silence. "How do you plead?" Auburn asked.

Dalila did not respond right away. She just looked down absent-mindedly. The seconds droned on into minutes and the fragile silence of the room thickened. Yet none of that made Dalila speak any faster.

"If you offer no defence on your end, then I will have no choice but to prosecute as such and charge you for being unwilling to cooperate," Auburn stated matter-of-factly.

Finally, when it seemed as if Auburn was at her wit's end, Dalila's first words came like a distant crackle.

"I do not know why I am being held here," she said. "Did I do something wrong?" she asked.

Auburn smiled. "You are a witch," she said, as if it were the most obvious thing in the world.

"But I didn't know that. I simply tried to help. All I did was heal my injured friend."

"And level trees with a scream," Auburn added, the gravity of her tone intentional.

"To protect my friends!" Finally, Dalila's voice became challenging, lively, lucid even.

Auburn suppressed a small chuckle as if not understanding the concept. "The law is the law, young one. It doesn't matter for what ends and purposes you used your powers, what matters is that you used them. If it is true and you discovered those powers within the forest, then you should have come forth and revealed your identity after the event. But you didn't. For all I know, you may have known about your true nature for far longer than you let on."

My fingers wrapped around the backrest again. I suppressed my agitation at Auburn's tone. It was clear that Dalila was a young and innocent girl, born to a testing fate, and not some plotting witch bent on burning the world to ash.

Dalila looked as if she wanted to say something but then held her tongue. I couldn't bear to watch any longer.

"It was my fault." I rose from my seat and heard Nora snarl beside me. Even Eric looked surprised; if it was because of the truth or because I so foolishly admitted it, I didn't know.

Nora tugged at my arm. "Sit down!" She hissed underneath her breath.

Auburn eyed me again. "Explain," she commanded. I matched her stare.

"I was aware of the truth when I met Dalila after the incident. She confided in me. I advised her to tell no one of what happened lest she face the dire repercussions," I lied. It was a cleverly hidden lie. I made sure to make no mention of Nora and her report, nor that Dalila's parents also knew of the truth.

Auburn's eyes narrowed deeply and her lips pursed till it looked like an arid fault line. "If what you are saying is true, there may be dire consequences for keeping such secrets. Are you sure, Erefiel Numyana? Son of White-Hawk, son of Lady Imrie?" Her words were slow and deliberate—she was asking me to reconsider, providing a chance to take back my words. The names of my parents were spoken to remind me of my station.

I wasn't going to back down.

"I am certain." Not an ounce of hesitation in my voice.

I knew that the cost I was to pay was a simple stain on my family's name. Father would disapprove and mother would be disappointed. I vowed to never have to rely on their status to get what I wanted, but I had to make an exception for Dalila.

Auburn sighed. "I respect your resolve, Erefiel, even if I do find it to be foolhardy. You leave me little choice. I will have to charge you on grounds of withholding information important to the state."

"I am fully aware," I acquiesced.

"He is lying," said the frail and timid voice of Dalila. "I said nothing to no one." Though sombre and melancholic, I was astounded to sense not a hint of hesitation or fear in Dalila's voice. Her words cut through the moment with an unexpected weight. Yet it wasn't bravery that came from her, but rather resignation.

Auburn pinched the bridge of her nose and squeezed her tired eyes shut, becoming irked by the show. "Little girl, I would reconsider. If it is true what Erefiel is saying, then your judgement may be softened."

"He lies." The words were spoken cold and quick. "He has nothing to do with this."

"But—!"

"That is enough!" Auburn raised her voice, cutting me short. "She has made her peace, Lieutenant General Erefiel. I suggest you do the same." The exaggerated way with which she spoke my name was with mock respect for my title and heritage. "Speak for the defendant again and you will be escorted from court." Her word was law, and I returned to my seat, defeated and deflated.

Nora's hand took mine and squeezed. I turned to face her, to reassure her, but was surprised to find the blazing fire reflected in her resolute stare. She hadn't given up yet. I smiled, remembering why I wanted her in my regiment. It was because of that infectious and seemingly bottomless resolve of hers. The battle wasn't over yet. Nora reminded me of that as she reminded others on the battlefield.

Questions were asked, and Dalila answered them to the best of her ability. She hadn't known of her powers before the day of the Morning Bell.

Dalila recounted what had happened: the healing, the screaming, and the loss of her love. Though in Dalila's version, Nora was not privy to her awakened powers and her friends had all lost consciousness. It wasn't entirely the truth and we all knew it. Jeremiah told her parents who passed on the report. But it was a minor enough lie to be ignored. Afterall, justice just asked for Dalila's blood, and no one else's.

"Mother Vinrie?" Judge Auburn addressed. The till now quiet Mother watched Dalila, her stare phlegmatic, her poise resolute. With the kind of composure expected of the pious and committed, Mother Vinrie made her calculations.

"I do not sense any malfeasance from the young girl's actions," she stated.

"That is not your call to make. I wish to hear about your professional opinions regarding her powers, and anything else that may be relevant." Auburn had a knack for robbing the wind from people's sails whenever they did something unagreeable. I surely respected her skill in constantly reasserting her position but this seemed like one case where it backfired.

"It most assuredly is relevant!" Mother Vinrie clapped back. "We don't just look at their potential for power, but also at their character. I know not if she truly did speak to Sir Erefiel about her powers, but it doesn't matter. What I *do* know is that she willingly refused Erefiel's chance at a lighter punishment because she didn't want to inconvenience the man. Selflessness is an attribute most highly valued among the Faithful. We serve selflessly and we do so gladly." The last part was spoken with the slightest hint of reverence.

Judge Auburn nodded. Her pressing was a test of character, and she found Mother Vinrie a good representative.

"As for everything else," Mother Vinrie continued, "the girl seems to truly have the power of an Inspired, barring of course, any sort of instrument used as a medium. This fact deems her to be classified as a witch. Would the church take her in?"

A momentary beam of hope. Perhaps Dalila wouldn't return to the life she knew, but at least she would live.

"The church would consider it, but there is still the question of responsibility. The lack of a proper representative makes it impossible to take her in. Witches of the past were represented by their family. Seeing as how Dalila was raised outside of Cleria's direct reach, I would need to find someone to take on that task. Only then can we teach her the ways of the Faithful."

"That won't be necessary," Auburn responded.

"Beg your pardon?"

"Dalila Reed, given to your title as a witch, you failed to comply with the law and give yourself in to the proper authorities within an acceptable time-frame. Due to the lack of representatives within the church of the Faithful at this time, you will be tried as a witch with intent to conspire against the state and to harm. It is with a heavy heart that I sentence you to burning at the stake." What a cold hag. I misjudged her. This was just the kind of case to elevate her position and Auburn was going for the kill.

Eric gave a long and blithe whistle at the statement.

"Wait!" Mother Vinrie pleaded, her previous composure broken.

"I will be her ward!" I jumped from my seat, my voice frantic and booming. Was I out of breath?

Judge Auburn's gavel froze mid-air; she was prepared to finalise her rule. Auburn stared at me and gave pause.

"What do you mean?" Auburn asked cautiously.

"I will take responsibility for the girl."

"You can't *adopt* her," Auburn clarified.

"I wasn't planning to. She will be bound to my name, to the name of the Numyana household. What she does will be done so with my reputation on the line."

"As well as that of your parents," Auburn reminded.

The mention of my parents gave me momentary pause. My fists clenched hard into my palm as I swallowed my pride. I nodded stiffly.

Auburn looked at Mother Vinrie, who seemed just as shocked.

"Well, is it possible?" Auburn asked.

"It is entirely unprecedented that a member of the Faithful, a witch no less, would be represented by someone of Erefiel's station. *No*—to be represented by White-Hawk himself." She gave herself a moment of pause to consider. "But it would be accepted. There is no greater representative than an accessory of the Elders themselves."

Perhaps I imagined it, but I would have liked to think that there was an air of relief even around Judge Auburn as she struck down her gavel.

"Very well, under the name of the Numyana household, declared by the present Erefiel Numyana, Dalila Reed is to be inserted into the church of the Faithful as one of its carers on the following grounds: Firstly, any action she takes part in is a direct reflection of the Numyana household, should she transgress on any of her duties, the Numyana household will take responsibility in whatever form the court sees appropriate. Dalila Reed will thus represent the church and the Numyana household to an acceptable degree, agreed upon by all parties. Equally, from this day hence, Dalila Reed is to never partake in witchcraft again. Breaking her pact will result in termination of her ties with all parties and result in immediate execution by burning at the stake."

There was silence at the decree.

"Any objections?"

There were none, and the gavel struck a final time.

Chapter Twenty-Three

DALILA

There are stories older than time. These are flames which have long since passed their glory days. One such tale survives as embers, shared from one cautious tongue to the next lest its fire be witnessed from Mount Morniar. Seven artefacts are said to exist, imbibed with the primordial colours which painted Minethria. Each weapon exhibits its own unique properties. If these artefacts do exist, none know where they have gone.

—HERETICAL SCRIPTURE OF THE EXILED SCHOLAR,
BY BRICIUS LIVVERY

Mother Vinrie was a curious soul. I could not discern her character outright, if she was good or not, strict or kind, cruel or gentle. She was built thin with rosy cheeks and a deepness to her eyes akin to the sombre stillness of glaciers. Her hair was hidden behind a curved, white habit with golden rim, including her draped stole which hung down to her chest.

After the trial was over, ghostly hands pulled at me for private conversations. Erefiel expressed concern and his promises were apparent, but I couldn't quite remember what he said or how I responded.

Upon exiting another backdoor to the courthouse, I came upon a lot where a fanciful carriage waited. Its edges were curled and deliberate, as if traced from a loose strand of hair in the form of an S. The construction was delicately framed with a golden rim all around.

The carriage sported double doors with a step to climb aboard, and when I was led to sit inside, I felt almost ashamed to sit on the most exquisite puffed pillows of vermilion I had ever seen. Especially with my still grimy nightgown. Mother Vinrie sat opposite me.

My hands were clenched against my knees, bundling a fistful of my gown to give shape to my twisted tension. My restless toes fidgeted, curling and tugging at their adjacent twins. My stare lingered on the floor as the carriage trudged along its path and joined the traffic of Cleria.

Not a great deal had been spoken between Mother Vinrie and me, except for her occasional comments and directions and my own wordless nods. I wondered what my own mother would say if she were with me at that moment; I felt she would give a slight tug on my ear and tell me to remember my manners.

"Thank you," I said coyly. Those were the only two words that I could think of.

Mother Vinrie nodded. "Don't thank me yet, child. You may soon come to resent me."

I pulled harder against my gown.

"Where am I going?" I asked, my voice resigned and furtive.

"To the Church of the Faithful," Mother Vinrie supplied.

I wasn't too sure about what the church was. My father did speak about them in passing at times, but never to me, and it was always done so with a sense of deference. Yet why did I get the feeling that everyone else knew something I didn't? I just heard it was an independent house of worship filled with women.

"Will I become a Faithful?" I asked.

Mother Vinrie nodded.

"What does that mean?"

"You will live as one of us, care for the shrines made in the image of Seeds and the Elders. It is a place of respect and worship. Some come to the church to ask for the Elder's ear so that their pleas may be heard and to show their piety. It is also where the great tithe is to be gathered and delivered to the lordships on the coming day every year."

I could hear the crowds outside the carriage. Just muffled laughter or spirited musings. It was all too jovial to be deciphered from inside the carriage, especially given my mood.

"Can I see my parents?"

That was the only question to which I was rewarded silence.

⌐ ⌐

The carriage came to a halt and the driver opened the doors. I was immediately struck with a remarkable sight. I gasped despite my stone encrusted heart.

It truly was like a cathedral made entirely of marble so white, I first mistook it for ivory. The front entrance sported immense double-doors which towered over the other surrounding buildings. It was hard to tell, but I judged the high walls of the place at five storeys and though the doors were indeed crafted as if for giants, it wasn't particularly wide.

On each door were carved reliefs of women facing each other, each facet done with meticulous detail from the lashes all the way to how their holy gowns creased and draped like a waterfall. The figures were on their knees, fingers wrapped over knuckles in prayer and their heads bowed in permanent deference. My eyes trailed the craftsmanship to the tensed strain of the chiselled feet, toes bent against the floor with perpendicular heels. I almost tripped on the rising steps.

"Careful," Mother Vinrie said as she almost glided.

I wondered who would open the great doors and give us entry. Surely Mother Vinrie was nowhere near strong enough? Did we have to knock? My childish musings were put to rest when I noticed a smaller and more inconspicuous door built to the bottom of the grand ones.

Upon entering, only women tread the long blanched halls, all of them clad in a similar white to Mother Vinrie to symbolise their devotion and purity. It looked like a turgid river of milk strolling through the austere hall. My gaze trailed up to the ivory sky, and I noticed a sterile odour.

"Hurry on up! We need to bathe you!" Mother Vinrie chided as she relentlessly pushed me into the coursing currents.

⊰ ⊱

The room I was guided into was bare, and I was relieved to find no one stationed to bathe me.

"Don't take too long, Mother Margaret will be here to help dress you. Find me afterwards." The door closed, and I jolted a little at the sound. The room was uncomfortably quiet after the constant barrage of sound. I was left to think on the events of the previous day, realising I didn't have a single moment to consider what had swept me into this moment.

I faced the contents of the room. A soft cloud of vapour slightly obscured the tiled flooring. At its centre, a wooden and curiously large tub awaited me. Stripping out of the nightgown and taking a moment to notice the dirt which smeared me, I made my way to the tub.

Gently, I lowered myself to the water's warm embrace and just let my body relax. The heat immediately did wonders to knead out the tension in my cold limbs and unfurl the anxious grip of my toes. I made waves in the water with the motions of my hand, and took note of the slish-slosh.

I knew that this was all fleeting, this moment of respite, this moment of privacy and quiet before I had to return to the outside world. I imagined what it would be like being a Sister of this Church, humouring ideas of praying and speaking with a serene cadence.

Caked dirt peeled from me and sunk in the pool, but not just dirt. Memories of the farm seeped from my pores and dispersed in the water, memories of disgruntled afternoons or time spent with my friends. I recalled how I sulked about something Fred did. Ben scraping his knee climbing the tree—he begged me not to tell mom and dad in between his cries. More and more of the memories on the water's surface distorted; pulled apart until there was nothing left.

"Mother said the Haar was endless possibility," I voiced out into the vacant room. I entertained the idea of being unmade, a scrubbed canvas to remake myself on.

Feeling I had used up the extent of my offered recluse, I started scrubbing away at the skin with a bristled brush to rid myself of the more stubborn muck. My eyes fell on the scars trailing my wrists. They told a story, a story about loss, about resentment, about love. I ran a finger over their bumpy tracks and tried my best to recount the days of their conception as if they were points on a calendar.

One, I recounted to be the day when Ben tried his best to be more helpful about the farm—obviously with his new feather tucked behind his ear. I recalled it because the cut was longer and deeper than the usual ones, and there was a brief moment of intense panic.

I worked my way down to another and recalled as if it were a distant memory when Fredrick offered me a piece of his bread wordlessly. I took it, not because I cared for the bread, but because it was one of the few times when Fredrick truly tried to reach out to me.

Somewhere among the tallied days was the first of them all, the day where I felt so withered and my heart was like a distant thrum, my breath so ragged that it stumbled over itself. I couldn't feel anything. That was the first day I let my skin bleed to bloodlet my sorrows and the rotting of my soul. It was somewhere in there, lost among the myriad of other cuts.

I traced further. Recalling when Father was wholly nervous and gifted mother her necklace. Then another distant thought struck me.

"My book!" I cried out loud.

I writhed within the bathtub, its waters splashing to the tiled floor, the distilled memories gone with the thrashing waves. Most of the steam had dissipated as I worked my way to the folded clothes waiting for me in the corner. I almost slipped.

I was supposed to call in another Faithful when I was done to help me dress, but there was no time: Eric had my book.

❦

I hastily dressed myself in the clothes and on the third frantic attempt to bind the habit I finally gave up and did a simple tie underneath my chin rather than tentatively around the bun of my hair. The seam of the clothing itself was lopsided.

My wet feet slapped the marble as I strode through the hall. The white, uncoloured rim of my shoes hanging in my hand as I cut through the deliberate and slow passing of my new Sisters who looked at me as if I were a wet dog that broke into their holy house.

My sprint showed purpose, the women moving out of my way as I ran past. All except for one.

Mother Vinrie stood stern and admonishing before me. "Where do you think you are going?" she asked.

Her frown parted when she took a good look at me. "I need to see Eric!" I said.

Mother Vinrie frowned. "The man who brought you? Why do you need to see him?"

"He has my book," I explained.

Mother Vinrie shifted towards apologetic, the heads of other sisters turning and slight gossiping whispers exchanged among their peers. Yet Mother Vinrie paid them no heed as she placed a hand on my shoulder. "You aren't allowed to bring any personal belongings with you on this journey."

"Please?" I begged. "It is a copy of the Kaseluda, and the only way I have to remember my family."

Mother Vinrie sighed and nodded understandingly. "I'll see what I can do," she said.

⋦ ⋗

Appropriately scolded for my behaviour, Mother Vinrie took me to Mother Margaret, who began to dress me properly this time. Her hands worked as if she were embroidering a work of art. She showed me how to fasten the habit and tie the loose seams, her tone patient and soothing. I braced myself for when she found my scars. She said nothing. Instead, her nimble fingers danced between the threads despite their age and before I knew it, the whole thing was pulled tight about me like a lace. I barely had time to admire the white robe—it was by far the most beautiful thing I had ever worn.

"Find Mother Vinrie, she still has need for you," Mother Margaret said with a warm smile before sending me off; I was too shy to ask where Mother Vinrie's room was.

I stepped out of the chamber and was made starkly aware of how much I didn't belong. I was a newborn, a blank canvas not yet ready for my colour. Without a single second to adjust myself to this new life, I was thrust completely into the middle of it.

It took a while of wandering before I found Mother Vinrie, or rather, when she found me.

"Dalila! I haven't got all day!" A hand grabbed me. It was Mother Vinrie pulling me into her room. "I know this is a lot in one day, but get it together!" She barked. I barely understood what she was saying. "Dalila! Are you listening?" She shouted.

I forced myself to pay attention as Mother Vinrie listed my responsibilities in quick succession.

First, I was to take care of the temple and be a shining and unquestioning servant of the Elders. Second, I would have classes daily whereby I would learn of our history and the truth of the world; Father would have been envious of such a chance. Thirdly, I would offer aid and help to all who needed it and represent the best and most selfless part of man.

It was the fourth duty, made only for me, that caught me off guard.

"I am not allowed to use magic?" I asked timidly.

Mother Vinrie stopped her explanation and turned to me. "Well, of course. You are a witch. Part of the amnesty granted to you is that you are to completely refrain from using any magic. Doing so will instantly excommunicate you from the church." Mother Vinrie hesitated. "It will also create a great deal of burden for Erefiel."

I hung my head. I didn't particularly care about the magic, nor did

I ever really consider using it outright. But having the choice taken away from me felt like being robbed of something important.

Mother Vinrie sighed, all the pent up tension left her. On a beat, her mood again shifted to a genteel and warm figure, underneath the façade of someone having to maintain her duties. She allowed herself a moment of vulnerability as she knelt and cast me with caring eyes. I allowed that kindness to ground me in the moment.

"Listen, Dalila. This world that you have been thrown into isn't fair, but it is what it is. You have a lot to think about, and I wouldn't wish this fate upon anyone. But this was the only solution, the only way to prevent you from being burnt at the stake."

Mother Vinrie made a slight nod, gesturing at my arm. "We all carry our burdens, and I won't ask you to talk about something you don't wish to. I won't be lenient, as I cannot afford to show any favouritism, but I do have sympathy for your situation. If you ever need to talk, I will try my best to be there."

I nodded, though I didn't fully grasp the meaning of her words, I did understand her tone. Mother Vinrie was apologising for her future harshness. Father did it all the time. I felt exposed as I withdrew from the woman.

"Are there others like me?" I asked softly, my head bowed and my hands twisting a knot into my robe. A habit Mother Vinrie quickly dissuaded with a soft slap on my hands.

"Witches?" she asked. "Yes, but none your age. The last witch to be born is already seventy years old and works as one of our longest carers. There used to be more, but fortunately, it seems they are a rarer occurrence." I felt hurt at that comment, did she suggest that my birth was undesirable?

"Can I meet her?"

"You will soon enough," Mother Vinrie commented.

Chapter Twenty-Four

DALILA

While Cleria may be the golden city of civilization and Museya the soul of art, the world of Bolton is an ugly but efficient machine. It wears a hat knitted from its spewed smog; the black lungs cough its corruption up into a diseased sky. It is said that within its streets, people walk smeared in soot and match the blackened bones of their homes. It is here where the containers for the Haar are crafted, so that the Haar can be captured for the mistmages of Cleria.

—SUMMARY ON BOLTON AND ITS ECONOMY

The chamber I was led into next was just as sterile and of blanched marble like the rest of the building. Pillars of opal white hugged the walls and half vanished into them. This part of the building was empty.

I mostly felt lost and confused, but there were a few pleasant experiences to go with this new world. Like the shoes I wore and how snug they felt.

I found my appearance to be a strange sight—never before was I privy to white clothing, the only other time I had seen such an attire was when women of the church strolled through Crowtown. I felt a soft tug at my heart when I imagined how my family would react to seeing such pristine garments.

Mother Vinrie returned my attention to the room where I beheld an old, withered crone who supported herself on a cane.

At the two furthest corners of the room stood two strange, out-of-place statues like guards from some gothic castle.

They stood at attention with two pronged spears in hand leading to a point. Their faces were hidden behind metal masks of such intricate and patient detail, depicting stoic and angelic features. Filigree sprouts curled upon the surface of the dull iron; the stems were braided at the edges to then take the form of spread wings.

The statues were dressed in white robes with faint imprints of falling feathers. A see-through veil hung from their backs like a cape.

Their complexion was an odd earthy blue, like the type born of mould over cracked and detailed skin. The hands, composed of three long fingers and a single thumb, were wrapped around the metal haft of their spears.

They weren't statues done in poor taste like I thought. Lifeless and inhuman eyes jumped to me from behind their iron masks. I vanished behind Mother Vinrie's body.

She chuckled. "Worry not, they are not here to harm you. They are angels, sent by the Grand Archon to ensure our church's safety."

I nodded but still couldn't come out of my cover.

"Come here, child. Let me get a closer look at you," said the old woman. She didn't seem to notice the guards in the back and simply waited in front of a rounded table of marble.

Rather than wearing the typical white of the church, her clothing was the darkest of blacks. Her wrinkled skin formed granules and valleys across her face, as her eyes hung sallow and yet still full of stubborn life. Her wrinkled and quivering lips trembled and pursed over missing teeth as she looked me over.

I hesitantly approached her. "What's your name?" she asked me, taking my chin into her hands, her eyes inspecting me rather than paying attention to my words.

"Dalila," I replied.

"Ah, that is a good name."

"Who are you?" I asked.

She chuckled. "Why, I am a witch, just like you. Lucia is my name, Lucia Gievan."

I frowned. "Why are you wearing all black?"

Now it was Mother Vinrie's turn to laugh. "Mother Lucia has served her time; she is now one of the Impure."

I turned worriedly to the old woman in obvious panic.

Lucia's cracked laugh was hearty. "Don't you worry, child, it is not a bad thing." She tugged on the hem of my robe and rubbed it with her wrinkled and withered thumb. I was surprised to see the condition of her manicured and groomed thumb nail which only slightly extended over the end.

"You see this?" she asked. "This colour, it is pure white. You still have so much of your purity to give to this house, to what it represents." Lucia pointed out towards Mother Vinrie. "The greater you serve, the greater you age, the more of your purity is given, until there is nothing left."

Lucia now addressed her own clothing. "I have given all I had to give. I have done my time, I now walk as someone unbound to the church. Or well… mostly unbound. It is a sign that my duty has been done." Perhaps I imagined it, but I thought to sense only the slightest bit of sadness at her correction.

"So, why are you here?" I asked.

"For you," Mother Vinrie said.

"Come." Lucia pulled me on my wrist, her grip tentative yet firm.

She walked briskly upon her cane, far quicker and livelier than someone her age had any right to, and pulled me up two steps towards a round marble pedestal in the corner that reached up to my neck.

Upon it lay a small cylindrical container of glass, its top and bottom sealed and closed off by bolted metal. Within, I could see trapped smoke curling and roiling as if it were vapour. The way it writhed, with such a slow rhythm, made it seem as if the coiling content was sentient. Next to it, I saw a bowl of the deepest, most virile blue I had ever seen.

My eyes widened after a moment when I understood what the objects were. There was a difference between the tales and experiencing something first hand. Up until that point, I had only ever heard stories, and that was all they were to me: stories. But at that moment, I was standing in the face of something I never expected to witness in person.

"Is that?" My question trailed off, refusing to even speak the words.

Lucia nodded. "The Haar." She hissed the word.

I now looked at the cylinder a second time and found the coiling mist more reminiscent of a serpent's movement.

"And this." Lucia turned my attention to the bowl. "Is ink; colour-magic."

"What is it for?"

"To test you."

I looked at her with obvious confusion, and then at Mother Vinrie. "I thought I wasn't allowed to use magic?"

Mother Vinrie nodded. "This will be the last instance that you will be permitted. Mother Lucia is here to provide support and providence, and to also confirm that you can indeed perform magic. She has also been permitted to use her abilities in this extenuating circumstance to ensure that nothing goes wrong. We wish to use the Haar and colour-magic to test the extent of your capabilities before we test your innate magic."

I looked at the strange and frightful angels standing in their corner and began to understand their true purpose.

Lucia seemed to notice as she leaned in to whisper only for me. "Don't worry," she said in hushed tones. "I won't let them hurt you," she promised. I believed her.

Hesitantly, I turned to the items and pursed my lips, my fingers wrapped around the cold marble of the table.

"What am I supposed to do?"

"Perform magic."

Lucia leaned forward and unwound a dial at the bottom of the cylinder. The hissing began as a distant whisper and then turned into a warning rush. From a small pin-size hole, the mists extruded and billowed into balls of white fog.

Unexplainable panic built into me.

"What am I supposed to do?" I asked, suddenly realizing how clueless I was.

"Mould it," Lucia advised rather casually. She didn't share my alarm.

I focused on the mist: a cat, a chair, an eagle, a well, a flower, a stag, a spider. Images and thoughts flitted through my mind in great flashes, yet still the mist did not take shape, simply whirling in on itself with fleeting patience.

"Child. Mould it." Lucia's command was sterner this time, the urgency trickling.

I glanced deeply into the mist, but my strained mind could make nothing of the shape. I gritted my teeth and grunted with pure effort.

I noticed the edges forming into straight blocks, colour bleeding into the mist. I felt relief at first, thinking it finally heeded me. But then I noticed that the shapes kept changing, a small-necked creature momentarily forming, its face pressed against the clouds mid-transformation as I watched the minute features of some horror groan. Claws trapped behind the walls of mist raked, then there came a thrashing tail, then the being shifted undecidedly between many bulbous forms. An eye poked through the mist and watched me with terrifying curiosity. The eyelid blinked and revealed itself to be made by writhing maggots.

Terror took hold as I dropped my mind and turned away with a shriek.

The threat was gone in a flash. I watched the mist suddenly break from its horrifying vision and turn into a miniature apple in the hand of Lucia.

"So," she began. "Perhaps not a Haar user." Lucia bit into the apple.

I cowered behind Mother Vinrie, and it took a few words of reassurance before Lucia could lead me to the blue ink. The only advice she gave was that blue was the colour of serenity, of calm, of healing and of caring. Yet even when she took my still trembling hand and made me dip my thumb into it, I wasn't able to evoke any kind of spell.

"Are you sure she is a witch?" Lucia asked Mother Vinrie, her tone almost sounding irked as if this were an entire waste of time.

"The reports are certain."

Lucia turned to me. "So tell me, what *can* you do?"

I thought about it for a moment.

Taking Lucia's palm and holding it over mine, I raised my free hand and called upon my light as easily as I evoked my voice.

"Unbelievable." Mother Vinrie gasped.

My golden light enveloped Lucia's hand, and her lips gave a frightful shudder as she watched her skin turn youthful. Sagging skin tightened about her fingers and the bony outline of her hand began to vanish. Lucia tore away from me and coveted the de-aged hand with its older twin.

She gawked in bewilderment. "Incredible," she said, echoing Mother Vinrie.

Just as promptly, her skin sagged and returned to fit its appropriate age.

"Like The Lady of Pain." Lucia gave a restrained nod. She took my hands in hers with such speed I didn't think possible. Her cane fell and clattered to the floor with a forgotten echo.

"You are blessed, my child, with a divine gift. You may not be able to use it, but it is a sign, a sign that you were born to heal, a sign of great things to come," my mentor promised. There was an uneasy fervour which stared through her wide eyes.

Chapter Twenty-Five

NORA

Some mortals challenge the Elders despite better counsel. Hegir the
Guile was one such man. He made a bet that should the Blacksmith
craft an indestructible shield, then Hegir would admit the Blacksmith
to be the greatest forgemaster. Blacksmith obliged. Hegir knew full well
that the Blacksmith would succeed and when he took the shield, he did so
with glee. What Hegir did not know was that all attacks phased right
through it. He never did get to deliver his praise.

—TALES OF THE MOUNTAIN, BY BLACK SUMMER

My sword hammered against Erefiel's shield. Again and again his defences denied me any meaningful strike. The most I managed was keeping the Nephilim on his toes. By the end, I was the only one left panting and drenched in sweat.

"Satisfied?" Erefiel asked.

"No, sir."

Erefiel raised his practice shield to parry another swing. It annoyed me that he had not used his sword hand even once.

I stumbled and fell to my rear, exhausted. My chest heaved. My sweat-matted hair stuck to my forehead.

"Now I am."

Erefiel gave an approving nod and did away with his shield and sword. He was barefooted along the wooden floor of his training room, his pants rolled up at the bottom and his loose tunic rustling in the light breeze from the open window. With the wind came the scent of dandelions and birds could be heard deep in song.

When first we returned to his home, a home he insisted was humble in comparison to his parents' estate, he invited me in for some tea. But when he saw my brooding, something changed in his approach, and instead he led me to this room.

It was a bare chamber with polished floorboards; it was enough to hold perhaps twenty sparring partners.

All around the edges of the sparring room were ornamental weapons ranging from maces to spears to slotted holders of swords and the occasional suit of armour to divide the decoration.

"Nothing like a good workout to get the emotions out," Erefiel said. I also tossed aside my own practice sword. "Where did you learn to fight?" he asked.

I recalled how stern and authoritative he was with me when we first met. Now there was an approachable lilt to the way he addressed me. Perhaps it was because I no longer served in his regiment?

When I didn't answer, Erefiel continued. "I am certain you didn't learn that in my army. We don't train our soldiers to fight like that."

"My uncle," I finally answered.

"Your uncle? What kind of uncle would need to know how to fight?"

I hesitated. "The complicated type."

"Ah," Erefiel voiced, surmising my meaning. "*That* kind of uncle."

He ambled across to find a seat beside me.

I looked at him and still was astounded by his overbearing features. The flawless white of his eyes, pensive yet beautiful, like a timid sheen of rime over a newly frozen lake. Then there were his long lashes, like branching pine needles encrusted in early snow.

A breeze rushed in from the window, and I was drawn to see what the fluttering dance the feathers on Erefiel's head would do.

He turned to me and smiled, and I caught myself staring before looking away.

"Thank you for reaching out to me today. If we weren't there, things would have ended a lot worse."

I didn't reply immediately. "What will happen to Dalila?" I asked.

Erefiel shrugged. "She will live as part of the church, serve the Elders by caring for their edifices here in Cleria, set forth to neighbouring human cities and provide aid wherever she can."

"What does it mean? Having her tied to your house, I mean."

Erefiel shrugged. "It's just a formality. I won't have anything to do with her. But should she transgress on the terms established, my house would have to bear responsibility." At that final bit, Erefiel seemed rather reserved.

"What do you mean by responsibility?" I asked.

"A fine perhaps. Most notably, it would become a stain upon our political status." Erefiel spared me a sympathetic look. "It carries more weight than you can understand. Let's say Dalila did become some nefarious witch that burnt everything to the ground. That kind of event would undoubtedly be held over my family's head forever. It damages their hold and reputation, in the eyes of the court as well as the people." His mood seemed to sour the longer he went on, only bouncing back with one final comment. "I have no doubt in my mind that Dalila would never become such a threat."

"She cannot use her magic, right?"

Erefiel gave a saddened nod. "Nor see her family; her life belongs to the Elders now."

I glanced about the room once more, a thought occurring to me during the unpleasant silence. Despite my best attempts at seeming subtle, Erefiel seemed to have noticed.

"What is it? What are you looking for?" he asked. The playfulness to the question suggested he knew the answer.

I looked down with slight embarrassment, as if I were a child caught trying to find the hidden sweets.

"Your sword, the blade of Bereniel." I didn't intend to sound as coy as I did.

Erefiel showed a rare and exuberant grin.

"Wait here."

I tried to stop him, but I barely got a word out before he jumped to his feet and left. I felt awkward waiting on the floor within the sparse and spacious room. Rising to my feet, I leaned against the wall, but then thought it too strange. I spent the next several minutes wondering how one normally did the practice of standing casually, but whatever I tried felt unnatural.

When Erefiel finally returned with his sheathed blade in hand, I abandoned all such pretence.

I had never seen Erefiel in action; he never needed to be. He would sit aback Zephyr and simply command the troops from his vantage point.

From what I had heard, Erefiel was truly a sight on the battlefield. Others had described him as a dancing feather that no blade could touch, a feather that transformed the wind about him into great, slashing razors.

When Erefiel unsheathed the blade, I was already mid-gasp and almost pleaded with him not to.

"Oh, it is alright. It's my sword, after all," Erefiel assured.

He placed the blade horizontally on both of his opened palms.

The glistening steel of it looked like it was polished with crystalized gems, the hilt adorned with a golden pommel, and the dark leather wrapping of the hilt left untarnished.

A brown marble finish to the guard spread wide and tapered to catch any blade, which slid down the steel.

It wasn't a remarkably long sword nor wide, in fact it looked standard in its design. Given the tales, I expected it to be larger, but nothing could prepare me for how it shone.

The only oddity I noted was the way in which the blade was made.

It seemed to be your standard double-edged sword, except for that one side of it sharply thinned away to leave behind an edge two-thirds the width of its counterpart; it looked as if someone had fallen asleep with one side pressed to a grinding wheel.

"Try it," Erefiel suggested.

I stepped back and raised my arms in respectful protest. "Erefiel, I couldn't possibly."

Erefiel chuckled, stepping forward and taking my hand to wrap around the hilt of the blade. "It's alright, trust me."

Its heft was no different from an ordinary blade, yet I was surprised at how balanced it felt despite its design. Not just balanced—I felt as if it would grow wings and fly the moment I let go.

"Swing it."

I eyed Erefiel consciously, fully expecting to be smitten by the Elders themselves.

I swung it once.

A slight sensation went through me. I looked at the weapon for a moment and then swung it again, harder this time. I could feel it more clearly.

Twice more did I strike, leaning into the sensation and the momentum until my hand suddenly felt empty. I stopped and looked at my hand, fully expecting it to be vacant. The sword was still there, the weight as true as when I first held it.

I frowned, incapable of grasping what had just happened.

"It felt as if—"

"As if it just vanished from your grasp, right?" Erefiel finished.

When he was tired of waiting, he simply answered the question no one had asked. "It becomes as light as a feather; that's where the name comes from."

"But my swings also seemed faster."

Erefiel nodded. "When you swing the sword, it gathers a gust of air at the tapering end that propels it even further."

I barely comprehended the explanation. Erefiel stepped to me, so close I could smell his sweat and a slight hint of lavender.

"This part here." He ran a longer finger across the thinner, tapering end of the blade. "It is designed to gather air and lend itself with a stream of wind to make the strikes ever faster the more you swing. Eventually, the vortex of collected wind makes each swing lighter than the last."

He took the blade from my hand.

"And if you are fast enough—" In a flurry of movements, the sword whirred past before vanishing entirely from sight, leaving behind a distorted glimpse in my periphery. When Erefiel stopped, the concealing winds unravelled and I could see the edge again. "—You can make it entirely disappear," he finished.

◁ ▷

When I finally took my leave from Erefiel's manor, it was with a calmed spirit and the gift of exhaustion. I was too tired to invest much thought into Dalila or my parents' contribution. But another thought occupied me instead.

I didn't quite know how to feel about the way Erefiel and I addressed one another. Since the day we met, I looked up at him with adoration.

The air about him, the respect he demanded. His reputation when it came to defending Greyhill made him an idol ever since I decided to join the army. Thus, when he took me into his regiment, no matter how short-lived that experience was, I felt incredibly fortunate. He was charming, forthcoming, and gregarious in all the right ways. But I didn't want a friend, I wanted a leader, someone to look up to and strive towards.

This and many more thoughts accompanied me as I took my leave. Along the way, Saru gifted me a sweet pastry for my troubles.

Just as when I had entered, I didn't quite know how to react upon seeing a shavinu. He wasn't as dirty as I expected. He was even more mannered than I was. I blushed when I realised I was staring at his scar. *An outcast,* I thought to myself. If my staring bothered him, he didn't show it.

I continued on towards the iron gates when I noticed a figure in pure white standing behind the intricate curlicue patterns of the gates. It was the same Sister who was at Dalila's trial. Her presence was a reminder of Dalila's situation and it did little to mollify me. It took me a moment for me to recall her name. Mother Vinrie.

As I went to open the gates, I noticed the woman's patient smile.

"If you are looking for Erefiel, he is in there," I said tersely.

"Actually, I think I'd prefer speaking with you," she said matter-of-factly.

Her disarming stance gave me pause. I considered that perhaps I was being unfair towards the woman. If it wasn't for Mother Vinrie, Dalila wouldn't have had any future to be mad about.

She held my gaze and did not falter.

"How is Dalila?" I asked.

Mother Vinrie nodded. "She is alright and will make a fine member of the church." A silence filled the space between us till it was dispelled by her introduction. "My name is—"

"I know who you are," I said.

"I'm afraid that I can't say the same about you."

I hesitated. "Nora. Nora Rawsom."

Mother Vinrie nodded.

"What is it that I can do for you?" I asked.

⋜ ⋟

Mother Vinrie urged me to find Dalila's Kaseluda. She had returned to the court building to discover that Eric had taken it when he left. She would have gone to take it herself, but Eric had already left the city, and I already had an idea of where he was headed. I had my own reservation about going there, but I owed Dalila at least that much.

The road to Bracken wasn't long but it was arduous on foot. I was fortunate enough to find an empty wagon with a fatherly faced worker who would give me a ride. I offered him chipped pieces of a silver token. The man's idea of small talk ended at acquiring my name. It was a pleasant change. I dreaded finding the ones who insisted on inane conversation.

The path took us up an elevated road where one could see the glistening of Delbour River snake to my left. The fresh air and open, wind-ing fields proved a welcome scenery to contemplate on recent events.

My thoughts occasionally went to Eric, wondering where exactly in Bracken I would find him. The safest and best bet was in the illegal fighting pits below establishments. If not there, then the brothels were a good second guess. He seemed like the type to stick his poker into any powdered opening.

I thought of Dalila and how listless she was. It left me dour. I mourned for the bright-eyed and lively young girl she used to be. I was always fond of her, especially more so when I saw her being protective of Jeremiah despite Beck's bullying. I'd even entertained the image of Dalila and Jeremiah marrying one day. It may have been a life wholly not for me, but that didn't mean there weren't women who found meaning in wedlock.

The pendulum of my thoughts swung to the future, and the world in my mind turned bleak. The paint chipped away at the corners and the portrait cracked, grime and muck darkening what used to be bright and vibrant colours.

Jeremiah was growing up, and I couldn't help but feel disappointed. Even after I made it abundantly clear what was at stake, he still betrayed Dalila and set her on a path never her own.

Though I didn't know what truly happened, and it was entirely possible—no—it most certainly was the case that Mother and Father squeezed the truth out of him.

I redirected my ire from my brother to my parents instead. I was wholly glad to have escaped that damning home of self-righteous trog-lodytes and their zealotry. A pang of guilt swept over me that wasn't there before. No—it always was there. I just chose to suppress it lest it keep me trapped inside that insufferable household.

Yet now that I was out, I couldn't help but feel as if I abandoned Jeremiah to those devils. Their insidious influence, originally shared between the two of us, was now wholly reserved for Jeremiah. All I could say was that when this business with Eric was done and over with, that I would return home with unpleasant tidings.

The thought of my rotten family made me think of Uncle Duncan. Perhaps I should visit him while I was in town? I humoured the thought and stowed it away for later.

Chapter Twenty-Six

NORA

Bracken isn't lawless, not by any means; the denizens are just more discerning about their goings-on. Does everyone know about the gambling halls and fighting pits? Of the brutish dog fights? Absolutely. They just pretend like it doesn't exist. All of it is swept under a rug till it forms prominent mounds one can peddle as an aesthetic rather than a problem.

—DEBAUCHERY AS A NECESSITY, BY PAUL RAIMEN

A town of industry and enterprise showed itself over a final hill, just as dusk stretched the shadows. Nestled snugly underneath a wreath of bounding hills as a perpetual air of smog rose from its top was Bracken. Delbour River ran gently along the wide valley to our left, down the steep drop from where the wagon trundled upwards.

Appropriately, Bracken was the closest town that led to Bolton and was like the snot-nosed little brother of the two.

I thanked my driver for his troubles and tossed him an extra silver for the taciturn company. In keeping with the service, he simply tipped his rimmed hat and went about his own business.

Again, I couldn't help but think of Uncle Duncan, knowing that he lived in Bracken. I shook the thought away. There were more pressing matters to deal with.

It was hard to deny the fact that he and I had grown distant over the years. Perhaps I would stumble upon him knee-deep in his liquor again.

I walked the streets and decided to deal with Uncle later. If Cleria was ostentation, then Bracken was crude practicality.

Paint costs money, gold costs money, space costs money. As a result, the streets were tight and the homes squeezed up to their neighbours. With no room to spread outwards, the buildings reached as far as three stories like constricted weeds.

At night, metal street lights hung their despondent heads and offered the barest of light. Even the huddled homes looked as if they were coveting warmth.

The buildings all were a deep and bare grey shade; lifeless and bland. Dirty brown made up the core of thatched homes and framed work. There was obviously very little love in the architecture.

A handful of souls travelled the strangled road. Men swayed on uneven legs. I questioned a few denizens and was led towards the Toothfairy. It was a supposed tavern barely able to make ends meet during the day. It awaited the truly desperate to wander in and serve piss-water for ale.

To the side of the building there was a set of stairs leading down to an innocuous enough looking door.

I could hear muffled chants trying to escape the building. I opened the door and braced against the bedlam. Next came the great stench of gathered crowds and sweat. The only hint of anything else was the sharp scent of spilt blood. The marriage of smells was truly repugnant—it was born from the union of gambling and fists.

I shouldered my way past crowds of the inebriated and the impassioned. These were folks chasing after the elusive mistress that was their addiction, the rare chance at being gifted a win like a soft and suggestive brush against one's cheek that sent one reeling for more. They loved the chase, and they were enslaved by it.

Within the centre of the pit, there stood a great towering man by human standards; his body made of a thick armour of muscle and fat.

His latest victim was a broken and groaning man. Surrounded by great paint strokes of his own blood, the defeated crawled through the sand.

With his ginger beard caked in blood, the winner roared and flexed his monstrous biceps. The crowds went wild. I couldn't help but snicker. How would they react if they saw an akar?

I found Eric sitting at the back of the domed arena. He was on a bench and looked unimpressed by the display. He didn't even seem to notice the people about him chanting.

I strode up to him. "Eric."

The man turned half-heartedly, seemingly surprised to see me. A cigar bud hung from his lips which trailed a smoky line upwards.

"Ah, if it isn't Erefiel's lapdog. What can I do for you?" He sounded genuinely amiable, but I did not doubt for a second that he was just amused to see me.

"It's Nora."

"I know your name, little one." He turned to eye me, betraying his disinterest before returning to counting his coin purse. "I just choose to ignore it." He took his bud from his lips and sauntered on to the betting stall.

I followed. "The book."

"The what?" Eric looked genuinely perplexed. He grimaced as if I had just asked him what the Elder King's eye was made of.

"The Kaseluda, Dalila's book. I am here to pick it up."

Eric appeared to suddenly understand as he snickered softly at his own private joke. "Afraid you are too late, little one," he said.

"Are you drunk?" I asked.

"Ta-da! You caught me!" Eric announced sarcastically as he turned to the man behind the counter. "All of it on that big guy." The man took the bet and bounced the weight of it in his hand.

"You sure?" the teller asked.

"Look, what do you mean by 'I am too late'?" I cut in.

"Read my lips, Erefiel's dog: You. Are. Too. Late." Eric accentuated and dragged each syllable, drawing ever closer so that I could smell the reeling stench of tobacco and booze on his rotten teeth. The bare lighting of this domed arena stretched his lips to an even wider sneer.

"No lover's quarrels; take your dame and leave," the teller said, passing over the ticket to Eric, who gave a drunken nod of thanks.

I was about to protest and list all the reasons why Eric would have a better chance at finding love within a sty, when I spotted a Kaseluda buried underneath a pile of papers at the back of the teller's desk.

I left the line and pulled on Eric's arm so he faced me. "You bet it away?" I asked.

"Hey!" Eric protested as his cigar fell to the floor.

"It belonged to Dalila! You had no right giving it away!"

Eric sighed. "Well, she left it with me! I wasn't about to keep it. How important could it have been anyway if she forgot about it?" Eric said.

A great, hot, searing flame awoke within me.

In the back, the announcer professed Giant Munasen's might and asked if anyone would be willing to face him next.

A brilliant idea unfolded itself in my mind. A plan so fortuitous and timely that I couldn't help but grin at what it promised. It just seemed too poetic and righteous to be true. I paced back to the teller, pushing aside the man standing in line and grabbed onto the desk. The teller recoiled.

"Put me in."

"What?" the teller asked.

"Put me in the fight. I bet on myself."

He blinked incredulously, trying to comprehend the absurdity of my request.

"Your payment?" he asked.

I unstrapped my blade and handed it over and gave him a purse carrying a total of ten silver pieces.

"I ask that when I win, I receive the book in the back there."

The teller turned to his clutter of papers and items and nodded when he finally got a glimpse of the Kaseluda. He turned back to face me. "Just the book?" he asked with a raised brow.

I nodded. "Just the book."

The teller gave a deep sigh as if I were wasting his time. He clasped a hand to the nape of his neck and rubbed before giving me an appraising look up and down.

"If you win, there will be a prize pool. The odds are—"

"Don't need to know," I cut back and turned on my heel.

Eric walked up to me with a cowl and hissed. "Nora, what are you doing?" The sudden wrench thrown into his plans seemed to have sobered him up enough.

My lips split into a vindictive smile at the mention of my name.

"Doling out karma," I stated. I wasn't thinking clearly. I did not consider my chances when it came to defeating the ginger brawler. All I saw was the promise of justice. That would drive me forward.

◁ ▷

The moment it was announced that I would be the next fighter, I saw hordes of beady-eyed and eager men run to the booth and throw themselves at the feet of Mistress Gamble.

The circular sandpit was illuminated by a hanging light of some form and infused with magic.

As I entered the pit, my feet bare so that they could feel the sand between my toes, I mentally counted the steps to the centre of where my opponent stood. I accounted for five long-footed strides before I could reach him.

I took note of the diameter of the ring and found myself pleasantly surprised at the amount of manoeuvrable space provided. Though seeing the man titled Giant Munasen, I wished for more.

Was this gamble fool-hardy? Perhaps, but it was too late to harbour any doubt. Just like Uncle Duncan taught me—if I was cornered, my only option was to tunnel my way out.

Eric came to mind. I imagined his expression after losing everything he had bet. I couldn't help but feel excited at the prospect.

I turned to Munasen. He was a balding bastard of ginger hair, his beard bristled and patchy. It mostly covered his jawline and turned into patchy clumps around his cheeks; like sparse trees at the edge of a forest.

A previous combatant must have knocked a tooth loose, for a trail of blood smeared his lips and faded into his facial hair.

The man's glare was hungry and ferocious, no mirth or pretence of being gentle. The betting men at the border of the ring goaded and cheered him on, prompting him to make short work of me—all of them were hungry for blood.

I looked about the room and suppressed a smirk when I saw the brief outline of Eric. He sat on one of the benches, his glare searing. His fingers clenched about his betting ticket so tightly that his knuckles turned white.

My hands constantly wrapped about empty air in search of my missing sword. How does one face a giant without a weapon?

I reacquainted myself with the brief list of rules that I was hurriedly told and the quick contract of liability I had to sign—though I had no idea what body of government would reinforce any such contract.

No foul play, which included no eye gouging or kicking in the groin.

No biting.

No leaving the ring.

The fight ends upon surrender or knock out or by disqualification for any of the aforementioned rules.

The announcer strode to me. "Hey girl, what's your name?"

"Nora."

"No…" the announcer had to purse his lips and collect himself as if he were talking to an idiot. "I mean, what's your *fighting* name?"

I suddenly understood what he meant and named the only name that came to mind.

"Simurgh," I said coolly.

The announcer blinked dumbly at first, but then his smile widened. His eyes glistened with a performer's hunger. The man appeared to see me in a new light, perhaps thinking that I had an appreciation for the spectacular after all.

And so he turned, a strange egg-like device of black marble in his hand that carried his voice over the sounds of the gamble-frenzied men.

"Welcome gamblers! Degenerates! I can see you are starved for some action! Presenting our newest victim, a rare treat for all you ravenous leeches: Simurgh, The Immortal Bird of Twilight!" The crowds erupted into frenzied chants, fuelled by the promise of my defeat more than anything else.

I neared the centre of the ring as Munasen took a few steps back.

The man before me stood a head taller than Chroma when I first faced the akar boy, and just like then, I only managed to reach up to Munasen's chest.

We stood a good distance apart where our fists and feet could not immediately reach.

There was no silence, there was no pause, there was no anticipation—just a deep and virulent hunger for blood. The moment stretched and continued to do so as if defiantly clinging to this single second.

"Fight!" The announcer called, and I was already on the defensive.

The hulking brute bounded towards me on heavy feet as I flitted away.

He leaned forward, his face wide open as I let loose my first punch to disorientate the man before quickly falling back.

His eyes shut reflexively and the man came to a halt.

After a brief pause of twitches to test each other, he advanced and threw his punch. I weaved under and took the split second of a chance to kick the man's thigh.

Munasen lumbered forward, almost falling to a knee, before turning around to convene his pursuit. He wouldn't fall easily.

Though large, Munasen didn't have much in the way of strategy.

Bone-crushing fists swung at me. Bobbing and weaving, I put distance between the greater brunt of hits, while the slower punches were slapped, brushed and rolled away by my body.

Yet I knew in an instant I couldn't keep it up for long.

I already worked up a sweat that very same day with Erefiel, and my own punches and kicks weren't amounting to much. My breath strained in my chest, and my mind raced as it tracked every movement, every muscular twitch that informed me of the next attack. A smarting heat blossomed from my heart.

Could Munasen keep it up? He certainly already had a few fights behind him.

The only thing I found fortunate was the straightforward approach of Munasen. No feints, no combos, no footwork. I slipped my way out of corners, my feet dancing and gliding across the sandy floor, just the way Uncle Duncan had showed me as a child.

"Stop moving, you slippery roach!" Munasen roared as a one-two combo of punches missed, and I landed a clean strike to his cheek. Hitting him in the torso was useless. I needed to get him where his defences were lacking.

Quickly, I slipped away and sidestepped to the centre of the ring, fists up, heels raised, and toes bouncing. I was ready to move at a moment's notice.

The audience booed and jeered at me. "Get out of there!" Shouted one. "Stop wasting our time!" My alternative option was letting Munasen kill me.

The giant charged on heavy feet, and I readied myself to dodge. I needed a choke hold.

His right shoulder twitched, but his left fist struck first. I didn't feel the initial hit, only the sensation of falling. My mind was dazed and my vision twinning.

Without a single second to compose myself, Munasen grabbed me by the hair and pulled me to my feet.

My toes dangled, barely grazing the sand below, when I screamed in pain.

"You thought me a simpleton? Didn't you?" His voice was just as gruff and unflattering as before, but there was a sudden intelligence underlying it all—I was played. The man sounded proud of the fact.

He turned and, in true showmanship; he displayed his claimed trophy to adoring fans and spectators. His hands were spread wide, one of which still held me, and I grimaced at the tugging pain on my scalp. His other hand waved and stoked the crowd's chanting.

"Munasen! Munasen! Munasen!"

He threw his free arm up and his grin said it all. The people cheered louder and louder, fuelling Munasen's ego.

Munasen turned and landed a solid blow to my face.

I recoiled and saw stars. A smarting warmth emanated from my nose as I was certain it had broken in-between moments of lucidity.

"Munasen! Munasen!" The cries of adoration were unrelenting as the words turned hazy.

"Munasen! Munasen!"

Another blow to my spleen sent me curling up into a ball and going limp all over. I gasped in agony, hoping that it didn't rupture. My breath caught itself, pained rasping sounds escaping as my feeble fingers tried fruitlessly to unclench Munasen's vice grip.

Another punch to my rib and I sobbed—the strikes were unbearable. My consciousness was slipping.

"Munasen! Munasen! Munasen!"

My left eye swelled with a throbbing ache.

"Munasen!"

Just as Munasen let loose a gloating and bellowing laugh of assured victory, I screamed like a damn demon. With blazing energy, I kicked and struck a toe into Munasen's windpipe.

I escaped his hold and the giant stumbled on wayward footing, choking on his bruised throat as he prostrated himself in the sand. I had crippled his air-supply.

I wobbled on rubbery feet, but my body would not rest yet. Pain spread all throughout me like ink on parchment.

With another shrill scream to keep me lucid, I clambered onto the man. My elbows and fists pounded on his balding scalp until blood was drawn. I ignored the flaring heat which spread through me, ignoring the broken rib which stabbed in my chest with each movement. I even ignored the pain in my lungs with each short breath.

All Munasen could do was cover his head with bloated hands.

The crowd's chanting died down into suffocated embers; barely even a glow was left.

My frenzy, my madness, my rage must have put an end to everyone else's revelries, for the quiet that filled the large, echoing chamber was deafening. I filled it with the sound of Munasen's breaking fingers.

A roar escaped, not from me, but from Munasen, who pushed himself up to his feet and sent me flying off his back.

Mangled hands tried to pound against my supine body, but I veered to my left and took hold of his offered limb. Twisting like a snake, I coiled around the appendage.

Munasen groaned and raged against my hold, refusing to fall to the floor.

I dared a chance. Swiftly I released my lock on his arm and delivered another kick onto the man's head. The first struck him in the face and made his head swing back. The second landed on his already accosted neck. He rewarded me with an agonising punch to my thigh.

My cry was brief before I cut it short and pushed through the pain; gritted teeth gave way to pooling blood.

Munasen's shock and pain and momentary distraction allowed me to return my arms into their lock and drag the giant to the floor.

My grip was true.

"Do you yield?" I asked, part of my question drowned in blood.

He roared, refusing to give up.

"Do you yield?!" I roared louder and tightened my grip, feeling the tendon's in his arms stretch, his thumb pressed in my hand as I twisted his quivering wrist, his purpling knuckles robbing him of any strength.

I did not ask a third time, but I did push slightly further until I was certain that I toed the line of truly claiming his arm for good.

"I yield!" he shouted, his words echoing louder than the cracking of his arm would have.

The borrowed energy fled my body all at once as I collapsed on the floor. Pain flooded to take its place. My ribs flared with agony; I could feel the promise of a bruise on my thigh and groaned at the thought. How was I going to get home in such a state? The sharp pain about my nose continued to blossom; the noisome odour of the chamber was completely replaced with blood.

The domed arena was truly silent as I stood. I turned and faced my onlookers. Each and every one of them was stupefied. The unwelcomed quiet made the rasping of my breaths all the more apparent. I spat blood onto the floor and despite my injuries, eyed the crowd with warning.

I turned to leave. My stiffening leg had me manage no more than a hobble.

The voice which addressed me was unexpected, and his words even less so.

"You fight well," Munasen said into the empty space as he groaned, rolling himself over to look at the flaring light from the ceiling.

"Thanks." I considered offering the same compliment in turn, but somehow it felt belittling to do so.

I limped through the sandpit. My ears rang. The crowds parted at my approach. I made sure not to look too deeply into their eyes.

I stood before the teller's booth. "My winnings." I stretched out an expectant hand.

The teller snapped out of his spell and gathered his wits. Frantically, the man put together more coinage than I had ever seen in my life. I repressed my urge to gawk openly and feigned indifference.

"And the book," I reminded.

The teller turned and looked entirely frazzled in comparison to his business-minded demeanour from earlier. He deftly passed over the book.

I nodded my thanks, strapped my sword to my shoulder and limped out on my way.

It was remarkably difficult not buckling under the weight of all those spiteful stares. I had to look forward. I had to stand true.

My winnings slowed me. I had a sinking feeling in my belly when I thought of how I was going to get out of here alive.

Suddenly, a hand violently grabbed my wrist as I turned to find Eric.

"Don't do this," he forced through gritted teeth, his eyes equally pleading as they were threatening.

I tore my hand from his grip. "You should have thought of that before giving away Dalila's book," I offered in turn, before making my way to the door.

My steps were the loudest they had ever been, echoing through the quiet hall of gamblers.

My mind raced. How would I survive the night? Should I run? Maybe I should stay there. No. It made no difference.

I had already lost count of the seething and furious glares pointed at me. I could tell they had every intention of robbing me the moment I left, especially in a sparse and empty road under the cover of night. None of these sad men would usually ever dare to challenge me, but as crippled and exhausted as I was, I would be easy enough pickings for a gang.

I hobbled forward, my feet limping, but my shoulders stood wide and proud, the bag of coins jingled tauntingly upon my shoulder.

I reached the door. So thin and insignificant, yet it looked more like death's door.

Someone stepped in front of me. Munasen. His breathing was hag-gard. He gripped the arm that I held in lock; it would certainly take a week before it was fully healed. I looked into his stony eyes, my breath raspy. I sighed. How foolish was I to think I could just walk out of there?

"Come," Munasen said. I looked up, uncertain of his meaning.

"I will walk you home," he offered, his eyes sparing a momentary glance of warning to all gathered in that hall.

Munasen opened the door and allowed me to walk ahead.

I hesitated only for a moment, wondering what I would do if he would attack me. But I knew it was worse to expose my back to the dozens of empty-pocketed gamblers inside the hall.

I stepped out into the night. It was surprisingly peaceful. I had a new appreciation for the calm.

Chapter Twenty-Seven

NORA

The veracity of certain gods is questionable. It is undoubtable that the Elder King and the other Elders do exist. By extension, it leaves little doubt for the existence of the Creator. However, other gods such as Oxular leave greater questions. Is this the manifestation of people's imagination or does Oxular truly decide to not reveal himself to the people? Greater question yet is how an unseen figure can become the deity for those who believe in the power of witnessing.

—A STUDY ON THE WITNESS CHURCH, BY JOHN MAURO

The pain came as a dull and distant ache before flourishing into a medley of injuries. I had no recollection of how I ended up on the sofa I was on, nor who it was that covered me in the felt blanket.

I groaned, my entire body sore as I removed the covering and sat up.

The last thing I remembered was the shine of a gibbous moon as I was escorted out by Munasen walking behind me.

When lucidity came, a thought invaded me and shook me fully awake.

"That snake!" I shouted and looked around. He stole my money!

"Oh, you're awake."

I turned with a grimace to the friendly voice and readied to give my captor another beating. What I did not expect was to find Uncle Duncan working his way to me with a steaming cup of tea.

"Duncan?"

"Who else?"

My cheeks flushed as I bowed my head. "Nobody." I made a mental note to give Munasen my thanks.

"How did I get here?" I asked.

"Your giant friend. You were both quite a mess."

I held my tongue when Uncle Duncan pointed to a tucked away bundle of bags, a book, and a sword pressed against a wall.

"He already told me what happened."

I let out a sigh of relief, accompanied by an equal one of exhaustion.

Uncle Duncan was a pot-bellied, balding man, though he emanated natural strength. He sported a decently tended moustache that cascaded into a full beard. His forearms were coiled monstrosities appropriate for a man working the factories and shovelling coal.

He wore a stained shirt made of woven hemp, a dark brown colour, archaic and despairing rather than carrying any note of comfort.

He came and placed a three-legged table before me of faded beauty. A tray of steaming tea set occupied the surface. Carefully, Uncle Duncan placed the plated teacup in front of me.

I stretched my limbs, fully allowing the pain to flow through my limbs so I could feel the strain of tense and sore muscles. My calloused hand and even the tendons in my arm complained as I worked my fingers.

I pulled the coarse blanket closer and took my steaming tea, blowing on it as Uncle took a seat on a single, pillow-less chair next to mine. He rubbed his stout hands together and waited for me to gather my wits.

I looked at the room and finally recognized its interior.

Light had very little governance in his home. Neighbouring buildings blocked out most of the coming sun. The walls were bare and of drab composition. The bed in the corner must have only had my uncle's drunken weight to comfort it. A small unremarkable wardrobe was tucked in another corner. And there was a small square table bracketed by two wooden chairs by the drab window.

On account of my broken nose, scent came last. I could most definitely smell that blasted hint of mature, distilled malt with its earthy aroma.

"How are things?" Uncle asked. There was no hiding the uncomfortable air between us. My last visit was years ago.

"Had something to take care of," I confided, rising to my feet. "Thank you, Uncle, but I best be on my way."

Duncan remained seated as I forcefully made my entire body drag itself, stiff and sore, to my winnings.

I sensed a question coming and hoped against hope that it never did.

"Where are you going?" He substituted one question for the real one.

"Home."

"Back to your dutiful station? I am sure the housing is good."

"It does the job," I said plainly, my back turned.

"And the food?" he pressed.

"How much?"

Duncan's words hitched.

I turned to him. "How much do you need? Let's get this over and done with." My query was cold as stone.

Duncan looked up at me, his eyes narrowing in an impressive performance. "Child, I am your uncle. Why do you think I would ask anything of you?"

I sighed and reached into my bag to scoop up a handful of glistening copper and silver coins.

"Last chance, take it and I will be gone, or have none of it and I will stay."

Uncle rose from his seat, his eyes remorseful.

"I knew it." My claim was spiteful. I dropped the coins to his floor and hurriedly dressed myself, my tears held back, for they were for me to bear and not a plotting uncle.

"Nora, please." He tried to placate me, his hands cautiously reaching for my shoulder.

"Enough!" I turned to him, one eye still mostly shut as I glared intensely through the other. "You were my hero." I turned away again, sniffing and damning the tears that threatened to break.

"When Mother and Father beat me; you took me in. You taught me how to take care of myself, to fight." It was too difficult; like breaks in the dam, my emotions bled from me.

"Now you're nothing more than a drunkard, a gambler, who took me in and waited for me to wake up to ask for money." My voice cracked—I cursed my weakness and vowed to be stronger, to never cry in front of those who didn't deserve my tears.

"Nora, that is just not true."

I heaved. I told myself to stop, to just leave. I belittled my foolish sense of hope. I turned to him, offering him one last chance.

"If you tell me right now that you want me to stay, that you won't drink yourself drunk, that you don't want a single fucking coin, then I will stay."

Uncle froze, his eyes searching for an answer somewhere on my swollen cheek, my bruised and broken nose, my open eye. But all his look begged for was forgiveness.

Mercy was not one of the things he taught me.

"Goodbye, Uncle. I wish you a good life."

I dragged my things and threw the sack over my shoulder, opening the decrepit door and limping down the stairs. When he finally broke free of his trance, he pursued me.

"Nora, you don't know what it's like, the fighting, the war. When I close my eyes, I still see them, the akar." His voice fell on deaf ears. "You were lying there, your coin fully bare for me to take for my own. It must mean something that I didn't take it from you!" I paused at the bottom floor and opened it to allow in the sound of industry. It was already noon.

I turned back to Duncan. "Well, aren't you are a bloody saint?" Those were the last words I offered as I slammed the door behind me.

Curse my family and its entire dysfunctional line. Curse all of this nonsense.

I hoped that, one day, Jeremiah would also snap to his senses and come with me to escape all of its ludicrous and caustic woes.

⋖ ⋗

Before hiring a cart to take me home, I stumbled upon Munasen outside of the fighting pit. His real name was James. I bid him my thanks and offered him a small sum of coins.

He was actually a well-spoken and intelligent individual, quick of wit and feisty.

His arm was strewn in a sling and apparently Daniel, the teller from the night before, was quite upset that his best fighter was out for a little while.

I promised to visit James again next I visited. I owed him a drink.

⋖ ⋗

I decided to indulge myself with my carriage of choice. The well-groomed and dressed driver seemed perplexed by my unexpected appearance, but he didn't complain when I offered coin. He did seem rather bothered when I placed the muddied soles on the empty carriage seat opposite of me.

⋖ ⋗

I first went about my task and returned Dalila's book to the church. I wasn't permitted to enter on account of my appearance and lack of membership.

When Mother Vinrie returned, she did well to hide her shock and surprise. She asked if I needed to be tended to.

I politely refused, and when she asked if I wanted any coin for my troubles, I again refused. I stated, rather arrogantly, that I had already been paid handsomely for my efforts. This left Mother Vinrie rather confused, or at least I thought it did—the woman was unreadable.

Next, I made a short trip to a small but similarly garish bank. Their highbrowed sense of superiority withered and died when they saw my comically large bag of coin I pounded onto their table.

"I'd like to open an account, please."

It took the teller a moment. The wiry gentleman made his impressively groomed moustache twitch like a chipmunk before returning to his task. "Of course, right away."

I filed for a small reprieve from my garrison. After getting my wounds tended to with some colour-magic, I stayed at a comfortable inn and decided to treat myself to some more luxuries on account of all of those gamblers within the Toothfairy.

Attached to the establishment was the soothing bathhouse where the waters ran and it perpetually steamed. From the carved head of unicorns placed into walls, steaming water would run and fill the tiled floors.

I entered the pools and just spent hours per day stretching my toes within the folding embrace of the bath, letting the heat of it envelope me like the warmth of a lover, gently kneading out the knotted aches of my body.

The prying eyes of regular patrons washed over me. I wondered if they ever saw a battle-hardened woman before. My scars told tales; I wondered how they interpreted them? I ignored them and found a warm bath to soak in and pulled small tides of water to my breasts.

Once my aches had partially ebbed and I found the pain nothing more than the slight ghost of what it used to be, I set off once more.

Just over a week had passed since my bout with Munasen. I found another form of transportation, more modest and affordable this time around. I made my way home to Basksin to give my horrendous parents a very unpleasant visit.

I arrived at Crowtown at night and made my bed at the Merry-Inn. It had been an age since I last saw Merry-Anne and it was nice to be reminded of her presence. It was frightening how quickly one forgets parts of their past when moving on.

The following morning, I walked the rest of the way to Basksin.

When I was younger, walking through the village streets left me with anxiety. Yet now, as I approached the open borders of Basksin, I barely offered a momentary glance to the arched bar of iron holding a great purple eye and instead wandered inside with searing righteousness.

I could still see the shadows of the past like a superimposed layer upon reality. Wherever I looked, I sensed its presence.

Anxiety had been my companion wherever I went as a child. I dreaded hearing my parent's footsteps tap against the wooden floor of our home for I wondered if I did something wrong again.

Shame.

Shame was my true friend in those days. Shame for the way I looked, shame for my unlady-like behaviour, my boyish proclivities, my appearance—all of it. My body tensed with the memories.

I recalled a version of me who felt trapped, someone who believed that they deserved that life, believed that they were wanting in every way.

People nowadays called me Simurgh, called me the Undying Flame, the Twilight Bird and all manner of other flattering and entirely exaggerated titles. Some would commend my drive and ask where I got that kind of willpower.

Of course, I would smile and jest, drawing out laughter from my comrades. But the truth was far less inspiring or patriotic than the people thought.

I recalled, still, the frightened little girl I once was, so furtive and withdrawn. "Yes, mother," I would say; "Yes, Father," I would say.

The thought made me sick, and I despised that young, terrified girl wholeheartedly. Despised how meek she was, how her body trembled at the sound of Father's belt against the table as if she were some trained whelp.

I allowed myself a smile saved only for me.

It was why I had such pleasant memories of Duncan when he took me in for a time, when he trained me how to fight, how to protect myself.

When I stood against a horde of akar before me, it was not that I was stupid or brave. It was not that I valiantly pursued the cause of righteous duty. It was fear that motivated me, fear of being found out. For everyone to realise that I was just a scared, vulnerable girl in need of help. I ran into the fray because running back into the shadows wasn't an option.

That lie enveloped me like a shroud but gave birth to another truth. I was in control, and the streets of Basksin couldn't penetrate the fortifications I had built.

When I still lived there, it was yet a small and unimpressive settlement of a dozen homes, sparse and strewn about, a Witness church being built with some serious money.

Now it looked as if it were a docile and deceptively joyful place. The residents here all were of some obvious repute, since all who wished to join had to make a sizable monthly donation, and that was nothing to be scoffed at.

The homes were like those at Cleria but with a more village-appropriate appearance. Rather than golden rims or extravagantly trimmed gardens, the homes were of simple muted-brown and blue colours; gardens were almost non-existent save the few strips of patched greenery to grow a small selection of flowers. A dash of lilac was added to the frames of the homes. The roads themselves were winding with cobblestone, yet no carriage actually went through them, given how small and accessible the entirety of the town was. It was not that the place was obviously grotesque, quite the opposite. It seemed homey and pleasant at first glance. Yet it was much like meeting someone with a gregarious smile, firm handshake, a visage pleasant to the eyes, well-dressed, and entirely sociable. But something was off. Something one couldn't quite place. Perhaps it was the fact that the smile was held for too long and seemed entirely unhinged. Or it had to do with those eyes, wide and peering with unbridled intensity.

Whatever the reason, something about Basksin gave it an unsettling aura.

"Good morning."

"Mornin'."

"Good morning, Sunshine."

"Be witnessed, my child."

"May you be witnessed."

"May you be acknowledged."

I walked through the town where villagers offered me their eerie greetings.

Some of them I remembered, and some I assumed may have remembered me, but gave no sign that they did. Their smiles were wide and full of heart—it was discomforting. I ignored their welcome and simply strode past.

When I walked up to darken my parent's doorstep, I found myself relieved that I harboured no anxiety at confronting them.

I knocked.

"Just a minute!" I heard my mother announce cheerfully from the other side. "Frank, it must be the pastries we ordered! They are here early!"

When my mother opened the door, I took full pleasure in seeing her smile falter and her plump and powdered cheeks deflate.

"N-Nora?" she asked as if unsure. "What are you doing here?" Mother tried her best to sound stern and chiding, but she couldn't shake her surprise.

From within the house, Father appeared through a sectioned corridor to the right.

"Who is it, honey? Is it the church?" Father's smile died equally as quick when he saw me.

Mother held her hands before her timidly as she stepped aside. "It's our daughter." She sounded almost apologetic.

Father was an equally portly man, but perhaps not as rotund as mother. His stomach was elegantly tucked away in a white shirt and handsome brown vest, his perfectly tailored trousers giving the appearance of a man with some coin to spare and his own goatee seemed groomed for some important occasion.

Looking at my mother, I noticed she too wore a long, puffy dress with a vile pink tone that assaulted my eyes. It went well with her wide hat and a transparent ribbon constricting the crown.

"What are you doing here?" Father demanded through gritted teeth. He approached with his finger pointed down to the exact location of his intent. "Shut that door!"

I sighed, stepping inside and doing as he asked. I eyed them both for long, silent seconds, feeling a righteous anger boil up inside me. Father seemed rather flustered that his tone didn't affect me.

"Nora!" I heard from the corridor as not-so-little Jeremiah showed himself.

My heart sank watching my brother limp with the help of his new cane. Though I couldn't help but also feel joy at seeing his loving smile meant entirely for me. Again, the boy had grown wider and taller, his body showing no sign of restraint.

I privately mourned for Jeremiah, pitying his fate. I didn't know what I would have done in his shoes. What I would do if I couldn't fight in the Clerian army anymore.

Mother and Father held their breaths in front of Jeremiah. None of us wanted him to hear us fight.

Jeremiah, wholly unaware, threw his arms around me and slightly buckled from the act. I had to half-catch him and chuckled. He'd grown over the years. My heart weighed heavy with guilt at the thought of all the years I had missed with him.

"Careful," I mused, helping him stand again.

My eyes danced about my brother, taking him in. Yet I avoided glancing too long at his injured leg.

"Jeremiah, leave us. We have something to discuss with your sister," father said flatly.

"But Father," Jeremiah protested.

"Now sweetie, just go up. We will leave soon," Mother said.

Jeremiah, too, was dressed in a well-tailored and handsome outfit, though his stout form gave more to mother's appearance rather than Father's.

Jeremiah left with his head bowed. He had leaned on me as he tried to reach for his cane. I picked it up for him as he limped out of the room, sullen.

"What are you doing here?" Father asked when Jeremiah left. The sound of his distancing cane became a marker for when it was safe to raise our voices. I knew for certain that Jeremiah was just on the other side of the stairs, listening in, hidden by the plastered walls.

"How did you do it?" I asked.

"Do what?" Mother asked, her hands thrown up in exasperation. During my older years, it was mostly mother who felt like she had to defend herself. The difference was that mother had not a single hint of shame in her.

"Get Jeremiah to talk about Dalila."

Father's eyes narrowed in a mixture of emotions: incredulity, hate, disbelief, anger. "That's what this is about? The filthy witch who injured your brother?"

I saw red filling the corner of my vision.

"Dalila tried to heal him."

Father threw his hands up. "Oh, and what good that did! Our son is now a cripple! Do you know how our neighbours talk about us now? How they see us with pity and smile as if everything is okay? We will be known as 'That family.' 'Oh, Frank and Martha? They are so wonderful! Isn't it a shame that they have to take care of a cripple?'"

I knew then for certain that Jeremiah hadn't left entirely. For we all went silent as frantic, arrhythmic strides of a cane and footsteps pounding upstairs, followed by a slamming door.

Father sighed in exhaustion and rubbed a hand against his wrinkled forehead.

"I will check up on him," Mother said meekly and made her way up the stairs, where she called out for her 'Pumpkin.'

Father returned his attention to me. "See what you do? You just bring trouble to this family."

"Me?" I gawked with disbelief. "You are the one that just said those awful things!"

"Oh please, Nora! I see the way you look at him. Those eyes were full of pity, unsure of what to say or do. You just look at him like some broken steed, unable to do anything; you just don't say it. You keep him at arm's length because you don't know what to do with him."

Like a small thorn, I felt an aching pain blossom in my chest. "That's not true..." I protested, though I didn't sound entirely convincing.

"He says so himself! Jeremiah asked me the other night if you love him less because he is broken now."

My heart began to shatter; no fracture, no break, just shatter out of nowhere.

"That is not true! I love him." Just a week ago, I made a promise to not cry in front of those unworthy of my tears, and I already feared I was about to break my promise.

"Oh, child. Where did we go wrong with you? We just wanted you to be a devout believer and Witness us all."

Father provided me a deep, crimson thread to weave my hate with. I clambered onto it. "It is a cult!" I declared, crying the word so loudly as to drown out anything else.

Father lifted a pointed finger, his eyes manic as he paced his way towards me. "Don't you dare speak heresy in my house or I will have your tongue."

"Look around! You all smile and wave, give great sums to a church you cannot leave, live by these rules that shun all others as you partake in ceremonies meant for you to be witnessed! It is feeding on your fear!"

Father lifted a plate from the table and seemed ready to toss it in a moment of pure rage. The only thing which gave him pause was the shrill scream from upstairs.

"Leave me alone!" Jeremiah screamed violently. I heard something shatter.

Father and I ran into the small opening and turned right to run up the stairs.

There, mother sat on a puddle of water with stranded flowers, and clay shards as she patted at the wound on her head. She kept tapping at it and looking at her bloodied fingers, as if expecting it to vanish at some point.

"Damn it," Father cursed.

"It's okay," Mother reassured, but her eyes kept blinking with every wince.

"This is a broken family," I announced, my voice just as broken as my claim, just as broken as the vase or my heart.

Father looked at me with such contempt.

"I rue the day you were brought to this world," he said, the words blistering. "I should have known from the start that you were good for nothing. That you would betray your faith, join those men in a life unfit for a lady. I should have just given you away when you were still obedient to someone who would have made a woman out of you."

The words should have hurt, but they didn't. They just hammered against a heart so callous that the impact formed diamonds.

"Mark my words." Father pointed his finger at me again as he looked up from mother's side, his eyes ablaze with conviction.

"You will regret this, all of this, you will regret turning your back on this family, regret taking part in a life meant for degenerates and the uncivilised, regret aiding those vile, demonic Elders and when the day comes that all will be forgotten. Only we…" Father tapped against his chest in quick succession, his neck straining forward to reveal the veins underneath. "We will be remembered, and you will not."

I did not offer any more words, nor did I voice my disappointment, my hate, or my lament. I could feel the tears coming and I had a promise to keep.

Hoping my eyes hadn't yet turned bright with tears, I turned away from them and left. I ran through the door, and kept on running through the village.

Nobody spoke any words of greetings but stared at me like mindless spectres observing something not supposed to be in their own world. Their smiles withered like discarded masks to reveal the maddening scrutiny in their eyes. There I was, an outsider, someone who brought conflict into their perfidious village. Their stares were scalding as I ran past.

When I finally ran free from the village and sprinted straight into a pasture far from any life and given to an audience of swaying grass, I finally allowed for release.

Falling into the field, I let loose a deep and tremendous wail.

I cried, I sobbed. My tears fell and turned to dew on petals in the privacy of that meadow. Wind passed, and it sounded like a choked sob coming forth as a hissed whisper.

If anyone could hear my ululation, I prayed they believed me to be a mournful spirit and to leave me to my sorrow.

My cries were interrupted by interludes of occasional whimpers before continuing. My throat strained at the force, my vocal cords trembling from its despair. I went to thoughts of my uncle, my mother and father, Jeremiah; I thought of the little frightened girl I used to be and now shunned.

Why was my family so broken?

Chapter Twenty-Eight

DALILA

It may be confusing to some how the cycles are divided. Consider that the first cycle began upon the growth of the first Evil after the establishment of Time's Contract as well as the attempted usurpation of the Elder King's eye. The first Seed, Xelxidon, was born eight hundred years after the Evil's ripening and brought the cycle to an end. Thus began the second cycle until the second Seed was born to conclude it.

—SUMMARY ON THE CYCLES. TAUGHT TO YOUNG SISTERS WITHIN THE SISTERHOOD OF THE FAITHFULL

During the little time I spent in the Sisterhood, I grew accustomed to the odourless marble hallways. The veined lines of the walls branched and reached up to its vaulted roof like roots.

What was a wholly new experience was the noise; a constant rush of chatter and gossip melding into itself.

Given time, I imagined the sound was like the sea. I never had a chance to see its waters, but my mother would tell me stories of great boundless bodies of water rising in tidal waves that could break on me like a hundred hammers. Or when they were tamer, mother described how the waves softly caress your bare feet in the sand as if craving your touch.

The sound within this abbey was more of the former, like a great striking wave threatening to pull me under. I tried to ride its rhythm instead of going against it.

Overall, the world was new and alien, intimidating and uncertain.

Other girls tried to approach me with welcoming smiles and pious greetings. Yet being torn from home and thrown into such a strange world made me distant; my lips sealed themselves no matter how pleasant the tidings were.

Eventually, the girls stopped their attempts except one who proved entirely relentless in her energy and spirits. She seemed oddly familiar at first, and as the days went by, I began to understand. This girl was me, or at least the version I had left behind.

Beaming and bright with hope, Yasmin was a cherubic young girl a year older than myself, her eyes were always wide with wonder and her cheeks were freckled liberally. I noticed on occasion that her hair was a deep rust-ginger on account of her rather unstable habit.

Despite her age, her attire was already fringed in a light yellow, telling of her dedication to the church itself.

I may not have given a great deal of replies, but even my one word comments to Yasmin were far more than anyone else had gotten out of me. I secretly thanked Yasmin for her persistence, for it proved a good distraction.

Her look on life was enviable, her desire and belief that everything could be well and good.

Given long enough, I had to excuse myself. The attention and interest Yasmin took in me felt undeserved. At times, she made me forget about Perry, at times, she made me forget about my magic that was kept secret from all the other students and most faculty.

It was a strange thing, to feel more comfortable with the familiar sensation of sorrow rather than taking the risk to be happy again. The idea of being entertained when all that was left of Perry had to be scraped from the forest floor felt wrong. It felt entirely wrong, allowing myself even a mere moment of joy in a world I knew could be so horrid.

During my first day, I entertained the idea of starting again, but I felt my soul stretch itself thin like scraped butter on toast. My past would not leave me. I moved on, taking a page from my father's book and losing myself in my duties.

Most of the hours in my day were spent learning of my responsibilities and duties, which consisted of keeping an orderly state and cleaning halls and making sure that the church remained presentable.

Though the entire establishment may have been referred to as church, the true church was an attached building with rowed benches, high verandas and balconies and a great rising plateau which towered over the chamber itself. The building could have easily held over thousands of individuals.

I saw little of Mother Vinrie other than when she was there to teach us how to appropriately hold ourselves as representatives of the church. My occasional classes with Mother Lucia were secretive retreats to imbed calmness and prevent the bubbling of my abilities.

My other classes had to do with arithmetic, languages, culture and, most importantly, history, especially the history of our world.

Out of all of the extra studies, I secretly had found myself growing ever fonder of Mother Margaret, who taught herbology, but it went far beyond just the study of herbs. We learnt how to stitch, mend wounds, diagnose illnesses, even so far as how one could concoct poisons in order to understand how one could treat its effects.

⊰ ⊱

It was one afternoon during the start of my second week when I entered the sleeping quarters that I shared with many of my fellow sisters and found a book waiting patiently for me on my bed.

My heart gave a reluctant beat as I realised what it was—my Kaseluda. There was a note scribbled on the top.

Nora returned looking like she had to wrestle it from an akar's grip. ~ *Mother Vinrie.*

I smiled tenderly and gave a silent thanks to Nora.

I rustled through the pages, barely even noticing the slight droplets of blood that found their way to the corner of pages and as soon as I saw the telling form of my blue trinket, I slammed the book shut before anyone else could chance a look.

My eyes strafed left and right to make sure no one had noticed. The other girls had begun to fill the room and exchanged gossip as they changed into their nightgowns.

Straightening out my own gown and trying to look as inconspicuous as possible, I gripped the book by its sizable spine before tucking it underneath my mattress for safekeeping.

Father and Mother used to tell me stories about Minethria and the Elders. But the tales were never whole. They were always patchwork retellings, its pieces taken from tattered remnants adrift at sea. I never did have the whole picture.

If the version told to me by Mother Elsia was the truth, I had no clue, but what I did know was that it was more fully formed than that which my parents had shared with me.

The world was as white as alabaster, formless, shapeless, made of nothing but the Haar.

One could walk its world and not fall through, but there was no concept of space, no concept of time, no concept of up or down.

The world was without its compass to orient oneself, and thus, one would walk aimlessly with no feeling of solid ground beneath one's feet. Sometimes one would wonder if they are upside down or perhaps walking sideways. Did you walk at elevation? Perhaps you were walking down a steep incline? It was impossible to tell.

The creator looked upon the state of the world and thought it barren and meaningless, so he sent upon the world his son, the King, the First Elder.

His crown grew from scalp and was of the brightest gold, as if forged by the flames of his own sun; his skin perfect and glistening like diamonds, his heart of incomparable majesty.

So the King did as the creator willed. From the Haar he formed the first trees; from the Haar he sculpted and made the first bird of such brittle wings to glide upon the winds that he blew into existence. Yet when the Elder King realised his reach had limits, he made his siblings from the Haar, those unbound by gender but who simply existed as an idea, as a purpose.

Next, the Elder King, in his endless wisdom, begged the Creator to form us humans.

The Creator did not understand. "Why my child? Why create a being unbound by us, why grant it free will and instil into it individuality?"

The King would argue thus: "It is precisely because they are unbound, because they are not tied to me or you or the other Elders, that they deserve such freedom. You created me because the world was formless. What form is there to something that is preordained? Is it not better to watch what path the world takes on its own? To not tangle the bend of the tree, but to let it thrive?"

Alas, the Creator obliged his son's wishes and brought mankind to the world: us. Bound by lock and key, he gave us gender so we may flourish untethered to the will of the Haar and the Elders.

When he saw us foolish and clueless to the nature of the world, eating upon poisoned berries and unable to see the truth of it all, he permitted us to share in the shine of his burning eyes and created colour.

So did the first sun rise up into the sky and reveal the beauty of the seven shades and their servants.

We were left to our devices and were the harbingers of war and hate, but also love and hope.

When the King wanted to give his subjects another chance, he created the first angel: the Grand Archon. It is said they are a great body of wheels spinning upon a central body of light. The wheels are covered in endless eyes. And within their golden spire, they formed the

Contract of Time to bind us mortals to its ticking clock.

Then there came more, the Elder King formed the lands for us to live in and created many other races such as the great Chitons deep within their mountain of Duran, insectoid beings, some even larger than the Elders themselves as their great, rotund Beetle King sits upon his throne. Large flies, colonies of monstrous wasps, great bodies of soaring dragonflies or even the ever ravenous mosquitos.

When, however, the borders could no longer be stretched, the Elder King created the first Seed, Xelxidon, her end of the cycle brought about the first spreading of the Haar and with it the zerubs. Beings with the heads of beasts, some may know of White-Hawk but there are many, many more.

The second cycle was led by Muriya the Protector, a great champion with hammer and might who swore to protect all beings. This brought about the raging sea monsters that roamed the pelagic depths and dissuade all who may wish to venture to the unforgiving waters.

The third brought with it the endless rage of the dragons: Kaelu the Strange, the silent, battled not with steel or hammer like brother and sister before them, but rather through whispers. Thin and sickly, withered and frail, with hair of algae green, Kaelu whispered the evil to death and ascended without having ever spoken a word.

Vikma the Congregator was beloved by all, carved in the image of a woman. He donned himself the mantle of man and swept through the lands with charm and panache, yet his cycle never did bring about another race to Minethria.

And so was it, too, with Nain of the Everglow, and again so with Jernun of Hivr. Marking an age with no new births.

Heyru of Dusk, with chakrams of the moon, danced the world into a new cycle. She ushered the coming of akar, who hammered mightily against their drums, the beating heart of their people resoundingly strong and demanding to be heard.

Kivran the Smouldering brought about the shavinu. People cursed with knowledge, seeing through their third eye their promised death.

Zaeo of the Lous left behind a nurturing light in the Lumari. Strange beings of the forest, with dainty bodies and a luminescent blue glow.

Accordingly, so too did Niefri of Blight midwife the Rashi: blood sucking monsters still hiding in their burrows away from human sight, far beyond the hems of civilization and past even the burning forest of demons.

≼ ≽

There was a certain bluster to these stories that was lost on me. Perhaps due to recent events which made me less excitable. Or perhaps being told about these old legends in a classroom robbed the stories of their appeal.

Regardless, I found myself often lost in the retelling of these events, my mind entering some delirious daydream where I would be taken by the ebbs and flows of Mother Elsia's story.

When she stopped her lesson at the telling of Niefri, I curiously recalled the untold and forbidden idea of the Eleventh Seed, the *true* Eleventh Seed. The thought vanished as quickly as it came, for I suddenly didn't feel compelled to entertain its mystery any longer.

One girl asked about the new Seed, I questioned her choice of words and thought perhaps that she also was treading lightly. I wondered how many girls, older and younger, suddenly harboured feelings of guilt due to an impossible task.

Mother Elsia nodded. She was not as old and wrinkled as others I had met, perhaps well into her fortieth year. There was still a spriteful and competent energy about her. She was a good teacher, focused, present, compelling and, more than anything else, incredibly astute. She did not reprimand students in that tasteless way some teachers did, but rather tentatively redirected and ushered one towards the focus of class.

Her attire was similar to ours, but the red hem told of her status and reputation as being a valuable member of the church, being a trusted teacher of their wisdom, and of being just wholly in its upper rankings.

"It hasn't even been a year yet since the Eleventh Seed has been born," Mother Elsia commented. I wondered if she subtly implied that it was okay to call the new Seed as the Eleventh.

"What is the new Seed's name?"

"No one knows yet if the Eleventh Seed has a name. It will be revealed when they are ready."

I frowned, not understanding. I raised my hand; my curiosity outweighed furtiveness.

"Yes, Dalila?" Mother Elsia seemed slightly pleased that I volunteered to contribute.

"What do you mean when you say that they will be revealed when ready?"

"Louder, child." Mother Elsia raised the volume of her voice as if to show me how it was done.

I cleared my throat and swallowed, engaging motion into my rarely used vocals and repeated my question; I felt as if I shouted.

Mother Elsia cupped her hands, her smile thin. "Well, the Seed is born as a vessel, a conduit for the cycle. As pliable and impressionable as a babe, they are raised within Mount Morniar until they form ideas, concepts, and beliefs. Once they do so, they are awarded with armour and blade made by the scorching blacksmith Elder who brandishes a new gleaming set made entirely for them.

"In time, the Seed will be given zerubs, yungbloods and humans of certain renown to help them on their quest of finding and slaying the Evil."

"But why?" asked another.

"So that when they return to the Creator, it is done so with wisdom and a view of the world about, they take their experiences so that they can share with the Creator. Alas, a creator is all knowing, but what can an all-powerful being know about what it is like to be mortal?"

⊰ ⊱

As we left the class and poured out the door, Yasmin caught up to me.

"Dalila!" She called. I turned to her. "Would you like to join me for lunch?"

"I'm sorry, there is somewhere I need to be," I admitted, though unable to mention Mother Lucia's name. Yasmin looked disappointed but spoke nothing of it.

As I made to turn, I caught an older Sister staring just like all the times before. She was in no rush to turn away. I asked Yasmin who she was.

"That's Candice. Comes from a well-to-do family. I heard she joined of her own volition."

"Do people usually not want to join?"

Yasmin shook her head. "It happens mostly with daughters who have no potential future." There was a sombre tone to Yasmin as she spoke. I wondered if I evoked memories better left buried.

Candice was older, her hair a fair and beautiful blonde but now hidden underneath her habit, her eyes a striking deep teal and her features fine and supple despite the slightly pronounced cheekbones. She was truly gorgeous.

But her eyes were always icy when they settled on me, her features barren.

She turned to her circle of friends and continued convening with them, and a slight smile resurfaced to her lips.

"Everything okay?" Yasmin asked.

"Yeah, it's fine," I said, making my way to Mother Lucia.

I did not quite understand where this uneasy sensation came from, why I would catch Candice staring like she did. Not once did we ever talk to one another, but since the moment I came to the abbey, I had tried my best avoiding her.

⋖ ⋗

Meditation had become one of the routines with Mother Lucia, a practice which instilled me with the rhythmic push and pull of waves. Once I anchored myself to that consciousness, she asked me to redirect it to my emotions, to sense the workings of my inner-self and toiling powers just beneath the surface.

I did not bother telling her that the numbness which dimmed the fireflies of my heart was more than enough to turn writhing emotion into snuffed out ash.

Truth be told, I appreciated meeting with Mother Lucia. Talking to her was the closest thing I had to honesty. Where I didn't have to pretend I was just like every other girl, it was the first time that I could voice my questions. Even the sentinel angels with their unmoving statuesque forms eventually became something I grew accustomed to.

"Mother Lucia," I said once the meditation had ended, and we began discussing my day.

Mother Lucia simply gave a slight 'hmm' to show she was listening.

"When did you first find out you were a witch?"

She blinked and threw back her head as she seemed to regress back to a very distant time.

"I think I was going through my eighteenth summer. Just like you, it was a story about love." As Mother Lucia recalled the memory, her voice grew ever more sombre and carried a brittle softness. "It's always love, always a story about love that makes us do what we need to do, that invites tragedy."

"Even Nayrien?" I cut in.

Mother Lucia hesitated for a moment, her lips pursed as she looked down at the table instead of to me.

Finally, she gave an affirming nod. "Even Nayrien. Her story was most tragic, not a love like yours or mine, but a sorrowful tale about her own sister who became infected by the rot and faded into decay. Her ever deep sorrow manifested in stormy clouds that filled the sky with bellied lightning and endless rain. Love can act as a catalyst to connect us with the power of creation. When the Elders tried to take her in because of her powers, she revolted… many people suffered because of it."

"What was he like?" I asked. "Your lover, I mean."

Lucia shook her head. "My love was not a man, you see, and that was where the problem began." A twitching smile stuttered across her features. "Her name was Grace." The name was handled gently, spoken as if its pieces would break and draw blood on her tongue.

"She was the most beautiful woman I ever met." Lucia permitted herself a single tear, carrying her sombre memory.

"She had this cleft chin." Her thumb and pointer finger framed her own chin to demonstrate. "Her eyes were wide things, and she had these full cheeks. She thought she was ugly. And maybe to some she was, but by god was she beautiful to me."

"What happened?" I asked, afraid to press too much.

Even Lucia seemed surprised to speak so openly. "Perhaps, another time," she said, her smile brittle.

Mother Lucia dismissed me on that note. I simply assumed she wanted some time for herself and was understandably exhausted.

Chapter Twenty-Nine

—the young girl born an Elder, brought to a deep slumber where her body became covered in roots and a tree sprouted from her belly. The tree grew branches, and the branches became walls that became the castle. The place changed as it willed, the same way the foundations of a dream may stretch. Mother Maiden was a projection of the girl's, a piece of her own gifted to those who required a guide through the endlessly shifting halls of Mount Morniar.

—MAKING SENSE OF THE SENSELESS—A GUIDE TO ELDER HISTORY, BY EUGEUNE MALIK

Within the endless halls of Mount Morniar, Ievarus was guided through its elusive belly. Their attire was one of dark blue, reminiscent of the colourless depths of the sea where the last few vestiges of light still graced.

Mother Maiden drifted along the cobblestone walls, their body hidden underneath the dragging mesh of robe like a tapestry of night, their steepled hands pointing downwards as Ievarus continued to follow whichever way they were taken. One mummified hand had extended itself from the midnight seam of Mother Maiden's garb to light the way.

They stopped at a door which appeared just like all the others, but when observed carefully, one could tell that it was angled oddly; was it leaning? Perhaps it was upside down? Or the halls itself wound and twisted in such inexplicable ways that it defied explanation.

This dream-like door opened, and within meditated the Preceptor, the same creature Ievarus had met in their father's throne room.

Preceptor was an oddly bloated and wholly spherical being who levitated in the midst of a runic circle. Long tentacles sprouted from pallid-grey cheeks, dancing and writhing, ostensibly of their own free will. The tentacles reached about the room to flip through opened leather tomes or to play with grails containing liquid of questionable complexion.

Preceptor's eyes were closed upon entering. As the door shut behind Ievarus, the Preceptor spoke their words. *"Art thou ready, Ievarus? To learneth of thy father's universe?"*

Ievarus stepped forward; it was their own act of affirmation.

"Very well, let thy knowledge expandeth."

Ievarus tentatively, and without any haste, stepped towards the inner circle, passing by bookshelves which contained hibernating wisdom. They stepped past the porticos guarding the middle. The dome above this centre shone and revealed motes of trailing dust. There was a circular depression constricted by three steps.

Drawn on the marble floor, a myriad of discordant geometry clashed with its neighbours, but it was true that there was a purpose behind the drawings. All around, along the steps and even within converging points of the diagram, there were white blocks of candles with their wicks burning, the wax puddling into white wreaths all around the clusters.

"What will I learn of today?" Ievarus asked, a question stated out of mild curiosity rather than any real passion.

The Preceptor's tendrils continued to work, paying their conversation no mind. Whatever there was to be said by Preceptor, it would be done so telepathically, yet silence was the answer that was given.

The being looked entirely like out of a stagnant and obtuse nightmare. The tendrils themselves wrapping around forked candles of gilded proportions while others dragged themselves diligently upon open tomes of knowledge, leaving behind a trail of slime. Preceptor's skin was just as sickly grey but the way their body swelled underneath the robes made them seem akin to a congested corpse, ready to explode with all their knowledge.

More of the tendrils sprouted from the floating being and extended.

Ievarus took a seat and crossed their legs. Milky and distant eyes tracked the worming tendrils.

One such tendril curled itself slowly around Ievarus' pale neck. The others dragged their weight across Ievarus' face.

Soon, one went through the corner of Ievarus' eye, the boneless limb stretching itself thin as it pulsed and wriggled. Another tunnelled inside Ievarus' nostril, a final one dug deep into Ievarus' ear. The tentacles found themselves a new home.

The world suddenly blanched and faded away like a distant dream as Ievarus stared upon a blank canvas.

There stood the king, their father, young and strong. The crown which grew from the Elder King's head was planted on a youthful and sculpted body of strength. Six arms were by the king's side and a staff of twisted oak was in his grip.

Raising a hand to the sky, the king fashioned the trees that rose from the mist; great, spanning land of lush green over distant hills.

The first of the Elders worked their way from the mist; beings of disproportionate design as if born from a painter's fevered dream. There stood Sielie, one of the earliest Elders that Ievarus had met with long limbs mounted on a wiry body. They wore a steel mask with slitted gaps for eyes. Black pearls peered out from them.

From the mist, there came the Chitons of Mount Duran, yet they already lived and thrived within the mist; mindless and without direction, they bided their time with baseless instincts. Like an endless, writhing swarm of monstrous insects, most held the form of normal bugs of larger size, but some, like the Beetle King, were anthropomorphic titans, a mesh of bug and humanoid form.

There was a girl, a young thing, diminutive compared to the monstrosities around her. She too was an Elder, an Elder lulled into a deep sleep as her dream took shape, building walls of shifting mortar and stone. She built Mount Morniar itself around her slumbering form.

The cycles came next.

Ievarus watched the retelling of history, great zooming distances coming into view to show the passing of ages.

Xelxidon of the light and the zerubs, a woman of such glow that one almost couldn't bear to look at her. She stood atop of a cresting cliff and raised her sword against distant threats.

Muriya the Protector, a great giant with a hammer that shattered the shells of writhing nightmares and conjured earthquakes.

The age of Dragons that came with Kaelu the Silent was a battle-field of scorched and scarred earth. The vision showed Zolas, the first dragon, as large as a mountain. A single beat of its wing caused great sundering storms and floods, its roar caused trees to be torn from their roots and for all of Minethria to quake underneath its force. Fissures ran its length and turned lands into islands that drifted to the distant sea.

Great passing images revealed a glimpse into the war and the hundred days of darkness where King Aemir donned both his eyes to face the dragon scourge.

Angels descended from atop of the Grand Archon's realm and even the remaining archangels, numbering seven, joined the fray. The archangels rode upon the back of a great worm brandishing several arms, it wielded swords and an infestation of eyes on its cream body. At the head of these angels stood Zeraphiel, with a face of such in-comprehensible beauty that it blazed like a piece of the Elder King's eye. He felled many-a-dragon who dared even look upon his grace.

Lightning split the sky, providing only the barest of light for the withering humans below to glance upon the chaos.

The Bugs of Duran arose as a swarm of their own, buzzing with amassing warrior wasps and other beings aback of flies.

Zerubs took to the fight while Yungbloods weaved their sorcery alongside the Elders.

The image left Ievarus and was replaced by another.

It was the quiet realm of the Ashen Forest. Ievarus veered their head to the sky and found a great ring of blazing fire. What drifted all about was not snow, but falling ash. It covered everything with silent acquiescence. The demons here were born at the end of Nain's cycle, before entrapping their fiendish kind within its pitted realm.

The Preceptor showed many more things, things strange and abstract, things caught by the fringes of their shadow; obscure and wondrous.

The rest of the cycle unfolded in a fevered flash until finally it was done.

Ievarus returned to the present as the tentacles receded. Another lesson instilled; another piece of Ievarus given so that they may become ready and conclude another cycle. And yet, Ievarus didn't appear any closer to their goal.

❧ ❧

Ievarus trained in many things. From start to end, their day was filled with lessons of history, of duty, and of combat.

Mount Morniar was a living place. Many doors led to entirely new worlds, new places dreamt up by the young girl who fell asleep on a rock. Yet no one could ever find her room since, not even Mother Maiden. Among the countless doors that spanned this mountain's dream, there was an Elder trapped in unending slumber.

❧ ❧

The surface of Mount Morniar was an incomprehensibly vast citadel of great bridges, ever-rising spires and dwarfing courtyards that proved entirely endless and impossible. Winding steps would drive most mad, as even the buildings themselves felt alive and watching.

Amongst its populace, Ievarus had met the CrowFather and LoreKeeper.

One would send out great flocks of crows that, when they returned, whispered tales and secrets of their journey to the CrowFather; a spindly and hunched giant.

CrowFather would then pass on this knowledge to LoreKeeper.

A being in perpetual trance, long and stick-like legs in a lotus position. Strange rat-like zerubs ran to and fro to groom and take care of the being. The LoreKeeper had no head but rather a single sprouting flower with its petals yet to blossom. But when CrowFather approached, the flower opened to reveal a giant ear to hear the CrowFather's whispers. Once, when Ievarus had visited, the flower blossomed a single eye for it to observe the new Seed with, before the petals wordlessly shut themselves closed.

Yet as odd as that was, the most noticeable aspect of the LoreKeeper were the many affixed arms attached to their upper body. They elongated endlessly so they could chronicle the CrowFather's whispers onto the blank pages of open ledgers.

Other beings included the Blacksmith, settled inside a domed chamber where the heat from the furnace immediately vapourised all moisture.

The being was made of cracked rock perpetually silhouetted by the blazing glow of a heat source inside his body. Affixed to the left peck was his younger brother made of a cold blue like that of ice. There was a hole as such where the heart would be.

There were many Elders among this world, strange beings of impermanent proportions and design. Maskmaker, Puzzler, Doll-Maker, Soprano, and yet others such as Silence, remained as elusive as ever.

To Ievarus, none of the strange and enigmatic within this domain could match the view atop of the courtyard. To stare out upon the ranging and bounding land of Minethria, a realm of permanence and assuredness—one could only wonder what went through Ievarus' mind.

Chapter Thirty

CHROMA

My visit in the akar settlement has opened my eyes to the truth. They are not beasts. I sensed loyalty, passion, and pride in these folk. The threat of the invading akar grows daily. If we wish to fight, we require the aid of their kin.

—REPORT TO COMMANDER ORSON, BY EREFIEL NUMYANA

J asper was unloading the last of the shipment, along with the other guards, when I neared the piled food.

"Let me help," I said.

Jasper had to do a double take when he saw me.

"You know, I still can't get used to how quickly you've grown."

I wasn't sure what Jasper meant until I looked down. It was true, four years had passed since the incident in the forest and I was no shorter than any other akar, quickly outgrowing my clothes as fast as Mother could make them. Yet I still lacked the width that the likes of Kolotha or Juta had.

"Don't worry, you will hit puberty too one day," I joked.

Jasper stifled a chuckle and motioned for me to leave with a dismissive wave.

I noticed two new guards grumble and mutter under their breath.

"What's with them?" I asked.

Jasper sighed. "Don't worry, lad. They're new here and haven't caught on to how things have changed."

There was a tense but noticeable armistice between the humans and akar. It was partially enforced by Erefiel's humanitarian program, but also given foundation because of the incident in Dreamwood. Jasper certainly had become friendlier since then. If it was due to our conversation or him feeling indebted to me, I was not certain, but I didn't complain.

"There are rumours of a large akar force invading from the highlands, and that has set everyone on edge," he said.

I chuckled. "A great force? That isn't likely. The tribes can't be united yet. Or that's what Mother said." Despite my comment, the idea did excite me. Father could be among the forces.

Jasper shrugged. "They are just rumours after all; no scout could get a clear enough number, but there is a force coming, and we have our men readying themselves to meet at Greyhill."

I nodded. I threw two stacks of rice over my shoulder and was on my way. I found Kolotha and Trem walked my way. Trem hadn't changed much. Kolotha had shaved most of his hair except for a single tuft in a ponytail bound with a collection of bones. White tattoos slithered on what skin they could find upon his scalp.

"Hi," I said.

Trem responded in kind, though Kolotha only snarled. I sighed as I passed them, thinking that Kolotha again was in some sour mood. It was impossible to tell if the akar was just constantly angry or if there truly was something that bothered him.

We moved back and forth, unloading the delivered rations into a storage silo built in the town itself. I tried my best to avoid making eye contact with Kolotha.

To break the tension, I decided to test the waters. "Should we report the refilled silos to Nokna?"

He shook his head. "Father is aware."

"Wasn't he made to wear that silly human outfit?" Trem teased.

Kolotha growled and bared his tusks. "I'd rather not have to think about that," he admitted.

Trem chuckled and failed to read the mood. "I don't blame you, the toga is unbefitting his form. At least he wasn't made to wear those suffocating clothes the highborn would wear."

Kolotha's fists clenched. "It is all an insult. He is chieftain and the humans dress him like one of their pets," he muttered.

"There you are," Siemeny said, walking over to us with Nedalya in tow.

Nedalya and I avoided looking at each other as she walked to Kolotha.

"Hello, my love." Nedalya's lips pressed passionately against her mate's. He wrapped his own thick arm around her and pulled her closer. My gaze found the floor.

I wondered if Siemeny felt suddenly threatened as she also took Trem's lips for a passionate kiss.

Trem's eyes bulged as he pushed Siemeny away. "Are you a Rashi? Trying to suck the life out of me."

Siemeny tried to not look flustered. I stifled a laugh.

We all had grown. Even the women sported strong and toned muscles.

"How was it?" Kolotha asked.

Nedalya spat on the floor as if it contained her opinion. "They make you learn how to sow, how to cook, how to be a good wife. Worse still, they make us learn about our exilers as if they were gods. It goes against everything we have ever learnt."

Siemeny gagged.

"It can't be that bad?" I asked with a chuckle, though I agreed that it left a bad taste in my mouth to be told that our mortal enemies were to be worshipped. The Elders were the only reason my people waged war at all.

"Of course, you would think so. We are warriors, Chroma, not human pets taught how to cook," Kolotha said.

"It isn't all bad; at least we get to be educated. To read, to write," I countered.

Kolotha scoffed. "You sided with them and killed one of our own. You fraternise with the Nephilim. Why am I not surprised that you are defending the humans?" Kolotha stepped towards me.

The others turned quiet. I felt everyone tense at the promise of violence.

I frowned. There was no pretence anymore; Kolotha was looking for a fight. "Kolotha, are you implying something? If you have something to say, then say it." I didn't shrink away. I stepped up to Kolotha and met his stare.

"Stop it," Nedalya said, taking a step between the two of us. She eyed her lover with warning.

My heart stung when she touched my chest. All it took was a lingering graze to make me step back.

"What Kolotha simply means is that all these changes are too sudden. Where will it end?" Trem said, siding with Kolotha.

I felt ambushed. "Are you suggesting I am one of them because I like to learn? Or because they provided us with food and medicine and teaching?"

"You are recognized as Baatar yet killed one of our own. You advocate all this change and it will eat away at our roots like a pest." Kolotha snarled, his tone deep. "You used to oppose our oppressors, too. What happened?"

I bristled. "You think me a traitor? Simply because I see value in knowledge? You have questioned me ever since that day. What is it? Do you think I don't deserve my title?" I challenged. I glanced over at Nedalya, who stepped away. I was the one who suffered at seeing my love give herself to another, so why was Kolotha the one attacking me?

Kolotha nodded. "You're more like them than you are like us. You don't deserve the title of Baatar." The last part was laced with venom.

My chest rose and fell with great breaths. My fist tightened of its own volition.

"I am a warrior." Kolotha slapped a hand to his chest with a passionate grunt. "My love is a warrior," he said and waved at her. Nedalya avoided looking at either of us.

"We are all warriors, proud of our heritage. But not you."

Nedalya found her voice again and spoke up. "That's not true!" Her protest was cut short by a biting snarl from Kolotha.

The shock was only temporary. She didn't back down. "Do not silence me! You won't like how it ends." She stepped between us, her back to me and her defiant gaze directed at Kolotha.

"We are *all* warriors. Chroma did what was right," Siemeny said. She harboured no emotion on the topic, simply only stating that which she perceived as fact.

I had nothing to say. Kolotha just glared at me.

Silence swelled until it was Siemeny who spoke and swerved the currents. "If you wish to settle things, you will do it in a way in keeping with culture."

Kolotha and I turned to face her, Siemeny's meaning clear.

"What?" Nedalya voiced.

"In the ring, fight to settle your differences."

The suggestion lit a fire in Kolotha, who grasped hungrily at the opportunity. "Fight me, Chroma. We will do it as our ancestors did." Kolotha's black eyes looked down at me. I could tell he craved for me to say yes.

Instead, I turned to leave.

⋞ ⋟

I made my way to my yurt, my mind a swirl of corroding thoughts. Mother sat inside tangling wicker baskets cradled upon crossed legs. Her muscular form seemed more apt for war than to weave.

"How are things?" she asked. I was sure my mood was written on my face. I took a seat beside her, taking up the toil as if to make sense of my disorderly thoughts the same way I made baskets out of woven strands.

"Kolotha is upset with me about something. Ever since that night with Nedalya, he has been distant."

"Isn't Kolotha always distant? He shows as much emotion as a rock."

I chuckled at the idea. "Yeah. I thought that I was just imagining it. Maybe he was just becoming sour with age? He has good days and bad days. Sometimes, he ignores me outright and other times he tries to help me. But today… he is angry with me about something." I let my thought settle before speaking it. "Even though he is the one who is with Nedalya."

Mother chuckled. "You are not owed anything, child. Not even someone like Nedalya." She nodded sombrely. "It is a shame, but a wild one like that can't be owned. You didn't believe in yourself, and she went with another. That's her choice."

I nodded; it hurt to hear but it was the truth.

"Did he say why he was upset?"

I shook my head. "Not exactly. He just said that I sided with the humans when I killed Ji'sura. That I don't deserve to be Baatar. I think it's also because of all this change in the settlement."

Mother nodded. "A lot of akar are having a hard time adjusting. As am I." She waved at the half-finished basket as if to make her point. "But I also know that sometimes, we need to adapt to our situations. Everybody knows that these changes are for the best. The extra food. The education. It may not be our way, but there are benefits."

She lowered the basket and turned to me. She took one of my hands in hers. In her eyes, I found comfort and stability. "You did the right thing, saving those children. Kolotha is a proud akar, he takes after his father and everything they represent. He has a lot of expectation riding on his shoulders as the son of the chieftain. Just give him time and he will come around."

My hands slipped from Mother's. I gave a brittle smile. "I don't know. Ever since Nedalya, I don't think things will ever go back to the way they were."

My hands wished to slip from her touch, so mother cupped my head instead, drawing me in for a loving kiss to my forehead. "We are akar. Passionate folk with deep and powerful emotions. That means we share in the deepest pits of anger, but also in love. That counts for something."

"You truly think so?"

"I know so." Unlike my own smile, hers was reassuring, unwavering even. It was these words that gave me the confidence to speak my mind.

"I have a question of my own," I began hesitantly.

"Ask me."

"Where do you disappear at night?"

Mother froze. She didn't know what to say. Her smile faltered.

"I noticed it first years ago, and since then, I notice it more often. They aren't taking you to the garrison, since you are still here."

"It's nothing."

"Well, they are having you do something."

Mother laid a hand on my arm, and fixed me with a pleading expression. This wasn't some game about love; mother truly was begging me not to persist.

"Okay, fine," I said sullenly, returning to work on the wicker basket as the rest of the labour went by in silence.

⊰ ⊱

Stealth used to be a simple matter when I was younger and smaller. It had become awkward the older I became. I trailed and stalked Mother. She was heading to the settlement entrance.

As long as it was within the vicinity of the settlement, the rules had become more lax in terms of who entered and left, though that was not the case in the midst of night.

I stumbled through and found the removable plank hidden behind Trem's home. The moment I heard what sounded like an argument, I tried my best to avert my attention, but curiosity got the better of me. I eavesdropped on a disgruntled Siemeny complaining about why Trem doesn't kiss her passionately. Managing to stifle a chuckle, I snuck my way out.

I was large, perhaps not as large as the likes of Juta or Kolotha, but I surely reached up to seven feet in height. Sneaking past the guards proved a more trying task as I had a select number of things I could use for cover, including piled containers of what I assumed were food and the occasional hut.

It occurred to me, then and there, that I had no idea what I was looking for or where Mother could be. But then I heard it, like a whisper, Mother's voice, locked in discussion.

I neared the house and found a space between two stacks of barrels. The window leaned open, and I could hear her inside.

"What is it?" I heard from the other side of the wall, but dared not look in case I gave my position away.

"I... Chroma knows," mother said worriedly.

There was a moment of quiet. "Did he say so?"

"Not quite, but he knows something is going on; asked me where I was going."

"Did you tell him?"

Silence followed. Mother must have answered with a shake of her head as Jasper continued speaking.

"I see. Well, we knew he was going to find out, eventually."

This time, I thought Mother to truly be silent. She sounded distraught.

"This isn't a good idea, Jasper."

"Zarien, please." The words were coaxing. There was a warmth to them that made me sick. An unpleasant truth started to dawn on me, a truth that thrummed into the beat of a burning heart.

"I treat you fairly, do I not?" Jasper asked, but no reply was given. There was a defeated sigh. "It is not without its perks." I heard the clanking of coins within a purse. It was a sickening sound.

"Okay, fine."

I knew it was wrong of me to listen, wrong of me to stay there and seethe with rage at hearing Jasper bed my mother with the promise of coin. I heard the ruffling of clothes, the kisses, the moans of my mother as she gave herself to this human. They writhed and folded their bodies into sweaty and tangled messes. The sound of their thrusting and bucking bodies was hell in my ears. I felt the room's light bleed into the night, taunting me. It tried to make me look inside as my mother was being defiled.

It suddenly all made sense; I should have known. It was so obvious.

There was no way mother was able to make enough coin to feed me more than most, there was no way she could afford such luxuries such as chocolate or whatever else she got her hands on, and there was certainly not a chance that she could afford to buy me such fine clothes.

I never questioned it. She said she was doing other work. I assumed it was some form of field work or perhaps the charity of some other member. I had never expected her to be selling her flesh.

I couldn't take it anymore. With my back turned to leave, I heard a knock against the wall that made my heart turn cold. Instinctively, I hid among the barrels around me.

"Keep it down in there!" A guard called out. The man was barely a stride away; his shadow stretched over as if to aid in hiding me.

The man laughed and left. Mother's moans turned ever louder.

I was going to be sick.

I couldn't take it anymore. I left and made my way back to camp and through the opening behind Trem's tent. Rage spread inside me and even behind the protection of the settlement walls, I could still hear mother's moans beat against my ear.

Sleep eluded me for most of that night. Even when sleep did come, I could hear the slapping of flesh against flesh, mother's carnal sounds and the vile clanking of coin.

⋖ ⋗

When I heard mother enter the hut and make her bed, I wasn't entirely sure if I was awoken from a fitful slumber or if my mind had just gone dormant with all the pent up rage inside me.

"Chroma, are you still awake?" Mother's voice was soft. It belonged to a whispering ghost, and her words were lined with apology.

With my back turned to her, I pretended to be asleep.

Mother lay in her bed. I heard her sob herself to sleep. I still felt hot from all the anger. It made me sweat and my heart beat against my rib-cage.

Come morning, I arose before Mother and went to find breakfast. A lot vegetables with a side of cooked rice and stale bread. I found a cosy place of solitude to down my food.

I ignored the morning greetings thrown my way. Akar understood generally that when in a sour mood, they were to be left alone. Though not everyone seemed to follow the advice.

"What has you in such a bad mood?"

"Not now, Trem," I said.

"Oh come now, you can always lean on Uncle Trem." He reached out with a casual hand to take a bite from my bread. "Is it about Kolotha?" His tone more sincere.

I grabbed onto his wrist and squeezed tightly till he dropped the loaf. Even Trem winced at the sudden pressure.

"Not. Now." The words squeezed through gritted teeth. My gaze never met his.

"By Googan; fine!" Trem caught an inkling of my sour mood and tore his hand away. "What is going on with the two of you?" he asked before leaving me.

I munched on the rest of my food and scanned the surroundings. I wanted something to direct my anger at. Kolotha's mention only made me feel worse.

Caustic thoughts kept me company. I bristled, thinking of how Jasper smiled and joked with me, all the while laughing behind my back as he made my mother his whore. How could I have been so blind? Accepting those gifts from mother, never questioning how she bought them.

For a brief moment, the image of Jasper was replaced by another. This body larger, skin darker, everything more imposing.

My spoon gave soft cracks before snapping in my grip. I looked at it. Splinters jutted from my skin. I numbly plucked them. Anger numbed any pain.

My chest heaved as blood leaked from the wound. My fingers curled into fists. My anger needed release.

I searched till I found the tattooed giant. His eyes riveted me. I stepped towards him with bundled fists. The image of Jasper fucking my mother sustained me. Kolotha straightened. He looked as if he'd been expecting me. Nedalya and the others were with him. We all knew something in the air had changed.

I stood before the chieftain's son. "I don't know what your problem is, but it doesn't matter. Let's settle this." I saw red, my vision fading between moments of lucidity and pure anger. At times, I imagined Jasper standing before me.

Kolotha didn't step back from the challenge. Though his temper was as cold as ever, it was obvious that he too desired this bout.

"I invoke the rule of Bah'Kha. No restraints."

"What?" the others rebutted.

Kolotha snarled. "Are you sure you wish to die?" His question was spoken deep and without inflection.

I stepped up to him, my eyes full of rage locked to his of calm gaze. "Shut up and fight."

The new fighting pit was modestly sized. Given its dimensions and the impressive size of the average akar, the square was only five large strides wide and did not give much room for combat. But it didn't matter, the ring served its purpose.

It was filled with sand. Akar of all sizes and sexes would pound against each other and bare their tusks.

Standing opposite me was Kolotha. He cracked his neck and rolled his shoulders, his form like an unmoving trunk rooted to the ground.

I stood with a ready stance and surveyed the surrounding sand. My eyes were on my adversary, drawing upon every exploitable weakness that I could spot.

A crowd had gathered about us, watching with anticipation. Their unusual silence inferred a sense of respect and attention to truly observe our promise of blood. Juta stood as referee on the side-lines, making sure that we understood the depth of our agreement, and that once it began, no one was allowed to stop it.

The rules were simple. The fight goes on until someone forfeited, was out of bounds, or was incapacitated through any means, even death. The invoked rule of Bah'Kha made it so that we could fully commit without any need for restraint. Death was not uncommon in these fights.

Juta looked at us and made sure we were prepared. "Engage when ready."

"Chroma! What are you doing?" I turned to find Mother in the crowd, standing tall and her expression full of worry. A brief flash of her defilement crossed my mind, and I growled, my fists curling.

I ignored her and turned back to Kolotha.

Siemeny was the first at mother's side, along with Nedalya and Trem as they tried to quell her concerns. Mother showed no sign of panic or distress. But I could tell she was confused. Her brows were bowed and knitted together. She was looking for an answer that didn't end in pain.

"I will prove to you that you are not one of us," Kolotha promised.

Kolotha's presence was akin to a beast's. Broader, taller, and far more menacing than I could hope to be. Tattoos scrawled him. His nose carried that horizontal piercing. His eyes were a deep and brooding darkness where the whites were barely visible at their horizon. His lower half was covered by a typical akar kilt adorned with even more bone while I wore brown pants and had my feet bare. I removed my shirt to not provide any hold. The difference in our size was laughable.

Kolotha glanced down at my more athletic and dextrous body.

We met at the centre and neither of us looked away. We took the starting stance of Baatar, bringing our foreheads together as my right hand gripped his nape, and he did so in kind. The fight hadn't even begun, and I already felt his monstrous fingers threatening to push me to my knees.

My left hand grabbed Kolotha's right for a crushing handshake. The heat from our bodies radiated and mixed. His eyes were bottomless pits that I tried not to drown in. His hold met mine, and I winced at the effort.

Our locked stares turned intense, an understanding dawning upon me that our fists would meet in a few moments.

"Commence!" Juta called, and the crowd turned lively. People shouted instructions, cheering one side or the other, some seeing me as the underdog, while others calling for Kolotha to end it quickly. The deep voice of Nokna resounded in the crowd, telling his son to be careful of his leg.

In between all my anger, I wished my own father could be there to cheer me on. The stray thought was already a mistake I would come to regret.

A great weight pressed against the back of my neck and pulled me to Kolotha's right.

The arena's border was just a stumble away.

My feet abandoned the floor and wrapped themselves around Kolotha's waist; I took the chance to strike with my elbow.

We were teetering at the edge, my strikes and weight making Kolotha bow ever so slightly like a leaning tree over a precipice. He roared, pulling us away from the edge and throwing me back into the ring's centre.

I jumped to my feet and charged for a grapple, wrapping my arms around his waist as Kolotha stretched his toes out behind him to brace. His fist struck my rib and robbed me of air. My hold weakened. Two more punches broke my grip, and I created some distance. Kolotha was a mountain bearing down on me.

His punch came and narrowly missed as I struck in return. The bones in my arms ached at the recoil, but I could not relent. Our punches became a flurry of blows that pounded into each other's flesh. Kolotha's swings felt like boulders as I almost keeled. Some savage thirst for this exchange kept me on my feet. I was tired, exhausted, Kolotha's compounding force threatening to cave in my skull. My heart beat to the rhythm of this exchange.

I felt it. My feet danced to it. Our fists made the music. It fuelled my punches and I could feel how my strikes challenged Kolotha's momentum.

Reflexively, I leaned into the storm where his swings had shorter range. My forehead crashed into his. I punched his hardened stomach. If the blows fazed him, he didn't let it show.

A returning hail came from Kolotha. I dodged by a hair's breadth and struck out with my own fists. The weight behind my punches felt true. But Kolotha was more than just muscle—he was uncompromising will.

His roar said it all.

I blocked another punch and created an opening with a head-butt—more stars trailed my doubling vision. Kolotha's head whipped back for a decisive moment as my free hand gripped his offered wrist. I pulled him in and twisted his arm as my feet abandoned the sand to find purchase about his neck.

We went hurtling to the floor, Kolotha's wrist in my hands, his arms like a reluctant lever pulling against my strength. His arm trembled at the effort, the bulging muscles and writhing veins straining against me. His overwhelming strength pulled me to a seated position. His bulging forearm was perpendicular to his shoulder. A desperate fist from his free hand swung and grazed my already rattled skull. The power was enough for my strength to loosen. Quickly, Kolotha grabbed my hair and pulled me in for a head-butt of his own. I relied on my built up ire to clamber onto consciousness while the scent of blood filled my world.

We contorted about each other. Punishing throws hammered against my ribs as a sharp pain flared.

I let go and rose for an uppercut that clipped his chin.

We moved about with our knees. I dove again at his legs and coiled myself around the limb, but my grip failed, and instead an elbow hammered against my spine.

I pulled back quickly, just in time for Kolotha to jump on top of me. He managed a half-mount. His fists pounded against my shielding forearms—I could feel my bones bend beneath the weight of his attack. I opened my block and tilted my head, narrowly dodging a strike. I pulled him close with the weight of his offered arm.

His outer leg was claimed by my own coiling legs as I took his head into a lock.

Did I just hear Mother cheering me on? Nedalya? I had almost forgotten the audience that encircled us.

"I won't lose!" Kolotha bellowed.

Fists attacked my already wounded ribs, and I abandoned my grip.

Kolotha rolled away, and breathed heavily as he rose to his feet. My breaths were far more laboured. The giant almost fell to his rear.

I rushed forward. My body was burning. Kolotha prepared to meet me in a grapple. I feinted as if I were going for another grab before jumping high with a knee to Kolotha's chin.

His knees buckled. I seized the chance and pushed him back. One step, two step. His footing slipped as the sand under his feet gave way and he ploughed great divots. I kept pushing.

A powerful roar sounded. Mine. The crowd roared back. Kolotha met my challenge. His movement halted. He teetered on the bounds, barely the length of his big toe left, yet he held on, he persisted. His growl was defiant, desperate even.

No matter how hard I pushed, it was now me who ploughed divots into the sand. He pushed back, sounding his own battle cry as I neared the edge. I broke our grips and landed a right punch that sent Kolotha's lips fluttering, giving me the chance to land two, three, four more.

A gash opened up above his left eye, unveiling a curtain of blood. I realised then one of my eyes was almost swollen shut. My body screamed at me to stop, but my spirit lost itself in the battle.

Kolotha gladly returned punches. His very body was a weapon, something designed to bludgeon and destroy, to overwhelm the opponent.

Ever deeper, I sunk into the primal trance, forgetting the very reason I engaged Kolotha in the first place. This was what I wanted, that sheer moment of blind, stupid numbness where my frustration, my pain, my anger was forgotten and the throbbing of my body became a distant lull, guiding me to the shores of cathartic release. I surrendered myself completely to the throes of carnage. On a sea of intense scarlet, I found the purest form of rage, a sensation that turned caustic emotions into fuel with such an intense beauty I had never sensed before—it was intoxicating.

Did I grab his wrist or he mine?

It didn't matter, neither of us would let go.

Our fists met over and over in some gratuitous celebration of blood.

Rhythmically, we pounded each other's faces as a carnal laugh and roar exploded from our lungs. I spat blood. He did too. It was our libation for this festival. We were lost in the Blood Dance.

The pain, the blood, the torn skin from our knuckles—*this* was what it meant to be akar. It was beautiful.

"Stop it right now!" I heard but could not see—they were human voices. Human guards rushed in with swords at the ready.

"What is the meaning of this?" Nokna asked, his voice like thunder.

"You tell me. Are you animals, after all?" I heard Jasper ask.

A deep, guttural growl escaped Nokna.

Guards closed in on us and tried to grasp my hand.

I wasn't finished.

My open hand struck a guard and sent him flying to the ground. My rage was directionless as I turned to newly offered flesh.

"Hold him!" More guards called.

"Chroma! It's over!" Mother called out from a distant shore, where the scarlet tide lapped at the sand.

"Stop it!" Cried Nedalya from somewhere far away.

I sent soldiers to the floor. My fists hammered into the men that closed in around me.

A deep gash bled from my arm and I could feel the warmth, distant but alive, pool along the contours of a boat within my red sea. Their charge met with my resistance. All until Juta stepped into the ring and handled me. Whatever he did sent me into the quiet.

The quiet was wrong; I longed for the heart-pumping release. For the Blood Dance.

Chapter Thirty-One

NORA

Thickwood is an uncontainable and direct consequence of the reced-
ing Haar. What remains of the sprawling cultures are now protected
behind Bravnicka's borders. But alongside Estria, it is believed the ruins
of old cultures and kingdoms still lay buried somewhere inside the forest.
And if not there, then it waits within the embrace of Haar.

—A STUDY ON THE LOST KINGDOMS BEFORE THE ADVENT
OF THE ELEVENTH CYCLE

My squadron paced close to my heel and numbered fifty men. Twelve were archers and another four rode alongside me on horseback; the rest were foot soldiers, pikemen and swordsmen, but no akar.

We departed from Cleria and made a stop at Fort Treb for provisions and gear before continuing. We needed to be prepared for the coming attack.

Reports spoke of a strong akar force amassing within Thickwood. I was rather sceptical that such primitive and simple-minded folk could organise such an army.

They tried almost two decades ago, and all they managed to do was separate a group of their dissidents and make them our problem. I understood that the rest broke into infighting, once more forming tribalistic bodies. Regardless, it would have been irresponsible to ignore it. I heeded Erefiel's call with my own humble company. Four years. Four years it had taken until someone of my status earned a company of her own, despite my supposed lack of certification in the form of a dangling phallus.

Our corner of Bravnicka was walled by mountains with a single opening that funnelled the invading akar. Greyhill.

I had a sinking feeling in my stomach the closer we got to Greyhill. Bradley cantered up beside me and whispered to me my fears. "Where are all the men?" he asked.

I didn't respond, and nicked my mare to speed up.

To our right, there was a stone fort. It sat on a far off hill and served as a watchtower. The opening of Greyhill was too large to construct any defensive wall to cover its span, so we opted for a normal defence.

I stared at Thickwood first and then turned to Bradley; my first recruit and second in command. Then there were Stamence, Howard and Victor. They were proven veterans. With a final glance at my hatchlings, who would get their first taste of akar might, I wondered how many of them would survive.

⊰ ⊱

The further I ventured into the encampment, the larger the sinking feeling grew.

"Unload the wagons! See what needs help setting up! Be on your way and find time to rest! You will need it!" Victor called out from his white stallion as the men nodded and went on their way.

Bradley paced to stand by my shoulder. "Is this a joke?" he asked, not even a hint of humour to his query.

I looked out at the scarred field. No green to carpet the floor, just dirt. I looked to the sky where the clouds swelled. I felt the promise of rain on my skin.

How many times before was the ground baptised by blood? How many more would lose their lives today?

I looked around, internalising and counting the stray souls wandering to and fro. They carried crates of weapons, gathered wood from felled trees. Leaning pikes were being planted to give some false sense of protection.

"How many do you think? Six hundred?" Stamence asked, bringing his steed to us as Howard and Victor joined right after.

"Less," I said. I couldn't keep the bleakness from my voice. "Maybe five hundred if we are lucky."

"And how many of them are actual soldiers and not some glorified squire?" Howard asked with obvious distaste.

"Let's go find Erefiel." I was growing restless inside but couldn't show any panic. I steered my mare to the stables.

⋪ ⋫

The situation was worse than I thought. What was originally supposed to be a force numbering as high as thousand five hundred was far less than that. I recognized none of the troops that came and could tell at a glance that most had not faced the threat of death often enough.

Following the trail of this failure to its root proved easy. I arrived at a grand white marshal's tent and wondered what nepotism awaited me.

I heard Erefiel. He was unhappy. I entered the tent.

"You!" I cried. Cassidy smiled as I entered. It suddenly all made sense. Erefiel stood glowering to the side.

"Ah, Captain Nora, such a pleasure to see you, how is your company?" Cassidy rested on a sofa of polished yew, cushioned with fitted velvet. The backrest formed a wave. He ate grapes like some comical emperor from a fairy-tale.

"How is your limp dick? Did your arm heal enough, or do you have to get one of your servants to get you off?"

There was a guard standing in the back like another piece of furniture. He snickered quietly before quickly tucking away his amusement.

Cassidy's smile vanished. "Careful who you speak to, whore; I am your superior." He threatened with a pointed finger.

"Yes, but don't forget that I am *your* superior, Marshal Cassidy."

Cassidy reclined back into his velvet couch. His tongue prodded the walls of his cheeks.

"What is all this? Where is the rest of the force?" I asked. I was sure Erefiel had already made his concerns heard.

"You have an army," Cassidy responded.

"*That* is a skirmish force, *not* an army."

"What's the issue? This number has never been a problem before."

Erefiel kept his composure far better than I could have hoped for, and sighed. "Yes, but that was before we received reports of an overwhelming force. I sent out a request for reinforcements."

Cassidy turned to Erefiel with a dumb, toothless grin and straightened his red robe. It was the perfect colour to conceal blood if I decided to gut him in his sleep.

"And I reversed that decision, Lieutenant General. You may be my superior, but that is only in title; you have no power over me." Cassidy stated casually. "Our taxpayers give out enough money as it is. I won't send out and ask for troops for a mere rumour. Nobody can even truly tell by just looking into the depths of that thicket." He waved dismissively towards the direction of the trees as he went to stand, making his way to a neighbouring shelf where he poured himself a glass of something dark. I had no doubt in mind that he was more worried about pocketing the money of his donors than the actual welfare of the common citizen. He wouldn't even need to step into the combat.

"Brandy? Anyone?" When neither of us responded, he offered some to his guard. He drank when the offer went unheeded.

"Cassidy Femur, and what if there is an invading force numbering in the hundreds? Will you take responsibility for all those who die at your hands?"

Cassidy sighed and pinched the bridge of his nose as if to block a coming migraine.

"Will you stop your whining? I sent another scout team. Told them to make certain there truly is such an organised force of akar; which, by the way, has never happened in the decade and a half since they have been organising. I think we will be just fine."

My heart stopped for a brief moment. But it was Erefiel that spoke first, finally showing the last thread of his patience gone up in flames.

"You did *what?*" he asked, taking a step closer to Cassidy who shrunk under Erefiel's glare.

"I… I sent a scouting team to check on the rumours." Cassidy's confidence waned.

"And did you think, perhaps, that you should discuss such a thing with your superior, the very man charged with the defence of Greyhill?"

"We-well—with all due respect, Erefiel, those were men from my division. I did what I thought was right as acting Marshal."

I could not quite hear what Erefiel muttered under his breath, but I could have sworn I saw his shadow thicken. I fancied even just a slight whimper from Cassidy.

Erefiel took a step forward and Cassidy took one back.

"So, the enemy could be organising a mass coalition beyond the tangled branches of that forest, they could be waiting for us to show our cards. Not only do you deny reinforcements, but you send in a second scouting team who, if they are caught, could tell the enemy that all we have to defend ourselves with is just five hundred men?"

Cassidy stumbled over his words before finally managing some semblance of decorum. "Arnold and his men are no third-rate amateurs. They will be wary," he stammered.

Drums played outside. The sudden bustle of men filled the air. Wordlessly, Erefiel and I shared worried looks before rushing out to inspect.

The world darkened even further. The scent of wet earth was in the air. A rumble of thunder echoed from the heavens as dark clouds knitted together just in time for war. The men gathered at the front where our barricades and defences were built, chests heaving as they silently observed the spectacle. All were silent.

I focused my eyes towards the edge of the forest and finally understood what everyone was looking at. A handful of akar stood there. As tall, wide and powerful as their kind could be. They approached from the cover of trees.

There was a leaner body in the mix, but no less foreboding. He stepped out into view and onto the scarred battlefield. His muscles bulged.

I noticed one of our own being dragged by his hair; kicking and crying in pain, hands clasped helplessly at the monstrous wrists of the lean akar which held him captive.

The akar tossed our man to the floor. Our soldier laid prone, unable to rise to his feet. I thought it was due to fear at first. I pushed forward for a closer look and noticed something was wrong with his legs. They must have been broken.

Cassidy approached from behind and numbly invoked the name of Arnold as a fading breath. It was the name of the supposed professional about to die.

There was some cry for help from Arnold, but it was barely audible as the akar reached for an axe brought for him. This akar held our gaze. He stretched the moment out into long, enslaved seconds.

Arnold whimpered. He pleaded for help. His words were drowned in his own tears as all others remained wordless. The axe fell and christened the battlefield with the blood of our kind; it was just the first of many.

A wet crunch sounded when the akar retrieved his axe, returning its heft to its original bearer. They retreated. Yet the boundless intensity of his glare would not let us be until the final moment when the shadow of the forest swallowed him and his men whole.

⚔ ⚔

Panic settled like an infection. Men ran to and fro, preparing final defences and palisades that would do little against the akar.

Eyes kept dashing from tree to tree where we expected the invaders to come any second.

I cursed the akar and their tactics. Something about the executor unsettled me. If they had the information, why didn't they just attack? They would have the element of surprise. Akar were rather straightforward. They didn't usually rely on battle tactics, at least not incredibly complicated ones.

A strange thought occurred to me, but surely I must have been reaching?

I turned to the men and saw some evidence to back up my concern. They were infected. Mania gripped the camp.

Did the akar do it deliberately? Plant the seed of fear to threaten our cohesion? Was the akar their leader? I had never seen him before. I cleared my thoughts. It mattered little if it was intentional or not; what I needed was a solution.

I was informed that two men were found trying to flee. I felt sorry for them, but this wasn't the time to get cold feet. They had to stand in the frontlines, as was their recourse.

Most of the preparations were in order and our squad commanders already organised the units and brought them to formation.

Erefiel was in the war room with a table and a map. The others stared at its edges in the search for answers.

Cassidy sat on one of the decorated wooden seats to denote his noble status. He had already changed into his battle gear made up of chain mail and plated armour. It sat awkwardly on his pampered body. He stared blankly at the table.

I found some comfort when I recognised a bard from the College in Museya, as well as a hooded mage in deep grey colours that denoted him as a Mistmage.

The bard I recognised as Maxin, the same one who took part in Perry's wake. His hair was a messy bird's nest with not an ounce of care. His eyes were sunken, but a deep cunning intelligence radiated from them as if trying to turn his understanding of the world into musical notes. His attire was in perfect form, tailored to uphold the College's class but be free moving enough in times of war.

Maxin wore a brown tie and was wrapped in a brown leather

vest; the shoulder had a diamond patch with the College's symbol of a lyre sewn onto it. He did not participate in the conversation and instead leaned against a wooden beam with his lute in hand and observed us all.

The mage stood with straight back and hands held in front of him. His eyes suggested a frightful keenness.

The rest of the audience was Lieutenant Hendrix, a notable friend of Uncle's and mine over the years. I may not have voiced it often enough, considering our professional relationship, but I had nothing but respect for that man. There were also other corporals and captains in charge of their own units.

"Nora, good timing. We are talking battle plans," Erefiel said.

"Battle plans? With all due respect, I don't believe we have the time; we don't even have enough information to have a battle plan!"

The mage turned his nose up at me. "Why is there a *woman* partaking in the discussion of men?" he asked with clear distaste.

I stepped forward and prepared to defend myself.

"She has earned the right to be at the war table more than you have, Magus Gurick," Erefiel said.

Gurick's eyes narrowed into heavy slits.

"Her involvement could compromise our objectivity," he groused.

"That's rich," I said, before Erefiel had a chance. "Coming from an old man. I mean, I hope you haven't gone senile yet. I assure you, this is not the bathhouse."

The man's glare darkened.

"Can we continue?" Erefiel asked, taking our stiff silence as affirmation.

Battle plans were discussed thoroughly and with attention to strategies. My nagging sensation only grew. Why didn't the akars attack yet? What were they waiting for?

Previous plans were thrown out as new strategies were offered. Some suggested setting up ballistas and troops atop the hills. Most ideas were shot down due to lacking time, or rather, foresight thereof.

Most of the focus was put on battle formations with only five hundred men.

Akar battle equipment was taken into consideration. No normal bow would have been enough to handle their strength. With the exception of a small tribe of akar but they didn't prove pressing enough to be factored in. What was most likely were their typical crude weapons, like clubs and some simple axes.

I could smell it in the air: rain was coming.

The men, too, became more and more frantic with their calls and their ideas, the weight of the coming battle urging them on.

Maxin's shadow lengthened in his sullen corner, his grip tightening about his lute.

Someone proposed a funnel formation to best control their numbers, but we did not have strong enough defences to stop them from coming. Arrows and spears became the best course of action, as they always were.

I looked up and fancied the first drop of water waiting to hit the tent. Rain.

"A moment!" I called for their attention, but the argument continued, heated and frantic, my words lost among its waves.

"I know when they are attacking!" Still, I went unheard.

I bottled my insecurities and unsheathed my sword, hammering it down onto the table, cutting into the wood and the map.

Cassidy floundered over the scene, his expression disbelieving as he tried to get out the first words since the meeting began. "That table was priceless!"

Cassidy was ignored, but I no longer was.

"I told you bringing her in here was a bad idea. Women can't handle the pressure," Magus Gurick said.

I directed a finger at him pointedly. "Shut it."

I planted a foot on the table and removed the imbedded blade; all ears waited expectantly for me and I relished holding their attention.

"I know when they will be attacking." My claim was spoken neutrally, without the need to raise my voice.

"When?" Erefiel asked.

"When it rains, sir," I declared.

"Do, pray tell, how do you know this?" Magus Gurick asked.

"The leader—"

"Leader?" Hendrix cut in.

I shook my head, clearing my thoughts. "The akar, the one who laid out the execution."

"Even if he is the leader, what makes you think he is waiting till it rains? That is uncomfortable weather condition for all involved," Erefiel pressed.

"It has happened before," I countered.

"Their honour made them continue fighting despite rain, not because of it," Erefiel said.

"Stupidity rather." Gurick chuckled alone at his own joke.

I considered the reason. "For cover, to cloak them and obscure their advances."

"Why go through the trouble?"

"To hide their numbers? Make our cavalry obsolete?" I offered, not entirely convinced by my own claim, but it did give Erefiel pause to consider.

I pushed forward. "Even if they don't have numbers, we don't know how much our men ended up revealing. Perhaps they want to use the cover of rain to make their numbers seem greater than they actually are?"

"Interesting theory," Gurick jumped in. "But I think you give the savages too much credit."

"Indeed, they are savages, but there was a frightening intelligence to the leader we saw." Even I had to admit that.

"Explain," Erefiel ordered, though I assumed he just wanted to see if we had the same thought.

"The way he killed Cassidy's man, Arnold… he wanted to instil fear into our men. It was calculated."

Gurick scoffed. "Oh please! They are straightforward beasts! It was a mindless execution! Nothing more!"

"No." Finally, the heaviest voice in the room belonged to the one who spoke seldomly. Maxin stepped to the table. "I agree with her." He nodded in my direction. "There was most definitely an intelligence to that akar. The way he moved, the way he held our gaze, made sure we were paying attention." Maxin shook his head, almost as if acknowledging the akar. "He is a performer. Every bit of what he did was theatrics to make sure we paid attention. The way he executed that man, he *inspired* fear into our troops."

Gurick groaned. "Are you trying to suggest he is an Inspired?"

Maxin shook his head. "Nothing of the sort—like you said, they are savages, and aren't inclined to the way of the Muses… but nonetheless, the effect is practically the same."

"But I believe there is another reason for their plan," Maxin added, his next words reluctantly barred behind pursed lips.

It dawned on me far later than it should have, and what I hoped would be one of our aces suddenly became obsolete.

"You won't be heard," Erefiel said. Maxin gave a regretful nod.

"Okay." The brittle voice of Cassidy cut in. "But how does that help us?"

The first sound of pitter-patter came from outside. First as independent and discordant drops, but then as a shower that filled the world with a constant static.

"It tells us that whoever it is we are facing, has a knack for strategy," Erefiel said unwaveringly. Like awaiting sentinels, we rose and made our way to prepare for bloodshed.

Chapter Thirty-Two

NORA

Some cultures believe that the spirit of death arrives with scythe
in hand to sever body from soul. Don't be fooled. Death doesn't
wield a scythe—it wields time.

—A NEED FOR DEATH, BY VISIAN PLUME

We stepped outside and saw our troops already getting in formation. We quickly instructed the heaviest and most competent men to take the forefront and provide a defence so that our own rear formation could fire arrows into akar lines.

The heavens rumbled with the coming of thunder. Lightning struck to sunder a lone tree atop a hill.

I had hoped to stand at the forefront and battle with my comrades, but Erefiel insisted I join him at the centre and allow Bradley to take the helm of my company. Once in position, I turned to my right and saw Gurick stand atop of a natural plateau guarded by a reserve of men. A tank of bottled Haar waited beside him.

Maxin was up there too, though standing underneath a tarp, his lute brushed with a brown colour to infuse it with an empowering spell. It was a desperate attempt to boost his music so he may galvanise and inspire despite the rain.

Regardless, Maxin coaxed a melody from his lute which penetrated the rain and distant strikes of thunder. It did not deliver its intended effect in its entirety, but it still weaved its magic, calming the soldiers and chasing away any thoughts of doubt or fear.

I felt it work its way into me and instil a calm. It brushed away nascent fears, providing me with a sense of confidence and clarity for what was to come. Like the design of an ambitious and wholly striving chef, I appreciated a subtle note, as if hidden underneath the aroma of confidence and serenity. It was a dancing dash of an exotic spice, a herb from distant lands like a gentle kiss; entirely magical. It did not over-power but accentuated the whole performance—that spice was courage.

Maxin may not have been a Muse yet, but I found myself wholly appreciating a man of such skill. I had heard long ago that a bard of such repute who played for an army was not someone who played firstly for the army, but rather for the music. It was an itch, a passion, a need to perform for any who would dare listen. Here was a man who played not because of a war, but because the music demanded to be played, even through thunder and lightning or the promise of death.

I looked around. We stood at the rear and stared at the back of men. Heads hidden under helmets made all the pike carrying soldiers look like statues. The only members which stood out noticeably were the twenty conscripted akar who fought at our side. Directly behind us stood the hundred or so archers waiting with their strung bows, and directly behind them were our reserves of a mere hundred men.

To my right was Erefiel atop Zephyr. His hawk-shaped helmet made him regal in comparison to his army. His blade of Bereniel was still sheathed at his side, and a kite shield of equally polished steel hung from his left arm.

The only other presence at our rear was a tight-lipped and tense Cassidy and several other men on horseback. Cavalry was out of the question given the conditions which would provide poor footing, but we still could use horses to deliver information quickly between the ranks.

I returned to look out at the plateau where army men opened the Haar container for Gurick. The valve turned and the tank released the volatile mists contained there-in.

Gurick pulled upon its threads and made the mist meander out. He exhibited a great show of control.

Hendrix traipsed closer atop his steed.

"Maybe you were wrong?" he asked me hopefully.

"Trust me." I cried over the storm. "Nothing would make me happier."

"Maybe we should w—" Hendrix was violently torn from his horse and nailed to the floor with the force of a monstrous javelin. The whole thing was a blur.

Shock filled me, blood streaked me, and my ears still waited for Hendrix to finish his sentence. His lifeless eyes took in a dark sky.

"Javelins!" Erefiel cried out in vain, his voice unable to reach the front of the line. But it managed to break me from my daze.

I looked to the forest and then my vision trailed to the sky, momentarily illuminated by a distant strike of forked lightning. Like tiny needles, there soared javelins, flying ever higher up before arcing forward and diving straight into our numbers.

My horse, as well as Erefiel's, paced restlessly on the spot; we were trapped by the surrounding men. Their front legs paddling high and slamming down onto the wet, muddy floor. The other mounts were equally stressed as more stray javelins landed around us and picked off men one by one.

Another commander fell, his cry cut short by the sudden frantic trampling of our mounts.

Gurick responded when he could, the mists trailing over to form a shield around the army, disintegrating the remaining javelins which struck its surface. But the damage was done, our horses distressed, the first blood spilt belonging to us, all because we did not know that they had the kind of craftsmanship or resources to build such weapons.

Lightning struck, and my own mount reared upon its hind legs and sent me plummeting to the mud.

I turned just in time to see through the rain. My horse raised its hooves over my body. I barely rolled out of the way in time as she slammed down.

Mud filled my mouth, my vision. I removed the helmet and tried to orient myself. The whining cries of the horses filled me with dread.

I speedily regained my footing and drew on my sword.

The akar hadn't shown themselves yet, hidden behind the canopy of trees as they threw their projectiles with monstrous speed.

Gurick's spell held, but Maxin would prove useless for the rest of the battle. I looked to the plateau and made a note to thank him in person. Another javelin struck thunderously onto the platform and skewered the mage to stone.

Maxin and the others were already quickly on the retreat.

Erefiel managed to calm Zephyr along with some others, yet I noticed that Cassidy and his decorated steed had vanished.

"Are you alright?" Erefiel asked.

"I'm fine!" I told him. "Help the men!"

"I can't risk an army without a leader!" he retorted.

"There won't be an army at this rate!"

The first sign of the invaders did not come as akar, but as monstrous bull-like creatures known as aurochs.

Four of them charged, their hooves hammering upon clumping mud and right behind them strode the akar. They did not run. They paced slowly, their eyes shining, umbral beads that glistened white with another strike of lightning.

"Fire!" Erefiel gave the order. A moment later, arrows flew from their bows and soared across the sky; a pathetic act of opposition when compared to the enormous javelins from before, and proven even more pointless when they met the wooden shields of the akar.

The aurochs came to a juddering halt as our allied akar grabbed upon their horns and planted their feet in the mud. At first I thought another strike of lightning resounded its thunder, but then I realised it was our enemy's roar.

The akar came from the forest like a deluge. Slowly their canter turned into full-on sprints with deep throated war-cries.

"Hold the line!" My cry was a futile act. I could only hope the line held, as I grabbed a discarded spear and rushed forward.

"Nora!" Erefiel's voice reached me in spite of the cacophony. I ignored him.

❧ ☙

Our arrows still whistled from above and picked off the occasional akar, but the enemy was naturally sturdy and even more so with their shields aloft. They continued to pour in; no way to tell how many there were.

Command was in disarray. Unit captains called to hold out their spears. The occasional panicked soldier shouted retreat, sending confusion down the line.

One allied akar was mistakenly killed by one of our men. The line between friend and foe became blurred. I watched as another akar battling an auroch fell to his own kind—a woman so grotesque I first thought her face was struck full of arrows.

I searched for my own unit, but all formation had unravelled as the battle turned into skirmishes. I prayed that Bradley still lived.

Our men were pushed back at an alarming rate, but not without putting up a fight. Outheld spears slowed the enemy. Erected stakes gave us enough time to strike back and chip away at their numbers.

The last time I charged foolishly into the fold was when I got my first taste of battle and acted with abandon. This time, I did it out of necessity: the line had to hold!

I struck forward as an akar's grotesque face peered out from behind the line, my spear burrowing into its eye. I retrieved my weapon and searched for more skulls to go spearfishing in. Their numbers piled literally before us as a defensive mound, yet still we were pushed back, our numbers falling in even greater swarths.

Lightning and thunder struck again. We could not stop.

A swift club broke our ranks, splintered spears and lifted men off their feet. I was sent tumbling to the floor, disoriented and prone.

Lying there before me were the two deserters from earlier. They stared into the nothingness of death. I picked up my spear as the first line of defence shattered. The akar stampede advanced and crushed the barely living. I stumbled to my feet when an akar came charging for me.

I stepped swiftly aside. I fell to a knee and the akar's wide swing went over me. I retaliated in kind, making sure that my sword found its mark underneath the fiend's exposed chin.

Another came at me. I weakened him with two surgical cuts to the knee and heel before piercing its heart. A female too drunk on blood was next. She raised her club too high over her head and invited me to slash clean through her throat. I pirouetted away from her falling body. Her blood bathed me.

I made myself a mound of their fallen and I called to its banner all who dared invade my lands.

One after another they fell to my blade, but I could feel my strength waning. My wrist ached. My knees groaned. The boom of thunder was like a lashing whip, forcing me to move forward. Blood and innards made each proceeding attack of mine heavier and heavier.

I couldn't keep up anymore.

An axe slightly grazed against my shoulder as if to have a taste. A slash to my hip drew blood and broke the leather strap holding my armour together.

The mud didn't give any clear footing. An axe broke through my sword. The rest of its weight slammed against my chest. If it weren't for the fact that I was already mid fall and still wearing my armour, my insides would already have been exposed.

I fell flat on my back. Was I bleeding? The rain and mud made it hard to tell.

The axe was raised for a final felling strike as akar ran past me. Our line was in chaos. Many died on both sides. How many hundreds had already died? I was about to join them.

Like a bird of prey in flight, silver blurred past me in one sudden brush. Erefiel jumped into the fray, his sword drawn. I had joined the Nephilim on the same battlefield countless times before, and not once was he ever made to draw his blade—until tonight.

His sword was a frightening blur. He soared and danced through the wading attacks—his speed and ferociousness inhuman. My eyes could barely make out his movements. The blade of Bereniel vanished and reappeared stained red with akar blood. The blade's coating of wind cleaned itself as if disgusted by what blood tainted its edge.

Erefiel appeared as an artist with a scarlet paintbrush.

Hammers, cudgels, axes, clubs, swords all rebounded off the surface of his shield, scratching away at the emblem of White-Hawk.

I was picking ticks with tweezers in comparison to how quickly Erefiel felled the monsters. Yet even he could not hold back the horde entirely on his own, nor was he trying to. What he did instead was buy us time.

The men rallied together and reorganised while Erefiel sprinted back and forth to where he was needed, his body quick and weightless despite the armour he wore, his snow-feathered hair rippling in a stormy wind without his helmet on.

I wondered if Erefiel claimed the lives of more akar than the rest of us combined as they fell. Our army reformed, archers fired, troops held their ground.

I rose to my feet, driven to do my part despite my body's complaints. I unclasped my cuirass. "For Bravnicka!" I howled.

But my cries were dually outmatched by the sound which came next.

The fighting stopped. A bleating and horrendous sound of nightmares that gave not just us humans pause, but the akar too.

We turned to the cliff and found the untended mist from before had escaped its containment and turned into the stuff of nightmares. Mage Gurick had become a part of this macabre painting, impaled to the side while the mists slithered and took a shape of its own volition.

A great mass of bodies formed into a spherical being of unidentifiable design. It was an entire amalgamation of arms attached to a multi-hued body; grotesque things peered from what only a fool would dare call faces.

Great bulging eyes, askew teeth like rotten stalactites adorning a scarred and monstrous lip spread across its entire body. The mighty boulder of flesh and gnarled limbs suddenly rolled down the hill. Its shrill cry made a mockery of humans.

It crashed into the akar lines. The enemy cried in panic, as blood spurt into the air. The carnage was hidden behind a curtain of bodies.

The familiar horn of retreat sounded as the creature tore into their numbers. Fear finally found itself a home other than just with humans. The akar abandoned their assault, and retreated over the bodies of our men and their own.

My eyes drifted along the carpet of the deceased.

The monster howled, grating, nightmarish sounds, its limbs seemingly boneless as they flailed and whipped into the akar. It pursued the retreating enemy into the forest.

Lightning struck from above, and not a single cheer of victory sounded from our kind.

From our people, there was only silence.

⋖ ⋗

When the rush of battle left us and the clarity came, we set to work beneath the rain. We looked for survivors among the dead. The groans of the dying were a siren, guiding us in our task.

Out of the original five hundred men, I wondered if even half survived.

I scanned the dead bodies and stopped short when I found Bradley staring back at me. His eyes cold and lifeless, his skin a pallid grey and the rest of him was covered underneath a mound of corpses. He jolted only slightly when another body was tossed to the pile.

I pushed aside the pile to get a better look at him, but found that only his upper torso remained. I rushed a hand to my mouth and looked away. Even clenching my eyes shut didn't help.

When I finally removed my hand and opened my eyes, I could not bring myself to look back.

Cassidy's steed was found rampaging along the boundary of the camp, riderless and frenzied.

It managed to kick one man in the chest and added one more dead to the final tally. The others managed to calm the horse.

As I suspected, I found Cassidy in his tent, frantically collecting his things. His armour lay partially abandoned except for pieces here and there. The vermin instead prioritised collecting the items which denoted his status as nobleman.

He did not notice me until my shadow covered him.

Cassidy made to turn his head, but I gave him no such chance.

Instead, I grabbed him by his lush, golden locks and hammered his face into the table once, twice, thrice until blood ran free and I was satisfied.

He slumped to the floor. It was the second time I broke something of his.

Trembling hands reached to his face as he shuddered in bewilderment.

"You fucking whore! You will regret—" I was in no mood for threats.

My fist struck true and silenced the incompetent man-child. I dragged him out by his collar and through the grime encrusted field. A few wandering soldiers paused to watch the show.

The war room was still vacant except for a brooding Erefiel and a few injured captains. The air which surrounded the empty chairs drew in more attention than the filled one's ever could.

Erefiel said nothing upon my entry. His usually pristine appearance was sullied with caked blood; it gave him a frightening presence. I threw Cassidy before the audience as if he were caught bounty at his trial. The worm was given a new coat of paint after I dragged him through the muck.

Finally, rousing from his slumber, Cassidy complained about his head and numbly scanned the room to find the lingering stares of those seeking vindication.

"Listen." Cassidy stammered. "We won, right?" His smile was frail and devoid of any charm it may have had.

No one said anything, all eyes turning toward Erefiel.

White-Hawk's son strode to Cassidy and picked him up by the scruff of his silk shirt, lifting him into the air as if he weighed truly nothing. I took satisfaction in the soft whimper.

Before Cassidy had a chance to say another word, Erefiel flipped him over his shoulder and onto the war-table. The wood buckled and the array of miniatures pierced Cassidy's back.

Cassidy writhed and whimpered in pain.

"We *won*?" Erefiel asked, seething. His hands clasped around Cassidy's cheeks to force his lips open.

Cassidy had no chance to explain as again, Erefiel displayed his inhumane strength born of zerubic blood and tossed Cassidy against the wall of the tent.

"We *won*? We didn't *win*, you ignorant, pampered infant; you suckle on your father's cock and think his influence will protect you?"

"You can't do this…" Cassidy wheezed, the air knocked from his lungs as he crawled away, his voice breaking and pathetic. "My father…"

"Your *father* is not here, is he?" Erefiel asked ominously. Again, he grabbed onto Cassidy's nape and flung him into the side of the table.

Saliva dribbled as long, blood-infused threads from Cassidy's lips. It slathered his muddied torso.

Erefiel strode to him, with a raised fist and frenzied eyes. Even I thought he was going too far. I wanted nothing more than to vicariously experience all that Cassidy had coming and more; the cathartic vindication was better than any ambrosia. But I knew the reality was far more costly.

I stepped in alongside the other bystanders. I held onto Erefiel's fist as others restrained him.

I had no doubt that Erefiel could have thrown his punch regardless. It was the act itself which gave Erefiel pause and made him reflect.

Cassidy's head was spinning, and his eyes glazed over. He seemed ready to prostrate himself like a worm.

"I can't kill the son of Jason Femur, but know this: *I* am the son of White-Hawk, I am Lieutenant General Erefiel who commands the defence of Bravnicka from the invading akar. I wield the Blade of Bereniel and have felled scores with its edge." The bravado backed by Erefiel's tone built upon itself like a rising storm. Cassidy gathered enough of his wits to truly wither under Erefiel's gaze.

"But you will be nothing more than an accessory, you will be a golden nut to dangle in the faces of people but with no power, no leeway. I will make sure that you return to Cleria and work behind the confines of walls and sign legislation without any power."

I privately wondered if someone like Cassidy would even complain of such a life, but the thought made his chastising no less enjoyable.

"Now get out of my sight." Erefiel hissed.

Cassidy stumbled to his feet, knocking over a chair as he frantically tried to exit. His rattled mind and fear made him fall prone before finally stumbling out into the pouring rain.

Chapter Thirty-Three

DALILA

The principle of magic is loosely defined and thus impossible to pin into concrete maxims. However, step far enough, and you find that even the most fluid of concepts have their edges and rules while the rest is exploitable. Colour magic comes down to will at the end of the day, and what is blood but potential, will, and colour all in one? But be aware, to use the blood of another for such purposes is shunned for a very good reason.

—Forbidden texts from the School of Sorcery in Cleria, by Unakin Plack

That very same morning, I notched another cut to my collection—my body had become a shrine to my suffering.

Sometime long ago, I would walk the world in a daze while an old spirit screamed murder from within me. The walls which surrounded the spirit were of cement and mortar; thick and obsidian, they absorbed the screams so that none heard her plea.

The screaming had stopped—if she still wandered those labyrinthine halls, it was as a lost spirit.

I roamed the waking world in a daze. My suffering was a silent pilgrimage in respect to those around me. The exception to that was Lucia Gievan, the only other witch and my teacher—my friend. She would stand by the shores of my isolation and stare out at my tiny island. I would look to her shore and feel it appropriate that her land was vast and plenty, but then I would see her upon an island of her own. My sea was stagnant, unmoving, given to resignation, which had an odd grace to its solitude.

At night when I slept, Perry visited me, either as an image of death or lively and spry with full cheeks and a brimming smile. Often it was with the company of that darned well. I tried peering into it, but could never bring myself to descend.

There was only one point during my waking hours where my mind was my own, a marriage between my submerged consciousness and my physical body. Only when I etched my sorrow to skin and made my suffering sing through the drained blood. It was my instrument, my paint brush; the razor my bow and the flesh my strings.

I awoke early, and found time within the privacy of bathing halls meant to be shared. I carved my indelible suffering onto the canvas that was my flesh. Yet when I dressed myself and walked the hallowed halls, my smile was nurturing, comforting, reassuring even.

I greeted younger students, still yearning for their new hems so that they may fulfil their duty as one of the Faithful.

Just a week ago, I received my own robes of the lightest blue, now belonging to the upper echelon of those recognised as a respected part of the church.

'Mother Dalila,' had an interesting ring to it, but I was aware of my other, less desirable title. 'Mother Fae,' they called me. A name granted because I spoke of fairies in my dreams and shared those visions with Yasmin upon my waking hour.

Fae: I liked the name.

The students praised me for my dedicated service. Months upon months I worked tirelessly, serving the meek and the starving, venturing forth aback carts to help those that needed it. I tended to the wounded and even watched people pass into eternal sleep with no one else by their side. I held their hands in mine until vacated vessels loosened their grips. I would watch them slip into eternal slumber, wondering if their ghosts still trailed after me.

⋜ ⋟

There was an ordinance to the Church of the Faithful, a coursing rhythm to its halls. So, when commotion stirred within, it would break the stream of white upon echoing marble floor and create a whirlpool of masses.

Last week it was when rumours of another offering were brought to light. Murmurs of a killer growing bold and leaving a ritualistic display of mauled corpses; supposed embellishments spoke of something infernal.

A month before that, the growing case of rot in Chamersburg called upon sisters to help.

I recalled how a year ago, all sisters felt collectively uncomfortable as we felt the touch of a forgotten; a name, a face, a body was shrouded in the blanket of oblivion.

Today, it was something new.

Proper etiquette was suspended as sisters gathered to see the rush of fully recognized Faithfuls gathering their contents.

I grabbed a passing nun, bringing her attention to me, her gaze was frantic.

"What is happening, Sister?" I asked.

"There was an attack at Greyhill, an entire force of akar tried to break through. There are many dead and many more wounded."

I looked at the flood of milk-white nuns bursting through the doors and filling wagons.

"I will come with you," I said, instantly wondering about all those lost lives and all those that could still be saved—I should have been there at the battle instead of biding my time within these walls.

"That won't be necessary; you have other duties." It was Mother Vinrie who spoke. She snuck up from the side and stood stern. Her tone was entirely level.

I released the Sister.

"With respect, Mother Vinrie. I graduated and donned the blue mantle. I must also help," I said with urgency as my Sisters trickled out.

"Mother Dalila, you may have risen to greater status and are seen as a Mother, yes, but that doesn't excuse you from your other… duties." She spoke the last word with inflection.

I frowned. "You wish for me to stay locked here and meditate? When there are people out there fighting? I thought this was what I was meant to do?"

"Know yourself, Mother Dalila." The statement was authoritative. "Our task is to make sure that you pose no risk to others; your task is to obey. Perhaps someday, we will see you display a modicum of control, which gives us the confidence of setting you out into the world."

"You already have. For months now, I have been helping people," I retorted.

"Not into a warzone, where the wounded suffer in such great numbers. The situation is dire, and this sort of bedlam is not something you are prepared for."

"But I am under control," I said.

"Is that what you tell yourself as you defile your skin?" The words were as sharp as my own instruments and cut through my sails, stranding me on the open sea. "I thought so," Mother Vinrie said one-notedly. "Mother Lucia is expecting you in an hour."

I nodded in defeat.

A tender and regretful sigh came from Mother Vinrie. The last of the nuns emptied the hall.

"I promise you; one day, you will be ready, and I will personally remove my yoke for you to go and help as you wish." She placed a hand on my shoulder. "You make our cause proud. No one doubts your conviction."

"When will I be ready?"

"When you have your emotions under control, like Mother Lucia."

"And when will that be?"

"When Mother Lucia says you are."

⋖ ⋗

The halls were drained as I walked to the library. Biding my time, I read more tomes about mending injured bones and tending fevers.

My mood didn't improve much since then. I sympathised with Mother Vinrie's position, but couldn't help be disappointed that I was left behind. It was there, Mother Vinrie's fears, her unspoken anxiety about what I represented. She tried her best to be tolerant, but it felt like the type of kindness born out of guilt. At the end of the day, she held dominion over my life. She was responsible that I didn't end up like the first witch. Despite being granted my blue hem, I felt more like a glorified novice than an actual Mother.

Increasingly irritated by the thought, I tread the path rarely taken to a wing fallen out of use. I stood before Mother Lucia's chamber. Mother Lucia waited in her chair. I was surprised to find the angels gone.

"What happened to the angels?" I asked.

Mother Lucia smiled. "Consider it a compromise," she said through wizened pipes.

I stepped inside, not entirely following. As if realising this, Mother Lucia filled in the gaps.

"It is an act of trust from Mother Vinrie. That you don't need guards standing in the chamber anymore and babysitting us."

My expression was puzzled. "Is that allowed?" I asked as I took my seat. Mother Lucia took it upon herself to serve me tea. As she poured for me, tea leaf strands floated to the top.

Mother Lucia shrugged. "Not strictly speaking, but it's not like anyone would question her."

"If she thinks me ready," I challenged, "why would she send me to you?"

"Because I haven't yet told her you are ready."

It was quiet as the unspoken was suggested. "You don't think me ready?" I asked.

"I never said that," Lucia teased. I held my tongue, not saying anything in turn.

"Congratulations on your new habit and robes." Mother Lucia stated in a vain attempt to change the subject. I did not take it.

She sighed, pouring herself a cup of tea as well. "Why would you want to go out there, anyway?"

"To help people."

Lucia made a dismissive gesture that took me by surprise. "Why would you want to help people?"

"Because it is the right thing to do," I said without hesitation, my brows furrowing at the mere question.

Mother Lucia blinked at me. "Yes, I suppose it is," she said, as if the thought never occurred to her.

"Do you not think so?"

"I do, but does that not include yourself in the process?"

I instinctively pulled the sleeves of my robes to hide my wrists.

"Hiding that which I already know won't help," Mother Lucia said playfully.

We spoke for a while, eventually landing on the topic of my studies.

"How does it go with your classes?"

I shrugged. "What is there to say? I value the classes with Mother Margaret. She teaches me how to treat wounds."

"There is always value in our history."

"How so?" I asked, not entirely invested.

"Whatever comes before guides the after. Only by understanding the past, how we were all created, can we ever hope to change things."

I was still not convinced. "I do not see how knowing about the cycles helps me change the future."

Mother Lucia's eyes narrowed at that. She leaned in on the table. "How much do you know about the cycles? Tell me about them."

I wasn't sure what Mother Lucia planned, but I decided to humour her. I told her about the Cycles, stopping at Nain, Vikma and Jernun to note a period of time known as the 'Vacantry'.

Mother Lucia shook her head. "It's not true."

I was pulled out of my recollections. "What isn't true?"

"The Vacantry."

"How do you mean?"

"There were new races born. All cycles will always have new races."

Something about the way Mother Lucia talked set me on edge. I humoured her despite my scepticism. "Which races are you speaking of?" I asked.

"Two of them, nobody knows. They are races still hidden from the rest of society. But one of them, I do."

Despite the fact that it all sounded like nonsense, I had to admit that I was intrigued by how slowly Mother Lucia let the question linger in the air.

"The demons."

"Demons?" I asked in disbelief.

She nodded. "The demons came with the end of Nain's cycle."

"Demons were born out of our most virulent evil, were they not?"

"Demons aren't all they are made out to be."

I frowned. "But Mother Elsia said—"

Another dismissive wave cut me off. "Don't believe everything you hear at the church, child. There are some truths better not associated with the Elders."

Respect for Mother Lucia made me offer her an ear, but what she said bordered on blasphemy.

"When the first demon came, it was of brimstone and sulphur, but its heart was pure and kind. A mortal, her name lost to time, gave herself a new name: Lillith. She saw the purity within the heart of this demon and offered herself to a being not sown with the seeds of calamity and hatred like her own kin.

"She became the mother of demons, bearing many children formed by Lillith's own vibrant imagination. Yet mankind detested them, feared them, and the Elders stoked that fire until the demons were banished behind the walls which now make the Ashen Forest." Her tone was sombre, deep, reflective; it was a tale drawn from a sorrowful pool.

"You cannot speak ill of the Elders." I softly reminded Lucia in a whisper, as if the walls themselves could hear.

She gave me an amused smile. "Child, we were made to come here against our will. Offering us a life of servitude in place of death is no great act of clemency." She sighed. "Make no mistake, peel away at these ivory walls and you will find that its foundations are just as black as any other house."

I thought about the words for a moment as Mother Lucia took a sip of her tea. "Now, shall we begin?"

Chapter Thirty-Four

DALILA

—*the ring of storm is one such item. It is said that a traveller took to the seas and travelled far and wide, in an age before the leviathans were born. In his travels, he discovered the boundary of Minethria and saw a realm of perpetual storms. Here, he placed a portal which connected the storm and the ring, so that the wind could be summoned wherever the ring-bearer wished.*

—TALES OF THE MASTER

After my session with Mother Lucia, Mother Vinrie bid me a visit.

"Come with me," she instructed.

The halls were less crowded and the sound of our feet more audible within the sparse white.

Mother Vinrie led me out of the church and into the streets filled with the commute of working men and the affluent. The sun climbed to its pinnacle. The strike of the Sisterhood's bell stood in agreement that it was noon.

Clear skies left people cheerful, though the remaining puddles on our cobbled streets were a reminder of yesterday's storm. For a moment, I fancied the lost souls from Greyhill looking out from within the pools.

I spared a thought for a family I had not seen in years. Father must have certainly been in a bad mood given the weather. I hoped their harvest was sound, and the rain didn't cause any major run off.

Yet here, Mother Elsia had taught us about the aqueducts which led the water to the ocean with our refuse clearly out of sight and out of mind.

Mother Vinrie didn't say where she was taking me. Our stroll was done in silence.

We reached a building of stony complexion and humble design: it looked like a modest and austere monastery in the middle of a city. Its architecture was framed by pointed spirelets, a rose window of stained glass, protruding gargoyles leaning ready for all threats and supported by the addition of bulging buttresses. The place had a gothic way to it, not needing anything gaudy as a humble house of worship.

My curiosity got the better of me. "Where are we going?"

"To visit our brothers within their own house. They are the Serving. An extension of our own body. They are deacons and priests who partake in all manner of responsibilities."

The steps led up to a large arching door of dark wood. Studded iron lined its body and a great ring of iron was mounted at the centre, far out of reach.

A smaller door to the side, however, opened to reveal a robed monk permitting us entry. The inside was reminiscent of a holy church as we took the side entrance into the atrium of the hall. The space was vacant, and only a few deacons were about.

Our valet was a holy man, his scalp made bare to mark him, and his robes of a thick, woolly brown. His wrinkles were cryptic hieroglyphs which told of his life and weathered years.

"Mother Vinrie." He bowed. "We have been expecting you."

The man turned to me. "And you must be our expected guest."

"Please, call me Mother Dalila," I offered cordially and bowed.

"Certainly." He mirrored me. "You may address me as Brother John."

Brother John led us through the nave of the holy halls, vaulted by the grey mortar which rose high into the ceiling. Each side was bordered by high windows letting light and air into the chamber.

At the end of the nave was the bema, crowned by its altar upon a high platform that made all devout crane their necks up to the sermon.

The Elders were higher beings, beings incomprehensible by human or mortal understanding, thus it was fitting that there was no symbol, no vessel or body meant to hold their eternal grace except for one: the spiral.

The Witness would make a circle with thumb and forefinger against their forehead to give the impression of sight, while those of the Faith would point at the outer reaches of their chest and spiral inwards to their hearts.

The depth and knowledge of Elders proved so endless, that no human mind could hope to grasp it; lest they fell into the pits of the spiralling whirlpool and split their mind in twain.

There it was, at the peak of the high arching stained glass window— a spiral nearing to a point.

To serve the Elders was to simultaneously lose yourself in their grace and virtue while not going too deep into the realm meant only for them.

"Brother John, what news have you?"

We turned to face the strong but coaxing voice. The man walked with the support of a cane. The individual in question was handsome enough, given his considerable age.

Though his cane wasn't the only evidence of disability; he too was blind. Looking about the chamber, his eyes drifted off into no particular direction, but his assuredness was no less impressive. The way he strode portrayed a sense of comfort within the house of worship, rather than denoting fear and prostration.

"Brother Clemence." Brother John nodded.

The man called Brother Clemence limped from in between the aisles. He had leathery skin and a salt and pepper stubble. It reminded me of a new-born chick. The man's eyes were a distant milky-white, but his smile was friendly.

"Ah, don't tell me. It is the witch that has come to visit?" Brother

Clemence wasn't particularly loud, but no less did Mother Vinrie stiffen and shift uneasily, her eyes scanning the room for any unwelcome ears.

"Brother Clemence!" Brother John leaned in, his tone carrying respectable rebuke. "Be careful what you say; not so loud!"

"Please, Brother John. I meant no disrespect," he offered as a balm.

"I worry not about your intentions, Brother Clemence, only about the intentions of prying ears." Mother Vinrie's tone was stern and heavy as a rock, but the pointedness of her remark was enough of an admonishment without insulting her host.

"You speak truth. I apologise." Brother Clemence's bow carried the weight of practice.

"Might I ask if you are Mother Dalila?"

"That would be me," I said.

"Ah, what a beautiful voice you have." His eyes unsettled me. They lingered in my direction, but looked right past me.

"You may address me as Mother Vinrie." I was saved from having to reply.

"Yes, I've heard of you. Devout, hardworking, selfless and a good Mother. I must say, your reputation precedes you."

"As does yours, Brother Clemence."

The blind man chuckled and turned, having us follow him in. "I appreciate the gesture, but really, I'm nobody. I will escort them to Father Maurice. You may excuse yourself, Brother John."

⊰ ⊱

The path led through a door and up spiralling stairs, which made way into a closed off hallway; narrow and tall. Stained windows bled light and exposed floating dust motes. Brother Clemence walked with a certain confidence through the halls, ostensibly having mapped all its corners and edges into his mind's eye.

"Brother Clemence, how was it that you could see Brother John?" I asked curtly.

Mother Vinrie was quick to chide me, but Brother Clemence

chuckled and reassured Mother Vinrie not to worry.

"This place is my home. Do you need to see your leg to know where it needs to be itched? Or perhaps you need to always look before reaching out to something with confidence? Just because my eyes no longer work doesn't mean I am totally helpless. I know the routines, my brothers and their schedules. I know the church because it trails like the topography of my own skeleton."

As if to completely discredit every claim just made, Brother Clemence walked straight into a potted vase where his sandaled feet clipped the edge.

"Ow!" He cried, massaging his toe with his free hand while the other balanced upon his cane.

I repressed a snicker. Mother Vinrie was a shining example of stoicism.

Brother Clemence apologised; I wondered if the display was intentional.

We walked the rest of the way in silence. I imagined Brother Clemence to have been humbled by his mishap. We came to a chamber tucked in between a collection of finely crafted doors etched with the elusive tales of old.

Inside, we found an open window. The stale taste of the hall was replaced by the scent of age; a rather musty aroma. I presumed, and privately so, that it belonged to the old monk before me clad in pure white.

"Father Maurice, I have brought for you Mother Vinrie and Mother Dalila."

"Thank you, child." Father Maurice was a worn-looking man, frail and grey with short steps and puckering lips that quivered just as extensively as his own limbs with the labour of walking.

The man was old, older than I had ever seen. Liver spots filled his desolate scalp like spread out islands. Tired and old, his brown eyes took in our sight lazily. His skin sagged and looked to be slipping from his face so that the moist red was exposed right underneath his eyeballs.

Father Maurice gave us a tired and friendly smile. His few remaining teeth, the last survivors of his old age like a morbid count for coming death.

His clothing was a similar white to that of our sisterhood, but had no coloured hems at its corners and its torso was embroidered with gilded threads depicting the rising sun and moon of the King's eye. His only other piece of attire being a stole draped comfortably over each shoulder and hanging low to just above his knee with fringed ends.

"Please, come on in," he said, a bony and fragile hand calling me into the study. Scrolls filled rhombus cubbies and books lined shelves or were stacked on the table.

It was when Mother Vinrie trailed behind that Father Maurice raised a stemming hand. "Only Mother Dalila will be required."

Mother Vinrie stood tall and composed, her hands folded in front of her waist as her eyes narrowed.

"I wasn't made aware of this," she said tersely.

Father Maurice shrugged, his smile apologetic.

"What can I say? I am sorry. But I wish to talk with Mother Dalila privately."

"May I ask why?"

"You may. It is simply because her case is an unusual one given her childhood. I understand she has certain properties that will make her more open if there wasn't someone from the Sisterhood watching over her shoulder."

Mother Vinrie wasn't happy, but she couldn't argue either—she had no power over the room. I knew little of why I was there, but something about the affair seemed non-negotiable.

"You are free to sit outside and wait if you'd like?" Father Maurice suggested.

"That won't be necessary," Mother Vinrie replied. "I will return to the Sisterhood."

She turned to me. "I expect you to return once you are done."

I bowed respectfully.

Acquiesced, Mother Vinrie turned and excused herself from the chamber, along with Brother Clemence.

Mother Vinrie shut the door. It had grown heavy due to the tension. Even when Mother Vinrie was gone, still the enmity screamed across a voiceless chasm.

Father Maurice breathed a droning sigh. "As if tensions weren't bad enough." He muttered entirely to himself.

I turned to Father Maurice, who immediately regarded me with a toothy smile.

"What do you mean?" I did away with any pretence. I had no ill intention with this man, but the exchange was obviously not cordial. It was plain to see how little say I had in any of this. I felt like a token, a chip to be bartered between the heads of these houses. I knew what I was.

There was a growing realisation that sprouted from fertile soil. It was like an egg, one so fragile its surface was cracked with the image of forked lightning. It harboured my frail, ominous existence as a sorry treatise. They saw me as a threat to humans, to the Elders, to the church and my Sisters—a very well hidden threat.

Within the hidden circles of these factions, they whispered about me like a nascent dark thought, never too far away from the light. It felt like a sorry attempt at parading around progress in the form of bondage.

I wondered for a moment; was this stray musing my own frustration or Mother Lucia's?

Father Maurice sighed but answered my question. "She will think I have spies in her church."

My gaze narrowed. The thought of my supposed Sisters spying on me was unnerving.

"No," he said, waving his hand as if I had made a silly joke expected of a child. "When I spoke of your discomfort, it was just a bluff. But to be fair, it wasn't an unreasonable presumption. Torn from your family at a young age and forced into the Sisterhood? Hard to think anyone would find comfort in that... at least anyone who isn't an Elder."

I eyed him coldly, but Father Maurice thought it amusing more than anything else as he gave a humoured chuckle and waved his frail hand. "Please, child. I have no spies in your Sisterhood. At least not in any capacity, you imagine."

"What capacity then?"

"Let's just say I have other means of acquiring information I need," he offered that small thread, that inkling of information to me with no hesitation. "There are ways in and out that not even Mother Vinrie knows." He made his way around his desk and to his seat.

"Why would you tell me that?"

"Think of it as…" he paused, his cane trembling as it toiled doubly as hard to hold Father Maurice's weight. The man lowered his aching limbs and finally let gravity pull him into the chair. A sigh escaped him before he continued. "An olive branch, an act of trust on my part. I hope it is acceptable."

I blinked. "People seem to be doing that a lot for me."

"Does that trouble you?" He frowned.

"It makes me feel coddled. But also lied to. I can't even do my duty to tend to those who need my help." I was surprised to find that irritation lined my voice. I wasn't unfamiliar with the sensation, but rarely let it show.

Father Maurice licked his dry lips and thought privately to himself. He stared at the foot of a bookshelf rather than at me.

He then turned around with his sagging, brown eyes. "What would make you feel not so coddled?"

"You could start by telling me why I am here?" I prompted.

Father Maurice waved to the chair opposite him. I moved as instructed. A waiting tea kettle, still steaming, was ready to serve me. After the one I had that morning, I politely declined—Father Maurice did not press.

"How is Mother Lucia?" he asked.

The question caught me off guard. "You know her?"

"When I served here, I was still just a brother, but Father Bruce, at the time, was the one who mediated with her. So? How is she?"

I wondered how to reply. "She is doing well."

Father Maurice chuckled, a fitful cough suddenly invading his lungs—it took a good while until the man calmed himself and took a sip of his tea to wet his throat.

With a quick apology, he continued. "I certainly hope that old fox is doing well! By the Elder's spirit, she had the energy of ten horses!"

I suddenly was more interested in what was being shared. "Was she so rowdy?"

"The worst! Oh, she would run through the halls, never listening to any of us! You are a model servant in comparison." I didn't know why, but something about his words pulled my spirits right back down and my smile weakened.

As if sensing this, Father Maurice offered me another balm, another piece of information. "It is another reason I asked for you alone, rather than along with Mother Vinrie. Mother Lucia was, at the time… combative and unruly when it came to the Sisterhood."

"What changed?" I asked.

Father Maurice shrugged. "She eventually calmed herself, became a model Mother and there were no more complaints."

Silence drifted between us; I felt as if I hung on Father Maurice's next word.

"You had a question for me," he teased, taking a victory sip from his cup. He suddenly didn't seem so tired and his eyes betrayed a keenness.

I tried to regain face. Father Maurice most certainly wasn't just a frail old man.

"Why am I here?"

"When a witch is taken into the church and achieves the rank of Mother, they are brought to us in the Brotherhood. The Sisterhood is the acting hand of the Elder's kindness, en masse. They go where they are needed to tend to those that need tending. We, the Serving, are the bridge to the Elders themselves. We ceremoniously handle the maintenance of this holy ground of worship and relay important documents to Mount Morniar."

My heart skipped a beat. The Elders were something ethereal, something distant, a concept so disconnected from our everyday lives that they may as well have been a fairytale. To be told that this man had ways to communicate with these otherworldly concepts was like being told he was one himself.

My shock must have been clear. Father Maurice waved dismissively and smiled. "It is not like I can send them letters daily. It is a complicated process handled by the king's men and government as well; but alas, the bridge is connected by me."

"I don't understand what that has to do with me," I said.

"Well, we are the spiritual bridge as well as the physical. It is required that I also get to see the witch, bound to the Elders and ensuring everyone's safety."

I withheld the thought that the safety he implied was not mine. I felt heavy. I was beginning to understand how little freedom I truly had.

"Now, tell me of your time in the Sisterhood."

Chapter Thirty-Five

DALILA

Upon the end of a Cycle, the sight of a Seed's ascension is a most wondrous sight. A pillar of light pierces down and pulls the Seed up into the Creator's embrace. It can be seen from the whole of Minethria.

—Father Maurice in his teachings to the Serving

I shared of my past, my youth, the incident in the forest made up of bare tatters and what others had told me. I avoided mention of my self-harm, but there was something about the way Father Maurice carried himself that alarmed me; his body may have been frail and withered, but I could no longer deny the sharpness of his mind.

I went on and shared about my time in the Sisterhood over the past four years, the adjustment of habitual routines, abstract and vague history, my time with Mother Lucia and our progress. But I thought it wise to omit the day's event and the absence of our angelic guards. It wasn't entirely a lie—he asked about my history, after all.

"Any dreams?" he asked casually.

I hesitated—his piercing brown eyes spherical and dark like the bow of a ship from the gaze of a passing fish. He sensed my hesitance. I knew there was nothing which could escape him.

I nodded.

"Of what?"

"In the forest… when we were attacked… the boy that was with us. He visits me in my dreams." The knowledge was forced from me, made to regurgitate itself from a swollen throat in the form of another fragile egg.

"Perry was his name?" he asked, and I nodded.

It was strange, hearing the name from his lips. It was spoken so casually, like a passing thought; a vase with beautiful imagery but hollow within. He spoke the name without consideration, yet when I were to speak it, it would be with care, appreciation, love, regret, as if the slightest error would turn it to dust. My vase would be tarnished and scratched, whatever images they once bore marred and covered in grime, but from my vase sprouted an entire verdant forest of thick roots and tangled branches.

"What do you talk about? In your dream?" he asked.

I blinked. It was a strange question to be asked. I never considered the content of our conversations but rather the mere company I bore.

"Life. How things are at the Sisterhood. What I hope to do."

"Do you blame yourself for his death?"

I went silent, not because I avoided answering. But rather because this particular egg refused to lay, forming a growing lump in my throat. I knew my silence spoke the truth regardless.

Father Maurice moved on. I was grateful. "And, Mother Dalila, what do you hope to do? What purpose do you wish to fulfil?"

I fiddled with my hands. This time I was able, eager even, to provide my answer.

"To help those who need it! I want to go to wanting villages and tend to their sick, treat the abandoned folk afflicted with rot, and tend to the wounded on the battlefield." That was my answer, and it was a beautiful answer, was it not? I was sure of it, the pureness, the truth of it all. If there was ever a shred of doubt before for Father Maurice, I was certain that he would be content with this answer of mine—for what cause is nobler than helping those in need?

"Ah," he uttered in stark realisation. "Like the Lady of Pain herself?" When I looked deep into Father Maurice's unfaltering eyes, I felt the confidence in my answer fade. "Would you try and remember all the forgotten?" he pressed.

I frowned, confused by the question. "I suppose, if I could," I stated.

"Would you inscribe each and every last one of them to your mind and etch their names onto the wrinkles of your brain?" His question was a test. Was he mocking me?

When Father Maurice recognised my confused expression, he provided me with the answer. "What about you, Mother Dalila? Do you fall into so noble a task?"

"The church states that we need to be selfless—"

"Selfless, yes—not masochistic. Not someone who fetishizes their own suffering."

My tongue was tied, made lame and impotent; I didn't know how to respond. I felt shame, as if my shell of virtue was torn from me to lay bare the self-hating woman that I was—a writhing fleshy worm of no worth.

"Have you heard the tale of Igura the Fractious?"

I shook my head.

"What do you think his title means?"

"That he was uncontrollable?"

"Yes, in a sense. The truth is that Igura was swift as if the winds themselves blessed him, always lending themselves to whichever direction Igura moved. His aim so true that he could shoot an arrow upon an airborne needle, meet its eye and pierce the target behind.

"But there was one thing Igura suffered from—his emotions. Bound by fears that played tricks on his mind and turned his quiet nights into fitful nightmares. His passion for things was uncontrollable. Always he would bound upon things and be distracted, and whenever he was faced with the same lesson, the alluring promise of deceptive hope made him repeat it all again.

"Fear, passion, hope, benevolence and will: these were the five aspects that made Igura who he was. Yet four of those things warred with each other, fed into one another, and made all of Igura's talents useless.

"So instead, he absolved himself of those emotions, expelled them into mortal coils to wander off and suffer alone. But as Igura travelled the world facing monsters, he realised the more difficult the challenges, the more foolish he was. Pure will: that was all he had. He had no fear to teach him wisdom when entering the lair of a beast, no passion to compel him forward when will was not enough, no hope to have him search in darkness what he could not find in light, and no compassion to mend the scars when the dirt settled and just a land of death surrounded him.

"So Igura set out on a quest to regain his emotions."

Father Maurice went silent—he wanted to gauge my interest. I would be lying if I said I wasn't intrigued.

"And, did he?"

Father Maurice had used the pause to allow himself the last sip of his tea.

"In a manner of speaking. Yes, he did. But his emotions had for far too long been separated from him. They became their own beings. They lived and dreamed and joked like Igura himself. They could no longer be one again. But that didn't mean they couldn't work as one. Face yourself, allow for your emotions to work in tandem rather than turning them numb to one another. With their wisdom and power combined, Igura was mightier than he had ever been alone and the world was all the better for it."

"Is this just another myth, or did this Igura truly exist?" I pressed.

"When it comes to legends, Mothers will tell you one thing and scholars another, but does it matter? The depth of this story is truer than any past event in history because it is *present*. Yet it is an old tale lost to the ages. I doubt anyone has heard of it."

Father Maurice extended his bony hands to me, just the tendons of his wrist taut and prominent like readied lyre strings, his fingers adorned with long manicured nails waiting patiently for my hand.

I knew without a shadow of a doubt his intention and offered my arm with very little hesitance.

He nodded, appreciating my trust as he pulled back my sleeve to reveal the crisscross map of scars that marked my suffering.

Father Maurice had a pained expression, not one of pity but rather compassion. He shuddered and his eyes began to water.

"You wish to save the lives of the unfortunate, but forgo on your own happiness all the while."

"How could I allow myself to be happy when Perry is dead and I am still here?"

"So that is what this is about? Penance?" he asked.

The word found its way into my own throat and felt rotten under my tongue.

"I want to do what is right," I stated, but my words held none of the same conviction as before.

"Then learn to love yourself, learn to believe in life and to help others because you want to. You are like Igura's compassion, aimless and alone you wander the world and fill your self-worth by making sure that others are happy. You give more and more of yourself until there is nothing left, like Mimir the Mad. You want to heal the world? Start by forgiving yourself and opening yourself up to the possibilities again."

⊰ ⊱

I left the brotherhood with much on my mind. Thoughts that no matter how vehemently I stirred, refused to settle to the bottom of my pot.

The sun was still high at its zenith and shone glaringly onto the city of Cleria. It was a warm and scorching day.

The words that Father Maurice spoke were a necessary confrontation; not because I agreed with him as of yet, but because I finally noticed the rot eating away at my beliefs.

I naively thought it would be easier than all this, thought that when I earned my habit and was named a Mother that I would find some value to my existence, but somewhere inside I always knew that to be a lie. Even when I first arrived, I thought I could wash away my muddied past and start anew.

My mask was torn for me. A voice spoke out from my exposed lies.

Liar, deceiver, imposter; so conceited to think that helping others, pretending to be virtuous would absolve you of your crime, rid you of Perry's blood. Blood that seeped its way into your pores to never be washed.

"Stop it," I murmured to myself, sparing a momentary beaming smile at the passing couple who bid me a good afternoon and praised the Elders. We shared in a momentary sign of veneration as our fingers spiralled before our chests.

They know your smile is a lie. They know your game of pretend, a child playing at virtuosity.

Tried as I might, the thoughts wouldn't fade. I knew they weren't mine. I knew them to be ridiculous, rotten fruit born from a sickened tree; withered and dark.

Oh Elders. Did the Sisters know? Of course they knew. Everyone knew I was pretending. None were fooled by my smile. They knew my vain attempt at seeming virtuous, treating the ill only to make my own light shine brighter.

What about Yasmin? Of course she knew, too. It was all a big joke to her. That's why she followed me around, gathering secrets to share with others. She must have been the reason everyone called me Mother Fae. ***Elders!*** *I am such a fool!*

My mind was in a frenzy, the broth boiling, bubbling into something caustic that ate through the metal of the pot. My forehead crumpled like wrinkled paper. A headache worked its way up while my robes conspired to suffocate me.

My airways tightened, air becoming scarce; I could not tell if I wanted to cry, scream, or breathe as a new vile egg swelled itself and blocked off my air.

I was breathing heavily, tightly; the world spun.

Oh Elders, they all knew! Everyone knew my lie. I needed to get out of here!

"Dalila." A word spoken in the darkness chased away the long reaching fingers of shadow and anchored me back into reality.

That was all it took, a single name to save me from the vertigo of my own fears, from the dark depths of my doubt.

I was doubled over on the floor; people walked around me and murmured.

There he stood, a friend I hadn't seen since Perry's wake. His expression was plastered with concern, a light stubble filled his chin and upper lip of brown complexion, his hair a loose gathering of wavy locks. His clothes were fanciful and a single lute case hung from his back.

"Dale?" I asked, realising only then I was gasping for air.

⋖ ⋗

We walked the plaza aimlessly, a stale awkwardness between us made up of doubt and nurtured by time. Dale had suggested a bar out of cultural habit, but then was flustered when remembering my robes. My robe stuck to me from all the sweat.

I was exhausted. I wanted nothing more than to return to the abbey and rest, yet something naturally compelled me to stay with Dale. It was in the act of seeing Dale all grown up and handsome in his leather get up that I was forced to face how much I had changed as well.

Dale was my friend once upon a time. I recalled distant memories where I was the tether: elastic and fair. I kept the group tightly knit, stoking its fires by elated and cheerful laughter, or reprimanding those who went too far.

Yet now, as I looked upon Dale, a new feeling evoked itself, one of sorrow at the death of who I used to be.

I didn't feel like Dalila, my own vase bland and hollow. I felt closer to the name spoken as whispers within the abbey: *Mother Fae.*

"So," Dale finally began to speak, assuredly one of many thoughts, queries, questions that had roiled in his mind until he finally settled on something he thought was appropriate, but not optimal.

"Joined the Sisterhood, huh?"

"Yes, I did." I was tired. I gave a strained smile.

"Five years, huh? How time flies. Do you like it there?"

"I suppose," I said. It was a heartless and empty answer. I may as well have made unintelligible sounds.

Did he know why I had joined the abbey? That it wasn't my own choice? I couldn't tell him even if I wanted to. I doubted I'd ever see this remnant of my past again anyway.

"Would you like it if I told your parents that we met? That you are doing well?"

I looked up at him and smiled; bland yet pretty. "No, but thank you."

He seemed confused. "But why?"

I blinked. It seemed obvious to me. "Well, they've moved on, Dale. I was nothing but trouble to Father and Mother. I don't want to remind them of that."

Dale was taken aback. "Bother them? They're your parents!"

"Please, Dale. Don't burden them." I lacked the energy he showed.

He nodded reluctantly and hung his head.

"How are the others?" I asked to change the subject.

"Well, Beck got married!"

The statement surprised me.

"Beck? *The* Beck? Who would insult and make fun of everyone? The one with a rat-face?"

Dale nodded with obvious nostalgia. "Ever since what happened that day, he changed. Became kind, gentle, giving. Wouldn't hurt a fly, that one. I don't know what it was, but he stopped being such an ass."

"What about Jeremiah?"

Dale shook his head. "Haven't seen him since the incident; his parents forbade it."

"Even now?"

Dale shrugged. "Considering all that happened and not being able to see each other for years—people drift apart. And I don't think he himself had any desire to make contact."

I nodded, wondering to myself if his remark was a subtle jab at me;

somewhere deep inside, that very real possibility hurt.

"What about you? How are things for you?" I deliberately avoided asking about the college.

"Well, things are a bit more complicated for me. I didn't get into the college at Museya. However, I did get invited into a school for those who are potentially gifted. Even if you don't end up being Inspired, graduating from there gets you invited to high table banquets and a chance to play for nobles of the highest echelon."

"You will get there, eventually," I reassured. I had no clue if Dale would ever become Inspired, but felt that he should at least hold his head high.

"Thanks." There was a distant look in his eyes. Was it doubt? There was no way to know.

With nothing left to say, we bid our goodbye.

I wasn't entirely present during evening dinner. I had forgone my usual evening ritual of bloodletting. Something about the deep, trance-like process was disturbed. I assumed it must have been my talk with Father Maurice, or perhaps my meeting with Dale.

There was an egg on my plate. My eyes trailed to it. Its shell was cracked, the top removed to reveal the firm yellow inside covered by a mantle of white.

The egg shell bits littering my plate reminded me of my chipped mask beginning to peel.

I wasn't hungry.

"Dalila?" Yasmin queried. She, too, had received her title as Mother and had asked that I sit next to her. I did so quietly, wordlessly, something that she had grown used to.

"I'm not hungry," I said and went back to my quarters.

My fingers felt limp, *uninspired* for the ritual.

It wasn't an unusual occurrence, but there still was a growing pressure within, an ache, an itch that was typically scratched when I scored through my skin.

I laid in bed, the long resting chamber soulless except for my own maudlin heart. I stared up towards the ivory ceiling, a brass frame made into filigree art stretched from one end to the other.

My finger twitched. I needed release, but the blade was not the way to get it. It spoke to me; there was a growing heat inside, spreading across my belly and loins in waves. I felt my cheeks flush, a heat coming over me. Desire grew.

My shell from that morning broke, shattered violently by Father Maurice—made to face myself. My caged emotions were free. Understanding dawned on me as my fingers worked their way down my body. Hesitantly, cautiously, they trailed the landscape white as snow, as if to approach the furtive rabbit that was my desire.

Slowly, finger by finger, I pulled up on the ends of my habit to reveal my legs, legs that began to restlessly squirm at the promise of what was to come.

My hand moved on its own, impatient, longing for a waxing heat that I had been denied for too long. The last time I truly gave myself over to such flame was on a stack of hay at the farm where privacy was hard to come by.

I moaned, gasping.

The chamber was empty, vacant beds my only audience. Dim candle light basked me in its timid glow.

The door was there. Dinner had only just begun, but anyone could have walked in at that moment.

My shell was broken, my sense of desire stoked and the flames nurtured; if anything, the fear of being discovered fed my sudden lust.

My fingers danced and explored, played over the unflattering fabric of my underwear in anticipation. With growing hunger, they found their way underneath. Who knew when the next time was that lust would so carefully stalk its way into me with the promise of release?

My moan cut itself short with a quick bite of my lip. My limbs shook with built up anticipation. The long months without release left my budding clit starved of love and sensitive to my touch.

Fingers played upon their instrument. It was a performance of love rather than pain. The glow of candles lit the chamber in bronze. The border of light trailed over my contours, lapping like waves at the shore of my body.

They danced, those digits of mine, made to mend wounds as they caressed my clit. I rubbed around in circles. My moan grew louder. It echoed across the sleeping chamber. The shifting borders of candlelights were fuelled by my display, the flickering more virulent as they warred for land on my scarred skin.

Reluctantly, I stopped to remove my robes. My bare, sizable breasts flattened across my chest. I removed my underwear to reveal the forest of curled blonde hair crowning the pink flesh I fiddled with.

The barrier was gone, my touch unbound.

I made no attempts to withhold my moans that echoed against those holy walls, my fingers dancing across the surface of my clit, my pronounced labia fiddled with liberally as I used my free hand to massage my big breasts.

My legs writhed, toes curled.

I wanted to savour it, the building pressure, the growing lust.

Any other time I would have repressed the urges that grew in me and I knew I would feel shame once I climaxed, yet I didn't care. Not about that, nor about who discovered me. I just chased after the promise of release.

My heart beat against my ears.

I could feel the pressure building, my fingers a blur as they worked. Warmth filled me. Words escaped me. Things I would never have dared to speak aloud, words that would have made Mother Vinrie blush.

I thought of a hard, beating cock between my legs. My lust almost fled when I even momentarily thought of Perry. Desperate, I clung to the image of Dale, the only other man I had met, a friend who was infatuated with me as a child.

Perhaps he'd have felt disgusted, knowing I used his image to pleasure myself, but it didn't matter to me then and there.

While my fingers continued their dance, I imagined him claiming me with absolute abandon.

I reached the precipice, an edge bound and forming into a whole. My toes curled before me, but extended within my metaphor as I teetered over the edge.

Release.

The sensation exploded from between my thighs and spread over my entire body. A flood to take away my noxious emotions, if only for a moment.

I panted there on my bed. A need for decency returned, but I was too tired to listen. Sweat bathed me, beads of my passion glistening in the soft candlelight that filled the alcoves. Their light softened after the performance.

I sat up, my mind in a haze, pulling the blonde locks over my ears.

I turned to the door and felt my heart grow frighteningly still. A shadow, a reflective bead of someone's eye watching me from the slanted door.

And as quick as a shadow did the figure flee.

Chapter Thirty-Six

EREFIEL

The Haar, for arguments sake, is akin to dough. It can be moulded and shaped to whatever is desired. It is unique to colour magic in that it can only create an object, it can never thus influence someone. It does bring up an interesting question about why untampered Haar forms into monstrous bodies with a desire to live rather than something inactive. Or perhaps the connotations are too horrifying to further entertain.

—SCHOLARLY MUSINGS ON HAAR AND ITS PROPERTIES,
BY E.L VENSTER

T he dust had not yet settled, not entirely anyway. A slew of Sisters came in like a white flood to blanket the dead. The Elder King's eye had a full view of it all.

It took an entire day to organise ourselves and regroup the remaining survivors. The rain had settled, clouds subsided, and we were left to behold the ruin. I didn't manage any sleep. It was a luxury I still had the privilege to complain about, while my fallen men did not.

A quick impromptu wake was held for those that gave their lives. Maxin, found in a daze, finally managed to clamber his way down the hill and back to our men. He now played a lament for the deceased, though one could feel his exhaustion seep into the notes.

My chest ached. A numbness took over me. I wanted nothing more than to bellow and mourn the death of a friend.

There he lay among the shattered corpses, tranquil and serene from the neck up, his moustache slightly besmirched and his skin a cold grey. But his eyes, his full cheeks, were still there—Hendrix was, to me, the greatest loss in this battle. A slight breeze came and rustled his fringed hair. If I didn't allow my eyes to drift to the absolute ruin that was his lower half, I could almost convince myself that Hendrix was only sleeping.

Nora stood with me, her heart heavy not just with the death of Hendrix, who vouched for her, defended her, but also her own second in command: Bradley.

Our mound seemed like a grotesque totem, an offering to the unholy gods hiding under a pool of tar.

Then came their drones; a swarm of buzzing flies as if hatched from the boggy mud beneath our feet. They already feasted away at our brothers and laid their eggs into exposed flesh.

"Burn them," I instructed once our moment of silence felt adequate enough.

"Excuse me, Lieutenant General." A man approached guardedly, his voice brittle.

"What is it?" I asked.

"My brother is amongst those men. We are Witnesses. Please, allow him a proper burial."

I groaned and noticed there were several other men that silently attached themselves to the man. They all came for the same reason. I sighed, allowing for my exhaustion to also expel my temper.

We lost a lot of good men—this wasn't a victory. It was pure fucking luck. Perhaps some men needed something to believe in times like these.

"Find your families, give them proper burials and sermons, but our numbers are cut short, so you will have to do it on your own." An inaudible but grateful round of murmurs came from the huddled men. With hurried bows, they turned to find their fallen brothers.

I made my way to the tent before anyone could see the wave of fatigue that came over me.

⋖ ⋗

The census was gathered. It was easier to see how many still lived rather than counting the scattered limbs buried under mud, or the bodies trampled until men no longer could be identified.

Of the original five hundred and forty-five men who were trained militia, only a mere two hundred remained, and added to that score was a mistmage—things couldn't get worse. One would think looking at the field that the numbers would have been higher, but my heart ached at the tally nonetheless.

It was *my* fault. No matter what action that weasel took, no matter how much I wanted to add one more to the dead, the responsibility fell onto me. I was their commanding officer, the leading commander, and I failed.

I was too concerned with holding the line that I allowed my men to die for me. At their final moments, they must have wondered where I was. Where the fabled Erefiel was, the supposed son of the White-Hawk—what a joke. If it weren't for Nora charging to the fore and inspiring our men, things could have ended differently.

As soon as the situation allowed it, I entered a carriage and made my way back to Cleria, where I had to explain this damned failure.

One thought in particular refused to let me rest. A grating, insistent thought that scratched at my skull: the javelins.

The size, the material, their design—wholly beyond the crafts-manship that mountain and jungle dwellers would have. Even as I continued to distance myself from the battlefield, the image of soar-ing silhouetted needles kept invading me. They were smooth, curved, glistening like flawless steel, a gloss so perfect one could see their own reflection stretched along its body. They protruded from the ground like mocking tombstones for the men they skewered. The more I tried to entertain the idea that akar gained the knowhow and resources to craft these monstrosities, the more ridiculous it felt.

Which made the alternative far more terrifying. Who was their new found ally?

⋉　⋊

The drapes were shut. Sunlight became an uninvited guest within my carriage. It reached with its dull fingers through the gaps.

I no longer had that grating habit as a child where I plucked feathers from my scalp like picking at scabs. I did instead rub them the same way humans tugged at their earlobes.

I was led through Cleria's bustling streets and into the welcome quiet of Strait district.

I went along with the pretence of progress we called bureaucracy. It was just a show. There would be no punishment, no smiting, no judgement.

This was just a formal report presented to the high court to do with as they wanted.

Judge Felicie Auburn was amongst their ranks, along with more ostentatious high-browed law givers nearing the ripe old age of death.

The representative from the king's council, Brutus, was a paunch bellied man with a gruff and professional exterior. Plithy, the viscount, reported directly to King Aston Tiemen and was administrator of militia events. This man was as thin and wiry as a thistle. Then there was General Commander Orson, old and not fit for combat any longer, but his reputation was frightening. He even fought alongside Father in his younger years.

The final seat belonged to my father and was naturally vacant.

My tone was tense, ornery, inclined to set loose a lashing tongue.

I informed them of Cassidy's incompetence in no vague terms, told them of the events that transpired, his reckless order that cost the lives of our scouts and betrayed our position and more.

I took note of Brutus' sigh of relief when I reassured them that Maxin had survived, though Magus Gurick was a grave loss.

A dark and brooding scowl was shared among them as I continued my report—bent helmet underarm, my armour grimy and completely unpresentable, yet I held my chin high and let my voice speak without inflection.

"You must be overthinking this, Lieutenant General," Judge Auburn stated, her remark hiding her intention—she was asking me to reconsider my statement, for its implications did not just have an impact on the battlefield.

"I know what I saw."

This was grave, not something that could be ignored.

"Son," General Commander Orson spoke, a man with white, thick mutton chops trailing down his jawline and arching over his upper lip.

"I'd prefer if you didn't call me son, sir."

The room went silent at my request; it was a brusque complaint that interrupted the general commander. But I was no human child to be scolded. As son of White-Hawk, they too knew what my station meant.

"Erefiel," Orson corrected himself, obliging my request with no noticeable annoyance. "I have been at this game for far longer than you have. That kind of strategic foresight is not something an akar I ever knew could muster."

"What about the one they call Muktow?" They went silent at the name. "They aren't stupid." I made no attempt to cushion my words. "What they are is *passionate.*" Orson didn't object but rather scoffed, as if I insulted him by stating something he already knew. I pushed forward. "Infighting, love, honour. Their emotions are always so close to the surface that anything can let these feelings loose. Our greatest fortune was this trait which caused infighting and tribalism amongst their ranks. To unite such people under one banner and instil discipline was what kept them divided, not stupidity."

"And you are suggesting that now, all of a sudden, they have come together with shared purpose? Holding hands and singing songs of peace?" Plithy asked facetiously.

"Songs of *war,*" I corrected. "And their alliance doesn't need to be an amicable one. It very well may be one of force."

The council murmured amongst them, momentarily high above their stands.

Judge Auburn spoke next. "You wish to suggest that the akar formed a coalition right under our noses and we didn't notice? Despite our scouts? That they have skipped pertinent phases in societal development and can craft javelins of steel before even mastering iron or building proper houses?"

"With all due respect, our scouts are as deep into their territory as a eunuch."

I didn't expect Brutus to chuckle. He quickly choked and returned to his previous austerity.

"If it is true what you say about the javelins, someone with that kind of knowhow may also be the one pulling the strings," Orson commented, trying to return the conversation to something more professional.

I hadn't even considered that. "It may be." I nodded.

Judge Auburn groaned and abandoned formality. "Erefiel, are you sure? About the javelin? About a coordinated leader?"

I bowed my head, but was glad I finally got through to them. "I'm afraid so."

Plithy scowled. "Excuse me! But the king expects to see a written report; you can't honestly expect me to just write up this nonsense and expect him to accept it! King Aston will be positively alarmed by the implications of this!"

"If I may, I suggest that we keep all of this a secret from the public. It would cause unnecessary panic and we need more information anyway," I said.

The others nodded in agreement, save Plithy whose animated features wrote tales about his disbelief. Plithy threw his spindly hands up into the air and let his ledger and stylus clatter to the table. "Fantastic, sure the king will be royally pleased," he groused.

I returned with open arms to the comforts of my home. The rest of the world was distant for a while and gladly so.

Saru met me at the gate.

The sun shone too brightly, a searing spotlight of judgement. The sound found its way into the cracks of my strained patience and left behind a migraine.

There it was, my home, balconies peering out with framed windows, groomed balls of potted shrubs standing sentinel at the staircase. Respite was so close. When I entered through the door and took in the smell of lacquered wood, I wanted nothing more than to just collapse then and there.

"Just a little more, sir," Saru urged encouragingly.

My fatigue must have been obvious. I turned to him. "Thank you." Did he hear my thanks?

I trudged to my room. As I entered my chamber, I removed my armour with the welcome help of Saru. I relished the freedom.

"You will need to commission a repair," Saru said.

"I need to commission new armour," I groused. A problem for another day. I threw myself onto bed with stained tunic and trousers. I lay there, hand draped over my forehead. For just a day, I dared to postpone my duties.

Saru pulled off my boots with no help from me. Without the added weight, I could feel my body again and it hurt. It reminded me that I was alive.

"I wish to be undisturbed until morning."

"That won't be possible."

I raised my head as much as I could and stared at Saru, hoping he was joking. I knew from the regretful look in his eyes that he was doing anything but. "What is it?"

"Your mother; Lady Imrie. She requests an audience."

"Of course she does."

I rose from my bed and rubbed my eyes. My mind was already leaning into a half wakefulness and dreaming of sleep.

Saru raised a hand, stopping me. "I'm afraid you will need to take a shower first," he said, almost uneasy at having to make such a statement. I looked at my grimy body and took a quick sniff of my armpits. "I suppose I do."

⊰ ⊱

Though reluctant, the bath was a welcome distraction. Perhaps not as tempting as the promise of sleep, but it was a strong second. It calmed me and dulled the ache in my limbs. Mother could wait as I permitted myself an extended stay within my cradle of warmth. At least for as long as I could afford to.

Even when the water turned temperate I stayed, if for nothing else than that it was a better alternative than having to get up and dry myself off.

Alas, all good things had to come to an end.

I rose, the ache and stiffness in my shoulders suddenly more pronounced as I dried myself and slipped into aristocratic clothes.

I wore a plain white tunic with frilled wrists and a jabot of lace forming a coned wave down my neck. My coat was a burgundy red as well as my breeches, though the shade was slightly darker. Saru insisted on a feathered hat, but I insisted that I wasn't a frolicking peacock. Not to mention it felt silly to hide my feathered white hair with more feathers.

A coach was waiting at the gate and the driver was an equally well-dressed man with a high chin and straight posture. I tried to hide my stiff gait. I even resigned myself to carrying a hideous cane of lacquered dark wood with the likeness of a hawk at its head made of silver.

I entered the coach and told the driver to be on his way.

⊰ ⊱

Palace Nostracie was a glamorous and entirely ostentatious display of wealth and power.

To the left and right of the garden were winding patterns of small mazes cut from hedges. Topiary animals poked their heads out to observe passing visitors.

The long and wide path was of arched cobblestones. The carriage neared the end of the wide cobblestone path and announced our arrival with the horse's hooves on stone.

Summer colours splattered the building from gilded balcony railings of filigree design, to the rose-red frames of doors and windows. I walked up the palace marble steps and in through the doors.

"Ah, Erefiel. Lady Imrie is expecting you."

"Joshua." I nodded my acknowledgement in a less aureate manner.

Joshua turned, his posture equally as straight and rigid as I followed. The rooms were filled with cushioned sofas that looked like the velvet strained from innards. Paintings lined the walls and depicted nobles known for uniting sundered kingdoms and creating the bastion known as Cleria. There were paintings depicting vague wars of long past ages. It didn't surprise me at all that the less grandiose conflicts like that of the Asamanian conflict were nowhere to be found. The most impactful work was the great, towering swarm of dragons that blackened the sky. The Elder King was hidden in this one, standing atop the back of a gargantuan stingray and only depicted as a silhouette within a cloud.

A long white carpet led me to Mother's seat. My mother was no queen, but she sure liked to parade herself around like one. Her heritage had gone from saviour, warriors, diplomats and merchants for such a long line that, at some point, our legend manifested itself as a form of veneration.

She was beautiful, arguably the most beautiful being that walked these lands, save perhaps the angel Zeraphiel.

My mother, Lady Imrie, was a woman of white; she reminded me of a white birch tree laden in perpetual snow. Her space undisturbed by all life as she would stand in her eternal stillness.

That was how I viewed the woman who sat upon her cathedra.

She was thin and long, her dress a work of unmatched craftsmanship. It had no embroidery, no special frill or belt, it was but a long and flowing dress, as if woven from snowflakes. Its folds fitted her body like a second skin.

With such dainty limbs, lithe long fingers ending in snow-white nails, her lashes an equal blanche like brittle twigs brushed with powdered snow. Her eyes a deep and consuming albino, as her skin was unblemished by any other shade.

Behind her throne there stood tall the Winter Tree, a marvel of magic taken from a part of the distant lands which long ago was reclaimed by the encroaching mists. It had no leaves, it simply spread its naked branches and yet motes of sparkling snow rained down from it and wreathed the cathedra in snow.

"You called for me, Mother?" I said as the chamber doors shut behind me.

The audience chamber was empty today, save for tending servants clad in their own robes.

"*What a pity that I need to call for an official audience to be visited by my own son.*" Mother's voice was brittle, like a soft crack spreading across rime. It was diluted, inhuman, and ethereal as if one day it would melt upon the ear of those who listened.

"Well, I apologise. I was preoccupied with my duties."

"*So I heard.*" Her expression was entirely stoic, unmoving in her regard. Her gaze was glacial.

Since her copulation with Father and works that even I was not privy to, Mother ascended into a being that toed the line of deity and mortal. Yet maternal was never a word I would have used to describe her.

"*Are you well, my child?*" she asked.

"Yes mother, I am well," I said coldly.

"*Leave us,*" she instructed.

Wordlessly, the chamber emptied itself of all servants. The bodies flooded out the entrances. When the last door was shut and the sound echoed with an unsettling finality across the chamber, it was only then that we regarded one another.

"*Why do you despise me so?*" she asked bluntly.

"I don't despise you, mother," I said truthfully. "How can I despise someone who I don't even know?" I wondered if passive aggressiveness even registered with her frozen heart?

"Do you wish to suggest that you do not see me as your mother?"

"Hard to do any such thing when you and Father are absent in my life."

"We are born with duty. I fear a normal family is one luxury we can't afford."

"That's an understatement," I muttered under my breath. I knew I was being uncharacteristically harsh, perhaps even unfair. But it was always like that. That cold, harsh exterior of mother, unchanging and callous, irked me like no other thing. I prodded and poked with my pointed words in hopes of picking at the ice, to find the one chink, the one fault in its design and earn an emotion from her, any emotion at all.

"Perhaps we can at least try; join me again within this home. It is your home, after all." Though I knew her words were meant to be loving, the colourlessness with which they were spoken made them fall flat before my feet.

"Mother, there is a reason for why I don't live here."

"Why is that?"

"You wouldn't understand."

"Humour me."

I considered it for a moment. Her gaze never left me as she sat from her high throne.

"None of this is me. The grand house, the eyes, the pillar upon which we stand as I am known to be your son first and general second."

"So you wish to distance yourself from this household?"

"That is correct."

"Then why invoke our name for the sake of a witch? Is this another stray you wish to take into your fold?" There it was, the source of that incessant and damned critique.

Her words swept my calm away and made my blood run cold.

Mother rose from her seat. The glittering motes of fallen snow shifted as she stepped down her dais.

Her long dress of pure white trailed behind her like a wedding dress. She stepped down the cold marble, her own pale feet seemingly comforted by the cold of the stony descent.

When she approached she looked upon me through those fine lashes; the coldness of her heart must have harboured some frigid idea of care.

Her movements were so slow, so deliberate as if she had all the time in the world.

"So you heard?" I asked as she stood face to face with me. She observed me with no emotion to read. "She is an innocent girl. What would you have me do?"

"I care not for your intentions, I care for your hypocrisy." That final word was not spoken with vigour, but it implied emotion. *"I have heard of the witch, of the akar, of even some unremarkable girl who you protected from a noble. What do you hope to gain here? You wish to distance yourself from this household? Fine. But do not pretend we are not a part of your life. Despite how I may now seem as Lady Imrie, Consultor of Ice, that does not mean I see you as any less of a son."* Mother cupped a cold hand to my cheek and caressed with her thumb. I could feel the soft layer of rime it left. It was oddly soothing.

"You are my son, and our lives make it impossible to experience life as other mortals do, but that doesn't mean we cannot try and find a way of our own."

I hesitated. "Why do you write me now and call for an audience?"

"Is a mother not allowed to worry? You never came of your own free will. Despite knowing fully that I wished for it."

"I knew nothing, Mother."

"Do you know that I still love you? A love that is cold and stagnant perhaps, but love nonetheless. My ascension may have morphed its shape, but the emotion is the same." Mother dropped her hand. *"I was worried for your wellbeing. I heard of the attack. I never wanted to force you to come here, but I needed to see you and make sure you were all right with my own eyes."*

I was tired, but I still could imagine how my stubbornness made the relationship worse. I wanted to hurt my mother the way she hurt me. There was a reason I felt compelled to fill that void, even if it resulted in a compulsion to help others.

"But remember, son, we have a name to uphold, a name that means more than most."

I looked at her, trying to discern her meaning. "Do you mean Dalila?"

"What will we do when the witch that lives because of us suddenly brings about ruin and desolation? What will happen when the changes you brought about the akar settlement fail? What will happen when a nobody that you tried to protect from the wrath of a noble makes us lose favour in the king's court?"

I welcomed the familiar anger. It made it easier to turn callous against Mother. I took a step back. "I know what I am doing," I reassured.

"I hope you are right, child. For it will be your cross to bear too."

Chapter Thirty-Seven

NORA

One of the greatest losses due to approaching Haar is that of Nepanta and its Grand Library. It is surmised that the Grand Library most likely still exists but is stolen by Thickwood's expansion. However, some sources suggest that the library and its denizens fell into disarray long before the approach of the Haar. What the cause may have been is uncertain.

—A REPORT ON THE LOST GRAND LIBRARY OF NEPANTA

Only twenty of my original fifty survived "The Massacre of Greyhill." I wondered what they'd call the next battle? The fallen thirty were replaced with new recruits, plus another ten men that I had to bring to shape. There were some among them who challenged me; nothing I couldn't handle. I enjoyed making examples of them.

The battle had swelled my reputation. Even my title of "Simurgh" was given further gravity by the rumours. Some said I downed fifty akar, others said a hundred. No doubt the numbers were conflated with that of Erefiel's. I didn't have time to squash the rumours nor did I particularly want to. If it garnered me further respect then all the better for it. Being a woman meant that I would always be put into question. I needed them to see me as a legend.

I regretted having no one to confide these thoughts. Bradley had died and so did Hendrix. And while Victor proved himself a competent lieutenant in things concerning logistics and organisation, that was the reason I had Bradley as my number two. I needed someone who would lend me perspective when I was too lost.

Regardless. I couldn't complain. I craved more recognition, more opportunities to rise in the ranks. When I was asked to venture past Greyhill and along Stoneseam I gladly accepted. Even if it was to intercept a caged demon for the Elders.

⋖ ⋗

Two months had passed since the battle as my unit marched. We took the north eastern path of Thickwood forest. I had the new recruits carry the bags of my veterans. A difficult task when done in humid heat. It was the last stretch of summer and the bothersome buzz of insects was lively and full.

The villages beyond our borders were depressing. The people inside Bravnicka were blind to the decay so far out. The shanty towns were made of disgruntled and weary-eyed folk. There was a listlessness to them as they submitted themselves to their work. We exchanged silent looks with the folk. Ours pitying and sorry as if they were already ghosts, while theirs full of spite for our full cheeks and polished armour.

Fortunately, we sighted no akar. After the Massacre of Greyhill, our scouts back home had forcefully placed an improved network deep in the forest. It was designed to alert Cleria of any coming attacks. Even so, we still had no grasp of the akar's true numbers or tactics.

We marched along Stoneseam, passing flooded marshes and thick forests with overgrown trees. On numerous occasions, our wagons carrying food and supplies for Whitshade got stuck in mud and it would take several of our men to free them. We passed another run down settlement near a narrow stream. The folks were mostly human, except for a shavinu. This one, too, had his Death-Eye mangled and torn. I called upon Stamence, who trudged closer.

"Yes, Captain Nora?" he responded. I didn't look away from the sickly man. I nodded towards the general direction of the shavinu as they broomed away within a chicken coop. I saw only feathers but no chicken. Eaten? "What can you tell me about the shavinu?"

"What do you wish to know?" he asked.

I thought back to Saru; Erefiel's servant. "Tell me about the eye."

"It depends. There are different tribes of shavinu. They used to be nomadic warriors before the Haar closed in again. Served as mercenaries to both sides of the Asamanian conflict, depending on what their envisioned death told them. When they come of age, their eyes open to reveal a glimpse into their final moments."

"So they know of their death." It was a statement to reaffirm my own understanding rather than a question.

"To an extent. It's complicated. But to summarise, all of the shavinu believe that the circumstances of their death need to be fulfilled. Once it happens, the eye closes and they are given an honourable burial. But from what I understand, these visions come vague and obscure, never showing the full event. The deaths are often mislabelled as prophecies, but they are more like a potential glimpse into one future."

"And if they do not fulfil their task?"

"The eye remains open. Even in death. An open eye is seen as an unfulfilled life, regardless of the tribe."

The shavinu I had seen was already left behind as we ventured along Stoneseam. "What about the one with the mangled Death-Eye?"

Stamence shrugged. "Some parents mutilate and abandon their children if they don't have a warrior's death in their vision. But usually it is done by the person themselves."

"How so?"

"Some can't handle the pressure, the constant dread of a death you wait for." Stamence went rather quiet, as if contemplating the idea. "Many self-mutilate and cut their eyes to free themselves from the burden. But they are the same people who are then cast out of their clans."

I, too, went incredibly quiet. The implications of such a thing were truly nightmarish. I wondered what happened to Erefiel's Saru?

◁ ▷

The humid air turned our armour into suffocating traps. The buzzing, noisome swell of bugs grew and was applauded by slaps against necks and hands. Lazy brooks continued to drool from small grooves and into the forest.

"Nora." Victor approached on horseback beside me as I turned to lend him an ear.

"Our recruits are lagging behind and complaining about the travel. They ask for a short respite." His words were for my ears alone as I carefully turned my neck to see them panting in the rear.

"We are almost there," I said brusquely. Victor nodded without protest. It wasn't that he sympathised for the men. After all, he went through a similar ordeal. Now there was a silent sense of respect shared between the two of us that didn't need to be addressed. His primary concern was preparation. The unlikely but possible chance of an ambush could mean death for our fatigued men.

"One more thing."

"Ask."

"That man." Victor nudged his head in the general direction of his meaning. "Do you know him?"

I turned to see Eric Richardson ride atop his own steed, one hand on the reins and a blade of grass between his teeth. He had been staring but was in no hurry to look away.

I turned back around. "Pay him no mind. He is simply here to deliver the payment for the demon and ensure the package will be delivered safely."

"Is there history between you two?" Victor pressed.

I turned to Victor and smiled. "What's this sudden interest?" I asked.

Victor looked ahead and shrugged. "I like to be aware of all factors. It helps me map all eventualities." Our horses rubbed against each other to wipe down their sweat. With a quick reprimanding nick, we pulled them apart.

"He is harmless, just mad that I robbed him of his money."

"You robbed him?" he asked surprisedly.

"It's worse than it sounds. He made a bet once in a fighting ring at Bracken and pushed all the right buttons to taunt me. I entered the ring and made him lose a great deal."

Victor seemed to ponder something. "Who did you fight?" he asked.

"Some big, large asshole. Looks as simple as a sack of potatoes, but damn clever, that one."

Victor's eyes swelled with recognition. "Great Munasen?" he asked.

"That's the one!" I found myself beaming at the mention of him.

"You've got to be kidding me. You're *the* Simurgh?"

I blinked, not entirely understanding. "I mean, that's what people call me."

Victor shook his head. "No, no. I mean in the ring! Your title was Simurgh as well?"

"Perhaps. It was a long time ago."

"You're a legend!"

I still didn't understand where all of Victor's excitement was coming from until he stilled himself to explain. "I wasn't there that night, but people couldn't stop talking about the woman who took down Munasen and robbed everyone of their money and just left."

"*Won* their money," I corrected.

Victor waved the word away as if it were of no import. "I can't believe that was you. Now everyone there keeps comparing new fights to your bout."

I smiled. I had never seen Victor so unrestrained when talking to me. I knew that his professional frame was a front more often than not. If he got to talking about something he was passionate about, he was like a child in armour.

"I never knew you were a gambler?" I teased.

"I never knew you fought in the pits," he countered with a teasing lilt.

I looked away to hide my flushing cheeks and urged my steed into a canter. "It was only once."

⊰ ⊱

Our final destination could not have arrived sooner as we climbed the final hill. I heard of Whitshade as a sorry town standing on its last legs. The years had not been kind to it, and though it was not due to the invasion of any akar or Rashi or other fiend found within the gates, they were running out of resources.

It was a truth that conveniently was left out of daily conversations within Cleria. The matter of the encroaching mists, the growing cases of rot outside of the borders, and the ever fading flow of resources. During the Asamanian conflict, the people from the west, who resided in their own empire of deserts and dunes, had to flee and come to our side of the mountains. However, given the sheer number of refugees, they weren't permitted entry into Bravnicka. Just like that, an entire royal line of kings and warriors gave into infighting. These parts never recovered from all the death and conquest in an ever-bloating forest. It had turned into a silent reminder, a cramped and huddled tangle of trees trying to escape the coming end.

It left a sour taste in my mouth that our kind was abandoned and yet we accepted akar refugees.

Whitshade came into view. The town was marked by a cluster of modest homes and a respectably sized house of worship. Except that it was all in ruin.

Smoke rose as thin pillars from shabby homes, many of the thatched frames had crumbled in and were left charred. Piles of ash could be found. A breeze of hot air worked its way through our troops and delivered the scent of burnt flesh.

"Victor," I called without flinching. Obediently, he approached.

"Gather men and deliver food and resources to the needy, take the carriages and see who needs tending to. Speed and efficiency are paramount."

"Yes, Captain," he said. He immediately started organising forces and working his way down.

Howard and Stamence came up behind me. "Do you think it was the akar?" Howard asked.

"Who else would it be?" I remarked with scorn.

"I doubt it. The akar would have no reason to raid such a place. What kind of advantage do they gain?" Stamence countered.

"You speak of them as if their kind acts on reason. They are miserable and needed food." My horse sauntered down the hill and my men followed. At the border, I ordered everyone to unload and dismount, offering help where they can unless I ordered otherwise.

Many were wounded, a lot of them fatally. The smell of burnt flesh clouded this place and stuck like cigar smoke to a drunkard's tongue.

Soft and depressing coughs echoed across the town of Whitshade; many were mummified in bandages. One man's stare followed me. He had an arm in a sling. Gauze wrapped diagonally across his right eye. There was as a listlessness to how he stared. He had no thoughts to offer at our approach. An ugly red splotch had seeped through the wrapping around his eye, giving the impression of some demonic red sphere observing us.

Howard reappeared moments later. "Victor is handling the relief and getting a hold of the situation."

"Who attacked them?"

"Vagabonds, a pack of raiders. Apparently, the soil is getting worse. Crops are harder to grow."

I bit my lip. People were getting desperate. Their ruin was just a matter of time. I felt a rage fill within me, wondering how Crowtown could offer succour to the very plague that brought all of this to us, but ignore our very own people starving out here by themselves.

"And our correspondents?" I asked.

"Not yet here."

Stamence appeared next. "We have a problem," he said.

I followed him to the church building. The side of its slanted roof to the west had caved in. A mound of charred wood remained at the corner of the church.

An unsettling heat wave hit me at the entrance, followed by the stench of the dying.

I heard coughing from inside. It was as if they were communicating with their dying neighbours to serenade the coming of death—the coming of Ankou upon his wagon.

"We can't trap a demon in here with all these people," Stamence stated the obvious.

I contemplated what to do. "Where is the abbot?"

"I am here. Abbot Tilbert is the name." The abbot's brown robes were stained by a barely visible cloud of red and other fluids I couldn't make out, nor did I want to.

"I am Captain Nora. As you are aware, we are here to pick up the package."

Fatigue took an obvious toll on this man, it seemed that the gravity of the situation kept him on his feet.

"I apologise, Captain, but as you can see, now is not an opportune time," he said, almost blithely, if it weren't for his exhaustion.

"Are all of these people wounded because of the invaders?" I asked in disbelief.

"Not quite; some of them have the rot."

My heart jumped into my throat. I stiffened. I took a moment to cool myself and consider my options.

"We will handle it," I assured.

"How?"

I turned to Stamence. "Set up my tent as well as all others that can be spared. Fill them with as many people as you can." He nodded and went on his way.

"Howard, organise a small group of the new recruits and see how many of the wounded you can promptly relocate to the new hospice."

I turned to abbot Tilbert. "Is that acceptable?" Abbot Tilbert seemed more overwhelmed than anything else as he nodded. "Good."

We cleared out the church and set up a makeshift hospice. A few holy men as well as three of our own medically knowledgeable medics got to work salvaging as much as they could.

I watched the wounded be carried and stiffened at the sight. There were those without arm or legs. Their empty gazes already belonged to the dead. It was too much. I turned away only to find another macabre painting: the rot.

Carried upon a stretcher to avoid touching the malaise was a young woman with her skin a pallid and sickly grey. Worrying thin branches of black veins scrawled across her inebriated skin, her lips dry and colourless, her cheeks cracked and dead skin flaking. A blackness filled her eyes as thick tears of tar rolled down her cheeks and down her lips of blackened gum and teeth. The scent that came from her was like mould wedded to infection; an acrid sweetness that made my nostrils flare and shrivel.

I covered my face in disgust. The sick woman stared at me blankly. My skin went cold as she smiled.

"How horrid," I uttered to myself. The woman was taken away.

"That's all of them," Stamence said, as he approached me from behind.

"Good," I said, trying my best to appear in control.

Chapter Thirty-Eight

NORA

Since the end of the Asamanian conflict and the disbanding of
the Unbound, it is believed that most Asamanian have taken onto a life
of demon hunting. As for the whereabouts of the prolific Ubar,
it is believed he has settled down for a simple life up in the
mountains of Stoneseam.

—A STUDENTS REPORT ON THE CHANGES OF MINETHRIA DURING
THE ASAMANIAN CONFLICT

We heard it before we saw them, like an earth shattering roar that upheaved the ground beneath us—it was truly demonic. I swallowed my fear; this was the first time I was going to see a demon. I couldn't show fear.

There was a glow, a burning bright fire. I heard the cracking of wood and could see the trails of sparking embers in my mind's eye. Like a ghost that haunted this town, the scent of sulphur and brimstone made itself known.

A cage rolled its way into sight. I saw a small team of men and women pulling a wagon. It contained a beast inside wreathed entirely by flame.

It stomped and thrashed, its arms like big lumbering trunks set alight. Flames were just shy of licking the frozen bars of ice that entrapped the demon. It roared and beat its chest to give the impression of an ignited gorilla.

The wagon creaked on its rickety wheels and drew into town.

A man walked to the front with three scars running diagonally across his face. He wore a protective gambeson with studded iron. He was armed with a short sword at his hip and a crossbow at his back. A robed woman, hood pulled over to hide her face, chanted mystical incantations underneath her breath as she meticulously worked a prayer spiral in one hand. The object was a looped wire in the symbol of the Elders with beads to flick up and down its length.

Then there was the armed woman with a monstrous crossbow on her back and potions of motley colours filling her bandolier. She sported many more belts, pouches and daggers, and had a wildness to her befitting a Demon Hunter. Most noticeable of all was the one side of her tanned scalp shaven to small bristles which revealed a worming red dragon curled around a ruined ear.

A giant akar dressed much like a human pulled the wagon. He had none of the tattoos or decorations typical of his kind. Lastly, there was a man with a piercing stare. An Asamanian. What remained of the Asaman delved into mercenary work as their kingdom was lost. Was he part of the Asamanian conflict?

His skin was the darkest black. His brown eyes matched his skin perfectly. He wore bound dreadlocks and carried a great over-encumbering glaive over his shoulders.

The demon roared. Embers came from the demon's maw like burning fireflies and the leering townsfolk murmured in excitement.

I approached the company and sighted Eric from behind a burnt down house. He tossed away an apple he had been enjoying moments ago to the foot of a dead-eyed resident. He clapped and wiped the juices from his gloved hands and stepped in front of me.

I caught a close look at the creature. It wasn't as tall as an akar as it rested upon its flaming fists, but it certainly was far wider than one. It huffed and exhaled heavily through its nostrils. Flaming beads for eyes observed us all with a strange intelligence I felt didn't match its appearance.

"You may not want to stare for so long," the Asamanian warrior suggested. I turned to find his own eyes prodding. "Makes it aggressive."

I nodded and avoided looking the demon directly in the eye.

The mystic approached the akar. Her white hood was still drawn over her face as she inspected her ally. I had only ever heard stories about mystics and was captivated. Demon Hunters were permitted an opening through the Ashen Forest in order to capture their quarry and return with prize in hand. The fact that the group before me had even one mystic on their team spoke volumes about their capabilities.

"You must be Seamus," Eric said, as the head of the band stepped forward.

Judging by their matching snarls, one would think they were related, but unlike Eric, Seamus did not have a blithe look to him. He just seemed perpetually sour.

"You got the money?"

Eric got the gist of the exchange and lobbed the coin purse to Seamus.

"Stoya." Seamus called and passed the coins to the heavily armed woman. She finally allowed her eyes to drift from the growing crowd and onto the purse.

Moments passed by silently except for the occasional infernal roar of the demon and the cracking of continually freezing iron-bars. The crowd of onlookers grew, with more and more townsfolk drawn in by the promise of excitement and danger. As if they hadn't already had enough.

"You." I turned to find the Asamanian warrior addressing me. "Are you the leader of these men?" he asked. I was surprised by the assumption. I tried to hide it. "That I am."

The warrior nodded casually to the swelling crowd. "I wasn't kidding when I said that you shouldn't stare; makes the beast uncomfortable."

"I thought the bars were meant to hold the demon?"

He allowed himself a bemused smirk. "It does, but why test fate?"

There was a cleverness to the man that I liked. I felt like a predator toeing the line of another confident animal, pacing back and forth, our eyes dancing in a language wholly their own.

I called Victor and Stamence forth and instructed them to do away with the crowd. There were objecting groans but none resisted.

"It's short," Stoya stated, before tossing the bag back to Seamus. The man lightly jolted the purse in his hand to feel the wanting clank of coins.

He smiled, unable to hide his irritation. "I thought your lot would have known better by now than to try and play us," he said.

"That's all the coin I was given," Eric said.

"Right." Seamus gave a disbelieving sniffle and tossed the bag back at Eric's feet.

"Let us know when you mean business. Come on, lads." He turned away, and the akar groaned. He rolled his shoulders to prepare for another trek.

"Wait!" Eric called, making private disgruntled complaints as he revealed a second purse, tossing it to Seamus along with the first pouch.

Seamus balanced the two weights and seemed satisfied before throwing it to Stoya a second time. "Eric, is it?" Seamus asked, his stare cold and sharp.

"Aye, that it is," Eric replied.

"Let the next person know that if you try to swindle us, we will just leave. No second chances."

Eric didn't respond. The laxness with which the band carried themselves showed a confidence that could only be born from treacherous trials. I had to admit, I simultaneously feared and admired whatever they had to go through.

Stoya tossed the bags back, and her curt nod made Seamus smile appreciatively. "Pleasure doing business," he stated, moving forward and clapping a hand to Eric's shoulder.

"What is your name?" the dark-skinned Asamanian asked as he approached me.

"Nora."

"Ah, like the sun's light," he said, as if it suddenly made sense to him.

He placed a scarred and sizable hand to his chest in an act of respect followed by a slight bow. He planted the blunt end of his spear into the ground like a flag. "I am called Rafik Dezak. It is a pleasure." There was a flirtatious brashness to the way he spoke, his eyes still engaged in their prowling dance, his voice a deep and coaxing purr.

"Hello." Now it was the mystic that spoke, her voice like chimes in a spring breeze; calming and soft. Her hood was still strewn over her features. I could only see feminine lips.

"This is Ida, our mystic," Rafik introduced.

"Gron! Hurry it up!" Seamus called further away.

"Yeah, yeah! Gron do this, and Gron do that." The akar groused with eerily human cadence.

Rafik chuckled. "The complaining one is Gron. The last two are Stoya and Seamus."

"Welcome. I hope the trek wasn't too demanding."

Ida and Rafik chuckled at the notion, a joke that I was not privy to. "As pleasant as it can be out in Thickwood," he commented.

Next it was Seamus who approached me.

"Hello. I understand that you are in charge? Captain Nora is it?"

I nodded. He reached out to shake my hand, his previous blasé demeanour replaced by a more professional one.

"Seamus, I presume?"

He gave a curt nod. "What happened here?" He asked, looking at the destruction.

"Raiders."

"And the church?" he queried. I understood where the worry lay.

"Roof caved in at the west, but the building still stands and the basement is unharmed."

Seamus nodded and looked at Ida, who smiled from behind the cover of her hood.

"It should hold," Ida commented.

"'Should' is not good enough; I want you to make sure."

Ida nodded.

From the corner of my eye, I noticed a young girl, unharmed but dirty. She demurely approached our circle—how scary the world must have looked to her.

I knelt down to her height. "What is it?"

She fiddled with her thumbs, head bowed, hair unkempt and wild. She looked not to me, but to Ida.

"Is something wrong?" I asked. "Where are your parents?"

When the girl said nothing, I tried another approach. "Do you wish to speak with the mystic?"

For a moment, I thought that the girl's tongue was still knotted tight; perhaps it was as she opted to nod timidly.

I stood to my full height, gently pressed my hand to the girl's small shoulder, and led her to Ida.

When the girl looked up at the mystic, I could feel her entire body tense. She backed into me. I looked at the young girl and noticed she went ghostly-white.

Was she shy? No, that couldn't have been it. I followed her stare to whatever she glimpsed underneath Ida's hood. Something scared her.

"Don't be afraid, child," Ida sounded like a large and undisturbed lake with only the slightest ripple at the surface. Ida went to remove the hood. Rafik's hand darted to stop her.

"Ida, there are people watching," Rafik said in hushed tones as if Ida weren't aware.

"Then let them see. It will instil caution." Reluctantly, Rafik loosened his grip and stepped away, permitting Ida to remove the white hood.

My own gasp was among those of the crowds as I looked at what Ida had been hiding. It was true. Her lithe chin and thin diminutive lips were like that of a doll's that evoked images of frail beauty, but that illusion was shattered. A ruinous and ugly scar of veiny flesh covered the upper half of her face as the result of some horrific burn; even her eyes had melted and meshed into the gut-wrenching brand. Despite the sharpness of our gasps, Ida simply smiled.

"Hear me, people," she raised her voice, though it still sounded as soothing as chimes. "This is the price of facing a demon; this is what happens when one underestimates their kind. Remember that when you consider approaching the beast's containment," she said. Slowly, the hood returned to cover her face. Ida turned to the young girl, who was still frightened. "Don't be afraid."

Ida knelt down to the child and took her hand in hers, and cupped them caringly. Next, Ida guided the young girl's hand and brought it up to her face, past the veil of her hood so that she may trail the lines of Ida's scars and see that she was still human.

The act instilled some calm into the young girl, though she still stood impossibly stiff.

"What's your name?" Ida asked.

"G-Gritta," she hesitated.

"Gritta, that's a beautiful name," Ida cooed. Bit by bit, Gritta seemed to relax. "Now tell me, Gritta. What is the matter?"

"My mother has become very sick. Could you take a look?"

Ida nodded. "Of course, Child." She placed a loving hand to the young girl's hair. "Now go, I will follow in just a moment."

Gritta allowed herself a weak but present smile as she nodded and left. Ida rose and turned in my general direction.

I suddenly couldn't bring myself to look at her.

"Please don't feel the need to pity me. I am far beyond that," she said as if sensing my discomfort.

I nodded, but I wasn't sure if I could keep that promise. How could one ever be okay with such a thing?

"Are there many injured?" she asked.

"Yes, in our tents; we made a makeshift infirmary."

Ida nodded. "I will see what I can do."

Next, she turned to the waiting demon. Its flaming chest heaved with contempt as its beady eyes glared at Ida. It was the kind of glare one expected from an imprisoned animal. "But first, we have a demon to transport."

I felt the demon's roar in my bones.

⋖ ⋗

The drawn cage was pulled through the landscape of homes. The towns-folk parted to make way for the wagon, their frightful eyes peered up at the spectacle with equal measure fear and curiosity.

The beast roared, and batted against the bars. Fire met ice and the demon drew back its fists to look at the waning flames of its limbs.

As we neared, the church doors were drawn fully open, the benches had already been moved to the corners of the room to allow space for the demon to be brought inside.

Where the roof had caved in there waited an ominous crow, its head turning to observe the spectacle for itself.

The hidden door to the right was pulled away, folding like a fan to reveal the rickety wooden elevator held by a pulley system. It did not entirely instil me with confidence.

Ida continued her chanting, blessing the body of the church as the akar known as Gron heaved and pulled the wheeled cage onto the elevator. The construction creaked with the weight.

Rafik had already explained that the horse they had lost its compo-sure and broke free, running down a hill where the panicked neighing faded and was followed by a distant echo. Then came breaking bones.

The church air was stale and thick. Eerily quiet too, as if haunted by the lost lives of the recently deceased.

The broken opening in the roof allowed a pillar of light to beam inside and reveal dancing motes of dust. A foetid stench clung to its walls, defiling what was once a place of hope. I felt like an unwelcome outsider, gazing over the nondescript patches of stained wooden floor. It looked like the souls of the damned had seeped into the building itself; their inaudible screams were deafening.

Gron lowered the elevator down with the use of a wheel attached to the beam of the structure. The demon lit the surrounding walls as they descended into the abyss.

I dared to lean over the edge, and stared at the lowering structure. The beast's roar echoed and resounded against the walls of stone. Its light dragged against its soon-to-be prison.

I worked my way down the spiralling steps to the left of the elevator, feeling entirely unconvinced about the integrity of the wood that sagged and groaned. I felt it became a voice for those who perished within the holy house.

Along with me came Seamus, Gron, Ida, Eric and Victor.

In a moment of realisation, I turned to offer my hand to Ida. She walked past me and ignored the offer. I followed after awkwardly.

Gron pulled the wagon to the centre of the room. We had no need for lanterns as the demon illuminated the cellar. Other than cobwebs, barrels of perishables and other resources, the room laid barren especially at the centre.

Ida pointed out the important measures to ensure that the beast was kept secure. The holy house was a conduit, a body of belief that symbolised the power of the Elders. That belief powered the runes carved into wooden posts and walls with intentional subtlety. Alongside those carvings were cleverly masked brushes of paint added to the scenery, made up of different shades of blue.

Before I could ask the hundreds of questions that rushed through my mind, Ida was already on her way to the faded ink.

I followed her as Seamus was doing a pre-check on the demon and explaining things to Eric and Victor.

I didn't care so much about how the cellar restrained the demon. My curiosity was aimed at something else entirely. "How do you see?" I asked.

Ida had taken her container of blue ink and was already restoring faded colours on the wall. Dainty and elegant fingers felt the coarse surface where the previous runes had faded. She turned to me as if taken aback. Lowering the container and the brush, she stood up straight and allowed herself to remove the hood with a tentative smile.

I grimaced, looking away.

"Are you uncomfortable?" she asked. "Would you prefer if I wore the hood?"

"Yes, I mean—no." I stumbled over my words while my eyes darted to and fro, glossing over the ruinous scar as if ever stopping to linger was an affront to the mystic.

The woman only smiled. "Why are you so flustered?" she asked. "Do you pity me? Do you think me less capable than you are?"

My tongue went rigid and my lips remained shut, but I realised silence was far more damning. It seemed obvious that I was more capable, but to say it aloud was wrong.

"Let me ask you this, do you find men treating you as lesser because of your gender?"

I suddenly felt entirely insulted. "That's different," I blurted without thinking and regretted it instantly.

Ida's smile faded and just a stern expression remained on her ruined face. "Do you think me broken?"

"Well, having lost your eyes, don't you need help?" I asked, treading carefully.

There was a soft and rather amused chuckle from Ida. "I venture past the bordered walls of Bravnicka and capture demons for a living, yet you think me frail?"

I realised the rush of blood filling my cheeks. "No! I mean—I didn't!"

Ida chuckled again. "Yes, you did. It's alright." She stepped forward. My eyes couldn't hold the stare. They constantly darted to the ruined mesh of skin covering the upper-half before focusing on her lips and nose—where was I to look?

"If I got upset every time someone thought me frail, I would never get anything done."

She took my hand in hers, and did like before, with Gritta. My fingers were made to brush over the bumpy mesh of skin.

"What do you feel?" she asked.

"Skin."

She then took my hands to her arm and made me brush over the smooth surface.

"How about now?"

"Still skin."

She relinquished her grip. "I am still human. I still live and breathe; I aid my brothers and sisters in the capture of demons within the Ashen Forest. Tell me, Captain Nora, why am I then deserving of your pity?" The query was an attack, spoken softly and with composure, but it was no less blunt with its delivery. "To answer your question: I cannot see. I sense and feel instead."

Without turning, Ida placed a tender hand and stroked the paint on the wall. "This is my work, my paint, which covers it. I navigate this place with such familiarity because I have been here before and I can sense the flow of magic, the aura given by things. I do not see as you do, but eyes aren't the only way to navigate this world."

Ida finished painting over the remaining spots and explained the process to me.

Blue ink could be used for many purposes, to calm and still, to relax, but it was also the colour of ice and water. In this case, it was used to create a barrier of cold and ice to imprison the demon within its walls, imbued with her intent and identity.

Upon the bars of the cage itself, there were small carvings of ice to encase the iron with a sheen of perpetual cold and the wood was reinforced with brown colours to strengthen its foundations.

We joined the others, Seamus summarised the explanation by bringing it down to two points: if the cage were to break within the basement, then the natural runes of the cave and church would imprison the beast inside, if the runes of all things were destroyed especially without the security of the church, then we are to flee for our lives and hope that we survived.

The only word of comfort was that demons usually cause little mayhem by themselves and would rather turn into an incorporeal form and return to their domain, rather than risk recapture.

I stilled any bubbling anxiety and nodded my understanding; Eric and Victor did so in kind.

❧ ❦

The humid summer day was waning as the Elder King's eye began its descent over the western mountains. My men were still busy with their relief efforts.

The groans and cries of the dying were a nauseating choir that filled the distant air. Without me having to prompt anything, Ida walked up to Seamus and stuck out her hand for Seamus to take. They spoke in hushed whispers until eventually Seamus looked at me.

"Ida wishes to tend to the wounded, so we won't be leaving, as of yet."

I gave a small and grateful bow. "Then you have already freed me from the awkwardness of asking."

Seamus smiled. "Shame, should have waited for you to ask and earn some coin instead."

I smiled in turn. "Perhaps food and lodging amongst my men will be enough?"

Seamus nodded to that. "We would be grateful."

Stoya passed with a drumstick lodged between her teeth. She munched her mouthful, and seemed to have caught the tail-end of our conversation. She threw an arm over Seamus's shoulder. "Rafik certainly will be delighted." She looked directly at me. I couldn't help but smile at the implication.

I turned to find Eric leaving, and it suddenly dawned on me how little we talked. I would just find him occasionally glaring in my direction. Not once did he make his thoughts heard.

At the time in Toothfairy, he had everything that was coming to him. Even at that moment I harboured not a single ounce of regret, but seeing how obviously he seemed to loathe me, I gathered I must have truly hurt him that night.

Chapter Thirty-Nine

NORA

The Faithful Church has many branches. The Sisterhood. The Serving. And then there are the mystics. They are the weavers of Haar and the wielders of ink. They are the only thing which keep the demons trapped within their Forest of Ash.

—Division of Religion, by Romana Rae of the Ravens

One of the truths I had learnt as a soldier was that a good leader was firm—something that most certainly should not be mistaken for tyranny. I opted to be fair, just, reasonable despite how much I demanded of my men.

Which was why when I told the new recruits that the night would be spent drinking and feasting from extra barrels brought with us, they all cheered in celebration. Of course, I couldn't allow everyone to indulge. I needed some to stand guard in case the enemy returned. But it wasn't just about my men. Whitshade also needed to be reminded that life wasn't just suffering.

The little festivity was formed an appropriate distance away from Whitshade upon a small hill that gave view of the town in case there was an attack.

The speaker of the town was called Bronden, but due to the unfortunate attack from the raiders, I never had the chance to meet him. In his stead, Abbot Tilbert took charge of the place. Abbot Tilbert was sharper than I had expected. He confided his concern on whether such festive banter and commotion were not a raging beacon to call upon the raiders and tell them of the new bounty once we were gone.

I reassured the abbot that once we departed, a good handful of my men would be left to dissuade the raiders from attacking, and upon reaching the capital of Cleria, I would file a request for reinforcement.

I was relieved to see that at least he seemed to believe my words, because I certainly didn't.

When you lived out here in such humble gatherings, it was easy to think the world was just as small, but Cleria did not care about such huddled masses and small towns. We kept our distance during the Asamanian conflict; Cleria wouldn't care about some settlement across the border.

At least Whiteshade was important enough as a pickup location for the demons.

Men got to work with renewed energy. We set up pots of bubbling stew, gathered wood for fire and prepared containers of smoked meat.

One team of men even returned from the woods with a family of boars as their prize and they wore their grins proudly. It earned them boisterous cheers. Of course, of those well enough to join us, the townsfolk were also encouraged and welcomed into our circle as the night began to set upon our island of firelight.

I glanced down at the town from the hill. Its own candle light was scattered and feeble, leaking through lonely windows where I imagined the curtains to look like saddened eyelids. Our banter and laughs masked the sound of the dying down below, like soft and muffled coughs buried under pillows to not ruin our jolly mood.

"Captain Nora?" I turned to find one of the new recruits standing behind me. He had a cup of ale in each hand and offered me one.

"Thank you, Recruit." I accepted the drink.

The recruit nodded, and I recognized him as one of the mouthy ones who challenged me when recruited. He turned to leave before I stopped him. "What's your name?" I asked.

"Sam," he obliged.

"How is your first mission going?"

He seemed somewhat taken aback by the question. "Good. Challenging."

"Do you still think my credentials lacking?" I asked bluntly.

Sam had to compose himself for a second. "No, Captain."

"What made you change your mind?" I pressed.

"Well, walking all that distance with that weight strewn on my back definitely made me think twice before talking," he admitted and earned a chuckle from me. "But, to be honest, it was the scenery of this place when we arrived. It was when I realised we were no longer in Bravnicka, that we could be attacked at any moment. But the way you handled everything made me realise how immature I was being."

I nodded, fully appreciating the candid response.

❦ ❧

Day transitioned into night. The starry sky spoke of the shambling undead from Estria. I found a sullen and brooding Eric sitting alone by the campfire's light. He was an island unto himself, as everyone else was already preoccupied with their own conversations or searching for one that didn't include him.

I suddenly felt a silly sense of anxiety at the thought of approaching him. Thoughts like those never stopped surprising me, having faced and felled numerous scrawls of akar. Yet, here I was, nervous about talking with a harmless human.

I wiped the sweat from my palms and, with a few sips of my ale, worked my way around to join Eric on the grassy floor.

He spared me a momentary glance as if to confirm my identity and then turned silently back to the raucous before him.

"You wanna talk about it?" My words were tossed into the space between us, a branch to reach out towards and take if he wanted to.

"What is there to talk about?" he asked flatly.

"You tell me? You're the one who keeps looking at me like you are counting the number of ways you can murder me in my sleep." I took a sip from my ale. During our entire exchange, our responses were spoken like poking jabs in darkness to get an idea of how the other was built, the texture, size, form, all of it unknown and explored with caution.

"Well, that's what happens when you have your entire livelihood robbed from you in a single evening and suddenly have no way to pay out your debt."

I fell silent, not out of guilt, *never* out of guilt when it came to Eric. I just didn't want the tension to continue between us and spread amongst my troops as rumours.

"Eric, if it were me in your stead that evening and you took all my earnings, would you have a single shred of remorse?"

"No," he admitted bluntly. "But that's the problem, Captain Nora. It was my winnings that you took—*that's* what made it unacceptable."

My attempt at reconciliation was laughable. Eric rose and departed to another lonely corner to sulk in. Not once was there a single drop of enmity in his tone. I could sense the cold rage just underneath the stony surface.

⋞ ⋟

The air was still humid and hot and caused my tunic to cling to me like a second skin. The wild had a strange sense of freedom to it. Cleria's rigidness had no reach here. As the shadows lengthened, my troops gave into a night of debauchery. All of us earned such an unbridled event once in a while.

I downed my ale. It loosened the bindings of my inhibitions as I worked my way to the team of Demon Hunters huddled in their own crowd. The audience was of curious townsfolk and my own men sitting like starry-eyed children full of imagination. They were being regaled by tales of what it's like hunting demons.

One story revolved around when Rafik's leg was stuck in a rockslide and Seamus was left alone to bait and distract a demon as thin and spindly as a mantis with pointed limbs that doubled as skewers for the living.

Another story surrounded Stoya. She had purposely inflicted a malaise upon herself with her potions so that a mist demon could possess her.

Rafik and Gron displayed the greatest level of competition, a match that Gron supposedly won on most accounts and that Rafik was just merely behind on. The difference being that Rafik's retelling of events was unconvincingly portrayed in a humble manner, which failed to mask the pride that he had in his achievements. While Gron attempted no such thing, and perhaps even embellished some of his tales. For an akar, Gron had an uncannily human way about him. Even his diction and prose were more reminiscent of a loquacious poet than it was a primal warrior.

"I swear it! A great demon! It had the heads of three crocodiles and spanned the size of fifty men!"

Seamus groaned tiredly. "We weren't there, Gron! You really want us to believe that you lifted such a monster by yourself and slammed it like a child's plaything?"

"Yes!" Gron cried desperately.

"Gron, please, no need to exaggerate." Gron sulked and crossed his arms as he took a seat, pouting like a child no longer in the mood to share his triumphs.

As the groups split into smaller crowds, I failed to notice that Ida had snuck up on me until she stood an arm's length behind. Her hood was down, the light stretching wormy shadows across her marred face, but her smile was as calm and tender as before.

I turned to her. "Do you want to sit?"

"Ah, Captain Nora. It's quite alright, I like to just bask in the fire's glow," she remarked, looking straight ahead.

"Perhaps then I could guide you to your friends?" I offered instead.

"That would be very kind of you." With our arms interlocked, I led Ida to the softly bickering team of hunters. She became my ticket into their circle.

"Why don't you join us, Captain?" Seamus asked jovially.

I hesitated, at first, until the remaining heads joined in on the request and welcomed me. I relented and joined their mirthful circle.

They asked about my past, my history, wanting to know more about where I grew up and how I managed to snag my own unit.

"What's he like? Erefiel? Is it true that he is covered entirely in feathers?" Stoya asked, hungry for gossip.

"Where did you hear that nonsense?" I retorted with a bellied laugh. "Erefiel looks human, just with white feathers sprouting from his head."

Stoya's eyes bulged. "So it's all feathers?"

"No! It's just *some* feathers; the rest is regular hair. Albeit as white as snow."

Stoya leaned back and returned to her casual and aloof demeanour. "That's disappointing," she said, as if I had just crushed one of her dreams.

"That must have been difficult, with your family," Rafik said absently. His eyes followed me hungrily.

"That it was, but surely not as difficult as what you do for a living." My smirk invited more banter.

I tried to be flirtatious, but it proved difficult surrounded by the other hunters. Eventually, the band broke off into smaller groups and it was just me and Rafik.

I wondered if everyone was aware of our intentions and orchestrated the entire affair. Perhaps I would have been worried about how it would reflect on my men, but I allowed the alcohol to do its work and rob me of sense.

When I caught Ida standing behind the licking tongues of flame, her image distorted but her smile ever present, I realised why she had asked me to walk her.

It was just me and Rafik at the borders of the camp. His midnight black dreadlocks were bound into a tight ponytail behind his head, his pauldron of steel and remaining armour removed to reveal the dirty brown shirt underneath.

We were lying on our backs on a patch of grass as we stared at one another. We sat closer than would be decidedly appropriate. I couldn't recall if I ever permitted myself to be so carefree amongst my men. Perhaps it was the promise of sex, the ale or even being so far from home: probably a mixture.

Rafik's eyes roamed freely over my body, taking in the view with a steady breath—I had no doubt he had done this dance many times before.

His beard was a growing patch of curly hair bound tight and close to his jaw. It fading into patches at the upper cheek like a forest transitioning to pasture. He smelled of dried sweat and natural body odours that made his closeness all the more tempting to me.

"Were you there during the Asamanian conflict?" I asked.

He chuckled. "Oh no! Don't tell me you are one of those girls?" His question was playful.

I smiled. "What? Of course I am curious!"

Rafik chuckled, knowing full well how common and predictable my interest was. Regardless, he obliged. "No, no, I wasn't. I was just a child when the conflict was nearing its end. But my father told me a bit about it."

"Care to share?" I batted suggestive eyes at Rafik, my gaze holding a whirlwind of promises in return for his inherited tales.

He didn't let it break his cool, a simple chuckle escaping him. "Fine. Not much to tell, really. The returning Haar chased us out from the desert. We lost our glory, our lands, our pride. We were forced to scavenge for food in a forest turning evermore perilous. Our people were proud; Father believed it right too. They banded together and began to conquer the woods. Their next stop would be Cleria."

"And then came the Unbound," I said regretfully. The Unbound were a crazed lot who professed themselves free of social constraints.

Rafik, seemingly knowing where my mind went, nodded solemnly.

"Yes, the Unbound thought it silly how seriously the Asamanians took themselves and revolted against them. It was all a big joke to them. At the end of it all, the Asamanians who were left broke into small clans. The Unbound fell into infighting and Ubar's own troops dissolved after that."

I nodded, recalling the three bodies which were integral to the conflict. "Ubar's a legend, even in Cleria."

"I met him once," Rafik said.

My eyes widened at that. "He still lives?"

Rafik nodded. "He's kind of a hero to me. Close to fifty years old now." His head hung a bit more sombre. "Though I suppose there is a good reason they say not to meet your heroes. He is a decrepit old man living with his family along the mountains of Stoneseam. Still, none compared to him in terms of leadership and skill."

Rafik seemed deep in thought at the mention of a legend. I decided to change the subject. "Ida, she was in on it, wasn't she?" I asked, looking back across the blazing bonfire to find her gone.

"In on what?" Rafik snapped out of his reverie.

"She asked me to take her to the rest of you as an excuse for me."

Rafik gave a wide and toothy smile like a child caught in a mild offence. "I would assume so. I don't know."

I leaned in, as if unsure what other ears might have been listening, but also so I could have a better idea of how my body shuddered at the proximity of his lips—but not yet; it was too soon.

"Is she truly blind?"

"In a manner of speaking. She can see things as trails of loose light, shady figures, or sense things in other ways. She can orient herself accordingly, discern the identity of someone she is approaching, but in a fight? Where hundreds of things are happening all at once?" Rafik shook his head. "Her vision just turned into dashing colours. She is powerful. Her grasp over colour-magic is unlike anything any of us have ever seen, and she could cast an innumerable number of horrors on us if she wanted to. But she needs the space, needs to be grounded and needs time to cast her spells. If things move too quickly, it is the same as not seeing anything at all."

I frowned. "Sounds more like a liability than anything else. Her having to rely on all of you to make it work."

Rafik seemed taken aback and leaned away.

"Sorry, I don't wish to offend," I said.

"I'm not offended… Just confused. What makes you think she is relying on us?"

I blinked, equally perplexed. "Well, you just said you need to buy her time to cast her magic?"

Rafik laughed.

"What?" I smiled, his laugh surprisingly endearing as it made my heart flutter.

"Ida isn't the one relying on us, *we* are relying on her: we are a team. Sure, she cannot see, but it's our responsibility to bring out the best in her. We all have limitations; what makes a difference is that we compensate for our comrades." My confusion must have been easy to see as Rafik sighed. "Gron is stronger than I am. Does that mean I am not needed?"

I frowned heavily. "Yeah, but he is an akar, that's not the same thing."

"And Ida is an invaluable mystic."

"Yes, but she's blind. It just doesn't seem worth the effort."

Bit by bit the tension between us cracked and stretched itself thin until the threads unravelled. Rafik distanced himself and sat up.

After a moment, I did so as well, and placed an apologetic hand to his shoulders. "I'm sorry. I'm the one who doesn't understand." I could feel the moment slip away.

Looking to another corner of the crowds, I found people cheering on Gron's display of might as he ripped apart a wooden log with his bare hands. He relished in the cheers of my men. I wondered if I should change the subject, but didn't think it wise to speak on a matter that may eventually also reveal my dislike of akar.

I decided to escape the present awkwardness and just relieve my bladder. Without a word, I left into the woods.

I stumbled into the copse of darkly shrouded trees, loosened my trousers and squatted down to the forest floor. As I heard the spray of fluids rush from me, a million thoughts ran through my mind.

Was Rafik upset with me? Would he still be interested? I was still giving myself slowly to the whims of the ale as I squeezed the last of my bladder empty.

I wondered what words I could offer to return to the previous sexual tension that pulsed between us? Wondered even then where I could take the man for some privacy.

When finished, I rose and pulled up my pants. I turned to head back to camp.

Rafik stood before me. He blended in perfectly with the night.

We didn't taint the moment with words. Our stares held. The sound of the distant crowd lost and in a realm left behind. I felt a lustful breath shudder from me. Our unspoken conversation mirrored the fullness of night, as again our eyes joined in primal dance.

A desirable warmth spread through my heart, spread through my warming loins. Understanding filled me.

We strode toward one another, no longer relying on words. Immediately, our tongues locked into a passionate dance, our hands exploring each other's dimensions with ravenous intent. I could feel my chin bury itself in his full beard. His petalled lips pressed against mine with want.

Rafik's chest heaved. His rough and encompassing hands took hold of me with firm desire. His hold slithered through the openings in my trousers and found purchase on my rear to pull me close. He took in a deep whiff of me.

The tide of our clash threatened to take us. I pushed my rear into his hold, burying my own head into his taut neck, where I took him in. My hips grinded of their own accord, trying desperately to provide as much purchase for the dark-skinned warrior. Rafik pushed me back, my booted feet stumbling over forestry until the bark of a tree braced me. I let out a gasp of pleasure and pain and smiled. Again our lips met, Rafik's wildness threatened to drown me. I accepted all of him.

With ease, he lifted me. I wrapped my legs about his waist. My curling fingers pulled on his shirt, freeing him from the layer so I could feel the touch of hard muscle. Rafik buried his head into my supple neck and kissed. My fingers clambered about his back, trying to grab hold on the sheer width of his being. I couldn't even reach the border of his spine.

I removed my shirt; Rafik gladly helped. The small mounds of my breast stood at attention, the nipples erect when Rafik moved from my neck to suckle on them. Like curling vines, my arms lifted up to the body of the tree as I panted and called upon the name of god. I could feel the wet tongue flick upon my nipple with such eagerness. The man's hips thrusted. Even though he was clothed, his body showed its impatience.

I cast another moan into the night for no one to hear. The distant sounds of my men aroused me even further, the danger filling me with excitement.

Rafik let me down as I frantically removed my trousers and he, too, quickly absolved himself of all clothing to reveal his erect cock.

All pretence of being anything more than feral animals was cast aside like moulted snakeskin. We stood there with our bodies fully in sight. Burn marks. Ugly scars across chests. Healed stab wounds. All of us was on display.

I went down on my knees and took his being into my hands. Tenderly, I stroked along his shaft. I admired it, the slight upward curve it had to its veined body. With voracious desire, I swallowed him, slathered him in my spit. My accompanying hand twisted along the shaft. Rafik let out a moan of passion as I looked up at him and stared deep into his eyes. I fell deeper into the moment. The mere erotic feel of it all served to heighten my own sense of desire. My spit slathered him with a reflective sheen. I slid my hand down my body. Between my legs. And slid my fingers into myself and conjured a moan. Desire claimed me, forced me to bury my fingers into myself.

I relented for a breath of air. A bridge of spit connected my lips to my object of desire. I looked up at the landscape of Rafik's muscles and stared into his eyes. I held that gaze while my hands continued to stroke. I relished seeing him moan.

Rafik stepped away and knelt to join me on the forest floor. He gently but firmly pushed me onto my back. He spread open my legs, revealing my untended bush. Without any hesitation, he buried his head between my thighs. His eyes also never left mine. I felt his tongue explore inside me. A maddening tingle swept over me, a sensation that made my toes curl. A sensation that made my arms stretch and go taut, grasping at dried leaves just to have something to grab onto. I gasped, my words turning barely intelligible as my mind reeled from it all.

Rafik's large hands scaled up my stomach and back down. I grabbed at the offered hands, my smaller fingers enclosing around stout and long ones, around calloused palms. With even more zest, Rafik committed himself to the act, his tongue exploring the outer rims, parting the seam to explore inside.

"Stick it in me," I said. It was half spoken as a breath.

Rafik didn't need to be told twice. Leaning back, he brandished took his sex into his own hand. Like a true tease, he rubbed its shape against my entrance and forced from me one more restrained shudder and moan. Without any more foreplay, the cock gently stretched open my walls. My mouth parted, but no sound came. My brows stitched themselves together in an expression of pure pleasure while Rafik inched ever deeper into me. I wrapped my hands around the man's strong neck, actually shuffling down to take in even more.

The feeling was that of pleasure and pain as we rhythmically gave ourselves to the moment. Our hips pressed into one another, my warmth spreading along his cock. A wet sound could be heard in our moment of union. We looked at each other wordlessly as Rafik picked up pace. My voice got stuck in my throat as I gave into the man's unrestrained thrusts.

My hands wrapped around his back once more, nails digging in, clambering as if letting go meant being torn apart. Rafik grunted and groaned. Skin slapped skin. I could feel it, the moment coming ever closer. A swelling pressure that then exploded from between my thighs. It came in waves. My eyes turned white from the pleasure, but the exchange never stopped. Rafik went harder. He gasped, his brows stitching together.

"I'm…" I knew what he wanted to say.

I pushed him away, out from inside of me, and the man fell on his rear from pure excitement. His cock twitched angrily, ready to burst. Before it could do so, I jumped atop of it and wrapped my lips around the shaft. I continued the eagerness he showed and Rafik flung curses into the unhearing night. His seed burst into my mouth, thick and long ribbons. I felt the cock twitch in my mouth and only when I was certain that he was spent did I pull away and then swallow. I looked him deep in his eyes.

"You are something else entirely," said a sweat-drenched Rafik as he collapsed on the floor and laughed.

Chapter Forty

NORA

There are mentions of a relic known as the Purple Crown. If it ever did exist, no one knows for sure except for perhaps the Lorekeeper. It is said that the wearer can bend subjects to their will. Further research references other variations of this crown. A question arises. Is the wearer in control or the crown?

—FACT OR MYTH? OLD TALES OF MINETHRIA,
BY LAY C. KONOVAN

Morning arrived. It was the harsh beams of a rising sun which burnt away night's revelries. The camp was filled with dissenting groans, and I started to question my judgement. My pleasure was had, my desire satiated; now I could afford to return to the old and austere captain that commanded her men.

Rafik had already left with his band, a fact that did not upset me in the slightest. Quite the opposite. He left me a note that I found in the pocket of my vest. It read simply, *"Had fun last night. Take care of yourself."* No signature. Didn't need one.

Good, another reason it was such a pleasant experience; no fear of misunderstandings or commitment.

Relief efforts commenced for another day before our band would set out and return with the demon in tow. Alongside the Demon Hunters,

Eric also departed, seeing as his part of the job was already done. Now it was up to me to ensure the safe return of the demon.

The ground shuddered, a barely noticeable thing; it gave me pause. Trailing my fingers into the dirt beneath me, I felt subtle vibrations.

My eyes went to the tree line. Raiders? They must have organised themselves after seeing our night's debauchery. There it was again, that soft tremble. I frowned. It didn't come from the forest. I followed the sensation, feeling for it. My gaze turned and lingering on the holy house behind me.

Again, another barely noticeable shudder. A loosened tile from the roof slid away and shattered on the floor. Fear came, accompanied by realisation.

There was a distant, fiery growl from the belly of that home. The sound of an ignited furnace ready to rupture.

"The demon!" I shouted. The souls about me were still in a trance. Groggy eyed, they wandered listlessly, not understanding my meaning. The guttural growl of the demon then echoed through the inside of the holy house, a deep and grating thing that quickly infected those about me. Their tired looks faded as fear took its hold. People started to scream, frantically running away or towards the building.

Now the growl came with the shudder, the house noticeably shaking, more tiles sliding from its broken roof.

It sounded like an entire frozen lake breaking at once, thunder hidden underneath its ice coming free.

"Captain!" Someone called.

"The building will hold!" I reassured.

The sound of the roar came closer. My heart felt faint and small within my chest as I realised the cage itself was in ruin.

Embers rose like fireflies, attaching themselves to the building's foundation, where they fed and swelled into infernos. There it was again, that bellowing cry. Fire claimed the holy house with a vengeance, ravenous in how it spread. A timber frame collapsed under the weight and turned the mound of rubble into a campfire of its own.

"Run!" I cried. My men turned frantically, looking at me as if I misspoke. "Everyone flee!" I cried.

The fires grew, and the demon's roars were no longer echoing. More and more of the building caught fire. I stood to ensure the traffic of injured folk passed by promptly when I noticed something that made my blood run cold. There, stuck in a trance, limbs locked out of sheer fright, was Gritta, staring up at the alight building as if it were a tyrannical deity forcing worship out of fear rather than love.

"Gritta!" I cried out. There was no response. I noticed the telling trail of liquid that ran freely down her lithe leg like veins of water down a cracked boulder. "Gritta!" Still nothing.

Another piece of wood broke and fell down, lighting the entire building into a sudden explosion of flame. Gritta finally managed a shrill and bone-chilling scream. The sheer intensity of the building's fire threatened to swallow Gritta whole.

"Oxular be damned!"

I sprinted forward, my body moving faster than I could think. The building was now entirely engulfed. The burgeoning flames stretched the shadows of the folk out as if it were tearing their souls from bodies; the girl was nothing more than a silhouette.

I found a strewn cloth that I pulled over my shoulders, and dove into a brackish trough still full of water; I ignored the sudden pain that came from knocking into its shallow grove. The trough tipped over. I rolled swiftly to my feet and pulled the cloak closer to myself.

"Gritta!" I cried a final time as I sprinted over into the searing furnace, my arm strewn about the young girl protectively as the raging flames grew ever taller.

"It will be alright," I promised.

The girl's eyes held only fear, tears trailing down her cheeks as she looked at me, terrified.

I never saw it, but I did hear it. The sudden eruption of inferno that radiated like a flash; searing hot flame lashed against my body, causing my skin to blister and break in an instant. The ravenous fire licked my skin and stripped away its layers with barbed tongue.

I grit my teeth as tightly as I could when the fire enveloped us. All moisture turned to vapour in an instant. My body was cocooned in the raging heat, the scent of brimstone heavy as it turned my nostrils into an arid wasteland. My throat shrivelled.

Flame became my entire world, flame that dug its nails into blistering flesh, threatening to break me. All I remembered in that final moment was twisting away from the wave of fire, an explosive roar that made my ears ring, and a young girl wrapped protectively in my arms.

I welcomed the darkness that followed. The inferno calmed into a grumble and all I could smell was burnt flesh somewhere far, far away.

Chapter Forty-One

NORA

The Magic of Minethria comes in three parts:

That of Ink, scrolled onto a surface to evoke a miracle relevant with its colour. Red births fire as much as it instils rage, while blue heals like the sustaining gift of water. Haar is the mist, it is potential, it is a weave to be spun into what one wishes to create. But the arts; they require submission, finesse. It is an unteachable talent which uses music to bend hearts, performs dance to sway armies, and recites poetry to instil courage.

—So you want to be an inspired? Museya textbook
on Inspired Magic Theory

A darkness enveloped me. I caught the occasional glimpse of the world as if through holes made by an infestation of moths. Rattled and delirious, I stared at the smeared faces of forming crowds. A crying child wept uncontrollably somewhere. Who were these people?

I felt my body strewn about the back of something; was it a horse? It had that familiar stable smell to it, though I couldn't be sure as the scent of something burnt still lingered.

A searing heat spread through the right side of my body as the horse galloped across fields. I heard the horse pant as it pushed its limits.

I could feel the numb pressure of its stride knock into my body. I barely noticed when I was strewn off its back and collapsed onto the floor. There was the soft feeling of wet mud bracing my fall, a coolness to it that just made the heat to my side sting more acutely.

"Nora!" I heard from far away; a voice trapped within limbo.

Everything was distant; my fevered mind delirious. The senses which typically provided a panorama of reality were undone, giving each of them a life unbound by their siblings.

When I finally came to a stop, I emptied the contents of my stomach onto a stone floor. The burning reflux filled my throat. Its stench was something else I could add to this improvised soup; the ingredients refused to harmonise.

My final glimpse of reality was made up of white shades hovering over me. They looked like souls who had come to mourn.

Their hands reached for me, fiddling with my body, stripping me naked and doing with me as they wished. "Stop." My lips were dry, the word as cracked as the hoarse nature of my shrivelling throat.

The gaps were filled. Darkness became my companion for such a time that it felt like it had always been my world. I caught glimpses of passing faces and worried voices.

"It's infected." I heard from far away. "We have to do it now."

The only thing that kept me company was the searing pain on my side, never leaving me to numbing depths in which I receded.

It was only when sensation returned to me like a crawling prick of needles that I realised I was still alive, and that this darkness was not my reality.

It came slowly, bit by bit, pieces of myself filled in from somewhere far away. My mind thought of wiggling toes and I could feel the stretch of skin only vaguely and the movement of bones. The feeling worked its way up, forming the rest of my body as I saw my shins from my mind's eyes, my thighs and then my chest. Yet still, only half of my body made itself known. I was being put back together, my consciousness reinserting itself into the vessel that bound and moved about the world.

As the prickling sensation finally moved itself up to my neck and planted me back into reality, my eyes opened. I had a dream while trapped in there, one where my head had been severed and the dangling strands of nerves were planted into dirt like roots.

⋖ ⋗

I was in a bed.

Being reinserted into my body brought with it the punitive ache that tormented me, no longer just some dull pressure too far to care about. The splitting headache was just the accompaniment.

My throat was parched. "Help." I tried to cry, but it came as a feeble wheeze.

I coughed painfully. My throat hadn't been used for a while. I looked to my bedside left and right and spotted a nightstand with a mug of water. Relief was in sight. I turned to reach for it. Again, I felt out of my own body.

Confusion settled, and then horror. Why did my arm not listen? There was a lacking fullness to my shoulder. I removed the covering blanket, and was suddenly stunned. I stared at what was left of my body. My mind could not make sense of it. My vision strained and flickered to fill in the gap.

My arm was gone; empty space all the way to the shoulder. I pulled the rest of the veil to reveal my absent leg. I felt my toe wiggle, like a distant mirage of a limb forgotten somewhere. My mind frayed at the edges, unravelled at the seams which held its idea of reality together. Like the binding spine of a book coming undone, the pages scattered freely into the wind.

Again and again, I looked to the remaining stump as if expecting to see something else. Again and again, the sight of my absent arm and leg left me at a loss for words. This was not the vision, the body I had known as part of my life, my reality. My throat croaked. I felt like crying, but not even one drop squeezed itself through my ducts.

I longed for it to be a nightmare, for it to be something I could awake from and escape. There was an uncanny sensation to the way I flexed my missing arm, the absent weight still not accounting for the uncomfortable sensation of moving fingers in my mind's eye.

I tried to cry, tried to scream, but the withered stem which was my throat managed only a groan. Soon enough, the ghostly shades of Sisters flooded in, calling for more when they saw me awake.

They had pitying looks as they worked their magic.

"Please," I said. I wasn't exactly sure what I was pleading for. If they heard my meek words, they didn't show it. Working quickly with their blue colour-magic, they brushed it upon my forehead and instilled me with calm.

Even as I faded back into welcome sleep, my crazed look never averted from these ghostly shades.

Chapter Forty-Two

NORA

There is a tale about a village from the eighth cycle. Even the village's name has been lost to time. Its denizens congregated and prayed endlessly, through day and night, until the plague of their village was forgotten. Whatever it was which urged such desperate measures will never be known.

—THE DARK TALES AND ITS SOURCE, BY HEMWEATHER

Time had turned into a slow drawl within this subspace. Previously rushing ravines turned into a stagnant pool upon which I drifted. The still waters were darkened with muck. The passing of time, which was once dictated by the entropy of action and exchange, was no longer of consequence here. I was mere driftwood infested with rot.

I caught glimpses of being fed soup by the hands of devout Sisters as they pulled me into a seated position. I listlessly let the contents dribble down my lip and chin, my throat swallowing whatever gruel was given without protest. Days passed sluggishly, my fettered mind unable to comprehend any of it.

Bit by painful bit, the waking world shaped itself into a tormenting tapestry. The dawning realisation of my removed limbs became such a stark presence. The fog of confusion parted eventually, the vapour thinning to reveal the smouldering fire hidden within.

I took in the confines of my austere room. A crutch carved for me like a taunting totem waited in the corner. A drab cupboard stood sentinel to the side. An unmoving door gave entry to permitted ghosts and closed shut otherwise.

On that third day, terror claimed me fully. I had been thrown straight into a nightmare. Bile rose and burnt my insides. Though what remained of me felt weak from being bedridden; I forced myself to sit up with my remaining left arm and left leg.

What a horrific sight it was. My one good leg was a pale shade, tangling itself in the strewn blanket while its lost twin squirmed in some other plane. An ailing sensation of knotted nerves plagued this phantom limb.

Both of the stumps were bandaged and tender. I tried to stay logical and calm. Thankfully, my dominant left arm was still intact. Yet, the more awareness returned to me, the further rage smouldered within.

This time, my throat found a new voice, powered not by words but by a most primal fear planted deep inside of me as I screamed a banshee's scream.

There I was again, that same timid, scared girl.

The door to my chamber burst open as three sisters strode in.

"It's alright! Captain Nora! Please relax!" one ordered.

It was too late. I had already lost control. Energy flooded my enervated limbs.

"Where is my body?!" I cried. My fear pretended to be rage.

"Hold her down!" the sister ordered.

The two remaining sisters went over to either side of me, one holding me down by the right side where my limbs were missing.

"Don't you touch me!" I was delirious, frantic, and in shock. The energy bursting from within was pent up from however long I was dormant, for however long the days slowly passed me by. I felt like a thin reed powered by the force of an explosion.

My free hand lashed out and struck one of the Sisters, causing her to stumble.

The sister to my left clamoured and grappled onto my arm, pulling me down as she revealed the leather straps that were to bind me. I thrashed and strained. I spat at the sister with all my contempt. Be it her sense of professionalism or whatever else one called it, the woman took the assault passingly onto her cheek and continued to tighten the strap.

As I was distracted, the other sister strewed her own strap across my chest and fitted it at such speeds that suggested she had done it a hundred times before.

"I'll kill you!" I screamed. Day after day, I simply wandered through my fettered sanity, watching these same sisters help my broken body; all I saw now were accessories to my plight. All that rage, all that contempt, not born out of hate, but rather fear, lashing out at anything, anyone, to distract me from the truth—I had become a cripple.

The bindings wrapped me like brown serpents, their teeth biting down at their own tails to restrain me. The last two straps for my absent limbs would have to go hungry, however.

The sister who had given the orders had retreated to a corner of the room and finally returned with a bowl in her hand which she stirred with a paintbrush.

"Calm, child. Calm!" She cried.

Never before did I come so closely acquainted with defeat. My arms were exhausted and hurting. Even if they removed the straps, my borrowed energy was gone, and I doubted I could even muster the strength to lift my fingers. Dead eyes stared into those souls as if my missing arms and legs had already traversed into the ethereal plain and I was halfway there myself—stuck in limbo.

My chest heaved, breathing pained breaths. I didn't care anymore about the parched ache in my throat, or anything else for that matter. My heaving turned into a throbbing ache. A blossoming flower of despair, of hopelessness.

My chin quivered, my vision blurred with the welling tears.

KIAN N. ARDALAN

I looked at the sister with her bowl as if she were the orchestrator of this torture and I'd be willing to give her anything to free me from it.

"This will help," she said, leaning over with the brush.

She wanted to calm me down, to lame me, to stop me from resisting. It didn't matter, I wouldn't fight any longer—I didn't even care.

She brushed its contents on my forehead and muttered an incantation to calm me like before.

"Please... kill me," I begged. Choice, I wanted choice. If I couldn't live my way, at the very least I could choose to not have to live as a broken cripple. She never did grant me my wish, but what she did give me was a close second—momentary relief as I was permitted to escape into sleep.

My dream was nice: I was in a tavern with my men. I was toasting with both hands, walking about with both legs. Howard had challenged me to an arm wrestle. I had to use my right hand because he was right-handed himself. I still won.

Bradley was there, too. I told him about everything. About my promotion, my unit. How I gathered an additional sixty men.

It was only when I said that I wished he was still alive that I realised I was dreaming.

I awoke, a small drawl, a process that I tried to drag out for as long as possible. Even when I was at the door and could open my eyes to reality, they remained shut. I wiggled my toes, moved my arm, and though I could clearly see myself doing it all, I couldn't deny the weightlessness, the absence like ghostly appendages of no real tangible form.

Tears welled and still I kept them shut, refusing to open my eyes. I didn't want this reality, I didn't want any of it. I wanted to return to the dream I had, to a world where I was unstoppable.

Eventually, the darkness became torturous and taunting. Slowly, hesitantly, my lids fluttered open. I looked at my covered body. The straps of the bindings were gone as I felt my left arm move freely.

364

It took time to grab the covers. A shudder escaped me. "It's okay," I muttered.

I pulled off the blanket. This time, I did not stare with rage, just profound sorrow. A clear thought ran through my mind. *They are truly gone.*

The door opened to reveal the sister from before standing there. Our eyes met. She seemed surprised to see me up. Awkward silence trailed between us until she gathered her composure and gingerly shut the door behind her.

There was another canter of water in her hands. She came and wordlessly set it on the table. Moving away, she worked her way to the foot of the bed.

"My name is Mother Merilda." I stared blankly. "How are you feeling?" she asked with a smile.

I didn't respond. I looked down at the right side of my body.

"Okay, then let me fill in the gaps. It's been two weeks since your accident. Stamence was the one who rode you here into the medic station at Fort Treb. Your body was badly burnt, and your limbs became infected; we had no choice but to amputate them. Since then, Victor returned your unit back."

"Casualties?" I asked numbly, my eyes not engaged in the conversation.

"A dozen, mostly your men," she obliged. Another sea of stillness passed us by until the next island of conversation. "The girl you protected, she got away unscathed." There was a hopeful inflection in that statement.

"What happened?" My own voice was cracked and emotionless.

Mother Merilda hesitated before retelling whatever information Stamence provided. Most of the evidence was charred and burnt, but apparently, there had been talk of faulty runes and colouring. The demon escaped its prison, turning into a trailing rope of fire that shot up into the sky and vanished.

An embarrassing flare of anger flickered inside me. *Ida.*

Of course. How could I ever lend myself to believing that a blind woman would be able to rectify, to ensure, to check, that everything was done appropriately? I cursed the momentary lapse of my judgement born from my need to fuck. We'd been conned.

I imagined Rafik and his comrades laughing as they delivered such a creature of mayhem into our lap. Watching from the safety of Thickwood as their malfeasance brought destruction.

Mother Merilda must have noticed the flaring of my nostrils.

"If you lash out again, I will have no choice but to put you under once more," she warned. I looked at her; she was serious.

I stilled my heart. The rage lamed, but present, so that it could numb the sorrow I felt.

"Is there something you can do?" I asked.

"What do you mean?"

"My limbs? You have colour-magic, couldn't you regrow them?" Mother Merilda tried to fold away a smirk. My request was ridiculous after all.

"I am sorry, there is nothing I can do."

"Someone else perhaps? A magus could form limbs out of the mist?"

Mother Merilda sighed as she stepped tentatively and took a seat on the bed. I flinched for a moment, about to tell her to be careful of my leg. Then I held my tongue when I realised how foolish I was being.

It was strange, being bed-ridden like that, having not moved for two weeks, not having eaten anything, being sustained with magic. I wasn't accustomed to being the helpless one, not since I was a child living under the suffocating watch of my parents, but the woman in front of me was the closest thing to my salvation that I could ask for.

"Nora, I know this is hard, but this is your life now," Mother Merilda said, in no loose terms.

I distanced myself, the words were meant for someone else, not for me. They were for some other poor sod called Nora, for someone else who lost their limbs. I was meant to be great, to do great things. Rise to the top of the ranks, stand over my parents and show them that I didn't need them, to show the world that it couldn't hold me down.

"Nora, listen to me. There is no way to get your limbs back."

I didn't respond, my glare darting to the bland and empty wooden wall; my nostrils flared.

Mother Merilda sighed. "I will get someone to bring you food," she said and left me to my thoughts.

◁ ✦ ▷

I laid in bed. Even the limbs I still had felt limp and fatigued, unable to muster the energy to move. The same arms that felled akar and had still boundless energy left; even they seemed like they were not my own.

Given time to adjust, I surveyed the room and found it austere and minimalist, with just a wardrobe, a sick bed, a nightstand with a Kaseluda on top, and a table with two chairs next to the shut door.

I found no sign of my armour or clothes anywhere. I wore a sleeveless tunic and white underwear. Wrapped bandages squeezed in my sweated torso. The only other thing I gathered was mine was the one crutch leaning against the wall to my left.

There were eerie moments where I still felt as if my missing limbs were still there, ghostly appendages moving in some ethereal plane but invisible to me. Sometimes, I felt a searing hot flame twitch and spasm on my side, like a nerve cluster being twisted ever so tight until I had to crumble into a ball. Other times, the pain was spread throughout my body as if I were skewered above a smoking flame.

Removing the tunic with some difficulty, I started to grasp a new sense of appreciation for how life was with two arms; how easy it was to remove articles of clothing from oneself. With my still remaining hand, I traced the shape of my body. I followed the same path that Rafik did just two weeks ago.

That bastard. I bristled at the thought of him.

I fiddled in-between the bandages that revealed the dark red and cracked ruin that was my skin. It looked much like the worming wound scrawled over Ida's face. I followed the wound all the way up to my neck; feeling the tenderness of pink skin. My fingers stopped there, reluctant to continue.

It dawned on me there were no mirrors in my room, and a greater pocket of despair budded. I was too exhausted, already too maudlin to give it any heed. It was too much to dwell on all at once. And yet, I wondered if the sisters didn't want me to see my own face? Was I really so terribly scarred?

The bed offered pernicious comfort. It whispered to me to stay in its embrace and forget ever standing again. My one wrist draped itself over my eyes. Perhaps it was to hide my new reality. Father's promise came to me from somewhere: did I deserve this? Was this my punishment for something I had done? The words belonged to Father, but were disguised by my own voice.

❧ ❧

Food arrived as porridge with flatbread and chunks of chicken floating within. I consumed it all ravenously. Perhaps it was to fill that emptiness with something that would never be satiated, but poetics aside, it was because of the fact that I hadn't eaten anything solid for the past two weeks while my body tried desperately to salvage what it could.

Eating was difficult. Balancing the tray upon a single leg was out of the question. I hung it over the side and lay the tray on the bed instead. Next it was eating with just one hand, gladly it was only soup, but I would usually cup my free hand underneath the liquid to avoid spillage.

I may have acted indifferent, yet each drop that spilled took with it more and more of my wounded pride. The one hand that was left to me felt alien. An awkward appendage that struggled to remember how one held a spoon. I felt disconnected from my own body, each remaining part dissociated from the other as I blew on the steaming liquid.

It burnt me. My finger spasmed and the spoon fell back into the bowl. The contents splashed me as punishment and I pushed the tray to the floor in utter frustration. All I could do then was cry.

The following day I awoke to realise I had wet my bed. My shame and embarrassment as the sisters changed my bedsheets without a single word of complaint came across as ungratefulness. Mother Merilda assured me that the mixture of pain and inactivity were to blame—apparently my bladder had begun to atrophy. Part of me wanted to laugh at the absurdity.

As more energy returned, it also reignited the ire harboured within.

The sisters were trying their best to take care of me; I could not afford to lash out at them. I was constantly in a sour mood but they never spoke of it. All it did was make me feel even more helpless. They wouldn't even scold me for being crass.

In time, I could no longer sit still. My body didn't realise that it could no longer bound the distances like it used to. My spirit was too wild and vast to fit within this shrivelled vessel.

Reaching out, I fumbled for the crutch. I had only used it once during the aforementioned cleaning of the bed and it took a remarkable amount of focus and pride to simply just rise and stand, but it mattered little as my first step ended with me on the floor and screaming that no one was to help me. Again, my pleas were ignored.

I let myself reimagine that event, feeling the memory, identifying what went wrong.

The sisters said to ask for their help when wanting to stand, but this was something I had to do on my own. There wasn't much left for me, but learning to walk again was something I could achieve by myself. Eyes glued to the floor, I focused, my heart beat at the promise of standing again. Great puffs of air inflated my cheeks and the toes of my remaining foot wiggled in anticipation.

All at once, I pulled myself up, groaning at the effort. All too soon, I reached the top, and realised my error. I put too much weight on the rise and it sent me falling to the floor. I grimaced, let out a hiss, and felt a pang of pain that distracted from the constant heat which overcame me.

There was a knock at the door. "Nora? Everything alright?" It was one of the sisters.

"Everything is fine!" I called back in-between pained breaths.

There was a moment of silence where I begged to whatever fiendish God would allow this nightmare to unfold, to at least spare me the pitying looks of these people. I let out a grateful sigh as I was met with an understanding response and departing steps.

Reaching out, I grabbed the crutch and pushed myself awkwardly to a seated position.

I spared a moment for what remained of my right leg. It was barely a stump and was bandaged at the very end. When the Sisters would change the bandages, I would be privy to seeing the ruined mass of black skin like the ends of a charred log.

"Come on, Nora," I roused myself.

With another grating groan, I fitted my good leg beneath me, balancing upon it, wobbling back and forth before shooting up with as much force that could be mustered.

I was standing, but only for a moment. My body contorted as I did little hops to find my balance. My breath was heavy, I could feel the thin reed on which I balanced. I hopped straight to the wardrobe as my leg gave way halfway through. It did not trip, did not get caught, it buckled like a folding blade of grass as I hit the floor hard.

I winced at the smarting pain, feeling a swelling ache come from my knee. My arm trembled when trying to push my body back up. A single cry of pain came from me. I dragged myself the rest of the way, coming to the foot of the wardrobe. With what dubious strength was permitted, I grabbed upon the jutting handle of the armoire. I pulled myself again up to my foot and leaned against it for support. My cheek pressed itself against the wooden surface.

I continued this trial of regaining my footing, waddling between bed and wardrobe, sometimes feeling as if my right leg would catch me to only then remember my reality.

Slathered in sweat and feeling it a pointless endeavour, I crawled my way back to bed like some pitiful worm while my crutch lay forgotten on the floor.

❧ ☙

A moderate amount of strength returned to me, but it came with an uninvited guest. Was I always this emotional? My mood swings were unpredictable and swung capriciously. I pranced between fatigue and rage, intermingled with tears when I knew I was alone.

My nights were uncomfortable. The searing flame of the church followed me. It surrounded me in its ethereal heat as my body burnt up in sleep and I was bathed in sweat.

I told Mother Merilda that I could feel my missing limbs burning; she said it was normal.

"By magical means?" I pressed.

She had snickered mirthfully. "By natural means," she had reassured and called it phantom pains. Along with that, I was plagued by things she referred to as 'phantom itches'.

When finally they allowed reflective surfaces into my room, I was permitted to see myself. They had eased me into it, talking about what happened and what to expect.

I think they were relieved to see that I did not react so strongly to the scar that marked me compared to how I reacted to my leg and arm.

I was never a wholly beautiful individual. I saw myself as rather plain. I had diminutive features, a slightly hooked nose, unremarkable eyes cramped tightly underneath the hood of brows and with thin lips rather narrow. I had a rather long face with a boyish jawline.

Now there was a trailing scar that scaled up the side of my neck and cheek, having burnt off some of the hair at the side of my head. I didn't care much.

Mother Merilda sat with me as the others left.

"You will be moving to Cleria tomorrow," she told me.

I spared her a look, finding that I was surprised at the statement. For some reason, I just assumed that this chamber would forever be my new world. I nodded, not entirely sure what that meant.

"Are you okay?" she asked, her tone now more familiar than at the start. "Stupid question, I know." I spared her a chuckle. "I mean, as okay as you can be given the circumstances?" she amended.

I sighed. "How can I be okay, Mother Merilda? Look at me," I urged. "What life is there for a cripple?

Her brows furrowed and she looked deeply into my eyes. "Listen to me, your life isn't over, there is yet still much you can do."

I scoffed. "Like what?"

"That is for you to discover."

"You don't get it. There is just *one* path for me: being a soldier. The fates took it upon themselves to rob me of that."

Mother Merilda went silent.

Another itch flared in my invisible calf as I reached to scratch it. My irritation became voiced as I groaned and slammed against the bedsheet where my leg would have been.

Mother Merilda looked at me and smiled. "Let me at least show you something," she said.

Taking the handheld mirror, she told me to hang my leg over the bedside.

I looked at her sceptically until she urged me again. I complied, turning so that my remaining leg hung over the side of the bed.

"Where does it itch?" she asked. I blinked, confused by what she meant. "Your leg. Where does it itch?"

"My leg isn't there," I reminded her, and wondered if the woman was actually senile.

She chuckled. "Just show me."

I sighed, deciding to humour her, and pointed to a supposed point where my leg would have been. Mother Merilda stood up and waved the mirror at the same height where my remaining good leg was.

"Do you see the reflection?" she asked. I nodded. "Good, now scratch your good leg where the itch is."

I suddenly realised what she was trying to do and followed her instructions. I couldn't believe it. It actually worked! Even if only a little bit.

With that small piece of knowledge granted, and a recommendation that a bigger mirror would work even better, she bid me goodnight and told me to prepare myself for the trip tomorrow.

Chapter Forty-Three

DALILA

It is said that there are seven archangels, with the Grand Archon being the first of them. Of the seven, one angel was born deformed and without eyes. Thus, the Grand Archon gifted one of his wheels to this child so that he may see.

—STORIES OF HIGHER BEINGS, BY MICHAELA DURITZ

I spent the last months drifting through these halls with sickening anticipation. Paranoia bore fruit to frightful fancies as I imagined the eyes that watched me, followed me, knowing well what transpired. Still, I did not know the identity of my voyeur, whoever it was that observed in my most vulnerable moment.

Masturbation itself was not a sin, nor was it necessarily celebrated, it was just a thing that people did and no one really talked about or questioned.

The unsettling part was the vulnerability I portrayed, the flux of unbridled emotions chasing release. To be watched during such an intimate moment was the same to me as when my brother caught me in that barn so long ago with shears to my wrist.

The first week was maddening. I proved inattentive, distracted, and wholly absent from any conversation as people questioned if something was wrong with me. I was convinced that they all knew what had happened.

Yet I smiled lovingly as I always did and reassured them it was nothing. I was hell-bent on keeping up the charade.

Only then, as I traversed the halls, did I manage to bring that frantic sense of panic down into a manageable bundle of unease. I looked forward to my escape as I commenced towards my morning routine with Mother Lucia.

Again she awaited me, her smile loving and tender, a fondness shared between us and even more so with the absence of the angels.

In a weird way, Lucia was the closest thing I had to a friend, even more so than Yasmin who I had come to grow fond of. Yasmin didn't know me, not really. I had nothing to hide from Lucia, capable of opening up entirely to her. It helped a lot.

That day, as we finished our tea and commenced in our soothing trance, she was the first to speak. "You seem distracted."

I flushed. "So you noticed?" She shrugged, reaching out for a plate of butter cookies and gently nibbling at them with what few teeth of hers remained. "Why didn't you ask me about it?"

Lucia shrugged again. "I considered it, but you didn't speak. I assumed you had your reasons."

I looked down. "I didn't want to trouble you with anything."

Lucia's brows furrowed with reproach. "There you go again, spouting nonsense. If you don't want to trouble me, then you will stop thinking so little of the both of us. Honestly, you think that I am so full of myself in my old age that I wouldn't help out a friend?"

My heart fluttered, and I looked at her in surprise. "You consider me your friend?" I asked.

Mother Lucia rolled her eyes as if I were a simpleton. "Naturally," she said, as if it were the most obvious thing in the world. She poured herself another cup of tea and refilled mine, too. The contents roiled a slightly green-hued liquid with rising steam.

"Two months ago, I left the cafeteria early and went to my quarters…" I hesitated, my tongue getting knotted up.

"Well? Out with it! I'm not getting any younger."

"Well, I pleasured myself." Lucia blinked, stunned. My cheeks flushed royally as I had to look away. I knew it, I shouldn't have said it.

"That's it?" she asked, almost disbelieving. I didn't know how to respond. "That's why you have been looking over your shoulder? Being all tense-like? By the Elders, girl, you really are an idiot." She took a sip from her tea.

"Well, there was also someone watching me from the door."

She blinked again and then gave me a toothy smile. "Maybe she just enjoyed the show?"

That only made me redder. "Lucia!" I called out in horror, my tone reprimanding, as Mother Lucia gave an old woman's delighted cackle at the depravity of her jest.

"So what? You masturbated. Nobody is going to burn you for that."

"Won't people gossip?"

Lucia put down her cup and looked firmly at me. "Even if they did, what does it matter to you?" I considered the question. "It's rhetorical. I already know the answer."

When it was obvious that I didn't share in her knowledge, Lucia offered to let me in on it. "You want people to see you as infallible, perfect. You want people to love you and have this glorified, angelic image of you."

"Well, isn't it good to be liked?"

"I'll be honest with you girl, I like you more when you are in here with me than when you are out there."

I blinked. A small part of me hurt at the comment. "Why is that?" I tried to hide my disappointment.

"Because, in here, I get to meet the real Dalila. The one who laughs, the one who masturbates, the one that admits she is broken rather than pretending she is okay." I didn't know how to respond. The idea itself seemed alien to me; why would anyone want to be with some-one who is broken? "Even your nickname, Mother Fae, I like it." She sipped from her tea.

I hung my head. "It's not supposed to be a compliment," I explained.

"So? What matters is what it means to you."

"Fairies aren't real. The other sisters mock me because of the dreams I had when I came here."

"Aren't real? Says who? Those dim-witted girls who find pleasure in gossip and mockery? Please. Most of them are trying to make up for their own depressing lives; born to noble families as seventh daughters only to be sent here is their own damned fate. They didn't choose this life any more than we did."

"Are you saying fairies are real?"

"Maybe," she admitted without a moment's hesitation. "There have been scarce tales passed along the ages, stories stuffed into corners to make way for more grand tales, like the war between Elder and Dragons or of the Elder Knights. Some say that Fairies do exist."

"Where do they come from?"

"There isn't much else to tell. Their own history is vague." She had to shrug. "And to be fair, there is as much evidence for them as there is for Oxular. Meaning not a lot."

After a moment, Lucia decided to change the topic. "I heard you will be going to Hartlou?"

I nodded. "I've been to rot camps before; this won't be anything new."

"Oh yes, it will. You haven't seen anything like this."

"Because it's bigger?"

"Because it is a lens into the abyss, a cloud of death waiting to pop. You have never seen such a large concentration of them just waiting to die."

The idea alone was depressing. "Is there really no cure for the rot?" I asked, remembering Mother Margaret's teachings.

"No, there is none. Only ways to delay the inevitable, and only two."

I was taken aback. "Really?" Despite the hopeless implication of what Mother Lucia had said, I still found hope in at least staving it off for as long as possible. "What are they?"

"Well, the first is the blood of The Lady of Pain. She lives in Chainhearth, realm of the yungbloods. It is said her blood can cure any affliction save for the forgotten curse and the rot. Though it doesn't rid one of the rot, it can lessen the symptoms."

I frowned. "That doesn't seem like something easy to gain."

"Oh, it isn't."

Suddenly understanding, I feared to ask about the second option, but I did so anyway.

"The Plague Knight can take away any illness and make it his own. That being said, the infection is never cured; the rot returns with time."

"How horrid," I commented, feeling for this ascended being.

"Truly," Mother Lucia agreed.

"Is there nothing I can do at the camp to help the afflicted? Anything at all?"

"I suppose there is one possible cure."

I felt my eyes widen as I clambered to the edge of the table, desperate for the reveal. "What is it?"

"Ascension."

Just as quickly, my hopes were dashed from me. Mother Lucia's smile was apologetic. "Yes, as you surely know. The rot cannot afflict those of higher born purpose. The yungbloods, the Elders. Even the Seeds are untouched. Beings such as the Elder-Guards or Knights used to be mortals who ascended. But it is not an easy method, nor is it the wish of most to become such a being. They would no longer recognise their previous selves."

"Why would anyone wish for such a fate?"

Mother Lucia shrugged. "For some it is fear, for others it is their pursuit of power… there are those that look for a purpose greater than themselves."

"What do you mean?"

"The Pain Knight gave in, not in order to be immortal or because of any such inane pursuit, but rather because of his lady."

"The Lady of Pain." I muttered; Mother Lucia gave an affirming nod.

"To protect Mount Morniar, where she resides in Chainhearth." Mother Lucia pondered deeply for a moment. "There is one thing."

"What?"

"Your magic."

I was stunned by her implication.

"But, Mother Lucia," I murmured in hushed whispers.

"Stop it." She slapped me over my head for my theatrics. "You truly thought I never use my magic?" She scoffed in disbelief.

"But… the church?"

"The church can't control everything. I am cautious, and I urge you to be as well."

When my confusion didn't fade, Mother Lucia continued as she took my hands in hers and looked me deep in my eyes. "It has come time to tell you the truth—we are not servants of this house, not really, we are its prisoners. And as such, I am a witch, and so are you."

"I don't understand."

"We've been given unquestionable power for a reason, power that can make us level cities and take on armies, yet we are made to believe that we are just like everyone else. This is the type of power that can heal, that can help those who can't help themselves. Be sly, cautious, cunning, but if you find a moment where your magic can make a difference, then do it."

"But this goes against the rules of the Elders."

"Bah!" She scoffed vehemently. "They act like gods above their mountain and levy gifts from our kind every year. They grant us more time in the form of months and call it mercy. They are not gods, they are *oppressors*."

The words struck me like a mallet across the head. I looked at the ceiling, certain that lightning was to strike us both down for such heresy.

All my life, people praised the Elders. Now Mother Lucia spat their name with such caustic contempt.

"I have to go," I said timidly. I withdrew my hands from her.

"Consider my words," she urged, the lovingness returning to her as I stood and made my leave through the chamber door.

⊰ ⊱

I was still in shock when I boarded one of the wagons leaving Cleria. There were five in total, all roofed with canvases serving as roofs. Metal rods gave it its signature shape.

Yasmin sat with me and I suddenly felt scared, as if my tongue would betray me and Mother Lucia.

"Did you hear?" Yasmin leaned over with the excitement of a child, her buck teeth more pronounced in adulthood and her freckles giving her the appearance of a typical farm girl.

"Hear what?" I asked in my usual demeanour.

"There was another murder!" she said with unrestrained excitement, sounding almost shocked that I wasn't in the know.

The tales of the murders had become more common. Cases happened twice or even three times a year. Even I, who felt as if the happenings were in a world far beyond my own, gathered a morbid interest similar to that of Yasmin.

"Apparently, it was an entire family this time, gutted and their innards used as ornaments for some insidious shrine. Whole families are falling victim now." I blinked. "The actual events are kept secret, but the guards are promising a reward for anyone who might have information."

"Is it really that serious?" I asked.

"I don't know, not serious enough to enforce a curfew."

"Not sure it would help if these people are being killed in their own homes."

It was a thought that didn't seem to occur to Yasmin. "That's true!"

Yasmin was holding back on another piece of information as she leaned in close to ensure that only I could hear it. "Some say that the killing is an oblation."

"To the Elders?" I asked.

Yasmin shook her head, stretching out the reveal. "To the demons of the Ashen Forest."

380

I entertained Yasmin as much as I could until we both decided to occupy ourselves with our own worries.

All the other sisters, graduated Mothers, either slept, read the Kaseluda, or delved into more conversations. Yasmin was one of the sleepers, her parted lips expelled a slight trail of drool that stained my shoulder—it didn't bother me.

I took one of the rough woollen blankets and covered her, making sure not to move too much myself.

My own thoughts went to Mother Lucia and our discussion. Given the space and time, I started to think that perhaps I overreacted. It was remarkably easy for me to simply believe that I was saved, that this act of the church was mercy, but it was just preferable to death. There was something she said that made me angry, not at her, but at the church; it didn't take long to realise what it was.

My magic.

There were people dying, suffering, left to their woes, and I could help them. My magic had the power to heal; in fact, it never killed a single person.

One didn't have to worry about the scarcity of colour, the limited supply of the mist that proved hazardous to gather from the encroaching Haar. I could save lives if only I was permitted to use my magic, or at the very least, ease the passing of those who were dying.

A part of me feared and absolutely rejected the idea entirely, but the other half entertained it with growing appreciation.

⋖ ⋗

The ride took about an hour since leaving Cleria. We arrived at a camp hidden away in the nook of bounding hills on one side and mountains in the opposite distance.

The first sign that we arrived was a revolting scent of sweetness like that of liquorice thick in the air. It tickled my nose hairs and made my nostrils scrunch up from the discomfort.

When Yasmin awoke, I found myself apologising as I tried so hard to keep still, but she reassured me it had nothing to do with me—I didn't believe her.

The second sign that we were nearing the encampment was the soft sound of revolting wet coughs. I could hear the thick phlegm that expelled itself as a ball of disgusting tar.

Finally, we came to a halt, and the sisters exited their wagons.

Within this place of death we were outsiders, our robes of untarnished white like ghostly shades of milk poured into muddied water. We flowed in an orderly fashion, drifting along the ground and around grey buildings towards the centre tent where the chorus of death played.

I had been in hospices where the wealthy could afford more comfortable treatment. Taken from their homes in Cleria, they spent their days lying on silk sheets and fed delicacies like a taunting reflection of the life they abandoned.

It was here, in Hartlou, where those who could not afford such things were discarded, and nothing could have prepared me for it. It was like a poisoned river, where the dying were carried on soggy driftwood into nothingness.

Bodies were left on despoiled sheets, organised into columns and rows with six feet apart from their neighbours. The heart-breaking cries of children calling for their Mothers and Fathers wedged nails into my already cracked heart.

That same scent of sweet liquorice was overwhelming. The heat from this huddled mass caused a nauseas sweat to break from me. Their groans were haunting. At the head of the assembly stood Mother Margaret. Though her expression was regretful and dour, she held her composure because surely she had seen this horror many times already.

Her age started to show more and more over the years, crawling slowly to the forefront as her body failed her. Her weight was supported by a cane, but she didn't let that fact slow her down. The woman expected much from us and had no patience for distractions or ill-mannered repose. She did everything in her ability to help where help was needed and even used that cane as a punitive instrument.

At the entrance of the tent, where many of our ranks shielded our noses with the sleeve of our robes, Mother Margaret continued to instruct us of the malaise itself and of the situation.

Despite the fact that before Mother Margaret we were all Mothers, we were just newly anointed; it marked the start of more demanding studies.

"Where does the rot come from?" asked one of the new mothers among our ranks.

Mother Margaret shrugged. "We don't know. Though contagious it can be, it has popped up among even those who had never had any contact with the rot."

Another asked how contagious it truly was. I could sense the trepidation in her voice and noticed not just her, but many others took a worried step back.

"That depends. Ingest the black substance that they discharge and you will be in danger. Wearing gloves here is mandatory and do not let your patients cough on you. If any of it enters through your orifice, it will get you infected. The healers who work here do so in rotating shifts to minimise exposure."

I raised my hand.

"Yes, Mother Dalila," Mother Margaret said.

"That sounds similar to your teachings on fungal spores, the fact that the by-product of this malaise can infect me so and replicate within a host would imply that it could be fungal? The black discharge is also indicative of that."

Mother Margaret seemed pleased by my observation. "How astute, Mother Dalila."

Despite our similar ranking, it proved hard not to feel flattered by the praise.

"However, that is where the similarities end; no fungal treatment has ever helped against this illness, and other fungal growths had never been found within the residents."

There were tales about the Midnight Bloom, but it didn't feel appropriate to speak about. I heard rumours of it from back-channels and sequestered alleys where the light of Cleria couldn't reach. Horror stories about people being forced to suffer through the rot in moist rooms and fed sugar until something akin to an umbral flower blossomed upon their skin. The petals were told to give the user an inexplicable high.

"What has been found?" I turned to find that it was Candice who asked the question. I recalled her giving me an undue amount of attention ever since I joined the Sisterhood.

Mother Margaret nodded. "Come," she instructed.

We made our way into an open space where a table was shoddily erected from branches knotted together. Upon it, there buzzed a cloud of noisome flies, wreathing the anointed dead.

Our group immediately began stating their disgust. I heard one of the Mothers wretch her morning breakfast and another reminding her that it was a bad idea to eat before coming to Hartlou.

On the table was someone who died due to the rot, and if it weren't the rot, then the fact that they were split open from belly to sternum surely would have done it.

Her body was entirely black and at first glance, one may have assumed charred if it weren't for the slathered tar that covered her. Her innards were removed, and left on a table next to the cadaver in an organised fashion. What remained of the body was a shrivelled black mass.

I gathered the body must have belonged to a woman given to the long greasy strands of hair that draped from inebriated flesh and bones. Her remaining skin was drawn over her body.

Inside her chest cavity, it was rotten black like the trunk of a rotten tree. The revolting liquorice smell was no longer present, and was replaced by decay.

"This is all that remains of those infected: devoured, defiled, spoiled."

"But, Mother Margaret, that doesn't make sense. You taught us that a disease wants to keep us alive as long as possible. It wants to survive, not destroy." It was Yasmin that spoke.

"Yes, you are right, but this—all it wants to do is corrupt. That fact hasn't changed since it first came to be during the third cycle."

Chapter Forty-Four

DALILA

It is currently unknown where the rot comes from. Some theorise that it originates from far below Minethria. I shudder at what its source might be.

—MEDICAL RECORD FROM THE FIRST APPEARANCE OF THE ROT. 3C212

O nce the tour was done, and long after many Mothers simply wanted to leave this place, Mother Margaret finished her teachings. She showed us not just the final phase of the illness, but also the sheer despairing sight of so many infected in one location.

When asked who would like to stay behind and help, very few were foolish enough to accept the offer. I was one of them.

Yasmin tried desperately to dissuade me of the idea, but my mind was set. I couldn't afford to hide behind walls when so many people needed me. I was surprised when it was eventually Yasmin who reluctantly decided to join me on this task.

Four others decided to stay, including the ever beautiful, yet stoic, Candice.

⊰ ⊱

A week: that was how long we had to work within the camp, except for me. Apparently, Mother Vinrie had made it clear that I was to stay no longer than five days. I repressed the anger and resigned myself to the order.

There were so many of them, so many dying. Their eyes simultaneously begging for help yet also so devoid of hope—it was a toxic mixture.

The best I could do was mitigate their pain, offer cloth dipped in cold water to offer at least some passing reprieve as I padded their swampy skin. Other than bringing water and seeing to their needs, there wasn't much else that could be done. One of the nurses was stunned when I asked her if they used ink to numb the pain.

"We don't have any, lov'. There are too many afflicted and the king couldn't spare the rare resource for such a thing," she admitted glumly, before leaving with two buckets of sloshing water in each hand.

❧ ❧

"Why did you stay?" I asked Yasmin on the evening of our first day.

She turned to me, surprised to see me standing behind her as we worked our way through the canteen food made for the workers. Stale bread and soup made from potatoes and turnips with some salted pork was on the menu.

"Why did you?" she rebutted, seemingly irritated.

"Because I wanted to help; these people need me."

Yasmin seemed almost embarrassed to tell me her reason. "Well, there you go. You know, it is very tiresome being friends with someone so selfless."

Was she annoyed with me? The idea that I had, in some way, irritated her upset me. She was my friend, my only friend amongst the student ranks, and I somehow found myself not wanting to lose that.

"Did I upset you in some way?" I asked as we took our seat at a table.

She sighed. "No, no, of course not. You never do anything wrong." Her glibness said otherwise.

"Yasmin…" I leaned in. "If there is something I did to upset you, please tell me."

"It's nothing! Alright?" She shouted, her fist slamming onto the table and spilling some of her soup. All eyes turned to us. The cafeteria went incredibly silent before our audience returned to their own conversations.

"Just—give me some time, okay?" Yasmin got up to leave. My hand reacted on its own and grabbed her arm. She stopped, looking down at me.

I don't know why I chose that moment to speak my question but I did. "Yasmin, was it you who saw me in the chamber?" It must have been Yasmin, anyone else would have already spread the gossip.

She tore her hand from my grip. "What are you talking about?" Her brows furrowed with equal measure confusion and anger.

I watched her leave. So she didn't see me? But why was she upset? I eyed the food jadedly, realising I had lost my appetite. Pushing it aside, I rose from my seat and snuck back to work.

⚔ ⚔

For several more hours, I treated the dying. The night light made the walk through the abandoned folk an eerie act.

The darkness had swallowed this place. The differing shades of pallid grey all the way to inky black provided a camouflage to the afflicted as they groaned and mumbled from the ground. A lantern's soft light was what provided me passage through here. I drifted among the dying as an uninvited guest: a white smear cutting through a canvas of black.

I stopped from person to person, my hands cleaning them, wiping away the turbid sweat with its sickly smell.

"Breshna, is that you?" asked one old lady as I approached her. The dark curtains retreated, releasing their closed fingers of night from the frail woman as I brought her into the light.

"I'm afraid not; my name is Mother Dalila," I said.

I looked at the woman and noticed the rot had already claimed her eyes. Milky white stared out and was tainted by black specks that distorted her pupils.

"Ah, I see." She sounded disappointed.

"What is your name?" I asked, trying to find common ground between our great chasm.

"Ingrid," she said.

"That's a beautiful name."

She scoffed, wet phlegm turning it into a raspy sound. "'Beautiful,' that's a word I hadn't heard in a long time," she said rather sadly.

"Well, I think you ought to hear it more often," I countered cheerfully. "You're a sweet girl."

I pressed one of the rags to her forehead. "That feels good," she said, her lost eyes closed shut and she appeared at peace for just a moment.

"There is more where that came from."

Her eyes opened, and despite being blind she looked at me, her skin a darkening grey, the rot spreading black, veiny roots across her cracked skin.

"I am not much longer for this world, child," she confided. I didn't know how to respond. "Just once. I wish I could see my Breshna again."

"Who is she?"

"My daughter."

"Perhaps I can find her for you?"

Ingrid shook her head. "That is sweet of you, but there is no need. She doesn't want to visit me. Too scared she will contract the rot."

"I am afraid visitors aren't allowed because of the risk involved."

She sighed. "I simply wish I could have felt her touch again, one last time," she admitted, the barest of cracks to her voice. Ingrid sounded like she let go of her final piece of misguided hope, a last selfish desire. A single pitch black tear trailed down her shut eye.

I removed my glove. "I hope this will suffice." I took the bare and unprotected skin of my palm to the old woman's cheek.

She was comforted by the act, letting out a pleased sigh. It took only a moment for her to realise what was happening as shut lids burst open.

"What are you doing?" she demanded with surprised and horrified whispers.

"It's okay," I said. The momentary act of human contact was worth seeing her face light up.

But Ingrid wanted none of it. She grabbed my hand and forced it away, black tar stretching like an adhesive between palm and my sleeve, cracked and brittle skin peeled away to reveal darkening flesh underneath.

Fear filled the woman's eyes. "Stop it!" she demanded; begged even. I drew away my hand. I failed again, and only made things worse. The woman was upset but calmed, eventually. "Are you mad, girl?" she asked.

"I was just trying to help."

"By infecting yourself?" I bowed my head. She must have sensed me turning glum. "Child, you have a heart of gold, but what good are you going to do if you get yourself sick because of an old crone who is going to die, anyway?"

I nodded. "You're right."

"Now go, before anyone finds you here and sticks you with the rest of us."

I extinguished my lantern and departed from the scene. The shadows mended themselves back together.

⋖ ⋗

The night before, I spent a good hour scrubbing off the peeled skin that clung to my sleeve. The foetid flakes were reluctant to let go, to depart from the living. Only thanks to the rough bristles of my brush did they finally relent and break apart to be washed away.

Hiding the apparent dark handprint didn't prove difficult within the dark quarters where me and my sisters slept as I changed into one of my other garments. The tension between Yasmin and me was still present the following morning. I thought it wise to continue giving her the space she needed.

I returned to the tent and helped appease the qualms of the suffering as best as I could.

When I made my way to Ingrid, my heart dropped when I saw

her place empty. Whatever fluids she discarded were now mixed and darkened her scarce bedding and the grass below it, too. The vegetation had wilted and turned dark from the corruption.

The next few days continued without incident, and it was on the third day that Yasmin finally broke the tension and approached me.

"Can we talk?" She was hesitant and bashful, as she avoided my gaze.

"Of course," I smiled tenderly. "About what?" I asked.

"Don't do that," she said, her voice stern.

Immediately I threw away my smile and turned apologetic. "Sorry."

I was cleaning what rags and supplies I could down by the river. One bucket was used to fill a circular tub of wood. I scrubbed best as I could to rid my robe of the rot. Yet, I couldn't help but wonder if such a malaise could ever truly be removed.

I joined Yasmin at an elevated mound on a jutting stone boulder.

She reached into her bag and offered me half of her sandwich. A thing she had done often in the past and just like all the times before, I politely declined. This time, Yasmin persisted. Not wanting to anger her any further, I took the offered half.

We were quiet for a time. It was noon and the middle of summer.

The bearing heat of the sun drifted. I wondered privately if the Elder King was watching my little private moment with Yasmin. I doubted it was of any interest to him.

There was a grove of trees just a little out, filled with apples ripe for the taking, and just a little further beyond the flowing river, the curves of a valley were visible. Before us, there was a field of tall grass filling the space between another gathering of trees and our camp.

A dragonfly fluttered on top of the shallow stream of the river and finally rested on a moss-covered boulder.

The scent of blooming summer was full in the air and it proved an adequate refuge from the nauseating scent of decay that was the camp. When Yasmin finally spoke, she did so in a way that I had never heard in the past five years that we'd known each other.

"I'm sorry I snapped at you. I know you were doing the right thing.

Deciding to join you was my own decision. That's what my mother used to say, you know?" She put on a gratingly high pitched voice to parody her mother. "'You can't go blaming others for your problems all the time! Make your own decisions! You won't find any man at this rate!'"

We both chuckled at the performance, but her tone was more sombre as she opened up, and it was then that I realised I didn't know anything about Yasmin.

"What does your family do?" I asked.

I think Yasmin appreciated me making the effort; she wasn't as beatific as usual. "My father is a businessman, handles the craft and distribution of paper. Most of it goes to Museya for the filling of scrolls, but a lot of it also is taken to the courts. People have a lot of use for good paper."

I never thought about it before, but it was true. Though being literate was a privilege few had, the uses for scrolls and paper would never fall short. The only reason my father hammered home the ability to read was so that I would understand the Kaseluda.

This time, Yasmin put on a low, gruff voice; I presumed she was parodying her father. "'The Canadere name is more than just a name, Yasmin! It is a responsibility! We provide paper so the world may function. Take your teachings a little more seriously!'" Yasmin comically shook her fist in supposed irritation.

I laughed. Not my brittle, humouring laugh meant to be polite, but rather a full laugh. Yasmin smiled, practically beaming at the sight as her eyes widened and sparkled.

"That's the first time I've seen you laugh," she said.

I calmed down, the sensation of grinning felt surprisingly unfamiliar. "What are you talking about? You've heard me laugh before."

Yasmin shook her head. "No, I mean like *really* laugh. Not that fake thing you do." I bowed my head. My cheeks grew hot at the comment as if I were caught in a lie.

"I wasn't one of my parent's later children with nothing to do. I was their second."

I turned to Yasmin. "So why did they send you to the Sisterhood?"

"Why? I suppose it was because they didn't see a future for me," she admitted. Yasmin sounded reflective, but not sad. It appeared that she had already come to terms with it a long time ago and simply hid behind that always cheerful smile of hers. I suddenly discovered a depth to her that I had never seen before and realised I had done wrong by not recognising it sooner.

"Clumsy, ditsy, ill-mannered, loud, un-lady-like: those were some of the choice adjectives they used to describe me. Seeing no place for me in the company and unlikely to ever find a spouse, they ended up giving me up to the church."

"That's horrible!" I protested.

She shrugged, her eyes staring out at the scenery, a gorgeous view that didn't seem to care about mortal struggles. "They tried," she said. "Tried to make me lady-like, stop making me so boisterous, more feminine and the like... just didn't stick, I guess." I didn't know what to say. "Dalila, the reason I wanted to be your friend from the first day we met was because you looked lost and alone. Just as I felt. You always seem so sad, like you are tearing up inside."

Was it really so obvious?

"I started to realise you were guarded, but I knew how hard it was for me all alone here, and I didn't want you to feel the same way. When we came here, and you raised your hand to volunteer, you confirmed what I have guessed for quite some time."

"And that is?" I was scared to hear the answer.

"You are selfless, beyond anything else. You help others without ever hesitating: it makes me furious."

I bowed my head. "I'm sorry."

"Don't be sorry!" She snapped, taking my hands in hers. "Do you consider me a friend?" she asked, staring deeply into my eyes, a sudden frenzy claiming her.

"Yes," I said.

"Then don't lie to me."

I nodded. "But I still don't understand why you decided to stay." Her hands slipped from mine, her conviction suddenly fading as it was her turn to look bashful.

"I wasn't angry at you. I was angry with myself. I'm scared, you see?" She clasped one of her hands that trembled feverously. "Yet you jumped into it without a second's hesitation. I thought that if you, if at least you were to not stay, I wouldn't have to feel bad either." Her eyes welled with tears. "I was just upset with myself," she admitted.

Within that moment, within the flowing stream, the swaying blades of grass, the rustling leaves of trees, all of them indifferent to whether we left or stayed—I saw Yasmin in a whole new light. She was my friend, and I felt more naked and vulnerable at that moment with her than I would have been if I stripped down entirely. The most remarkable part about that was that I didn't feel scared.

"Yasmin, I think it is time I tell you about myself." She seemed puzzled by my remark.

I confided about everything: my home, my time at the farm, the events that took place in the woods and even the fact that I was a witch. There was not an ounce of doubt when I opened up to her.

Chapter Forty-Five

DALILA

Beware, ye' who deny the wisdom of Elders. The Kingdom of Estria shattered an eye of the Elder King and are now bound to the rising moon. They cannot die nor can they live. Upon the rise of night, know that the stars are the remnants of the stolen sun, and know that each one sparkles to indicate the undead rise once more in their parish of bones.

—PROPAGANDA FLYER IN CLERIA

The time I didn't spend treating the ill was spent with Yasmin, though I did so guiltily. It felt wrong to be enjoying myself while there were people dying. But my relationship with Yasmin had changed for the better. I could be myself with her, and she'd scold me for being so self-sacrificing. I appreciated that. Accepting myself was difficult, but Yasmin made it a lot easier. I even found myself reacquainted with feelings of contentment, something I hadn't had in a very long time.

I told her of many more events and being able to be open with her was so freeing that it bordered on addiction. Other than Lucia, Yasmin was the only other person I opened up to. Though the identity of Lucia was not mine to give away, so some secrets I had to keep. That included the landscape of scars that marked me, for I knew that all it would do was discomfort her.

But I did share in the private night I had, a fact that had Yasmin giggle like a child and yet simultaneously blush feverously. I finally confirmed that Yasmin wasn't my voyeur, which made the mystery all the more curious.

It was my fourth day working, and I found myself surprised that my time was coming to an end. Not because of my desire to help the sick as best as I could, that was obvious, but rather because this little retreat and moments with Yasmin turned into an unexpected delight that I even looked forward to!

I had two more days until I had to return before Yasmin did. The claustrophobic, austere walls of the Sisterhood would provide a suffocating and bland contrast to the open air.

⋞ ⋟

During my fourth night, I was compelled to spend more and more time with the sick and less and less time with Yasmin or on breaks.

I was eternally grateful when Yasmin did not scold me or make me feel guilty for brushing her off; in fact, I found our new relationship made her more understanding of my compulsion. I still thought of Ingrid and found it a shame that I could not see her for one more night.

Yasmin had asked about my magic, and I confided about its healing properties, but also told her that it was the most grave of secrets, and that the use of my magic was strictly forbidden. Her response was much like my own—indignation. It was a shame to have power to treat the dying, and yet be forbidden from using it. In my mind, I dangled the key to a peaceful death, taunting them with my white robes and practised clemency as I dabbed with a damp cloth, yet it was a balm that did nothing.

Out of that sea of inflicted, there was one in particular that caught my attention.

Her calls were desperate and pleading, not meant for me, but they drew me in, regardless. She kept calling for her mother in-between sobs. When I neared her, she looked at me with pitch black eyes and streaks of thick tar that trailed down her temples and clumped in her hair. It formed a vile halo of black. It reminded me of a bird clumped in too much tar to take flight.

"What's your name, child?" I asked as I knelt beside her and readied my bucket and cloth.

"Rebecca," she managed.

"That's a beautiful name," I said as I dabbed her forehead with the cloth. "I'm Mother Dalilia."

The title seemed to remind the girl of her longing. "I want my mommy."

Gently, I pressed the cloth against grey skin, soaking up the small beads of sweat squeezed through clogged pores.

"Is she here? In camp?" I asked.

The girl sobbed, the question seemingly making her even more uncomfortable. "I don't know." She sounded scared.

"It's okay, it's alright, Rebecca. What's her name? Where can I find her?" I queried.

"I don't know." She sounded even more terrified by the notion, her voice cracking and the words distorted as if drowned in her own turbid tears.

I bit my lip; one of the symptoms of the rot was delirium. The corruption found its way not just into the heart, lungs and other organs but also into the brain. It ate away at it until it was nothing but a black puddle. That tar would trap cherished memories and steadily pull it under; the girl didn't have long to live.

"I want my mommy," she said again. The pain in her voice broke my heart. There was nothing I wanted more than to help her, to soothe her pain.

It was night. The torches erected in an orderly fashion to provide some dimly lit vision for us sisters. I looked around. Nurses and sisters spread among the weary and the dying and offered scant relief. I removed my glove.

"What are you doing?" The girl asked.

"Shhhh." I summoned it.

A power I hadn't used in years since I moved into the church, a power made to heal and save.

I coveted the light glow that enveloped my hand. Luminous motes danced like distant fireflies of warm, yellow light, its blurred edges as if visible through a fog. I lowered that hand to the girl's forehead.

I looked over my shoulder to make sure no one was watching. As my hand rested on the girl's forehead, the motes grew in size.

It soothed the girl, her eyes closing tranquilly. Any pain or discomfort she had melted away with the light, even her complexion seemed to improve.

"Mommy," she said, but not in that pained and scared way like before, but rather as if she thought her mother was present.

"What are you doing?"

My light died in an instant and I pulled back my hand. The voice came from behind me.

"Nothing," I replied, as I inconspicuously put my glove back on.

I rose and turned, displaying my most mannered posture and giving no sign of my panic. Candice stood before me. She wasn't convinced, leaning to the side to find that Rebecca had fallen sound asleep, even with a smile on her face.

Brushing the topic aside, she faced me. "You've been sent an important message. I was asked to inform you of it."

I frowned. "An urgent message?" I didn't know of anyone who would contact me.

"It's from Mother Vinrie."

My curiosity grew. I followed Candice out of the tent, the noisome and sickening smell left behind. As we walked, Candice turned to me.

"What was it that you were doing back there?" she asked.

I held my tongue. "Nothing."

"Didn't seem like nothing. That girl looked like she was at peace." She leaned in towards me. "Did you sneak in blue ink?" she whispered.

I froze. Should I lie? If I said yes, then she would have an acceptable reason; but if she reported it to Mother Vinrie. "No," I said.

I knew she didn't believe me, but she didn't press me any further and turned to leave.

"Mother Candice." She stopped mid-turn and looked at me again.

"I have the feeling you don't like me. Did I do something to upset you?" I asked, treading cautiously.

"It's not that I don't like you, it's that I don't trust you," she said bluntly, and took a step towards me.

"Why is that?"

Before I could react, she grabbed my arm and pulled away my sleeve in one swift movement while not once breaking eye contact. This was an interrogation.

"Why does someone who is supposedly so sweet and kind, so self-less in her pursuit to serve, hate herself so?"

I tore my wrist away and pulled the sleeve back down.

"I don't trust you because I know that smile isn't real. I've known it since you first joined the Sisterhood."

She had been watching me. I suddenly felt so vulnerable, so exposed at the thought that I was caught in such a private and intimate moment. It was then that I finally solved the mystery that plagued me for months.

"It was you," I said with dawning realisation.

"What?" she asked.

"You're the one who saw me in bed. That's how you knew about the scars."

Candice's cheeks blossomed a violent red. I could practically feel the heat of her embarrassment on my own skin. She couldn't look at me and turned. "Let's go," she said.

⋖ ⋗

I didn't have time to delve into the revelation as I opened the letter addressed to me:

"*Dear Mother Dalila,*

It is uncouth and prohibited for me to deliver news of anyone from the outside world, but considering the events and the favour owed, I have decided to make an exception.

Nora Demiel Rawsom has been gravely injured during one of her missions.

After extreme care and uncertainty, she has recovered and there is no longer fear of death. However, the incident has resulted in life-altering injuries that make it impossible for her to return to her former duties.

I understand you still owe her a favour and I trust that you would have liked to be informed of her situation.

There is a coach waiting for you if you decide to take it, otherwise, you can return this letter to the driver and send him on his way.

Regardless, I thought you should be made aware.

Best regards,
Mother Vinrie."

"What is it?" Candice asked as she stood behind me. I shuddered at the news and sprinted towards the coach.

Chapter Forty-Six

*Within the realm of the Elders, there are three trees of import. The
first being the tree of Knighthood, where one either becomes an Elder
Guard or Elder Knight. The second tree is that of parturiency, from
where those mortal women rife with dormant magic are turned into
surrogates for Seeds or Yungbloods. Upon the surrogate's demise, new-
borns will suckle sap from a branch. The final tree is that of ascension so
rarely harvested from. The White Lady is the most recent receiver of
this gift and now embodies the winter storm.*

—Excerpt from the "The Elder Wisdom." Taught in the
Sisterhood of the Faithful

I evarus, the Silver Prince, had earned mastery over every scrawl-
ing inch that made them; from skin to flesh and bone. An Elder
Guard stood opposite Ievarus in the sand pit. They were there to
test that mastery. Wind moaned through the balconies of the ever-rising
tower. The wind had a voice. Less and less Yungbloods and Elders had
come to watch the latest in a line of successors.

Long was the time that passed since Ievarus' birth, and their daily
life consisted of battle and history to ready them for their destiny. Now,
even the White-Hawk struggled to keep up with Ievarus in battle. Their
naturally one-track mind, void of anything other than the bland nuances
of flowing battle, was truly something to witness. Thus, it was appropriate that Ievarus had reached a point where they needed an ascended

being that grazed the power of the Elders if they were to slay the Evil.

The towering Elder Guard stood as an elegant work of art, stretched long and reed-like. Their body glowed a soft, azure blue. They wore a long shoulder cape of blue gossamer which draped down the left shoulder. A masterful mask of steel was embellished with the symbol of a tree. Perhaps the same tree from where it received their fruit of knighthood. The mask began from the brow and tapered down to a point at their chin so only the sides of lips were visible.

The Elder Guard brandished their weapon. A rapier held by two dainty right arms, while the remaining left arm was concealed under the cape. Their hair looked more like luminous blue seagrass and even bobbed as if held in a body of water. The sword's guard was a coiling pattern made out of electrum. The rapier's edge shone with reflective dreamsteel.

Ievarus' toes curled about the sand, gripping at crumbling nothing and feeling the grains against their uncanny anatomy. They carried masterfully crafted swords of typical fashion, one being a longsword and the other a short. With emotionless and pearly eyes, Ievarus blinked while the Elder Guard hissed a sound like steam from a furnace. Their rapier was gripped by both right hands and held vertically before them.

Ievarus darted in a sudden blur, relaxed rubber feet turning firm at the exact moment of advance to catapult forward. The sudden speed at which they clashed, at which their jerking movements beat steel against steel, impossible to follow with a mortal's eye. Blades met and sparks flew.

Ievarus' feet only ever met the floor briefly for a gentle kiss before taking flight again, keeping aloft by juggling their weight with the help of the guard's banging blade. The way their movements mingled together truly was like a choreographed dance. Ievarus was like a spore in flight, the grounded Elder Guard a reed. There were no sudden lashes of the sword, but rather graceful shifts in stance and balance in the flowing arch of a sword swing. Though still, the Guard retreated.

Rapier skewered forward as Ievarus seamlessly contorted in mid-air, spine arching concave at such a harrowing dimension for a human. The Silver Prince leaned into the momentum to turn into a flurry of dancing strikes, like a winged nut where the leaves were replaced by blades. The guard hissed.

Another swirling spin. Ievarus' silver hair turned rigid at contact, and joined the clashing of swords. Hair upon hair battered against the lean rapier like sickle scythes.

Elder Guard glided away, a single purposeful step giving distance, so that Ievarus was forced to meet land again. Elder Guard sprung forward, sword pointed true to pierce. With such blinding alacrity, Ievarus' curled toes shot up and caught the blade. Hardened digits held the rapier tight and pulled down. With an eagle's grip, Ievarus pulled their weight up with just the strength of their toes and brought their free leg hammering down onto the visored head of the guard. The guard slammed down into the sand and was made to prostrate by force.

The bout was over before it even began.

"Enough," called out a voice from the rafters.

Sirmy the Informer stepped into the orange light of burning torches which lined the ever rising balconies.

This enigma was the same headless Elder, having instead worming hands that sprouted from the neck. One large eye in one hand and parting lips into the palm of another.

Two more arms sprouted and grasped onto their own collar. The rest of its body came free with a lurch from within the humanoid vessel, coming out like some overfed parasite and leaving a trail of stretching slime behind. Sirmy's true body was long and fleshy. Hands ran down the length of its wormy flesh. The fingers acted as legs for the extending, boneless body. Sirmy crawled down the wall with help of synchronised fingers. If there was ever a tail to this form, Ievarus had never seen it.

"Ye has't grown strong, my liege."

"When will I be ready?" Ievarus spoke the question blandly.

Sirmy's fingers formed waves as the hands which held mouth and eye stretched out like antennas towards Ievarus' height. The rest of

Sirmy's form skittered along the sand. *"Not yet, though thou showe'th skill with thy steel, one need'st more to fell Evil."*

Ievarus bowed their head. "What do I need?"

"A soul, an idea." Sirmy's wet eye leaned in until it was but a breath's length from Ievarus' own pearly gaze—the thing was the size of Ievarus' head.

"A spark so that thou may be worthy. Thus tis time for thy lesson with Preceptor."

⊲ ⊳

Preceptor's tutelage had become a common enough occurrence. Whatever discomfort was to be had, became part of the process. Invasive tendrils slipped through their orifices and sent Ievarus into a fabricated world of Preceptor's making. Appendages prodded, scoured the unregimented landscape which was Ievarus' reality and activated centres of the Seed's consciousness to evoke images deep within.

Preceptor's voice rung as an echo within the recesses of this world, vibrating along the invisible threads.

"Wherefore doest the cycle convene?" Preceptor asked.

"To protect the Creator's world and push back the Haar."

"Wherefore doest needeth a Seed?"

"Because only one of Elder King's blood can defeat the evil."

Like parting water-colours upon a canvas, the mist within this realm opened up and revealed the great Seeds that came before: the greatest examples of what could be done in the face of evil.

Ievarus watched Xelxidon with her blade of light, infused by the rays of the Elder King's own burning eye. The blade was encrusted in gold. Just beyond the hilt guard, was a golden circle with a hole. Golden teeth pointed inward. An open chasm ran through the centre of the blade.

Atop her hill with an army behind her banner. Xelxidon lifted her shield emblazoned with the sun and pointed her sword outwards. Rays of pure sunlight shot down from the sky and skewered the first evils' blight—duty compelled her.

Muriya the Protector was gifted the hammer of creation by the Blacksmith himself. The Hammer would strike down upon the world and summon great, jutting pillars of earth—family compelled him.

One by one all the Seeds were listed within the mindscape alongside something which motivated them. Even Kaelu the Silent was motivated by something, even if it was a secret never shared.

"I am powerful, just as they are."

"Tis not about power, Child of Silver Willow."

Suddenly, within this landscape, Ievarus was gifted a body to manipulate, to move in, to traverse with as they pleased. Then there were small humble walls of wood crafted all about them. The roof had caved in and the scent of burning was apparent in the air.

Suddenly, there came the noise of chaos, of pain, of bedlam. People, mortals, a sound so simple, so unrefined and primitive that it was entirely new to Ievarus. They heard the cries of tortured men and women all around. There before Ievarus was a boy, glassy eyes peering up. The ichor of life was flowing from a slit belly as he grabbed his stomach.

"Please, help." The language was simple, yet still Ievarus did not comprehend as the boy stretched out a hand.

Screams billowed and filled the starry night sky. Embers sparked and people screeched in horror just outside the torn down home. Tattered curtains swayed and blocked whatever tragedy was unfolding.

Ievarus knelt down to the boy, eyes blinking listlessly, a mere observer, curious about what was unfolding. With small deliberate movements, Ievarus grabbed the boy's hand and looked at it as if expecting to find something hidden along its lines.

Up above, suddenly the screeching sounds returned, but this was that of an otherworldly creature.

A dragon soared up from above, mighty leather wings beating as great streaks of flame blossomed from their maw and burnt all asunder.

Ievarus let go.

"Why?" Ievarus asked.

"Save us." A small girl appeared hidden underneath the bent boy's belly. The girl's eyes radiated desperation, a concept beyond Ievarus' understanding.

Ievarus blinked. "This is not my destiny," Ievarus said. "I have to slay the great evil."

The boy and girl's visages morphed into straight faced disapproval. The world bled away and the white realm returned.

Instead of the children there now stood the Preceptor, thin and tall instead of bloated like before.

The thoughts rang inside Ievarus' mind, but Preceptor was unmoving. Abyssal beads looked forward, tentacle beards writhed. *"Thou may has't formidable strength, but what thou requireth be purpose."* The Preceptor showed Ievarus the rest of their history, the sacrifice of the one who would become the Pain Knight; a frightening figure covered in protruding spikes to symbolise their torment. The emotions and the tide of Seed's past and their ties with humanity.

"I don't understand, Preceptor," Ievarus said. "I understand my purpose. It is to fell the Evil and convene the cycle."

"No, Ievarus. That be thine quest, yet thy purpose is thine own to discover."

❧ ❧

Walking along the open and vast courtyard of the Elder's home, Ievarus looked out at the vast world. Yet still, the vista that expanded, bracketed by a sea on one side and mountain range on the other, was a sight to behold.

Ievarus was capable of discerning facts, seeing the shapes of things, discerning colour; Ievarus knew that a blade struck into one's heart meant death. But Ievarus did not understand what death itself meant, did not know of things like love and rage, or something as simple as what it meant when a wounded child stretched out a hand.

The issue wasn't the fact that Ievarus didn't help the mortal children; it was the fact that Ievarus had no reaction whatsoever.

"Ievarus."

Ievarus turned to find Aeolus. Aeolus was a curious and rare spawn, born from an Elder's spawn of a spawn. A surrogate was granted to one Yungblood from which Aeolus came to be.

This one had a pinkish skin like newly mended flesh and walked on three-toed digitigrade feet where the ankles bent to provide strength for great strides. A long and waving prehensile tail ended in a fork, but the protruding spikes were sheathed beneath the surface. Aeolus was lithe and thin, slitted feline eyes peering out from an equine head.

The only other notable feature were the horns with a rather expressive quality to them. They shifted and changed independently, occasionally morphing from spirals reaching upward and bending their way into pointed bull-horns or curled ram-horns. Branches broke and forked and took unique shapes of their own.

"How were the lessons today?" Aeolus asked. Ievarus blinked and turned back to the distant lands. Aeolus coughed. "My liege, as per my instructions, I am to remind you of human etiquette for when you have to leave our borders. Thus, when someone asks you a question, you are required to respond."

Ievarus turned back to Aeolus. "And what if I have nothing to respond with?"

"You do so anyway."

Ievarus was a blank sheet. Nothing about their unchanging features relayed any information.

"It is the same as ever. I still do not understand what you all want."

Aeolus grew curious. "Does that frustrate you?"

Ievarus blinked listlessly. "I assume that this feeling is… frustration. I do not understand this world, given a quest I am not allowed to fulfil. Am I not allowed to feel frustration?" Ievarus asked plainly.

"Quite the opposite; that is a warranted emotion, albeit very human. Elders do not have those kinds of emotions."

"Why?"

"Time. When one lives for so long, such things can become wasted. Hate, love, those are such fleeting things to a timeless Elder. Why spend energy on a transient flicker? But they still have purpose; conviction that transcends beyond emotion."

"Do you have emotion?" Ievarus asked.

"Well, I am not like the Elders."

Ievarus blinked. The shifting horns of Aeolus framed his equine face until finally the Yungblood spawn answered the question.

"Yes, Ievarus: I have emotion. A desire to fulfil my duty for my lineage and for the Elders."

"Like Xelxidon?" Ievarus asked. The word 'duty' trailed in the air.

Aeolus chuckled. "Not quite the same, no. Her duty was something unmatched entirely."

"So even one duty could be different from other duty?" There was a brief moment when it looked as if Ievarus had captured a concrete idea, but no sooner did that also slip away. Of course, it was difficult to discern anything from their hard lines.

Aeolus took note of this apparent contradiction and provided Ievarus with something else. "What about your smile? Have you been practising that?" he asked, tail swaying back and forth.

It was agonising to watch Ievarus piece the process together, the facial muscles jerking like a spasm. First, feeling the tug at the corner of their lips, then pulling on them to reveal teeth and gum underneath. The corners had to curve upward.

Aeolus watched the process and saw it was akin to rotating cogs and pulleys trying to display emotion. With the stoic indifference of pearly eyes and the rest of Ievarus' poreless face remaining unchanged. The sight was truly horrific until it became comedic.

Aeolus laughed, watching Ievarus grin so fiercely that it turned into a painful grimace. Gums showed as long as the parting lips allowed. Ievarus' tightly bit teeth looked like a primate's threat and everything else about the taut skin made it torturous.

"Needs some work."

"Did I do it wrong?" Ievarus asked, perplexed.

"Wasn't the best."

The equine figure departed back into the embrace of the transitory veil, their shape bending and falling into the scenery of these congested buildings that seemed endless in their dimensions and depths.

⌐ ⌐

Ievarus walked along the courtyard, watching the passing black shades stretching like shadows and passing over bridges. Rising spires and spikes filled the gothic architecture of this otherworldly place with rose windows peering out from their multi-coloured stained glass. The structures yawned forebodingly with indiscernible dimension. The expanse managed to dwarf all who passed through there. The structures leered down upon the passersby as if purveyors of judgement.

Out, at the boundary of the courtyard, one could look down to see the next echelons of Mount Morniar protruding as an extension from that realm.

The second level of Chainhearth carried homes of cobblestone huddled close together. Soot-like colouring clambered onto the baroque architecture. It was a place of brick and mortar homes with tiled roofs and smoking chimneys. This was the realm of the Yungbloods, creatures spawned from the blood of Elders. It carried an air of regality now marred and hidden by the thick layers of soot so dark that even the Elder King's eye could not pierce this perpetually dark realm.

The third tier was a distant place, nowhere near as otherworldly as that of the Yungbloods and the Elders, but still a work of marvel.

It housed the zerubs with remarkably well fashioned homes the likes of Cleria's nobility.

In the sky, there soared flying manta rays that glided with only rare moments where they felt the need to gracefully flap their fins and stay aloft.

"Quite a sight, is it not?"

Ievarus turned and beheld a figure they'd never seen before. This one was not as large as a typical Elder; in fact, the figure proved even shorter than Ievarus. They wore a deep brown wool robe similar to that of a monk, but their face was shrouded in darkness and hidden behind a hood.

Instead of a face, there was a spider, its web made upon the arched curvature of the hood as the arachnid moved about its net.

"Who are you?" Ievarus asked.

"You may call me 'Master'," the figure stated. Their voice was an abstraction. It came across as more a trick of echoes and caverns rather than something shaped by tongue and teeth. Whatever it was, it originated from within the wreathed shadow of their hood.

"No one is my master," Ievarus countered.

"Is Elder King Aemir not your master?"

Ievarus blinked.

"The king is my father." Ievarus stated hollowly, not seeming to grasp the meaning behind the words. "Are you another Elder sent to teach me?"

"I am no Elder," the figure stated.

Ievarus turned. "A Yungblood?"

"Ah, so you are capable of being curious?" When Ievarus did not respond, Master continued speaking. "I am not Yungblood either, nor zerub, nor Nephilim."

"So what are you?" Ievarus prodded.

"I am me," Master said matter-of-factly, as if it were obvious, though there was also a teasing lilt to the statement.

"I don't understand."

"Of course you don't," Master cut in. "You want everything to be given a label, a context to make it easier to grasp," the figure said.

"All of you speak in riddles."

Master sounded amused. "Is that irritation I sense? Curiosity and now annoyance. Perhaps you are not a lost cause after all."

The figure turned, hidden feet gliding about the cobblestones as Shades traversed the realm. Ievarus stood unmoving but faced the rescinding image.

"Well, you want some answers, don't you? Come with me," Master said.

Without the Maiden, it was an almost impossible task to navigate the maddeningly unmappable walls of the castle.

Venturing through one of the open doors and down the spiralling stairs, Master led Ievarus with such a relaxed but purposeful gait that one would think them a Maiden. And so, through winding paths, suddenly shifting angles where one felt as if they were walking up and down walls, any concept of verticality became obsolete within the belly of the sleeping mountain.

Master illuminated the path through a summoned flame in their wrinkled hand. Finally, the two reached an inconspicuous door resting upon the wall.

"In here," Master said.

Ievarus followed behind and entered a new chamber with air so ancient it was forgotten. Again, it was a long and winding path, but the roof of this chamber was far taller, with slightly more berth to the sides as well.

Master raised their hand and sent upwards their flaming ball of light, the borders of its glow lightly teasing out the contours and shapes of shrouded murals. Suddenly, the ball stopped. There was a brief moment where nothing happened and then it flared, expanding in a flash that violently tore apart the clambering shadows and revealed the curves and shapes of the walls.

To the right, there were standing great statues of stone. Enough of the darkness was done away with to reveal their design.

It took Ievarus a few moments to decipher the identity of those shapes. "The previous Seeds," Ievarus said.

Their weapons were either stabbed into the ground before them as a salute or missing altogether.

"This is the hall of your predecessors," Master announced.

Ievarus turned and looked at the opposite wall to their left. It was a timeline. But something wasn't right; whatever comprised the first gigantic mural was now just an alcove of rough stone. Whatever image it had once held was torn asunder, only to continue on towards the creation of the Grand Archon and the time with the Seeds coming after.

Ievarus paced towards the missing mural.

"What happened to it?" Ievarus asked.

"It was destroyed. A part of the Elder King's history, buried."

"I know of the past. Preceptor taught it. The Creator and the Elder King made it all, fashioned humans out of nothingness even before the first cycle."

"How do you know for sure that is the truth?" Master prodded.

Ievarus blinked without an answer, the rhetoric nature of the voice lingering in the air. Ievarus was a sapling, a babe who only had one source of information and that came from the Elders. There was no reason to question them.

Ievarus followed along the walls, eyes peering up at tales and wars that waged across Minethria, taking note of the lost lands reclaimed by the Nif, previously occupied by rapidly expanding humans and other lesser known races.

Eventually, they reached the end of the hall, another rubble of stone at their feet.

"What is this?" Ievarus asked, turning to see the last of their predecessor not stop at Niefri the archer but at an eleventh statue broken at the hips and missing its upper half. Ievarus spun around to face the statue's reflection. Its mural was also scarred and barren. "It's... angry," Ievarus said, with a startled voice of recognition.

"Yes, good. So you *do* understand," Master said.

The first wall was destroyed, turned to rubble because someone wanted to hide it. It must have occurred to Ievarus that this final mural denoted rage; the defacing of names, the destroying of the images, it wasn't just hidden—it was erased.

"You are not the first Eleventh Seed," Master said.

"Explain," Ievarus commanded.

The spider upon the hood gyrated as if preparing to speak the truth.

"There was one before you; another."

"What was their name?"

"No one knows." Master pointed towards the carved out scribblings that spanned the wall. "The Elder King erased all knowledge of their existence."

"Why?"

"So that the true Eleventh Seed may turn forgotten."

"I don't understand. Why did the King do this?"

Master was seemingly amused. "Why indeed? Why would a father do such a thing to their child?" The term 'father' was spoken loosely, as if to mock the notion after how carelessly Ievarus had used it. Master pointed out towards the start of the hall now basked in darkness. "Why would one hide the history of how the world came to be?"

Ievarus looked back to the murals and noticed the defaced being of it all.

"The Eleventh Seed turned traitor to the King, never did accomplish their purpose and fled as a result. No one knows what happened to the Seed, only that the King ensured that they would disappear and vanish like they never existed."

When Ievarus turned back to the mural, their glossy eyes peeled and focused on it. Ievarus must have felt compelled to discern, to draw out any vestige of the last Seed's face or name—some form of identity.

"You are the final piece, meant to replace the last Prince."

Ievarus turned to find they were alone. Master was no longer present, and the drifting ball of fire gradually dimmed, the hungry shadows reclaiming murals the same way the Nif continued to reconquer land. As the last of the light vanished, all that was left was Ievarus, who became just as much a fitting relic as their surroundings.

Chapter Forty-Seven

CHROMA

Curses are more than just magic. They are contracts. No curse is unbreakable for each is written in the ink of condition. Find the condition and you can break the curse.

—Introduction to Curses. Introductory study to
magecraft in Cleria

After the bout, I awoke upon a bed of hay surrounded by our shaman and guards. It was a nursing tent.

The guards gave me a warning? I supposed it wasn't much of a surprise. It made sense—the relationship between us and the guards had never been this amicable and easy. I played a big role in that. I bridged the divide between our cultures, which made things easier for everyone involved.

Mother was waiting to scold me the moment she made sure I was okay. When we returned to our yurt, she demanded to know what possessed me. I looked at her, my anger still bristling. It was time to speak my mind.

"Mother, I know that you have been keeping Jasper company at night," I said, tending to a sensitive, swollen bruise on my cheek with a damp cloth.

Zarien stepped back in shock. "Chroma, I already told you there is nothing—"

"I saw you, okay?" I cut in.

Mother turned speechless.

I sighed, allowing the rest of the words to dribble out. "It was night. I followed and found the two of you fucking."

Zarien couldn't deny it any longer. "Yes, I have been giving myself to Jasper."

I stared at her. All I saw was shame. "Why?"

"When I arrived here, I had nothing. I needed a way to support us. You were newly born, and I had to feed you. The other men volunteered for hard labour to nourish their children, but what was I to do? They wouldn't accept a woman akar to help them. It isn't their way. I needed to feed you with Muktow far away. The other men volunteered to help, but I was too proud to agree."

"And now?" I pressed, feeling that though the rage was gone, a deep guilty sorrow replaced it instead. She didn't have a reply. "Do you love this human?" I asked.

"Jasper has done right by us."

"That wasn't my question."

She hesitated. "No," she finally admitted.

"I want you to end things with him," I said.

Mother's brows furrowed in indignation. "You *want?* You have no say in who I sleep with. Being with him allows us to live comfortably. Without it, we can't do anything."

"It's my turn to provide. I will volunteer for the labour work and provide for the both of us. I don't want you to whore yourself to some common guard for money; you are a warrior."

Mother nodded after a moment, her head hanging. "I haven't felt like one in quite some time," she admitted.

Mother was an adept fighter and competent compared to most; I hated seeing what human culture had brought her to. She was never aggressive or boisterous like others, but I never thought her to be so submissive. Part of me felt at fault. I walked to her and wrapped my hand behind the back of her head to bring our foreheads to touch.

A shuddering sob finally escaped her. "I'm sorry," she said, trying to choke down her tears.

"It's okay mother, you did what you had to," I reassured her.

"Please don't think less of me."

"I'm not," I lied, and hated that. But I knew, with time, I would see my mother again for who she truly was: a strong and reliable akar meant for more than just offering her flesh to humans for money.

⋖ ⋗

A long three months had passed since that event and things had returned to a sense of normalcy. As promised, I had set myself to work on any hard labour work to earn for our family.

The days would come and go. I was taken further than I ever was from the settlement. It was a secluded building operation where I, and two other akar, carried large logs for the builders to fashion defences made to kill my own kind. I understood that the western mines were where the real money was at, but given the cramped space and nascent distrust among the human folk, I gathered that I would likely not be welcomed to work among them.

Within the settlement itself, most of the infrastructure was finished, and we all had settled into our new lives. But not everything had returned to the way it was.

Jasper joined Kolotha in avoiding me. I took it as a sign that mother truly did end things with him.

It was a curious thing, seeing how the dynamic amongst our people had changed. If it were a couple of years ago, Jasper's men would have jumped on the chance to make our lives harder, but it wasn't that simple anymore.

The relationship between our people had become friendly in the loosest terms. Erefiel's insistence on a more sustainable infrastructure made it so that we were easy to work with, and there was no longer this suffocating tension in the air.

Jasper couldn't just make my life harder and not expect anyone to care. He was clever and subtle about it.

He pushed me as far as he could before anyone could raise questions about it. I didn't mind, my body was built for such work. Plus, the news of Erefiel's visit lifted my spirits as well. I found myself shocked, but pleasantly, so that the arrival of someone who was part of this oppressive system would put me in such a good mood.

I entered the yurt where my mother was weaving another one of her wicker baskets.

"Why the big smile? Is it a girl?" she teased.

"Erefiel is coming."

Mother dropped her hands and played at disbelief. "Chroma, I'm sorry, but I don't think akar men are his type."

I turned to Mother with a raised and questioning eyebrow, prompting her to continue, but she simply smiled and tried to hide behind her work.

"Rest assured, he isn't my type either," I replied. I was shocked to find this new side to Mother. Ever since ending things with Jasper, she was more confident. She seemed relaxed and jesting, elegant with her tusks and warm eyes. Even the way her fingers danced between the crossing wicker strands was done with contentment.

Just last month, she even took part in the pit and won. I hadn't seen her more alive than when she threw her fists into the air in victory and her chest heaved and her tusks gleamed along with her smile.

As an unspoken rule, we simply avoided bringing up Jasper in conversation or anything that had to do with her affair. I only asked once who else knew about her and Jasper. She was rather avoidant, but she assured me there was only one. Though people whispered.

Despite the topic being dropped, Mother didn't stop from trying to match me with others.

Nedalya was no longer an option as her relationship with Kolotha continued. Mother understood how strained my relationship had become with Kolotha and spoke no more about the matter.

"One of these days, you are going to have to find a partner," she insisted.

"I will find someone when you do." She glowered slightly. I spoke my mind before she had a chance to. "Father is far away. It is time you find someone."

Mother paused. "Not just one," she said.

"What?"

"I have been spending a lot of time with Juta and Sukin, and they seem to enjoy my company." Mother's announcement was cautious and hesitant, almost as if asking for my approval.

I blinked. "Really?" I smiled in excitement.

"It's too early to tell," she cautioned.

"Well, maybe if they get to know you."

"Oh, they already seem to know me *very* well."

My mother's meaning dawned on me and made my brain wrinkle. "Stop it!" With a chortle, I stumbled out of the tent and could still hear her laughter.

Erefiel was supposed to arrive on the morrow, and I had a lot to prepare for.

◁ ▷

I finished work early that day. Since Jasper wasn't there to torment me, I went home with my reward of bacon and vegetable broth to share with Mother. I found her outside. She was arguing with Jasper about something. Their whispers were harsh and elated. Mother towered over him and stabbed a finger at his chest. She did not hesitate to bear her tusks. They hadn't noticed me yet. They were arguing at the entrance, far away from eavesdropping akar.

I was about to walk in there myself, but hesitated. Something that Jasper said made my mother freeze. Her tense muscles relaxed as she returned to her timid self. Jasper also seemingly softened, taking mother's drooping hand to his own and whispering some comforting words too far for me to hear.

Mother tore away and grimaced in disgust. Jasper smiled. While mother's body tightened his body language proved more relaxed. He looked up into her eyes. They walked together and out of the entrance into the guard stations.

I had seen this exact thing transpire years ago, and back then, I was too naïve to discern the meaning behind it. This time, I knew full well what the scene meant and found the clay bowl crack under the weight of my grip and the contents pool to the floor. Why couldn't I move? I had to go stop them. A deep but thin fissure opened upon my heart and I felt myself falling through. I had to help, had to stop and save my mother.

So why couldn't I?

Numb and in shock, I fell into bed alone, feeling disgusted with myself, thinking about Jasper's pleasured moans as he used my mother.

The anger bubbled somewhere in my stomach, but I was too tired and in shock to act on it.

I permitted the private tears to flow, knowing that mother comforted a man against her will despite being from warrior blood. I was supposed to stop this, help her escape that prison.

My deepest fantasies made me hear their moans despite not being anywhere near.

With an empty stomach and absent appetite, I headed home and gave myself to sleep. I wanted nothing to do with this reality.

⊰ ⊱

I awoke to the sound of clucking chickens. The events of last night crept slowly to me. I turned to my side and found Mother hadn't returned. Perhaps she couldn't face me? I knew I couldn't. I laid there for a while and just stared. Part of me wondered if it was all a dream, but I knew that what I saw was real.

I got to work to distract myself. I axed away at wood and unloaded my frustration on my long line of victims. I only remembered that Erefiel was visiting thanks to a guard who informed me. Just the day before,

I was full of giddy excitement at the news. Today, I was too distracted by Mother's situation to even care.

Erefiel was waiting in a lounge room where, on a table, he surveyed the bound and open ledgers to piece together the progress of his program. He turned to me and a smile split his face. "Chroma!" he said and walked up to me. "My! How you've grown!"

I was entirely unprepared and even took a hesitant step back as the man wrapped his arms around me. Last we met, we stood at the same height. I now towered over him a good length, but that didn't seem to faze him at all.

Parting to stand at arm's length, he let his arms fall to his side. "It is good to see you, Chroma. I trust things have been going well since my departure." His tone shifted to a slightly reprimanding note. "Though I heard that you caused quite a commotion a few weeks ago."

"It is good to see you too, Erefiel." And I truly meant it, even if my tenor lacked his energy. "I can't thank you enough for all your effort."

He waved my formal comment away. "Please, it is quite alright. It is not just for you. The wellbeing of your folk benefits us all. Being able to work in unison rather than against one another will make us all better off." Erefiel's smile wilted, and his brows began to furrow when he noticed my sour mood. "What is it?"

My tongue wouldn't unfurl. "It's nothing." Why didn't I just tell him?

Erefiel moved on, and approached the table. "Well, perhaps you will be in better spirits when I tell you that everything is right on track." He practically beamed with his debonair smile.

I was truly grateful. The ability for my folk to tend to their own chickens and even handle their own cows for dairy was an invaluable gift. Even small gardens were shaped to grow our own vegetation, all thanks to Erefiel's efforts.

"But there is something else." Erefiel eyed me teasingly, holding back on exciting news.

"What is it?" I frowned. Something about how he spoke had my attention.

"Chroma, since my efforts here and the promising collaboration of our people, no matter how small, I was able to convince the council to continue on this path for an even greater project."

"What is it?"

Erefiel's tone turned serious. "Your kin's invading force has grown bolder, more dangerous, especially with their latest attack. We would like to introduce your kind into the army to protect these lands."

I didn't understand. "But, we already do fight for you?"

Erefiel shook his head. "That is simple conscription. And to be honest, your potential is being wasted. However, if one of you were to join as an *official* soldier. Well, I think there is real progress that could be made. For the image of your people and for our task of keeping the invaders out."

Something irked me about the idea. "What difference is there when you force our kind to fight for you?"

Erefiel shook his head apologetically. "No, I'm sorry. I should have made this clear. The right for your kind to *willingly* join was something that I insisted on. As another bonus, forced conscriptions for your kind will be forbidden. Anyone who would wish to join would do so of their own volition and have a chance at being integrated into everyday life." His eyes were wide with excitement. "Do you understand what I am saying, Chroma? Your people could live as a valued citizen within the walls."

I blinked, finding myself almost dumbfounded at the sheer fantasy that was being displayed. For the first time ever, I had the sense that I must have been growing up, because all that was being spouted sounded entirely naïve. A world where akar and humans could walk side by side without conflict? Impossible.

"Don't you find that a bit naïve?" I asked.

Erefiel shrugged. "Perhaps, but the point is that even if such a world isn't possible, at the very least this will improve the image of your people and further improve your quality of life."

I bit my lip. "You expect us to kill our own kind? This isn't our fight."

"Chroma, the land of Bravnicka is now as much our home as it is yours and your people's. We have given you much, don't forget that," Erefiel said firmly. "Despite everything, we have given you a home and fed your people, and now that there is hope for a peaceful and mutually beneficial life, there is even more reason to protect that. If they break in and attack us, do you think they will welcome you with open arms?" I lowered my head. "You have yet to see what a horde of them can do. You faced just one of them and barely made it out alive when they were wounded. How do you think you will fare when they all break through?"

Each stressed point made things clearer. "You're right," I admitted. After a moment's consideration, I wondered who I could recommend. "Perhaps Juta would be willing to fight alongside you?"

Erefiel shook his head. "Actually, we were hoping that you would be the one to join us."

My eyes widened. "Me?"

Erefiel nodded. "You are the bridge between our folk. If you were to join our ranks first, and show our people your values and candour, I believe everyone else will also naturally fall in line and we can start adding more of your kind to our defences."

I was stunned. "Are you sure?"

Erefiel nodded. "It is the best course of action. You won't be taking part in the actual combat to begin with. It would be a shame if you were to die on the first day." He gave a teasing wink.

"I don't know what to say."

"Say you will join."

I hesitated. A thought struck me like lightning—would Father be among the enemy? I would be made to watch as my supposed brothers were culled and killed, clothed in Clerian armour and waved about like a taunting banner to my people from the mountains.

"I accept."

Erefiel allowed himself a wide, pleased smile as he nodded. "Good! We will wait until my return and you will declare your intentions to all. It is important that this comes across as *your* decision, so keep it between us."

"On one condition," I cut in.

"Name it."

My hesitation lasted a mere moment until I found my voice. "It is about one of the guards," I explained. "And Mother."

Chapter Forty-Eight

NORA

*If colour-magic comes from ink and mistmages use the Haar, it begs
the question where the Inspired get their magic from? It is suggested
that any accomplished creative taps into an untouchable pool of creativity which is shared between all the people. They bring back from this
'beyond' their art. I, personally, think this is all a bunch of rubbish.*

—Spoken by Mistmage Gurick during a lecture

I had time to practice balancing on my crutch, each step a weight-
ed hop as I leaned to my left and braced myself with my new
and wanting limb. I hopped forward, practically tensing the
heel of my foot with each drawn out step—I discovered it was a far
more difficult practice with shoes on and without the help of my toes
to balance the weight of my body. Naturally, the sisters offered to help,
but I refused.

It was an unspoken and obvious result that my time in the army
had come to an end. I didn't dare speak it out loud, and I was glad to
find Mother Merilda and the other sisters did so in kind.

I had to deal with things one at a time as I processed my new reality. My fight wasn't over; I'd find another way.

As I wobbled and swung forward, each step was the equivalent of
ten strides when I still was whole. I bit my lip and concentrated wholly

on not toppling over. Mother Merilda and her company of three sisters trailed behind. There was one who stood at the top of the stairs.

Their presence unnerved me. I could feel their lowered arms waiting tensely for me to topple over, prepared to leap into action the moment I failed. The weight of their anticipation made my task all the heavier, regardless of if I still had two feet to walk with or not.

Of course, their belief was warranted. I was half the person I used to be. It would surprise no one if my body simply decided it was too much and collapsed. But another part of me, the part I tended and nurtured ever since abandoning my previous life, wouldn't let me give up.

Mother Merilda stepped forward and whispered in my ear. "If you use the wall to lean on, it might be easier to move forward." The advice was a loophole in a game I never knew of.

I retorted with a response of my own, only slightly louder and spoken with whatever conviction I could reserve. It was only then that I realised I was out of breath. "There won't always be a wall to hold me."

I continued swinging forward, trying my best to ignore their stares, waiting for me to fall.

As I finally reached the end of the path and readjusted my crutch, I was rewarded with an aching wrist, tense shoulders and rigid leg. I looked down the steps and again was forced to confront my broken self. Were there always this many steps? Did they always look so foreboding?

My voice was feeble and meek. "Please, could you help?" I felt disgusted for asking.

A carriage designed for the noble caste waited for me. It wasn't a visually assaulting one with rich colours, but rather fair and modest. Intricate filigree festooned the door in silver. The rims were an auburn shade as if leached from last autumn and the curtains mimicked a strong brown reminiscent of aged oak.

I allowed for the sisters to support my weight from the door to the carriage, instead of making them wait because of my wounded pride.

KIAN N. ARDALAN

Fear of being spotted by my old colleagues added expediency to my step. I had no doubt that news of my predicament already spread to every corner of the barracks. I imagined what terrible whispers now worked the ranks.

"So the twilight bird is mortal, after all."

"This is why women don't fit amongst our ranks."

I imagined how my unofficial moniker of "undying flame" would now be spoken ironically.

The ride towards Cleria was done silently. I closed the curtains so I could brood within the dim light of this cushioned interior. My crutch had to be stuffed diagonally so that it could fit. Having nowhere to bury or direct my shame, I punched the cushioned backrest. The softened blow only reminded me of my broken fangs.

My eyes welled with tears. I looked to the front where my driver would be and wondered how soundproof the walls were. Who was I kidding? I knew they could hear me.

Yet I convinced myself that since he'd never actually see me cry, that I could make an exception. It was a feeble attempt at compromise because the tears came whether I wanted them to or not. This was exactly what I feared—to be no more than that little girl who tried to be something she was not.

⋨ ⋩

Upon arriving at Cleria and cantering through its streets, I dared a peek through a small opening in the curtains and noticed that we weren't at Strait district. Instead, we went through an austere and greatly crafted building belonging to the church of the Faithful.

As I opened the door before the driver had a chance to do so himself, I beheld a gathering of sisters. They stepped to help, but shied away when I held a dismissing hand. Just like before, they stood there agitatedly, waiting for me to fail. With crutch in hand, I shimmied to the edge of the seat and dangled my one foot over the end, aiming it at the step before me.

I slowly slid off of my rear and was relieved to find my foot plant upon the metal step.

I prepared myself for the next move, leaning my back against the carriage as I squatted down and lowered myself to the floor. My leg was sore and aching from all the new manoeuvres, but it held. The flexing of my toes sent the soft ghost of a cramp waiting to happen.

Finally, I kicked my foot out from underneath and allowed the step to catch me—it didn't. I slid and fell with my rear onto the floor and felt bone collide with stone. A startling pain lanced through me. On cue, the saintly shades stepped forward to help me all at once. Dressed in their spotless white robes as their ensemble of digits stretched and pawed at me.

"No!" I cried, holding up my crutch as if it were a warning. My pleas fell on deaf ears, my requests no longer worth respecting. They fell upon me like ghosts. Their forms cast above me until all I saw was their faces framed by white habits.

"Leave me be!" I shouted, I dropped the crutch and swung my fist at the nearest sister. How hollow my punch felt; just a shadow of my previous strength. I was hollow, disempowered, my words were just as impotent as my fists. I was helpless as they pulled me to my foot.

"Are you alright?" one asked. I glowered at the woman and saw her blanch because of it.

"I can walk! I don't need someone doting on me and carrying me as if I were some child!" I cried out, a pitiful attempt at regaining some face, to be seen as more than just a cripple. With crutch in hand, I eventually composed myself and leaned against the crutch's body.

The one sister nodded. "I apologise." Her words were hollow, but I felt as if the other sisters followed suit in reluctantly respecting my wishes. They bowed their heads. If anything, the acknowledgement felt condescending.

"Lead the way," I muttered bitterly, but my breath was laboured again and there was an annoying fringe of hair obscuring my vision. I could hear my taxed heartbeat through paper-thin skin, an unwelcome warmth and sting coming from it as my body could no longer contain my fervour.

The sisters led me to the patio where stairs awaited me, a number which was of no matter to the average person, and a burden to me. I could feel the sisters staring, unsure of what to do should I fall again.

I hopped and jumped each step with the help of my crutch, using wide movements—I was sure it looked even clumsier than I felt. The tension from the sisters dissipated when I made it to the top. Finally, there was a stretch of steps leading up. One of the sisters blushed a deep and rosy red as if only then realising the dilemma.

"I'm sorry," she said. "There is also a room downstairs for you."

"No, it's fine," I said.

She looked up the flight of stairs and then at me. "Are you sure?" she asked, obviously uncomfortable with the idea. The crux of the issue was left unspoken, but it practically screamed in the mind of everyone present. I ignored her, looking up at the climb before me, imagining several ways that I could make my way up.

Mother Merilda's advice came to me as I looked at the wall.

I gave my crutch to one of the other sisters, sparing her a warning look, and leaned with my left palm against the wall. Each step upwards was a gruelling testament to my stubborn pride.

I already felt my rear ache with the earlier impact as I squatted and cleared another step. A cramp was beginning to form in my leg. With each following jump, I would let out a breath of relief. I wasn't even halfway up when my footing slipped and I fell hard against the steps. My chin banged against the wooden protrusions. Stars danced across my vision, my body pained, my leg felt numb underneath me as I reorientated myself.

The frantic and worried cries of the sisters burst from their lips as if already nocked upon their tongues. They hurried up the steps with enviable ease.

"Stop!" I shouted, turning back at them. There must have been something about my look, an intensity that became undeniable as they froze. The sister I had reprimanded earlier stretched out a stopping arm, and brought the others to step away.

I failed—of course I did. I wasn't able to climb it by myself. But of course I couldn't—I was but half a person. Their unspoken words filled and rattled within the confines of my skull. Nothing about the way things turned out seemed to surprise anyone present. It was simply the way of things.

I propped my one arm below me and dragged myself up the steps.

The pain of bruises made themselves known across my body as stars continued their dance across my vision. My remaining leg flailed and pushed step by step. I had to be careful with my stumps, which smarted at any leaning pressure.

The gruelling minutes passed in silence, filled only by the sound of my scraping knee and strained groans.

Finally, I made it to the top of the stairs. Great, heaving breaths came from me, and I was lathered in sweat. I looked down to the bottom of the stairs where the sisters stood in shocked silence. I felt vindicated; it was a subtle and hollow victory, but still it was there.

One started clapping. And then another. They all joined in with thunderous applause that left me stunned. There was a frenzy in their eyes, a sense of inexplicable admiration at what had just happened.

My moment, my crawl, suddenly felt tainted. All I did was climb some stairs, a task that never before warranted any praise. I wanted to show that I could still walk, could still climb stairs like everyone else. It was about embracing the mundane. Their laudation was an insult, showing how little people had come to expect of me.

⊰ ⊱

My room was much like the one before, with the exception of mirrors.

After gathering my strength again, and being motivated by my disadvantage, I practised walking until the motion became second nature—it never did. The movement was clumsy, and steps took much longer than they usually should have as I laboured through the interior.

The following day, I had a sister remove my bandages and leave me be. Of course, they asked me if there was anyone they could inform of my situation, to which I made them swear that they would tell no one. Yet that didn't stop the first company of visitors from knocking on my door as I learnt to navigate around the cramped space.

The door opened to reveal Howard, Stamence and Victor announcing their entry.

Upon seeing me, their smiles turned pitying and dour. I felt naked. Naked in such a way that even having all my clothes torn from me never would.

I swallowed my embarrassment and sauntered over to my bed. I allowed gravity to do the rest. The air was tense—I had to break it. "You boys finally decided to come and visit me? I thought I had to stride all the way there and teach you some manners again. Hope you aren't being this tardy with my men."

"Wouldn't dream of it," Victor said in that stern way he did when at the job.

What was this dynamic? Was I still their captain? Their leader? They seemed equally confused about how to address me.

I could see, despite all their efforts, how their eyes would drift to my injuries before veering back to me. They seemed unsure of where to look. Was this how Jeremiah felt? I was awash with guilt. Instinctively, I slowly took more and more of the bedcovers and pulled it over my right shoulder. My right leg-stump was already hidden.

Stamence sat on a chair drawn close to the bed. Victor leaned by the door, noticeably tense and uncomfortable, as if ready to bolt at any moment, and Howard stood by my wardrobe.

"What happened? After the incident, I mean."

None of us had yet addressed my injury, instead getting over small talk as I was comforted to hear that the unit was still whole and functioning. Victor spoke the least of all, and I was ashamed to find that I preferred it that way. I wasn't ready to hear that I was no longer part of the army, let alone that I had to give up the unit I spent years forming.

Howard scratched the nape of his neck. "Well, the town was more than just a little singed, the nearby buildings were in ruins and the church was completely destroyed."

"The demon?"

"It escaped, turning into a trail of flame and vanished up into the air."

Stamence chuckled. "You should have seen Howard over here. He was screaming like there was no tomorrow, completely off his rocker."

Howard blushed a bright red as he mumbled a private complaint—their banter brought a nostalgic smile to my lips. I absently wished that Bradley could also be here. Stamence took a lit candle from the corner of the room and played as if he were trying to scare Howard. Howard turned stern, clearing his throat and nodding in my general direction. Stamence cleared his own throat and looked immediately embarrassed.

"I'm sorry, boss. Humour helps me in times like these."

"Please." With a placating wave, I let the cover slip from my shoulders. Who were we kidding? Just because we didn't talk about it didn't mean it didn't happen. "It's alright. I don't want you to watch your words around me. Plus, I'm not your boss anymore." When I said the words, it felt like a stake hammered into my heart. Though speaking it aloud didn't prove as difficult as I had suspected. It felt more akin to relaxing my grip on something that was already shattered. Once my knotted tongue relaxed, the words practically slid off my lips, limp and obvious.

It was silent for a good while, until Howard seemed to remember something. "Oh! Right!" He reached into his hidden pocket underneath the leather vest which did a humbling job at hiding the man's belly.

Eventually, Howard unveiled a pouch that he opened and stared into. The man grimaced. He mouthed the words 'sorry' and pulled out a crushed flower—it was a tulip.

"What is this? I am sorry, Howard, but you are not my type; plus, even with only an arm and a leg, I am still way out of your league."

Stamence gave a roaring laugh, and even Victor let a smile slip through the cracks.

I was hurting, hurting over a wound that wouldn't stop bleeding; it only made it worse seeing my men hurt on my account. I wanted to save them that discomfort.

Howard stepped to my left and placed the flower into my opened palm.

"You had one job, you brute!" Stamence chided, and Howard only shrunk further.

"It's from the girl you saved, Gritta." Howard explained as he closed my fingers about it. My calloused hand was obviously laboured, but they seemed so vulnerable next to the man's stout fingers, as if all these years I truly had only played pretend. "I'm sorry it ended up being crushed. It was a hard ride."

I shook the sentiment away and found, to my surprise, welling tears. "It's alright, thank you."

I set the flower by my nightstand next to the canister of water. "Is she alright? The girl?" I asked.

Victor nodded. "Thanks to you."

"Good." I permitted myself a smile.

I turned my attention to darker matters. "Did you discover anything about what happened at the church?" I asked.

The group fell silent, sharing private looks with one another where once I was part of that circle. Now it was as if I didn't even speak their language.

"All the evidence went up in smoke," said Stamence.

"Was there any evidence of shoddy workmanship?" I pressed.

"Not any that we could find," Howard answered.

"And what about Seamus and his gang?" Again, they shared private looks. "Speak!" I demanded, my scorn surfacing. How quickly we did away with the friendliness.

"They vanished. After the incident, we sent a rider to the Mystics and the Demon Hunter guild. None of them had seen the group."

"Of course they didn't." My remaining fist clenched about the bed sheet. If I were still whole, I would have hunted them down myself.

"I bet you it was that Ida, she must have slipped up. The damage was their fault."

"You don't know that." Howard cut in.

"Who else could it have been?" I challenged.

"The church was already damaged," Stamence supplied.

"That shouldn't have mattered if that blind bitch did her job!"

"Boss, stop it." Now it was Victor who joined the conversation, his tone dry and monotonous.

"I want you to keep searching for them! They are responsible for the destruction of that town."

"Boss." Victor's voice turned more authoritative as he stepped closer.

"They need to be brought to justice."

"Nora! That's enough!" Victor's own voice boomed to challenge mine. I was stunned, as were Howard and Stamence.

"Victor, let it be." Howard tried to calm him down.

"That's *Captain* Victor to you," Victor rebuked.

I scoffed. "Oh, so now that you have my position, *my* unit, you think you are in charge?"

"This has nothing to do with the town," Victor declared.

"Yeah? Then enlighten me. What *does* it have to do with?"

"You! You are mad about what happened to you and want someone to blame. You think I want this job? Everyone looking at me and not seeing their captain? If I could give you back your arm and leg, I would do it in a *heartbeat*. But your men look up to me now, and I will not risk their lives by sending them on a wild goose chase just so you can have your vengeance."

I broke down. I was tired of breaking my promise.

Never before had my men seen me cry. Years upon years I built my reputation as infallible, indomitable. All useless now. They saw the true me, the girl who cried through the night when her parents locked her in her room. How quickly the shell crumbled down.

Even then, I tried to pretend as if my new body was a mere nuisance and nothing more.

"Tell me what I can do, Victor? Howard? Stamence?" One by one, I turned to face them as if looking for the answers somewhere in their pitying gazes. "Tell me!" My call was a deep and raw cry, distorted by my straining throat and intermittent sobs.

"I am the one who is responsible for what happened." Victor's words were familiar, sounding just the same as when I finally admitted I was no longer their captain.

"Don't." Stamence tried to intervene but was silenced by a raised hand.

"You tasked me with seeing to the logistics, making sure everything was rightly underway, protecting it all. I should have paid more attention to the structure as well and seen it for what it was: a hazard. I let my guard down."

Howard and Stamence stood with Victor. "If Victor is at fault, so are we all," Howard said, and Stamence joined them. There wasn't even a flicker of hesitation in them.

I wiped the tears from my eyes with my remaining wrist and used the covers to wipe my snot.

Still, my vision was blurred from the crying, and I could feel my chin quiver. "Just promise me you will treat my men well," I said timidly.

The three of them nodded.

"You will always be our captain," Victor voiced as he went rigid and slapped a fist to his chest to salute.

Howard and Stamence joined in, both of them at attention and waiting for orders.

I sobbed, no longer carrying any authority in my orders. "Well then, you are dismissed."

Chapter Forty-Nine

NORA

*Ludwig the Battle-Inspired followed the example of Heyru of Dusk
and found inspiration in war. He flourished his weapons and developed
forms to bring art into blades. His dance controlled the flow of conflict
and even provided a keener edge to his attacks. The school of Ludwig is
said to still exist beyond in Thickwood.*

—Esoteric histories, by Branlis Norf. 8C304

Eating had become a tiresome and unnecessarily taxing affair as a tray with collapsible legs became the surface from which I ate.

On that day, I had the luxury of baked beans with eggs and fried bacon, along with some sourdough. One is somewhat familiar with the eating hand, but only when I was limited to that one arm did I realise how much the rest of my body contributed.

Holding the tray steady, sitting upright, repositioning the tray and my body, and even balancing on my rear with the help of my leg. Learning to manoeuvre with this limited range of mine showed me the number of muscles that had gone unnoticed along my years.

The phantom pains had only gotten worse, especially at night. I would feel a searing, hot pain radiate from my side and stab needles into me. When I finally braved myself to shower, I found the experience tiring. I had to sit within the circular wooden tub and push my one leg against the end of it. I used my shoulder blades to crawl out and grab the bucket of water. Simply having to position the heavy bucket in a way to pour the water required long minutes and arduous ingenuity. I almost overturned the entire tub the first time.

It was in these insignificant and private moments to myself where I so sorely noticed the absence of my arm and leg; although I had never even saved a moment's consideration when I was still whole.

⊰ ⊱

One of the sisters tended to me. Her hemp towel dipped into ice cold water to soften the ceaseless pain that radiated from my side. The cold was a bitter-sweet release. It simultaneously stabbed tiny needles into my tense form, but also dulled that ethereal heat following me.

At first, the common treatment was using warm cloth, which only seemed to make me sweat even more. I finally requested to try the cold instead. It didn't matter in the end.

The sister gently massaged my scarred side to relieve some of the tension.

"May I ask you something, Mother Sara?" I asked, going against the usual custom of her visits. I convinced myself that it would help distract me from the discomfort.

"Of course, Miss Nora, anything you'd like," she said. Her eyes and hands never lost their stride as they worked their way down my ribs. How strange that title sounded. *Miss* Nora. No longer Captain.

I winced as Mother Sara's hands grasped a particularly tangled mass of nerves.

"I'm sorry," she said. Mother Sara's accent was surprisingly rustic and not indicative of a high-caste, though I didn't press her on it.

"It's alright," I reassured, as she returned to her task. "The day I arrived, while I climbed up the stairs, you all started clapping." Mother Sara stopped. "Why?"

She looked me in the eye and an affectionate smile split on her

436

lips as if she only then realised who she was talking to. "Why, because of your perseverance, of course."

"My... perseverance?"

Mother Sara nodded. "Climbing up those steps in your shape; I could sense your will, your determination. You wouldn't let it stop you." Her hand cupped my cheek as she looked lovingly into my eyes. "You are very brave and strong of will. It inspired us all."

I scoffed; an act which seemed to insult Mother Sara as her smile faltered and she revoked her hand. "It was just climbing stairs. It's not such a big deal."

"Oh, but it is. The fact that you managed to do it in your state."

"Please. I felled scores of akar and led my own military unit. I have accomplished far greater feats."

She blinked. "Yes, that is also impressive. But that was before your accident. The fact that you climbed those stairs despite your injuries is even more admirable."

I blinked. There was an awkward silence that trailed the distance between us, an awkwardness I couldn't quite grasp. I had achieved so much in my young age, against all odds, to now be reduced to *this*? I had protected these lands and stood upon a kill count so great that it dwarfed that of many others, and yet, I suddenly wasn't even expected to climb an Elder-damn staircase?

"Please leave me," I said quietly, not even sure if Mother Sara had heard me until she began to speak again.

"Nora, I am sorry if I—"

"Please... just leave." I didn't raise my voice. I was too tired to do so. Finally, Mother Sara nodded and got up to leave, taking her bucket of equipment. As she stood by the door, she paused and turned.

"Miss Nora, before I leave, I was informed to let you know that you will be discharged in a week's time." There it was; that great inevitable question that would come, eventually. Where would I go? What would I do? It seemed even that choice had been taken from me. "Your parents have been informed of your situation, and you are to be transported to their estate in a few days."

I jolted slightly at the news; I must have misheard."What did you say?"

Mother Sara bowed her head as if rueful she had to deliver the news.

"I thought I asked that none know of my predicament."

"I am afraid that wasn't possible. The laws dictate that you need to be passed into the care of someone, the closest family you have being your own parents."

"Get out." My rage bubbled, and Mother Sara didn't need telling twice. She left quickly.

⋇ ⋗

In between curling up into a ball due to the blistering pains on my side, sleeping, and relearning to walk, there was not much else to do during my day. I had finally filled my suddenly vacant schedule with books.

On account of it being Cleria and within a building of the Sisterhood, the books that were supplied recounted great stories of old battles and the past Seeds—mostly things that weren't permitted when I was a child.

A peculiar passage revolved around Heyru of Dusk. Just as Xelxidon's weapons were fashioned from the light of the Elder King's eye, so too were Heyru's chakram infused with the moon's light.

With the body of a contortionist, she danced and swayed in combat. Her chakrams soared as great bladed disks that would arc in the air and return to her wrist and ankles. There was a strange feeling of envy as I read about her, the ease and natural grace with which she used her own body. I shortly fantasised of being able to do so myself, imprinting my own image onto that of Heyru.

When I read of Muriya the Protector, I just read about a monstrous brute who caused seismic calamities with the brunt of his hammer. He had a gentle heart and became a symbol for justice.

When I read of Kaelu the Quiet, I understood their powers to be world altering just by whispering wordlessly to existence.

The next story I read had nothing to do with the Seeds but rather with the Lady of Pain, a term I heard in passing but never quite knew about. Legend had it that the Lady of Pain was once a mortal ascended to live on Mount Morniar.

She was part of the Sisterhood, and when it was discovered that her blood had the incredible property of simply healing any ailment, she felt compelled to travel the world and treat all wounded souls. Her cause was selfless. Her reason to be was to nurture the ailing wounds of people spread far and wide. But her story was also tragic.

The want of man was ravenous, devouring, bottomless. People came to her begging for more blood. But her strength had waned; she had given more and more, but it was never enough. Famished, simply skin on bone, she would sit upon her cathedra of bondage and bleed in a bowl at her feet.

Mothers came with their dying babes and others with plagues unlike anything before. Each taking more and more. Enough was enough; the Lady of Pain was dying, so she took a retreat. The people couldn't, wouldn't, accept that.

They beat her, cut her, ripped her apart until every drop of blood could be used to save a life.

The Elders above saw this cruel, unending greed and took her broken body up to Mount Morniar, where she was born anew as the Lady of Pain: a martyr for the dying.

It is said that out of the goodness of her heart, she still offered her blood to those who needed it: what a fool. I could not comprehend nor understand her motivations. Looking at my broken form, I wondered if her blood could repair me.

There was a knock at the door. I closed the book and left my forefinger to mark the page I was on.

"I said I didn't want to be disturbed." I called out.

The door opened anyway, and I rolled my eyes at the sight of another sister.

"Hello Nora," the figure said.

"Listen, I just want to be left alone. I will be out of this place soon enough." I turned back to my book, but the woman remained standing.

She was an abnormally pretty thing, even with the habit which hid her hair. She was tall, her eyes compassionate orbs staring out, her supple lips forming a cautious line. Her cheeks were full and rosy, forming a perfect oval face that curled to a dainty chin. Her advance was cautious, as if not wanting to upset me.

"Can I help you?" I asked.

"It's me. Dalila."

My eyes went wide, and for a moment, I was awash with joy as I saw that little gentle girl had turned into such a dazzling sight. "My word, Dalila! It has been too long."

"It has." She closed the door behind her.

"I am sorry we weren't able to meet under better circumstances." With the book still in my hand, I waved at my ruined half.

"Please." Dalila frowned and she gave a slight shake of her head. "I am just glad to see you are alive."

I sighed and returned the book to my nightstand along with its neighbouring stacks. "Can't say I feel the same way." After a moment of awkward silence, I decided to change the subject. "How did you know I was here?"

"Mother Vinrie informed me."

"Who?"

"She is the sister who asked you to return my Kaseluda to me."

"Ah, yes." I smiled timidly.

"May I?" she asked.

I nodded reluctantly as she drew a chair to sit by me.

I smiled. "You've turned into quite a wallflower," I said. Seeing her this close, Dalila had become strikingly beautiful, albeit in an innocent way. She seemed timid and easy to scare, with her deep blue eyes, curling lashes, supple lips and pronounced breasts; she would become a target for many nefarious men.

She blushed at my comment and even seemed to hide her features.

"It's a compliment," I reassured, if she didn't get it the first time. "You know, when you were a kid, I secretly wished that you would get together with Jeremiah, make him a good man." Dalila seemed shocked by the admittance. "But now I see that you always deserved much better than what my family has to offer."

Dalila chimed in to defend my brother. "Jeremiah was always the sweetest!"

I nodded. "Yes, but my family attracts disaster. After the incident in the woods, Jeremiah had never seen anyone his own age outside of Basksin. He even stopped writing me letters."

Dalila smiled privately to herself. "Well, perhaps we all are doomed to having difficult lives."

"Tell me, Dalila, how has life been in the Sisterhood?"

Dalila hesitated for a moment, looking down at the book in her hands before looking back at me.

"It's been good. Been trying to help people as much as I can. The rot is worse than I ever imagined. What about you? How are you?"

I scoffed. "As good as can be." I made to lift my non-existent hand and felt strange and uncanny movements in my shoulder. Dalila shirked when realising how silly of a question she had asked.

"I don't know what to do, Dalila." I felt the tears coming again, but something about Dalila didn't make me ashamed. "I achieved a lot. Hard to believe that it was all taken from me in a single day." I asked the one question I hadn't spoken aloud to anyone, even myself, because I knew it didn't matter. "Why did it have to happen to me?"

My eyes turned rheumy. I sniffled and felt my lips quiver. Dalila remained quiet and simply listened. I looked at the ceiling as if to drive my tears back into their ducts.

"I was told that I had to return and live with my parents. And… I don't know what to do."

"It could be worse," Dalila said. They weren't the right words, but I couldn't imagine what anyone could say in such a situation.

"Please, how could it be any worse? My life is ruined. I'm a broken cripple with nothing to offer. Have to live again with the same people that think I'm a terrible daughter. How could it be any worse?"

Dalila was quiet.

"Please, tell me. You were taken to the Sisterhood, you also lost much. How did you deal with it, Dalila? How did you deal with your magic?" A great thunderous streak split through my mind as a revelation. I went quiet. "Your magic," I muttered, my tremourous voice seemingly levelling out.

"Excuse me?"

I looked at Dalila with hopeful eyes, but hers were filled with confusion.

"Your magic. It heals, right? Mend me. Make me whole again, bring me back my arms, my purpose."

Dalila stood up immediately from her chair and retreated.

"Nora, I can't."

"Why not?"

"I am forbidden from using it. I don't even know if it will help."

"Please." I had no shame, no pride to hold me back. I was a woman with nothing more to lose. If I had to grovel like a worm before her, I would—no price was too great.

"If you are fixed, they will know; Erefiel's name will be smeared."

"Please." The word was barely audible as I spoke it, my voice fading with each refusal, with each reason Dalila presented to deny me this release. Never before did I feel so shameless, so desperate as I did in that terrifying moment.

Dalila's brows knitted together in deep contemplation. Her sea-blue eyes darted about in search of an answer. I tried to still my sobs; my crying bubbled up as hiccups instead. I could see a private conversation unfold itself behind her stare. After a moment, her look of doubt became one of conviction.

"Let's try it."

All at once, a lively shudder escaped me; I felt hopeful for the first time since the accident. "Thank you! Thank you, Dalila! Be blessed!"

She hesitantly stepped towards me, my own impatience causing me to reach out and grab her greedily, pulling her the rest of the way in. I was trembling, my one hand grasping for my saviour with zealous gratitude. My missing limbs writhed in some other plane.

She took her seat once more and looked to the door to ensure that no one was there.

"Don't worry, no one will be walking in," I promised.

Dalila focused, her hands coming to life with a golden aura of light that cocooned it. She first brought its light to my shoulder, and I felt its warmth bereft me of the pain. It was working; it had to be. I felt life. I was being made whole again. My mind detached itself and sprinted across an open plain.

Seconds passed, then minutes.

Still the light danced and my pain eased, but my shoulder remained unchanged.

I pulled away from the fantasy, fear gripping me. "Why is nothing happening?" I asked, hoping for an answer. Dalila didn't reply, simply looking at my shoulder with stark concentration. A livid fear came from the receding darkness to claim me.

A few more moments passed, and the light faded. Her hand fell.

"I'm sorry, there is nothing I can do," Dalila admitted.

A great tide of rage ruptured. "Try again." I did not plead. I ordered.

"Nora, I'm sorry. It doesn't work that way."

"You heal, don't you? Your magic heals? So heal my limbs!"

"There is nothing to heal! You aren't bleeding, you aren't dying; I can't make limbs regrow!"

"You're lying!" I accused, grabbing her wrist with a vice grip.

She winced. "You're hurting me."

"Heal me! I know you are just pretending! Worried that the Sisterhood will know; it's okay, I'll protect you, just heal me! Make me whole so that I can protect you." My voice felt like it was drowning in my sobs. I didn't even recognise the desperation that filled my very being.

"Stop it!" Dalila shouted. It made me come free from my rage before it took me further. Dalila stood, nursing the part of her wrist where I grabbed.

"I'm sorry," I said, my voice back to its soft and hopeless tenor. "I think it is best you leave."

Dalila stood from the seat. It was silent for a while, as her frightened breath filled the air. I couldn't even look at her from shame at how I behaved. Before she left, Dalila reached into her bag again and brought forth a Kaseluda, opening it to one of its pages.

"In the woods, when we were attacked. Before Perry…" she trailed off. "He gave me this flower, a bluebell." Taking the pressed flower from between the pages, she placed it on my bed before me. "It gave me strength when everything else in the world was against me. I hope it will help you, too."

Without another word exchanged between us, Dalila turned and left, leaving behind just this one pressed flower with its faded blue colour. It proved to be a wanting balm as I spiralled deeper into horrifying realisation.

Chapter Fifty

DALILA

Do not be fooled, my sisters. It is easy for the non-magical to align themselves with Elder teachings for they are not victims of their designs. Our magic is what makes us ripe to be made into surrogates. Never forget, clemency in the form of subjugation is no clemency at all.

—UNKNOWN

The church of the Faithful was just a short walk from where Nora was being treated. I drifted with a certain numbness. The summer air was waning and the telling chill of autumn made itself known. I wanted to help Nora, I really did, and watching the maelstrom of her emotions eat at her made it that much worse. I wanted to run back in there, tell her I'd take care of her, tell her that everything would be all right; the only thing stopping me was a blaring instinct that said it would do more harm than good.

As I took the long, white-washed steps, I thought about how difficult such a climb would be for Nora. If I could give my limbs to her, I certainly would.

I reported to Mother Vinrie first, who sat in her office going over some paperwork. She kept the conversation short, asking me about my experience in Hartlou. I expressed my overwhelming sense of helplessness at seeing all those suffering. Next, she asked me about Nora, to which I stated that she was still coming to terms with her new injuries.

When I left, I did so to meet up for another session with Mother Lucia.

Yet this time, I found myself reluctant. My body stiffened at the thought of approaching her, sitting alone with her. I was surprised to find that I actually preferred the company of the angel guards if for no other reason than to make Mother Lucia watch her words.

⊰ ⊱

When I entered, Mother Lucia awaited me with a toothy smile and soft eyes crowned by wrinkles. I sat composed, but I knew it wouldn't fool Mother Lucia.

"You seem uncomfortable, Dalila. Is it because of me?" I didn't have a response. "Is it because of what I said?" I bowed my head as if ready to be chided. Mother Lucia sighed. "Dalila, child, please look at me." I did. "Do you think me a bad person?" I thought about the question and then shook my head. "Then why do I unsettle you so?"

I leaned in to whisper despite the room being empty. "Because what you spoke of last time is heresy, and it can get us both killed."

Mother Lucia found my caution to be unwarranted. She smirked. "Well? Did you use it?"

I considered my answer; was it a trap? When I realised that my silence had gone on for too long, I finally nodded. "Yes."

"And? What happened?" Mother Lucia asked, her eyes trained on me as she took an anticipating sip of her tea.

"There… was a girl. She had a lot of pain. I simply numbed some of that pain."

"How did it feel?" Mother Lucia asked.

I remembered the moment: the smile on that plagued girl's face, the foreboding black veins noticeable over the backdrop of sallow skin. Her comforted smile; it felt good to appease her, even if for a moment. "Good. It felt good," I admitted.

"Magic is magic. Nayrien had her reasons for doing what she did.

She caused all that destruction, not the magic itself. Magic is neither good nor bad. It is the wielder who defines its worth."

"Do you sympathise with Nayrien?" I asked.

"Of course I do!" Lucia proclaimed.

I tensed at the statement. "She used her power to destroy and kill so many."

"Because she was to be offered up to the Elder beings against her will." I shushed Mother Lucia loudly, looking to the walls, convinced that I would find ears poking through. "Oh, please! Nobody can hear us."

I turned back to Mother Lucia, my own emotions matching hers. "You shouldn't blaspheme the gods."

"They aren't gods. They are tyrants."

I stayed silent, worried that the more heated our discussion, the more likely it was to be overheard.

Mother Lucia gave a defeated and long sigh. "Look, have you ever wondered about why other forms of magic never have been contained? The Haar mages, the bards, the poets? Ink users?"

I blinked. "Because Nayrien showed the potential for destruction without a medium."

Mother Lucia scoffed. "That's all propaganda. Our constraint is a symbol of power. To show that we can be tamed puts the church, and the lordships of Cleria, in greater light. It quells thoughts of rebellion against the Elders."

I wasn't sure how to contest that claim and continued to sit in silence.

"That's the thing about belief: the stronger it is, the harder it is to break, and even harder to repair. I was perhaps a good few years older than you. I visited the home of a suffering girl, hurting from an infliction nobody could identify.

"She had a fever, felt weak and constantly secreted fluids from every orifice. None of us were certain what was wrong with her, as she would become better and return just a few weeks later with her parents, who were awash with worry."

"So you healed her with your magic?"

Mother Lucia smiled. "It's not that simple. I can't heal the way you can, not even close. I can create links, wield the magic of ink, and apply curses." I wasn't able to follow. She continued, suppressing a choked sob as she recalled the story, and her old eyes turned rheumy and red. "It was her parents. One night, when the young girl was alone, I spoke to her about a bruise I found on her thigh. When I asked if it was her parents, it was like her tongue had swollen in her mouth, as if her throat itself tightened and refused to let her speak. But those eyes were generous with the truth."

"That's horrible," I said.

Mother Lucia nodded in agreement. "None of my supposed Sisters believed me. Each week, she would return. Each week I would have to treat her and pretend like those disgusting parents were good folk who cared so much for her child." Mother Lucia's contempt was palpable. She seethed with the memory, spitting the words like venom as she recalled the event. As the rest of her story unfolded, I remained stock still, even feeling a sense of righteous vindication as the tale came to a close. "I cast a curse on the girl, a curse to protect her. The next time someone were to feed her any form of poison, the culprits would receive it too. The girl survived, the parents didn't."

"What happened to the child?"

"She joined the Sisterhood."

I blinked, wanting to ask who it was. Yet I assumed that it was none of my business, and that if Mother Lucia had her reasons to stay quiet, I would respect that. "So, Dalila, I need to ask. If you are in a room and your magic will save someone. Would you keep following the rules or actually use your abilities for good?"

I hung my head. "I don't know."

Mother Lucia left it at that and tried to steer the conversation elsewhere.

"Tell me of your time in Hartlou."

I smiled. "Well, I became close with Yasmin."

"Who?"

"She is a friend of mine—I mean, has been for a while. But this was the first time that I actually felt like I could be honest with her. I told her of things."

Mother Lucia turned unnaturally guarded. "What kind of things?"

I shrugged. "The masturbation. My need to help people. My fears."

Mother Lucia's stare deepened. "Does she know about your magic?"

"No," I lied instantly, the weight of her stare made me consider my words wisely.

"Are you sure, Dalila? Does she know of me?"

"No!" I cut in, indignant.

"Are you sure?" she pressed, worry in her eyes.

"Yes. I would not put your life as well as mine in danger like that."

Mother Lucia seemed appeased by that. "Good." Her smile returned to its usual softness. "Listen, Dalila. I am taking a risk in confiding the truth of our nature in you, and I do that because you are a witch and because I like you."

I frowned. "'Our'?" I emphasised.

She bit her sagging lip in contemplation. "I will tell you more when it is time." She left it at that.

Chapter Fifty-One

NORA

Over Minethria's extensive history, there have been some creatures whose veracity is difficult to prove. The Simurgh is one of them. All we know about it is that at the advent of every cycle, this colourful bird bursts into flame and is reborn again. A more scientific lens would suggest that this legend is a representation of the beginning and end of each cycle.

—Monsters: The lies and the truths, by Balaby Phox, 6C902

Hopping down the steps was, as usual, long and difficult. As I fought my way towards the wagon, my entire body stiffened when I saw my parents. Many emotions fought for dominance: shame, anger, indignation, remorse. Yet when Father and Mother came running to me with such obvious worry. I was disgusted to find relief.

Mother was wearing an exuberantly purple dress with a wide-brimmed hat and matching feather. The puffy dress was engorged to match her bloated cheeks as she fanned her pasty complexion. Father, on the other hand, wore a well fitted vest with his coat draped over a fore-arm, his shirt a deep burgundy to distinguish himself as a businessman.

"Oh, sweetie! Look at what they've done to you!" Mother embraced me without any restraint.

I was taken off my foot and relied wholly on her to keep me balanced. Eventually, she distanced herself and wiped the tears from her eyes, which threatened to smudge her lavender mascara; she looked up to prevent the colour from running.

Father approached me next. "Nora, dear. How horrible. I knew that this life was nothing for a flower." I was too exhausted and felt too exposed to offer any rebuttal. Mother and Father seemed happy to jump at that. Strong and independent they could not contest with, they could not bend or control. But as I was weak and unimposing. They knew how to handle that.

"Listen, Nora. This is good," Father whispered into my ear coaxingly. Mother stirred his words into the pot; her hand stroking my back. "Things will go back to how they were, we will be happy. I only want the best for you, my child. You'll see, this is for the best."

I shrunk at the seditious promise.

"Come, hurry. Let us leave this perfidious place and go home," Mother urged in her high-brow accent.

Without missing a beat, Father and Mother hurried me down to the carriage, their haste urging me faster than I could manage as my cane and foot slipped, sending me into the door.

"Oh dear! Nora! Please be careful." Mother pleaded.

"You really need to watch where you are going, Nora."

I swallowed my rage and turned my exterior to stone. No tears, no anger, no emotion—I would not give them the satisfaction, especially not among the sisters who watched.

I finally stood again with Father's help while my mother fanned her sweating self.

"Are you alright, dear?" Father asked her.

"Oh, it's just this whole ordeal! It really upsets me."

"Let us be on our way then." Father hurried me to enter the carriage, after which he guided Mother and then joined us. The doors closed, the curtains shut and the coach was on its way. Father took the seat next to me while Mother sat opposite.

"What a gaudy place." Father scoffed, rubbing his moustache with parting thumb and forefinger. He removed his top hat to reveal the receding crown of his hairline. Here I was again, thrown back into a life I had crawled my way out of; it was almost funny.

Most of the ride was done in silence, except for when Father had to complain about my incessant sweating.

Even sitting proved torturous as the wagon rattled over the beaten road. I had to tense my rear muscles to ensure that I remained in place. I eventually leaned against the door frame to support my weight, but the constant bumps along the way knocked my skull into the wood until I became nauseated.

It wasn't long before I had to shout for the driver to stop the wagon. I collapsed outside and fell just in time to expel the contents of my stomach.

"Nora! Control yourself!" Father scolded.

"Frank, go easy on her," mother insisted.

"Look at her, Martha! Our daughter is a cripple. I knew I shouldn't have let her leave and be corrupted by those vile apostates. We need to be harsh on her and set things right. Purging herself in public is no way for a lady to act."

I spat out the last bile and wiped my chin against my shoulder. I considered trying to stand but didn't have my crutch. Instead, I shamefully crawled my way back to the carriage to which my father rolled his eyes and came to help. "Stop pretending and get a hold of yourself! You are not some ragged urchin begging on the streets!" he scolded bitterly, before roughly picking me up from the floor.

I hopped to the door as Mother reinforced Father's lecture, but insisted that he still ought to go easy on me for the time being. I didn't care either way, I knew what I was in for. Pulling myself up with just my one hand and hopping my way into the carriage. Father and Mother grew silent and returned to their own seats.

Father took his folded coat in a frenzy and the driver snapped the horse reigns that set the wagon back into motion.

The coat found its way around my shoulders and, for a moment,

Father's scent wrapped me up and comforted me. It smelt of abuse and dependency, of confusion. I found it nostalgic.

All of it was ruined when Father opened his damned mouth. "At least hide your shoulders, dear. It will draw eyes. Plus, it upsets your mother."

To obey was easier than arguing. "Yes, Father," I said softly. Father puffed through his nose in approval. In the past, I could have the final say by simply walking away from a conversation. Something told me I no longer had that option.

⋖ ⋗

Finally, after many painstaking hours and an incredibly sore rear, we arrived at Basksin, the place I rued to call home. Father tried to convince the driver to ride into the village, but the man insisted the roads weren't meant for horses.

After some grumbling and complaining, Father simply wrapped the coat around my removed limbs and offered himself as support. He hastily urged me through the streets packed with nosy onlookers.

I couldn't see their faces on account of being covered by Father's cloak like some unused furniture, but I could hear their chattering as they whispered to one another.

"Father, slow down," I urged.

"Hurry it up," he said harshly under his breath.

Mother called from behind, telling us to wait up. I could hear her frantic and laboured breaths.

Finally having had enough of their ever growing mass of onlookers, Father swooped me up into his arms like a child and carried me the rest of the way. I blushed at the act, not realising how much lighter I had become.

The door opened and Father put me down on the floor before leaving again.

I could hear him calling out for mother. I removed the cloak from my head and looked about.

It seemed bigger from down here; all the furniture, the old ticking clock adorned with a peering eye, the table that reached to my collarbone. The air was thick with a musty scent reminiscent of my parent's old age but there was also a familiar odour which filled the place—filling me with the complex mixture of dread and comfort. Going from the hot weather outside into the brown walls of this furnished but closed in house was disorientating.

"Close the door, fool! Or do you wish the neighbours to see?" I turned to find Father pushing my gasping mother inside. She carried my crutch and dropped it on the floor beside me. Mother plummeted into a ready armchair.

She fanned herself, her cheeks a rosy red and sweat patches had formed pools underneath her armpit. I ran my arm through the opening of my crutch and then grabbed onto the nearby armchair to hoist myself up.

I turned, hopping on my crutch and leaning to face my parents. It was only when I looked up that I saw their pitying eyes and faltering lips: they didn't know what to say.

"Where is Jeremiah?" I asked. The last time I saw him was when I stormed out of this place and it had also been years since I received any letters from my little brother.

Father smiled proudly. "He'll be here soon enough," he promised.

� ⋗

Stairs had become my bane: stairs to walk down since my first care, stairs to climb back up at my second resting place, and stairs to climb up to reach my room.

And yet my pride had become a stubborn and unrelenting force to keep denying any help offered my way. For some, it was because I didn't want to be a burden; for others, it was because I didn't want their pity. For my parents, it was simply because I didn't want to give them the satisfaction of hearing me ask for help.

After continuously insisting that I could do it on my own, I strained every piece of my willpower and focus to climb up those stairs. The task took a good couple of minutes of hopping, but that didn't stop me. I was glad my parents didn't clap like those Sisters did. They grumbled instead. Father complained about my undue stubbornness and how ungrateful I was despite them taking me back in.

My room was left much as it was, to my parent's credit. My bed with its austere but no less pricey structure rested against the timber wall with its sheets faded. There was an armoire filled with feminine and modest clothing that no longer fit me.

There was a dresser to my left when I entered. For a time, I entertained more traditional ideas of womanhood. I tried new hairstyles, embellished my skin with copious powder, made my young lips pop with gawdy red, and then complained about the crookedness of my buck teeth. It was the closest I had ever been with my mother and the only time we could connect on anything. That was a long time ago.

I looked onto the faded wood of my dresser and thought of how it looked far smaller than I remembered; it seemed just as decrepit as I did.

It took only a few more hours until Jeremiah arrived home, his return announced due to Mother and Father's booming elation which crept up as muffled sounds from below. I tensed, thinking about how my little brother who I hadn't seen in years was just downstairs.

It wasn't long until the sound of heavy, limping steps drew closer and up to the second floor. The owner of that gait now stood opposite my door, I could hear the clunking of a cane as clear as day.

There was a pause, a hesitation on the other side. I held my breath. The knock finally came.

"Come in," I called out. The word was held ready ever since I heard my brother enter the house, and yet still it sounded cracked.

The door opened slowly, the hinges creaking. I saw my not-so-little brother on the other side with affectionate yet sombre eyes. "Hello, Nora," he said.

Jeremiah was still a large set individual, but his growth spurt had given him a sudden boost I would never have expected. Easily standing as tall as the tallest man or shortest akar, he entered my room clad in the black robes of the Witness church and with a stole sash draped around his neck.

His own brown curls had only become more prominent over the years as well as his portly chins.

Jeremiah was larger and more rotund in every way, but the air about him did not hold that same lack of confidence. Everything about him was larger; his height, his posterior, and even his presence. His eyes still held that blue gentleness they always had—small tiny beads set deep within an overly round face.

I looked at his large hands adorned with rings and found his cane head to be garishly fitted with a peering blue gem within a silver egg to give the impression of an eye.

When I finally broke out of my initial shock, I finally found words to speak. "Talk about a growth spurt."

Jeremiah gave a deep, throaty chuckle, even his laugh seemed weighed down compared to his previously exuberant self. "I suppose it has been some time since we saw each other."

I barely recognized him except for his eyes and familiarly freckled cheeks and bone structure. The man before me took a seat from the corner of the room and brought it to the foot of my bed.

"How are you?" he asked.

"I'm tired of answering that question," I admitted.

Jeremiah scoffed and used the cane to tap against his bad leg. "I know what that's like."

I looked him up and down closely. "Jeremiah, what is all this?" I asked.

"Well, I ended up going through the church program and am now an official Watcher."

I blinked, not sure how to respond. "Congratulations," I said meekly. "Since when?"

"Closing in on a year."

I couldn't keep playing along, not with Jeremiah. I shook my head.

"I'm sorry." I bit my lip as if to seal the rest of the words wishing to be spoken.

"For what?" Jeremiah frowned.

"A Watcher? Really? I thought you didn't buy into this whole cult nonsense."

Jeremiah's sudden growth gave him an imposing presence as I felt the man tense at the claim.

"Things have changed," he offered, hoping that I would take the hint and let it be.

"Jeremiah, did you forget how horribly our parents treated us? How abusive they were? Why did you go along with this drivel?"

"Nora, stop this." His hands clenched about the head of his cane.

"It is a cult!"

Jeremiah closed the distance with such speed, one would doubt his disability. His hand struck along my cheek, the weight of those rings banging metal into my thinning flesh and sending me into the wanting comfort of my bed.

I turned, cheek hot red and for a moment, I reached with my missing arm to caress it.

His finger pointed threateningly at me, his pale cheeks turned a furious red and his previously loving eyes now filled with warning.

"Heed my words, Nora. *You* are the one who left this family. I had no other choice than to be the good son my parents wanted me to be. And guess what? I am *good* at it. I finally found my purpose and I bring joy to believers so don't you dare try and lecture me, don't try and take *this* away from me. You have no right after abandoning me here."

"I told you to come with me!" I protested, suddenly feeling incredibly helpless.

"And do what? Leave my parents all by themselves?"

"Yes!"

"I was but a child!" Jeremiah boomed and turned away from me. "Mother and Father were right about you." The words stung deeper than anything else he could have said.

"Look at you, Nora. Look at where your independence got you. This *is* your penance for trying to escape your faith."

"Says who? Father?"

"Me!" Jeremiah thundered the declaration from within the belly of his swollen conviction.

I was afraid. For the first time in my entire existence, Jeremiah frightened me. I saw Father's wrath in that expression of his, except this was much, much worse.

And all at once Jeremiah stilled the tempestuous churning of his storm and returned to his former decorum. In one swift movement, which again made me completely forget about his lamed leg, Jeremiah lowered himself beside my bed and helped me back up into a seated position.

"But it's not over yet, Nora. This is a sign, a sign from our faith that you have a chance at redemption, to return to our fold and be remembered forevermore."

I looked into those eyes and realised that it wasn't compassion I saw, but rather an icy coldness like frosted rime. I should have taken him with me when I had the chance.

⋖ ⋗

My days confined within the room were spent getting used to this new form I took. Contact with the outside world became limited, a fact that became evermore apparent as I never even left the house. This time of self-reflection allowed a chrysalis from my doubts and fears—I felt exposed and needed to find a way that I could move forward.

I practised walking, and started to feel empowered as moving around the room became easier and easier. Jeremiah, whenever he was home, proved to be a caring and compassionate brother, yet I watched him dubiously. He would share his own journey with his leg and talk about how regularly he had to massage the tense knots that built up and how some days were better than others.

On all accounts, he proved himself reliable and forthcoming, massaging my own spasming side and helping me get used to balancing on my one foot.

Other things I had to learn on my own; like how to defecate cleanly into a bucket which would then be disposed of by Mother or Father. I insisted that it was something I could do by myself but they refused to let me step a foot outside, not for my sake but rather because of what rumours would spread amongst the people.

Jeremiah was right. The pain was worse on some days than others. No matter how much I prided myself in willpower, it didn't matter if the pain caused my body to lock itself stiff.

Father reluctantly tried to help me move to the bucket.

"Come now, Nora!" Jeremiah wasn't there so Father lifted me. Much of my weight had withered and my form was that of a lanky reed. Yet still, being bunched up into a ball made Father's task toilsome.

"Oh please, Nora! Stop this act!"

"I'm not acting," I managed through gritted teeth. The stiffness of my claim was born out of shame, out of pain, out of a reluctance to admit that I was reduced to a creature who needed help simply to defecate. This sense of utter helplessness, to have to rely wholly on someone as caustic as Father was all I could bare.

It proved too much—Father managed no more than two steps before tripping.

"My back!" He wailed, keeling over with the back of his hand to the small of his back. I was sent banging to the floor. The pain I was already subjected to made me barely feel the fall.

"Nora! This is unbefitting! Stop pretending and get a hold of yourself."

No matter how much I strained, my locked limbs refused to obey. Even my jaw was shut in place from pain and anger, leaving me without a response.

"Fine! Have it your way! Defecate all over the floor where you lie! But you are cleaning it up yourself."

With a temper, Father left me in my room and shut the door behind him. I could barely strain my neck enough to see the distorted edge of the bucket just out of reach.

Just stand, I told myself. It didn't matter; my body refused to obey. I did just as Father wished, the pain and mental toll I took on made me defecate in my gown as I was curled up on the cold, wooden floor. I did not know how long I was subjected to that foetid stench, how long I lay there in my own filth until Jeremiah came home to help.

⊰ ⊱

My reluctant but unavoidable reliance on my family proved incredibly disempowering and conflicting.

I spent years proving to them and myself that I didn't need them, that shallow desire was what drove me to such excellence. It was that harshly self-critical image of myself that constantly made me strive for more and more, as if they were right on my heels, waiting for me to fail. All of a sudden, I had no way to contradict them, to prove them wrong. The reason I had become so furtive, so obeisant, was because I could no longer prove my point in action; even my family's ludicrous claim that my predicament was the act of some higher being was something I could no longer argue. Defying them would mean being thrown onto the streets.

So when they told me I couldn't leave the house I nodded and complied, when my belongings from Cleria were delivered they confiscated my savings and burnt anything that was deemed sinful.

When they discovered the Kaseluda which I smuggled in from the Sisterhood, I was denied food for three days which made my warrior's form wither further within my reflection.

But worse than even denying me nourishment was being cut off from human contact as their uncompromising force locked me in my room. I was left with one terrifying and irrefutable truth: I was entirely at their mercy.

If one were to keep peeling away the layers of a person's sense of self, make them desperate, reduce them to nothing more than an animal, the value of their pride also plummets. I was supposed to be Simurgh, The Undying Flame, The Immortal Bird of Twilight—I didn't feel that way as I wept until my throat grew hoarse and pained, knuckles pounding against the locked doors as I crawled my way to it.

The knotted tangles of nerves on my side flared, and I felt the ethereal and invisible flame continue to lick me with barbed tongue, especially so in my sleep—a realm that I often escaped to for release but even there my moments of respite were scarce and short.

Time.

I had no idea how much time there was in a day. Just a few months ago, I would curse at how quickly the day passed, now I thought it maddening how slowly it went by. Given very little to occupy myself, I scoured for anything that would make the days go by quicker.

The dust covered dresser that I hadn't used in so long now seemed like apt company as I hopped my way to it with two quick strides of my crutch and sat on the low dresser.

As I looked at the truly piteous display of items that gathered dust on my counter, I once again had a moment of brief lucidity through a fog-covered lens. I vaguely noted how broken I had become, but was too tired and hungry to care at all.

Testament to how long these items had gone untouched, I struggled to open the lid of a flat and round container. It was clamped tight, and without another hand to hold it steady, my fingers simply shook at the strain. I slammed it against the table until the lid cracked and came off on its own.

What had been an applicable layer of lip-colouring now was dry and cracked, whatever saturation it once held faded to grey. I sniffed it, then placed it back on the table to try and poke at its arid surface—all I got was ashen powder covering my finger. I smeared it on my gown.

I found my reflection for a brief moment and thought at first a stranger looked back at me—I was ready to weep if it weren't for all the tears I already shed screaming at the door.

The woman who stared at me was someone I barely recognized.

Her cheeks prominent from wilting fat with grey and disparaging rings fitted around lifeless eyes. Her brunette hair was a matted mess of clumped strands. A great ugly mesh of burnt skin climbing its way up her neck like pink vines wishing to strangle her. I was a withered husk, half way into my grave.

I took that old forgotten brush from the desk and decided to comb this sorrowful girl's hair. Tugging and pulling at her scalp, I tried to free the matted strands. I had to try hard not to keel over with every pull. Like pulled weeds the brush groomed my despoiled self, thick tangles forming a ball within the bristles.

I looked down at the brush and rolled its handle upon my palm. There was a certain unbearable torture to boredom, a thing people tried to escape. Even then in my half-lucid version of reality, that blaring instinct kindled within. Memories flashed, a momentary escape, a bare flicker for something that I recognized and humoured.

Another form of escape presented itself that blossomed like a newly kindled forge. A heat spread between my loins, and I suddenly longed for a sensation I hadn't even considered since the accident, since Rafik. I bit my tongue and felt my lust flare ever so slightly remembering that accursed night.

My primitive side wished for such a passionate night again, but I drowned that desire. Rafik was a conspirator in my ruination.

Regardless, I tossed the brush to my bed and hopped to it. I was surprised to find an eager, and even lively, step to my stride. I felt myself becoming enslaved to that growing desire, an offered distraction to save me from my dour self.

A strange and shaming thought occurred to me. Was I allowed to pleasure myself?

After all that happened, after the ruin that befell me, was I ever to be an object of desire again with my broken self and scarred body? I didn't take the time to entertain such dark thoughts and willingly lowered myself into my pooling lust.

The past month of insecurity and uncertainty had turned the experience into a wild and turbulent affair. So much tension had built itself into my flesh and bones, so much tension that distended my body and wished for an out.

I had fostered intimate relationships with emotions I never had given much attention to: shame, regret, envy, pity; the constant flux of these experiences now melded into a single virulent pot of motley colours as I found myself falling deeper and deeper into longing.

I was already loosely clad as I doffed just the underwear which girdled my one leg.

My loins radiated a heat unlike the one that quailed my body—it was comforting; primordial in a sense. I wielded the handle of my brush and guided it towards the source of the heat, stoking the flames. I was there, I was still present. Banished were the phantom limbs that haunted me, I felt the remaining bone and muscle in my stumps writhe out of pleasure, the stoked flames fueling barren limbs.

I braced against the coming sensation. Quivering and relishing every moment of it as an escape from the reality of my life. The days were a stagnant river having turned murky, but that singular moment swelled and stretched itself into the kindle that brought me out of lethargic stupor, even if just for a moment.

Life flooded within me, a liveliness that granted my flicking wrist even more enthusiasm. The heat, the stark sensation blossomed from between my legs and spread outwards, enveloping me. It was like a drop of ink in water.

My body bucked and reeled, my leg contracting, a tenseness running through my arm. My stumps flexed and clamped down on nothing. This was mine, this one moment left to me was still mine. To pleasure myself, to be in control of my own budding climax. There were still things I could do by myself.

I felt the flooding warmth encase me, felt the built tension and turgid emotions seep out from my pores, felt it in my sweat. My hand took on a life of its own, my body arching as the crest neared.

When my orgasm blossomed, it did so as an explosion, a rising tide that hammered against my inner walls.

It was a private moment, spent with myself in a body that was still wholly my own. I still had a body, a thought I didn't quite consider yet. A body that could feel pain, pleasure, comfort—one that could still achieve glorious release. It was empowering to have such clarity as I lay panting, my eyes glued to the spotless ceiling, however fleeting that clarity may have been.

As I lay there, sweating and hot, panting at the sudden release, I smiled. It wasn't over, I would find a way out. My gaze fell to the door which entrapped me as I slowly started to consider my options.

❦

When finally the door was opened and Jeremiah came to me loving and concerned, I played along. In truth, I was love starved, so pretending to be indebted and dependent on them wasn't so difficult. I reminded myself that this wasn't who I was, as I wept onto his stole and he patted my back. For some reason, it was easier to believe this time around.

Rumours had spread like an infection through the town and presents were brought by the handful to my parent's doorstep with well wishes. Father complained and grumbled about the townsfolk's pity and how the entire household was being looked down on.

Mother, on the other hand, kept opening up gifts to reveal steaming pies and even one bag containing a generous fistful of sugar.

"Sugar?" Father repeated incredulously as his moustache crinkled with distaste. "I bet you it is the Horandaise family! I tell you! That man thinks himself better than the rest of us. Just because his company manufactures a great portion of carriages sold to the wealthy. Pah! He is an instrument to their despotism."

Mother seemed to not have heard anything that Father was saying as she greedily unpacked one gift after another to feed her insatiable excitement. She gasped at the next round of presents and her smile filled her full cheeks and had her eyes recede underneath her brows and fat. "Frank! Look!" She revealed the gift which was a gold item made into the likeness of a scale except holding one bronze and one silver egg on each end of its hooks. "Salt and pepper shakers!"

I watched from the side, sitting at the dining table at the far end of the room with convincingly defeated eyes. I was biding my time, observing, eating greater portions of food and privately training in my room.

More so than the weight of my body and stagnant weeks, it was the faltering of my will which proved difficult to regather. As eye-opening as my private moment was, the sort of motivation it awoke faded all too soon until only its hollow shape was left. Regardless, bit by bit I reclaimed my strength. I would not allow for my family, nor myself to drag me down.

"That reminds me! Nora!" Mother turned towards me with pure excitement in her eyes.

I smiled meekly at her.

"I've got something for you!" Mother proceeded to jump up, another one of her plump dresses billowing with every skip as she went to a corner and withdrew a hidden box. I had to admit, my curiosity peaked.

Mother opened it and withdrew a modest dress. It was a very dark blue which at first sight could have been mistaken for black. It had a buttoned up collar with three buttons blending into the fabric, the collar itself smooth and round edges and its sleeves long with frills at the end. The skirt was puffy and large but not to the extent of mother's pleated attire. For all intents and purposes, the offered dress seemed rather nice.

"Try it on!"

I groaned inwardly and smiled outward. I stood, and with some practised ease hopped my way over to her where I took the dress.

Something seemed off.

"What is this?" I frowned.

"Go and try it!" She suppressed a giggle; pure excitement in her voice.

⊰ ⊱

I sometimes wondered if my parents plotted ways to disempower me: this was one of those times. I hopped out of the kitchen where I had gotten changed. The only witness to my change were the religious eyes of Oxular on the walls.

When I returned, mother was practically clapping and giving out a high pitched squeal. "I love it!" She exclaimed.

"Yes, you look positively lovely," Father affirmed.

What was hidden from me was the fact that I was forced into a dress with a custom filled sleeve and fake hand fitted at the end of it. It served to give the momentary illusion that I still had both arms.

"It does look better, but do you think you could do away with the crutch?" Father asked me as his hand cupped his chin contemplatively.

I was speechless; mother took that to mean that I loved it.

"I know! Isn't it wonderful?"

I forced a smile, realising that this would be far harder than I first thought. "Yes, it is," I lied.

"Oh good! We bought several more for you." She revealed the boundless dresses stacked in her arm. "Let's go and try them all on!"

I held back a sigh and did as I was told. "Of course, Mother."

Chapter Fifty-Two

CHROMA

Why did the akar come to us? Records show that when pressed, the
akar spoke of some sort of conflict within their ranks. But it's not so
simple. These are warriors. What kind of madness could have possessed
them to seek refuge with the enemy? We suspect that they remained
tight-lipped on this matter.

—THE AKAR REFUGEE PROBLEM, A SUMMARY REPORT FOR
COMMANDER ORSON

As I returned from my day's work at the construction site, I found Nedalya waiting for me.

"Hello, Chroma. Can we talk?" Her approach was amiable, though her smile told me she harboured something I needed to prepare for.

I hesitated for a moment, pretending as if my heart did not beat with longing.

"Sure," I said casually, offering a friendly smile.

Nedalya and I walked the outer perimeter of the settlement. A few other akar also stretched their legs and trained. Running laps or simply loitering in private huddles or sparring.

We remained silent for quite some time. There was the occasional sound of hesitant breathing never fully forming like a stillbirth.

"How are things for you?" Nedalya asked. "I heard you became close to that Nephilim. Erefiel, right?"

I nodded. "He is a good man, means well."

Nedalya scoffed. "I mean, surely there must be something in it for him. I don't believe that anyone outside these walls truly cares for our people, even less so the son of White-Hawk."

I was about to defend Erefiel, when I remembered what he had planned for me, what he planned for all the akar living here.

I just shrugged. "Perhaps give him a chance. He might surprise you."

Nedalya gave me a curious smile. "Perhaps you are right."

"What did you want to talk about?" I asked, fully contemplating all the things that still went unspoken between us. Like the fact that though my desire for Nedalya had waned, it was never truly expunged. Or perhaps the fact that her lover seemed to still hold contempt for me.

"We are meeting later today, wanted to ask if you'd join."

I floundered. "Sorry, I have things to do, still really busy."

Nedalya sighed. "It's about Kolotha, isn't it?" There was even a hint of guilt in Nedalya's voice.

I looked away, feeling silly that I thought we could avoid the topic. My only affirmation was a reluctant nod.

"That is actually what I wanted to talk to you about."

Nedalya had my attention. The two of us took a seat at a protruding plateau of earth and looked out towards the stagnant noon. The clouds parted up above and in the distance, the hooded cluster of Dreamwood had the canopy sway with passing gusts of wind; it carried the scent of mature earth to us.

I started off the conversation. "I thought Kolotha was upset because of all the changes that are happening. Or because I sided with a human."

Nedalya almost chuckled, her bulky frame seemingly out of place as she picked a blade of grass. A passing wind made the decorative bones in her hair rattle like bamboo chimes.

"In truth, he would have acted exactly as you did. He wouldn't admit it, but he actually supports the changes here. They all do. What Trem and the others said wasn't them agreeing with Kolotha. They wanted to diffuse the situation."

"What do you think?" I asked.

She shrugged. "Making us learn to sow and cook and mend rather than fight is humiliating…but it is also true that our settlement has prospered more than ever before. I mean, look at us! We are sitting casually outside with no fear of being beheaded. It may only be a few steps away from the walls, but it makes a world of a difference." Nedalya breathed in life, breathed in the summer air that spiralled all about us.

I was thankful, thankful to hear that I hadn't just made things worse. A weight lifted itself from my shoulders I didn't even know was there.

"So why is Kolotha upset?" I asked cautiously.

Nedalya wet her lips, the soft protrusion of tusks showing their tips.

"Remember when you saved those children?"

I nodded.

"What did our people chant when you returned?"

"Baatar," I said.

Now she nodded. "Kolotha is envious, and that envy festered. He convinced himself that the true reason for his contempt is because you sided with a human. In truth, it is because of the fact that you gained the title of Warrior before him." She fiddled for a moment, looking almost ashamed. "I think we were all a little envious. But him more so."

"Why?" I asked.

She scoffed. "You really have to ask me that? He is the son of Nokna, there is a lot of expectation that comes with that." Nedalya considered her next words. "Imagine you are the son of a great akar, your father a man of great power and reputation."

"You mean like Muktow?"

Nedalya looked at me and nodded. "But imagine that your father is actually here, a man that everyone looks up to. Reliable and strong. People come to you and tell you how they expect great things because you also grow formidable with the body of a true warrior."

I nodded, following thus far.

"Now imagine what happens when another steps in and takes the title of Baatar before you."

I grasped Nedalya's implication. "Especially when that person is the weakest in the tribe."

Nedalya averted her gaze. "I didn't say that."

"It's okay. It's true. Back then, I was so full of doubt, seeing all of you outgrow me. I felt like something was wrong with me…" the next words were caught in my throat. "It was the reason I ran out on you—" Nedalya's hand on my arm gave me pause. I looked up to find solace in understanding eyes.

"I know. I knew back then, too. I'm sorry. We were both hurt," she said. We left it at that.

"You think you are lesser than us for some reason, lesser than me, Kolotha, Trem, and Siemeny. I don't understand why. None of us have memories of the outside world, yet you managed to see more of it than any of us. The changes you brought to the settlement… Kolotha tried to accept it and be supportive, but it just ate away at him. Made it harder over the years. But as you also grew and your recognition grew to challenge even that of Kolotha's father. Well, he didn't take it so well."

I entertained the idea of Erefiel's project; if it all went well, then perhaps Kolotha would still earn that title.

"It took me a while to get that information out of him. I had to put together bits and pieces—Kolotha is not exactly the talkative type."

"Well, thank you for telling me. I hope it hasn't affected the two of you."

Nedalya went silent. "Actually, Kolotha and I have parted ways." The words, the way they were spoken felt like it made my heart blossom with white pain and pleasure. The callouses I built were chipped away and fell like a loose stone into sea.

"What?" I asked, looking at the woman, equal measures of disbelief and hope. My heart pounded.

"Chroma. Please don't look at me like that."

I flushed and looked away.

"Kolotha was great at the beginning. But before your fight, he tried to use me to hurt you." She shook her head. "I couldn't accept that. Things ended soon after."

"Why didn't you tell me?"

She chuckled. "When? You never spend time with us anymore."

I bowed my head. "I suppose that's true."

Nedalya sighed and continued. "I think I am done for now with all this passion. I wish to spend some time by myself, discover the kind of person I am." She turned to me with a smile I hadn't seen in years, a smile that reminded me of that young akar I loved. It made my heart melt. "We can't all be like Chroma." And with that, she departed.

⋞ ⋟

Four nights later and four copper richer, I returned to the settlement atop a trundling wagon when only a sliver of sunlight was left. I indulged in some dried jerky I had stowed for a special day.

Trem had been keeping me company at the construction site that day, filling the time with groans and complaints about Siemeny's incessant needs. Part of the reason he had come to work on the defences was because it was the only way to get some distance.

Though I felt it was better to have someone to complain about than to have no one at all.

I roamed through the entrance, finding the guards were staring with an unreadable intensity. It was only when I approached home that I knew why—Jasper was back.

He wasn't wearing his guard uniform, or any uniform for that matter, just a simple faded tunic and brown trousers with a vest. He was in some form of argument with Mother.

"What is going on?" I asked. Jasper turned to find me looming when I noticed the odorous stench of alcohol radiate from him and heard the familiar slosh of a bottle in hand.

"O'... good... if 't isn' th' golden boy himfelf. Come! Come 'ere!" His speech was slurred as he stumbled, a limp hand waving me closer.

"Jasper, it would be best you leave."

"Why? I am jus' like one o' you now!" he proclaimed with a drunken smile, his torso swaying back and forth as if balancing on stilts.

"You are not welcome here."

Jasper seemed wounded at my claim and simply hung his head with a weak nod. "Fin'! I just wanna know why your mothe' betrayed me. Dat's all!" He found that same blithe smile on his lips again.

"I was never yours to betray," mother stated, her posture unbending.

"I dreated you well!"

"Jasper, you need to leave." I went to grab his arm, but he pulled away, almost falling over.

"Oh, the grea' Chroma. Always there to loo' after your whore mo-tha." The man barely even reached to my chest as he stumbled towards me. His lips peeled back into a vile sneer. "Think youself so amazin', so love' by all: a strong and prou' akar."

"You will never be worthy of my mother." Ire boiled within me, but my words were like a cold fire. Jasper hurled his drunken insult, his eyes showing the depths of drowned loathing.

He chuckled manically. "Worthy?" he emphasised. "Le' me tell you about *worthy*."

"Jasper, stop it." Mother pleaded harshly, carefully stepping forward, but something made her hold caution.

"You think your mother so great, so pure, well I fucked her lustful pussy every day, and she *love*' it."

The bones in my hand pained with how tightly they formed a fist. My jaw locked tight out of fear that I'd bite and rend given the chance.

"What will you do?" he asked. "Strik' down you' own father?"

I froze. Shock stunned me. The word bounced around my skull and tried to slot itself into some version of reality that I could understand. "What did you just say?"

"Jasper!" Mother cried and stepped forward, her own fists bulging and ready to silence the man. Yet the drunk Jasper stumbled back, braced by an erect wooden beam where he drunk himself another swig and eyed me with such frenzy that I found it contagious. I felt my world melt, the sludge of colours draining through gutters at my feet until only violent red remained.

"Dat's right! I'm your papa! Son of a human. Thought yourself so grea', huh? Born to the legendar' Muktow after all!"

I looked at mother, but it was the bottomless shame in her eyes that told me it was true—she couldn't even look at me.

"Come to me, my son! Give me a hug!"

I did as was asked and stepped towards him.

"So, fuckin' gre—" I silenced the man with a quick break of his neck.

Despite the tumultuous rage that claimed me, the act was cold. I had not even a drop of emotion when I took the man's life. The world was a lie, the foundations of it all revealed to be rotten as everything came crumbling down.

I looked at my mother, her eyes streaking tears. She was speechless, her lips parting, but all that came was a croak.

I heard first my people step out from their yurts, their eyes unreadable as they went from Jasper's limp body and twisted neck to my stance. Kolotha appeared from the clusters, his dark appearance unreadable as he simply watched.

Next came the rushing steps of guards who found me standing over the body of one of their own.

Chapter Fifty-Three

DALILA

If the Haar can be used to make a chair or a volley of arrows or a house, why not use it to create a wall which spans Greyhill? Only the Elders possess the knowledge for such grand architecture. The one time mistmages attempted such a feat, the wall grew mouths to swallow its guards.

—LIMITATIONS OF THE HAAR, BY GURICK ZILIEN

As my friendship with Yasmin flourished, I allowed her to become my voice of reason when it came to self-indulgence. There was much about her that I came to cherish, my only regret being that I hadn't given her the chance sooner.

I learnt that I had undervalued her, thinking her simple and impressionable when it came to matters that did not fit her rose-tinted view, but I couldn't have been more wrong.

The weeks that I got to know her showed that it was I who wallowed in dour sentimentality and pessimism. Yasmin was still a bright-eyed romantic, hopeful that all things would go well, but not because of some immature fancy. She needed that optimism or what was the point of it all? Despite being rejected by her family, despite everything, she still smiled.

So during one of our breaks where we were excused from the Sisterhood, she convinced me to join her at a theatre performance within the city. The amphitheatre was just outside the town square and evidently not too far off from the pious portion of the city.

The performers were from Museya, a city I still did not have the fortune of seeing for myself. I heard it was truly a testament towards artistry. It was said that they knew of a truth that could not be expressed academically, but rather through poetry, dance, song and all other performing arts.

Yet the price to partake in such a spectacle was a small fortune, for performer and audience alike.

Thus, those with a more humble budget wishing to make a name for themselves would partake within Cleria, and the Clerian people would bury their prejudices of Museya for more affordable entertainment. Even many of Museya's own citizens travelled to Cleria to escape the steep costs.

Yasmin had decided to invite me, insisting that I didn't need to pay.

The play was titled "The Futile Resistance of Mellezi." It was their third showing, and Yasmin had already barraged me with how spectacular the show was said to be.

I worked my way through one of the pamphlets which was stuck on every post, tree and corner where traffic flowed. The pamphlet showed a rendition of a decrepit and desolate land on one side and green on the other, showing the transition from proliferation to destruction. At the very centre, there was a winding flight of steps carved out of a grand castle with a great throne at its peak and a skeletal king with a crooked crown at the top. At the very base, there climbed a clueless and intrepid young man; I assumed the figure was Mellezi.

I was intrigued, not just by the concept of the tragedy itself, but also by the tangible excitement radiating from Yasmin. She was somehow drawn towards something which uncompromisingly promised despair. This truth was made even more apparent upon seeing the deluge of heads in a sea of people that came to watch this play themselves.

Despite the promise that this story would not have a happy end, people still came wide-eyed and excited. Was it a morbid sense of curiosity? A fascination for the disparaged and the hopeless?

I would make a bet with myself that none present would ever wish such unfathomable tragedy for anyone, yet wanted to entertain the concept through theatre.

The play began in most typical fashion as our Mellezi stepped onto the stage to address his father, the king.

The king dismissed the young prince's concerns and said that the crops would return in earnest at the next season. They did not.

Again the boy returned, and the father assured a second time that surely the crops would grow the season after. They did not.

Eventually, the kingdom fell into destitution, and the king's people were dying.

Famine stretched along the lands and the depression of this make-believe world trickled down onto the audience, causing a sombre and sympathetic silence.

The bard approached the stage, lute playing softly and adding melancholic irony to the progress of the play. All of it will fall and nothing will be saved.

I looked at the bard and felt my immersion break under its weight.

"I know the bard," I said loud enough for Yasmin to hear.

"You do?" she queried incredulously, herself yanked out of that realm with me as she craned her neck to see.

It was an uncomfortable and grating feeling at first, but my doubts were put to rest the moment Dale stepped to the front and sung his soliloquy. His character was supposed to be a court musician to the king, forced to watch in acceptance as the world shattered all around them.

"He's cute." Yasmin blurted out almost teasingly as I looked at her and she gave me suggestively fluttering eyes.

I felt myself blush and decided it best to not indulge her. "Just watch the play," I said instead, as we turned our attention back to the stage.

Eventually, the King died, still convinced in the fifth year that the world would return to normal.

Thus, Mellezi climbed to the top, becoming king and fighting against the plague with his own efforts.

There it was, the glimmer of hope, denied from us the audience so that when offered, we took it hungrily and unquestioningly.

"Perhaps there is a happy end," we convinced ourselves. "Perhaps it does show that a good king brings progress."

The land started to bear crops, and the people began to prosper again as the king's own coffers grew.

How easy it proved to crush the audience's hopes as again we were reminded of the title of the play: "The Futile Resistance of Mellezi."

In a sudden twist, the Wanderers came, horrific beings of yore. During the early times when the mists were still strangling the few lands that the Elder King ruled, the Wanderers were among the entities that were present from the start.

Legend had it that they were ten at first, but then there were three. Obelisk-like, hairless and thin creatures, three times taller than an average man, wearing long, dark, transcendental robes which covered them from neck to feet and dragged behind them to create streaks of withered life as they wandered without discernible purpose. Three long and deathly fingers on each pallid hand. Ovate and hairless heads the colour of grey stone and no face on their ominous forms.

This was the version told by the people, but upon that stage, they were the size of regular men and their faces were hidden behind black veils.

The king begged, pleaded with the mighty powers as the Wanderers travelled patiently and wordlessly through the land; one in front as the trailing two stood on either side.

Here came the horrified gasps of the audience as the people turned against each other. The pitchforks previously held to protect their neighbours suddenly became the instrument of their demise as they tore each other apart. The carnage was mindless, passionless; the Wanderers did not pause, did not flinch at all as they continued on.

So, too, did they reach the castle walls. The gates raised by those robbed of their own will and a river of red paved the way to the king's throne room.

Soon enough, Dale stepped forward and gave his final soliloquy; the kingdom fell into ruin. The resistance of Mellezi was futile as the end of his home was fated. But there was more. Eventually, as the King had said, the crops did return, the land healed, and new people came to take over.

The curtains closed and the audience burst into explosive ovation.

The curtains opened at the end for the cast to bathe in our praise, which was when eventually Dale caught my eye within the audience and suppressed a smirk.

⋖ ⋗

After the play, when most of the audience departed, Dale approached me and Yasmin.

"That was quite a show," I commended.

He bowed humbly, seemingly pleased to see me.

"It was fantastic!" Yasmin cheered, still wiping the tears from her eyes. "So tragic! To try and be a good king for his people and for it all to just come toppling down."

I chuckled. "Dale, this is Mother Yasmin. Also from the Sister-hood."

"Pleasure to meet you." Dale curtsied. "I'm really happy you were here! I hope you enjoyed it."

"Yes, it was very tragic. At least it ended on a hopeful note."

"You think so too?" He pressed, his eyes coming to life with inten-sity. He took a step towards me.

I nodded, suddenly taken aback at his energy.

"I think so too!" Yasmin agreed.

"Oh, thank my days! The others were adamant that they wanted this whole thing to end with the Wanderers and, on a dreary note. I don't blame them. It is tempting to be overly dramatic about tragedies, but one can be overly dramatic. Don't you think?" His grin overflowed with excitement as he prompted for our opinion.

"Completely agree," Yasmin affirmed. I wasn't even sure if she understood the question.

"I don't know; I see the other side of things. Things in life don't always play out well nor have a hopeful end."

"Yes, but don't you think that it is important to look optimistically towards the future? No matter how dark the present might be?" Dale objected.

I wanted to say that Perry never had that option, never got a chance to look to a brighter future. I wanted to mention Nora, about how bleak and dark she viewed her remaining life.

Yasmin saved me from making a choice as she chimed in. "Do you think I could take a look at the set?"

Dale shot up at the prospect. "Of course! I could also introduce you to the cast."

And just like that, the illusion of brighter days was shattered with a shrill scream from behind the stage. The moment of silence was gone in an instant as curious murmurs spread among the few still present and people huddled worryingly amongst themselves.

Dale and I ran towards the theatre, both for reasons of our own.

"Dalila! Where are you going?" Yasmin called from behind me.

"Control the masses and lead everyone out. See if you can get the guard!" I called back, not waiting to see if she followed through on my command.

Running through and into the shaded backstage full of props and other devices, I let Dale take the lead.

Dale ran towards the back stage. There was a huddled cluster of the cast blocking off a room. Upon the floor, there sat a young woman, her hands trembling uncontrollably and tears of her ruined makeup running down.

"Sharon, what happened?" Dale asked, but she didn't answer.

Another man from the cast tapped Dale's shoulder and regretfully pointed him towards the source of dismay.

"Step aside, please. I am a Sister and can help." Almost instantly, the people parted, but I knew upon seeing the bodies there was nothing I could have done.

Inside, there were three clad in the same black robes of the Wanderers from before. Now their faces were revealed to show warped expressions frozen in horror. Lifeless gazes drifting about us on-lookers, as if we were the new audience for a different kind of performance.

The walls were splattered in great strokes of blood that came from the exsanguinated victims; wreathed shadow had made itself a home in hollowed sockets, while red tears trailed pallid cheeks. Weird and crude symbols were scribbled onto the surface of the chamber in a runic language I did not recognize.

They drifted gently in place, their bodies supine. The ends of their umbral robes rippled; they were tattered flags in the night sky.

Chapter Fifty-Four

NORA

One of the greatest honours given to a woman of the Witness church is to become a seer. They tend eternally to the house of Oxular and its catacombs at the cost of their eyes. The eyes are then taken and are preserved to prevent decay. For who requires eyes when Oxular becomes their guide?

—TEXT FROM THE MANAICHIA, THE WITNESS HOLY BOOK

On one hand, I found myself entirely loathing the life I was forced to return to, as Jeremiah's seldom but wholly present involvement added to my oppression and disempowerment. On the other hand, it was precisely the driving force I needed to escape this hell.

That was always my secret: fear. Fear of being that insignificant little girl, fear of being in fear. Fear of those more powerful than me.

Suddenly, being under the oppressive thumb of my family seemed a far more urgent concern than my crippled state. It compelled me to become familiar with my new body, and I used that terror as fuel.

The days passed quickly from one to the next as I trained with renewed fervour.

The pumping of my blood from withering muscle was truly intoxicating and gave me the energy I needed, as well as improving my mood altogether. It was strange to consider how much of a difference it made to have a goal.

Push-ups with a single hand proved impossible as my entire body weight leaned onto one side and trying to improvise didn't prove auspicious either.

However, I started to lean against the footrest of the bed with my arm and use my knee as a fulcrum to push my body away. The diagonal position of my push-ups compensated for my shortcomings. I also used a small stool to balance my right-leg stump, so I didn't tip over.

When my body got strong enough, I would advance towards using the chair of my dresser to lean in even lower until my knee ached and bruised.

With my hand braced on a table for balance, a wall to lean on and pure uncompromising will, did I manage pitiful squats with just the one trembling leg. The slow, deliberate motions felt as if they were going to snap my remaining foot from below me until the pumping acid burnt an intensity that contrasted that of my sides.

Mother was excited to see me wear clothes of her choosing, leading her to believe that I was coming around to their way of thinking. I indulged their fantasy, wearing makeup and acting with such decorum and humility befitting a proper lady. In reality, I found Mother's choice of clothing hid my noticeable growth and they didn't question my growing appetite, as it seemed like a sign of life and virility. They were even glad to see that my face was becoming fuller.

One night, as I left my room to stretch my leg in the hall, I happened to hear chatter on the other side of my parents' door.

"Who would want to marry her?" Father asked.

"She is still a sweet girl, and is finally beginning to see things our way."

"She is a cripple, my love. Her skin is ruined and burnt; who knows if she is even able to still bear children. Hell, I don't even know if she *can* copulate."

"Frank! No need to be crude!"

The rest of their discussion faded into silent mutterings, and that was fine by me—I didn't want to hear any more of their plans.

The concept of wedlock was never a concern of mine. I had never even spared much thought for love. My position in the Clerian army and the freedom it provided were all I had needed. On the rare occasion that I longed for sexual release, I would indulge in passionate and spontaneous nights. I never wanted anything more than that.

Returning to bed and tentatively massaging the short stump of my right leg, I lost myself in deep thoughts about my own future. My mind still reeled, but the fog had cleared enough so that I could contemplate such things.

No profession, of which I would like to commit myself or otherwise, would be accepting of my condition. I felt a sudden stark fear bud within me, but I repressed it immediately—I could not give into hopelessness.

Did I want a partner? To settle down? No—it would just be another way for someone to take care of me. To be indebted to someone. The complete and utter sense of vulnerability at having someone take care of me was something that I had never experienced before. To be entirely at the mercy of someone else, to not be able to enact my own will, had an unspoken and primal terror to it.

Yet I certainly couldn't return to the military, nor was it easy for me to commute.

Could I have worked as a holy person? Perhaps, but again, I found that I took an option not because I was fond of the idea, but rather because I was being cared for.

Deciding that delving deeper into such thoughts would simply leave me miserable, I instead faded into the comfort of sleep. As I lay in bed and stretched out to extinguish the still lit candle, I paused to notice the dried and faded bluebell flower.

I wondered for a moment how Dalila managed to overcome her own trials, to have her whole life upturned the way it was.

My thoughts went to when we last met and shame filled me with a spreading warmth; I grimaced at the memory.

⊰ ⊱

On most days, Father would leave for work and Mother would indulge herself at home; yet on that day, mother was excited and positively tripping over herself as she got ready for a tea party with the 'ladies'.

On account of the house being empty and myself having grown rather comfortable with my new method of walking, I decided to venture out in the fresh air after months of growing pale indoors. I wore one of the darkly coloured dresses mother had gotten me in another shade of very deep auburn red and slipped on an elegant flat.

Moving down the steps wasn't a sweaty and mind-fizzling ordeal, but it still took me a noticeable amount of concentration as I hopped down one step at a time.

After a few minutes, I repositioned my crutch and loosened my wrist, making my way out the door.

Most of my fortune was confiscated, assumedly never to be seen again, but I still saved a few coffers in my own personal belongings that hadn't been found. I found comfort at the weight of loose coins on me.

Being within the fierce season of autumn, a drab coldness swept through Basksin as droopy clouds swayed overhead.

I started to understand my mother's choice of colour for me as I traipsed through the streets. It was the dark shade that made my entire body blend in on itself, making the loss of my limbs even less apparent. The fake arm fitted onto my right was fully extended as I limped through the crowds.

No sooner was I out the door did murmurs follow me and eyes trail behind.

"Isn't that Nora?"

"Frank's daughter?"

"Poor Martha."

"First Jeremiah and now her? Oxular bless and acknowledge them."

I ignored the incessant voices which wove into one another and I knew for certain that Mother and Father would eventually hear about all this. I didn't let that stop me. In truth, I was ecstatic—being able to roam around as I did was something that I hadn't indulged since my injury, and I found that roaming around had become a lot easier.

Finding a bakery, I stood in line to buy myself a small loaf of bread. I wasn't hungry, nor did I crave anything in particular. But I had a certain longing for things which others considered entirely menial; such as being able to walk to a store and purchase something. I longed for that independence again.

The people in front insisted adamantly that I go ahead. I found myself confused. I gave a friendly smile and declined. This only made them more persistent. I had no doubt that my appearance prompted the act.

I yielded reluctantly. "Thank you." My smile was stiff.

I didn't just get a loaf. I was given an entire basket of food from the baker. He was an affable, moustached man with a round and kind face, and a comb-over tried to hide his receding hairline.

"I just want a loaf," I interjected.

"Please, just take it." The man pushed the items onto me.

My mood was souring. I accepted the offer.

Leaning against the shop counter I could feel the crowd grow uncomfortable, gazes avoiding me while restless feet shuffled. It took me under a minute, but still, the steps I took to procure my purse were far too long for everyone else.

I took the coins to recount them, feeling their weight and surface from within the stitched bag, and pulling out enough for the one loaf I wanted and a good quarter of the rest.

"No, please," the baker pushed out with his palm. "It's on me." His smile was practically beaming with pride. Agreeable murmurs swept through the crowded line.

"I insist," I imposed strongly, my extended fist holding the coins, my smile forced.

"Please, you need it more than I do."

A livid anger flared inside me that I bottled. I dropped the coins on the counter, threaded my arm under the basket handle and swiftly turned to leave.

I hopped as quickly as I could, feeling the basket swing at my elbow with each prompt stride.

Two men came to my side and offered to help.

"I don't need help!" I snapped.

The men froze, confused by my reaction.

They lingered behind, trailing my shadow and waiting for me to rightfully falter. It would have been easier to accept their help, to simply let them feel better about themselves so that they would leave me alone. But a greater, prouder, part of myself refused any help that I didn't need; I didn't spend weeks and months trying to get used to my new body just to stroke someone's ego.

As the weight of their gazes burnt into my back and I reached the end of my patience, I turned to them; two, three hops at a time.

"Why are you following me?"

The men blinked. "In case you fall o—."

I cut them off. "Why do you think I need help after I told you I am fine?"

The men stuttered, eyeing each other as their stares would occasionally drop to my obvious limitation. All three of us, all the people who started to watch this interaction unfold, knew exactly why the men offered their help, but nobody was comfortable to speak it out loud.

I hopped closer to them.

"Here is the truth: you want to help me because all you see is a cripple, someone miserable and in need of your gracious help. But let's be honest, you aren't helping me, you are helping yourself. This is just another way for you to feel good about yourselves in the eye of Oxular."

They were dumbstruck, not just because someone like me had the apparent gall to defy their act of kindness, but also because they probably were never reprimanded by any woman like that.

Their stares suddenly were glaring and dour as they turned to leave, muttering amongst themselves out of earshot.

I finally found a seat upon a bench when the crowd dispersed; it was like the parting of grey clouds. My mood lightened as I enjoyed the filled bean buns from the bakery.

The curious gazes of the folk diminished with time, yet they would give me pitying looks before passing on. At least I didn't have to worry about sharing the bench with anyone.

I did receive eventual company, not in the form of a person but rather a medium sized dog with a coat the colour of golden honey. It sat on its hind staring at me, its dangling tongue hungry for whatever was in my basket.

I smiled at the thing and after holding the bun between my teeth, I used my freed hand to pet the animal, working my way around to under its chin where the dog leaned back to lick my palm clean.

Leaning back and with my teeth holding the bun, I would tear small pieces to toss to the canine.

"I think she likes you."

I turned to find a little girl on her tiptoes leaning over the backrest of the bench.

"Her name is Dea. She's my dog," the girl said in light conversation.

Turning back around, I looked more closely at Dea, who still had her tongue sticking out, my offering already devoured.

"What's your name?" the girl asked.

I found myself suddenly caught off guard by the casualness of the conversation.

"What's yours?" I turned back to her.

The girl scowled and pouted—her lips in a thin line. "I asked first!" She protested.

I chuckled, pleasantly surprised that I found the moment uplifting. "Fine, I'm Nora."

"My name is Donna, but my friend's call me Don."

"Don?"

"Yeah, because I am always done with everything." She gave me a wide and ugly grimace where her gums peeled back to reveal still growing and crooked teeth.

I chuckled again, handing the girl one of my loaves. "Thank you!" she exclaimed happily and climbed onto the bench of her own accord.

Tearing a piece off, she handed it to Dea, who eagerly started to chew. Don giggled enthusiastically. She wore long length stockings and a puffy brown dress. Her gloves fitted to keep her hands warm and her hair braided into two pigtails.

The girl turned. "What happened to you?" she asked casually.

I was taken aback at her curtness, but happy that Don wasn't being overly cautious.

"An accident," I offered.

"What kind?"

It was strange opening up to Don, someone who didn't seem to pity or judge me, but was genuinely curious. "I was a soldier—"

"A soldier? Cool!" She cut in, all interest in my deformity gone. "What kind? Did you fight the akar?" she asked, leaning in closer and closer.

I smiled. "Hordes of them! I lead my own company, you know?" I indulged Don, whose eyes went wide with admiration and respect. In doing so, I found my own spirits rising at being able to relive my previous life.

"Are you still a soldier?"

I hung my head. "No… not anymore." My smile was sombre; wilting slowly.

"Why?"

"Because of my accident, I can no longer fight."

"Well, my mommy says that if there is something you *really* want and give it your best, then nothing is impossible." The girl's fist tightened and her eyes shut tight as she emphasised the point.

I smiled encouragingly. "You're right." Although inwardly, I wasn't so sure. I could only hope that whatever it was that this young girl wanted to do, she would achieve it, even if my own problem wasn't something easily overcome.

Don left with her dog. I took that chance to leave as well.

❦

Returning home, Mother and Father were unsurprisingly upset with my leaving the house without talking to them first. I tried my best to seem reprimanded without over playing my part. "But Father! I have been stuck inside for weeks! I needed to get out."

"The entire town is talking about you! Apparently begging for handouts because of your injury."

There was the slightest flare of anger; more so than the lie, it was the implied pity that irked me.

Mother had warmed up to me over the past few weeks as we bonded over more feminine interests; I gathered that she would do anything to not lose me again.

"Frank, perhaps it is best to not be so harsh on our daughter. She does need to go out after all, and the people already knew about her—keeping her a secret just made it seem like we had something to hide."

Mother's voice was coaxing as she stepped in front of Father, quelling his anger.

Jeremiah was standing at the back of the living room, watching our engagement unfold as a towering judicator. His gaze unnerved me; the boy I remembered as my younger and warm-hearted brother now had the look of a calculating predator about him.

"Perhaps this is a good thing," Jeremiah cut in.

"How so?" Father asked.

"Mother is right, the people know Nora is here. Hiding her just shows that we are ashamed. Are we ashamed of the fact that Oxular has returned the last piece of our family to us?"

Out of all the people present, Jeremiah was the youngest in the room. Yet for some reason, his direct involvement in the church held a powerful sway in the household that was capable of muzzling Father and Mother—naturally, I was pushed to the very end of the hierarchy.

"Of course not, son. But the people will talk—"

"Then let them. Their words mean little in the grand scheme of things. Oxular grants us his great eye so that we may be seen, what may be heard is of no consequence."

Father gave an affirming nod. "You are right, my son."

Jeremiah nodded back with a smile of his own. "Thank you, Father." The spoken title was hollow. The entire dynamic was surreal, Father's pretence at control merely a farce as it was truly Jeremiah who held dominance. I wondered if my father was even aware.

"So what do you suggest?" Mother asked, truly looking to Jeremiah for guidance.

"I suggest we take Nora with us to the church, show that she is part of this family, part of this community. Her presence is nothing to be ashamed of. It is a reminder that now we are whole, that Oxular has brought back my sister into the fold."

My smile was unbearably painful as I was backed into a corner; it felt like little thorny brambles sprung from my cheeks and pricked my lips into a contorted attempt at happiness.

I knew what was being implied, and I held no power to work my way out of this.

"I think that is a great idea," I lied.

⋞ ⋟

Mother and Father no longer tried to stop me from wandering around town. Every once in a while, I indulged the chance to experience the open air without feeling trapped. On one occasion, Mother kept me company and tried with such conviction to make me try on some new dresses. I assured her I was fine and instead wanted to simply roam around.

During our walk, she unloaded an entire flood of bottled up gossip over the years that she never got to mention to me.

"Do you remember the Bethannies?"

I did not.

"You were so young, but they always were so fond of you! Unfortunately, the family ended up losing their fortune and had to leave." The last part she whispered to me behind the cover of her hand, giggling at the tangy gossip.

"And do you remember Meredith? Such a sweet thing! Found herself a bit of fun outside of the town. However. with some lowly farm boy! Rumour has it that she became pregnant and her parents sent her away. Just don't say anything. Her family said that they sent her off to Museya to learn how to play instruments."

If there was one thing that I took away from mother's never-ending drivel, it was about the nature of wives gossiping. I was certain that in the same malicious way she took joy from judging other people's lives, that they too judged mother and me.

I never did understand that about them; these people's constant need to put up a friendly front, talk with such high esteem amongst one another, only to turn and feast gluttonously upon the other's failure.

How did the others talk about me? About mother? Was it done with that same loathsome passion? Did they talk about me when I fled? Talk about how ungrateful I must have been as a child? How my parents failed?

What did they say when Jeremiah broke his leg? "Serves him right for playing around with non-believers"?

I had no doubt that they saw my accident as punishment, penance for leaving their church.

Eventually, mother and I found space on a bench and I realised how oblivious mother was to all the stares. She recognized one such group and waved excitedly. They averted their gaze and hurriedly absconded.

"That's weird," mother commented.

"It's because of me; people are still uncomfortable."

Mother turned and understood. It was only then that she recognized the weight of the leering stares trying to dissect us—I could only imagine the tales these people spun to compartmentalise our household.

All of a sudden, mother's effervescent and sunny disposition withered. I sensed how tense she became as she rubbed at her nape.

"Let's get going, Nora," mother noted hurriedly.

"You go ahead," I said. "I will sit a little while longer and come after."

Mother didn't even try to hide her sudden discomfort as she looked around to catch lingering stares.

She smiled fraily at me. "Don't be too long; wouldn't want you to catch a cold," she offered as a suitable reason.

I wasn't in any hurry, and in fact enjoyed the moment of privacy—even the stares soon enough became white noise in the background. Part of me secretly hoped to run into Donna and her dog. When the company never came, I returned home with a sense of contentment that I hadn't felt in a long time.

⊰ ⊱

A month had passed before I finally joined my parents, and the town, in church. During that time, I had learnt to adapt and even would turn to the kitchen to cook and prepare food. It wasn't at all easy, and daily activities, which in the past were simple daily chores, suddenly became laborious obstacles.

No longer could I stand at the counter, so instead, I sat on the floor with a tarp draped before me.

Using my left foot to hold the ingredients steady, I learnt to unevenly chop before adding them to a stirring pot to create big chunks of simply boiled items. It dawned on me that I didn't know how to cook before my injury, but the simple act of doing it gave me a mountain of confidence.

There was a calmness to the household that was becoming dangerously placating.

I didn't fight with Mother and Father and instead learnt to become compromising and manipulative in my desires. This resulted in them offering to buy and reward me with new articles, jewellery, or whatever else that they believed I wanted.

It would have been easy to lean into this life, a life without any more strife, where I could pretend our family wasn't a rotting body.

Perhaps in another age, this would have been my life. I would have been obedient, amenable, doing all that I could to appease Mother and Father. I would have married into a life not my own, but it would have been easy.

The idea of how alluring and tempting it was terrified me, another emotion I had to privately keep to myself as I smiled.

My mother dressed me in one of the navy blue outfits she bought and sat with me to colour my cheeks and smear gloss onto my lips before doing my hair in a braid.

It was surreal watching my reflection with depthless eyes—in many ways, I no longer recognized the woman staring back at me.

Although I had regained some meat to my bones, I was still comparably leaner than before. The gnarly scar that ran up the right of my neck and tickled my cheek was still present despite mother's best efforts.

Yet as mother embellished me in women's products, I found that I didn't stare at myself with that same disgust or hopelessness that I originally did. Nor did I look upon the same Nora I used to be.

It wasn't the makeup or the done up hair or the clothing—it was me.

I saw myself in a new light; there was a fierceness, a cold, smouldering heat on the surface. I felt in control of it, in control of my body in a more defined and precise way than I ever had, and all it took was stripping me down to my lowest form so that I could learn to adapt.

For the first time in a very long time, I was surprised that I held out hope for a possible future as the year was coming to a close.

"Mother?" I turned to her, my hand reaching across my chest to gently halt her.

"What is it?" she asked, smiling comfortingly at me.

"I have a request."

Mother seemed taken aback and on guard. Whenever I used to voice my desires, Father and Mother were typically against it.

"This… arm." I lifted my shoulder to address the fake limb mother had made on my right. "I would like it removed for today."

"Are you sure? People will stare," she said, as if I were the one oblivious to that fact.

"I am. I want people to see me as I am, and if we have nothing to hide, then let's show that," I said.

Mother seemed convinced at that notion. "If it is what you want." Though hesitant, she honoured my request.

❂ ❂

It was snowing outside; soft, white flakes dancing in a slow fall to blanket the world. Moving through that snow with just my one leg was no easy feat. I practically ploughed a path through and onto the street.

Jeremiah had already gone ahead. Father, Mother, and I merged with the passing crowd and made our way to the building.

At the centre of Basksin was the church, a large building with a slanted and tiled roof, and a dark shade to its outer walls. Its architecture was in many ways identical to the Church of the Faithful, with slight alterations to give it its own features.

A rose window of stained glass was centred with a great circular purple eye staring outward, the rest of the panels depicting concepts and ideas of a religion built on primordial and existential fear.

Groups of holy monks standing with their fingers forming the eye of Oxular, but their faces were blank and expressionless.

At the very top of the rose window was Zeraphiel The Angel. Zeraphiel was said to be born from and equal to the Grand Archon. Ranking highest among the Seven Archangels, they were depicted with eyes covering the entirety of their six wings, their face was wreathed in golden flame because of their incomprehensible beauty.

"Keep up," Father urged privately as I shuffled into the flowing crowd. The people naturally gave me space as I drew closer, creating a small moat between them and us.

The entrance was a grand, arched doorway with its double doors of dark wood swung wide open.

Stepping inside, I noticed how stale the air inside was. Up above, there were more glazed windows where sunlight peered through and into the long space. To the left and right were rows of benches.

"Nora!" The sound was instantly familiar. I turned to see Donna run excitedly and wrap her arms around me.

Mother and Father were stunned.

"Hello, where is Dea?" I asked.

"Outside, pets aren't allowed," Donna admitted.

"Donna!" I looked up to find a woman jogging over with obvious horror.

Reaching down, she took Donna into her arms and pulled her away from me.

"I am so incredibly sorry! Stella is the name; I am the girl's mother. She doesn't know what she is doing." The mother apologised profusely, practically begging for my forgiveness.

After a moment's pause, I could sense that Stella wanted to say something, and I begged that she didn't.

"I must say, you are really incredible, living as you do. I am sure you must be really happy to have parents who take care of you."

I found myself at a loss for words until Father cleared his throat. My teeth grated.

I gave my best practised smile. "Yes, I am blessed," I lied.

A little after, my parents and I found ourselves a seat at the back of the church.

Banners painted with eyes hung from the ceiling and long curtains repeating the symbol, giving the walls vision so that they may always look upon us and acknowledge us.

At the end of the church, there was an erected stand with a short set of curling stairs on either side. There at the centre was an altar and a pulpit just behind it.

A Watcher came to the front with soft purple robes. His name was Watcher Glenn. He had noticeably aged, with white hair on a balding head and sagging skin. He hunched forward, but his voice still boomed with controlled confidence.

"Welcome, Witnessed."

Almost in perfect synchrony, the masses took made rings with pointer fingers touching their thumbs and pressed it onto their forehead to show the eye of Oxular; I was flustered and rushed to mirror their act.

"Thanks to Oxular, the merciful god, we can now see." The priest turned and waved up at the great marble carving of a vertical eyelid slightly open to stare out at us.

"It was with the coming of Heyru that Oxular began to shut his eye. Day by day, we were becoming despotic, vile, and unworthy creatures. It pained Oxular, so the great eye wept and was blinded.

"He could watch our corruption no more, as we dug ourselves deeper into this hedonistic and blasphemous life. It is thanks to our devotion, our praise, that his eye opened once more and watches us. We are graced by his great sight and thus will be saved when the rest of the world becomes forgotten."

The man held all of our gazes, looking down at how the audience clung to each pernicious word slathered in promises of salvation. Absolution was held over our heads, dripping onto outstretched tongues as if it were honey. I could sense the terrifying veneration that radiated from the crowd.

"Mrs Johnson, if you could please stand." Watcher Glenn tactfully raised his arm before him. In response, a well-dressed woman rose from the seats and wiped down at her crinoline skirt. The thing had a deep lilac colouring to it with a large, white bow constricting the collar. The woman seemed somewhat mollified and at peace, almost as if through the influence of some narcotic.

Her skin was pasty white and porcelain-like due to whatever compounding layers of cosmetics she had stacked on top of each other. Yet no matter what she did, it could not entirely hide her weathered features nor the frenzy in her eyes.

"She has been with us now for only a few years, her impious ways leading to her very son being forgotten." There were disapproving and affirming whispers among the onlookers. It didn't seem to faze Mrs

Johnson, who stood with a beatific smile.

"Now she has joined us and seen the truth! Her loss is a reminder of Oxular's great love and benevolence."

"Thank you, Watcher Glenn, for saving me, for showing me the light of truth! If only my son..." The woman trailed off. Her smile faltering, her lower chin quivering until the layers of cosmetics cracked like dry clay.

"It's alright, Mrs. Johnson." Watcher Glenn said with such convincing warmth and understanding as he delicately lowered his hand to motion for Mrs Johnson to sit.

"Thank you." The words came out as a sob as Mrs Johnson lowered herself. Nearby hands pawed at her with intended comfort, but it looked more like the damned coming to pull her back into their fold.

"*May you be witnessed.*" I couldn't tell if the words were supposed to be comforting or a threat.

There were nods and murmurs of approval from the crowd.

"Today, I want to give the stand to Watcher Jeremiah, a man many of you know, of truly uncompromising faith."

With the help of another Watcher, Watcher Glenn was helped down from the steps and Jeremiah approached the pulpit with a formidable presence.

"As many of you—if not all—already know, my sister has been returned to us."

Another wave of approving murmurs rose and were quickly stemmed with a simple dampening motion from Jeremiah.

"For too long, my family had been taken apart and incomplete. Tempted by the pernicious allure of decadence from the people in Cleria, worshipping monsters atop their vile realm on Mount Morniar."

Still, the murmurs were of agreement and taking a passionate form.

"Avarice, tempted by the promise of foul arts, those people turn to ruin!"

The chants now were elated and no longer simply murmurs.

Jeremiah had his audience by the balls as he stretched out the silence to ensure that we hung on the edge of his every word.

"One day, when the time comes, all will be forgotten. Oxular will close his eye and look to none except us, his chosen."

My heart stopped as Jeremiah waved his hand out. "I would ask that Nora, my sister, so courageous and repenting, to come and join me up here as one of god's chosen."

The people turned, and all stares suddenly fell upon me—in that instance, I wished to be forgotten.

With the judging weight of those stares, I rose, staring contemptuously up at Jeremiah who watched me with trained love and compassion. The hall was silent, none in a rush as all observed me until I shrunk under their zealotry.

"Behold!" Jeremiah exclaimed when I finally went to stand beside him. "Oxular, in his eternal mercy, decided to lead my sister back to me. But not without a price."

Jeremiah looked at me. "Show them," he ordered. His voice was not even remotely loving.

I blinked in utter shock. "What?"

Instead of waiting for me to react, Jeremiah took it upon himself to pull back the hanging frill of my dress. My balance faltered and just as I was about to fall, I felt two pairs of hands grasp me from behind to hold me erect.

"Stop it!" I exclaimed.

"There is nothing to hide, sister."

I struggled helplessly and felt a terror take hold. I screamed, but it did nothing, the skirt was pulled away and the audience gasped upon seeing my missing leg. My brother pulled down the dress at my neck to reveal the ruinous scar and the stub of my shoulder.

"This may be cruel, but this is a reminder of Oxular's graces! By offering her limbs, my sister has been granted a second chance at a virtuous life. Believe in Oxular, and you will be saved, for his love is endless."

Finally, Jeremiah let go of me. I would have fallen if it weren't for the disgusting hands that held me.

The eyes lingered, they peered with scrutiny to determine the verdict. Ashamed, I bowed my head to hide my reddening cheeks, and, though my eyes did water, they did not cry.

"Now, let us all take a moment to pray for my sister, and to thank Oxular for bringing her back to us."

All heads bowed accordingly and, in silence, their prayers were made. My presence is a mere medium to unload their zeal onto. All I felt was disgust and fear—I was entirely helpless within the centre of their piety.

Chapter Fifty-Five

NORA

*It is unknown why the forgotten curse afflicts those that it does.
It appears random and indiscriminate. Yet at the same time, the forgotten curse is suggested to also be bargained with. Does it make
it an unknown god?*

—Making sense of the forgotten, by Alziery Demensh

Within this holy house, my spirit felt defiled, and I couldn't have absconded quickly enough. Rigid and exposed, I kept pulling down the hem of my dress as if the audience could still see the source of my shame laid bare.

Finally, when Jeremiah thanked me for joining him and had me excused, I hastily climbed down the steps with my gaze fixed to the floor, striding towards the double doors we had entered.

Silence trailed the hall save for obfuscated murmurs. My breathing hardened as I could feel my mind go hot; I was feeling light-headed.

Quick and rasping breaths escaped me as I strode faster and faster to the back of the church. The banging of my crutch on the stone floor became the irregular heartbeat of my panic.

As I reached the end, a man moved aside so that I could pass. I leaned against the door and found its heavy body unmoving without two feet to hold me steady. My one leg trembled. I inhaled the air of this zealous crowd. I felt their judging stares burn into me.

The door finally pulled itself open as I leaned back. I toppled onto the floor, my wooden crutch rattling. My gaze was wild and fixed—I refused to look up, too scared to look into the eyes of these monsters.

A gust of cold wind howled through the open door and enveloped me. With trembling fingers and volatile panic, I struggled to my foot, the crutch in my hand as I went out into the snowy open.

I tottered to the side. Someone closed the door behind me; I didn't know who.

Scaling down the steps with such haste was painful, feeling the surrounding cold battle with the radiating heat of my ruined side lathered me in sweat.

My breathing eased the more distance I created. My mind was no longer swollen with a nascent fear, but my heart banged with such a fervour it wouldn't calm any time soon. My vision was frantic, jumping from one snow-covered home to the next, trained on windows where I expected an audience to my suffering. Still, I felt Oxular's eye peer into my back as I stumbled on.

I wandered far. Far enough behind another building to avoid the peering eye of the church following me and then into a small copse of trees sequestered in the corner of a park.

There I sat on the ground. The cold enveloped me and caused my one hand to stiffen. I shuddered in shock. I crossed my good arm and set the hand against my right side, the discomforting heat thawing some of the cold.

I sat there for a while. The lucid part of my mind that I had trained was still there, something that made me fully aware of the frayed part of my brain. My confidence, my frail sense of self that I had been building up was threatened and at risk of being undone; I couldn't allow that to happen.

Time passed out here in the cold until the snow no longer fell, and I was still hidden in my small refuge. A soft cover of snow tucked me into itself. The cold numbed the shock, the pain, but also my mind. Dampening whatever caustic thoughts roiled within.

It was when I heard the sound of approaching footsteps that I started and fell to my side, my left arm keeping me up.

I expected it to be Mother, perhaps father, or even Jeremiah coming to scold me, to further turn me into an object of their devotion.

What I did not expect was to find Dea sitting there, fur thick and tongue hanging out in expectation.

"What do you want?" I asked, unable to keep the trembling from my voice.

The dog cautiously got on all fours and approached me. I recoiled slightly, but when Dea gave me a loving lick her presence stilled me. Dea rubbed herself against me, her soft fur against my cheeks. I even laughed when the licking turned more lively.

"Stop it!" I chuckled in between my frayed composition. The tense thorns of my shame began to unravel slightly. Dea's presence imprinting some calm.

I pushed myself back up into a seated position within the snow and began to pet Dea. "Good girl," I said.

"Bitch spending time with her own kind; how befitting."

I spun and found two men looming over me. Within the secluded space of this snow-covered spot, they leered with insidious grins.

"Who are you?" I asked harshly, as I began to force myself to stand.

"Don't you remember us?" the man asked.

It took me a moment, but then I did remember them—they were the same men who tried to help me at the bakery.

A thought began to dawn on me. "You are not from around here, are you?"

"No, ma'am," the closest man said. At first glance, there was absolutely nothing remarkable about them. They seemed like ordinary men in their forties, one with a rugged, stubbly beard and the other long-faced and wiry.

Dea, sensing the tension, started to growl.

"Nora, the Undying Flame, the Twilight Bird, Simurgh. You have earned many titles during your short career, haven't you?" The rugged man's words were drawn out, slow, deliberate, taunting in their design.

In a moment's desperation, I flung the crutch at his head, which he easily ducked under.

They didn't have to lift a finger as the sudden lack of support sent me falling forward and all he had to do was step aside.

Dea began to bark at the two men. I hoped that there was someone to hear it and come help, but I knew that everyone was praying away in the church, blind to the events happening outside.

"Shut that mutt up!" The rugged man shouted to the wiry one.

Though, as the thin man stepped forward, he hesitated. "You know I'm not good with dogs."

Seizing the moment, I turned around and swung my second crutch behind the older man's knee. But the weight of the crutch proved too heavy from just one hand. The second swing was caught and my only method of moving was removed and broken over the man's knee. In a strange way, it felt like losing another limb.

Dea continued barking.

"Danny, shut that damn dog up before someone hears it!" The older man climbed over me as I scrambled desperately to get away with my one arm and leg.

I heard as a reluctant Danny finally inched over to Dea, who barked louder and louder.

There must have been a knife, for I heard the familiar sound of wet flesh being rended followed by Dea's feeble whimper.

I screamed such terrible profanities from the depths of my carnal being. The man on top slapped his hand over my mouth to silence me. As if filled by Dea's spirit, I bit hard onto the man's hand until I tasted blood.

"Bitch!" The man tore away his blood soaked digits.

"I'll kill you!" I swore.

Both men laughed. "Yeah? How?"

I felt a sudden fist strike me across the temple and send stars into my vision—that was all it took for the contents of my stomach to expel and smear across my face.

Again they laughed. "The great Simurgh, you aren't as amazing as the stories say you are."

Suddenly, I felt the man's hand grab upon my clothes and tear at the fabric.

"Wait, stop! Please!" I begged, but the man simply pressed my face back into my vomit and laughed. Bit by bit he tore away the last shreds of my dignity, leaving me lesser than the vomit that puddled around my cheek. My mind was tearing itself apart, stretched so thin like sausage over a butcher's table.

Tears came and there was nothing to hold them back; it was not a sudden burst of sorrow but a slow, gradual trickle.

The cold mixed somewhere with the rest of my toiling emotions, a fugue coming over me as my mind fell deeper and deeper into a numb darkness.

Like an observer trapped within my own body, simultaneously disconnected from it all, I felt the man tear away my clothes until I was laid bare and offered no resistance.

"I will enjoy making good use of your little hole," the man bragged sadistically.

"Hurry up, Regan. I want a chance too!"

"Don't rush me, Danny!" Regan snapped back.

I did not resist, did not move; my body was not my own.

Somewhere far away I felt the vague sensation of fingers feeling out my loins and trailing up my leg.

My mind receded, secluding itself into some crevice as my reality blurred; I barely felt Regan's finger explore my exposed sex. Someone spat.

"It's okay, captain. You can still serve the people just like this."

I wept openly, a numb and continuing trail of tears as I lay on the cold snow that wreathed me. The purged contents of my stomach lost colour as it seeped into the snow, the sharp scent so very distant from where I was.

The man's member slid inside and stretched me open, squeezing further tears from me. The pain mixed with shame. I could no longer contain my sanity. Regan grunted, his hips nudging me forward as his free hand forced my face further down. Skin slapped against skin.

"You know, in fact, I think this is a far better improvement! You don't even need those extra limbs."

A primal and desperate fear gave me voice again.

"Please, stop it! Don't!" The words came from somewhere deep inside me and sounded just as distant.

"He wanted you dead, but this is *so* much more satisfying for him." They laughed. Just as I fell deeper and deeper into the recesses of my own mind to protect me from this defilement, so too did it seem as if Regan and Danny gave themselves further to the spirit of depravity, finding unfiltered glee in my torture.

As one fucked me, so too did the other bury a heavy blade into my arm just below the elbow. The smell of blood wafted in the air, a hot unbearable pain burst from the spot.

"Stop it!" I cried.

They didn't listen. The blade sawed through flesh, strumming bone to nurture a blood-curdling scream.

"Shut the Elder-damn up, you whore!" Again, my head was buried into my fluids to stop the cries. The putrid acid bubbling from my frightened gasps as I re-inhaled the burning pool. The weight from behind knocking into my rear over and over until it pained and burnt. The more I tried to cry, the more I swallowed from the vomit.

I was left helpless as the rape, the pain, the eventual consequences of this monstrous act would follow me into tomorrow.

Bit by bit, I was taken apart, torn into unrecognisable shreds until there was nothing left of Nora.

When all was said and done, the pain overcame me and the passing of time escaped me. I felt no hand move or toe twitch until Regan eventually pulled away to cover my naked body in his filth. A pooling warmth encased me; the scent of my scarlet blood thick in the air, as if it also taunted me. There was a dour sense of despair as I felt the pain that came from my freshly dismembered limbs.

But it wasn't over; Danny had his turn too.

My world collapsed, my mind frayed. There it was, Nora the Undying Flame, Simurgh, The Twilight Bird left broken. With the last vestiges of myself still left, I was granted one final offering of knowledge.

While Danny indulged in his vile and carnal defilement, Regan leaned in to whisper a truth which became the core of my suffering.

"Cassidy Femur sends his regards."

Chapter Fifty-Six

DALILA

Cleria exists as a division of districts. Most of what can be seen by the common folk is grand and befits the golden city. However. The castle of the kingdom and its central body is beyond the capabilities of mere humans. It is unquestionable that the impossible architecture and confounding properties of Castle Belmore were made by people who had keen understanding of Elder design.

—THE UNTRACEABLE HISTORY, BY KIERLOU BRAGIN

I stayed until the guards arrived. The scene of the massacre left unperturbed to truly reveal the macabre design of the killer.

There was a hint of recognition upon seeing the dead, floating bodies encircled by the cryptic runes of blood. Not in the sense that I knew the artist, but rather that I gleaned the hint of passion instilled within—the perpetrator was an Inspired.

As soon as the first guard stepped to the display, he uttered, "Elders save us." And collapsed right outside to expel his stomach.

Due to the magical and insidious nature of this display, the Sisterhood was summoned to analyse. Mother Vinrie was naturally first on the scene, along with another who I did not recognize.

"Mother Grace, see what you can discern," Mother Vinrie calmly instructed and turned to me.

Her eyes narrowed curiously. "You were here when it happened, Mother Dalila?"

I nodded. The pointedness with which she addressed me was not born out of suspicion, but rather bellied anger with no one to direct it at.

I told Mother Vinrie everything: the play, the end, the scream. The only part I conveniently left out was my conversation with Dale. I wasn't sure how she would feel about me connecting with a small piece of my old life, but I didn't wish to tempt her wrath, especially when she was in such a sour mood.

The woman known as Mother Grace, who was a rather plump middle-aged woman, returned.

"Definitely the work of an Inspired."

"Medium?"

"Blood magic."

It was already obvious, but just because the evidence was present didn't mean that they were related.

There was a weight to those words: "Blood magic." The source of life, the elixir of mortality, held a dormant power. It was a conduit instilled with the life lived by the person who embodied it. The blood of a newborn had power because of potential, because of how pure it was. The blood of an old general was tinged with experience, aged because of it.

Colour-magic used ink to perform great feats, and though Red was most commonly drawn from flowers, it wasn't so uncommon to use blood as a replacement.

"But this is different," Mother Grace explained.

"How so?"

"Whoever is doing this is growing drunk with power—this was a work of passion."

I joined in on that perspective. "The killings have gotten more frequent; there is growing confidence here."

"Or brashness," Mother Vinrie provided.

"Blood magic is Red magic. Typically used to instil feelings of rage or passion, or to evoke flames. It can also be used as harnessed energy for some other purpose."

"What has this killer used it for?"

"*None* of those things. In fact, it didn't seem like they used it for something other than writing symbols and making his victims float."

Mother Vinrie's eyes narrowed. "But you think there is more to it, don't you?"

"Those runes, drawn into the wall—I don't recognize them."

The gravity in Mother Vinrie's voice heightened. "You don't know the language?"

Mother Grace shook her head.

The implications carried unspeakable dread. There weren't many languages which spread across Minethria, but there were even fewer languages unknown to human tongue.

"Do you think it is *their* tongue?"

Mother Grace seemed hesitant. "It's not impossible. Should we report it?"

"Absolutely not! Not until we have more information."

I was noticeably confused. "What is it?"

I never saw Mother Vinrie hold such fear in her eyes. Her stare danced about until an affirming nod from Mother Grace gave her the encouragement she needed.

"There aren't many languages Mother Grace doesn't speak. Some of them are lost to the ages and others only meant for higher beings."

Her meaning began to dawn on me. "The language of angels is one example or the tongue of the Chitons. Otherwise, it could also be the hidden language of the Elders."

"And if that were to be the case, it would mean that someone among us mortals has the ability to invoke spells in the tongues of Elders."

The fear I felt wasn't out of acknowledgement for the sheer immensity of Elder power. It was because of the sheer *unknowability* of it. The presence of an Elder regarded things steeped in myth; very few mortals had ever had the privilege of seeing them in the entire history of Minethria. I couldn't even begin to imagine what sort of power those runes could hold.

⊰ ⊱

Yasmin was still in shock for the following days, and, once everything had settled down from the night of the attack, she kept to herself most of the time, which I obliged.

My own nights were restless. Nobody seemed to notice the guilt that I battled, but I had become formidable at hiding my emotions.

The night of the killing, Perry visited me. He was a guest I saw less and less of over the years. There I was again, in the woods where he died. It had taken a more vigorous form in my dreams. The trees were taller and wider, more birds sounding from the canopies and yet nowhere to be seen. The light that bounced off the forest floor seemed to be perpetually stuck in twilight.

I appeared as I did in my daily life, wearing the white robes of the Sisterhood with the tranquil blue hems.

Perry appeared from behind the tree.

"It's been a while since you visited me," he said.

"It has."

"I thought you moved on."

"I will never move on, you know that." Perry nodded; I sensed guilt in that.

"Do you at least have my flower?"

I shook my head. "There was someone who needed it more than I did."

"It seems to me like you are just putting others before yourself again."

This form of Perry still looked just like I remembered him. He was handsome and young, but the languid and aloof way in which he addressed me spoke of a calm confidence I didn't remember.

"So, why are you here this time?"

"Some people died."

"And you were present?"

I remained silent, my head bowed.

"You couldn't save them?"

Nothing.

"They died, and you lived?"

"You already know the truth, so why taunt me?"

"Because you won't speak the truth."

"It's illogical, but why do people keep dying around me? Why do I have to live with the fact that, in spite of my powers, I can't save a single person?"

Perry stepped towards me, the space between us a clump of rocks covered in growth as he reached the jutting stone on which I rested.

"How do you hope to save anyone if you don't even value your own life?"

⋖ ⋗

I didn't know when the dream ended, if it was just moments before I awoke or hours after. But when it did, I slipped back into that decrepit shell of mine and tugged at the corner of my mouth to present my hollow smile.

Mother Lucia had been awaiting me as always, and I realised that I didn't look forward to our meetings like I used to.

I didn't talk much, and instead Mother Lucia engaged me. "I heard of what happened from Mother Vinrie; what a tragic thing."

I looked at Mother Lucia. Her eyes weren't forceful or judging. She had no intention of forcing me into conversation.

"Would you like to tell me what it was like? Finding their bodies?"

I tread cautiously. "It was like opening one of those pop-up books for children. But instead of something loving I was greeted with wrath."

"Was the book angry?"

"No... it was celebrating."

"Celebrating what?"

I sighed. "I don't know... I have a question."

"Ask it," Mother Lucia said.

"Blood magic... what is it good for? What can the killer be hoping to achieve?"

Mother Lucia shifted in her seat. "There is a common misconception that the colours can only perform feats in their respective shades. So only blue can heal, only red can evoke flames."

"Isn't that true?" I cut in.

Mother Lucia didn't appreciate me interrupting her. "Well, blue magic can heal. But so can green. It is the colour of nature, after all. Some things cannot cross boundaries. Purple can convince you that you feel calm in a deceptive sort of way, but only blue can instil true calmness. All colours convey energy and are able to evoke lightning as energy too. Blood magic can be used to harness energy for all kinds of purposes. You said it felt like the scene was 'celebrating'? Well, perhaps the killer already has what they want."

"And what is that?" I pressed.

Mother Lucia shrugged. "Who can say? But to have discovered such a power must have come from a place of deep longing. You don't discover an affinity for blood magic unless pushed towards that path... perhaps someone lost something. They are celebrating that they regained it? Or maybe they are celebrating the deaths of the fallen. An offering, so to say."

Mother Lucia gave me much to consider. Something lost and recovered? Were these sacrifices a way to achieve that? Perhaps a lost power? Or position? I couldn't say.

I gazed up at Mother Lucia. "I don't think it was a coincidence that the three Wanderers were killed off."

"Why do you think that?"

"It carried a sort of weight. Something symbolic?"

"What kind of symbol?" Mother Lucia pressed.

I slammed my fist on the table. "I don't know! Okay? I don't know everything!" From somewhere within me, there was a crevice where my emotions bled—I promptly closed off the opening.

Burying my frustration, I looked at Lucia with her gaze full of concern. "I'm sorry. I have been a little on edge."

Mother Lucia gave me the time I needed and didn't respond. "You said there are other witches. Do you know any of them who could have done this? Anyone in the coven who had lost something they could regain with blood magic?"

My mentor turned stern. "We want to show the people that we are champions of good; what good would the killing of innocent actors do?"

"I don't know? Maybe it would be a challenge against the Elders?" I went silent at that notion. An idea blossomed in my mind, a sudden connection made on its own.

"What is it?"

"The Wanderers, the stories. The killer is challenging the Elders."

I looked at Lucia, my suspicion granted further gravity. "You have to tell Mother Vinrie where the other witches are."

Mother Lucia was insulted by my suggestion. "I will do no such thing!" She rose to stand.

"People died!" I rose as well to meet her gaze.

"Death happens all the time! What about the bigger picture? We are made to be the servants of monsters and chastised by the contract of time."

"The people are in danger! Not the witches!"

"I *am* talking about people! Witches are people too, and we just want to live without having to be ashamed of that, to be burnt alive, hiding underground or forced into servitude!" Mother Lucia's features softened gradually like thawing ice. "This isn't about me. Soon, I will no longer be for this world, but I wish for you to be able to live without having to choose between bondage or death."

"I get to help people. What greater honour is there?"

"Is that what you tell yourself? You were never given a choice, taken from your family when you were just a child."

"This is my family!"

"Please! Do you think any of them would cherish you if they knew who you truly were? They would see you as a monster."

"Yasmin doesn't!"

The moment the words escaped me, I instantly regretted them.

"What did you just say?" Lucia queried.

There was no backing out. "Yasmin knows, I told her."

"But you said—"

"I lied." My mentor was speechless. "She knows nothing about you, but she knows about my powers, knows that I used them for that child."

Mother Lucia leaned in. For the first time I could see anger in her expression. "You don't know what you've done. You've put us all at risk."

I had enough. I turned and stormed out of the room before anything else could be said.

⋖ ⋗

In a moment of desperation, I found that I needed to be heard. Yasmin's own distancing cautioned me from reaching out, and, with Mother Lucia's emerging truth becoming a dangerous revelation, I decided to seek out Father Maurice at the Brotherhood.

I was in a deep daze as I wandered through the snow-covered streets, dealing with many thoughts proving impossible to untangle until I came onto the small congregation of Brothers.

Already having been there once, I wandered through the halls until I came across Father Maurice's office, but found it vacant.

"Who goes there?" I turned around to find the blind Brother Clemence addressing me, his gaze a good ways off and his eyes now hidden behind a bandage.

"It is Mother Dalila. I was hoping to see Father Maurice."

"Ah, I am afraid he has been absent for a while."

"Where is he?"

Brother Clemence shrugged. "He comes and goes as he wills, dealing with things we are not privy to. Perhaps I could help?"

I offered him my hand as I became his eyes to walk him through the halls. We came to a small, square garden stripped due to winter. A deciduous tree dressed itself in layers of snow; the garden itself divided the main church building and Father Maurice's office. I led Brother Clemence to an empty bench.

Snow had settled here from a few days prior and blanketed the garden, though it was one of the days where the capricious sun decided to burn patches of snow away and reveal the soil beneath.

"Why the blindfold?" I asked the man.

"Oh, I'm sorry, would you prefer I removed it?"

"No, no. Just, I was wondering why you wear it. Last I saw you, you weren't covering them."

Brother Clemence smiled. "Yes, well. Apparently, some of our visitors were a little uncomfortable with the sight—didn't know if they should look directly in my eyes or not."

"I'm sorry to hear that."

The man chuckled affably. "Oh, it's no matter. A small thing for me—I'm blind anyway. The covering won't make much of a difference. What has brought a devout Sister such as yourself to this holy place?"

I hesitated, wondering how much I could convey; evidently, Brother Clemence seemed to have already gathered a theory of his own.

"I suppose you came here to seek a confidant, perhaps in Father Maurice?"

I nodded to confirm his conclusion when I remembered that he could not see my affirmation. I voiced it instead.

"Perhaps you could confide in me?"

It took me a moment to gather my thoughts. "You know of my predicament?"

"That you are a witch? Yes, I do know."

With Father Maurice absent and my own loneliness nestling within me, I decided to confide in Brother Clemence as much as I could.

"Could I ask you something first?"

"Anything," the man obliged gladly.

"How did you end up serving the house?"

The man smiled. "I was a painter once."

"Truly?"

"Yes." His smile was feeble as he recalled the memory, his unremarkable cane leaning against the chair to his side.

"I was a good one too, not enough to ever be an Inspired. Nobles asked for my services, granted, I proved to be more prodigious in spending my earned wealth rather than saving it." The way he addressed his past self was critical though also wistful.

"One day, I noticed my vision kept... fading. Black spots filling my eyes. Soon enough, it all vanished. Just a stark white left behind."

"Did you try to see a healer?"

The man nodded. "Aye, but the disease kept coming back, faster and faster each time, until I had no more of me to give."

There was a slight hesitance. "I eventually found out that my friend did it to me. Poisoned me over time because of envy. Lost everything because of that."

"I am sorry to hear," I offered solemnly.

He licked his lips and his tone became more upbeat as he moved on from his past life.

"The church found me. I have been in service of this brotherhood ever since. It has been a good thirty years, I believe."

The man turned towards me. I couldn't help but feel as if his lingering gaze could actually see me.

"I am all better for it, you know? Being a part of this church has been the best thing that ever happened to me. I didn't see it that way at first, but I certainly do now. It has given me the opportunity to heal. And I have learnt how there is power in suffering."

I suddenly felt as if I were to be judged and scolded by a man so unmovable in his devotion.

A surveying, aged hand rested lithe fingers on mine. Brother Clemence's gaze stared outward, and his smile offered some reprieve. "I know better than anyone that faith isn't easy to come by. If anything, it is something to be earned every day. If you have your doubts, I don't fault you."

I found myself opening up. "It isn't easy to be appreciative of the church when it was either that or death." I spoke Mother Lucia's words.

"Is that why you have come here rather than talking to your mentor?"

I froze for a moment. "Something like that." I collected my thoughts. "Growing up, my father was so unwavering in his devotion to the Elders. Mother and my brother fell so easily behind that, but I never did." Recalling my youth felt so alienating, like recalling the memories of a stranger. I was so stubborn, headstrong, always questioning the stories of the Kaseluda. Not because of doubt, but because of pure curiosity.

"Now, even within the Sisterhood, Yasmin of all people has every right to hate the cards fate had dealt, and yet she smiles, approaches each day with such optimism and even follows through with her duties to the Elders. I can't confide in my mentor, let alone in my best friend. I just don't feel like I belong."

There was a pause. "Tell me more about this, Yasmin. She sounds important to you."

"She is," I admitted. "I feel as if I found a constant, someone to rely on without ever fearing that she will betray me. She is honest. Even on my worst days, when I have to pretend, she sees right through it all and tells me what I need to hear."

The man chuckled, ostensibly pleased by how I described my friend. "I am glad to hear you have someone you rely on so much. You know, you remind me of myself when I first came here, lost and unsure. Though to be fair, I was also resentful and full of spite, thinking none of this was for me. Unquestionable faith isn't possible, child; you aren't broken."

"How did you accept it?"

Brother Clemence pondered. "I guess I didn't, or at least not in the way you imagine me to have. I took the parts that worked and made them my own, found a way of belief that fits my own narrative so that I can show devotion in my own way."

"I am not sure I understand," I said.

"What is important to you, Dalila the woman, not Dalila the Sister?"

I pondered the question. "To help those who need my help."

"Well, there you go; that is a big piece of your puzzle."

I was glad the man couldn't see the disappointment in my gaze. "That doesn't solve my problem; what does the church, the faith, mean to me?"

"I think you are thinking entirely in absolutes. The Sisterhood, the Brotherhood, they are what they are as a body. There is nothing dictating any finality."

I considered the idea when Brother Clemence said something completely unexpected.

"Your suffering is beautiful, you know?"

I turned to the man with deeply furrowed brows. "What do you mean?" I asked.

He chuckled disarmingly. "I don't mean anything by it. Suffering can be beautiful. It brings despair and melancholia, but there is a purity to it that bears unmarred authenticity. The kind that motivates you to help others. Your suffering urges you on, powers your need to help. There is a maudlin beauty to that."

"Thank you," I said sombrely, not exactly sure what to say in turn.

"Who would you say matters most to you in life? Who do you feel as if you've wronged?"

At first, I felt the murky image of Perry rise to the surface before I ushered it away. "My family, I suppose." I was slightly rueful at the remark. "I haven't seen them since I came here. They went through so much because of me. I don't want them to suffer anymore than they already have."

"What do you think your parents would say if they were to see how you've grown?"

I shrugged. "I don't know. Call me a burden, maybe?" Though inwardly, a malicious voice whispered with such rotten intimacy. *They would curse you for all that you've wrought, for the suffering you brought into their life. So ungrateful.* I knew the voice to be that of a deceiver, but that didn't stop it from inserting its barbed tongue into my ear and twisting.

The blindfold about Brother Clemence's eyes creased and bunched up to indicate a frown. "Why do you think they would see you as a burden?"

I shrugged again. "All that self-pity, all that melancholy. Mother looked so hurt to see me in pain and didn't know what to do. Even before Perry's death, my father was always upset at the nonsense I spoke. Wanting to be like Xelxidon and such. Would tell me it was our place to worship, not to dream of a station above our standing. Besides, I can't visit them anyway as I am bound to the Sisterhood."

"Perry... who was that?" Asked Brother Clemence cautiously, as if not wanting to scare me away with a tender subject.

Hearing his name didn't trigger any raw emotions nor did it pry at old wounds; on brother Clemence's tongue, it sounded like the name of a stranger. "A boy I loved. He died because of me that night in the forest."

"When you discovered your powers?"

"Yes."

"It is a shame he died. But again, there is power in that kind of suffering. I know all too well." He waved casually at his blindfolded eyes. "It is what gave you your powers, powers that can now be used to tend to those less fortunate. That isn't nothing."

Brother Clemence's pursed lips rubbed against their petalled halves before speaking. "Perhaps one day you will find the courage needed to visit your parents. And, perhaps then, you will find the missing piece that makes you feel whole once more."

There truly was something empowering about his philosophy. To turn this infected hurt into a force for healing. "You have given me much to consider, Brother Clemence." I rose to stand.

"Please, your company was delightful enough and has given me questions to meditate on myself." The blind man seemed mollified by our exchange, a content smile to weary lips.

As I vacated the building, I pondered on the message delivered. To find my own faith? To use my suffering as a power? I was no closer to bridging the chasm which Mother Lucia had wedged within me.

One thing did appear clearer, however, and that was my own waning trust in Mother Lucia.

Chapter Fifty-Seven

EREFIEL

Be ware, be ware
Don't stop to stare
Blink by blink,
Your friends aren't there.

—NURSERY RHYME ABOUT THE FORGOTTEN

S top it," I chided Zephyr as we strolled through the road. My steed threw back his head and gave a complaining flapping of his lips.

"I know it is cold; just get it together."

Due to the winter month, Zephyr showed more of his temperamental and unreasonable side. On most days, he proved more languid, and it took longer to get him warm.

I didn't blame him; the season had a way to chill the blood within me also, and leave me drowsy during the waking hours. I sometimes wondered if it had to do with father's affinity to a bird of prey.

Finally, we approached the akar settlement, and I felt my own body tense. I wanted nothing more than to gallop quickly after I had received the news, but Zephyr's stubbornness forced me to still myself and the closer we came, the more my impatience resurfaced.

I was supposed to return to the settlement in another two weeks' time, but the letter I was sent informed me of the travesty.

Steadily, I approached the heavy air and took note of the leering guards which sought me for guidance in their unrest.

"Lieutenant General Erefiel." A young man saluted me as I dismounted Zephyr, while another promptly came to take him to the stables.

"Where is he?"

Without any questions asked, the guard led me into the same underground basement where I first met Chroma.

With lantern in hand, I told the men I would go in alone and took the steps down into the dark and damp chamber full of rusting iron bars and mildew; the air was stale and mixed with the sweat of akar detainees.

I noticed Chroma immediately. A ball of intense and bottled heat radiated from him. I stepped forward and forced Chroma into the light. Upon his wrists and ankles were chains which rattled with each movement.

This was not the young man that I knew; his stare was intense, though it did not linger long on my shape.

"I guess I am not the model akar you thought me to be." His tone was without inflection, but I could sense the flaring embers beneath. I was sympathetic towards the boy and took a seat at a shoddy table where I could rest my lantern.

The subtle but persistent sound of water dropped to the dirt covered floor.

"What happened?" I asked glibly.

Chroma didn't speak at first and, when he finally did, there was contempt in it; not directed at me, but for the world in general.

"They didn't tell you?"

"All they told me was that Jasper appeared drunk, and that you killed him for approaching your mother again."

Chroma didn't deny the tale, but I knew for certain there was more.

"Chroma, I can't help you if you don't talk to me."

"Does it matter? I am locked in here. My life became forfeit the moment I killed that man."

I didn't counter his claim. But it impacted more than just Chroma. I worried the tension between akar and humans would only worsen as a result.

This was a worst-case scenario. The volatility of the settlement would rise to lengths unlike before, and I feared the consequences. I needed to actively prevent such a scenario and, for that, I needed the truth and the whole truth.

"Did you know?" Chroma asked, breaking me from my thoughts.

"Know what?"

With animalistic fury, the boy pounced upon the bars, his hot-blooded side left fully bared. The chains that confined his ankles and wrists to the far side of the cage shattered upon his powerful leap. "Don't you lie to me!" His growl was from a furnace; any pretence at him being harmless fully dispelled—his grimace that of a rabid beast's. His brows furrowed to contort his features into a primitive snarl, his eyes full of passionate hate, his tusks bore themselves.

"I don't know anything unless you tell me what happened!" I stepped towards the bars, in no way intimidated.

His rage tempered into a smoulder, the fire covered with a lid but no less volatile. Chroma removed his locked grip from the square bars and stepped away.

"Jasper was my father," Chroma said, his wide and heaving back hiding whatever expression he had. His tone was undeniably sad, sadder than any voice I had ever heard. The words dripped as tepidly as the droplets from the ceiling.

"What?"

"My father was never Muktow. Mother conceived me with Jasper's seed."

I blinked, unsure of what to say; suddenly the events of that night didn't feel so hard to imagine.

"I'm sorry I let you down." The gravel tone to Chroma showed that, despite his very real regret, that the anger within him did not subside and perhaps never would.

That was when I noticed the drops of blood scraped from knuckles and dried upon the bars, the dented form of this raging akar so internally wounded with no way to let it out.

Chroma kept talking. "When I was younger, I always felt like I didn't belong. Smaller in size and tusks, weaker than my friends, even lighter in skin. Never once did I stop to consider that maybe it was because I wasn't one of them."

"That doesn't mean you should have killed a person."

Chroma turned to look over his shoulder, his one presented eye a glaring, bottomless pit while the other half of his face was wreathed in shadows. "I warned him." His words were spoken coolly and without remorse.

"Chroma, there is nothing that I can do for you from here. What you did, it will not only affect you, but your mother and all your people—"

"They are *not* my people!" Chroma cut me off with a threatening snarl.

He turned and walked to the end of the cage, his eyes looking down. Not once did they settle on me again.

"Leave. There is nothing left for you here."

"You have no one else to turn to. Shutting me out isn't the best course of action."

With the lowest, deepest growl belonging to that of a wounded beast with nothing to lose, Chroma repeated himself. "I said leave."

I turned, feeling a hot anger of my own rising, which I quickly had to quell.

Before I did depart, I left Chroma with one final thing to consider. "Perhaps you are more akar than you think."

⋖ ⋗

Desperate, I strode back through the winter road, my path long and tenuous. My mind was scattered. Before I left, the captain of the camp informed me that tensions were high within the settlement and that it was only getting worse.

Chroma was the only hope of bringing about any form of lasting agreement between our people; ironically, his half-blood self would have made him the perfect bridge. But that was the danger of building a foundation upon just one akar; it made the entire relationship tenuous at best.

Despite what Chroma believed, the akar adopted very human tactics to get back 'one of their own'. Partaking in worker strikes and refusing to build the defences. They even refused to pay any of their taxes.

Privately, I asked the captain who knew the truth of Chroma's conception. Obviously disconcerted, he said that most of the men who were there since the beginning knew of it, but they had kept it a secret.

I was at a loss. What could be done? It was unfortunate, but the law was clear; Chroma would face death and, as sympathetic as I was to him and his people, there was nothing I could do. What repercussions would there be? I could not imagine the people to simply sit there and accept it. If the akar joined together with their two hundred strong, the guards wouldn't stand a chance.

Should they be exiled immediately to re-join their people? No. They would have gathered a decade's worth of information about us.

For a moment, I considered the unthinkable; when all other options seemed growingly implausible, I had no choice but to entertain it.

Did they all have to be imprisoned? Or executed?

That would just give them the cause to retaliate and protect themselves.

"I need a drink." I voiced out loud, my breath misting before me as I strode straight into Crowtown.

⊲ ⊳

I was wearing a thickly padded Gambeson with wood-brown greaves and thick leather boots. Upon my shoulders, to keep me warm, was a fur cowl with the hood draped over my head to hide my distinguishing feathers as I strolled inside.

Zephyr was accepted by a young barn boy who kept blowing into his palms and rubbing them together.

"That be a pretty horse, mista; boy or girl?"

The young lad was perhaps fourteen years of age and eager to make a coin.

"Boy; his name is Zephyr."

The child nodded. "Good name for a horse. My paps and I run a stable, we'd be happ' to tend to your mount."

I tossed a solid silver talent to the young lad.

"This be too much," he hastily protested.

I appreciated the young boy's honesty and smiled underneath my hood.

"Keep it. Consider it my investment for future stays." The boy nodded excitedly and began to pull Zephyr along.

My sword and other belongings were hidden underneath a secure, warm covering.

"No need to brush him, just provide with good water and some pasture. I won't be here long."

Promptly, I bowed my head low. My height made it difficult to avoid attention. Still, most gazes gave me no more than a moment's consideration before moving on.

The inn was called Merry-Inn and proved to be a small but cosy establishment.

Inns within Cleria had the precedent that bigger was better, yet this place sacrificed room for hominess. I had to admit I preferred it. I imagined most small folk living out here preferred the alluring idea of expansive halls with everything dipped in gold, fancy ballroom galas and overly garish party-wear.

It was for that very reason that I felt drawn to this simple décor.

My entire life had been full of grand expectations, claims of being more than human, wondering how the son of the White-Hawk would live up to their father's legacy. For all that, I barely ever saw my father, even more so in the past couple years, as he remained upon Mount Morniar.

My entire childhood was decadence and sparkle. I wondered what it must have been like to have a simpler life, with a humble mother who would smile warmly at me as she tasted dinner, only to notice me staring. Or perhaps a father coming back late from work, exhausted but still excited to see me. Instead, I got a father who lived among gods and a mother with a heart made of ice.

I could hear my mother's chiding voice. Her warning came back to me. One of my strays had turned rabid during a time when everything was at stake. There was no way of knowing when the next akar attack was coming.

"Excuse me." I brushed past a narrow path made by two chairs from opposite seats and made my way to the bar.

A fair woman approached me at the counter, her smile wide and friendly.

"Running from the law?" she asked playfully, referring to my donned hood.

I chuckled. "No, just not in the mood to draw attention."

To give the woman some ease of mind, I revealed only a glimpse of my snow-white brows and hair, along with the feathers jutting up above. The woman was taken aback for just a moment, but quickly recovered her footing and cleared her throat.

"I understand. Is there anything I can get you?" she said, her eyes still noticeably alert.

"Just an ale will do."

Without skipping a beat, she was on her way and promptly returned with ale in hand.

As I reached to pay her, the woman stopped me. "No need, it's on the house."

I slowly returned my pouch, and the woman explained further.

"Word goes around, especially when it concerns the son of White-Hawk."

I found the remark to be quite sour. "Usually it only goes around *because* of that," I complained.

"Well, not this time." I looked up at the woman, her figure plump and her complexion cheerfully golden, like a sunflower blooming in the wrong season. Her eyes were a deep auburn and the corners of her lips creased when she smiled.

"I heard what you have been doing for the akar living in their settlement. Father thought it a fool-hardy decision, but I saw the value you provided for them."

"Well, I am afraid there are not many that agree with you."

I took a sip from the ale and instantly felt the frothing surface film to my lips like sea foam to a cliff. There was a note of nutmeg powder on top, along with a generous tang of honey within.

"This is wonderful!" I exclaimed.

The woman blushed and gave a small curtsy. "Thank you! It is my recipe."

"Are you the owner of this place?"

She shook her head. "My pa is."

"And why is it called the Merry-Inn?"

She shrugged. "No reason. Just catchy, you know?"

"So family owned?" I clarified.

"Just my pa and myself and some help in the kitchen, you know? We get a musician to come here once a week to regale kids with stories."

"And your mother?"

"Never knew her, unfortunately, and dad's memory isn't what it used to be either, I'm afraid."

I nodded.

"Georgia! Another round!" called a nearby table.

"Coming!" Georgia exclaimed and excused herself.

I looked about the neighbouring tables and only then recognized another militant from the Clerian army. His banner was that of a guard but rather bore the insignia of a bird with three sprouting feathers like sprigs from its scalp.

I recognized the man instantly as Howard, one of Nora's men. The memory of her crashed over me; I hadn't seen her in a very long time. Joyed at this auspicious chance to hear about her, I took my ale and ordered another for the man.

As I took my seat with him, the paunch bellied man first looked at me and seemed apprehensive.

Unable to see my face through the hood, Howard spoke cautiously at first. "I'm sorry, but I don't want any company," he said, his gaze cautious.

Again, I did the courtesy of only slightly lifting up my hood to give away not my distinctive feathers, but rather just my familiar face.

"Captain Erefiel!" All of a sudden, the man floundered.

"Please! Lower your voice! I don't want to attract any attention."

The man's cheeks quickly reddened. "Of course."

I pushed my extra mug of ale to the man, to which he said his thanks.

"Is everything alright?" he asked.

"Everything is fine, just some problems with the akar settlement."

"Well, I heard of all the good you did for them."

"I doubt your captain sees eye to eye with you. How is Nora, anyway? Is she still doing well?"

Howard went incredibly silent all at once, the uncomfortableness radiated from him.

Suddenly, I was filled with concern. "Did something happen?"

"So you didn't hear?"

"Hear what?" My query was almost an order as I easily slipped back into the role of superior.

"Nora made it very clear that she didn't want me to say."

"What happened?"

I knew Howard wanted to speak, and the plain dominance that came from me made it easy to break down his walls.

He told me everything, the trek to Whitshade, the caged flaming demon, and then the accident.

"She protected the young girl, but paid for it dearly."

"Is she still alive?"

"Well, yes, but she lost an arm and a leg on her right side."

I suddenly felt very saddened by the news, thinking about the unstoppable and driven woman having gone through such a tragedy.

"Where is she?"

"Captain, she made it very clear that she didn't want you to know."

I emphasised each word as I repeated it. "Where. Is. She?"

Finally, through his pursed lips, the man broke. "Last I heard, she was to be sent home to live with her parents in Basksin. I was actually sent here to oversee a new order for horses and thought I could visit her in the meantime—but her family was adamant that I wasn't allowed anywhere near her." Howard sounded defeated as he told me of the truth.

I was still stunned by the news. "Thank you, Howard."

Immediately, I rose from my seat and drew my hood lower over my face.

All other matters became trivial in the face of the news I just received. I was suddenly urged to go and see to Nora.

"They won't be welcoming you!"

I ignored the man and burst out through the inn doors and made my way through to the stables.

⟨ ⟩

Zephyr was still in a sullen mood, but my haste must have been infectious, for he begrudgingly sped through the slowly falling curtain of snow, galloping through the open road like a wayward wind.

When we arrived at Basksin, and my cold lungs pained at each breath; I dismounted Zephyr and forcefully brought him to heel before tying his reins at the gate.

Quickly, I went from one stand to the next and questioned passing folk. I didn't realise until halfway through that my hood had been blown fully off and eyes followed me endlessly throughout the camp and rumour began to bud. Those I questioned watched me with bewildered shock, too entranced to give me my answer in a timely fashion.

Finally, someone was able to point me to the Bray household.

It took three fully harsh and pounding knocks until the door opened and a disgruntled man stood on the other side. His eyes looked at my chest before craning up to see my notable zerubic features.

"Good day," my smile was short and forced, and my speech even more curt. "My name is Captain General Erefiel Numyana, tied to the Clerian army and son of White-Hawk and Lady Imrie. I understand that Nora is under your care? I consider her a friend and would like to see her."

The man's puffed cheeks quickly reddened with anger. "I send away that uncouth soldier and they send me a half-blood? I don't care who you are! I will tell you what I told him. Nora will *not* be seeing anyone from your uncivilised cohort, and I ask that you remove yourself at post-haste!"

I promptly braced against the door before the man could shut it in my face.

The man gasped at my action. "How dare you! If you don't leave this instance, I *will* inform the guards."

I was in no mood to play at being reasonable, as I shoved the door back open and ducked underneath the frame and into their house. Though not as vast as my own establishment in Cleria, or most other establishments, there was wealth within this home with handcrafted furniture and flashy design.

"I don't think you understand." I tried to keep the rage out of my voice. "I *am* the guard."

"Frank? What is going on?" I heard a woman call from upstairs.

"Nothing, my sugarplum! I'm dealing with it." Frank tried his best to sound confident, but the franticness in his voice betrayed him.

"Move." I ordered, and when the man did not, I simply brushed past him.

A smouldering calm radiated from me as I climbed up the stairs.

"Sir! Sir, you cannot step in here! This is our house! Sir!" The more the man spoke, the less power he held. Each word spoken louder and louder only to reveal how hollow his threat was.

I strode up the stairs and turned. A woman was caught off guard and screamed when she saw me.

"Frank! Who is this man in our house?"

"An uncivilised brute from the army!"

"Excuse me." I pushed forward and found there to be no one else in the house.

Though I knew that Nora had a brother, he didn't seem to be present. I entered the only room with a locked door and immediately froze in my tracks at the sight of my friend.

Chapter Fifty-Eight

EREFIEL

*As one can surmise from my report, Erefiel Numyana stated that
he and his men successfully pushed back the onslaught of invading akar.
Though it is veritable that the akar have learnt the art of cohesion and
stratagem, I do dare say that the threat is negligible. Due to the clever
tactics of our own Clerian men, a creature moulded by Mage Gurick
was set loose on the beast before his own untimely demise.*

SIGNED—PLITHY JULIAN MANNES THE VISCOUNT

L aying upon a bed, hollow and broken, was the strongest
spirit I had ever known. I shuddered in horror. She didn't
just lose her right arm and leg.

I gathered the wounds on her left were new due to the bandages
that covered them. Her right limbs were completely gone up to the
shoulder and pelvis, yet her freshly dismembered left limbs were cut
off just below the joints.

"What happened to you?" I asked, yet Nora didn't even seem to
notice me. Clear dribble ran down her chin as her eyes glazed over
like fogged glass.

I turned instead to the parents, who looked upon their daughter
as if only then realising what happened to their child.

"What happened to her?" My voice boomed.

Frank was taken aback, but the mother was not. "She's been like this ever since..." her voice caught itself in her throat. With a shudder, she pushed on. "Ever since the attack."

"When?" I asked.

"One week." Frank finally gave in and answered my questions. "We had someone from the church come and even a doctor, but there is nothing that they can do."

I looked at Nora. She wore a nightgown, her depressed skirt outlining the contours of her ruined body. Her brown hair had formed a sombre halo about her head as dead eyes looked past me without even a hint of recognition or acknowledgement.

"She doesn't talk, doesn't move, doesn't do anything. We have to feed her soup, so it runs down her throat and she doesn't choke on it."

"Did you catch whoever did this?" I asked.

"We were all in church when it happened," Frank explained.

"And she was attacked in your home?"

"She was out in a small, secluded patch within a garden when we found her bleeding like that." Frank suddenly balled his fist and seemed to burst with rage.

The woman noticed and placed a comforting hand on the man's fist. Begrudgingly, the mother looked at me and spoke shamefully of what happened. "It wasn't just her limbs that were removed, we found her covered... in something."

"What?"

"My daughter was defiled! Raped out on the streets!" Frank's anger burst from him, a sense of frustration lining his cries.

I turned again to Nora. I wanted to ask who did this, but all I saw was a hollowed-out shell of a friend. Whoever did this planned it so that nobody was watching. Someone wanted to desecrate her, to defile her, to punish her.

"I knew she never should have joined your filthy lot! This is her punishment! It is *our* punishment." Frank voiced.

Completely ignoring the man, I walked to the side of the bed and, for a moment, I hoped that she would turn to me and speak. But even standing so close, I was of no consequence to whatever was left of Nora.

"I will take her to Cleria." Bowing down, I lifted Nora in my arms and almost toppled—not because she was heavier than I expected, but rather the opposite: Nora weighed nothing at all.

"Over my dead body you are!" Frank turned and obstructed the door.

"Move."

The man stood strong despite my cold, seething gaze and domineering stature. Though I still noticed the slight tremble.

"Frank, maybe they will be able to help her."

"No, Martha! I won't let them defile her even more! To use their foul arts!"

"I don't care!" Martha finally broke and wept without restraint.

She practically howled and grabbed onto Frank as her knees buckled and she fell before him. "Please, I don't care if she has to be taken to demons, or even to the bloody Elders themselves! As long as my baby comes back to me."

I suddenly became a spectator to their performance, completely forgotten. Frank knelt to his wife. "She will come back to us," he promised.

"Look at her! Look at our child!" She pointed to Nora, who lay motionless in my arms, the sleeves and skirt draped like limp curtains about her as her listless eyes looked out without recognition.

"I will take her with or without your permission," I insisted. "But I would much rather it be with." My tone was softer.

Finally, befallen by a weeping wife and a half-blood Nephilim, Frank nodded. "Do what you will. She is no daughter of mine anymore. Just take her and leave."

I felt as if Martha wanted to complain, but her weeping was too much as Frank picked her up and led her away to give me free passage.

As I roamed through the snow-covered streets of Basksin. The people filled the space all around to create a bordered path before me.

Still, Nora was quiet, not speaking a single word as I carried her in my arms.

The snow spotted her and me—it was like a scene from an abstract painting with no story, just emotion.

Me, a strange being with white feathers sprouting from scalp and hair of pure white; her, a human broken and dismembered with a gossamer white gown hugging her wilting form and draped over her dismembered limbs; the road before us, a carpet of laden snow made to bring us away from this place of pain.

The blanched flakes drifted from above like mourning petals. The crowd watched with impartial gazes, a valley of souls watching me depart from their religious haven. Taking with me proof of suffering as it had no place within their lives.

Chapter Fifty-Nine
DALILA

Rumours can sometimes be harbingers of truth. It is well known that Cleria is not just that which is seen above ground. Some are thoroughly convinced that ancient tunnels and aqueducts run throughout the bowels of Cleria. These constructs hint at a lost culture. Though if any of this merits truth is still questionable.

—A STUDY ON CLERIA'S RISE AND WHAT CAME BEFORE,
BY HERMAN FALLS

I t was a cold winter dawn, the kind where the previous night's slumber was impossibly deep and evidently wanting. My waking was a slow and sluggish endeavour. My eyes heavy and a slow haze clouding my thoughts.

Regardless, I partook in my rituals while everyone still tossed and turned within their own nightly cocoons.

I found access to the bath an undeniable luxury in comparison to my past life. Red runes were drawn onto the tiled walls and served to heat the cisterns and its waters. My gown shed itself like a second skin, sliding down my contours as now the billowing mist of the steam enveloped to conceal my scarred temple.

A sponge scraped across my skin, purifying the sanctum before I took my concealed razor to skin and bloodlet my caustic self-contempt. I watched it mix and thin with the spiralling water until it was gone from sight, as was my libation.

⤳ ⤳

Late in the afternoon, as I read the Kaseluda within a private reading room, I suddenly heard a bustling commotion on the other side of the door.

"Stop! You can't be here!"

"Where is she? Where is Dalila?"

I was instantly drawn to the living as I jumped from my seat to open the door.

"What is happening?" I asked.

There, on the other side, was a young student, a Sister not yet turned Mother.

"I'm sorry, Mother Dalila! I tried desperately to tell him he can't come in here, but he demanded to see you." The speed with which the young maiden spoke betrayed her fluster and distress.

Just behind her was a tall man clad in regal clothes, though the rich colours were hidden underneath muck and snow.

He turned to reveal himself—I could never forget that face.

"Erefiel?"

I looked down into his arms to find a woman. At first I thought her dead given the glazed expression; a gown draped over her body like some spectral bride. Glassy eyes stared out listlessly. It was only then that I noticed it was Nora.

"What happened?" I asked, striding through the young Sister and up to Erefiel.

"I don't know. All I know is that she was attacked in Basksin."

I looked up at Erefiel in disbelief. "By her own people?"

He shook his head, his own frantic haste infecting me. "Someone outside of the village. It was premeditated; someone wanted to make her suffer."

"Nora, can you hear me?" After a moment of no response, I looked at Erefiel for answers.

"She has been like this since I found her."

I placed a hand on her forehead.

"She's ice-cold!!" I turned to the Sister standing behind me. "What's your name?"

The girl seemed caught off guard. "J-Jane." She stuttered.

"Okay, Jane. I need you to go find Mother Margaret. Tell her that there is a young girl who is going into hypothermia. Tell her to meet us in the east wing nursing room for guests."

Jane nodded, the severity of the situation steeling her as she went on her way.

"I considered warming her up at my home before we came here."

"It's a good thing you didn't, might have done more harm than good." Erefiel nodded.

"Tell me everything," I told Erefiel as I led the way to a separate room.

⋙ ⋘

Within the room, I had access to a small tool kit of surgical implements. Though Erefiel had covered Nora in his cloak on the way here, her gown was still damp as I began to cut through it and remove her clothes.

Erefiel sat on a chair in the corner, his eyes glued to the wall as he told me everything that took place.

It took him longer than expected to arrive here, given the fact that he had to strap Nora to Zephyr and be gentle when galloping back to Cleria. I looked upon the ruin of Nora's form and forlorned. Her left arm and leg cut beneath the knee and elbow, her right leg and arm burnt to shoulder and hip.

In that moment, I would have rather she looked at me with hatred, with spite, with despair, or sorrow or any other emotion. It was the listless gaze that peered past me that left me despondent.

Dismembered and naked, her brown locks forming a halo about her head, her small round breasts left fully to bare upon an unmade warrior's body. I could not contain my tears.

"Who could have done this?" I asked.

Erefiel remained silent, his own speechlessness speaking volumes about our sorrow. Finally, the door burst open.

Mother Margaret gave a reflexive prayer at the sight; she had probably not expected this severe of a case. Quickly, she collected herself and forced Jane out, who tried to peek a look at Nora's splayed sanctity.

"Is she even alive?" Mother Margaret asked as she turned back to Nora.

"She is, but she has lost a lot of heat," I explained.

Mother Margaret nodded and brought forth her own warming cover to wrap around Nora. Nora's expression remained unchanged, even if her lips quivered as a natural bodily response. Mother Margaret correctly identified the cause of the wounds and assessed it as being unrelated to her present scars.

"What a horrible fate this woman has lived. I pray to the Elders that they bless this child and protect her from further harm," Mother Margaret beseeched as she patted an absorbent cloth of warm water upon Nora's forehead.

Jane eventually returned with a lukewarm pot of water, using it to gently guide small sips down Nora's throat.

⊲ ⊳

Eventually, Erefiel and I were taken to Mother Vinrie's office to discuss what had transpired. She did not address Erefiel warmly and was quick to admonish.

"You know that it is against the rules to enter this house without an invitation as someone who isn't a Sister? Even more so as a man," Mother Vinrie said to Erefiel.

Erefiel stood at the opposite side of the table alongside me in lieu of sitting. It was a sign of deference.

"With respect, Mother Vinrie, given the pressing urgency of Nora's state, I didn't consider the rules to hold precedence over her life."

Mother Vinrie banged her fist on the table. "And you know what is permissible and what isn't?" she challenged. "Believe me, Erefiel, if you weren't son to Lady Imrie and White-Hawk, I would have been well within my rights to ask for your immediate incarceration."

Erefiel held his tongue and repressed whatever retort he wanted to speak.

"Besides, as much as it pains me to say this, that poor girl is gone. She is no longer within that body. Whatever horrible travesty that took place was obviously too much to handle… for anyone." Mother Vinrie gave an exhausted sigh as she leaned back in her seat. "Perhaps it is even best that she stays that way."

"Not Nora," Erefiel cut in.

"Excuse me?"

Erefiel took in a calming breath as he gathered his thoughts. "No one, and I mean *no one*, has the kind of iron will that Nora does. She will make it."

"Look at her! I understand she has quite a reputation as a soldier, but what kind of life can she live even if she does return?"

The words were a punch in the gut. "Mother Vinrie!" I cried incredulously.

Erefiel also spoke up with more practised composure than me. "With all due respect, you know not of who you speak. Nora wouldn't wish to give up, no matter the circumstances."

Mother Vinrie chuckled almost blithely; something I'd never seen before. "See reason! She has no arms! No Legs! What is there that she could *possibly* do? You expect me to ask one of our Sisters to take care of a woman with no future? Someone who will never respond again? And even if she were to wake up…" Mother Vinrie's words trailed into nothingness before shaking her head with absolute assuredness. There was a glimmer of pity in her pursed lips. "No, I'm sorry, there is nothing we can do for her."

There was a pressing and final silence, which accentuated the reality of the situation.

"What if I were to take responsibility?" I asked.

Mother Vinrie's eyes narrowed, readying herself to deny my request.

"I am locked and bound to the church anyway and I would do it with unquestioning diligence. If I have nowhere to go, I might as well use that time doing something that is right."

"Mother Dalila, I know your heart is in the right place, but I can't have you helping someone with no future. I wish for you to help those who need it."

"Nora *does* need it," I rebuked. Mother Vinrie seemed unaccustomed to my sudden stubbornness. "I am a Mother; it is our duty to help those who need help and provide aid. It wouldn't be right to deny that to her, even considering her situation."

Obviously annoyed, Mother Vinrie turned to Erefiel with a fake smile. "What are your thoughts, captain?"

Erefiel looked down at me and then to Mother Vinrie. "I believe I was correct to represent Mother Dalila."

Mother Vinrie gave a dissatisfied growl but acquiesced. "Fine, from now on, Mother Dalila will take care of Nora; one of our nursing homes will be provided."

My spirits rose with that announcement.

"However!"

No sooner was my elation halted. Mother Vinrie continued. "If Nora does not awake in five months, I won't have you wasting anymore time on her."

Chapter Sixty

DALILA

The fastest way to cripple the work of an Inspired, is to reveal their secrets to admirers and show exactly why the art works. Even more dangerous is to reveal these secrets to every promising student and watch them cripple their own work into derivative nonsense.

—Dangers of Teaching, by Joshua Shuh

The home provided was a narrow two-storey house with a private room downstairs for the caretaker and the upper floor for the one who needed the care. However, given the impractical design of the stairs, I decided to take the sleeping quarters on the second floor and leave Nora below.

Having my own place and away from the plain marble walls of the Sisterhood was a pleasant change, and I surely valued the privacy. The only thing I regretfully missed was access to the showers, but that seemed of little consequence when I considered the good I was doing.

Already on the third day, I took it upon myself to absolve Nora of her hair, cutting away the mid-length wavy locks bit by bit as if it were part of herself. What was left was an inch long, which suited Nora's reputation as a rugged warrior, or at least it befitted a shadow of her past-self.

My daily responsibilities were cooking, cleaning, making sure I turned her body regularly and got as much blood flowing through her as possible to avoid any bed sores. The last part was anxiety-inducing, as Nora's inactive self had made it impossible to know if she had anything to complain about or not.

Though she wasn't entirely unresponsive. At times, I would turn to find a lone tear course down her withering cheeks. Other times, listless eyes followed me in a haze, as if observing me from a vast distance I could not bridge.

On days when I fed her a thin broth, I made sure to hold her up as best I could and brought small spoons to her lips. Her body reacted with minute responses like swallowing or even providing a slight inclination of parting her mouth as little as was needed to eat or drink; the cloth I fitted into her collar I used to wipe clean the dribble that poured down her chin.

When I had time for myself, I appreciated the chance to remove myself into my chambers and, upon a bucket, provide another libation poured from my drawn blood. One such night, I stared upon my reflection naked with pure, unbridled disgust.

My contours were that of a voluptuous woman, my expression unreadable, my body telling a story of self-hatred. My temple was one of shame, the notched carvings on my skin chipping away at the foundation to mark its contemptuous piety.

I hoped against hope that my helping of Nora would grant me worth, show how selfless of a being I could be, show how I truly repented for the death of Perry so long ago.

That was the reason why I would carry her, dip her body into a warm tub and scrub away at her skin. That was the reason I willingly removed Nora's diaper to clean the extremities that came from loose bowels.

At some point after that first month, I began to wonder if Nora would someday return to this realm. I spoke to her at times, wondering if she could hear me. Four more months. The nascent presence of ticking time was a slow and voiceless thing; a hibernating fear, waiting.

I divulged my deepest and darkest secrets, not stopping to consider the repercussions if she were to eventually wake.

Nora would just look at me with those listless eyes, limbless and resting against the headboard as I fed her the beige liquid that sustained her.

Most of my confessions concerned how I had missed Yasmin. I didn't get much of a chance to see my friend often since being delegated to this house, but she would visit and help when she had the chance.

I told Nora about the one time I masturbated out on my bed and was caught by Mother Candice. Still, I did not know how to feel about that woman, though I had heard she had a firmer position within the Sisterhood.

One thing that I did not realise, until I confessed to Nora, was how glad I was to no longer see Mother Lucia. My duty and service made it difficult to continue my meetings with her. I told Nora of the murder I had witnessed, and my thoughts on Mother Lucia's knowledge.

I didn't think Mother Lucia was capable of doing such a horrible act, but I felt she put too much trust in her witches, a fact that would cause many more unfortunate murders.

"Should I tell Mother Vinrie?" I asked Nora. As always, she simply blinked without a hint of a reaction.

It pained me to think how slowly this chasm was being wedged between me and the only other witch I had come to know; the only woman who comforted me since the moment we met.

Not to mention, the last time we talked, I revealed the fact that Yasmin knew of my secret. I don't think Mother Lucia believed that I left her out of it. I couldn't help but feel uneasy about it. Did Mother Lucia think I divulged even more information? Perhaps revealing that there was a coven of witches? The more I lingered on the thought, the more it unnerved me. I focused on Nora instead.

⊰ ⊱

During my many musings and sole company, I wondered if there was a way to help Nora recover. I then heard a voice, a seething vile thing that whispered doubt into my own ear.

What if I just wanted Nora to recover so that I would be free of my burden of taking care of her? Was my intent selfish?

A contradiction ailed me as I fought internally with my desire to be good. During my nights, I would be forced to face the truth that the only reason I wished to aid Nora was to feel worthy of something—that in itself was selfish.

I battled with my own demons the same way Nora did. Silently, stoically, without anyone to hear our suffocated screams.

The snow of winter had thawed, and the streets cleared, the weather leaning towards spring in the midst of a new year and a new beginning

I had commissioned a wheelchair to be made for Nora. It was delivered within a week's time and was of no mentionable design. The frame of the body was made with twisted metal and carved oak, while the wheels and spokes were fully polished and lacquered wood.

I had carried Nora down and taken it upon myself to wheel her through to Strait District. The dress she wore I had commissioned along with the wheelchair. It was a loose fitting and simple dress the colour of darkened rust. The sleeves were rolled and pinned up so they wouldn't flail and the hem of her dress was fastened to the seat along with Nora's torso.

Our path was filled with the whispers of onlookers who pointed and pitied the non-responsive Nora. I ignored them, doing my part as the lady in white who was poised to lead her charge through the road. I was caught off guard when people walked up to us and praised me for my kindness, stating that I was truly a good and virtuous woman to be taking care of such a wounded soul.

They did not know the pain in Nora's heart and so spoke to her only to be ignored. I explained that Nora was not in the best of moods and to not take it personally.

On two such occasions, I had to sincerely decline any form of coin that was being offered.

I was supposed to feel vindicated, satiated, when they showered me with such self-serving praise—yet all I felt was dirty. I leaned to the side and looked at the woman who was supposed to be my friend, awash with guilt. It felt like I was parading her through the city for myself.

⤛ ⤜

We arrived at Strait district and, after a very troublesome battle with the hostile architecture of the establishment, I managed to carry Nora to the top of the stairs where I propped her against a wall. I then carried the wheelchair up to her—the task proved laborious and the last few steps were made easier by a passing soldier that rushed to help.

I pushed and strained against the wheels that dug through dirt and into the garden where new recruits trained. I paused underneath the shade of a veranda.

I hoped the sight of something that once filled Nora with such life would once again stir something within. Yet nothing; we watched for close to an hour as men cried and shouted, blades clashing and hollow shields catching blows. I leant to Nora's side. Even then her empty eyes seemed to barely take notice of the event before her.

"Nora, I don't know if you can hear me, but I thought maybe hearing the clash of ringing swords would bring you back to us."

Nothing.

We continued to watch. Her limp, unmoving body strapped to the chair, our presence hidden underneath the veranda.

Nora never did respond, except for one single tear which ran down her hollow cheek.

"Let's go back home," I said, fearing that Nora would perhaps never return to us.

From within, the vile, caustic voice spat its seditious venom again. "*Is that a problem?*" it asked me.

Chapter Sixty-One

Among the inspired, there are those whose magic takes rare forms.
One such example comes from those who have committed themselves fully
towards acting. It is said that when such an Inspired performs, that
they transform completely into their character. Some legends speculate
that actors with more questionable motivations may be employed as assas-
sins for their transformation can fool even the sharpest eye.

—THE MASTER

I evarus had roamed the plaza daily since meeting the Master.
Yet there was no sign of the hooded figure with a spider nestled
as a face.

The plaza was a vast and scaling place, the buildings all made in the
image of gothic mediaeval architecture with grand and towering design.
Each yawned and stretched as if observed through a contorted lens.

The insides were colossal works with plenty of room to spare. The
altars on which hymns would be sung were high up into the air and the
chamber would be filled with the congregating souls of higher beings.

Finally, as a stormy cloud drifted over from behind Mount Morniar
where the Nif reigned, a voice appeared of which Ievarus had been
searching.

"It has been some time. I trust you have been doing well, young
Seed."

"Where have you been?" Ievarus asked, unfazed by the unannounced approach.

"Here. Waiting."

"Waiting for what?"

"To see if you would speak of me to the Elder King."

Ievarus blinked. The stretched being of carved alabaster did not comment.

"There is a storm coming," The Master said, though Ievarus had no way of knowing the truth behind those words.

Thunder crackled close from above like a whip hidden within those roiling clouds.

Master stepped to the edges of the balustrade which barred them within the plaza. Looking beyond and down below, they could see the swirling spiral of congregating stingrays.

"I see that you still make no progress with the Preceptor," Master said.

Ievarus stepped to stand beside Master. "I know not how to instil an idea. I do as I am told to do. Why can't that be enough?"

"I will tell you a story," Master began. "There was once a man named Igura the Fractious, a mortal of unparalleled skill. He was truly gifted, able to outwit any opponent, always a step ahead of the competition.

"Yet the man was not without flaws. Fear held him back, hope made him careless, compassion made him impressionable, while rage made him uncontrollable. The man, convinced of his own limitations, expelled these parts of himself and left behind only his indomitable will."

Ievarus blinked.

"It took Igura a long time to realise these emotions were a part of what made him great, so he set out on a quest to retake them. Alas, they could no longer be drawn into the man. It had been too long for such a thing. Instead, they became a band, fought as one, and Igura was stronger than ever."

Ievarus blinked. "Is there a way to find Igura and learn how to absorb emotions?"

Master did something akin to a chortle. The spider spun its web to mirror the elation. "It is just a story." The spider seemed agitated by the remark and spun a new pattern upon its web.

"I don't understand how a story is supposed to help me."

"You cannot find an idea because you have no emotions to instil in them—you live among Elders, immortal beings devoid of such earthly concepts. If you wish to have an idea, a motivation—" Master waved out towards the great landscape of Minethria, small and far from Ievarus' reach.

"Then meddle with mortals, learn from them, allow them to teach you what it means to fight."

Ievarus blinked. "I am not permitted to leave until I am ready."

"Ievarus, how do you expect to be ready when all you do is as you are bidden?"

Ievarus looked out to the sprawling landscape. "And where would I find such a human?"

"There is one." Master revealed an object from the hanging sleeve of their robe. It was a circular disk with shifting iridescent colours upon its surface.

"This will lead you to one called Dalila, a Sister of the Church. She will teach you of compassion and perhaps lead you to the other four concepts."

There was a tug, a sensation beckoning the spawn to venture forth and see what could be found. Ievarus accepted the circular pendant and draped its chain around their neck. Without a moment's hesitation, Ievarus hopped up onto the railing of the balustrades and looked down.

Another rumble of thunder came from overhead. The cries of the stingrays echoing spectral chimes as they spiralled.

Ievarus leapt from the end.

Below there jutted the stacked buildings of the Yungbloods, and just below that, the humble residence of zerubs. The structures blurred past like streaking paint on a canvas. The impermanent and ever-shifting world of Mount Morniar would fade and the permanence of land would present itself.

Ievarus fell, the air around them rushing and howling as it swept past their ears.

Ievarus picked up speed at their plummet. A black mote at the root of Mount Morniar divided the mountain and the lands beyond.

Wind tugged and dragged upon Ievarus' spread body.

Ievarus hardened, landing upon an unsuspecting stingray that temporarily broke their fall; the large beast shrieked from the pain, before plummeting to the reaching black tendrils where the wyrms thrashed.

Ievarus leapt from one to the next, sharpened fingers piercing into leathery flesh and slowing their descent. The nails clawed their way down one fin, tearing through the lopsided stingray. Ievarus continued further and further. Lightning cracked the sky.

And so did the spawn of the Elder King walk among man.

Chapter Sixty-Two

EREFIEL

There is a sect of shavinu who upon receiving their vision, abandon all connections with their friends and head out into the unchartered woods. Wherever it is that these shavinu head is unknown, but it is suggested that they share in some unknown future of Minethria only they are aware of. Even now, they wait, for the day of their collective deaths.

—THICKWOOD AND ITS UNKNOWNS, BY LINEN FRICH

I n my yard, I donned my armour and swung my blade with great flourish. Sweat glistened upon my brow and skin, and the feathers upon my scalp rode upon the rushing winds at each explosive turn and strike.

"Doesn't seem exactly practical to be training with that heavy armour. Father used to say that the shavinu need to be unhindered at all times." Saru retold with just a hint of indignation. If it was for my need for armour or for still evoking his neglectful father's platitude—I couldn't tell.

My flow was broken as I turned towards Saru. He stood in his servant's attire of black and white. The gnarled slit upon his forehead looked like scowling lips, judging my performance.

I walked to him, accepting the towel offered to wipe myself down. "Well, I won't be fighting without it on the battlefield, so there is no point in training without the armour on."

Saru nodded; the logic was sound, but I was sure that he still deemed it a liability.

"So, what is it?" I asked, wondering what would compel him to approach me so.

"It's your father," he said. I lowered the towel and affixed my attention entirely to his next words. "White-Hawk is on his way home."

❧ ❧

I dressed myself with great haste, absolving myself of my battle armour and donning the ceremonial piece.

Armour was supposed to be practical, not encumbered and adorned with spikes and high rising pauldrons and heavy chest pieces with great exaggerated reliefs. But—when there was cause to celebrate and rile up the crowd of patriotic citizens to assuage the payment of taxes—we dressed to impress.

My ceremonial armour was an intricate mesh of glistening steel and golden rims. The helmet was shaped in the form of a hawk's head with just more exaggerated plumage jutting from the top. Unlike my battle armour, the beak head was polished gold. On each of my shoulders were intricate metal feathers, alternating between silver and gold. My chest piece was emblazoned with a relief of my father's head. Instead of feathers, my greaves sported chiselled images of snowflakes upon their shape and the knees themselves were fashioned to show a golden sun on the right and a silver moon on the left. A silver cape finished the look.

When I approached the stable, I found the stable boy frantically gathering up all the pieces of ceremonial armour to dress Zephyr, and the fact that Zephyr seemed to be rather temperamental made it an even harder endeavour.

With little time to waste, I opted for a simple saddle and leather reins before riding off to stand at the welcoming party.

Given the rather short notice, the welcoming party was a messy and uncoordinated blunder as a half band of trumpets filled an alleyway. The skies were not divided by triangular pennants connecting the buildings, nor did flowers shower the path.

Even the escorting party was just four present soldiers who weren't otherwise preoccupied elsewhere, holding aloft great towering banners which presented the spiral of the Elders.

News travelled ravenously as people crowded their balconies and streets. With self-plucked petals from their own tended gardens or pots, the citizens tossed their offerings onto the streets while father rolled into the city.

The only other notable visitor was a strange creature; ostensibly also a zerub. They walked like a decrepit hermit, their robes a sagging and enveloping mesh of opal black, not entirely ebony, with a deep sea-blue colouring to the hems.

The hands of the creature held a twisted oak staff with a bulbous head. Their towering stature and presence spoke for itself.

Scaly, avian talons with two fingers and a thumb wrapped themselves around the staff. The only distinctive feature was a vulture-like hooked beak protruding from under the draped cloth about the head.

How they could see was not clear, but nonetheless, the creature led the way forward.

Father's escorts were angels, three of which walked with their expressionless steel masks and held halberds. The remaining three angels hovered with the help of their gossamer capes turned into transparent wings; they were reminiscent of an insect's.

At the end of the path, through the roads of admiring and screaming onlookers, there was the town square. A marble set of stairs reached a standing and wide square plateau for just such an occasion.

Father exited his wagon and with his features left fully to bear, the crowd ululated with loving cheers while more petals rained down as if bidding for Father's attention.

Father, as well as the large and round mystic creature, scaled the top of the stairs with no hurry at all.

Eventually, at the top, I stood opposite my father and wanted nothing more than to rush into a hug.

Mother was there too, the White Lady standing taller than most humans. Her glistening dress was even more extravagant than my own cape. It sparkled as if stars were sewn into the fabric, layered over and over atop each other and again seemingly brittle, as if made entirely of rime. The dress covered her from neck to toe. The sleeves widened at the wrists, while the end of the dress dragged behind wherever she stepped and left just the kiss of frost. Her lashes were curled and long like the leaves of a yule tree brushed with crusted snow; her lips were a glistening gloss of ice, her skin pale and frozen.

I did not rush forward but instead stepped with diligence, still wrapping my arms around my father. "It is good to see you," I said so that only he could hear me.

His hand patted my back. "Likewise, my son." His feathers brushed against me and by all accounts he had that earthy smell common with animals.

Next, mother stepped forward, almost gliding serenely like a spectre. Her dainty and tended hands held together before her.

"My love," Father spoke with affection as he took mother's hand and beak-kissed her icy flesh.

Mother gave an acknowledging and expressionless nod which, as far as we were concerned, was a great sign of affection.

Father turned towards his guest. "This is Hachen, The One of Twisted Tongue, The Feeder of Faith, a zerub of the highest order and one who has the honour of serving the Elder King."

The introduction held with it such grand weight that the mere idea of being in their presence almost compelled me to kneel.

Hachen was the word of the Elder King; practically the word of God.

Hachen spoke, his voice a hoarse and guttural thing. "**I thank ye', House of Numyana, White Lady, Erefiel, for your gracious welcome, despite the abruptness of our visit.**" The being looked at us from under the cover of his cloak, Hachen's movements were slow.

"Why do you visit us, Hachen? Is the Elder King displeased?" Mother asked.

Hachen made a sound that one could have called a chuckle. "**Nothing of the sort. I was just to escort White-Hawk back to you and bring gifts.**" Hachen turned, the avian talons waving to address the assorted angels of six, now all standing with halberds at their side in columns of two and rows of three.

"**Perhaps I could visit the holy houses to see what mortals now worship in the Elder's name. Truly, it has been five hundred years since last I saw of their ingenuity.**"

Along the narrow streets, we were escorted to the doors of Nostracie Palace.

The angels and Hachen were taken elsewhere, further into the centre where a home was made for the rare guests of Mount Morniar.

As mother glided and excused herself to her throne room, I went along with Father to his private chambers.

The more I walked with him, the tenser he seemed. Unease radiated from him as he looked about himself and his frantic gaze jumped all around us. Still, he upheld his composure, bottling the growing pressure inside that was about to erupt.

We entered his room together when Father asked to give him some privacy. I gently shoved him inside and closed the door behind—he couldn't contain it any longer.

A great heaving and desperate gasp expanded from him.

"Take this off me!" he pleaded, the stoic frame gone as he was ridden with panic.

I rushed to him as he tugged at the coif and collar of glistening armour. Father tugged at the metal as if he were covered in a suit of vermin. Bit by bit, we pulled and tore down the chastising armour until he was left bare in his sweat stained tunic and simple greaves, his feet open and bare as his human toes curled and strained.

Father leaned against the bed canopy post and slid down it, his expression pained and panicked.

"Father, what's wrong?" I joined his side, his breathing laboured as he still gasped for air.

"Water." He begged.

I rushed to the side, a canter of water and glass at the ready. Father avulsed the canter from me and drank straight from it, his gullet an endless pit devouring the contents to the last drop.

Finally, he tossed the canter to the side, the morphed metal rattling against the carpet and chiming as it hit the wooden floor just beyond.

"Father? What is it? I am worried."

The man didn't look at me, instead staring down at his feet.

Minutes passed by, his breathing calmed until eventually he seemed in control but no less disturbed.

"It's just—I have been up there for quite some time. Returning here always takes its toll."

"What's it like?" I asked, sitting with him so we were level.

Finally, his eyes met mine, they were bloodshot beads, the gold around the black pit turning into scarlet.

"That *place* is alive, it is nothingness, it is *more*. It is… a feeling, a crawling sensation that creeps onto you at night." Father was shaken at the thought. "It is not for mortal men; it changes you, whispers to you. It is a constant and feverish dream with no end." He looked puzzled. "Did I even sleep?" The question was addressed to himself.

I nodded, sympathising though I could not understand. Mount Morniar was the realm of greater beings, of practical gods; it wasn't made for mortals. Born from the first cycle, acclimation for the zerub was easier than with other races; it was the irregularity with which Father came and went that made transition so difficult.

"Father, you are as old as the second cycle. I would have thought you were used to the place?"

"It is not staying there that is difficult, it is returning to these planes, that is. My mind needs time to adjust."

"And Hachen?"

Father scoffed. "I'm not even sure. Perhaps he has given more of himself to Mount Morniar to ever be free of its permeable clutches." My father paused for a moment. "That place... it changes you. I return to you now and this place too seems strange, odd to say the least. It never changes, it is permanent, no longer fluid."

"Is that why you came back? Because you need to rest?"

Father shook his head, noticeably exhausted. "No. The Seed is gone."

I stood up in a sudden shock. "Gone? What do you mean?"

"They vanished. It seems they ran away from Mount Morniar; that is the real reason I came with Hachen and the angels. We are searching for Ievarus."

Chapter Sixty-Three

DALILA

The Elders deserve remarkable credit for how they have found ways to subtly bind mortals to time without it ever being questioned. Despite the Elder King being a god beyond the inconveniences of time, he has a remarkable talent for tracking its passing with the rise and fall of his golden eye every day. And even the seasons are a constant reminder of our ticking clock.

—HERETIC MUSINGS OF INSICHIA, THE FETID WITCH

I t was a stormy night, the kind where I retreated to my chamber to avoid its tempestuous mood. Rain battered against the building, while distant thunder strummed notes for the leviathans of the sea.

I had already finished tending to Nora when I climbed the stairs to my room.

With the window left open, I buried my head into my Kaseluda, tentatively stroking the pages and thinking back to the bluebell flower that used to fill it. I couldn't help but wonder where the flower disappeared to; certainly it was lost somewhere within Nora's old home. I couldn't bear to think that her parents would have already thrown it aside, believing it to be nothing more than a wilting and unimportant flower.

As I turned to blow out the candle beside me on the nightstand, a flash of lightning outside revealed the outline of a figure perched upon my windowsill.

I shrieked, terror enveloping me, my hands and feet trembling from the sheer shock.

Was the creature human? No. What was it?

My brain tried its best to make out the contours of the beast; drawing lines and shapes around it to grasp its form. Finally, the lightning faded, and I stared upon the presence of an unordinary being.

Perched upon the windowsill was a barefooted figure, impossibly tall, perhaps just as tall as Erefiel. Its arms were long and lithe, white strands of hair hung straight from its scalp like woven silver threads. I looked upon their face and saw inset milky pearls looking back at me.

The creature stepped inside, presenting a pendant and a circular object with iridescent lights dancing upon its surface. It shifted to a shade of calming blue.

"D... Dalila."

Was it a question? Or a statement? I could not tell.

"Are you... Dalila?" The being's voice was softly worn stone at the bottom of a river bed, without inflection or emotion, without discernible gender.

"Are you Dalila?" They asked again.

"Yes!" My response came out frantic.

I fell out of bed and dragged myself to a corner. The being's stare was unusual; though there were no pupils, I could tell its gaze rested entirely on me, focusing, making sure to catch each shade and detail.

"Who... who are you?" I stammered.

"Ievarus," the being said, as if I were supposed to know what that meant.

It came closer and closer. The way it looked at me was like a curious child stumbling upon a novel sight.

"Are you... the killer?" I asked it.

It tilted its head. "Killer?"

The creature looked confused, naïve even. It lacked that wrathful

and passionate presence that dripped from the macabre display of floating bodies. I still pondered if this was what had committed the crimes.

"*What* are you?" I asked.

"They call me the Seed." Lightning struck like a final note upon
the reveal.

The only other thing that could have shocked me more was if
Ievarus had said that they were the Elder King himself.

Before me stood a piece of Mount Morniar, a vestige of gods and
elusive higher beings. Just that day, I heard of the commotion: White-
Hawk had returned with an entourage.

As the towering Ievarus worked their way towards me, they knelt
into a squat and took their long hands to graze my cheek. I shuddered—feeling the skin of a Seed felt like blasphemy—I was making
contact with the very being I was to serve.

"Di—did you come with White-Hawk?"

"I came with no one."

I looked behind Ievarus and noticed the storm had picked up, the
deluge of rain covering the sound of their presence.

Quickly I went to stand, brushing past the still squatted Ievarus
as I closed the shutters of my room and pulled close the curtains. A
puddle had formed under me that led wet prints across to where Ievarus
was now. I bit my lip, taken aback by the surreal nature of the moment.

"Wait there," I said.

I quickly returned, finding that Ievarus had taken my instruction
too literally as they hadn't moved a single muscle, still squatted as their
eyes followed me with a deep sense of curiosity. Hesitant, I swallowed
my concerns and walked over with a towel in hand to dry Ievarus.

"Can you even catch a cold?"

"A cold?" Ievarus parroted, noticeably confused. "I don't understand."

"Can you get sick?" I rephrased my question.

"How does one catch a feeling?" Ievarus asked, obviously perplexed.

I smiled to myself, finding the innocence of this esoteric being to
be endearing. As I did, Ievarus rose, their fingers prodding onto the

creased edges of my mouth, pulling my lips into a grin.

"You smile?" Ievarus asked.

It took me a moment to process their query.

"I found what you said funny," I explained, taking Ievarus' hands and gently lowering them.

The being towered over me, my height reaching their chest as their head almost scraped the roof. They must have been taller than Erefiel.

Ievarus once more presented the pendant. "Are you compassion?"

I didn't understand. The pendant was round and wide, covering the entirety of Ievarus' palm. A golden pattern filled the outer reaches of it and a domed glass covered the roiling colours inside. Or was it Haar?

"What do you mean by 'compassion'?" I asked.

Ievarus continued to explain a story, a story that I had heard before about Igura and his divided self.

"Teach me about heart, compassion." Was it a question? I still could not tell.

That night, I kept company with Ievarus, and only scratched the surface of explaining the vast complexity of the human world; yet to me, it was the enigmatic world from which they came which I couldn't explain. Despite this odd encounter between a god's spawn and a mere mortal, I found Ievarus strangely endearing with their naiveté.

I asked what Mount Morniar was like, but Ievarus didn't understand the question.

As I ran my towel over their body, I noticed how elastic yet taut Ievarus' skin was, as if made of rubber. Their hair was also rather curious. I ran my fingers along the impeccably straight strands, which drooped like the flora of a weeping willow, threads swaying into their neighbours. The hair had a weight to it, simultaneously rigid and yet malleable as the sombre candle light glossed over them.

I suddenly felt a flaring cut upon my finger tip and removed my hand in shock, looking to find a barely noticeable cut that did not bleed but still stung.

"Did I hurt you?" Ievarus asked.

I gave a sombre and reassuring smile before shaking my head. "No, you did not."

Again Ievarus was taken by my smile and prodded its corners.

I chuckled. "Stop it."

"Why?"

I found Ievarus' innocence endearing.

"You wish to learn about emotions?" I asked, pushing the Seed away.

Ievarus nodded.

"Who sent you?"

"Master."

I quickly decided that prodding Ievarus for information about Elder beings seemed like a waste of time, let alone wrong in an unspoken way.

"Master told me that you can also help me find other parts?"

I pondered on that and quickly came to think of Will.

"Perhaps there is one that may be of help."

Chapter Sixty-Four

EREFIEL

Heyru of Dusk held mastery over the flow of combat. With her six arms and eight chakram, she partook in dance and sent out her ringed blades. It is said that when she performed in her Battle Dance, that the blood of her victims joined her.

—Passage from the Kaseluda

That very same day, I escorted father after he stilled himself. Mother waited within her audience chamber, sitting beside Father's own seat, made from twisted and tangled oak to give it a fae-like appearance.

The years living amongst the humans and going back to Mount Morniar seemed to fracture the man in two, presenting a vulnerable side of Father that I had never seen before.

Once again, I was offered a seat of my own and declined—I wanted to stay away from the politics as much as possible. Mother chided me in that cold, icy way of hers, but father didn't fault me for it.

When the tide of guests and their tithes finally stemmed, father retreated to his private quarters with mother—I could only imagine what for. Though I was sure he told her everything, just as he had told me. The new Seed, Ievarus, was somewhere in Minethria and had yet to be found.

I took my leave from my official duties, passing them to my lieutenant as I wandered most of my day deep in thought. As the hours passed, I made my way to my parent's chambers.

I found father lying in bed without mother, wearing a new set of plain clothes. He wore no boots, just naked feet and wiggling toes as he looked up towards the canopy of his own bed.

"Can I come in?" I asked, knocking on the door and disrupting my father's musings.

"Yes son, come on in," he said in a levelled tenor through avian features. Father pulled himself up into a seated position, though he still seemed distracted by whatever plagued him.

"How are you feeling?"

"Like I am finally sober after a decade. The world seems so... still all of a sudden. I constantly am expecting the walls to stretch or move or do anything at all."

I could tell these were the words of a man on edge—father still had much that occupied him.

"Now I dread the day that I visit Mount Morniar," I admitted.

He looked at me, hearing these words for the first time.

"You wish to go to Mount Morniar?"

I shrugged, strolling to a canter of water at the side of the room and pouring myself a glass. "Why not? Being in service of the Elder King himself, that must be something incredible. Let alone having been constantly by his side for several millennia." I pondered the idea. *Elder King.* Father had known his kind for so long, yet I never asked what the figure was like. "What's he like? The King."

Father was taken aback at my sudden query. "Erefiel! You know it is forbidden to ask!"

I chuckled. "We are within our own four walls; who is to know?" My casualness was enough to assuage father's concerns.

He considered his words wisely and then frowned. "I'm... not sure."

"Not sure?"

"The Elder King... is unlike anything I have ever seen. In a lot of ways, he is ineffable, indescribable. It is no wonder Hachen turned out the way they did. Constantly being in the presence of such a being—it fractures the mind. The shape, the contours… they dance in your vision, stretch and morph as if we are looking at him through a tear in reality. It's as if his own shape writhes with a will of its own. The only way I could survive, to not truly go mad, was to sleep. To give myself to the inexplicable nature of the king and simply submit myself to him numbly. And his eyes…"

Father paused at the memory, tentatively remembering what it felt like. "One carries a sun within; it flares and burns if I were to look directly at it… it radiates pure power. But when he wears his eye of the moon… I barely see him, I barely notice him. His form is transient, impermanent, just like his castle."

I recognized father's rising anxiety and decided to veer away from the topic. "Perhaps you can take me with you when you return."

Father looked at me as if he had forgotten I was there. "No, son, not yet. It is not for me to decide, only a higher being can make that choice."

"So how do I prove myself? There is only so much I can do here against the akar." I wasn't able to keep the frustration from my voice.

Father reached out, his hand laid on top of mine. "Trust me, you are in no rush to visit that place."

"It's not about Mount Morniar."

Father didn't seem to grasp my meaning.

"It's…" I hesitated, father's albino eyes looking up at me.

"Nevermind. I just hope you stay for a while. Maybe we can spar like we used to? Or just spend time together. I don't really mind."

Father nodded. "I'd like that." There it was, an answer, but not a promise.

❧ ☙

That night, I slept within the palace for a change. My own room, though similar to how it was during my youth, was embellished with added furniture and a new bed to compensate for my large size. The next morning, I was saved the hassle of trying to keep myself busy when I was delivered a letter from Dalila.

She had invited me to her residence where she took care of Nora with post-haste, and I suddenly couldn't help but feel a sense of panic overtake me.

I wished to walk, but Mother insisted that a driver would escort me. Soon enough, I stood before the residence and hurried to the door, knocking.

Did something happen to Nora? Is that why I was summoned so urgently? Why then not report it to the church? Perhaps Mother Vinrie would still feel it a waste of resources?

Eventually, Dalila opened the door, her brows furrowed. "Erefiel. Why do you look so perturbed?" Dalila asked.

I waved the crumpled letter in front of her. "You told me to come quickly."

"Yes, I did." She still seemed rather confused.

"Is Nora alright? Are *you* alright?"

Dalila suddenly grasped the reason for my worry, her eyes widening apologetically. "Sorry! It's not about Nora. Come in, quickly."

I did as I was told. Dalila closed the door behind me. She seemed on alert.

"So what was it that had you summon me with such urgency?"

Dalila steeled herself. "Before I tell you, I need you to remain calm."

Unsure of what was waiting for me, I nodded obligingly. Dalila turned to lead me upstairs. I had to duck under the protruding frame of the ceiling half-way up the stairs.

"Where is Nora?" I asked.

"Downstairs."

"Can't we see her first?"

"I promise I have taken care of her just before you came. She can wait."

"What could possibly—" The rest of my words got stuck in my

throat when Dalila swung open the door and within I saw the most curious being.

Immediately, I reached for my hip and grasped at air, realising I hadn't brought my weapon.

I stepped forward at the ready.

"Wait! Stop. They mean you no harm."

"Who is that?" I asked.

"The Elder King's spawn: the Eleventh Seed."

This time, I took a reflexive step back. "What?" I exclaimed.

"Their name is Ievarus."

In a sudden hushed whisper, I bent down to Dalila. "*What* is the Seed doing here? My father was sent to find them!"

Dalila spoke back in hushed tones. "I figured as much; don't worry, Ievarus is here for a reason."

When we turned to face the still Ievarus who sat cross-legged upon the wall, milky white eyes observing us. It was Ievarus who finally broke the tension.

"Are you my Will?" Ievarus asked plainly.

⋖ ⋗

Dalila shared with me the tale of Igura, a figure I had never heard of, but I quickly began to put the pieces together. For whatever reason, Ievarus needed to understand human emotion if they were to slay the festering Evil and unfasten the choking ring of Haar.

The Seed was entirely different from how I imagined. Rather than carrying about an aura of enigmatic power and destiny, the being looked like a confused toddler in everything but form.

Constantly, Ievarus would be distracted by items in the room, wandering about and poking the simplest things, like a candle holder or rustling through the wardrobe.

"This is none of our concern," I informed Dalila as I kept sparing a glance at Ievarus. "My father has been sent to take them back. This is beyond our station."

"What?" The surprise in Dalila's voice was apparent. "Send back the Seed? They came seeking *me* out. Don't you think we have a duty to follow along with whatever the Seed requires?"

"Not behind the Elder King's back! Are you insane? I put my family's name on the line for you. Do you have any idea what will happen if they find out? They are not some eloping noble; this is the Elder King's Spawn we are talking about."

"So it won't be behind the Elder King's back. Let us help Ievarus. We will seek an audience with your parents and present our interest in helping."

Dalila presented the round disc pendant. It was larger than the span of her palm. When she pointed it at me, the ever shifting iridescent colours instead blended into a solid brown.

"What does that mean?" I asked.

Dalila smiled. "That you *are* their will."

⊰ ⊱

On very short notice, Dalila had beseeched upon her friend, Yasmin, to look over Nora as we went on our way to Nostracie palace for an audience.

There was no cloak long enough to entirely cover the long-limbed Ievarus, even so his monstrous stature would still alert prying eyes. So when the coach was brought close enough to the building, Dalila and I quickly ushered Ievarus inside. Yasmin stopped us on the way out, physically peeking above Dalila's headline to peer at whoever we were hiding.

"Is that Erefiel?" I heard Yasmin say in astonishment. "And who is that tall man you are hiding? Is that another zerub?"

I couldn't quite hear the rest, but Dalila had left to deal with Yasmin, curtly admonishing her into silence. When Dalila got into the coach with me, we sat side to side facing the direction ridden while Ievarus' cramped frame was squashed against the roof of the coach.

I wasn't faring much better, cramped tightly with Dalila sitting next to me as we started to sweat from being on high alert.

"What did you say to her?" I asked.

"That I would explain later, and to not speak so loud."

The coach rattled on as it trailed through the road.

Ievarus eyed us tentatively, curious fishlike eyes jumping from me to Dalila and then back again.

"Do you think anyone saw Ievarus?"

Ievarus was a good head taller than me and, I imagined, matched the height of any akar. "You kidding? Pretty hard to miss. Pretty sure our driver went as white as a ghost. Good on him for staying quiet."

Dalila started to chuckle. It must have proved contagious, for I joined in.

Ievarus simply stared at us with placid inexpression. Then Ievarus tried to smile, the corners of their lips spreading and curling upward. The end result was a crooked thing which grimaced awkwardness instead of joy. It just made the moment all the more surreal, and our laughter took on a life of its own.

Ievarus seemed drawn in, their fingers reaching out to prod at our smiles. It brought an end to our laugh.

Dalila lowered Ievarus' hands. "Ievarus, we talked about this."

Ievarus leaned back into their seat; it would be a lie to say that they seemed admonished.

"What a situation. The Eleventh Seed of the Elder King, a power so great and divine destined to slay the festering Evil, and you just scolded them." I couldn't remember the last time I had such a good laugh. Everything as of recent just seemed so dark that I never even had a moment to pause and think.

The energy died down when Dalila turned towards me. "I never got a chance to thank you properly," she said.

"For what?"

Dalila's smile was warm. "For betting on me. You took responsibility when I was a child. I would not have been here if it weren't for that. You are a good person, Erefiel."

Coming from Dalila, her voice soothing and harmonic, it instilled some joy in me that I welcomed. I had made several bets. One may have fractured a tenuous relationship with our akar refugees and another may never wake up again. It was comforting to know that at least Dalila turned out the way she did.

As we trundled along the path, silence filled the space once again, a fact that didn't seem to bother Ievarus the least as they took the role of a non-partial observer. On more than one occasion, Dalila had to scold Ievarus and tell them to not pull back the curtains.

"You know, I think this is a good chance for us to do something right. Maybe all this suffering, all this nonsense will finally end if we can help Ievarus finish their quest. Maybe it is the Evil that causes all this rot and death and war. The akar would then have enough space and maybe all this invasion and nonsense will finally end."

"Is that hope I am hearing?" I teased.

"No. She is not hope, she is compassion," Ievarus corrected.

I looked at the being sitting opposite of us. Still their voice was without inflection.

"Maybe it is Yasmin that got to me," Dalila admitted.

I considered her words. Dalila wasn't wrong, and I too longed for an opportunity to prove myself in the face of all this suffering. The longer I entertained the thought, the more it occurred to me that this is exactly what I wanted: a way to show my worth, to enter Mount Morniar, and prove myself to father. And if the Evil was slain, then perhaps the akar conflict would dissolve by proxy.

"It's not over, you know," Dalila said. "We still need rage, fear and hope to complete the aspects."

Like a receding tide unveiling swallowed land, a thought surfaced slowly to the forefront. "I don't know about fear or hope, but I do have someone for rage."

More and more, I became convinced of the potentiality of what was being offered.

"What are we going to do about their height? The moment we step out of the coach, people will be suspicious," Dalila voiced.

Ievarus blinked. "Should I be shorter?" Before waiting for a response, Ievarus' body gave from it quiet, cracking sounds. The skin rippled, fingers contorting, face crushing inward through increments until the provided cloak practically draped itself over Ievarus.

There stood not a tall humanoid being of indiscernible gender, but rather a young teen with silver strands of hair curtaining their face.

"Is that better?" The voice remained unchanged. Dalila and I watched on in shock.

Chapter Sixty-Five

EREFIEL

There once were two men who played a game. The first told the other that it would be played to completion and no one could leave the challenge. With a hefted axe, the challenged would strike a single blow upon the challenger. Once done, the challenged would return the blow. Both were divorced from their heads.

—TALES OF THE BROKEN KNIGHTS

Within Nostracie Palace, we stepped up to my parents, the White-Hawk and Lady Imrie, and the odd representative Hachen, and unveiled the young form of Ievarus.

Elated murmurs rose from both sides of the audience chamber. But as expected, no one waiting at the top of the dais broke their composure.

I spoke my bid and made my claim. Ievarus even stepped forward, body contorting and crackling back as something underneath rippled to return Ievarus to their former height.

Though not exactly eloquent, Ievarus still was able to express their point.

When the audience went silent and pondered what to do next, Ievarus took it upon themselves to smile—an act that turned into a grimace and looked rather like an expression of pain.

Dalila stepped forward and, in hushed tones, scolded Ievarus.

"But I'm smiling. It is a good thing?"

"Not now."

I sighed and took the lead.

"Ievarus is a pure soul, one that wishes to do good. Hachen, it has now been six years since Ievarus' birth. Yet still, they do not have any ideas or notions of their own."

Hachen stepped forward. I perceived that the figure seemed rather indignant at how casually I addressed them. **"That is correct,"** the figure said in their vulture-like voice.

"We believe that we can help with that. The Haar is closing in, the rot spreads quick. The Elder King's loyal subjects die daily from akar invaders." I paused for effect, an act that didn't go unnoticed in father's eyes. He nodded approvingly.

"How long until there is no one else to fight for you?"

"*Watch it, child.*" Mother's voice echoed as if through a hallway of ice.

Hachen raised their three fingered hand up as if to wave away the matter. **"To be frank, this is beyond my power to decide. The Seed is to discuss such things with the King himself."**

"Then we shall go with Ievarus."

"Absolutely not!" Father snapped and rose from his seat. Mother, instead, went icy cold.

Hachen grumbled.

"I am afraid I have no jurisdiction in making that decision. No one is simply permitted to come and go as they please."

Even Dalila seemed in shock as she came to my side and whispered harshly. "Are you mad? I am a Sister! A Mother! I cannot simply go to the land of the gods."

Ievarus spoke up. "I... need them," they stated. "I won't go back without them."

Hachen pondered for a while. **"That is a surprising development."**

"What is?" Father inquired.

After a deliberating pause, Hachen finally spoke, both hands leaning upon their towering staff. **"The young prince had never before expressed a desire that didn't have to do with defeating the Evil."**

The chamber remained quiet.

"Very well, but let it be known that your guests are _your_ responsibility, Ievarus. I have no intention of losing favour with my king."

⤙ ⤚

At the very first chance I received, I went on my way to recruit the aspect of rage. Dalila, on the other hand, remained with Nora to tend to her, and Ievarus was kept within Nostracie.

There were already plans to parade Ievarus through the crowds. We hoped it would spark hope into the people.

In my recruiting of rage, I asked for an official document, sealed and notarized, to impart Ievarus' mission to collect potential people who presented images of the aspect of Igura. But not in so many words. The existence of this arrangement was still very much a secret.

My impatience was obvious; I itched to ride towards the akar settlement.

Chapter Sixty-Six

DALILA

Xelxidon did not originally wield just a sword, but also a shield. It was imbued with the power of the Elder King's eye and as such, the golden plate with its shut rendition of an eye was called the Sun Shield. When opened, it would sear through all in its gaze with blinding radiance. Where the shield is gone or why Xelxidon abandoned it, no one knows.

—Theory and Speculations, By Monyr the Scholar

Returning to my residence, I quickly dismissed Yasmin, who was tortured with curiosity. Even if I had the energy, I couldn't tell her a single thing. She did pout, but eventually relented, stating that I owed her.

Everything was still so incredibly surreal; I hadn't had a chance to process any of it. Ievarus, spawn of the Elder King. I certainly did not expect them to be so innocent and naïve. There was something entirely endearing about Ievarus; as pure as the strands of silver hair that adorned their scalp.

Was this it? A chance to prove myself? What greater glory than tending to Ievarus. The one who would bring about a new age of prosperity.

I entertained heavy, self-serving fantasies, imagining what a glorious end I would have if I sacrificed myself so that Ievarus may serve their duty. In that way, I would have long since paid my due and perhaps live on in the memories of others. Yet the shadow of Mount Morniar cast itself over my thoughts, numbing whatever excitement it would have brought. I looked back to my childhood and at the sheer cliff walls of that place. It was a tidal wave, still so distant. To enter that realm was unheard of. What majestic horrors would I see?

⋖ ⋗

The following day, I couldn't help but feel coursing excitement despite not sleeping at all the previous night. I had spent time trying to describe emotions to Ievarus, the concept of will, of compassion, of rage.

Now that I returned to my chores with Nora, I couldn't help but be distracted constantly by the thought of Ievarus and even felt myself turn hot when I considered going to Mount Morniar. Part of me entertained meeting the Elder King himself, a thought quickly and violently banished.

I turned to Nora, who sat there as she always did: listless, disconnected, a hollow shell where, once it harboured a storm in a bottle.

I had her leaning against the end of a wooden circular bathtub as I scrubbed and tended to her. I didn't need to, but I found it calmed me as I scrubbed away her skin with a sponge.

At times, I would glide my fingers along the contours of her wounded flesh, feeling the writhing, gnarled skin that put itself back together. I would feel the stumped ends of her shoulder, of her arm, feeling the difference of one which was burnt away and one which was brutishly hacked off.

I paused, my hands dipped into the stagnant water of the bath. Had Mother Vinrie been right? Day by day I considered more options to bring Nora back to us, and I wondered if Nora wilfully refused to do so, preferring to lock herself away into some recess of her mind, a crevice of her own making. Time was running out.

"Nora," I began softly. "I am sorry I wasn't present the last few days. I hope Yasmin took good care of you." I permitted myself a soft chuckle. "I'm sure she did."

I dipped the sponge back into the pool and continued to scrub during our one-sided conversation.

"I met the Seed, you know? Their name is Ievarus, child of the Elder King—not as awe-provoking as one might think, but still, it was a surreal experience.

"They had a sort of... innocence. You know? As if born yesterday. Brought with them a tale, that of Igura. I don't know if you have heard of it before—I only heard it once. Anyway, the Seed wishes to take me as an aspect of humanity, to teach them what it means to feel, to believe in something. It is supposed to help prepare them for the slaying of Evil. I wonder what machinations await me on Mount Morniar."

I hesitated as I prepared my next words; could Nora even hear me?

"Nora, I won't be here any longer. If I am sent away to Mount Morniar and join Ievarus in their quest... I will try and find someone to take care of you, I swear."

Something miraculous began to happen. Were Nora's eyes blinking more frequently? They seemed less languid and more alive. Was there a shine? A sparkle returning to their surface, a gloss reminiscent of thought and intelligence rather than passively watching the world pass by.

I was dumbstruck. Was she returning? A livid fear claimed me at the possibility. What would she say? How would she mourn?

Her shoulder twitched, the stagnant pool of water sending the barest of ripples. The waves grew. The stagnant water coming alive with waves that crashed into its container.

Eyes blinked in quick succession, as more and more life creased into Nora's withered face. She seemed dazed, confused as to where she was, a languid head processing her surrounding lazily. Finally, her gaze rested on me. She processed it all sheepishly, taking her time to return. It was like a ship-wreck lost at sea finally being spat out with gradually rescinding waves.

When she spoke, it was evidently through a throat that had turned vestigial from lack of use. Her words were a soft and brittle croak that I barely understood.

"The Seed... is here?" she asked. It was a question that came from a place not yet present, but on its way. Perhaps I imagined it, but I think that was hope in her voice.

Chapter Sixty-Seven

NORA

Have you heard of Selena's blade? It is said that once she took to the skies with weapon in hand, her feet never found the floor again. She was the most gifted of Ludwig's students. It is thus a shame that he found himself skewered to her sword.

—ANONYMOUS DRIVER ON THE ROAD

I felt so lost, broken pieces of myself drifting endlessly within a boundless void.

There was a window, a glossy and fogged surface through which I passively watched the world spin. I was numb, forced into a cramped cocoon where my broken mind receded.

So too did the pieces of myself drift through the abyss, passing by each other endlessly. But there was something that was lost, something that I had no choice but to accept—my limbs were gone and they were never coming back.

That was it: my playful fantasy, thinking I could go back to my old life if I tried hard enough. A dream that inevitably got dispelled. Yet, within that darkness, a word peered through, a sound from without.

"The Seed."

Then another: "Mount Morniar."

I began to stir awake from within a bottomless pit, instinctively clambering onto those ever elusive words as if threads. I was in a realm of black where everything was covered in glossy tar, all of it reflecting a shine like metal. Cracks formed from where my remaining conscious-ness could peer out—even here I had no arms, no legs, but still I wasn't entirely gone.

The *Seed*.

A possibility presented itself, a way to make myself whole. Images evoked from the Kaseluda took vague shape within my abyss, misshapen ideas that told of the Elder might.

⊲ ⊳

My eyes had been opened. They scanned and peered and in the very simplest of ways they could *see*. But not really; they observed, but they didn't account, didn't acknowledge, just simply glossed over an indif-ferent world from a disconnected body.

But now, I climbed out of my shell and crawled back to claim the reins of my body. There before me sat Dalila.

It pained me to speak. My throat cracked and dry but still I spoke with my hoarse voice. "Did you say… the Seed was here?"

Dalila was dumbfounded, her eyes blinking as if she just watched me return from the dead. I instinctively reached out, wanting to grab and shake her; but that was impossible.

"Dalila, listen to me. Is the Seed here?" My words drawled. Now it was my turn to be patient with her; a luxury that I could not afford.

Finally, Dalila nodded. "Take me to them," I said.

⊲ ⊳

Dalila didn't expect the fervour with which I ordered her around, and I hid the fact that a splitting headache ailed me. My body ached; it felt weak from falling out of use. From my paper-thin skin I could feel my weakened heart pump blood like a withering fruit.

Bit by bit, the world which I numbly looked over started to reshape itself. I felt a distant shoreline contain my disjointed and murky memories in its pool as my mind hopelessly tried to put together the events of the past month with an elusiveness I couldn't quite grasp. A fugue clouded my thoughts. All I knew for certain was that Dalila had cared for me with such unwavering diligence and attention. I felt guilty for still ordering her around after all she had done; yet the mention of the Seed sustained me like a maddening idea and gave me haste.

I bit my tongue, holding back on lashing out at Dalila as she hurried to prepare my wheelchair. I was disgusted by the object. It was just another form for my body to take, for me to be pushed around in. It didn't matter, all that mattered was meeting this Ievarus.

In a rush, I asked Dalila to tell me of Igura, and so she did.

"Where is that damned coach?" I complained, as we waited behind the door, cutting her off in the middle of the story.

"Nora, are you sure you want to meet Ievarus? It can wait. You need to rest."

"I want to wait outside," I commented, my gaze practically burnt through the door; another everyday object that became laborious to me. Despite the water Dalila made me drink, I still sounded like someone who corrupted their innards with years of smoke.

"Are you sure?" Dalila queried. "It won't make things go by quicker and—"

"I told you I want to wait outside!" I tried to scream. My atrophied vocal cords faltered at the strain, the second half of my cry turned into a pitiful whimper.

Regardless, Dalila became apprehensive. Without another word, she took me outside.

❧ ☙

Folks stared without restraint, but I ignored them as we waited. Dalila shied away on my behalf. I was restless in that seat. What remained of my limbs writhed painfully and contorted with unused muscles. I was glad that my singular focus made me numb to my appearance.

Finally, when the coach did arrive, the driver seemed flabbergasted and unaware of how to proceed. His eyes danced and flitted between me, the seat, and Dalila; I scowled at him.

Eventually, Dalila carried me into the coach while my chair had to be stuffed into the compartment with us; it splintered a frame of the door to the driver's dismay.

Dalila and I had to sit opposite each other on account of the wheelchair occupying an entire side of the seats.

The wagon trundled over the cobblestone street. I could tell Dalila kept eyeing me to make sure I wouldn't fall over, but on account of my left arm being slung through one of the spokes of the wheels to hold on to, I was confident I would manage.

Already I began to regret being so callous and rude to Dalila, the woman who took care of me all the while I was just some broken husk. As I was about to summon the courage to apologize, it was Dalila who spoke with that meekness of hers.

"Nora, why do you suddenly want to see the Seed?" she asked.

I briefly hesitated. "I was gone for quite some time… wasn't I? Even now I feel like I am asleep. None of this feels real anymore. Yet when you mentioned the Elders… the Seed. I thought maybe, *just maybe*. If someone can do something about my situation, it's them."

Dalila's surprise was obvious, even if she tried her best to curtail it. She tread carefully with her next words. "And what if they can't?"

"They will."

"Nora…"

"They have to!" I cried. My throat aching with the sudden force. My eyes shot towards Dalila, arresting her attention. My tears flowed. "They just have to," I said, my tone softer.

Dalila veered away from the subject. "Nora. Who were the people who attacked you?"

I blinked, a pause as she awaited my answer. "I'm sorry, I don't remember anything," I lied. There it was, that fierce raging and bellied anger inside me, a roaring flame that swelled with new life. If anyone were to seek out vengeance for what had happened, it was to be me.

It seemed like the wrong time to apologise now.

❧ ☙

Upon arriving at Palace Nostracie, a practical miracle in terms of avarice and design, I allowed for Dalila to lead the way.

Dalila and me were openly led through Nostracie palace with relative ease and left in an empty lounge to wait.

It reeked of opulence. Golden seams framed curved wardrobes and fashionable carpets spanned the entire floor with filigree patterns. Festoons accessorised the arched walls around. Gossamer curtains billowed softly from tall windows that reached from roof to floor.

Finally, Ievarus entered the room. The figure wore a long ivory chasuble vestment with barely discernible patterns woven into the fabric, its entire length draped and hung to show the woven patterns of Elder history.

Dalila was right. Ievarus was the strangest and most surreal creature I had ever seen. Such pearl-like eyes, long strands of flowing silver hair, a poreless, pale complexion to their thin and undefined features.

"Dalila. Have you come to teach me compassion?" the being said flatly.

"No, Ievarus. I have brought someone for you."

Dalila wheeled me towards the being. "This is Nora."

Suddenly, the towering being bent down and extended a hand as if to shake mine.

"Um, Ievarus, no. Not like that."

The being blinked, but there was no readable emotion. "Did you not say that this is how people greet each other?"

"Yes, but Nora has no hands, so…"

"But she can still shake."

The being gently bent down, and as if dealing with the brittle wings of a butterfly, Ievarus took my left stump and shook it.

My heart fluttered for a moment. This seemingly unimportant act made me partake in what most deemed a trivial practice, and that meant the world to me.

If I were to speak, now was the time. But the simple act of speaking to a Seed proved more intimidating than I expected.

"Ievarus, spawn of the Elder King. I beseech thee to make me one of thine aspects."

There it was, that drawn out, suffocating silence. I was a fool. Of course Ievarus would say that I couldn't become a warrior. What use did a Seed have for a cripple?

"What can you teach me?" Ievarus asked.

I suddenly considered the statement. "I will fight for you, teach you anything you'd like to know."

Ievarus didn't say anything for a long time, their eyes unsettling as they studied me.

Dalila leaned in and whispered into my ear. "Ievarus wants to hear what aspect you'd represent."

I didn't know what to say. An aspect? I was so focused on simply getting my body back that I didn't stop to consider anything else. "I will be any aspect you wish as long as I am made whole."

"I don't understand," Ievarus finally said. "How are you not whole?"

I was taken aback by the statement and floundered over my words.

"Nora had lost her limbs a while ago," Dalila answered for me.

The Eleventh Seed blinked. "I see. I only saw her wholeness as is. I did not consider the worth of limbs."

Ievarus reached into their robe and removed the hidden disk. Slowly, they reached out with the pendant towards me. At first, the domed, glass surface shifted in iridescent colours but then came a searing red-hot colour like scarlet rage.

"No." Ievarus' words sliced through the buoyant moment. "I already have rage."

As if it were a simple and unremarkable declaration, Ievarus returned the pendant and turned to leave the chamber.

"Stop!" I roared—I could not let them leave, not let my only chance at being someone again be taken away from me.

"You have nothing to offer," Ievarus said.

"I don't care!" I leaned forward, straining against the belt that held me in place, my neck veins protruding.

"You can't leave me like this! I will do anything! Just fix me! Give me arms to fight with, legs to run with! Anything!"

Ievarus stood there watching me sideways, not in any way unnerved by my plea. I was an insect to be studied under the stare of their milky eyes. Though at least it wasn't a look of pity like with all others; theirs belonged to a being outside the scope of mortals.

I thrashed in the seat, feeling bellied embers glow from within. My glare seethed and burnt, but it did not faze the unmoving Ievarus.

"I don't care if you have someone for rage! I will be your aspect!"

Ievarus peered from above. "I don't need you."

"Then let her be hope!" Suddenly, it was Dalila that cut into our conversation.

I turned to her. "Stay out of this!"

She ignored me. "Let Nora be hope."

Ievarus didn't seem to comprehend. "The disk said rage."

Dalila walked up to Ievarus and tugged at their robes, looking up to their alabaster face. "That is something you don't understand, Ievarus. People are complicated, *emotions* are complicated. What you see is just the colour of the disk, but there is more involved here. Nora has lost something, something that made her who she was. She is trying to put herself back together, to have hope that there is a chance to have more in life despite what has happened to her."

There was a moment of reflective silence in Ievarus' eyes.

"Isn't that everything that Igura is about? Putting yourself back together?"

Ievarus' emotionless eyes lingered on me. My chest heaved as I held my tongue. Ievarus blinked.

The Elder King's spawn knelt down, their willowy silver strands cascading like enamel curtains to frame the opal pearls that served as eyes. "I will do as Dalila wishes, to see how rage can also be hope."

The being rose to leave, ducking under the low hanging doorframe until it was just me and Dalila. "Thank you." My attempt at gratitude was rather stinted considering my anger. But I had to push through. "For everything." It was all I managed.

We turned to leave the quaint lounge, and, as we did, I heard an all too familiar voice that sent fear galloping through my blood.

"Go," I whispered harshly to Dalila.

"What?" she replied.

"Just go!" I said, a little louder.

"Where is she? Is it true?" The voice became clearer behind a turn in the passage. It was undeniably Erefiel. The tall and pristine Nephilim turned the corner, frantic eyes searching desperately until they settled on me and I shrunk under his gaze. His own smile swelled into a beaming grin.

"By the Elders! It is true!"

I tensed within my seat, feeling my stumps clench tight as if trying to pull on the chords of tendons no longer present.

Erefiel strode to me, seemingly oblivious to my discomfort. The man practically knelt before me, his gaze searching for my elusive eyes. His hands clasping on my shoulders. "You're back!."

"Erefiel," spoke Dalila hintingly, a sobering tone to her. Erefiel looked up at Dalila and then took a step back, looking at me.

"What's wrong?" he asked.

"Nothing." I bit my lip, turning my gaze away from the man and refusing to look in his eyes.

"Nora?" His voice was now pained. "Why won't you look at me?" His query was full of hurt.

I turned to the man, my voice breaking. "It's nothing." I tried to force a smile, but it was brittle and shaking.

"Nora? What is it?"

"Nothing, really. Please, can we just go?" I told Dalila.

She looked at us. I couldn't see her but I could feel it. She was hesitant, unsure of what to do. "She had a long day."

"Long day?" Erefiel repeated, then scoffed.

"Yeah, that's it." My voice was so unusually timid. I caught a glimpse of passing souls turning away and leaving us to our awkward island.

Finally, although with reluctance, Erefiel nodded and provided a sombre smile. "Then rest. But first, I need you to tell me who did this to you? I will bring them to justice." His promise was resolute and unwavering.

I shook my head. "Already told Dalila. I don't remember."

Erefiel blinked confoundedly. "Are you sure?"

I nodded.

He paused for a moment. "Nora, try to remember. They might try to do it again. And I can't protect you if that happens."

My voice turned grating. "I don't want your protection."

"But Nora—"

"Stop it!" I reprimanded him. Erefiel stopped, his gaze distant. "I will be coming with you to Mount Morniar. I will be remade there. I can protect myself."

Erefiel frowned. "Remake you? How?"

"I don't know yet. But if anyone can save me from this plight, then it is the Elders themselves."

I avoided his eyes throughout it all; awkward silence filled the space. "Please, just leave me be... I don't want you to see me like this." If Erefiel heard the last part of my sentence, I wasn't sure. But regardless, he rose from the spot.

"Take care of her until we reach Mount Morniar... anything she needs, our house will provide it," he said to Dalila.

Chapter Sixty-Eight

DALILA

The Sword of Bone was said to have been made by the remains of an Estrian undead. The bone still lives and its cutting edge is said to be the only way to permanently sever the connection between an undead and the stars.

—WEAPONRY LOST TO THE AGES, BY CORNYTH ABENHAUR

In a week's time, we were on our way to Mount Morniar. We rode within a carriage seemingly with no driver nor drawn by any creature but by an invisible force of its own.

The border past Bravnicka to the guarded domain of the higher beings was blocked off by an obsidian stone wall which spanned left and right. Lining the walls was a tribe of hook-beaked zerubs.

They were Calatay, a specific type of zerub engineered in Mount Morniar. They were all fashioned tall, with hands and feet that were eagle-like in design. Three digits on each hand, with one being an opposable thumb wrapped around their tribalistic spears. Their other weapons were feathers which sprouted across forearms into a scythe-like armblade.

At first glance, one would think the feathered cape attached to their forearm was some sort of uniform before realizing it was a part of them; spreadable wings to fly with or at the very least glide.

I had heard of the Calatay, as they were part of many tales that mothers told their children. But seeing them for myself brought them into reality.

Within the carriage sat Erefiel, Nora and myself; a harness was built to keep Nora in place.

Tension grew within the carriage as Erefiel tried to commune with Nora, but she wasn't reciprocating. Was it embarrassment? Shame? A feeling of vulnerability? I didn't blame her for the reluctance and I could feel that she trickled with anticipation. Her only thought was to fill the hole left behind.

I asked Erefiel who he had found for rage, a mystery not yet answered.

"Chroma," he said.

"Who?"

A sudden realization seemed to go through Erefiel. "Do you remember when you were attacked by the akar in the woods?"

I nodded.

"Chroma is the same akar who assisted in protecting you."

My eyes went wide. "Are you sure?"

Erefiel hung his head. "There are some things that have changed."

Slowly, I turned to Nora, expecting her to have something to say, but she kept silent. Strapped to that seat and with palpable impatience, she simply looked out the carriage window upon the strange straw huts of these Calatay.

At the end of the path, we were greeted by a serene display of soaring, great stingrays who spiralled above. With a slow and deliberate flap of their fins, a few glided down to the soil. Exiting the carriage, Erefiel and I were already coordinating who would get the wheelchair and who would carry Nora out.

Instead, the door opened with Ievarus on the other side, reaching in and taking Nora out on their own accord.

"What are you doing?!" Nora cried.

"Watch your tone, human!" Hachen warned from somewhere in the vicinity.

We exited the carriage to find Ievarus had taken it upon themselves to organise everything, and sat Nora upon her wheelchair.

I rushed over, finding the short-haired Nora visibly flustered as I began to fasten her to the seat.

I looked about at the traipsing tall beings who walked upon the roofs of their homes. A passing gust of wind made their vibrating feathers look like a threat.

"Are they opposed to our visit?" I asked Erefiel privately.

The Nephilim shook his head and leaned in. He too eyed the creatures attentively. "Father explained that when Ievarus departed, he killed several of the stingrays. I would assume they are not too happy about that."

I watched on towards the black wall of Mount Morniar in awe—it was a high rising and directly vertical thing that yawned endlessly. Even when I craned my neck, I couldn't see the end of it. A light ribbon of fog obscured the view halfway up. Something about the cliff face seemed alive. The rough crags where shadows nested, peering outwards, moving as if they were alive. I felt as if it tried to speak, to communicate. My heart lunged into my chest at the thought of entering the Elders' domain.

I heard the sound of rushing waves, heavy and anchored. The air before sprayed inky water and, instead of a salty tang, I tasted a fetid stench. I moved closer to the edge, past where the stingrays had landed.

"I wouldn't do that," White-Hawk warned. I buried my surprise at being addressed by this legend and turned to him. Up close, there more certainly was something majestic about his presence. His head was truly that of an albino hawk with sharp eyes and presence. Yet something about the way he held himself was uncannily human.

"White-Hawk. It is a humbling honour to meet you." I addressed the cliff. "What is in there?"

The zerub joined me. "After the Elder King had his eye stolen and taken to the Kingdom of Estria, he spread apart a wide chasm, dividing land and mountain so that no human could scale its walls again. Now its depths are filled with writhing nightmares called wyrms, large and long like eels with rending stalactites for teeth."

"Wyrms?" I pressed.

White-Hawk nodded. "It is a creation of the King, unnatural off-springs of Volar birthed like maggots. They carry dragon blood, but are no different than giant larvae that gnaw at the base of Mount Morniar for sustenance.

I braved a glance over the edge and clasped my mouth in shock. Underneath, there were beasts just like White-Hawk described, slosh-ing through a thick pool of umbral black. Their cries were like ethereal metal being grated against itself.

"How horrifying," I noted.

❧ ☙

We were seated upon the stingrays. A large leather saddle made to span the entirety of its back as we grabbed onto offered holds. When the beast began to beat its fins, slowly we rose up from the ground, and I felt my heart clench and my breath lodge itself in my throat. It felt like wading through water.

Up and up we went, the air becoming thinner by the moment. Not simply just because of the altitude; there was something else at play. Something about this abstract realm for higher beings was as if we had ventured to the end of the world where the fabric of it all was undone. We rose past the fog and to the higher stations. There were pristine buildings with arching bridges holding aloft even more stacked homes. A bronze gloss covered this first tier of zerubian architecture. At the very centre between the huddled buildings was a grand, bronze statue of Kerubiel, leader of the zerubs. Its head had the face of man, lion, ox and eagle at each corner.

Next came the congested buildings of Chainhearth with narrow streets. Its diversely dimensioned denizens strolled through dreary buildings. Baroque architecture turned muted and robbed of colour in this bleak shadow cast from Elder light.

Erefiel tapped me on the shoulder. "Look," he told both me and Nora as we turned around.

The sun was rising, a luminous orb that was the Elder King's eye from the horizon at sea, the glistening water reflecting its burning light. There was our world, a truly astonishing and indescribable sight. There, among our own obstructed realm, was Bravnicka, made up of Cleria, which appeared as a glistening gemstone in the distance; Museya, on the other hand, was an even further blue marvel like a pearl. One could see the rising cloud of smoke from Bolton: beyond that were the lawless and deadly realms of untamed forests and beasts, the mountains and planes upon which the akar reigned and even further down one could see the mesmerising ring of fire that floated above the Forest of Ash. If one strained hard enough, one could notice the first hint of suffocating fog which tightened about the remaining lands.

⋘ ⋙

Upon reaching the pinnacle, I found that I was holding my breath. I didn't know what I was expecting, but if I had to guess, it was a majestic and truly awe-inspiring world of unimaginable majesty.

Instead, what I saw wasn't some big and bloated realm of riches and power, but something that triggered some vestigial part of my brain. It was a sight upon shifting waves, rippling on unsteady foundations with some semblance of gothic mutedness.

When I stepped off and tread onto this divine world, the thought became indubitably apparent: this wasn't so much a place as it was a feeling. I felt like I was in a dream, a vague and abstract dream that left me uneasy and short of breath. The idea of buildings and structures blending into one another to give a sort of shape to madness. I felt as if it would turn to smoke the moment I reached out.

Everything about my surroundings was stretched. There were yawning cathedrals with rose windows made in the spiral of Elders. The buildings were swollen with edges and contours I couldn't quite grasp. There were large domes that looked like an infectious boil grown upon this landscape.

I saw grand buildings with flying buttresses and spires larger than I ever thought possible. It made me feel like a snail trying to scale the side of a basilica.

The towering arches we were led through were like gaping maws to swallow and spit us out again, their overbearing height weighing down on me in an unspeakable way; all to make me feel as insignificant as the child who would stare up at the mountain every morning.

I turned to the streets and noticed the first figures in my view, like monstrously stretched out shadows gliding across the ground.

"Are those Elders?" I asked White-Hawk. The zerub scoffed at the suggestion, as if such an implication was absolutely ridiculous in the face of the real thing. Even he became more dream-like in my field of vision.

"No, those are shades."

"What are shades?"

"I have no idea," White-Hawk admitted.

Along the path, there was a sudden, incredibly deep divet, though not very wide. I could tell at the bottom that there was a narrow stream, like a vein running through it.

We walked over the cobblestone street and past archaic buildings filled with an ineffable presence that pressed against my chest.

Hachen turned to address us. **"Ievarus will be taken to see the King; in the meantime, I will do as instructed and guide the mortals known as Dalila and Nora to the Blacksmith. White-Hawk, I trust that your offspring will be your responsibility."**

White-Hawk nodded.

From a seemingly innocuous and unremarkable door which opened up to a wooden room no wider than a closet, there now stepped out a creature that truly took my breath away. I had no doubt it was an Elder.

They were a being cloaked in woven night from head to invisible toe, six thin and bone-white arms steepled upside down and an unreadable face of porcelain portraying perpetual sadness upon that mask. From behind the seam of this clothing protruded a mummified arm carrying an ornate lantern.

The being towered over all of us and was as tall as the passing shades, if not taller. When it bowed, I noticed its entire body bent as if without bones.

Its face neared us, and I felt as if my mind was beginning to fray. Trying to comprehend this being proved impossible. They never did say a word, instead *gliding* to the side and allowing a new sprouting hand to wave Ievarus to the door.

I could not tell what was on the other side because conniving shadows veiled it.

⋖ ⋗

Hachen guided us through meandering paths of claustrophobic alleys. The high rising walls looming over us. I could already tell a splitting headache had worked its way to me. I was exhausted. The world seemed to tilt itself on an axis.

There was a drowsiness as if I had been awake for weeks on end—I noticed that suddenly—all the truths, all the realities that I had gathered since my moment of birth began to unravel within this space, like ink parting from drowned paper.

Everything suddenly seemed impermanent, of no apparent consequence. This was the edge of the world, and I saw how truly fragile it was.

We approached a large dome made up of surrounding mortar, a plume of smoke rising from the top. The structure was incomprehensibly large.

I leant in down towards Nora, who sat silently upon her wheelchair. "Are you alright?" I asked her, wondering if she felt the same disillusioning effect.

"I'm fine." I could hear the grinding stubbornness in her voice, the bubbling rage underneath that gave her the strength to stay lucid.

Upon entering, we were greeted by a nauseating wave of heat; the very space before us distorted by the burning furnace within. I pushed Nora along with Hachen still leading the way.

Inside this dome was a place of potential, of creation, of primordial and molten fire waiting to be forged into something divine.

The walls themselves were of stone, reaching up to an opened vent. Yet below us, the floor was made out of an iron grate and just below there steamed a pool of blinding lava, bubbling and splattering in its roiling eddies.

The Blacksmith awaited, his presence clouded by the encompassing heat. He was known as an Elder of legend who fashioned countless artefacts. Some were said to have found their way to the hands of Seeds, while others were given to the world of Minethria, waiting to be found once more.

At first glance, I would have thought this being was a product of nature, a serendipitous result of rock formations and volcanic discharge that just so happened to form some likeness to man. But then this force of nature moved and struck a veined hammer to anvil, evoking sparks like a primordial god.

The giant was made entirely out of molten rock, where glowing fire flowed between the cracks of the charred, sediment flesh. We were to the being what ants were to us, as a simple press of the glowing thumb could completely crush us.

The Blacksmith was suspended in air, their lower half replaced by a spherical solid boulder, hooked chains spread from its corners and were mounted into the stone dome.

Their beard was made of flame, like a perpetually burning nest that birthed ember; their head was entirely encased by a mould of rock except for the eyes that pierced out like smouldering coals.

The Elder had four arms, two on either side, entirely of moulded earth with crags of lava running through. Where perhaps a human heart would have been there instead was a smaller figure, like a disfigured dwarf. This one was not made out of flame, but rather teal-blue water with a watery hole just below where it sprouted.

Their work station was a circular table of silhouetted marble that ringed around the Blacksmith's upheld form.

"**Great Blacksmith,**" Hachen began. "**I bring you a mortal who wishes for a new body as per the wishes of the Silver Prince, Ievarus.**"

Their brightly burning hammer struck several times upon an artefact. Sparks flew from it like birthed stars, which quickly faded into darkness.

The burning ember eyes deigned us for a moment before returning to their hammering; each strike sent vibrations through me. "*No,*" the being bellowed, their voice birthed from the depths of the earth and just as sonorous.

"*You heard him, that's a no!*" The being that spoke was the smaller growth upon the Blacksmith's chest. It cackled with childish amusement.

Hachen spoke before Nora had a chance. "**Please, oh great Blacksmith. They have come a long way, and it is the prince's wish.**"

"*Thou mortal wilt perish.*" The blacksmith's voice was just as tempered as the controlled length of its hammering, yet also just as deep as the encumbering inferno bubbling below us.

Nora interceded. "Then so be it!"

"Nora!" I scolded her in hushed tones. It was wrong to talk to Elders in such a way. I knew that long ago because of what my father told me, because of the Sisterhood's teachings. Yet now, I understood it on a more instinctive, more profound level. Talking to such a being was like talking with primordial flame. There was a divineness to this creature that my mortal self could never comprehend. To even try and fathom its existence came with trepidation.

Nora bit against her harness, her left stump bringing its strap to her mouth so she could rip it out.

"What are you doing!?"

Before she could answer, the buckle came loose, and she fell to the floor, the iron bars already burning hot upon her landing as an excruciating bellow escaped her. The scent of smoking flesh rose to fill my scathed nostrils.

"Nora!" I cried in sheer panic.

"Help me, Blacksmith! I will die regardless of what you choose to do. Help me. Give me a body to fight with, to destroy with!"

As Nora crawled forward, patches of her skin peeled and melted off to stick to the hot iron—yet it was the uncompromising rage that kept her moving. I could still hear her pained cries be muffled down to restrained groans.

"*Should thou live, thy vessel will never be as it once hath been.*"

Nora didn't reply, no doubt in part due to her seared flesh and agony.

"*Interesting this one,*" commented the blue being and chuckled like a child.

"*Quiet, Dwarf.*" Boomed the Elder with indifference, yet the disfigured Dwarf looked properly reprimanded.

The Blacksmith watched for several moments, soaking the scene in from up above, watching Nora's tiny form drag across the floor the same way we may watch an unwelcome insect. Like pieces of themselves, like specks of fleeting stars, embers crackled and sparked from their primordial body, their defined form hanging from the boulder as Blacksmith observed Nora's uncompromising will. Their look was purely one of indifference as all waited for the Elder's response.

"*So be it; a conduit shall be provideth for thy fury.*"

Nora's wailing cry echoed and wrung true within this raging furnace. I could not tell if it was a cry of vindication or one of pain.

Chapter Sixty-Nine

NORA

Some insist that the fabled dragon city of Krem absolutely does exist. From this city came the first of the fabled dragon warriors. They drank from the blood of dragons and took upon dark rituals to transform into DragonKin.

—TALES OF LOST CITIES, BY FATHER LANCET

E verything was gone, my consciousness, my hopes and dreams, my memories of better times and thoughts of friends, and lust, and love; all that remained were the smouldering coals of rage I tread. In the end, that too was taken from me, thrown into the furnace to stoke the pieces of my new body.

The burns I suffered upon that iron floor were mended by Hachen's ink. I could see the wild design of these otherworldly beings. I would not retake my old form but be reborn from the ashes in a new vessel.

Day after insufferable day, I stayed with the great Blacksmith. Neither of us talked as I withstood the constant heat that made me hallucinate, all while his hammer evoked sparks from glowing dreamsteel.

The hollow banging rung endlessly as the days blended together and my mind was a roiling soup of consciousness. The numbing shock, the anchoring rage, my conviction stoked by bellows, pumping fear as fuel. All of it melded into one in this dream-like place.

I looked back to that young girl turned servile by her parents.

Thought about a brother grown into a tyrant who far surpassed my parents in their cruelty.

I looked at my time in service, being one of Erefiel's warriors, Cassidy's vile and twisted smile as he taunted me. I imagined what sadistic glee the man felt, thinking that my due punishment was justly enacted. The rage it sparked kept me going, stopped me from truly being lost in my maudlin realm. If only Cassidy could know what pain I would bring upon him when I rose from my ashes.

I sometimes saw Cassidy there with me, his flawless features sneering, mocking me. I would talk to this product of my frayed sanity, whisper back worse threats to this shadow I created. I promised things, vile things; things which were born from this unconstrained domain of ever-shifting dimensions; it brought a horrifyingly vivid creativity to my promises.

Danny and Regan: their names never left me. I would repeat them in private, replay the fractured pieces of my defilement. During my days in shock, where I was an unmoving doll and everything went by in a haze, those names stayed with me.

There was a caustic and festering intimacy that I developed for those names, ideas, dots that kept me going, that kept my spirit burning. I longed for our destined reunion; for a chance to return the favour of their noxious passion.

These disgusting figures kept me company in these unlucid days. We would break into mad laughter, talking about all the horrible things I would do to them. The Blacksmith paid me no mind, simply hammering away stoically like the embodiment of creation that they were.

When the Blacksmith spoke, it was to tell me what was going to happen. Their voice was like a harsh melody, rhythmic and transcendent, though pure in its coarseness. I wasn't always sure what they said.

My heart was removed, the frail thing as crimson as a beet in the large hands of that creature. Even removed from my chest, it beat with a certain desperation. The momentary glimpse I had of it awoke something maternal within me; how small my heart seemed, how intrepid and stubborn for such a small thing. It felt apt to call that thing my heart; a scared little girl hiding in the skeleton of an imposter.

The gaping hole in my chest was like a distant ache. Something I was supposed to panic about, but the sensation never came. There was a certain terror from being in such a state. The world of Bravnicka was permanent, and it had rules and foundations that could be relied on. Yet here, I felt as if even my own mind and emotions were unconstrained, distorted and left to roil.

With delicate prongs, a ball of luminant gold like molten rock was inserted into my chest. My body fought, contested with this raging concoction of liquid fire that poured through my veins and burned me from the inside. That was an understatement—I felt like someone had lit a fire in my belly and was roasting me from within.

"Thy new heart hast been born from sacred tree. It feedeth off thy will, and shall sustain thee through it. It shalt turn thy form into a worthy vessel for its swollen gloat. Yet, I prithee; a word of caution. Feed its ravenous hunger with all thine ambition, and behold as thy fruit explodeth, spreading its seed in a glorious scatter of flame. Shalt it blossom, the fruit will turn thee and all else into ash." There was a reserved calmness to the Blacksmith's poetics, a sense of reverent beauty to the bomb that filled my chest. Be it due to the nature of this frenetic realm or because of my own, I wholly accepted the heart which beat in my chest.

The day passed with my undying screams. The lava poured through me, while my throat felt constantly aflame. My nostrils bled from the cracked dryness. First I bled, then I oozed the bright burning fire itself like trails of molten gold. I wondered how much more my mind could take; perhaps I was already insane.

I could feel it as I writhed on the giant's work desk. The flame, the fire, it consumed me—the lava coursing through my very veins. Eventually, I stopped screaming. Had it been hours? Days? I could not tell. My mind, my sanity, was stretched thin and kneaded on the worktable.

The Blacksmith was surprised to see I survived, and though weakened, I was still whole. I felt the warmth spread just underneath my skin, pulling me apart. When I craned my neck to behold my naked and scarred body, I saw the lines of heat coursing through me just below the surface. It looked like a forking network of glowing roots.

The Blacksmith's Dwarf bent over to me, its disfigured hands of teal-blue caressing my scalp. "*Come, my human pet.*" It began to shush me. "*You are doing so well for a mortal. Don't you dare break now.*" It cackled again.

My parched throat was a withered stem that could not speak. Yet my eyes tried to burn with the same ferocity that I felt underneath my skin as I eyed the Dwarf.

"*Shhhhh.*" The Dwarf's cool touch sizzled and steamed on my skin, as the pudgy hands of water went to part of my lips. Dwarf's deformed head stretched open its gaping maw, from where the coolest and most revoltingly fresh stream of water poured into my withered gullet.

⋖ ⋗

Where there once was a heart, I now had a gaping circular hole. From it burnt a blindingly hot light. The spherical glow was encased inside a metal cylinder.

I regained my strength bit by bit. My broken mind was held together by stubborn callouses, but still it was frayed. Madness and rage leaked in through the cracks to sustain me. Did I even sleep? Time seemed of no consequence in this place. It felt like being trapped in a painting.

The power that coursed through me was stronger than anything I had ever felt during my mortal life—it was intoxicating to a fault. I felt a restlessness work itself in me, as if the fire that coursed through my veins was armed with pokers that stabbed beneath the surface and urged me to action.

In a haze, I was delivered to another Elder—the Engineer.

This was a wildly terrifying creature with a prawn-like face and prodding pincers running down its neck. The digits poked and electrocuted. Their humanoid hands disassembled me, taking me apart and tampering as they saw fit. My back was ripped open, peeled like the skin of a tangerine to expose my spine. The ends of my stumps were shredded. What remained of my limbs were defiled and played with.

In the end, I felt my spine strengthened, stretched even taller as it ran down my back. There were jutting parts exposed from the re-knitted skin at the end of my stumps.

I stared upon the molten rock of Blacksmith and wondered when I was to return. Was the prawn-faced Elder another trick of this world? I found that my mind was in tatters. My sense of self stretched so thin, I could see through it into this maddening world.

"Elder," I spoke. The one word made me realise how agonising it was to speak.

"Thou hast address'd me?" Blacksmith asked.

"Am I still alive?"

"Yes, yes, you are." Cackled the Dwarf, as if finding pleasure in a joke I was not privy to. *"I hope you stay alive until we have the final piece."*

"The... final piece?" I queried. Blacksmith was the mountain, the volcano. Committed to their labour with no part in the Dwarf's conversation, their hammer birthing stars which quickly faded.

"The final piece..." Dwarf chuckled, pausing to first compose themselves. *"Comes from Vol'tar's scales!"* Dwarf's laugh was insanity.

⋘ ⋙

Vol'tar's roar was the one thing that grounded me, the one event which brought with it a spark of lucidity into this wild and fevered dream to make me consider the wild mutilation of my body. I was grateful it only lasted a moment.

The deafening roar coursed through the bones of the entire mountain. The roar raged, it sundered, and it threatened to burn the world to the ground. What a mighty and terrifying sound that came from the bellow of this dragon. I could only imagine how mountainous Vol'tar had to be. Its cry alone sounded like a force of nature.

"Ahhh, Vol'tar feasts!" Dwarf said with a crazed sense of awe. The teal surface of their body rippled. His deformed hands rubbed together

as it looked up at the open roof where the gas escaped. *"I wonder how many died to procure its scales."* Dwarf laughed again.

⤞ ⤝

The scales were like ebony gems, shimmering and reflecting light off their blackened surface.

Blacksmith got to work immediately, hammering away at them. Bit by gruelling bit, Blacksmith melded scale with dreamsteel until the final product was like glossy obsidian.

The pieces were prepared, and bent ever so finely by hand to form into black gauntlets of destruction. The blue pool swirling underneath the dwarf embraced the forged limbs. Gas escaped from the enclosure and rose.

With the diligence and patience due a mountain, Blacksmith pieced together my vessel. The giant being set before me my new appendages that gleamed in the shifting light of the smouldering cauldron.

I stared at the things as if they were made of glass, each one placed just beside each corresponding socket. I was afraid—here it was, my final chance at salvation.

There was no more reason to hesitate: I stretched out my left arm towards the socket. This prosthetic was not as big as its bulkier counterpart and had an elbow guard to protect my transformed arm.

Like sharpened teeth, the object bit into my flesh and whirred. I cried from the pain, feeling as if it were a writhing metal worm trying to devour me.

With gritted teeth I huffed, my spit launching itself onto the table and evaporating in an instant. This new arm, this extension, didn't feel like it belonged to me. It felt alien, a crutch not wholly my own.

It writhed, the surface made of tiny little scales that rippled and oscillated from finger tip to stump. I got a glimpse just below the surface of the molten gold, which poured from my veins into the device. It was exhilarating!

I put on the next arm, the shoulder locking in and biting hungrily against my mortal flesh. This time, the pain was welcomed, intoxicating even. I could feel the inner machinations of Blacksmith and Engineer's design start to rumble.

This arm was bulkier and heavier. I noticed quickly that it had even less mobility to it. Moving the elbow alone on this device was a slow and deliberate experience that I had to consciously enforce. I recognized the difficulty with which the fingers moved.

Yet, in the grand scheme of things, it didn't matter; that was the most feeling I had in months. The very fact that I had fingers at all overwhelmed me in a way I could not express. I wasn't done. Finally, I donned and allowed for my new legs to bite down on me and latch like metal leeches.

Yet, I knew full well this body wasn't mine; at least, not yet.

Steam rose from the grated floor. Blacksmith watched me break through my chrysalis through smouldering coals. I rolled to my side. Dwarf clapped with excitement. My left foot planted itself under me. I pushed up to stand, the right leg dragging against the surface. A part of my unravelled consciousness expected the legs to vanish beneath me. I stood for only a moment before they gave way and I toppled on legs that did not obey me. It felt like trying to balance on stilts; I knew then that I had to relearn how to walk.

As I fell forward, I did not collapse on my face like I naturally expected to, but instead fell to all fours as heat radiated from my new limbs. The objects rippled and oscillated with the tiny scales which ran its entire obsidian body.

⋞ ⋟

I was admiring the elusive landscape of Mount Morniar when Dalila came to meet me outside Blacksmith's domain.

Being removed from that boiling chamber suddenly made the entire world seem impossibly cold. A soft breeze caressed me and whistled as it passed through the openings in my sockets and appendages. I was sensitive to the touch, shying away from the forgotten cold.

I leaned against a wall and felt at times like the masonry was alive. Part of me was convinced I could sink into the architecture inch by inch. Only by turning around to check I felt sure that it wasn't the case.

Wearing my new limbs, I stood so that I could meet Dalila eye to eye. She approached like a distant spectre in a vista she didn't belong to; much like a stain on a painting.

"Nora! Is that you?" she asked, drawing closer. The quality of her human voice brought with it something familiar.

"Not even I can be certain in this place!" I made a show of my new body, stretching my arms out to my side. I attempted desperately to not move. My heavy legs held me upright as I leaned against the wall for support. How did I even come to stand here?

The limbs weighed on me. The movements slow and laborious as even my right arm failed to rise above my shoulder. My right leg pressed into bone as if trying to devour me; my entire hip ached from it.

"What happened to your chest? Your body!" Dalila shrieked in concern as she rushed to me and inspected the transformation.

"What happened? I can move! That's what happened!"

Dalila stepped back suddenly and looked me in the eye. "Nora... did you get... bigger?"

I hadn't noticed on account of everything else, but it seemed so obvious, especially considering how I towered over her white form.

◁ ▷

Being taken away from the constant fumes which had left me in an endless fever. I began to take note of the more transient and tepid feel of Mount Morniar. It felt like we were in a dream, but the way that Dalila and I interacted with the world was almost as if we were intoxicated. Many of our inhibitions, our reasoning of the rules of all were dampened like a portion of our minds had gone to sleep.

The days after acquiring my new body proved triter than I expected. Dalila wheeled me away. The sensation was uncomfortably familiar. From some recess of my consciousness, I remember watching as Dalila wheeled me about the city while I observed everything in a haze. I repressed my impatience and allowed her to guide me.

In the meantime, a golem of stone was tasked with delivering my encumbering limbs.

I told Dalila of all that happened, the procedure, the pain, and the awkwardness of my limbs. Yet the more I tried to explain, the more surreal and dream-like it all was. Within my chest beat a miniature fruit that burnt like a sun. It sent liquid fire through me. It was comforting to talk to Dalila in this impermanent place. The air loosened our tongues. There was an openness between us.

Dalila thanked me for returning her Kaseluda so long ago.

We were stationed in housing built for mortal visitors. It had a total of two hundred and eighty empty rooms, and only one would ever be occupied for the odd visitor every odd century. It felt like a mockery of the highest human architecture with far reaching arches above each door. A set of rooms in a hallway where one would reach the end and turn, only to find themselves at the next floor without the need for stairs.

A deep velvet rug covered the floor and each door appeared to wait with anticipation to house a new guest.

Yet there was a sense of permanence, and more regimented dimensions to this building. The rooms were fashioned truly for visitors of grand renown among humans; though I was sure that given all their lordly might, erecting such an accommodation was of no difficulty to the Elder beings, and if it humoured our proud kiln, then all the better for it.

⊰ ⊱

It was when Dalila was trimming my regrown hair to the length of a thumb that I suddenly summoned the courage to speak. This place muddled my pride, made it so that I was not as ornery or tight-lipped as usual. I took advantage of that and spoke my overdue thanks.

"Dalila, I never had the chance to properly thank you."

"For what?" she asked, seemingly confused. I couldn't tell if her eyes settled on me or not.

"For everything. These past few months, I was taken apart in so many ways, and yet you helped me." The words came from the heart, no longer spoken with callousness. But that also made them sound alien on my lips.

A distorted sense of shame came over me, thinking of how Dalila took care of me, of how vulnerable I had been in that state as she fed and bathed me. I thought of how she must have taken care of me when I soiled myself and bit my lip.

"Nora? Are you okay? Did I cut you?" She inspected the scissors for blood in a dazed sort of way.

I chuckled, truly finding this woman endearing. "I'm alright," without my new limbs attached, I raised my left stump to her precious hands so that she could lower them.

"Truth be told, I have never been better. And if it weren't for you, I may not be here right now." Some lucid part of me knew that once we returned to the mortal plane, that I would never be able to speak again with the same honesty I did at Mount Morniar.

I lowered my head. "Thank you, truly, for all that you've done for me. I mean that. And I am sorry for how I treated you. I fear that once we leave this strange place, I will return to the same grating Nora you remember. I hope you will forgive me then, too."

Dalila smiled and nodded, her eyes turning rheumy as the first tears flowed. "I am just glad to see that you are okay," she admitted.

I looked over at my obsidian limbs stacked against the room wall. "I have one more favour to ask you," I said.

"Ask away."

"Will you help me grow accustomed to this new body of mine?"

Dalila chuckled. "I thought that was a given."

❧ ❧

Once the exhilaration of being provided new limbs faded, I was left with only the impatience to hurriedly master the new prosthetics. Every chance I got, I would wear those limbs, feeling time and time again how they bit into my flesh.

I began with my left arm attached to my elbow as I sat on a chair. All my other limbs watched from the side-line as I slowly grew to tame them.

At first, I practised with small objects, holding them in my hand. It was a task that proved increasingly awkward, as they would either slip or break under my unfamiliar grip. Feeling the texture of items, touching or grabbing anything felt disconnected and uncanny.

Next, I donned my right arm and tried to use them simultaneously; each hand flexing so that I could curl my fingers sheepishly. I found the use of both arms to be rather difficult.

The right appendage had a sagging weight to it and was bulkier to boot, but I noticed that when powered, the surface would ripple. My chest would heat up and a strength flowed into the arm, ready to strike with added power.

Still, if there was one thing I had learnt over my years as a soldier, it was that power was overrated, especially if it was clumsy and imprecise.

Dalila had requested a set of rails for me to hold on to as I walked.

A task easily provided to us by a fox-headed zerub. He acted as the establishment's concierge and was called Fylax.

⋖ ⋗

Within a small square courtyard, I tread forward, one foot after the next, as I felt like I was using somebody else's limbs. There was an unexpected benefit from my therapy in Mount Morniar. This place felt weightless, in a way, like wading through water. That fact alone and the sleep-like nature of my brain made the task of learning to walk more accessible, but certainly not easy.

My left foot moved easily enough, rising and bending at the knee as a leg should. Though my ankles lacked the mobility of flesh and moved only at the rise and fall of gravity's pull.

It was my right foot that dragged behind me almost literally.

Each step was more of a hop as I lifted its encumbering weight.

It did not raise by force of my thigh as one would expect, but rather by a swing of my hips, hips that often ached and cramped as the thick behemoth of a prosthetic pressed into my sides.

I would waddle, my arm prosthetics removed so I could focus solely on the rhythm of my legs until I found my stride in intervals.

Still, I did not relent, still I stepped forward. I would take breaks; unsure if an hour had passed or just fifteen minutes. Dalila had learnt to curtail her concerns, overseeing my slow and gruelling progress in absolute acquiescence. I stumbled closer and closer to making these limbs my own.

Again, one might say that I was a body of pure unrelenting will, but the truth of the matter was that each step I took, each time my metal claw-like hands wrapped themselves around the railings, I envisioned my goal at the end of it—vengeance.

Chapter Seventy

NORA

*There aren't many who are known from the kingdom of the Chitons.
But Kyelisier, the Vesper Knight, is renowned across Minethria as
one of the fiercest fighters. In the form of a humanoid wasp, Kyelisier
strikes forward with his rapier. His ferocity is matched by his visage.*

—TALES OF DURAN

Finally, it was time; we departed from Mount Morniar.

As guests of Ievarus, we were not privy to the politics of Elders. Accordingly, Dalila was to have met two Elders during her stay while I had my entire body taken apart and reassembled in the design of these beings.

White-Hawk and Hachen remained in Mount Morniar as the rest of us descended. We departed from the lordly world of higher beings. I felt the lucidity of stationary life return.

It was during this moment that I admired one of my attached limbs. How it reflected a distorted image of the rising sun off its surface. Each of the rippling pieces the size of a fingernail were made up of the fractured scales of Vol'tar.

I wondered privately of Vol'tar's magnitude: of its sundering potential, of all the things that I could only imagine. I felt oddly indebted to the beast, but knew that even if I was able to get an audience with the chained creature, I wouldn't have any more parts of me to offer lest I wished for death.

As we came closer and closer to landing, I felt the encroaching desire of Erefiel to speak to me more and more, and yet, the more and more I tried to avoid it.

Last I saw him, he saw me broken and helpless, without any limbs, and being dragged around by Dalila. I didn't want him to see me so, to think of me as someone who needed saving.

Day in and out, I was constantly driven by a roiling rage inside. Now that rage took the form of this golden heart pumping fire through my veins. I barely had a chance to simply stop and process everything.

Yet I felt like if I did take a moment to reflect, to try and process how much my body and my mind had changed over the months, I would crumble to the ground and never get back up.

As we descended and the strange air of Mount Morniar was left behind, I could tell that we all felt certain parts of our minds reawakening from their slumbers. A certain lucidity returned to our gazes. It came with a sense of relief, escaping that realm of limbo, but it also left me feeling empty. How could the triviality of normal life ever compare to the wonders of the Elders' domain?

⊰ ⊱

With our feet planted beneath us, there certainly was a feeling of groundedness. I also became astutely aware of the encumbering weight of my new limbs as I slid down from the leathery skin of the stingray and collapsed clumsily to my knees, leaving tiny craters punched into the dirt.

As I sheepishly tried to regain my footing and climb to my new feet, Erefiel approached me.

"Need help?" He asked.

"I'm fine," I said coarsely.

Erefiel hesitated. "Nora, can I talk to you?"

I was reluctant to answer. Whatever I said, I knew that he wouldn't let it be, despite the fact that Erefiel approached me the way a well-meaning man would approach a wounded dog.

I pulled myself to the stingray and used its body for leverage, slowly rising to stand. "Listen, Erefiel. I am grateful that you took me away from my parents." *And my brother,* I thought privately. "But I have no interest in talking about what happened. I just want to move on."

Erefiel stood there, somewhat dumbfounded, while Calatay brought forth our coach.

"I need to know, Nora. What happened out there? Who attacked you?"

"I don't remember," I said, not looking at him and taking a moment to feel a fresh breeze pass over the vast, treeless pasture and caress my scalp. I couldn't recall ever feeling the wind touch me so tenderly. Not just my scalp, but there was a slight whistle as it rushed through the small openings where prosthetics met flesh.

"Nora, try to remember. If you do, we can try and bring them to justice! It doesn't just have to do with you; the second attack leads me to believe that someone else was involved at Whitshade."

I turned to leave, still trying to get some practice and move towards the coach in my new body.

"It was an accident," I lied.

"I know you are hiding something," Erefiel said calmly.

I turned to him with slow, deliberate movements. The man was calm, his expression full of concern as he watched me, hoping I'd let him in. Without the air of Mount Morniar to impair our emotions, there was a stark tension in our exchange.

He continued. "You were so adamant that it was the Demon Hunters, that it was Ida's poor work that caused it all. Yet all of a sudden you insist it was just an accident?"

My surprise must have been obvious.

"I did some digging after finding out what happened," he said. I silently cursed Victor and the others for their loose lips.

I decided to coolly double down. "It was; someone made a mistake."

He stepped towards me. "*Someone?* Not Ida this time?" His tone was accusatory.

My words got stuck in my throat, so I turned to leave, limping awkwardly with a slower right step. Why couldn't I say her name? Why not blame it on Ida? I could ponder on that question for a long time, but I knew the truth and, in a strange way, it shamed me.

Looking at my new body, my new form, I was exactly that which I had pitied and judged, feared so naturally as death itself.

Here I was, able to move, able to walk and step forward, to grasp and hold things. By no means was it perfect. I still wished I could feel how my fingertips would depress when pushed against a surface. I wish I could move each digit independently and feel a satisfying itch scratched rather than clanking metal to metal. I wish my hip didn't have to feel the prosthetic press onto its bone each time I took a laborious step forward or even that I could move a proper wrist rather than this inelegant replacement.

But I could move and, more importantly, I could still fight.

I thought of Ida, of Jeremiah, of so many injured as if they were already dead and just didn't know it yet. There I was among their kind, and I could see that I wasn't useless, not until my very life would be taken from me.

"I don't remember," I lied coldly and headed towards the coach.

⊰ ⊱

I almost entirely forewent any sustenance on account of my new pounding heart. The core sustained me, pumped its liquid fire through my veins and powered me like some sort of machine. I couldn't forgo food entirely, but didn't need to eat as much. The nights themselves proved restless as my frayed mind was pulled apart, held together by a thin stretch of sanity. I would thrash, my body still adjusting with my impermanent vessel, struggling to discern when I wore limbs and when I was naked.

The heat from my core as well bled into the clustered nerves on my side. My body had come to know heat in a dangerously intimate way. Constantly reformed from one fire to the next: learning from the fire of a demon, smothered within the flame of the Blacksmith's forge, and now filled with fire that coursed through my veins. This infernal trinity made me wake in a puddle of my own sweat every night with clumped nerves and pulsing warmth below my skin.

Over the next few weeks, I reserved a private quarter for myself where I trained. The costs were of no consequence since Ievarus' scouting of mortals had gone public and my needs were covered appropriately.

I was to be used as an Empowered Soldier, tested and tempered to master my new limbs so that I could aid Ievarus when the time came.

To ease and make my new form more comfortable, I was provided straps and harnesses of leather which, when taut, would pull the prosthetics closer in so that I didn't have to hold my arms by neck strength alone—my back and neck were tenser as a result.

Having to learn to eat by myself wasn't easy either. Most spoons either didn't wish to obey me as the contents dribbled down my chin or poked my cheek; that was if the utensil didn't just outright break in my grasp.

Other things I still lacked the confidence for and relied on Dalila to help with as she did weekly visits.

My body needed to be massaged regularly to rid myself of the spasming nerves and tense muscles.

I had grown large, wide and tall in stature due to the natural task of holding onto these heavy limbs but also due to the power of this molten heart.

My breasts had practically vanished entirely on account of my defined chest and my abdominals now clearly revealed their contours.

When finally I had grown relatively accustomed to moving, I decided to test the limits of my strength. My heart would ache and burn with the flame, the heat even slightly distorting my field of vision as embers sputtered out.

Rearing back my right arm, I felt its surface bulge and ripple with the instilled power before striking. The leather straps snapped instantly under the explosive power. Not only did the sculpted head of Judicator Felicie Auburn crumble into dust, but also the marble stone of the podium—the strength behind that punch was exhilarating.

Finally, feeling confident enough, I picked up a sword from the stack. The mere task of bending over to grab the blade from its rack had my weight almost stumble forward, but I was happy to find how quickly my left leg stepped to catch me.

My bulky and stump metal digits wrapped themselves around the blade's hilt, only with patience and focus, but bringing it out from its slot caused the other weapons to tip over and clatter to the floor.

I eyed the strewn weapons and ignored them with a defeated sigh. Simply cleaning up the mess would take me considerable effort; I doubted I could even return them to the stand. I turned and instead focused on the blade.

Seeing as I preferred my left hand, I switched grips and began to swing forward with the sword, feeling the weight of each thrust in my shoulder and back; what I didn't feel was the blade. It was off, clumsy, forced and completely lacklustre. I was too slow.

With each strike, I needed to bend my wrist to extend the cut and each long and slow movement meant that I wouldn't be able to block any incoming attacks.

"What's the point?" I groused; tossing the weapon aside.

I wondered, was it better to just go with my arms rather than with a sword?

Suddenly, the arm rippled as if by its own accord or as if it sensed my intentions; it was rhythmic. I felt a pattern from finger tip all the way to my stump. It felt alive.

The arm morphed, flattening itself as the entire metal prosthetic turned into an elongated blade.

"Fascinating," I murmured, eyeing the obsidian prosthetic with wonder. I made slow, deliberate turns, trying to discern its dimensions. It hummed from grazing the wind. With my free arm, I allowed the stout metal digits to tap against the blade's edge. There was a vibrato to the way it sung. I swung the blade, feeling the air itself vibrate with each cut. Everything about it sounded metallic and heavy. The movements were slower than what I was used to, but it certainly held a satisfying weight to it.

Next, I turned to my other arm, focusing on that too, but imagining something a little more extravagant.

It started to morph; the scales shifting and gliding about its surface like a glossy ant-colony armoured in metal, moving in perfect synchrony until my hand vanished, and in its place there was a whip made from dragon scales and dreamsteel.

Each blade was an arrowhead pointing outwards, flat and wide, all linked by a thread made from my molten heart.

In a moment of excitement, I lost myself and swung the thing to whip it forward, cutting through one of the pillars that held up the veranda about me in this small square.

I winced, hoping that the building would still stand as the one pillar fell apart.

I returned the limbs to their normal shape, the tiny pieces assembling into arms and digits; I felt a sort of connection to their being.

⋞ ⋟

Five months had passed in a flash. The most I heard from the outside world was the constant buzz of Ievarus' waiting quest and a foreboding rumour about the akar forces growing.

Dalila was to visit me today; I couldn't help but feel a morsel of guilt when she found me already gone. Would she feel upset? Probably concerned, more than anything else.

My relationship with my new prosthetics was tentative at best but it held. I'd grown accustomed to the bulky and uncomfortable weight they bore on my bones. Whatever waking hour I had was spent mastering my new body. I could walk with a comfortable enough gait that, to the unassuming eye, it appeared as no more than a casual limp.

As I stepped onto the streets, the hood of my cowl was pulled up and my metal body was hidden underneath its drab colours. I avoided any stares and kept my head down, casually strolling out of the Clerian gates and onto the road.

I found quickly that walking on even footing proved far more forgiving than walking along winding paths and rising hills.

Regularly, I took breaks at the side of the road behind trees and boulders to avoid the gaze of the occasional passerby upon their cart of goods.

It was the indecisive pass over from spring to summer, a constant mix of more stubborn winds and gleaming sun.

Today, it was decisively more akin to summer, as the harsh heat above beat down on me and used my limbs to cook me.

I had removed my right arm and placed it into a long hemp bag carried over my left shoulder, yet still I felt the sweat pour from me and the uncomfortable prosthetics rub and chafe against my skin. It was about the fifth time that I was walking along after another break that a trundling wagon snuck up from behind.

"Good day, miss. Where might ya be headin'?" The haggard and boorish voice of an old man spoke out.

I turned, allowing for my hood to conceal my features.

"To business that is of no concern of yours."

The man chuckled. "I highly doubt that! Otherwise I wouldn't be here. Well, hop on in. Perhaps I can get you there faster," he coaxed.

I didn't pay much mind to the old man's eccentric rambling. "That won't be necessary, I will find my own way there."

"I insist. Whatever it is you are hauling in that bag don't seem very light. And I can't just pass on by when someone obviously requires some help. Consider it a personal courtesy—can't let you die out here on my account."

I tilted slightly to look up at the man. His skin was loose and hanging with whiskers of salt and pepper. As if sensing my scrutiny, the man flashed a toothy half-grin as if plastered on a corpse. Whatever his rickety wagon hauled was covered in a tied down tarp.

A single horse of ashen colour pulled the wagon. Its bones protruded from the animal's paper-thin skin and it was plagued by flies; the animal looked to be on the verge of falling over

"Your horse is a bag of bones. My bet is you'll be joining me down here soon enough."

"You mean Pydru?" The old man pointed towards his horse. The poor animal gave a protesting puff through its nostrils. "Please! Pydru gonna outlive a lot of them other prize horses. You trust me on that! Ain'tcha boy?" The man chuckled, leaning over to slap Pydru's rear as the horse nickered in agreement.

The man chuckled. "Now, you joinin' us? Or are we gonna stand here until I got to toss you in the back?"

The man seemed harmless, and, as the sun continued to beat down on me, I felt my new body plotting to wear me down before I ever reached Bracken. I looked over at the horse at the front.

With slow and deliberate movements, I stepped up and onto the wagon, feeling the entire thing lean slightly to its side on account of my weight.

"Woah! You a hefty lass, ain't ya'?" Just like that, the man set his horse in motion.

"You know, you ain't allowed to say that to a dame," I chided, somewhat finding the curt and unfiltered comment refreshing.

Looking closer at him, he had deep brown eyes with lids that plotted to sag until he could see no more. He was wearing a tall black and wide-brimmed hat, along with a vest over his shirt and doublet.

"You ain't no dame. I can tell you that much."

I went quiet for a moment. "You don't find me suspicious?" I queried.

The man shrugged. "I ain't one to judge. I just want to take you to wherever you be goin'."

I didn't know if it was a ruse of the wind or just having the stench of my own sweat clog my nostrils, but I suddenly took note of the slight pungent smell that wafted from the wagon behind me. I turned to find it wreathed by a cloud of flies. I didn't need to imagine what it held—it smelt of death.

"What are you transporting?" I asked, suddenly getting ready for the trap to be sprung.

"Oh, nothin' special. I am just a body collector. Been rather busy, you know? With the rot and all. Keeps me and Pydru on our toes!" the man supplied affably.

As the man's wagon trundled along and a gust of cool air soothed my aching limbs, we sat there in silence, the scent of the dead lingering just behind us. Pydru relieved himself quite liberally as his tail wagged to make room for the liquid brown to dribble from its anus.

"Charming." I wrinkled my nose.

The man gave a rowdy and coarse chuckle at my comment. "Aye, my princess do be havin' a quite sensitive digestion. Drama queen, that one. Yet never fails to sniff out the dead, sometimes even before the people know it themselv'. Wherever death be, Pydru follows!" The man gave another hoarse chuckle that turned into a livid cough. "Apologies."

It was then that I realized that I hadn't even told the man where I was going.

"Where are we heading?" I asked.

The man looked over at me, seemingly perplexed. "Well, I am taking you to Bracken, of course," he said, as if it were the most obvious thing.

"How do you know I want to go to Bracken?"

He chuckled. "When you've been in the business as long as I have, you know a thing or two about where people ought to be goin'." The man gave a wink from a dreary eye, the lid drooping like a second skin.

There was something disconcerting about the man, odd, but not threatening either.

"Where are you headed?" I asked.

"Oh me? Wherever there are dead to be collected. Wherever Pydru deigns to take me. At this moment? I am headin' to Bracken." He gave me a toothy smile with whatever teeth still remained.

"Whatever." I decided to leave it at that. The man didn't appear to mean me harm, and if he got me to my destination in one piece, then

I didn't mind a little bit of eccentricity. It was then that I looked about and noticed how empty the road had become. The sun was blaring from above, yet still the quiet of the surrounding trees was unusual; not even a single bird chirping about.

As more and more of the distance was left behind and the still terrain with closed-in valleys passed by, I wondered how I ever thought that I could travel the distance on foot.

"I am glad you found me when you did. Don't think I could have made it," I admitted.

The man chuckled again. "Don't thank me, thank Pydru," he said. Pydru nickered in agreement.

"What do you mean?" I asked.

"I told you, didn't I? Pydru has a knack for sniffing out death, and you reek of it, lass."

I was momentarily stunned, wondering what to say in response when we reached the crest of the hill and looked at the drab and clouded exterior of Bracken. I shifted and subtly tried to massage my cramped limbs.

"It's uncomfortable, I imagine," the man said.

"What?" I asked.

The man nodded towards my limbs, the obsidian gloss of my left arm peaking through my cowl, which I quickly dashed away.

"Who are you?" I pressed.

"I told you, just a body collector," he supplied.

Admittedly, I was glad to dismount from the man's wagon as I felt solid ground beneath my metal feet.

"Nora, one more thing." I turned at the sound of his voice. "Try your luck at the Toothfairy, you will find what you are looking for." He winked.

As the man made to turn around his wagon, I called to him.

"What is it that I want?"

The man seemed taken aback by my response, but then gave me a haunting grin as if to a private joke. "Well, what you want is revenge."

"And what is it that you want?" I added.

"To help you find it."

The man tipped his hat. The grin turned into a cryptic. Something chilling was implied there. As Pydru turned around, I saw half the horse's face was nothing more than exposed bone and flesh.

Though as strange as my driver was, he had eventually gotten me where I needed to go.

While my surroundings was undisturbed, I took my right arm from the bag and reattached it, wincing slightly at the sudden clasping teeth around my shoulder.

I stumbled into the Toothfairy. Few people spared me a glance. There wasn't anyone in Bracken who didn't have something to hide.

Truth be told, Danny and Regan weren't the only names that kept me company during my restless nights.

There was more to this than was apparent on the surface; a realisation that became all the more crystallised when Erefiel voiced my suspicions.

Cassidy Femur had organised all of it. Danny and Regan made sure that I knew that much, but that wasn't all. Somebody sabotaged the church at Whitshade and hoped to count me among the casualties. It was obvious that this was orchestrated. The most suspicious suspects of all were still hunters who vanished after completing their part of the deal, yet I jumped to conclusions once before; I wouldn't make that mistake again. Danny and Regan owed me answers before I would dole out punishments.

Chapter Seventy-One

NORA

It is a rather clandestine part of Elder history, but not all Elders have aligned themselves with the Elder King. What sources I can find suggest that the Blacksmith was once a most noble Elder who forged the weapons of the gods. Now, the Blacksmith lays imprisoned; forced to forge the very chains which bind him, he continues to labour for his king.

—HERETICAL DISCUSSIONS ON FORGOTTEN HISTORY

A bar within such a despot stank exactly how one would imagine; the lingering scent of ale, vomit and smoke that wedged itself into the foundation of the entire place. The floorboards groaned trying to hold my weight as I stepped up to an empty table in the corner of the room and surveyed the patrons.

Now more than ever could I smell my own lingering sweat, but that wasn't all. The scent of brimstone wafted, and I made an effort to wrap the cowl closer around my chest, to not let the light of my new heart bleed out.

All I ordered was an ale. When next a waiter came, I ordered their boar hind with baked beans—suffice it to say it was dry and bland. I coveted the meal and formed the appropriate fork and knife out of my prosthetic hands; it proved easier to eat that way despite the odd angle I used to cut the meat.

I scanned the room, surveying every single person who came and went.

A few times, I thought I saw the wiry and long-faced look of Danny or the older appearance of Regan, but I knew that I simply tried to etch their likeness onto the faces of others.

At one point, I even saw Munasen enter and leave. Part of me wished to approach and greet him, but not enough as to abandon my quest of finding Regan and Danny. My owed apology and drink would have to come another time.

In a weird way, my molten heart ached and burnt akin to a skipping heartbeat when I finally recognized their vile expressions upon their entry. It was like some perversion of intimacy, of corrosive longing, like seeing a lover again after being away for a long time. What remained of my mortal skin prickled. My breath paused. A shiver ran down my back and I felt my heart pick up pace.

"Rounds for everybody!" Regan announced enthusiastically.

Tankards of ale were raised into the air and salutes came from all, even I joined in.

When I was delivered my drink, I simply sat there and observed the two of them with a calm and seething rage, a worming leviathan that slithered underneath a still sea waiting to spring out. My eyes never left them as the two started to drown themselves in drinks and chanted exuberantly at one another. Making blithe calls to neighbouring tables.

Finally, when the guests began to stem and most patrons called it in for the evening, I took my forgotten ale and joined them at their table, my hood still pulled over.

"Mind if I join you?" I asked, trying my best to sound forthcoming.

In most cases, a stranger completely shrouded in a cowl raised plenty of alarms. But, given their rather stunted reasoning, they seemed to see me as just another clandestine citizen of Bracken.

"Please, sit." The one called Regan instructed.

"Though if you are here to hire our services, I must let you know it be best to handle such matters when my partner and I aren't so drunk."

I smiled under the hood.

"I would just like the company," I said, taking a seat with them.

"Missy, I must say, you have quite a beautiful voice; I wonder if the face underneath be just as grand." Regan stretched out an arm to pull away my hood.

I leaned away from his reach. "Nuh-uh! All good things come to those who wait."

His burning red cheeks rose from his amused smile. "Oh, a tease! I do quite like that."

"We would both like a turn," Danny said with a sadistic look in his eyes as his arm strung itself around Regan's broad shoulders. A memory flashed. I remembered all too well how they both took their turns. The foetid ecstasy as they penetrated me from behind, burying my face deeper in vomit.

"Bah! This kid! Took him out on one job months ago and now he thinks he is the best!"

I smiled, feeling the coming finale that only I was privy to. "What job?"

"Oh, it was great! Someone got on the wrong side of a noble up there in Cleria, paid us handsomely to dole out some punishment on the one who did him wrong!"

"Oh, a noble! Must have gotten paid well."

"That we did." Danny cut in, his statement full of pride.

Regan leaned in this time. "You know, I've never been with a woman as large as you. I think that would be quite fun."

I gave a forced chuckle as if I was bemused. Neither of the two vermin seemed to catch on. Again I recalled the roughness with which they raped me, the fissures I felt opening below.

"Tell you what, I am feeling rather frisky tonight. How about I take you both on?"

The two men shared quick looks and, just like that, they both agreed.

"I have to warn you though, I like it rough," I said.

"Wouldn't have it any other way," Regan smiled hungrily.

Rather than waiting until they took me to whatever abode vermin like this called home, I decided to have our fun within a secluded alleyway.

With my body as it was, it would tire out quickly. My new prosthetics were clumsy and inefficient, holding a lot of heft, but with no real alacrity or range of motion. Any fight that I engaged needed to be planned out and won as quickly as possible. But for the drunk and clueless duo, it was over in seconds.

It was like a banquet for my catharsis. The sound of their breaking bones was music to my ears.

My right arm wound up as its light bled through my cowl. I had grabbed onto Regan so tightly that just my grip alone shattered his shoulder.

Danny, caught in the shock, stood defenceless as I pulled him into the dark alleyway.

The dragon's flame bled through my outfit.

"My shoulder! She broke my shoulder!" Regan cried out as he fell to his rear. None along the outer streets cared about the deafening cries—it was just another day in Bracken.

I stood over them, light bleeding through and colouring the tight, obstructing walls on either.

"What do you want from us?" Danny cried, tears in his eyes.

"Who sent you? Was it Jordan? I told him we'd pay him back!" The sudden pain that rushed through Regan seemed to have sobered him up.

With Danny's leg laid out before me like a twig on a forest path, I stomped down to hear it snap. The boy wailed in agony, grasping onto his leg until he bit his lip to stifle the cries. The tears now came fully as his head rocked back and forth.

I did not answer.

Instead, I pulled my arms from underneath my cowl, their obsidian sheen giving off the distorted golden light underneath as I gingerly removed the cowl from my head.

Regan's lips quivered, his eyes wide with primal fear. "It can't be."

My expression was a calm, cold rage as I stared down on them with festering contempt.

"Look—I—we're sorry. Please, let us pay you. We will give you the money." Regan stammered.

Holding back the strength of my limbs, I swung low with my right leg, initially just planning to knock Regan back into the wall—I did not expect to hear his raised arms shatter from my half-hearted kick.

Again, the man wailed pitifully. His back must have cracked from the impact as his torso folded over and he fell to the floor.

Regan's following breaths were raspy and pained. I left him for the time being and turned to Danny. The boy winced and shuddered. Whatever he saw painted on my expression made him blanch.

"I will ask you this once: who set up the trap in Whitshade?"

It was like a rabbit frozen in the path of a hungry wolf.

Danny's lips trembled. "P… please. I don't know," he muttered, a sudden puddle forming underneath him; I simply watched with indifferent disgust. "Regan was the only one who was in touch with them."

Without even a moment's hesitation, my left fist swung and struck along the cheek of the weeping Danny. The crunch of broken bone filled the air followed by a wet slosh. His partially eviscerated skull embedded itself in the brick wall beside him.

As I removed my obsidian fist clumped in viscera and blood, I looked at Regan. Fear returned him to the present. He stammered. Words were trying to be formed through a frayed and terrified psyche. It was coming. I waited patiently for the words: Demon Hunters.

"Eric Richardson!"

There was a stunned silence.

"Eric did this?" There was hurt in my voice.

"He was the one who sabotaged the church! The delivery, the Demon Hunters. It was all a lie to ruin you!"

Eric? It suddenly all began to make sense. He was the only other person who was there to hear what the process of containment was.

Only he had access to the cage and was sent with me on purpose. That was why he left so early.

I stepped away. Danny's still embedded skull now sliding and leaving behind a stroke of scarlet. Loose bricks clattered to the floor.

"Please, I told you what you wanted to know. Please. I—I'm sorry." Regan sputtered in-between sobs, snot running down his nose and his eyes glassy behind the tears as he looked at me for mercy. "I was just doing what I was paid to do! I will give you whatever money is left. I will even help you find Cassidy!"

I raised my fist, the scales of my arm forming and shifting until it took the shape of a very long, thin blade.

The man's eyes livened with fear. "What… what are you doing?" he asked.

"I told you: I like it rough." Any mirth in my voice was gone. Only a glacial and unmoving desire to hurt left.

Chapter Seventy-Two

NORA

*Out of all the Seeds which came and went, it is said none could match
the power of Muriya. A single strike of his hammer could sunder entire
kingdoms and pock great valleys. Some weapons of the Seeds were never
retrieved for they were lost. Muriya's hammer was never retrieved
for none since him had enough strength to raise it. It still waits at the
Cornais ruins in the Swollen Swamp for a successor.*

—Excerpts from "Lost History of Minethria"

I strolled through the barracks; the off-duty guards did not spare
me even a single, wayward glance in those Spartan halls. My
cowl provided me cover, coveting the bleeding light on my chest
and hiding away my face. My steps were heavy as I climbed up the
stairs one notch at a time, the left leg taking the mechanical lead while
my heavier half moved with the swing of my hips. I asked a passing
guard about Eric's room. The man didn't seem to question who I was
and waved me along to one of the many identical doors that lined the
hallway. The door was unlocked when my metal grip found purchase
on the handle. Eric was in his room. The only audience to witness his
death was a gathering of empty bottles. The man looked defeated, his
eyes a dull and vapid expression waiting for the end as he gazed up at
my vengeful form.

"I knew it was a matter of time," he said, his smile maudlin. "Can I offer you a drink?" he asked, turning around, searching about his place for a bottle that hadn't been emptied. "How did you find me?" he asked, still searching.

"Asked around. They said this was your place."

He chuckled. "Wonder if they realised they were sending death to my doorstep."

I removed the cowl and let it puddle on the floor, my writhing prosthetics left fully to bare.

He turned to me, obviously inebriated. Still, there was a sense of awe muddled somewhere in that gaze. "If I may, the whole metal limb thing looks good on you, especially with the short hair," Eric plopped himself back onto a chair, his eyes peering listlessly.

"What happened to that drink?" I asked.

He lifted his arms. "Sorry, can't seem to find it." The man chuckled, his greasy locks hanging from him as he swerved his head around in a daze.

I could tell that he hadn't slept in days. His eyes were claimed by a certain frenzy. The heavy bags implied sleepless nights. Eric was consumed by fear—he knew I was coming and numbed his trepidation with a sea of liquor.

I stepped forward. Eric observed me with resignation.

"Why did you do it?" I asked.

"Do you remember?" he began suddenly, his voice taking on the sort of inflection as if he were about to tell me a story. "Do you remember when you came to the Toothfairy? You fought against Munasen, had me lose all my money. I warned you… didn't I?" Eric was too drunk and tired to sound defensive.

In that moment, with his drenched and filthy clothes unchanged in days and perennial snarl, I couldn't help but feel sorry for this broken man.

"I told you not to do it; I owed money, lots of money. That was going to be my way *out*." There were now tears in those eyes that accepted death. "I didn't want to do it, I really didn't. But Cassidy promised to make all my problems go away, to pay away my debt."

The man sobbed freely. I no longer saw a shrewd and heartless drunk, but a broken man who could only dig himself a deeper hole, no matter what he did.

"After the attack, he asked that I meet you, that I defile you. He no longer wanted you dead. He wanted you dismembered *completely*, to be raped and destroyed, he wanted you to know that it was him who caused all this."

I frowned, suddenly realising his meaning. "But you didn't, you *couldn't*... that was why those other men were sent."

Eric nodded sluggishly, tears trickling down a sallow face.

"I suppose they're dead? I want you to know that I didn't want to do it. To pay the raiders. To set up the trap. I didn't *mean* to. But no matter what I do, things just get worse and worse. When I heard that you were being taken to Mount Morniar, I knew what was going to happen... and I was relieved," he confessed.

I stopped in my tracks, looking deep into the eyes of this man. There were no more tricks, no more lies; all he wanted was forgiveness, not so that I would spare his life, but so that I would understand how deep a hole he had dug for himself.

The mistress of gambling truly did make Eric give everything. All that was left was his life.

"Does Cassidy know?" I asked.

Eric nodded.

I stepped forward, arms winding up as Eric slumped in the chair and did not resist.

Bottles shattered underneath my feet or rolled out of the way.

As my obsidian hands reached out with their cold touch, grasping and wrapping themselves about Eric's head, I felt him grow stiff and a shudder escaped him. His eyes were windows into a hollowed out man full of regret and pity.

"I hope you can forgive me," he said.

My arms tightened. It was terrifying how easily his neck snapped from just a little pressure. But the sound was barely audible, like a thin twig.

Eric Richardson slumped in my grip.

"I cannot," I admitted.

❦ ❧

It was all almost over.

While Danny and Regan's death felt akin to some depraved orgasm born out of my fractured sanity, that of Eric left me feeling sullen. It was too easy. That cathartic release I desired turned out to be a disappointment. Long after, I felt his fragile form in my arms, how easily he broke under my grip with barely a snap to signal his passing.

The man was exploited, used by Cassidy who assuredly knew full well what kind of predicament Eric was in, and how he'd be willing to do just about anything.

I had waited until the streets were empty and everyone went to their respective residences. I did not return to my accommodation, knowing full well that there was already a party searching for me; I could only hope that Eric's body had still gone undiscovered.

Biding my time within a secluded alleyway, I practised my breathing.

It was calm, rhythmic, the undulating stretch like a capricious tide pulling in and out of shore. So too did my new body pulse with my breath, the scales vibrating and fluttering at each exhale like a dragonfly's wings.

Finally, when the streets were empty, I donned my hood and went on my way.

As expected, there was a body of guards awaiting my arrival, and it was pretty much unavoidable that at the helm of them stood Erefiel.

I seldomly approached the centre of Cleria. Yet I had no choice if I wanted Cassidy's head to roll. A full moon shone a spotlight onto the climax of my vendetta. As I stepped past the vacant plaza, I was met by none other than the man I admired most, even when I was still just a child with a dream.

I approached. Erefiel stood with his battle armour donned, including sword and shield.

His supporting company numbered only about two dozen men.

"Nora, stop this madness."

I smirked privately for a moment underneath my hood, unsure of who I was trying to fool. Gingerly, I removed the hood, but to my audience it must have looked like slow and deliberate movements.

"Move," I said, the only command I was willing to speak out.

"Nora! We already found Eric's body. You can still walk away. But if you break down the Femur walls and kill anyone in there, there is nothing I can do."

"I am bound to Ievarus, as are you; the laws of man don't apply to us anymore."

"Yet kill Cassidy and you won't be welcome here; in fact, if we were to kill you, Ievarus will just find someone else."

The man stepped forward, removing his helmet as if seeing his pleading expression would make me reconsider.

"You were taken in to be hope because of Dalila's instance. Don't make her regret that. This blood isn't just on your hands—it is on hers."

I had to admit, I never considered how my rampage and lies would affect Dalila, but it was only a minor annoyance. It was too late to regret anything.

"Then so be it. Cassidy needs to pay for what he has done to me."

"And then what?!" Erefiel challenged pointedly.

"Move. I won't ask a third time."

With a defeated sigh, Erefiel donned his helmet again and drew his blade from his scabbard. "I won't let you kill anyone else."

The distance between us spanned over a hundred and fifty feet within the square of laid cobblestone and erect Cleria banners. It was a distance perfect for a crossbow.

So when Erefiel closed the distance, it was done so in a frightening flash.

Quickly, I calculated a point of attack, my usual and old tactic of speed and distance now seemingly impossible as instead I channelled my arms to transform, powering my fiery blood into limbs.

My right arm became an obsidian kite-shield, which covered me from head to armoured shin, while my left arm extended into a short sword.

Trying to fight Erefiel in this form was impossible; my lumbering body trying desperately to keep up with a weapon that gathered speed the more momentum it had. More than once did my left leg manage to keep me from falling over while my right appendage dragged behind like an anchor. I lowered my centre of gravity even further to use that weight to my advantage.

As I held out my shield, I felt the light touch of passing wind graze my scalp as I instinctively turned to find Erefiel had jumped over my form as if lifted by a gust of wind.

His blade was impossibly fast, my shield never able to catch the haft of his strikes and slow nicks against my flesh. Golden blood flowed through the wounds, trickling and sizzling against the floor.

Erefiel was toying with me; deliberate shallow cuts made to tire me out as he knew my body would not be able to last long enough with all the energy I was expending. His turns and gyrations were sharp, making sure to constantly stay at my sides.

I could feel the gust of air cocoon around us, venting through the flat side of Erefiel's sword.

My scales rippled, chittering excitedly at the chance of letting loose.

Wind's touch grazed my skin, my nape, stroked the hair on my neck like a light breeze caressing blades of grass. The incisions were artful, opening shallow gashes to slowly bleed me out.

It was coming. Quickly, I transformed my weaponized appendages into regular arms. I breathed in, allowing my heart's light to brighten as power poured itself into my bulkier right arm.

This was a gamble, a feeling, a slight nudge guided by the wind's rhythm.

I turned and felt the scales stand on end. The burning hot inside me lit a small island around our fight. With my left hand free, I quickly smeared some of the scalding blood from a gash and flicked it to my side; I had intentionally left it open. Erefiel's momentum was arrested. His shield rose to catch the droplets which sizzled against the polished surface.

Now was my chance.

I struck with my empowered right. Momentum carried me forward despite it being a clumsy attack. I realized then how much power I imbued into my punch until it was all too late. My fist landed and the air ruptured.

A shock wave sent me to my rear, pain lancing through my entire body, starting from my right shoulder. I heard something clatter. The view was obscured by a cloud of dirt.

Turning, I found my right arm giving off vapour just a few feet away.

One of the wooden banners snapped, toppling over and landing at my feet to show the insignia of Cleria in the form of a sun. Yet Erefiel was nowhere to be found.

I heard loose bricks clatter on top of each other. The dust settled. My chest tightened as I held my breath. In the distance, masonry rolled down a pile. The wall of someone's home was demolished. Erefiel stepped out from within, coughing. His shield had a large concave dent that slipped right down his unmoving arm. Blood ran down his scalp, and I could tell he panted uncontrollably. The arm must have been broken, but I breathed a sigh of relief at seeing him alive.

I didn't notice when the rest of the guards encircled me, spears and swords trained on me as fear plastered itself on each and every single one of their expressions. The pointed ends of their weapons trembled.

I looked away from the terrified gazes, any appetite for punishing Cassidy ruined.

"I yield," I said reluctantly, falling supine.

Chapter Seventy-Three

The history of Minethria is quite discordant and difficult to regiment. It is theorised that part of this issue is as a consequence of the forgotten. If a single person would be tied to important events, it is possible that when stricken from existence and memory, that their tied history is also tampered with.

—AN ANALYSIS OF MINETHRIA'S DISCORDANT HISTORY

Within the room stood the four aspects Ievarus had gathered; all except for fear.

Ievarus found that what Dalila had said was correct. Humans took on many forms when it came to emotions.

Within the small room, both Nora and Erefiel expressed rage, but Erefiel most of all at that moment. What were the signs? Erefiel's neck had stretched itself taut and revealed bulging veins. His features were twisted. He shouted with an elevated voice.

But Chroma sat in the corner with nothing to say, simply appearing as a wide bodied and quiet individual.

Perhaps not being able to understand the complexity of it all, despite being in the midst of it frustrated Ievarus even more. But the path that Master had set Ievarus on already showed potential.

Dalila told Ievarus of what happened, the fact that Nora had sought revenge for her injury; she then had to explain what revenge was.

Like the long-limbed and willowy being that Ievarus was, they observed the explanation emotionlessly.

"Will revenge bring back her body?" Ievarus asked.

Dalila leaned into Ievarus and spoke clearly of one insight of her own. "Emotions are not supposed to make sense, they are just there. Same with the aspects. Hope can oftentimes just lead to more pain."

"So why hope?" Ievarus asked, while Nora and Erefiel continued their argument. Ievarus kept an eye on the two.

Instead of answering Ievarus directly, Dalila pondered for a moment and tried another tact.

"Ievarus, what is it that you want from us?"

Ievarus blinked, looming over Dalila. "To instil in me an idea, a reason for hunting down the Evil."

Dalila nodded. "What if we couldn't teach you that? What if you won't gather an idea from one of us?"

Ievarus pondered; the answer appeared to be simple. "I would find another way."

"And what if there is no other way? What if you will never have an idea?"

Ievarus froze, and remained so for quite some time. There was no emotion to read off their sculpted features. It was the closest thing Ievarus had shown to distaste.

"What if you will roam forever? Never able to fulfil your purpose?"

Ievarus uttered no response.

"That is why we have hope. You *hope* that you will learn about emotion. You hope that you will have a purpose towards slaying the Evil. Because if you lose hope in that, you have no reason to continue."

The concept was something new. In very basic terms, Ievarus *wanted* to slay the Evil, not because it was the right thing to do but because it was the only thing laid before them since the moment of their birth.

Ievarus vocalised their epiphany. "I… hope that I will have an idea."

Dalila nodded approvingly.

Chapter Seventy-Four

EREFIEL

When Kivran the Smouldering was born, it was with such an uncontainable power that even their visage was ineffable. Thus, The Blacksmith forged for them a new vessel. Upon his battle with the eighth Evil, he had no choice but to abandon his body if he was to triumph. Ever since, a crack ran through the vessel where molten gold flowed and granted him his title. The only thing left to mark the sight of this battle was a black tree and a sundered crater. None of his allies returned.

—AN ASSESSMENT ON OLD SEEDS

My fight with Nora died down.

Due to the fact that no one else perished, especially not someone as important as Cassidy Femur, Nora had been given a week's house arrest and had her limbs confiscated during that time.

A quick trial was convened to suggest that the law was upheld. The case of Nora's tragedy was blamed on those who already died. Cassidy Femur was mentioned not once during the entire trial.

I remembered her explosive impact. The way it shattered my arm a dozen different ways and sent me flying through a wall. I had never seen anything like it. It gave me the confidence that Nora was a force to be reckoned with with her new vessel. Thankfully, my otherworldly build ensured that my broken arm healed in a matter of days.

Nora kept apologising in her own way—meaning boorish and insincere. I didn't care about my broken arm or the fact that I almost died. What bothered me was how brash her actions were. The first thing she did with her new body was kill the men who assaulted her. I couldn't fault her for it, but it was a blasphemy towards the god who made the vessel.

I sighed before stepping up to the round table in which Ievarus and all the other aspects circled around. The way Ievarus stood, the way their milky eyes observed us, and even their eerily slow movements unsettled me with no end.

"It is official. We are now tied to Ievarus, The Eleventh Seed, The Silver Prince, The Elder King's Spawn. Notarized and approved by Cleria's King: Aston Tiemen, and seemingly upheld by the Elder King's Council as well. We are to be representatives of Ievarus. Ievarus will occasionally follow and observe, but is for the most part not to involve themselves with the problems of us mortals.

"Accordingly; I, Erefiel Numyana, son of White-Hawk and Lady Imrie, am to be their Will; Dalila of the Sisterhood of the Faithful is to be their Compassion; Chroma of the akar is to be Rage." I paused, trying to come to terms with the last mention, even more so with the next.

"And Nora is to be hope." I spoke her name glibly.

"Now, while I have you all here, there is something I would like to discuss," I said. "Nora."

Nora turned towards me in surprise.

"There have been growing reports and concerns regarding the outer reaches of Thickwood. We believe that the akar are amassing a new force to strike soon. I can't send in anymore men, but I can send you. Separate from the army and tied to the Seed, as well as having…" I simply nodded towards Nora's appendages. "I believe you are the best option to scout and report back."

Nora stood straight and proud, even giving a heavy salute.

"However, you are not going alone," I nodded towards Chroma, who sat in the corner.

Nora looked towards the akar and back to me with an indignant scowl. "I can do this alone!"

I banged my fist on the table. "Come on, Nora! You almost killed me, and now I am bending over backwards to give you what you want! To ease you into the forces through scouting. You will go with Chroma or not at all."

Nora kept her stare on the silent akar while Chroma brooded; his eyes unshifting.

"Fine," Nora acquiesced. "On one condition."

"What?"

"I get to take someone I trust with me."

I was too tired of the back and forth. I pinched the bridge of my nose and waved my indifference.

"Nora, this is a scouting mission. With your new limbs, I think you will be best in a pinch. If something happens, I want you to *run*. Chroma over there will make sure you return in one piece and can speak the akar tongue if need be."

Nora looked over to Chroma with loathing, but didn't protest.

Ievarus now stepped forward from the shadows.

"Aspects. I ask you for one thing," Ievarus said, hunched and still towering over all.

Ievarus produced four containers, all containing ink.

One by one, Ievarus worked their way to each individual, marking them in their respective colours.

Compassion received the colour blue for stillness and tranquillity, brushed with a thumb against Dalila's forehead.

Rage was passed onto Chroma, the red in striking contrast to his charcoal skin.

Hope was passed onto a reluctant Nora, the orange similar to that of a setting sun promising its return.

And, finally, Will was given to me, the strong and unfaltering brown: a colour that assured resilience and strength.

Chapter Seventy-Five

DALILA

Nain of the Everglow was made into two people. Come day their hair turned golden and the pit on their chest radiated sunlight. Come night, their hair darkened and their chest reflected the moon. It is said that during Nain's ascension and the dark marriage of the eclipse, that Mount Morniar trembled.

—APOCRYPHAL ACCOUNT OF A MUSE

Nowadays, I was no longer sure of the state of things. For one, I was not surprised to find that Nora had departed from her estate. In my heart of hearts, I knew she went to dole out punishment for those who played a hand in her tragedy. Yet it was also true that her form was whole, a new way for her to get about despite its many shortcomings.

I couldn't help but wonder; did I abet Nora in her vengeance? Did I enable her, nudge her forward, knowing each step brought her closer to fulfilling her macabre pursuit of catharsis?

I saw Nora again. Her rage had turned into a smoulder. I was relieved. Relieved in a way that was immediately followed by guilt. Three people had to die so that a woman I admired had some semblance of peace, one who had dragged me away from home when I was just a child. I didn't know how to feel about that.

When the meeting was over, and I bore the blue ink across my forehead, I returned to the residence where I had taken care of Nora, one last time, and spent a private moment to imbed three cuts into my skin for the three men who died.

My days from then on passed without consequence. I returned to my former duties, all except for one: I no longer visited Mother Lucia and avoided our sessions entirely.

Considering that Mother Vinrie didn't approach me about the subject, I assumed it was either something of little importance or Mother Lucia spoke nothing of it.

So, when I was finally called into Mother Vinrie's office and found Mother Lucia sitting there expectantly, I found my breath caught in my throat.

"Dalila, please take a seat," Mother Vinrie waved towards the free chair opposite her desk.

I saved just a momentary glance for the purse-lipped Mother Lucia, who showed just enough hostility for me to notice.

Finally, when Mother Vinrie spoke, it was with a long exhale.

"Mother Dalila, I don't know what to say. This is rather unprecedented." Mother Vinrie's tone wasn't full of reproach. It rather came across as relief. Yet still I braced myself for the scolding.

Curiosity gripped me. "What is it?"

"You are no longer bound by the church; you are allowed to use your powers as a representative of the Silver Prince."

My confusion was noticeable. "What? I don't quite follow."

Mother Vinrie produced a page and, with her glasses nestled securely on her nose, she continued to speak.

"Mother Lucia brought something rather interesting to my attention. According to the state's commandments and the rules of our kingdom, any member who serves directly under a higher being with sway in Mount Morniar is beholden to their laws and decrees. So, by extension, though you are still a witch and still a part of this Sisterhood, you are no longer required to restrain your abilities."

I bit back a response—I wasn't even sure what to say. "Thank you," I finally managed.

"Don't thank me, thank your mentor. She is the one who brought this to our attention and argued on your behalf."

I looked at the old woman, her expression saintly. Yet I couldn't shake the feeling that she had her own stake in all this, hidden underneath all that supposed sanctimony.

"Thank you." My words were hollow and forced. If Mother Vinrie noticed, she didn't comment.

"There is more." Mother Vinrie began, the next part seemingly coming a little harder to speak out. "By extension of this timeless decree, you technically can visit your family and return to them if you so choose."

"What?" This time I was truly taken aback by the news; it felt as if I were being told I could return to a life that had no place for me.

"You heard Mother Vinrie, child. You are free of this life, if you choose. But you are still bound to the servitude of the Silver Prince until their task has ended."

"And if I choose not to serve Ievarus?"

"Then you automatically return to our service."

"And once their task is finished?"

"Well, technically, you are an accessory towards that end. You would no longer be bound to anyone and would have the option to ascend."

The words were so alien and otherworldly, spoken by people who didn't understand the weight of them. I absent-mindedly trailed off into quiet reflection.

"Just know this, Mother Dalila." Mother Vinrie's voice trembled only slightly. The old woman leaned forward on her table and held me in her wide eyes. Her wizened pointer finger tapped on her desk. "You are still part of the church, but if you so choose, you are permitted to leave it all behind."

I saw a rare moment of vulnerability from Mother Vinrie, the same woman who had met me and took me in at my trial. This was it, my chance, an opportunity to slip through the bars which pretended to be my home.

"Thank you, Mother Vinrie." I even turned and nodded. "Mother Lucia." I wet my lips before continuing. "But I have no intention of going back."

This news seemed to surprise Mother Vinrie, but not Mother Lucia.

"I have been too long gone; no longer the daughter they once knew. I would rather spare them the pain of seeing me again."

Mother Vinrie chuckled. "Dalila, think about it first. This is a chance no other witch before you had ever been given."

"I really appreciate it, but I don't need time to consider. I get to help people here, get to make a difference."

I twiddled my thumbs and bowed my head. I reflected on sweet Perry, on Nora, on young Rebecca with her rot infested body, on Ingrid who just longed for a person's touch again.

"This life is all I know now. I would rather stay here."

Mother Vinrie's movements were hesitant; she was obviously not expecting me to stay.

"If that is your wish," she said, unconvinced.

"I will talk to her," Mother Lucia said.

⊲ ⊳

Leaving the office, Mother Lucia addressed me instantly. "So you still live; just decided to avoid our little sessions."

"What are you trying to do?" I whispered harshly towards Mother Lucia, finding myself full of distrust.

"This is your chance!" She said sincerely.

"My chance for what?"

"To change people's opinion of us. You serve the Elders, you *represent* them. Show that you mean well, change the image of us witches so we can come out of hiding."

"I thought you disapproved of the Elders?"

"Not so loud!" She chided, pulling me to a secluded corner so we could continue. "It doesn't matter what I think. This is about improving the lives of others who are persecuted just like you. You think you are the only witch who has been born? I found every other little girl like you, scared and alone, and hid them. I want them—I want *us*—to come out of hiding and be free of all this madness."

"So, that was your plan? That is why you found a loophole for me to use my powers?"

Mother Lucia scoffed. "Why do you always mistrust me? Just believe that I mean well."

Then it was my turn to scoff. "I am sorry, but I find it a little hard to believe when there are people being murdered on the streets."

"I checked my coven!" Suddenly, Mother Lucia had to still herself on account of her raised voice. Once collected, she resumed. "I checked my coven after all your infectious doubt and bickering, and I found no evidence of the killer being among our kind. Yet I heard of your act."

"And what act was that?"

"You helped your friend regain a body just so that she could go and bring down judgement on those who defiled her."

I held my tongue.

Mother Lucia, her calm and motherly exterior, suddenly shed to reveal a scornful and indignant woman.

No more words were said as she brushed past me and walked down the hall.

⊰ ⊱

Again, I was lost. Despite Mother Lucia's accusations, I felt no remorse for the death of those men, and it was precisely that which made me sink deeper into my own self-hatred.

Was it because they had what was coming to them? No, that wasn't true. Yet maybe I was just glad that Nora was back among us; I found some form of comfort in helping with that.

I truly was pitiful.

As I strolled aimlessly down the halls like some spectre, I heard livened commotion spread from within. People ran, whispers spread like invisible spores from one lip to another and lured in more and more Sisters to its source.

I followed the bait, dragged along the jogging folk.

"Excuse me, please move." I pushed my way through the crowds, making space as I closed in on the sleeping quarter of Sisters.

It was finally when I entered that I grasped what the commotion was and the strength in my legs abandoned me.

"No..." the word came from me as a brittle breath, carrying with it another chipped piece of soul.

There, splayed violently before me, was the desecrated body of Yasmin. Her body stripped bare, floating recumbent upon empty air, her uncovered hair swaying like virtueless tangles of fiery red water.

A deep red cut spread down from each collarbone like a V, down her breasts and her midsection. The skin peeled open like a curtain to expose organs. Again, emptied eye-sockets looked out in terror.

Despite her floating form, her bowels were pulled out, her guts hanging until they coiled onto a bloodied silver platter. It looked like she was ascending, turning into some higher being who no longer needed such organs to weigh her down.

One by one my friends were being taken from me.

Chapter Seventy-Six

CHROMA

Jernun The Fury was an unstoppable force. Rage became his dogma as he took upon battle. He forwent the weapons of the Blacksmith in favour of his fist, and when his battle trance was fully realised and the eye upon his chest awakened, then everyone joined in the festivities.

—Excerpt from the Kaseluda

When I sunk into my new surroundings, and my mind turned blank amidst the darkness of the prison of iron and stones, I did not expect an exuberant and breathless Erefiel to burst right in and free me.

An aspect of Ievarus? The embodiment of rage?

Even as I prepared myself for the trek beyond the forest borders, to get a glimpse of people who I never truly belonged to and never would, I still found myself in a haze as Jasper's words played over and over in my mind.

I was not the son of Muktow.

Crack.

I was a bastard.

Crack.

Again and again, each thought was punctuated by the brittle snap of the man's neck. How fragile and delicate my father's life was as it slipped through my fingers; like a newborn chick with slitted eyes yet to open.

After being released, I asked to be taken far away from Crowtown and the settlement, far away from my people. I didn't have the strength to face my kind, not yet.

Erefiel explained it all. This was my final chance to prove myself. He sounded hopeful and emboldened, though all I felt was hollow and simmering rage.

During this dreary month, I simply slogged along to daily routines. My nights were fitful and restless, as my rage had become a boiling quagmire that dragged me deeper and deeper into its embrace. I thrashed and hammered against my despair—I was drowning.

Yet this sudden change of events brought more pleasant musings. For so long I dreamt and imagined leaving Bravnicka to return to the unbridled whims of the wild where the true akar were from. My mind swayed between states of fancy dreams and unavoidable truth. Could I truly discard my past? Find a new beginning out there among people that I always imagined?

The closer the days came, the more I entertained the concept—I was to enter Thickwood forest and meet with tribes of old.

I was still half akar. If I were to venture forth into Thickwood, I could still find my father. No. Find Muktow.

I bit the shame away and focused on what mattered: I *could* join them, join my people and be one of the akar.

Only for a moment, my mind went to mother, to my friends. I shook the thoughts away and felt them dissipate like smoke. That life, the life of an unwanted vermin born to a race of warriors, was something I no longer wanted to return to. Kolotha's words haunted me. Did he know the truth when he said I wasn't one of them?

It didn't matter. I would join the true akar beyond our borders.

This was a covenant made onto myself, one pledged with sharpened knife and a bowl of water as I ritualistically trimmed at my scalp; this was a new beginning.

❧ ❧

The day after, I met with the woman-warrior, Nora, and her human accomplice Howard. Howard was a paunch-bellied man but a competent fighter with a glint of cunning in his eyes. It was inside a war tent that we met; I assumed the scarred desk with curled scrolls spoke of courted battles.

Nora had changed since I last saw her. No, that was an understatement. She was an entirely different *being*.

All those years ago in the forest, when she first struck me with such enmity and where I aided her against Ji'sura, did no justice towards the foreboding air that emanated from her now. She was like a fed furnace, constantly radiating such heat that it threatened to scald the moisture in my nostrils.

I looked even closer; the woman was far broader and gained height, her body a tapestry of converging scars like a constellation of pain and war.

She had trimmed her scalp so just a bare bristle of short brown hair remained, and her expression was full of ferociousness that it even gave my own rage a moment of doubt.

I still towered over her as she stood just below my chest, but the gleaming obsidian metal that shimmered just underneath her cowl revealed the subject of circulating rumours—dismembered and robbed of her limbs, she was granted weapons by Elder beings.

"Want a closer look?" Nora had caught me staring, and her calm threat made me match her gaze. The woman raised a fist to accentuate her point.

I didn't respond, holding her gaze. In the end, I was the first to look away, not out of fright but rather indifference. I strode over to the awaiting Erefiel.

Erefiel was going over some scrolls when he gave me a slight glance to acknowledge my presence and then did a double-take. "Like the look," he said flatly in regards to my shaven scalp.

"Sir," Howard clunked forward in his gambeson armour and then saluted.

"At ease," Erefiel said. Despite being a Nephilim, Erefiel appeared exhausted and preoccupied more than anything else; something was bothering him. Or perhaps it was simply the stretched and hostile tension within the room that made everyone's mood so sour.

"Erefiel, I must insist again. I can do this alone. I don't need an *akar* to come with me." She spat the word with such contempt, to make sure I heard.

"I heard what you did to those people, how you nearly killed Erefiel."

Howard hung his head and scratched at his beard, knowing full well the direction this conversation was heading in.

"Oh, so *it* speaks? I have no interest in being lectured by someone who committed patricide."

I looked at Erefiel, who took a step back from the bickering, offering his attention to the scrolls before him.

"Oh, don't look at Daddy to save you. You didn't think I would look into someone I was being assigned?"

She was intentionally taunting me, trying to get a rise, and, though I once would have walked away, the currents of my anger swept me where they willed. I slammed a heavy fist on the table, splintering its end and snarled my tusks towards Nora. "I won't be belittled by someone with just half a body." I retorted.

Without missing a beat, Nora took a heavy step in order to face me, posing as if she were going to leap over the table. "I can show you what I am capable of with just half a body." Little obsidian scales on her arms and legs rattled like pebbles.

"Enough." Erefiel's command wasn't loud or reprimanding; if anything, it was exhausted and worried. That heaviness, that depth, was what made us turn and put aside our rising scorn.

"You fight and bicker amongst yourselves while an army amasses just beyond our borders."

Erefiel looked up at us, his albino eyes holding our attention. "I will be honest. There is a reason I have called upon you both. Howard is a liability but one that I will respect since he makes you more reasonable, Nora," he said to the woman patronisingly; but she did not lash out. I was certain she carried a great deal of respect towards this man, despite what I had heard about their fight.

"I am *desperate*. There is no denying it; the akar are forming a force so formidable that our own defences look like sticks. The scouting network hasn't gotten back to us in months. We have already requested reinforcements from both Museya and Bolton, including as many mages from Cleria as we can afford to summon."

"When will they arrive?" Any brashness from before was gone in a flash as Nora returned to being a loyal soldier.

"We believe in two weeks."

"And the akar?"

He shrugged. "Perhaps a month, at least."

I hung my head and found a seat. My heart suddenly beat faster, as Nora and Howard exchanged worried looks.

"We don't have much time, and we have even less information. Nora, I initially did not want to send you out there, but with your new body, I am certain that you can handle it. I imagine if it comes to it, you can run away quickly?"

Nora nodded, though something told me that running wasn't necessarily her favourite option.

"Chroma." Erefiel held my stare for a while longer and, though Nora's glance did not bring me to heel, Erefiel's look of pleading trust humbled me. I began to understand why this man commanded such respect among those who knew him personally. I felt sudden shame at abusing that.

"Chroma, I am sorry, but things have changed. I need your people more than ever to fight in the front lines. The reason I want you to go with Nora is because I want you to protect her and the fact that you could blend in with the enemy if need be is auspicious. But it is also to provide an argument towards letting your people fight with us."

I rose to stand. "Are you conscripting them?"

"If need be," he admitted coolly.

"You said my people deserved more than that!"

Erefiel's calm was like brittle glass cracked all over, its contents leaking through, shattering when he slammed his fist against the table and rose in kind. "If they don't fight, there won't be a kingdom to defend your people!"

"What about the Elders?" Howard asked.

"We sent a letter, but it is the Elder way to not meddle in mortal affairs. We can't rely on them."

Erefiel turned to Howard. "This is a perilous task that I am sending you on. Both of these individuals have ways to survive. Howard, are you sure you want to risk your life?"

Howard stepped forward proudly. "With all due respect, General Erefiel. I would follow Captain Nora to the Haar and back." He looked at the scarred Nora with unwavering fealty, an act that made my own decision form. I was a fool for having trusted Erefiel. My people were all the same to him.

"Fine. I will help how I can," I said, though they did not see the seed which took fruit within me. My people won't be made to die for this human cause.

I spoke of duty, of fealty. That I would serve Cleria and their king. Yet, in truth, I decided then that I would do anything to free my people from their bondage, even if it meant joining the akar horde.

Chapter Seventy-Seven

CHROMA

Out of all the races born from the cycles, none are as terrifying as the
children of Niefri. The end of the tenth cycle and the beginning of the
eleventh birthed the Rashi. They are no more than immaculate, scarlet
marbles which walk on their many thin tentacles. They find a host
and implant themselves through these horrid tentacles. The orb grows
as it feeds on their blood until it replaces its victims head entirely. The
Rashi become vampiric abominations. They still fester in their burrows
somewhere in Thickwood.

—A REPORT ON THE STATE OF MINETHRIA EARLY
INTO THE ELEVENTH CYCLE

Treading into Thickwood was a commitment I hadn't been prepared for. A scatter of guards witnessed our departure with very little confidence for our return. True to its name, the trees of this forest quickly clogged up the path and revealed nary a road to guide us with.

Tangled branches formed a canopy above our heads to chase whatever sunlight tried to slip through.

Howard trailed behind, and Nora in front.

Already the scent of earth and leaves tickled at our nostrils. Twigs cracked underneath our stride—even more so for Nora, who left noticeable depressions in the soil.

I remained sandwiched between the two. My own weapon of choice was a great axe, as I was made to wear the garments of one of my fallen brethren. It was a fur kilt wrapped around my waist embellished with the skulls of fallen humans, beasts and even akar tusks; they rattled like the hollow chimes of death, still locked in combat.

My shoulder was protected with a fur pauldron, and the rest of me remained at the mercy of the elements. The axe I carried bore a curious heft to it—I never wielded such a weapon before, yet I was comforted to find how easily it slipped into my grip.

Looking ahead, Nora attempted a steep path upwards and dragged her heavier right leg along. I noticed the whirring sound of her limbs and her laboured breaths—she tried desperately to hide it, but the woman was exhausted. Her new body wasn't made to scale such terrain. Scattered leaves robbed her of her footing. That happened more and more often the further we tread.

Howard ran to her. "Do you need a break?"

Nora pushed him away and went to stand. "I'm fine," she said, her breathing heavy. There was a limp to her right leg that I noticed once Nora had removed her hood. The larger prosthetic must have been pushing into her flesh and bone. As I watched, I slowly realised the truth of her new form. The body did not strengthen her; if anything, it encumbered.

The version of herself that pronounced such precise alacrity and speed was the fierce warrior that I remembered. Yet the woman before me was an indomitable soul incapable of giving up, trapped within a makeshift body.

"Elder-damn!" She cursed, slipping to her rear and clasping her left leg.

Howard ran to her side again. "What is it?" he asked.

The woman winced, her prosthetic fist pressing against her meaty thigh.

A pained breath of air blew itself from puckered lips as her forehead creased from the pain. "My leg cramped."

Howard started to massage the spot, an act quickly rejected by Nora as she clumsily pushed him aside. "I'm fine."

"By Googan's eye," I groused, stepping in front of Nora with my back to her. I went to my knee.

"Get on," I said.

She scoffed. "Yeah, right. I'm fine."

"Look, you are dragging us behind. The sun is already setting. We won't make it in time at this rate. Just climb on board."

Nora's cheeks flushed. "Do I look like I am someone who needs help?" she challenged.

"What are you trying to prove here? Your pride won't be worth a damn if you slow us down."

Still on my knees with my neck turned towards them, Nora and Howard shared private glances.

"Fine, but if you try anything I will end you," she said and climbed on my back.

I was shocked to find her crushing weight press itself on me. It wasn't enough to slow me down in any meaningful way, but she certainly was far heavier than I first expected. I felt gratified to find my strength, so often attributed to akar, to be so formidable. I allowed it to embolden my belief in my heritage.

Despite our quickened pace, breaks along our path were a common enough occurrence. During one such respite, Howard returned from scouting with discarded akar implements. Soon after, we passed by fallen souls.

We came by a trail of blood and corpses which grew in size the closer we got to the heart of this massacre. The scent of decay filled this place, swollen from the masses that lay dead.

Bodies of fallen akar littered the floor.

"What happened here?" I asked.

"Nora," Howard called out.

"I know," she said. "Chroma. Let me down."

I obliged, lowering the warrior as her limbs unfurled and the scales rippled from being put back into action.

"That's the first time you called me by my real name," I commented with a chuckle.

Nora looked away. "For the time being, we are allies. But give me just cause and I will end you without batting an eyelash."

"So you keep telling me."

Nora stepped forward. The two of them obviously knew something about this place that I didn't.

"What happened here?" I asked, but my answer was given to me as we turned around the bend of a boulder and found the mound of dead akar; there were dozens.

At the centre of it all was a horrid abomination, a mass of coalesced flesh and bones, with hands and legs sprouting like mushroom stalks. A body of mouths covered its entirety, the obtuse and bloody teeth stained with akar blood.

The thing seemed to be sagging and deflated, but horrendous to look upon as a boulder made entirely of olive flesh.

"What is that?" I asked in horror.

"Last we had our battle, there was a contained body of Haar which escaped and turned into this monstrosity." She paused. "Truth be told, if it weren't for this... *thing*. We would have died and our defences would have crumbled."

Nora placed a metallic palm onto it. "I suppose we owe it our thanks."

An arm flinched. My heart stopped as the thing began to roll. We jumped back and readied ourselves; Howard with his sword, me with my axe and Nora's arms whirring to life.

But the thing just rolled an inch, turning over and fell into a small divot in the ground.

"It's fine. The thing is dead," she said, not sounding entirely convinced.

I turned to our surroundings, suddenly on alert. Was this an ambush? If an akar came, I needed to be quick when I betrayed Howard and Nora.

"Nora. This doesn't add up." Howard stepped towards the swollen mass of bodies.

"What do you mean?" she asked.

Howard knelt down towards the dead. "This horde numbers dozens, yet our battle was a year ago. These people died recently."

"How recent?"

"Perhaps a week? Maybe less? The bodies only now show signs of decomposition except for the big one." Howard pointed at the abomination.

"Was it hunting them? Maybe the creature was too much of a nuisance, and they needed to cut it down?"

I stepped towards the dead creature. The wordless remnants told me of conflict, but not of its essence. The intrigue bit at my mind.

"This killing wasn't an act of desperation," I clarified, looking at my surroundings. "This is a celebration."

"Celebration?" Nora asked.

"The akar weren't being hunted… they were the hunter."

"Good, that means fewer savages to smite," Nora made as if to leave.

"You don't understand." I turned towards the two of them. "My people hunt. To be the one who slays an unslayable beast is to garner the respect of all. You shouldn't ask about the hundred akar felled in battle. You should ask about the one who dealt the killing blow." I was walking around the beast, trailing its sides and stepping over the corpses of my people.

There I found it, on the other side of its body.

Nora and Howard stumbled over to me. "My god, what is that?" Howard blanched.

"The killing blow," I said.

What we stared upon was a dented mass of flesh punched in. The body had crumpled inwards and what remained was a disgusting black bruise covering the entire side.

"Whoever killed this being will garner the respect of the rest." I turned to look deeply into the eyes of Nora and Howard. "Enough to rally the rest of the tribes under one banner."

Chapter Seventy-Eight

DALILA

During the fall of the Asamanian kingdom and the fast return of the
Haar, the strife between Cleria, Museya and far off kingdoms seemed
less pressing. The strife was done aside in return for a truce. But
peace built on the grounds of self-preservation is a temporary solution.
With the threat of impending death and the fear of oblivion, the nation
of Bravnicka invested in a rebirth of culture and the Renaissance.
Museya became firmly the pinnacle of artistic soul and connection while
Cleria became a bastion for civilisation and advancement. Bolton, in
turn, became the black sheep.

—Accounts on the change of Bravnicka
since the coming Haar

gain, someone else died because of me. Again someone
who mattered most to me was defiled because I couldn't
do what had to be done.

No more.

With tears streaking down my cheeks, I strode through the marble
austere halls and burst into Mother Vinrie's office.

Inside, I found Mother Grace and Mother Lucia deep in sombre
conversation, showing equal measure concern yet respect towards my
friend as they discussed how it could have happened right under their
noses.

I realised that I had interrupted them.

Mother Vinrie shot me a chiding glare, yet she gave pause as she took in my knotted features; their faces were all distorted thanks to my tears.

"This better be important, Mother Dalila. I know full well that Yasmin was your friend, but you cannot enter unannounced!"

I raised a violently trembling finger to Mother Lucia and spoke my words with disgust. "Mother Lucia has betrayed you, has betrayed us all. She harbours a secret coven of witches and practices magic!" I ululated.

Mother Grace shot to her feet. "How dare you!" She cried with her own pointed finger. Lucia pursed her wrinkled lips and planted her cane, her eyes looking away, unable to meet mine.

"Do you have any proof?" Mother Grace asked.

Mother Vinrie, on the other hand, was unfazed. Perhaps something about the severity of the accusation made her composure turn to stone.

"Mother Grace," she called out, stopping the scholar from her accosting. She turned around to face the accused.

Mother Vinrie did not speak to Mother Grace again; that silence was all that was needed.

"Is there truth to what Mother Dalila says?" Mother Vinrie went to match Mother Lucia's gaze. Mother Lucia was too tired to meet the question head on and turned away.

"Answer me, Mother Lucia." The query was glacial, void of any inflection, but the gravity behind each syllable weighed down on all present.

Finally, after a long pause, Mother Lucia nodded reluctantly.

"No." Mother Grace gasped, pure disbelief in her exhale. "That can't be."

I had imagined this differently. Slowly, as I watched over this scene, I realised that the endless sorrow at having witnessed Yasmin's desecration compelled me to betray Mother Lucia's trust.

I held onto that fleeting anger, but it was already infested. Its roots rotting away from the infection and turning into empty sorrow. This wasn't the rightful vindication I sought; it was just meaningless betrayal.

"Explain yourself," Mother Vinrie commanded.

Mother Lucia went entirely mute, her head hanging in submission. In a moment of desperation to undo as much as I could, I pushed past Mother Grace and knelt at Mother Lucia's side; tears did not even streak her cheeks, but rather dropped one by one like pieces of herself onto her lap.

"Lucia, this can be fixed. Tell Mother Vinrie where the coven is located. If you help us find the one responsible for all this, then your life can be spared." My own voice was breaking, tears flowing to match Mother Lucia's.

The woman turned towards me with a sombre smile. "These tears are not meant for me, but for you." She paused. I could sense her disappointment, a fact that further served to divide my already torn heart.

Mother Lucia sat up.

"It is true. I am a witch, and I still practise magic."

Mother Vinrie steepled her long fingers and narrowed her eyes. "You know the implications, do you not?" she asked, her tone authoritative.

Mother Lucia just smiled sombrely.

"Wait!" I stood up, floundering to undo this mess made in a moment of passion. "We can make a deal! I believe that the perpetrator of these crimes is someone within Mother Lucia's coven. If we can find where it is, we can bring the real perpetrator to justice. All the others who aren't part of it can be brought into our fold! To serve the Elders!" I knew what I spoke of was a far-fetched fantasy, not spoken for Lucia's sake, but rather my own.

Before Mother Vinrie could even voice her thoughts, Mother Lucia intersected. "No." If her voice was full of unending pity before, it now was resolute and unbreakable.

"Mother Lucia, be reasonable. You know this will mean your death."

Lucia scoffed. "I am a withered old crone with one foot already in the grave. My body aches daily. Death would be a blessing."

Mother Vinrie turned to face me. "Yes, but I could also put Mother Dalila to death. I have no doubt that she had known about this truth for quite some time and didn't speak out."

Mother Lucia shook her head and chuckled. "No, in fact she had only known a week ago," she lied, a fact that was pretty obvious to everyone in the room but didn't matter.

"I could still have her burnt alive alongside you if you don't tell me the truth. Did Mother Dalila practice witchcraft while she was under your care?"

"No." Mother Lucia's words were spoken without an ounce of hesitation.

"Yes!" I jumped in, the word bursting from me. "I did! Just tell them the truth, Lucia! If they know where the coven is, we will both be spared!"

All eyes turned to me.

Mother Vinrie was the only one to address my statement, and she did so with noticeable disdain. "You would actually offer up your life to save another person?" For the first time, I noticed her composure break. Was it disbelief? Or disappointment which I saw in her eyes?

"No." Again Lucia spoke with such indomitable clarity. "She is no longer beholden to this church. Her path is now attached to that of the Silver Prince. We both know you have no claim to her life, and that you have no choice but to kill me."

How helpless I felt at that moment. For the first time, I truly witnessed how resolute and iron-clad Lucia was. Often, she would complain about her clicking hip with a husky chuckle and shake of her head. Yet in that moment, it was her in control.

"So, is this the part where you use your magic to escape?" Mother Vinrie pressed, not backing down.

Instead, Mother Lucia smiled and went to stand, extending her wrists. "Let it be known that on this day, the supposedly insidious witch plotting to bring ruin upon all offers herself willingly, without any resistance. Yet the world decides I am too dangerous to live."

Mother Vinrie's eyes narrowed. "You wish to die a Martyr?"

Lucia shook her head. "No. A *symbol.* If the cost of freedom for all witches is what remains of my pitiful years, then so be it."

Chapter Seventy-Nine

DALILA

*Some parts of Minethria's history are intentionally left in the past.
The Rot Knights were one such part. History still suggests that their
adoration of the rot was almost fanatical. They would find the rot within
the tunnelled depths of Mount Duran and coat their weapons in it. As
such, the Rot Knights were a scourge upon the lands. Unsurprisingly,
most sources suggest that their very downfall was the rot.*

—History of Minethria from 4c to 5c, by Jallen Ainsworth

L ive executions were a strange practice within Cleria. It was a
practice of a forgone time. Yet perhaps such primitive rituals
were what satisfied man's need for violence? Mother Lucia's
execution would be scheduled in two weeks. A fact that constantly followed me as I boarded a coach to visit her.

Accompanying me was Ievarus, who had again shrunk into a more
inconspicuous form, clad in their cowl to obscure features. Ievarus
had heard of what happened, and apparently the event was intriguing
enough to warrant an observation. Truth be told, I wanted to be alone
in my suffering, but that wasn't an option. So, instead, I pretended as
if the alabaster-skinned prince wasn't even there.

Ievarus produced their disk pendant and raised it to me; a quiet rage simmered within, being so directly observed during my melancholy felt like an invasion. Yet curiosity did get the better of me. I watched the disk's surface shift from the roiling swirl of colours into blue. It was not the deep, strong blue of compassion; it was something more faded and turquoise.

Ievarus stared at the colour for quite some time, unmoving except for vapidly blinking eyes. The sound of the trundling wagon on cobblestone kept us company.

"It's broken," Ievarus finally said.

"It's not broken," I replied, looking out towards the passing folk, who were completely oblivious to the plight of the bleeding world.

"Why did it change?" Ievarus asked.

I sighed. It was easier to simply give what Ievarus wanted.

"I am sad."

"Sad?"

"You know when I smile?"

Ievarus expressed their understanding as fingers poked into the corners of their mouth and stretched lips into a sheepish grimace. "Smauf," Ievarus said through contorted lips.

It earned a weak chuckle from me.

I nodded. "It is the opposite of happiness. If I am sad, I feel melancholy. I feel weak and empty." I considered how else I could describe the emotion. "If I feel *bad*."

Ievarus went impeccably still, dull eyes blinking at the thought. I could see the alien concept straining their mind.

"Why?"

"Because my friend died." I hung my head in regret. "And I betrayed another."

"But what about compassion?" Ievarus queried.

"Emotions change, Ievarus. I already told you. So do aspects. That is part of what it means to be human. It is not always about happiness or hope; it is also about fear and rage. It is about everything."

❧ ❧

When we finally arrived, the posted guards were expecting us. They took a wide birth from the strolling Ievarus.

Underneath the prison was Lucia, her robes of black confiscated, and instead she wore a regular stained tunic and trousers with bare feet. The woman really looked pitiful. Her entire body smeared with filth, her hair of deep grey a wild tangle and her arms locked in a restrictive yoke with rare colours of purple smeared onto it to negate any magic.

"I was wondering when you'd visit," she said, sitting on an unremarkable chair in the corner of the room.

When she looked closer and found Ievarus had removed their hood, Lucia seemed positively impressed. "I see you brought with yourself a most notable guest," she jested facetiously. Lucia held no love for the Elders or their extensions.

She offered me a glance. Her eyes suddenly rolling in their sockets. "Stop staring with such pity, Dalila. I am not the one you should feel sorry for."

"Please." I grabbed onto the iron bars. Any attempt at appearing phlegmatic was gone. I was simply desperate to help as much as I could. "Please. Just tell me who is responsible for these killings."

"I can't tell you what I don't know."

Again I sighed, moving away to slump into a decrepit chair.

"Why did you do it?" I finally pressed.

"Do what?" Lucia asked quizzically.

"Admit it. I was rash, compelled by anger. I had no proof either way."

She chuckled. "Please. Once you open that door, there is no way you can close it again."

The room went silent for a while, before Mother Lucia decided to turn my visit into another one of our sessions. "You know, one of the best things I ever learnt was that if someone puts the blame on you, the best thing you can do is own it. Give the person nothing to tempt you with. If I had dragged it on and I would have been found guilty—probably would have—then I would always be remembered as that 'lying witch.' But this way, people will someday see a witch wrongly put to death; a proud and honest witch."

I narrowed my gaze. "You really do believe that you are doing the right thing, don't you?"

There was a deep and considerable pause. "I could ask you the same thing, you know?"

My eyes trailed to the floor.

"Is our guest not going to say anything? Maybe about how merciful the Elders are? To be grateful for all they've given us?" Lucia was speaking to me, but the glib query was directed at Ievarus.

"They are just an observer."

"Curious," Lucia said.

I wondered what to say, but Lucia stepped in instead. "I will make it easier for you, child. My time has come. If I need to die to show that witches are harmless, then so be it. But I won't betray my coven."

"Fine." I stood to leave. My visit was brief and with nothing to show for it.

As I climbed up the stairs, Lucia called out to me one last time. "Dalila, I hope that someday you will see the truth for what it is and embrace your heritage. And I hope serving the Elders will be the key. My only regret is not being able to see it for myself."

"Goodbye, Mother Lucia."

Chapter Eighty

CHROMA

Intechu is a usurper. The fungal god found their prophet and
imparted the gift of a single mushroom. Infected with the spores, the
prophet returned to his people and blossomed into a cloud. And so the
usurper stretches their influence.

—THICKWOOD HORRORS, BY ALATAN MIERSH

The first few days of travel were tiring. These forests were not our own. Mother had told me stories of Thickwood. Of how the enclosing Haar created the swelling mass. What remained was forced to live in its cramped quarters. My brothers were forced to retreat to deadly forest lands and up the mountains to the west. Equally so, the forest proliferated at an unmanageable rate. Trees forced into such thick groves until they became a tangle of competing vegetation.

Finding my stride with Nora was most cumbersome of all, as her constant distrusting glare would burn into my back, while I carried her up and down uneven soil.

When we crept even deeper, we found old scouting stations turned to rubble and anything of value had been scavenged by the akar. None were left alive during these raids. Howard and Nora called them guerrilla squads, no more than six to eight to creep up unannounced and pounce like the silent night itself.

We rummaged through the wreckage for provisions. But, other than dead Clerian scouts, we found no food or weapons. At most, we found a few barrels of mouldy bread, while Howard stocked up on arrows for his crossbow.

Further within the forest, we found the remaining men hanging like ornaments from trees and gently swaying just enough to hear the constant groan of the branches that held them. Flies buzzed and formed halos of death about their desecrated cadavers. One body was visited by a crow that poked at a rotting eye, plucking it out to swallow. Other corpses had parts of them scavenged.

Howard spun the spiral at his heart, an act of deference before moving forward to cut the men down.

"Leave them," Nora interjected callously.

"We can't just leave them here. They deserve proper burials."

"If we take them down, the akar will know that we are here. The longer we go undetected, the better."

Nora had already dismounted, her derogatory jabs were pocketed. The woman opted for ignoring me instead—I took it to mean a reluctant form of thanks. She stepped forward, her legs clanking and snapping roots and vines beneath her heavy stride.

She turned to me. "What do these runes say?"

I stepped forward for a closer look. Upon the corpses, brushed in some form of crusted paste, I noticed familiar runes from my days of playing Janaham.

I pointed up. "The blood of Kho'shah." I turned to another. "The skull of Ankou." I got the glint of one faded symbol almost hidden underneath the grime that covered them. "That's the eye of Googan."

"And?" Howard pressed.

I shrugged. "They don't mean anything by themselves. The akar don't have a written language, the runes are symbolic; you derive meaning from context."

"And what does this context mean?" Nora amended.

"This is a warning. An offering made in blood, but also a border to let us know that we are being watched."

Nora scoffed. "This is intimidation. They are trying to dissuade us from entering. Their bodies are mostly whole. I would have expected a little more savagery and mutilation."

I shook my head and couldn't help but chuckle.

"Something funny?" Nora asked, her tone warning.

"You constantly make the mistake of thinking us savage; we are not: we are warriors. Chop up parts to leave them to dangle? What good would that achieve? They left them whole so you would recognize your own kind, even better if you know the person by name. This is done with purpose."

Still, I looked up at the bodies and found my mind following along the trail of my thoughts.

It was true that akar tactics were cold and meticulous, perhaps even gratuitous at times. Juta had shared countless stratagems within that same philosophy. But this wasn't just a cold and pragmatic display. It was a conversation. *"Stay away or die."*

We moved on, leaving the corpses to gently sway like macabre talismans.

❧ ❧

That night when we made camp without any fire to huddle close to, just like every night since we had ventured into the depths of the forest. The first sign of living akar was hunters tracking down wild boars the size of bulls. We made our camp a good breadth away from where they were discovered.

The succour was made underneath a jutting block of stone, where natural creeping vines acted as a veil to the entrance. Inside, we ate our rations; except for Nora, who insisted that Howard keep it to himself on account of her self-sustaining body.

Within that sweat inducing night, where insects preyed on our flesh, we listened to the erratic chirps of grasshoppers and distant predators of the night.

For the first time since treading into the dense forest, Nora felt safe enough to remove her limbs, starting with her right arm that dislodged itself with a heavy clank. Then she removed her clothes until a thin white shirt covered her. The blazing heart I had heard of flared in her chest; the light brightened like an undulating pulse to illuminate her ravaged self. I could now more clearly make out her battle-scarred form, and the unrelenting visage of rage that she was; she held no semblance of hope.

Next came her legs, plopping off one after another within the humid and suffocating air of our abode.

"Why don't you always keep them on?" I asked Nora, who sat there with just her barely visible silhouette present. I could discern the close cut of her hair, the bare outline of her limbs set aside with some form of order as the rest of her dismembered form leaned against the wall.

"Despite it being capable of carrying me around, it still isn't my real body. The metal keeps chafing onto my skin and leaves me with aches and burns all over." There was an odd smoothness to her movements now as she shifted and positioned herself with the help of her stumps.

The woman looked at them. Her left arm gently pushing against her body to ostensibly force out clumped nerves. I just barely noticed the creased pink folds and sweat that sheened the dismembered ends.

I looked away once I realised I'd been staring. There was something truly captivating about Nora's ferocity.

"Have something to say? Out with it." Her tone wasn't scornful, but callous.

"You know, when the rumours began to spread about your bout with Erefiel, they described you as many things: The Metal Dragon, The Undying Flame. They said you were like a beast of pure obsidian rampaging and sundering the place with the power of the sun."

The crickets chirped. A soft breeze passed and made leaves rustle outside our hideout.

"I didn't expect your body to be such a burden."

Nora chuckled. Howard had nothing to say and instead snacked on his rations at the entrance as he kept one eye trained towards the snoring forest.

"Aye, perhaps it is a burden. But in truth, I am grateful. If I have the ability to walk and fight, then that is all I need. But these prosthetics can never make up for the speed, precision, and duress that I had with my real body."

"Erefiel doesn't know that, does he?"

Nora went quiet, the silence between us now personal.

"If rumours have already spread and people think I am some unstoppable machine, all the better. But the truth is that my little clash with Erefiel was pure luck—there is no way I would have won that if he went in with the intent to kill me."

I bit my lip. Nora's kind words were unusual. It felt as if she had grown more at ease with me. I decided to address it. "And yet you trust me enough to open up?"

"You misunderstand; we are in enemy territory. If we come across danger, it is important that my allies know my weaknesses. My promise from earlier still stands."

⊰ ⊱

As Nora faded into a heavy sleep, Howard joined me with an offering of dried jerky and berries. It was easy communicating with Nora. Her coarse manner made it so. I felt no conflicting need to try and be friendly, but that wasn't the case with Howard.

The paunch-bellied man sat beside me, and we simply filled the silence by eating.

When that was finally done, the man decided to open up.

"What is Ievarus like?" he asked.

"Didn't Nora tell you already?"

"She did, but I just thought I would start some conversation."

"Not interested."

"Come on! The only thing I saw was an owl."

When I didn't respond, Howard opted for another approach. "You know, I heard what you did for those kids, for Nora's brother. I even used to be stationed at the akar settlement."

I squinted my eyes. "I don't remember seeing you."

He shrugged. "It was a long time ago and only lasted a week. Point is, I know the akar aren't bad people." He shifted, his eyes glossing over Nora as if to make sure she was asleep. Her glowing heart had slowed and the rhythm dulled into soft pulses.

"Don't tell the captain, but I get it."

"Get what?"

"Your situation. After all that has happened to you, to your people. It's not easy. Just know that you are doing the right thing coming with us."

I went silent. "I'm sorry, but the last time I trusted a human, it cost me dearly." I felt like those words were meant more for me than for Howard. I had to remind myself of the end goal. I rubbed my hand against my trimmed scalp to remind me of that.

Howard stayed. "You don't have to answer, but is it true that you are the son of a human?"

"A human that I killed," I said, my voice full of warning.

The man chuckled hoarsely. I turned to him, shocked at the reaction to my threat. Howard suddenly started to swing his arms about his chest theatrically. "*A human that I killed,*" he said with a teasing pout.

I was stunned at the satirical display. He quickly collected himself. "I'm sorry. It's just that I know when someone is pretending to be intimidating."

"I killed my father. A human." My tone betrayed my defensiveness.

"Yeah, I heard about that." He considered his words for a second. "You are supposed to be Rage, right?"

I nodded.

"To be fair, this is all wrong. It is the captain that should be Rage. You seem more appropriate for hope."

Something about being confronted like that made me falter.

"You are suddenly quite talkative," I said, trying to brush aside the line of questioning.

Howard reached out to me with his waterskin. "Here."

I sniffed the top, noticing the stench of earthy wine creep up. When I looked at Howard, the man shrugged. "Calms the nerves."

I took a swig and handed it back. It wasn't anything fine, but the earthy and bitter complexion was like a lost lover's kiss.

"Look, I've been there. When I was a boy, it was just fat and no self-confidence. My father was a harsh man. However, he taught me to never show my fear, to scream and shout and bite until no one else would mess with me."

"Wise man."

"Foolish man," he corrected. "Dug himself an early grave with all that drinking of his, was so obsessed with hiding his fear that he drowned in it. All I am saying, is that I know what it's like to lash out at the world because you are scared."

"You don't know me," I said indignantly.

"Let me ask you this. Did you visit your settlement after Erefiel freed you?"

"I have nothing left there," I countered defensively.

"Right, there it is again. You didn't go; not because you are angry, but because you are scared."

A chip of my heart broke, and I suddenly felt a statement that was most certainly a lie fit itself through a lock. I was so sure that I left because of their betrayal, because of the years of constant lying. So why did Howard's words leave such an impression on me?

"What choice do I have?" I stated. "I don't belong there." Whose words were these?

"What are you talking about? You were raised there. Fought against them. You were able to analyse and read the runes of your people and gather their intent. You are akar through and through! Scratch that. You are part of that settlement, the one who became their bridge to a better life. There is a reason Erefiel puts so much trust in you. If anyone can bring our kind together, then it is you: an akar."

I sat in silence, considering those words.

"There is something I don't get," Howard added, interrupting my rumination. "If you so strongly believe that you no longer belong to your people, why did you set out on this quest? Why come at all?" One question after another forced me to face the truth.

Suddenly, I turned my gaze to the slumbering Nora who stirred in her sleep. I decided to change the subject.

"Why do you follow her? You don't speak kindly of Nora's actions."

Howard hung his head sullenly. "Aye, her anger is something caustic. It will fester and eat her up on the inside. Even before all this, it was like she fed off of her contempt of your kind. But truth be told, there is an unconditional force behind that power, and also a fierce companion to be had.

"I mean, look at her. She went through hell and back to gather a makeshift form to fight in battles. I am not sure if anyone else would have been able to do that, but she never gave up. You heard one of the names they call her: the 'Undying Flame'. That's because she never relents, and that kind of aura is contagious. Makes us all want to fight with her, to the death, if need be."

Howard went quiet, as if to truly add weight to his next sentence. "Once she is on your side, there is nothing that can't be achieved."

Chapter Eighty-One

CHROMA

The primordial colours are said to be the first colours which came with Elder King from beyond the Haar. It is ink which never fades and is more potent than any other drop of its diluted descendants; for these are the divided essence of its pure origins. It is also said that upon the rise of Xelxidon, the Nightmares rose from Black and only her sword of light could burn past them.

—Scholarly analysis of Kaseluda retellings

As I stared out towards the black night, where the wayward forest remained still and sleeping, I couldn't help but ruminate on Howard's words. Was I truly just hiding behind my fear? Bearing my fangs like some wounded dog?

When I was brought before Ievarus, the Silver Prince, and stared upon that strange visage of silver-wiry hair, alabaster skin and deep pearly eyes, my rage was most certainly affirmed by the round disk in hand.

Yet my talk with Howard seemed to have lamed that rage considerably. Was it doubt? Perhaps, if I were observed now, Ievarus would find a frightened mutt hidden underneath all that anger?

I struggled breathing.

I ran from our hideout, looking about myself to make sure that the path was clear before I ventured forth. My eyes naturally adjusted to what scarce light was offered, allowing me to traverse the uneven terrain that often tripped Nora during our trek.

The summer night air came with a humidity which squeezed sweat from every pore. Gnarled trees locked branches like bucks in combat. More and more, I was filled with longing for home: for mother, for friends, for all of the settlement.

Yet here I was, beyond the border to seek what I always desired: return to my true heritage. Perhaps I would even get to meet Muktow and learn what it meant to fight under his wing.

I shook the childish thought from my mind, a thought born from all the years I fantasised meeting him as my father and having him take me in, pretending he was proud of me. That was all this thought was; a way for me to keep the musing alive.

As I mindlessly wandered deeper into the forest, my mind unfurling a thread in my wake so that I could find my way back, I heard the first sounds of akar beside myself.

I crept through a small brook closed in by a raised mound on either side, hearing the harsh tongue of my folk grow cruder, until I turned a corner and pulled myself up to get a better vantage point.

There, standing in a circle, was a formidable party of four; all of them battle-scarred and ready for combat. The man at the centre spat harsh words in heavy akar, sounding like a chisel chipping away chunks of a mountain.

Though they did speak akar, it was a harsher, more guttural version than my folk. There were words I didn't understand, but I understood enough.

"Anything?" The ostensible leader asked, wearing a leather strap across his chest with a stringed longbow on his shoulder; the longbow was large and akin to the size of a ballista's width.

The other three stepped forward. "*Nothinnnnng.*" Her voice was like a serpentine snarl. Unlike the others, she did not travel on two feet but was squatting; moving on all fours like an ape. I could barely make out the sharpened and tapered black claws on her hands and feet, her digits stretched and long, as if born for such a primitive art of combat. Her clumped mass of hair gave way to reveal a deformed and crushed face that turned even more grotesque when she smiled with crooked teeth.

The other fighters were both men, one wielding a club with a shield of tied wood; this one was the largest of them all, reminding me of Juta.

The last carried a heavy axe, like my own.

This was it, a company of my own people. I realized then how ridiculous my disguise was. They would see right through me. I consider jumping in front of them, telling them of my intentions and the truth. They could take me to the rest, to Muktow. I would provide them with the information they needed. Certainly I was invaluable. The information I had could better serve their assault.

So why wouldn't my body move?

Would they even believe me? Or slaughter me? I tried to inch forward, but my squatted thighs were locked. My heart beat faster in my chest, trying to tell me something I couldn't understand.

I heard a sudden rustle of leaves from above and instinctively shrunk into the surrounding foliage. What descended was an owl so silent, one would have thought its wings were woven with the night itself. It landed upon the arm of the centre man.

There was a satisfying grunt. "Neyt found something," the man said. "Lead the way."

The squatted, bestial woman gave a hoarse and excited laugh, before the owl took flight and the scouts prowled.

As I shadowed them, I found the doubt within me spread. Step after step, it festered.

The owl hooted from somewhere up high where the Elder King's moon-eye provided blind light.

The quadrupedal warrior scampered across the forest floor.

I tread softly from my own shifting cover.

My heart beat to the sound of my query: *Do I join them?*

"Human!" One of the akar growled with malice.

I peeked over the cover to see Howard stumble into the clearing, his front wide open. The akar drew his bow. The owl hooted up in the distance and the arrow was knocked and ready. My body moved before I had a chance to fight it.

Jumping with axe in hand, I gave a battle cry that startled the akar. Their heads spun to take in my falling form. My axe plummeted, failing to strike flesh but successfully breaking the monstrous bow in two.

The other akar were still trying to gather themselves, stunned as to why one of their own assaulted them.

Stop it.

"Howard! Run!"

I want to join them!

My mind screamed at me as I flung my axe wildly at the akar in front. Soon enough his larger and broader stature stepped forward, seeing me as an obvious threat. I swung my axe, its haft burying itself into the wooden shield of the club-wielding akar, who used the momentum to rip my weapon free.

From my blind spot leapt the squatted and hunched woman, cackling with a husky voice as her claws dug into me. Her skewed and twisted features wild with manic ecstasy. I countered by contorting my body, my legs moving of their own volition as I transitioned into a hold like a constricting snake, squeezing its prey.

I grabbed and pulled and rolled away, leaving the woman crying as her arm was left broken. I looked upon the damage and found my body striped with countless stinging wounds. Blood seeped from my form.

Then came the large akar, his club swatting in a wide swing that sent me flying through the air and into a tree. My head spun from the impact, and I felt the rations shared between Howard and me tickle my throat with an acidic burn. When finally I collected my surroundings, the leader approached me, hand tightening around my throat and pinning me against the tree.

"Who are you?" the akar asked; the woman was still writhing somewhere in the background.

The axe wielding akar stepped forward. "Must be one of the akar fighting with the humans we heard about."

"Deserter…" the leader hissed, his grip tightening. He held out a hand, a gesture immediately understood as the haft of the axe found itself in his comfortable grip.

"Go and find the mortal and bring me him, unharmed." The mountainous akar gave a snarling growl and then departed.

I gripped at the arm, my throat squeezed so tight that I couldn't speak, let alone breathe.

"Googan will have no place for you amongst us."

Spots bloomed across my vision as sudden steps thundered in the air. One. Two. Three.

A machine whirred, a small mote of light poked holes into the darkness.

From the corner of my eye, there flew back the body of the giant, sliding onto the ground with a caved-in chest.

The other two turned towards the source; it was Nora. Her arms were oscillating, with smoke trailing behind her left appendage.

The moment of distraction was all I needed as a sharp punch to my opponent's throat loosened his hold. Next, my legs shot up and wrapped themselves about his arm.

In one swift motion, I twisted and took him with me to the ground, before pulling the claimed arm to my chest to snap it. In desperation, the akar flailed with the axe. My eyes were clenched tight when I felt the metal edge imbed itself into my arm and stark pain filled me.

I rolled away. The axe ripped out and left behind a burning flesh wound; blood gushed freely from it. As I rolled to my feet, so did the akar. He grabbed his own arm. He too did not escape completely unscathed as I must have been mere moments from tearing the ligaments within.

From my peripheral, there dove the large owl like death on wings. The talons at its feet scratching and clawing at me.

Just barely I ducked under a swung axe. I kicked out a leg, causing the leader to lose his footing as our hands both grasped for the weapon, and we wrestled.

Our strength matched as we pushed and pulled for better leverage. Yet blood poured from my arm endlessly, pooling and causing our grips to slip on the handle. The axe clattered to the floor and my fists flew forward against the face of my opponent. Panic filled me. I tried to ignore the smarting gash on my arm.

On the side, Nora had changed her right arm into an obsidian kite shield and her left became a blade.

The previous owner of the axe now wielded his dead friend's club. The weapon clashed against Nora's shield, who swatted it away, her twisting torso parrying the momentum rather than just her clunky arm. The fact that Nora didn't collapse with the strength of each strike told volumes about her new found power. Though it all came at the cost of mobility as she failed to nimbly manoeuvre her body between strikes. Each step was slow and clumsy rather than quick and precise.

Howard shuffled forward out of the cover of trees, crossbow at the ready and an arrow knocked as it pointed at my opponent. "Halt!" We stopped, entirely out of breath.

"Get on the floor!" The akar didn't listen, simply watching with a deadpanned look of opposition.

The akar's gaze shifted to Howard's side. Suddenly, the woman whose arm I broke leapt, one hand still capable of shredding and killing as it clawed away at Howard, while the other dangled misshapen and twisted by her side.

The bout between my adversary and myself continued. The leader resorting to digging a sharp thumb into my newly cut wound. I roared thunderously, pounding against his head.

There was the sound of something wet being cut into. The head of an akar flew through the air—it was Nora's adversary. Nora stepped forward towards the rolling Howard and the hunched woman. In one rigid motion, her metal leg kicked outwards. The leg brimmed with light underneath the rippling scales, proving strong enough to shatter every bone on the side of the female akar and send her flying up to be tangled in the canopies.

Blood slathered me, the scent of iron heavy in the air. My adversary slipped out from above. Howard readied his crossbow. He, too, was prone, but his crossbow held its target in sight.

But instead, it was Nora whose legs turned into the bow-like limbs of a panther before springing forward with explosive force. Her direction was true; she could neither turn nor change her course as her metal knee crashed straight into the body of the akar and knocked the warrior to the ground.

All was silent; the last akar lay unconscious on the forest floor. Only our panting filled the quiet and a serenade of crickets chirped.

I could feel the tension leave me. Howard sprung to his feet, crossbow aimed at the waiting canopies. I fell to a knee, arm clasped at the gushing wound.

"Leave it, the owl is gone," Nora said as she slumped down a tree.

"Damn it." Cursed Howard.

The rustle of leaves caused us all to snap our heads in freight, alert to any sudden movements as blood pumped vigorously through our veins. The dead body of the animalistic woman dropped to the floor. Her side had turned a gnarly black as it was mostly dent in.

Nora's limbs whirred down, the chittering like from pebbles ebbing. She turned to face me. "What were you doing?" she asked, all four digits of her prosthetic hand addressing me.

I stood there, somewhat unprepared for the inquisition. Instead, I slapped her metal hand out of the way and stared her down. "I went for a walk when I found them; I shadowed their movements after."

"Really? How do I know for sure you weren't going to betray us?"

"Because he saved my life." Howard stepped towards us, his entire body covered in bleeding cuts that dripped from him and stained his garments. His look was fierce. "He jumped in the path of their leader when he drew out his bow to fire. If he hadn't distracted them and told me to run, I would have died."

I wanted to look away in shame. If only he knew what really went through my mind. Instead, I hung my head and leaned against a tree to calm myself. I could feel Nora eye me suspiciously.

"Is that true?" she asked.

I didn't answer.

"It is," Howard insisted. "I would have been dead if it weren't for him."

Nora took a second to look at Howard, then me. She relented. "Get the rope, we need to tie up the akar, see if we can get any answers from him."

"We need to tend to Chroma's wounds."

"I will be fine." I waved dismissively. Though I did feel lightheaded, I knew that I wasn't about to fall over yet.

Promptly, Howard and I used his hemp rope to tie the akar to a tree. He had a more ashen hue to his skin in comparison to the charcoal typical of our kind.

Once finished, I walked up to Howard and checked on his wounds as well. I pursed my lips and lightly took one of his arms, smelt it, then my own. "I need to treat you."

"Treat me? Your wound looks far worse," he said.

I looked quickly to my arm, where the wound still bled. The flex of the tight muscles had actually managed to stem the bleeding somewhat, and if I didn't move around too quickly, the light-headedness from before wasn't so pressing. "I will be fine," I reassured levelly.

"You still have some water?"

"Back at the cave," Howard said.

I nodded. "I'll go get it."

"No, you won't." Nora protested. "You will stay where I can see you."

"It's fine. I will get it." Howard insisted, giving me an appreciative pat on my arm, careful not to hit the wound. "And the bandages."

In the meantime, I had foraged for some herbs to help treat my own wounds as well as Howard's. Nora stayed with the still dreaming akar but instructed me to not wander off too far. If it weren't for our captive, I was certain that she would have followed me like a shadow.

I was happy to have found some yimroot, a plant growing close to the ground and always at the base of a tree where its deep roots attached itself to its overbearing protector.

I took the leaves and also managed to find hayreem, the plant of a vine growing close to the tree. Suddenly, I thought back to Mother Margaret and her lessons and realized how long it had been since I had seen her. At no point did it dawn on me that she was no longer a part of my life. It was as if she slowly faded away, and only now did I remember all the lessons she taught me. I bade her a silent word of thanks. Finally, I took for myself one of the leather strips of clothing from the dead akar.

When Howard returned, he did so with all of the supplies. "I guess I have to live with the fact that we won't get any sleep tonight," he complained to no one in particular.

I went to mend Howard. But first, I made sure to tend to my own cuts and slashes inflicted by the talons of the female akar as well as the axe wound. I drew the salve over the gash on my arm. I chewed the remnants of the yimroot to fend off any fever that may have wanted to plague me.

First, I used the water to wash away the depth of the cuts and the grime from my hand, as well as a quick splash on the akar clothing I salvaged—a task that ended up with the waterskin empty and Howard disgruntled. The leather clothing I tore into strips and bandaged about my arm tightly, using my teeth to make sure the knot held. I glanced up at Howard, who had a suppressed expression of worry. Another one of Mother Margaret's teachings came to me: telling people what I was doing would help calm them.

"You know the feral akar who attacked you?"

"Chroma, I don't think I will ever forget," he said with a note of terror.

"Juta had told me about her tribe. The Masakansie. They purposefully stunt their own growth to take on a more primal form. Thanks to their deformed backs, they cannot stand up straight, but their long arms allow them to move from treeline to treeline more swiftly. They purposefully groom and take care of their nails."

"Why not just use a sword?"

I looked up at the man. He seemed to be calming down as I handed him the root and leaf of the two plants. "Chew on these. Don't swallow." Howard obliged.

"Oh, this is horrid!" he mumbled.

I obliged his answer. "They believe a weapon that can be used to kill you is a traitor in waiting. A weapon that is part of you, however, can never betray."

Nora chimed in, slightly distanced from us but still leaning into our conversation. "Wise words," she said.

"But that's not all. They take part in ghastly rituals to kill their prey."

"How do you mean?" Howard asked.

"There is a reason I am cleaning out your wound right now. I already did so for my own cuts. See?" I showed him the wounds smeared with paste.

His face went a ghostly white. "They dip their hand into poison?"

"Not just poison—faecal matter."

Howard wrenched in disgust. Nora actually gave a humoured chortle.

"Hold still." I scolded. I put out my hand. "Spit it out." Howard first looked at me as if I were insane, but finding no mirth in my eyes, he allowed the clumped and wet ball of paste to slide out of his tongue like some snail.

I proceeded to rub the paste into his cuts. "They allow themselves to be bitten by venomous beings to make their claws more potent."

"I don't think that is how it works," Nora commented.

"It's not. But other than that they dip their claws into poisonous concoctions."

With the last bit of paste remaining, I decided to rub even more onto my own wounds. I was no longer in danger of falling unconscious.

Howard looked at me, his eyes suddenly deep with concern.

"Don't worry," I said. "You'll live. But you will be weak for the following days. You can't continue with us."

"That's not your call to make," Nora objected without hesitation.

"I can still fight." Howard jumped in.

Now I turned to Nora. "He will be a liability. If he comes with us, he will be sick for days and just slow us down. Or worse, he will die. He needs to stay in the cave. We will bring him enough water and food to last him until we either return to get him, or he is well enough to return on his own."

The two of them went quiet. One final question presented itself: did Nora trust me?

"I am still coming," Howard cut in.

"No, you're not," Nora objected. Her gaze affixed to me, calculating her decision.

"You will stay at the cave until we return, or you are well enough to return to Greyhill alone and report to Erefiel," she ordered.

I had expected more resistance from Nora. Howard seemed to have done so, too.

The discussion wasn't yet over. "Chroma, why is it that I haven't seen this type of warrior on the front lines? Or the bow wielding one over there." She tossed a glance at the restrained akar. "If the enemy has bows, why not use them?"

"Most wood would snap underneath the weight of akar strength. The knowledge to craft such a bow which withstands akar strength... Only one tribe is capable of it. The Kinitari; it means 'hunters'."

I began to realize something as I looked at the fallen akar. I had to make sure I wasn't just imagining it. More and more, the evidence began to present itself. "The Kinitari and the Masakansie are solitary tribes. They keep away from the affairs of other akar."

"Yet here they are, one cohesive unit." Nora waved about herself with her prosthetics as if simply trying to bring out of me the conclusion she already settled on.

"It is true, there is an alliance, and if the Masakansie and Kinitari are part of it, it would stand to reason that they all are."

"So you are saying they will be building archery units?" Howard queried.

"No. I think they already have," Nora said, her voice heavy like stone.

⁂

Finally, when we had enough of waiting, we awoke the sleeping akar with a solid metal strike to his face. The giant groaned and snarled awake, shaking his bald head and bearing tusks as he reoriented himself. As his vision focused, and he looked upon us with understanding, the giant casually spat a clump of blood in our direction, which missed terribly; the rest dribbled down his chin.

"We want information," Nora said impatiently.

The akar chuckled and spoke his words in harsh and threatening akar. He strained against his binds.

"What did he say?" Nora asked.

"He says he doesn't understand your 'weak and pathetic language'."

Nora looked at me with humourless eyes.

"His words, not mine," I clarified.

"Ask him how large their force has grown."

I did. "He says enough to break down your defences."

"I want numbers."

I asked in akar. I bit my lip at his response.

"What did he say?" Nora asked.

After a moment of silence, I translated. "That he will not commune with a human's pet. Wondering if I have no shame."

The akar chuckled hoarsely. I wondered if the embarrassment in my voice was audible.

"Shame, huh?" Nora stepped forward. "I know a thing or two about shame." Her left arm rippled, slowly having the scales shift and realign themselves patiently into a blade.

"Tell him to bring us to his army."

685

I held my tongue.

Nora turned to me, a seething heat to her tone. "Tell him."

I did so.

The akar laughed again before looking up at Nora and mockingly spoke his taunts.

"He asks if you think he fears death. He is a proud warrior and welcomes it gladly."

Now it was Nora who chuckled. "Death? No, no. Nothing like that." She softly ran the tip of her bladed arm across the akar's bare chest without drawing blood; it was almost sensual.

"I was like you once," she continued. "I believed myself unstoppable, for if someone doesn't fear death, then nothing can stop them. But there is more than one type of death. I know that now. I went to that place and managed to return. Shame: shame can be far worse than death." Nora now placed the sharp edge to the akar's right shoulder and applied just enough pressure to draw only a bite's worth of blood.

"I wonder, do you think you could return from that place?" Her cadence was lustrous and teeming with implication. There was no need for me to translate; the glacial steadiness with which Nora held the akar was enough to deliver her intent.

The akar spoke, his voice now soft and robbed of its resolve. "He says he will show us."

Chapter Eighty-Two

DALILA

For whom are these tears I unknowingly shed?
Searching my mind where broken mirrors 'flect,
Their name eludes me; it has suddenly fled,
Lament the memory plucked from my head.

—STOLEN MEMORY, BY TRACEY WINTERWOOD

Day after day, I was tortured by the ever nearing execution of my mentor: Lucia Gievan.

Stripped of her title and excommunicated from the church, Lucia had nothing else to her name except to provide some macabre entertainment to a sea of supposedly civilised onlookers.

The last burning of the stake was more than two centuries ago. There was an unspoken pretence that the practice had served its purpose and humanity had moved on thanks to such a necessary evil. It was just another way to justify cruelty.

The whole event stunk of pretentious sanctimony, as if this was a necessity to ensure that we didn't return to some dark-age.

That morning, I forwent my typical arrangement of white robes and instead donned the one single assortment of blue that I had. It wasn't the typical blue, not like that of a bright ocean that instilled serenity, but rather a faded and depressed shade. The last time I wore such a thing was for Perry's funeral.

Yet it was not to mourn the death of a sister; not quite, it was to mourn the need of the event. It was another symbolic wound that said: "You made us do this." To say that, even when Lucia was to be burnt, she had forced our hand. Though it wasn't the case for me. In my heart of hearts, I truly wore this blue to mourn the death of a mentor; despite the fact that she did force my hand.

Ievarus shadowed me; I couldn't remember the last time they hadn't. They observed and preyed on my sorrow. It wasn't done in some malicious and questionable way, but rather in their own scholarly pursuit. Nonetheless, my silent observer was practically attached to my hip and trailed behind with listless but curious eyes as we passed through the town square and towards the military district.

It was the first day that showed that summer was nearing its end, as a timid and brisk morning promised a coming autumn with just a meek bite.

I thought for a moment back to my father. If he were here, he would preach about how this was a necessity; standing with unwavering faith. It seemed ridiculous.

There was once a time when I was brash and loud; I spoke whatever was on my mind. That version of me seemed like it was from a dream. It was true, sometime long ago when I still harboured the innocence of a child, I questioned the Elders. Did I rediscover that same girl? Or were these seeds of doubt that Lucia planted?

We arrived at the modestly large square plaza where the onlookers streamed in at the break of dawn. People noticed Ievarus, who now walked without any cowl to hide their features. The commotion had shifted from heated and unbidden whispers to a simple glance and acknowledgement. Even after ten completed cycles and another to be added, novelties wore off quickly for mortal lives.

I had drifted to the front row that was filled with uniform Sisters clad in their sombre-blue robes. Ievarus found a place beside me.

I took in the sight of wealthy folk dressed in more modest attire. No longer did they parade around in thickly frilled collars and tight corsets to give them a wasp waist, nor did the men wear motley coloured doublets or velvet coats. Instead, all wore some semblance of blue with a more respectable appearance, though still with some focus on fashion and presentability.

Before us, I looked upon the erect wooden stake at which Lucia would be burnt with a stack of dry hay piled at the base. It occurred to me, suddenly, that I had front-row seats to this spectacle. I was reminded of the play, the inevitable fall of Mellezi and his kingdom, the tragedy of those actors.

I entertained the idea that perhaps Lucia was the murderer. Perhaps she had engaged in such dark rituals and led us all to believe otherwise. If it was so, then at least her death would hinder the killings of others. If not, I hoped that it would dissuade further acts of murder from whichever witch committed these crimes in her coven.

I looked about the encircling congregation of onlookers and wondered if perhaps the killer was here, watching, filled with scorn that their mentor was about to die? Perhaps they would act out to protect Mother Lucia? If so, there was a unit of soldiers present and a high-ranking mage to protect us all.

There was a drabness in the air, the kind with the overbearing threat of rain that would make one's head crane upwards. A part of me goaded the rain.

Finally, the broken and wizened form of my mentor was brought from her prison with her wrists bound in yokes. My heart sunk when I looked upon her. The time within that cage did not do her well. Her skin was filthy and covered in grime. The dress that was previously a lively grey was now faded and discoloured, the shoulder strap slipping to reveal sagging skin. Her frazzled hair was clumped and wild and even her eyes seemed to have been void of any hope.

The two guards dragged Lucia forward. Her arms were yoked with a rectangular block of wood, and her ankles were restrained by iron chains, which limited her already weak stride.

I felt my tears well but kept it to myself: I had to stay resolute. To me, Lucia seemed like a kind and well-meaning sage, but to all others, she was just a witch, a conduit for everyone to unload their righteous beliefs and burn away.

The guards removed the bindings, their eyes never meeting Lucia's, as she had her own head bowed in resignation. Next, they tied her to the post, her bare feet shuffling and slipping upon the hay below her until she found the wooden surface.

The one who stepped forward to give the decree was the face of indifferent justice, the judicator, Felicie Auburn, with a heart of stone. The equally lithe and withered woman who decided over my fate when I first arrived in Cleria.

"Lucia Gievan, you have been tried and found guilty of being a practicing Witch. You covet more of your kind and hide them from our justice system and from the laws of the royal King Aston Tiemen. You are thus sentenced to burning at the stake. Speak now of your coven's whereabouts, and you will be able to live out the rest of your days in prison."

Judge Felicie Auburn was dressed in a judicial robe of dark purple and spoke from a wooden platea with herself and Mother Vinrie in another chair. There was one more seat meant for Ievarus, but which was refused, as they had a greater interest in watching my reaction to the spectacle instead of the show itself.

With her back turned, Lucia said nothing. Instead, her eyes scanned the sea of onlookers. All of us awaiting her coming death, when finally, her gaze found mine. She smiled for a moment and nodded. I did not know what the gesture meant. Was she telling me it was okay? Was this her forgiveness? Whatever it meant, it made my heart ache.

"I take your silence to mean you choose death." Judge Felicie concluded as she returned to her seat and waved casually towards the guard, holding a lit torch.

A part of me died again, chipped away like the other pieces; a cracked fingernail kept scraping at the dried paint.

The guard lowered his hand, the fire from the torch taking a ravenous hold on the dry hay. I gasped quietly. A sound immediately cut in half as the remainder was stuck in my throat.

My mentor's eyes held onto me. There was a calmness in her smile. When the tears came, I saw only love and suddenly felt so bitter. What had I done? The only other woman who ever knew what I was going through, and I betrayed her.

Quickly the fire spread and devoured, hungrily the violent flames reached upwards, scaling the offered body of Lucia. She screamed. Her moment of professed calm was gone and in its stead was a wail that instilled such vibrant horror into all of us. She cried. Cried with such agony as if being torn in two.

The curtains of flame rose to obscure her bubbling skin. The scent of cooked flesh spread through the crowds. Some quickly realized that they didn't have the stomach to bear this cruelty any longer and absconded. Others gave righteous chants as if cheering the flames on.

When it was all over, what was left was simply a charred corpse bound to an ashen post; the fire vanished as if properly satiated.

Soon enough, the crowd scattered. Even those who were swept up in this sudden carnal sight were drained and empty, wandering back to the comfort of their privileged lives to leave this dark stain and pretend it never happened.

Ievarus had remained silent, spoke of nothing and simply watched. Good. I had no intention of conversing with them and truthfully wished that they would finally leave me be. Yet, unlike the fire, Ievarus' curiosity seemed bottomless.

I turned to leave when I was suddenly drawn in by the sight of Brother Clemence sitting on a bench. The draft of exhausted crowds bent around his position, draining through the narrow roads in-between unwavering buildings. Brother Clemence sat there with his usual black garments, his white blindfold pulled over his eyes and a cane at his side. The man reminded me of a younger Lucia, his pose stoic and unflinching despite his wizened body.

In spite of my reservations about conversing with anyone after the tragic event, there was something alluring about Brother Clemence's loneliness that made me approach him. As if he were the only one who shared in my sullen mood. Perhaps there was something about solitude that sought kindred spirits.

"Hello, Brother Clemence."

His head craned to the side, his blind gaze trailing several measures over my head and up to the sky.

"Who am I regarding?" he asked.

"Mother Dalila. We met when I had come to visit Father Maurice."

"Ah yes! Of course. No need to explain. There is no chance I would forget someone like you."

"Someone like me?" I queried.

He gave an amused chuckle. "The one witch who serves in the abbey? The one recruited by the forces of Morniar to fulfil the Eleventh cycle? Who *doesn't* know of you?"

I felt a warmth rush to my cheeks at the remark, but said nothing of it.

I turned towards Ievarus, who stood behind me. "Speaking of which, the Silver Prince known as Ievarus shadows me... just so you are aware." It felt awkward, notifying Brother Clemence of Ievarus' presence. Was I warning him? Was there a need to announce my escort?

Brother Clemence smiled reassuringly. "It is no problem at all," he said.

I hesitated a moment before joining Brother Clemence at the bench.

"How did you arrive here?" I asked.

"Brother John had escorted me after much convincing. He warned me, however, that he didn't have time to stay and guide me back. Truth be told, I think he had no interest in witnessing the execution, same as Father Maurice."

"So, why are you here?"

"For the same reasons you are. To pay proper respect to an old friend." His smile was frail.

"It's not just out of respect. I am responsible for her execution. I betrayed her."

"I heard. I am sorry about what happened to your friend. I know how much she meant to you. Hell, I even told Father Maurice about it when he returned to the house. He was glad you had such a close companion," Brother Clemence said, his statement honestly remorseful.

"Thank you, Brother Clemence."

"I can't imagine what you are going through. First with Yasmin, and now Mother Lucia?" He shook his head and tsked; his lips pursed. "What's it like, to lose those close to you?"

I considered the feeling. "I feel light. Not because some weight had been taken from me, but rather as if I have been hollowed out." I looked at the dreary world and then the sky. "I feel as if a simple gust of wind could pull me from my feet."

Brother Clemence nodded. "That sounds truly terrible. Yet, I must say, you're not the only one who feels responsible."

"What do you mean?" I frowned.

Brother Clemence fidgeted with his fingers, lost in thought. "When I first came to the Brotherhood for my sight, Mother Lucia was much like you, a devout helper who tried her best to aid all those that she could." The next part formed a lump in his throat, reluctant to be spoken. Eventually, he pushed through, accompanied by a single tear that escaped the white blindfold. "She tried to restore my eyesight, you know? It was madness; she could have been killed. Although, I'd be lying if I said that it mattered to me at the time. I would have done anything to get my eyes back." Remorse filled his cracked voice, followed by a shudder.

"She was a good woman, helping all that she could. We grew close back then as she helped me find my footing in this new and unknown realm. She already spoke to me about her doubts with the Elders. I tried my best to silence those thoughts, but she was hell-bent. She even told me about a witch she had found. Initially, Mother Lucia was going to report her, but when she found that young girl… she said she saw herself: just a child confused and scared." Over and over, an unstable smile formed and faltered on his lips. His chin crumbled and robbed his smile of its foundations.

"I never knew that; she never told me," I said.

Brother Clemence shrugged. "Naturally. She was trying to protect us both. Not to mention, we had a falling out, eventually."

"What happened?"

"She went too far, that one. I told her to stop her madness, lest she got herself killed. She insisted that there was no way she could stop… that she would not stop." Brother Clemence fidgeted. "Now I think that I was the one who was in the wrong." His smile was sombre.

Silence filled the air. The scent of burnt flesh trailed our surroundings while we spoke of the dead. Ievarus simply stood unblinking, an impartial observer to our exchange.

"Do you believe her?" My lips moved of their own volition.

Brother Clemence craned his neck towards me, though his gaze was off. Judging by his lips, he seemed rather stunned. "Believe what?" he pressed cautiously.

"Mother Lucia's doubts, about the Elders?" I did not know where this line of questioning was coming from.

The man bit his lips as if to prevent their disobedience. He then spoke in hushed whispers. "The Seed is right there." The fear was palpable.

I turned towards Ievarus, who watched, unwavering. They might as well have been a stone column.

"Do not worry, Ievarus doesn't involve themselves with our opinions. They simply care for me." The last part was spoken almost with distaste.

Not entirely convinced, Brother Clemence still pushed onwards. It began with a shrug. "Aye, perhaps? I share some of her concerns, maybe. The contract of time being obvious perfidy… and what has been done to you witches, too. I sometimes think that a true benevolent ruler would grant me my sight back, not stay on their mountain with indifference."

It was like Mother Lucia was speaking through him; though this time, I felt no avulsion or shock at the implications.

Finally, he shrugged. "But what are we going to do? Fight the Elders? Please. Human history across the entire existence of Minethria has been filled with tyrants and lords. The difference is that our oppressors now live upon their mountain without getting involved."

"Do you doubt your service?" I pressed.

"I do what I must because this is my life now. I have resigned myself to it. I mean, when your friend, Yasmin, died; how did you feel?"

I considered the question. It felt like a very private thing to ask. "Empty... I guess that's the best word I can find. Like a part of me, a part of my life was robbed, and I forgot how to breathe, how to stand, how to laugh."

He nodded, seemingly satisfied with my response, as he sighed. "That was how I felt when I lost my sight, except it was a true and endless loss. However—" Brother Clemence rose to his feet with a strained grunt. "If it weren't for my lost sight, I wouldn't have found religion in the first place. It took a long time, but I think I finally found my place among all this." His smile was sombre but honest. "As I keep saying. There is power in suffering."

"If you could get your sight back instead of serving the house, would you?"

This smile was truer, unblemished by any form of doubt. "Without a second's hesitation," he admitted.

There was a long pause as we looked outwards at barren ground. No souls remained, but the charred body of Lucia still hung untouched. I couldn't stare more than a second. Brother Clemence turned towards me. There was suddenly a grave look to him. "Dalila. I must tell you something."

"What is it?"

Brother Clemence's hesitation was palpable. He finally found the strength to speak, though his words were spoken in hushed tones so not even Ievarus could hear. He leaned in. "There is another witch in the church."

My eyes widened. "What do you mean?"

"It was not just Mother Lucia and yourself. Another Sister, perhaps even a Mother, is also a witch."

The implication terrified me. "Is that the person who has been committing these murders?" I whispered back. I thought back to what Mother Lucia had told me. Was there anyone there who had lost something? Someone who celebrated having it back?

"Maybe. I do not know. Nor do I know who the witch is. But be careful." That was the last thing Brother Clemence offered.

Chapter Eighty-Three

CHROMA

There is much terror which unfolds beyond our sight in Thickwood,
all of it hidden under the swollen forest. Yet it pleases us that the Rashi,
as unpredictable and formidable that they are, remain sequestered to
their own burrows in the north. And the Lumari are as ever shy and
secretive as they are known to be.

—SCOUT REPORT ON THE ACTIVITIES BEYOND GREYHILL

N ora had no choice but to trust in me. Not enough to have me watch over our captive prisoner, but enough to have me gather the necessary resources for Howard. At the same time, given Nora's destructive capabilities, she was the obvious choice to keep watch over our hostage.

Howard certainly felt weaker and needed to hydrate himself quite often, but his body wasn't in peril and he could still move about—he would be fine.

"Didn't you also get clawed by that bitch? How come you're fine?"

I gave a gloating smile. "Akar are made of harder stuff." Some form of insult rode his lips, but I was gone before I could catch the entire thing.

When it was all settled, we unfastened the akar while Nora's blade was at his neck, and I refastened his binds around his torso and arms.

Nora had mounted my back, transforming one of her arms into a thin, metal rope coiled about the akar's neck, as if he were on a leash.

The akar revealed his name to be Juki.

❧ ❧

It was the following day when Nora's complaints and winces became more prominent.

"Sit down. Let me take a look." Binding the akar to a tree, I found that Nora had been hiding a noisome wound at her hip formed by the constant friction of metal. The brash and shallow cuts were infected and leaking puss, though it seemed corrosive as the material sizzled upon the ground.

"I'll be fine," Nora insisted.

I looked at her dubiously. "My body is made sturdy; it heals faster than normal," she said.

"True, but you aren't giving it time to heal."

"I will rest when we are done with the mission."

I looked back over my shoulder at the bound Juki. His eyes showed a frightening sense of guile, like a hunter observing their prey.

"How much longer until the army?" I asked in akar.

When Juki answered, I turned to Nora. "He says we are almost there. Once we have scouted and have the information, we rest and turn back." Nora stared me down, but my gaze held steady. Finally, she relented and gave an affirming nod.

❧ ❧

As we continued to roam through the forest, the akar hurled insults. Nora would ask what he said; her breath was warm and brushed against my ear.

"He is asking me why I debase myself to be a human's mount… says I have no honour."

Nora eventually pulled sharply at her rope-like arm, quickly resulting in a gagging sound and the akar to stumbling back.

"Tell him to hold his tongue," Nora instructed coolly.

Juki grumbled but reluctantly said nothing for the rest of the trail.

It was nightfall and Juki no longer had to guide the way as little motes of light trailed and danced in the distance, followed by the swelling sound of life.

We tied Juki to a tree and even gagged his mouth before leaving. The giant did struggle, and I could only hope that the binding held.

We heard it first, a great growing mass of growls and sounds. The light of torches danced like fireflies before us between the trees. The closer we got, the greater the mass of intersecting voices became. Nora and I cautiously crept up towards an overhanging bluff, where we looked down past the columns of trees.

There it was: the akar horde.

For the first time ever, I saw Nora instinctively raise a circle made by curled metal fingers and thumb to her forehead. "By Oxular," she said.

I was equally stunned. Before us, towards an incline of jagged stone cliffs, was a sea of akar. Tribes from all types meshing and working together. Logs were being dragged with uniform rhythm, and the distant clashing of hammers could be heard. Lit torches formed islands where some akar were barking orders and others heaved great tree trunks or carried supplies. Everything about what took place before me planted a fear that I couldn't quite place. Akar tribes were usually no greater than fifty. The kind of recourses and management required for anything greater was impossible and went against the tribalistic nature of my kind. And yet here they were, working in perfect unison.

"There!" Nora spoke quietly and pointed. I saw what she meant. There were great steel javelins and piles upon piles of arrows and bows. Further to the right, though slightly obscured by the cover of trees, I noticed a Kinitari archer. He trained akar from other clans who stood in a single file, as they loosened arrows into wooden masts. *No.* Not just wood. I barely made out a human's leg fastened to the tree.

The akar barked the order to fire. The arrows hissed before piercing flesh.

We heard the deep cry of an auroch and saw upon the mountain crags a pen of the herded beasts.

What was more, this wasn't just a couple hundred akar, this was several thousands by a glance. The light shone and glistened off their sweat swaddled bodies. In the distance, there was the sound of war drums being played from within the mountain, as if its own vocal chords took part in some guttural throat singing.

"Erefiel was wrong," Nora said.

"What do you mean?"

"They aren't going to be attacking in a month's time. They are ready to move, now." The trepidation in her voice was hard to hide.

"We need to move."

"Wait!" I told her. "Who is that?" I pointed towards a figure who emerged alone from a cavern. There was something about their aura demanded to be noticed.

Nora seemed to recognize him immediately. "The leader."

"Leader?" I asked dubiously. The akar seemed barely older than myself, but there was a chilling cunningness to his appearance. That couldn't have been Muktow.

"What is that in his hand?" Nora asked. She leaned forward on the dirt and braced against my shoulder. We strained our eyes and tried to piece together what little we could see.

I noticed it too. A pitch black cudgel of equal measure to Nora's own arms minus the glossy shine. The weapon widened at its striking end and was studded with uniform steel bumps.

"I think I know," said my lips, though I didn't want to believe it.

Nora looked at me expectantly. "Mother told me stories about it, a weapon so strong it could cave in mountains. With each strike it gains weight, but also power, making each consecutive blow heavier."

"An artefact," Nora said.

I nodded. "It is said to be made by the Blacksmith."

❧ ❦

We returned promptly to where Juki was still fastened to the tree, his face contorted into a dour expression as he saw us.

"We need to go back, now," Nora said.

"We can't; you need to give your leg time to rest. Let the infection bleed out and we will continue. If we get into a fight, and your injury compromises you, we will both be in trouble."

Reluctantly, she relented. The woman fell to her rear, leaning against a tree where she removed her right leg comprised of an entire prosthetic. We bade our time so that she could heal.

In the meantime, I approached Juki, finally finding a moment alone.

"I have some questions," I said in akar, removing the knotted gag.

Juki chuckled. "You may speak my tongue, but you sound just like one of them," he noted harshly.

I decided to ignore the insult and turned to find that Nora had actually dozed off. She must have been pushing herself and was more tired than she was letting on; her right prosthetic rested beside her as she found a cosy tree preceding the bluff's overhang.

I turned back to Juki. "Where is Muktow?"

Juki stood alert at the mention of the name. "Muktow?" His tone was suspicious. "Who are you to him?"

"He is my f—" I caught myself, feeling my cheeks warm at the mistake. Softly, I amended my statement. "He is someone important to me." That was the best alternative I could think of.

Juki appeared disarmed by how I spoke of Muktow. "Muktow is dead, has been so a long time."

My eyes widened to betray my surprise. "Are you sure?"

Juki chuckled. "I don't know what he means to you, but I am certain. I watched him die."

That man was never my father, never someone related to me, and yet remained a great cornerstone of my identity. My entire youth was built around that man. If anyone would affirm my place among the akar, I thought it would have been him. My hope was dashed from me. It felt as if I had lost someone important.

"Who are you to him?" Juki queried cautiously.

"No one." I must have sounded crest-fallen.

Juki nodded and grunted, the act of reminiscing seemingly lowering his guard. "Muktow had few close allies; I remember looking up to him. And his son."

"Muktow had a son?" I pressed, feeling jealousy take hold.

Juki was taken aback at the sudden question. With a slow blink, the akar nodded. "Sun'Ra is his name. Child to both Muktow and Zarien."

My mother? "Zarien birthed him a son?"

Juki nodded. There was suddenly an awkward sense of kinship between Juki and me. We weren't clear on the details, but there was an unspoken truth.

"Who are you?" Juki asked, void of any contempt or disdain.

I looked again to Nora, who was sound asleep. "I am the son of Zarien."

Juki's eyes widened and then bowed in understanding.

My heart ached. What more did my mother hide from me?

Juki continued. "I was young at the time, but Muktow was heralding a great force under the call of his banner and was close to uniting the tribes. However, when Sun'Ra was born, Muktow was betrayed and killed by one of his bones."

"Bones?" I asked, not familiar with the word.

Juki fumbled for an explanation. "Like a second in command."

I nodded, and Juki continued. "Sun'Ra was spared, but not out of mercy. It is not in our kind, not since Muktow." The name was spoken with sombre fondness. "The boy was forced to serve as a slave to his father's murderer, chief of the Barni tribe at the time. It was the final slight towards Muktow. Your mother, her tribe and other supporters of Muktow fled; they had no other choice."

I was in shock; *everything* I thought I knew was a lie. Was I the only one in the settlement who didn't know the truth? I wondered if Kolotha and the others were kept in the dark as I was. It made me furious.

"What happened to Sun'Ra?"

"He eventually had his revenge, killed the usurper in his sleep and paraded his body through the camps. There were many tribal wars in the past years, but Sun'Ra is a calm and decisive leader, greater than even Muktow. Our last failed attack took far longer to return from. The years have been difficult, but since finding the Black Conduit, nobody dares question him anymore. Now we charge forth so that our people may live without fear of death, so that we can bring down the Elders."

I considered this. I had a brother? A half-brother perhaps, but he was still blood.

"Why do you help this filth?" Juki asked cautiously under his breath. He was no longer insulting me, rather a sense of familiarity filled the gap between us.

"From where I am standing, they are just trying to defend their home."

"They aid those who exiled us." Juki growled.

I looked back a final time at Nora. "I wish to join my people. Take me with you."

Juki considered my words. "I will, and I will take you to your brother. But first, you must free me so we can kill your master."

"Master?" I repeated questioningly.

The giant gave a nod in Nora's direction. "The human with a body of metal. She can't be allowed to live."

I drew back. "Can we not leave them be? I will free you. All you need to do is take me to our kinsman."

Juki's expression hardened again, his chest expanding faster and faster as his breaths had shorter and shorter intervals. He had a look of indignation.

He strained against the binds, causing me to stumble back. "You aided them in killing our kind... *your* kind. They were my friends. People your *brother* valued." He spoke of my blood as if it were some bad joke. "You will either free me and help kill that wench, or I will tear from these binds and deliver you to Sun'Ra as a traitor."

My soul was conflicted. I stepped away.

"You will *never* be one of us!" Juki declared at my departing.

Nora eventually awoke with a wincing groan. She placed a hand on her hip and then on her limbless leg. I sat with her. Under thick night, I could tell whatever machination she brought from Mount Morniar also improved sight in the dark. Her eyes shone as if having trapped amber.

She winced and groaned, metal hands rigid as they tried desperately to grasp and untangle knotted muscles and nerves.

When finally she quieted down and her aching body didn't warrant her groans, she permitted herself a chance to speak.

"It isn't easy, you know. My nights are filled with horrible aches and pains. Sometimes, I can still feel the flames eating at my skin as if there were splinters embedded beneath the surface," she said, void of any distrust or caution.

"People see me as unrelenting, unwavering. Think that this new body of mine makes me even stronger than I was before. They're wrong. Every day is a mixture of pains and aches, feeling my new limbs press into my soft flesh. Each step forward, I have to swing my hips, move my torso just so my legs obey me. I have to focus with all my strength to avoid breaking underneath my awkward grip. My wrist didn't even allow me to wield a sword, nor can I run like I used to."

I didn't speak; it didn't feel like my time.

"To think that I am even forced to entrust my life to an akar." She chuckled, as if the mere idea was ludicrous. The way she said those words, it was like an apology, an admittance towards her constant distrust. "I owe you an apology, Chroma. If it weren't for you, Howard would have been dead, and I wouldn't have even made it this far," she said.

My heart swelled with guilt until the pain was intolerable. If only she had known of the things I plotted behind her back. Did that prove her right? Was her prejudice warranted? Still, I juggled the thought of betraying her.

I couldn't reply, so instead, I rose to my feet and wandered a good distance away from both Nora and Juki.

I found my own spot against another tall tree and had a good view of both.

My thoughts were muddled and tormented with doubt. It was obvious to me that the brother Juki spoke of was none other than the leader that Nora had pointed out. The same man who wielded the Black Conduit in his hand.

I thought back to Mother; why did she hide so much about the truth? About Muktow? About all of it? All those years, to have had a brother and to have been left in the dark. I was certain that Juta, Nokna and all the others who came with Mother at the time knew about the truth. When my mother's belly swelled, did the others know? Or did they just not question who the father was?

Did Kolotha know? Siemeny? Trem? Nedalya?

I fell deeper and deeper into this pit of conflict. Who would I choose? I could see my brother, join my people. There was so much that I could do. But to abandon Nora? Howard? Erefiel, who offered me a second chance? Given a chance to calm myself, I found my conviction faltering. I was no longer certain of what I had to do. I felt even my rage to be muddled and distorted since my talk with Howard.

I thought of Googan, of akar deities. Muktow. I knew I was not his son. Nonetheless, I asked for his guidance.

As I pondered on my answer, my eyes wandered to Juki and a feeling of unease filled me. I didn't know what it was at first until my eyes settled, and I saw the telling form of an owl behind Juki's back.

My heart stopped for a moment.

"Nora!" I called out. It was too late. The bindings were damaged enough by the owl for Juki to tear through the rest.

The akar came to his feet running, his forward momentum propelling him even faster as he charged unrelenting towards Nora. The woman was taken unaware, still stunned with her removed prosthetic by her side.

My body charged before I had a chance to think, my feet pounding and straining against the forest floor.

Nora was in arm's reach when I tackled Juki, his outstretched arm grasping until it claimed Nora's removed leg, taking it with him as we dropped over the cliff's edge and plummeted into the trees below.

Chapter Eighty-Four

CHROMA

Not much is known about the politics of Chitons, but it is widely accepted amongst scholars that a form of hierarchy does exist. Each divide of bugs, from the flies to the beetles to the mantises are governed by their own lords. Yet rumours arose that somewhere during the fourth cycle, the Flymother disappeared from the mountaintops. Where she went, none know.

—BOOK OF THE CHITONS AND THEIR HISTORY, BY ANON

Within the depth of night we fell through the air like tangled hawks. Painfully, a canopy of trees broke our fall. One by one the proceeding branches swatted and snapped against our momentous weight.

I felt my neck whip back upon landing; my entire body was in pain.

Juki was already rising to stand, wielding Nora's rigid prosthetic leg. His own hands were wrapped around the ankle as the thick stump of the thigh was held like a club; I recalled the encumbering and absurd weight of Nora when I was carrying her. I did not doubt the effectiveness of this improvised weapon.

I rose to my own feet, withdrawing my axe from its holster.

"So you have picked your side," Juki said, regret and disgust intermingled in his claim.

"No. I said I would come with you; it's not too late, we can go without her." We circled one another, careful to lay out our surroundings, lest we tripped on an exposed root or uneven ground.

"And if you were to meet her on the battlefield? What then?"

I hesitated for only a moment, but that was more than enough. "I would kill her," I said unconvincingly.

Juki pounced forward, arms swinging the clumsy, lop-sided leg. The large thing bit chunks out of the surrounding trees, the slimmer ones completely breaking in half and toppling to the floor.

I couldn't afford to shield or parry with my axe lest I wanted to fight without a weapon. But I noticed how awkward of a weapon Nora's leg was. Juki was a hunter, back muscles sculpted through constant use of monstrous bows. They weren't designed for clubs. On top of that, Nora's leg didn't offer a substantial grip due to its sleek polish, and I had no doubt the sweat which clumped her ankle only made it a matter of time until Juki's grip faltered.

Could I disarm him?

Just narrowly did the strike miss my head. As I ducked and fell back, I noted the dent where the leg struck the tree.

I bided my time, waiting patiently for a single error until it came. Juki swung too wide, leaving his side exposed. I took the hooked end of my axe's steel and used it to pull Juki's leg from underneath him, causing the sweat encased prosthetic to elude his grip.

Juki landed hard on his rear. Whatever vegetation carpeted the place suddenly exploded into the air. I pressed my foot to his chest and lowered the axe to his neck.

"Go. Simply leave, and I will let you live," I said, almost pleadingly.

Juki looked at me with something akin to sorrow in his eyes. "A warrior doesn't fear death," he said. The words sounded almost like a promise as he looked me deep in the eyes.

Before I could do anything, Juki grabbed the other pointed end of my axe and pulled it into his throat.

I stepped away in shock, axe falling from my grip. Juki held my gaze though blood pooled and sputtered from neck and lip, bubbling and curdling. His chest convulsed while wet coughs spat out more blood.

It took pain-staking minutes until the light in his eyes faded.

His body lay there limp, unmoving, scarlet ichor continuing to spill from his lifeless body.

It was over. Barely did I know Juki, and yet emotions toiled within me. The answers I wanted, the chance to belong to a people who I wished so dearly to be a part of. I knew I was never going to get another chance like this. This short but nonetheless present sense of understanding between us made me feel as if I had just lost a part of myself, as if I had lost a friend.

I could have met my brother.

I walked up to Juki, fingers trailing to his eyelids and closing them. "May Ankou take you to Googan's side."

When all seemed maddeningly silent, and I felt Juki's blood pool about my feet, I heard the cries of conflict from up above the cliff.

Chapter Eighty-Five

NORA

It is said that the flame knight and frost knight were twins in their mortal days. Now, as Elder Knights, they share such a bond where upon their union, their kindling brings forth a power to be reckoned with.

—Tales of the Elder, by Nuniya

I t all happened so quickly.

I tried opening up to Chroma, to perhaps allow myself to trust him despite his roots. My own pilgrimage of the soul had me grow and become more tolerant, to see Chroma's heartfelt acts for what they were.

Yet when he walked away, I couldn't help but feel as if I had ruined any chance for that.

As I tended to the soft and puss-exuding side of my hip, I failed to notice the charging akar freed from his bonds. I was frozen in place, unable to stand and defend myself on account of my removed leg.

Yet Chroma was there in an instant, knocking aside the charging akar as they both plummeted down the side of the bluff and into the darkness below.

"Chroma!" I dove just in time to watch their dark silhouettes blend with the night.

I was careless. Quickly, I collected myself, turning to put my other leg back on and only bracing against the sensitive pain it would continue to cause. Except my prosthetic was no longer there; I went cold with realisation.

The stygian owl belonging to Juki suddenly accosted me, flapping its silent wings and hooting as its talons scratched against my metal arms. I swatted clumsily, time and time again, I tried to get to my feet, only to remember that one of my legs was gone.

Finally, my left arm caught hold of one of its wings and pulled it in. A small terrified cry came from the owl as its head was enveloped by my fist and nothing came after but the crunching of bones and the sound of wet viscera staining my palm.

The owl drooped lifelessly before I relinquished my hold, falling with spread wings to the ground. I turned to the plummet and crawled to its edge, wondering how I could get down there. Even my improved eyesight provided no glimpse of anything but a dark blanket at the very bottom.

I heard noises. Looking to my right, I saw the dancing light of lit torches followed by the intermingled, guttural language of the akar.

Panic filled me—I quickly devised a plan.

The light on my chest beat. Though the akar wouldn't have known what the light meant, I knew that it at least conveyed the idea of life; the kind of idea I needed to hide.

Promptly, I dragged myself a good distance from the edge and went limp on my stomach to hide the pulsing light of my heart. No doubt the trail I left showed I was dragging my body, but I doubted, or rather hoped, that the nearing akar wouldn't read into it.

I could hear them. They must have had a plain sight of me, speaking in their harsh and guttural tongue. Even staying still proved a mighty task. I could feel my pulsing heart beam radiant light into the soil. Whatever critters tunnelled below me must have looked upon a muffled glow through the dirt.

I tried to place the position of each voice depending on how clearly

I could hear the rolled syllables and deep grunts.

One of them was barely discernible and even more so a second after—they must have looked away at the overhang of the bluff. Of course, the broken tree branches and signs of a scuffle would make it clear that someone fell over.

In total, I counted three. No. Four akar.

I could not stand. There was no way I would be able to take them all on from the front, especially if I gave up my element of surprise.

Chroma and Howard were also nowhere near me; I would have only one chance at this.

One of the akar neared me. Was the unsteadiness in his voice indicative of doubt? I wasn't sure. I could feel him practically above me—it took such a ferocious will to not move.

I felt a foot nudge me on the back, prodding and shoving to see if I were a trap in the waiting—I was. He must have thought me dead, for eventually his large, beefy hands trailed over my metal arm and then my back.

When I heard him say something again, and his voice momentarily grew more distant. I saw in my mind's eye him turning to say something to his comrades.

Now was my chance.

Slowly, carefully, I turned until I saw him looking back at his comrades. I kicked out with my left leg, pushing the giant's own out from under him and bringing him to his knee. I heard bone break from the impact. His pierced features fell towards me with wide eyes, in perfect range for my arm to transform and free head from shoulders.

I was right, there were four in total. Now only three. The severed head fell to the ground and rolled without protest.

Two of the akar faced me, momentarily bewildered, while the last was in the midst of turning around.

Sitting up, my left arm transformed into a bladed flat whip. I swung it around the neck of the unaware akar. The giant was pulled off his feet, dragged through the dirt in a moment as my whip shortened instead of me having to pull. My right arm whirred to life and punched straight through his back. Ribs broke like twigs. I felt what must have been his heart burst like a wet fruit.

There was a wet choking sound, followed by a sputter of blood. I retrieved my arm.

The two facing me broke from their stupor and charged. Both of them towered over my seated body; I was at a major disadvantage.

First came the thrust of a spear. The dead akar in my grasp bodied the piercing attack, the spear-head coming out of his back. I grabbed on and felt the weapon splinter. My left arm took the form of a thin blade, the transition from whip- severing the dead akar's head as I pulled in the spear with a powerful tug.

Stumbling, the spear-wielding akar came forward. My left arm-blade skewered to find purchase in his eye socket.

I noticed too late the axe that came swinging from the side. It took everything I had to simply raise my left elbow-guard in an impromptu act of defence. I was flung from my place, rolling disoriented until my back hit a stocky boulder.

There was a seething and terrible number of burning cuts along my face and flesh. It was then that I noticed the axe-blade had shattered upon my arm, and pieces of it were embedded in my flesh, turning their shrapnel ends into smoking points of hot metal.

The akar didn't relent. He dropped the axe and picked up the cudgel from his comrade, charging me with a terrifying roar. My arms transformed into two halves of an obsidian kite shield and slammed together to absorb the force of the strikes. I could not see anything, but I truly felt the force behind each swing hammering down onto my raised defence.

Again and again my shoulders smarted with each slam, as I felt myself being pushed deeper and deeper into the ground. It was only a matter of time before my body faltered.

A swing to my right flipped me onto my stomach. My shoulder ached and smarted while my back was exposed. I turned my shield back into arms as I felt the full force of the cudgel slam down onto my back. A stunted and gasping cry escaped me at the unbearable bludgeoning. If it weren't for the Blacksmith, I would already have been dead.

With a defying roar of my own, both of us regressing into some primal instinct, I allowed my blood to flow freely and felt my arm whirr itself into life. The scales rattled with anticipation as I thought back to how I nearly killed Erefiel.

My empowered fist slammed into the ground despite being a mere inch of a distance and made the entire floor explode beneath us.

Dirt and soil went everywhere. The akar and I flew through the air. Only a smoking and ruined crater was left where I struck.

My shoulder burnt, and I felt my left prosthetic go limp and dark.

My body extolled beyond its capabilities. I watched as the akar clumsily rose to his feet and in a daze; he kept swaying from one side to the other. A misshapen and dented cudgel was in his hands and a gash to the beast's forehead allowed a streak of crimson to run free. He turned towards me. My own vision was compromised, my entire body burning up.

My limbs refused to listen; only the lightest twitch of metal fingers flicked at the effort. I sat there watching up with hazy eyes. *So, this is it?* I mused. *I thought I would last longer than that.*

From the side charged Chroma with a terrifying roar. He took my opponent to the ground and started bludgeoning him with my leg. Blood splattered everywhere as Chroma gave a primal cry of rage. The frenzy in his eyes alone was terrifying.

I couldn't help but chuckle. It was funny seeing the last of them being battered to death with my leg as tattered ribbons of blood sprayed the air. All I could hear was the sound of exploding tissue and caving bone until all that was left was just a wetness.

⊰ ⊱

I must have passed out.

When I awoke, I was in a daze and unaware of my surroundings.

All I could tell was that I felt weak and nauseated. Feeling as if I had slept for years on a bed of rocks. I filled in the gaps—I was in motion. I felt the trundling sensation of movement that lightly tossed me up and down. First, the memory of the battle returned with dread, then I noticed the charcoal tint of skin before me. Panic gripped me as I noticed I was strapped onto the back of an akar, but only for a moment until I recognized the familiar shape and scent.

"Chr...oma?" I said meekly.

It wasn't yet daylight, though the pitch black of the forest had softened into a rousing grey.

Chroma looked behind his shoulder tentatively. "Rest," was all he said.

The motion and exhaustion sent my stomach reeling. I expelled the contents of my stomach onto Chroma's back. He didn't complain.

Eventually, Chroma took his own advice as we stopped at a ravine where he drank from its coursing water and cleaned the vomit from himself and me. He offered a drink of water from his cupped hands. Tentatively, I drank from it, my eyes never leaving his as I finally realized how much of my life I had entrusted to this man. I had to admit, being forced to face a hateful prejudice that I had for so long wasn't something I was ready for. It left me conflicted and unsure. I allowed myself a compromise: Chroma I did trust.

Finally, I had regained some strength and some of my bearings. When I had fallen unconscious, the limbs attached to me plopped off by themselves. Chroma collected a bag and some resources from the akar who attacked us. He used it to carry my new limbs, along with creating a makeshift carrier out of other bags and some vines for him to carry me on his back. He had informed me that the embedded metal had actually come free by itself. The pieces inching out of my closing wounds when I was unconscious.

It was now daybreak, and I could tell we were both exhausted. Sleepless nights and all this fighting made rest a luxury we couldn't afford.

I suddenly groaned. "Oh, my head." I pinched my eyes shut as tight as I could to mitigate the headache that swept through. I raised an ethereal hand to the tender spot and winced when I found a boil.

"The akar must have hit me harder than I imagined."

Chroma was making a small campfire on account of it being day and suddenly looked away from me. I felt there was some resignation.

"What is it?" I asked.

Chroma hesitated, his stare lingering. "Well, when you were unconscious, I tried to create a carrier for you. Except that the first one wasn't very successful." He paused, pursing his lips as if wondering if he should continue. "The strap broke, and you fell pretty hard on your head." Chroma readied himself, his body tensing as if ready for a scolding.

There I sat, without any of my limbs affixed, leaning against a tree and seated upon a boulder.

I laughed. I began laughing so hard that my chest hurt. I laughed until tears welled in my eyes and I was afraid I would topple over, but by Oxular—I couldn't stop.

When I finally calmed down, the aftershock of my fit coming forward with the occasional residue of light chuckles, I saw Chroma smile and give a chortle of his own. "What's so funny?"

I tried to collect myself, but I couldn't promise anything. "The last thing I remember is you beating the akar to death with my own leg. I am just imagining my limp and unconscious body sliding off your back and my head hitting the floor. You must have been terrified!"

Chroma laughed more heartedly. "I was. I secretly hoped you died so I wouldn't get a scolding."

Again, I started to laugh, and this time, Chroma joined me with just as much vigour. When our moment finally died down, Chroma returned to more pressing matters.

"Nora, there is something I need to tell you."

I gave him my ears; he had earned them.

"When I climbed up the mountain and killed the last akar, you were unconscious at the time, so you didn't notice. But the akar army is already on the move."

My eyes went wide. "What?" All humour now turned to vapour.

Chroma continued. "That is why I went ahead and created the carrier for you. We need to return to Bravnicka swiftly."

I thought it over. It was too early. Even if we managed to beat the akar in time, it would not be enough time for Erefiel to gather the resources he needed. He would know of their advance even before we'd arrive home.

"Chroma, help me with my body. We need to go home."

"No," Chroma objected.

I couldn't help but be affronted. "Excuse me?"

He looked at me, resolute in his standing. "You need your strength. Let me carry you. I will be your legs. When we return home, you will need to be at your full strength."

I pondered as our gazes held. Finally, I was the one who relented; to an akar, no less.

I gave a defeated sigh. "Fine, but then you better hurry up." I couldn't help but smile.

Chroma shared my smile. "You better hold on tight—you won't be of any use to anyone with a cracked skull."

Chapter Eighty-Six

EREFIEL

Shayley was the first Nephilim. Born to Gazzey, the deer shaman, Shayley set off to make her new home in Thickwood. With her own assortment of glowing antlers, she meditates and blends in with the burgeoning forest, waiting for whoever seeks her wisdom.

—THE FIRST NEPHILIM AND THEIR HOME, BY VILLY ZOME

Secretly, I had hoped that father was here. I imagined what it would have been like to fight side-by-side, father and son. I even smiled like a daydreaming child, imagining what tales would be spun about us, entertaining phrases like "birds in flight."

Yet father returned to where he belonged, by the Elder King's side. I was sure he had already grown accustomed to that place again. I had gathered an idea of what father was saying. During my short stay, it truly felt like I was inside a dream, the foundations and walls all around me shifting and contorting as if a simple touch would unravel it all.

On that very morning, an emergency meeting was called, and General Commander Orson promoted me to Commander of Greyhill; my position was now made official. Before returning to Greyhill, I decided to spend the rest of my day within my own four walls, away from the clumping sweat and earthy grime as troops marched back and forth in uniform.

This would be my final day in my own home before waiting anxiously for the inevitable attack of the akar.

I had given my workers the day off. Saru was the only one who decidedly refused. With my yard to myself, I resigned to the training space bracketed by the stone wall around my property and the inner wall of my house.

Upon an erect wood post, I swung the blade of Bereniel, dressed in full armour and fastened shield. This exercise made me truly aware as to the pent up stress and anxiety within me.

It had been over a week since Nora and Chroma left. Did they find anything? Did they die? I shouldn't have sent Nora. I hoped Chroma was protecting her.

Lost within the tangle of strangling thoughts, I felt my arm swing harder and faster, chipping away splinters from this wooden mast until finally I cut straight through. My sword had become a wisp of smoke from all that gathered speed, and as I looked down at the severed stump, the blade had enough time to allow its cloak of wind to fade and reveal its shape.

"What did that poor mast ever do to you?" Saru asked.

I turned around to find him holding a tray of steaming tea and a canter of water with biscuits. It was mostly a sunny day today, but the bite of cold did not lag too far behind.

"Made the mistake of insulting my honour." I joked in between ragged breaths.

Saru gave me a rare smile, the violet corners of his lips creasing. He moved to lay the tray on a small coffee table.

I removed my helmet and strode over. "You know you are dismissed, right? Why is it that when I actually want you to be on hand, that you are nowhere to be found? Do you just enjoy defying me?"

Saru smirked. "Well, what else am I to do? The people in this city would recoil at my presence. The only reason I am tolerated outside your four walls is because of a piece of paper I carry around saying that I am your property."

I frowned gravely, feeling insulted. "You are not my property." I sounded sterner than I would have liked.

"I know I am not. But I am to the people outside these walls." He tapped the scar of his third eye. "Father would have surely agreed with them."

I sighed at the mention of Saru's father, never quite knowing what to say.

"It's not your fault." How nostalgic the words sounded. The last time I spoke them seemed so long ago, before all this madness.

"Stop it." Saru protested, shooting me a chiding glance. Even at twenty-two, Saru seemed too calm compared to how I remembered him in his youth. Even if it had been over a decade since I had taken him in. "I'm the one who is supposed to take care of you. Remember?"

I smiled nostalgically. "You were adamant about that ever since you came to live with me. Said you wanted to earn your keep despite your lack of grace." I took a seat on a white chair with its backrest carved into filigree patterns.

Saru looked somewhat indignant at the comment. "I wasn't that bad."

I had to stifle my laugh. "Please! I had to replace half of my kitchen after everything you broke."

Saru chuckled reluctantly. It was a hearty thing. Saru took a seat of his own. "It gave me a purpose. After my sight was robbed from me, I didn't know what to do. Then you found me and took me back with you." Saru sounded conflicted.

"There is so much you can do!" I protested.

"Erefiel, you don't get it. You try so hard to fix everything so that it fits your view. Stop for a moment and consider a life where you were told that this—" he waved casually at the mangled eye on his forehead. "It will dictate your purpose in life. Give you meaning. When you blossom to a ripe age, a vision of your final moment is granted to you. The idea instilled pride in my parents, thinking I would have a meaningful death. Now imagine your vision does not show a warrior's end. Imagine your vision shows you dying of old age instead." As Saru continued, it seemed almost as if he were reliving the events as shadows being cast against a cave wall. The chirping birds and lazy clouds above, proving indifferent to this dark memory.

"Your father took away your sight… banished you… marked you for all of your kind to know." I finished the retelling. I knew the story all too well.

Saru let out a rare and brittle shudder from him, a sputtering thing as if repressing sobs. "Erefiel. If you die out there… I know how dire the amassing force of the akar is. The people within the safety of these walls may not know, but I saw the extent of their savagery."

I smiled at Saru. "I won't die. I am not going anywhere."

Saru nodded, his movements frenetic. "Stop trying to take care of everyone. I keep hearing of the sacrifices you make. For Nora, Dalila, even an akar! You keep finding wounded pets to tend but forget about yourself." It was implied that he was also one of the wounded pets.

We went silent for a while. The subtle stinging of my eyes caught me by surprise as I felt the first welling tears. Seeking the approval of a father was something I knew all too well. "You know, last time Father was here, we promised to joust a bit. Just to spar. Something we hadn't done since I was a child. Even back then, he wasn't very present, but I remember those rare moments so distinctly. Yet Mother," I shook my head, "people would tell me that she was so loving and warm when I was just a child. All I remember was how cold and distant she became with her transformation. The older I was, the further she withdrew until I saw only orbs of ice staring back at me.

"You're right," I continued. "I am broken in a lot of ways. I suppose I see the likes of Cassidy leeching off of their birthright like a breastfed parasite, and I dread becoming like that, too. If I can make a difference, then why shouldn't I? But more than just that, I wish to make my father proud. To live up to the name of White-Hawk and stand alongside him at Mount Morniar. Even if it doesn't happen with the akar defence, it most certainly will once I help Ievarus slay the Evil."

I turned towards Saru and felt a creeping warmth in my cheeks. "I'm sorry. I don't wish to burden you."

"Of the many things my parents got wrong, being able to express your emotions wasn't one of them. I fail to grasp why being open and vulnerable is something frowned upon amongst people of your station. Consider this: go too cold and you turn into your mother. Bottle it all up within and perhaps at some point it becomes too much to handle."

Saru didn't know, but the final comment reminded me of father's breakdown behind the walls of his chamber, a side to him that he even hid from mother.

"You know, if I fail, it's not just Greyhill that falls; all of Cleria will be at risk. No. All of Bravnicka. I can't fail. I'm not going anywhere, I promise."

A deep and sombre quiet filled the space between us, as we both brooded on our cathartic exchange. The stillness was like a stagnant lake beginning to freeze, the cracking of its crystals audible.

Suddenly, from my arched gate came a loud rattling followed by panicked cries.

"Erefiel! Commander Erefiel!"

I stood immediately at the call of my name and ran to the gate where a sweat clad and heaving young soldier awaited me with desperate eyes.

I slipped into my role. "Report," I ordered, though I already knew what he was going to say.

"The akar are coming!"

Chapter Eighty-Seven

DALILA

Legend says of a warrior riding down from the heavens upon a yellow steed. From their yellow bow, they fire the embodiment of lightning itself.

—TALES ACROSS MINETHRIA LOST TO TIME. AN ANTHOLOGY

W ith Mother Lucia gone, I reassured myself that the killings were finally done with, though I wasn't entirely convinced.

Yet things did quiet down; no pointed messages written in blood stated otherwise. I couldn't help but wonder if it was because Lucia was the killer herself. She knew that Yasmin was privy to my existence and seemed convinced that I had betrayed her identity as well. It was no secret to me that she wasn't fond of the Elder gods reigning upon their mountain; perhaps the murders were an act of defiance?

Was this all some grand ploy? Did she try to come across as loving and considerate to hide her darker side?

I did not know. What I did know was that I truly missed having someone to open up to, to listen to my concerns even when they were often half-truths and lies to tell me what I needed to hear.

This time, Father Maurice was present at the Brotherhood of the Serving and sat in his office.

No one had guided me there, but nonetheless, I believed he was expecting me.

"Ah, Mother Dalila. Please, take a seat. Brother Clemence had told me that you came to see me once before?"

I nodded and stepped forward, shutting the door behind me.

"I see you have brought a guest."

I turned towards Ievarus, still in their shorter form. I was so used to their constant shadowing I had forgotten all about them.

"Shall Ievarus stay outside?" I asked.

"Nonsense!" Father Maurice retorted, rising as swiftly as a man his age could.

"This is a house of worship specifically for their ilk! It is an absolute honour." Father Maurice shambled forward around the table and went into a curt bow.

Ievarus, nonetheless, blinked indifferently. They looked to me as if for guidance, but I wasn't too sure myself. So instead, Ievarus gingerly tried to mimic the bow, and I quickly struck their arm as if to dissuade them.

Confused, Ievarus rose and so too did Father Maurice.

"How fascinating, to see a Seed follow and study us mortals."

I nodded. "It actually came from your tale of Igura," I supplied.

"Curious," was all that Father Maurice said, returning to his side of the table and plopping down with rickety knees.

"Where did you disappear to when I was here? Brother Clemence mentioned you are gone quite often?"

Father Maurice nodded. "Sometimes for months at a time."

"Is it Elder business?" I asked.

Father Maurice gave me that piercing look of his. "More... personal matters," he said, as if not finding a better word to fill in the space.

I eyed the man suspiciously, but had no time to delve further.

"It is a shame what had happened to Mother Lucia." His wild and unkempt white brows furrowed in disapproval. "Such a crime," he said while rubbing his thighs.

"Yes," I admitted, taking a seat while Ievarus remained standing just behind.

"I understand that she was a witch?"

I nodded. "Practising witch, yes. I reported her after finding... a friend of mine dead."

"Ah yes, it really is such a pity. Do you really think she was the one responsible for the killings?"

I shook my head. "No. But I do think she is hiding the one who is." I kept hidden the worrying news Brother Clemence had confided in me. There was a witch within the Sisterhood. It would have explained how they were able to kill Yasmin without being detected.

"Ah, yes. Her secret witch coven," he said glibly. "What makes you so certain that they were involved?"

I looked at the man as if he had just asked why I was so certain the sun would rise every day.

"They're witches. Throughout history, witches had given in to their power and passion and torn the world asunder."

Father Maurice nodded. "Well, was Mother Lucia such a force?"

I recoiled. "No."

"Are you such a force, Mother Dalila?"

I blinked, unsure of how to answer. "I don't mean anyone any harm."

"And you suppose someone within that coven does?"

I shrugged. "A single witch with the intent and means would."

"Dalila, why have you come here today?" Again, there was that frighteningly sharp stare of Father Maurice; nothing was hidden from those peering eyes.

I contemplated my answer, knowing full well that Ievarus watched my response tentatively. "With Mother Lucia gone, with Yasmin gone. I feel like there was someone I needed to talk to."

"Why?" he asked.

I twiddled my thumbs as my hand absently trailed to my forearm.

"Because I felt like I needed to."

"That's not really the reason, is it?" Father Maurice asked pointedly.

"Mother Lucia sought a safe haven for girls like yourself. Girls who were exposed to a life where they were no longer their own masters. She had good intentions. The real reason you came here is for me to tell you that you made the right choice."

I felt lost. "Didn't I?"

"Mother Dalila, did you know Mother Lucia and I were good friends?"

I blinked. "I did not."

"Well, we were. She told me about her plans to absolve you of the church. She did that for you, you know? To give you the right to use your magic, to heal the wounded just like you wanted. To visit your parents. You are the first witch to ever receive those rights. Now tell me. Have you used your healing powers since being granted immunity?"

I hung my head.

"Did you visit your family?"

"They don't have to go through all that again," I murmured timidly.

"I heard of what happened to Yasmin, your friend. Brother Clemence had originally told me of her relationship with you. That she meant a lot. You trusted her, so why not your parents?"

I remained silent.

Father Maurice sighed. "Mother Dalila, I assume you came here for comfort. Well, I offer you truth instead. I speak what I see. If you decide I am wrong, then so be it—I am wrong. But all I see is a woman too scared of returning to her parents. Not to protect them from herself, but to protect herself from disappointment."

I shot up from my seat, bristling at the words; tears ran and my voice cracked. "You know *nothing* about me!"

Father Maurice nodded. "No, perhaps I don't. Perhaps, I took a gamble on you. But you seemed to be sure about Mother Lucia as well."

"What if my parents die next? What then? What if I return home, and they perish, just like Perry? Just like Yasmin?"

"So that's what this is about? You feel like you are the witch responsible for their deaths?" Father Maurice's query did not try to soften its edges.

Without another word, I turned and left, my shadow following right behind me.

◁ ▷

I was undoubtedly upset and, instead of leaving, I went to the small square garden and wiped my tears there. Ievarus in the meantime offered no words of consolation, and, quite frankly, I grew sick and tired of their presence.

As I wept, I was greeted by a familiar voice. "Know that I cannot see you, but I know a hurt soul when I hear one," said the calm and soothing voice of Brother Clemence.

I sniffled. "Ah, Brother Clemence. Forgive me, I didn't wish for you to see me so."

Brother Clemence raised a halting hand and used his cane to find his way forward. He stood there as he usually did, still wearing the white blindfold across his eyes.

"May I?" he asked.

I nodded.

"Just to remind you, I need verbal affirmation."

"Ah, yes! Excuse me. Of course, you may sit."

The man plopped onto the seat and stared out, unable to see the statuesque Ievarus in the corner observing us. For a moment, I considered making their presence clear, but truth be told, I liked to simply pretend as if the Silver Prince was absent. Additionally, the last time I had brought Ievarus up, Brother Clemence seemed rather on edge.

"I am assuming the voice I hear belongs to Mother Dalila?" Brother Clemence clarified.

"That it does."

The man allowed himself a self-praising chuckle. "I'd never forget such a tempered voice."

I smiled.

"What ails you?" he asked.

"A lot of things. Mother Lucia died because of me. My best friend was killed. Now I am not even sure what to do."

"Well, what did you want to do?"

"To serve, to help those in need. To save those who are important to me."

Brother Clemence nodded, head pointed to the floor. "Then do that."

"Well, what if Mother Lucia was innocent? What if no one in the coven committed the murders? How could I go around and do what I do, knowing I got someone killed?" The knotted pain in my chest twisted its aching roots. I came to Father Maurice for the truth. Perhaps he said exactly what I needed to hear.

Brother Clemence considered his next words. "At the time, you probably felt like you had to do something. You acted doing what you thought *needed* to be done. There is something pure in that kind of conviction, even if others may frown upon it."

"Father Maurice doesn't seem to share your sentiment."

Brother Clemence chuckled. "Father Maurice can be quite strict."

"Where does Father Maurice go during his retreats?" I asked.

"Nobody knows, he can be quite an enigmatic man. Many think him frail and senile, but he is still quick in mind and body."

"When I first arrived, he told me that he has connections to the Abbey."

Brother Clemence smiled. "He has his resources, I suppose. But he knows that what you did was done because you thought it was the best course of action."

"And if I was wrong? If I sent someone to their death?"

"Then you make the best of it. Make amends. Sitting around in self-pity doesn't change the reality of things," he recited. "Avoiding your fears and running away simply because you are scared of the consequences won't help, either."

"There is power in suffering." I echoed Brother Clemence's adage.

A thought came to me. Perhaps Father Maurice was cruel in his statements, but once again, I found that the wizened man struck a truth

I hadn't considered before.

"Remember when I told you that Mother Lucia and I had grown close?" he said, leaning into me so that I could catch the scent of musky pine and smoky incense on him.

"Yes."

He seemed suddenly hesitant, as if afraid to breathe life into the ghosts of the past. "There are secrets out there, you know. Secrets of which few know except for the Elders." His tone became hushed whispers, foreboding even. "Mother Lucia secretly uncovered these secrets."

"What kind of secrets?" I asked.

"'Not all is as it seems', she would say. One such knowledge she vehemently believed in was the creation of the demons. Where do you think demons came from?"

"From the cruelty and sins of man."

"Ah, to Mother Lucia, that was not the case. She said of how Lillith grew to be the mother of demons, nurturing them and tending to them."

A distant memory returned to me from one of our many exchanges. I nodded. "I remember. She said something of the like to me."

Brother Clemence shrugged. "Mother Lucia was a good soul, but her fanaticism for these remnant truths made her frightening. If she was the killer, her motivations may have been misguided, but I have no doubt they were always pure."

I nodded. "Do you still think my suffering beautiful?"

"In a tragic, melancholic kind of way. Like warm honey spilt over frozen water. It thaws the ice and draws in a sense of tragic suffering. Like 'The Futile Resistance of Mellezi'."

The man paused for a time before continuing. "I may be blind, Dalila. But I can sense your hurt. It drips from you as if secreted in your sweat. That kind of hurt doesn't go away by itself, definitely not when you are alone. You left your family, your parents, and went on to live by yourself. You can't process that kind of hurt without aid."

I fidgeted for a moment. "People keep telling me I should visit my family. But I keep having this nightmare. What if I return and find them dead? What if bringing them back into my life brings just more suffering for them? I can't allow that." I shook my head.

"Tell me about your family," Brother Clemence softly prompted.

I looked back to a past that was no longer my own. The images played out on a stage, and I was the only member in the audience.

"We had a farm. Nothing big, but we made enough. Father was tough on me, but he meant well. He'd have liked you; he liked anyone who was a servant of the Elders. Mother always had her hands full with all of this. Except maybe Fredrick, he was always rather good at being obedient." I was surprised to find a wistful smile creep its way onto my lips. I hadn't realised how vehemently I had shuttered away this past of mine as my tears came freely. I had an inexplicable longing to see them all again.

A shudder escaped me. "I thank you, Brother Clemence. I know what I need to do." The truth instilled equal measures of terror, but also excitement in me.

"And what is that?" he asked.

"I think it is time I visited my family again. I can't do this alone." My declaration wasn't resolute but it held firm.

The man nodded, pleased to hear that. "Maybe then your powers will truly come through in a most wondrous fashion."

Chapter Eighty-Eight

EREFIEL

Within the wide spread history of humanity, the reason behind
Museya's divide with Cleria has been lost to time. Some foundations are
so old, that they become lost under layers and layers of history and are
never to be found again. The layers cement into culture and tradition
and nobody cares about its buried foundations.

—A TREATISE ON WHY MUSEYA AND CLERIA HAVE DIVIDED,
BY SULIVAN SENTU

I rode swiftly atop the back of Zephyr to Greyhill. The young soldier still green behind the ears had difficulty keeping up.

The only word on Nora and Chroma came from Howard. The man returned with ill tidings and was worse for wear, stumbling and vomiting the report together with whatever vitriol spilled from his stomach. The foot soldier who had come to collect me said that Howard was being cared for. Apparently he had been poisoned by some akar.

Howard gave a comprehensive report while on the brink of delirium: the attack, Nora and Chroma's decision to pry deeper into the woods. I put together the abridged version given to me by the soldier, but I still needed to hear the rest from Howard.

When I scampered into the infirmary tent, I was greeted by a sallow and sweat-drenched man. His skin was a sickly yellow, his eyes threatening to shut completely. The man's chest rose and fell with great, laboured breaths. Howard filled in the gaps as best he could. His lips were cracked and dry. The Sister who treated him said he had expunged much of his contents and was dangerously dehydrated.

"It was a real pain, alright. After the attack, Chroma treated my wounds, warned me about the poison," Howard chuckled hoarsely. "I think the damn bastard underplayed it."

"The akar, Howard. Tell me about the akar." I struggled to keep the panic from my voice.

Howard's nod was a weak thing; he tried to wet his lips. "I heard it, never did see it. But that was enough: the tremor of earth as a great force marched through the lands. I sensed it; the air itself was alive with the promise of conflict, as if the forest was rising up. I could *hear* their war drums in the distance. It sounded like the beating wings of a mountainous locust, each powerful and sonorous. I rushed as quickly as I could, but I don't know if it was enough," he confessed; a weak, deflating wheeze blew through his parched lips.

"How many?" I asked reluctantly.

Howard tried to shake his head. "I don't know," he said. "But what I do know, whatever we have, it won't be enough."

I leaned in. "Nora and Chroma?" I whispered these words for him alone. The man simply shook his head almost violently.

Howard grabbed my arm and looked me deep in the eye with his affliction. "I don't know where they are. But I know in my heart that they still live." Suddenly, his cheeks filled and the man bent over the side of his bed to expel another bucket's worth of fluid.

"Commander, you need to leave," a Sister said, pushing me out. I did not impose and settled my eyes on the fighting Howard.

Before I left, I halted the woman and looked down at her, my white eyes meeting hers. "Whatever you do, make sure he survives."

She reassured me that Howard would live.

I inspected our defences and had all the captains report to me. Our own force hadn't been twirling their thumbs, either. We had amassed a swollen body of ten thousand men, though many of the glancing faces were new and inexperienced recruits with fear clearly etched. It was a number that deserved respect. Despite Howard's concerns, this gathering of forces was no small feat.

What provided the most reassurance was the fact that our numbers were reinforced by four muses and ten archmages, one of which would strengthen the sound of our Inspired musicians. On top of that, we were gifted five dancers, of which two were partners. Their coming meant that Museya was just as concerned about the akar as we were.

I immediately allocated the dancers into pertinent positions within the army formation to work as bolstering. Their performance in the midst of battle would maintain troop formation and prevent utter chaos.

The only things that were not ready in time were our built defences of ballistas and trebuchets and many of the palisades. I cursed under my breath at the loss of the akar builders. Their efforts could have helped with the wall. Now we didn't even have any to reinforce our ranks.

I sighed heavily. The only thing I could do was hope that Howard was wrong, that his delirium impacted his report. And perhaps the Elders would see it upon themselves to intervene—no, I couldn't afford to hope for help that may never come.

◁ ▷

Three painstaking days had passed, three days where howling wind whispered of death like a seductress. The air about the camp was tense. Soldiers squatted in circles gambling with their tossed dice, hollow laughter supposed to distract us from what was to come. Our weapons were always within reach, the edges practically shaking with anticipation. The skies themselves were clear and showed no sign of changing.

A fly swarm had gathered, encircling our stables and feasting on the manure of our horses. They would await our fall, so that a cloud could feast on what was left and plant their eggs.

I could practically feel the agitation all about me, trying to seep in through my pores. Fights would break out among our troops as the waiting turned maddening. The turgid air flayed against our sanity.

Again and again, war room meetings were held to go over the plan, the defences and the training of recruits reminded of their duties. All of it done to repress the knotted sense of unease within.

Thus, when we heard the sound of the enemy marching in during the afternoon, all of our bodies tensed simultaneously. I could feel it, the way our gazes wordlessly danced from one to the other. The sound of a distant tree groaning as it was brought to the ground and birds broke free from their canopies.

We prepared for war.

⊲ ⊳

There were many heavily clad knights of Cleria seated upon their own steeds in glistening silver and golden armour. Atop the adjacent hills were the robed mages in their deep grey.

Already, in a swift afternoon, everyone gathered at their stations and stared out towards the lingering trees like a womb waiting to birth carnage.

I waited atop of Zephyr at the forefront while men to either side of me prepared for the first sign of conflict, with spears at the ready. There was a chill breeze which cocooned us, married to a radiating and soothing warmth from the Elder King's blazing eye above.

Hours passed, only the occasional cacophonous crunch within the forest depths telling us of our invaders. Night was coming as the sun tried to draw out its sluggish descent, and the world was painted with twilight strokes. Shadows lengthened, their long fingers stretching over our even longer expressions.

Then the drums started, a soft and foreboding thrum like that of an awakening beast. The rhythm fading softly with each consecutive strike before bursting to life again.

THRUM, thrum, thrum… THRUM, thrum, thrum.

I heard men gulp among the new recruits. "Hold steady! Don't let fear control you!" I ordered. Zephyr was restless under me, his hooves shifting on the beaten soil.

The dancers dispersed among the troops must have shifted in their place, rehearsing choreographed motions and figures for different moments. I imagined how they must have steeled themselves, blocked out any thought that they would be in the midst of war and focused solely on the dance that was to be had.

Then it came—the stampede of feet through the veil of the clustered trees. The drums had stopped. Silence, such a deafening silence that my ears burned from the absent drums. When finally the light of the sun had faded and only our torches breached the night, they came. A force of black and terrifying bodies built for war approached. The surrounding fire of our torches glistened off their hides to grant them further presence. Yet they never advanced too far past the shadow of their trees. Their black, beady eyes glistened like stars.

My army numbered up to ten thousand men. All the captains proceeded over their units and awaited the charge as we looked out towards the treeline. It was impossible to tell how many there truly were.

Their leader was not stupid.

The cover of trees, the drums, the marching of their feet. They wanted us to think their army was larger than it already was, to truly make us afraid of an outright attack. Except for a slight, audible shuffling, the silence gave birth to chirping crickets and the crackle of flame from torches.

"Steady!" I roared into the swelling night, my voice trying to instil bravery in our men.

Or maybe they truly were so large and were trying to make me doubt it?

Elder-damn.

Regardless of which it was, we had no idea as to the true number of their forces.

Somebody roared a command in akar. In response, the forest came alive with such a deep and ferocious bellow that the ground beneath our feet shuddered and flocks of birds burst from the canopies. But not just birds. Suddenly, arcing way up into the sky, came a rain of javelins just like before, but not just javelins. There were arrows in the mix this time. I shuddered, thinking about the implications of their utility.

My heart went worryingly still for a moment until the spears and arrows either recoiled or splintered upon colliding with the invisible wall.

I could breathe again; the archmage wall was holding.

More of the projectiles arched and rained down, colliding against nothing. There were defiant and impatient growls from within the shadowed treeline that vibrated against my skin. But then it stilled. The silence was an unsettling one. It suggested a sort of ordinance, discipline in the face of someone.

This silence did more to unsettle me than the entire horde of akar roaring in unison.

Out from the shadows stepped a familiar figure—the ostensible leader of this marauding horde—as the light of the surrounding torches peeled away one half of the shadows that covered him.

There was a sharp and twisted intelligence in the akar's eyes. His midnight hair was long and draped about his shoulder. His body was clustered with even darker tattoos and his face was decorated with bone piercings. He walked with such a confident gait while the restless horde shifted among the trees.

He wore a large, circular shield on his left arm, and in his right hand there dragged a black cudgel.

The weapon was carried with effect, with intent. He wanted our gaze to shift to it, for it to ensnare our attention. The show unsettled me down to my very core. I could have sworn the akar was looking at me, blinking with uncaring stoicism.

The world went silent; who knew what large swell of souls had congregated here, and yet one could have heard the trickle of a brook in this maddening silence.

Recognition dawned. I remembered tales of one of the many artefact weapons scattered upon Minethria, all made by the Blacksmith himself. Among them was the one weapon gifted to the akar several millennia ago. The Black Conduit. It dragged behind the leader like an entity all its own.

"No…" I muttered under my breath.

The leader approached the barrier, his expression lingering on the sea of mortals that faced him. He stood there alone, one man upon desecrated soil. Soil which had tasted blood countless times before and knew of nothing else. We awaited with armour and steel crafted by the sharpest minds of Cleria, stood alongside warriors who knew the touch of a sword from the moment they could walk. We represented the culmination of humanity's scholarly pursuit and progress. Yet he met all of our eyes without faltering.

The figure stretched out his hand with practised stillness and felt the pushback of the invisible wall. There was no crease but rather a ripple visible in space. The fabric revealed iridescent shades at the corner of his dark palm. Wordlessly, he stalked back and forth from the perimeter like a mad panther, fingers digging into the manifested wall, his gaze never leaving us.

Finally, the akar came back to face me. He was young, perhaps no older than Chroma. To have garnered such a loyal following and turn these war mongering tribes into one single force; my fingers tightened about Zephyr's reign. He could sense my unease, and it infected him. Maxin was right, this akar knew how to put on a performance.

His cudgel hammered against the barrier.

Suddenly, my troops laughed, feeling the tension crack just as much as the iridescent fabric of the barrier.

"Go home, animal!" Called one, galvanised by seeing the barrier hold.

"You are not getting through with that pea-sized brain of yours!"

"Die of the rot, savage!"

My troops erupted into cacophonous laughter, all of them raising their weapons in premature celebration.

"We're not afraid of you!"

"You can't enter!"

The chants picked up speed, but so too did the strikes. I could feel the tremors in my bones.

Again and again the cudgel struck. The tempo of the swings held until too much weight was contained. Each strike hammered with more pause than the last. The akar's focus was steady, unperturbed by jeering and insults. His eyes looked far past even us.

The cudgel struck another time and then another. Suddenly, the weapon's bludgeoning end fell to the ground. Slowly, the akar raised it with greater effort, his muscles straining and bulging.

"Getting tired?" Shouted a soldier.

"Just go home!"

My grasp on the reins tightened. Zephyr must have felt my unease.

Again the thing struck, and there was a crack in the ethereal fabric. The laughter died, deflated into a whimper. Fear spread through our men like a fire.

The akar picked up where we left off, not with chants or jeering of their own, but with the beating of their war drums from within the forest. It was the beating of a heart which spoke for them—the heart of an animal.

Again the cudgel struck, again a crack formed.

The akar was panting on the other side. He raised his weapon nonetheless, his bicep muscles straining at the weight.

From deep within the forest, chants now accompanied the drums. The monstrous, dark troops began to spill from the treeline one after the other.

"*Husa Bok Nala, Husa Bok Nala, Husa Bok Nala.*" The wartribes chanted, charcoal hues and war paint and builds of all kinds spewed forward.

Again another strike, and the barrier vibrated like brittle glass, the crack spreading further.

The akar picked up their pace, weapons in hand with axes and shields and spears and clubs. From the rear came charging aurochs goaded forward by their rear-men. The barrier seemed to falter at the sight of the encroaching force.

The cudgel lifted itself for one final strike. Its wielder strained, roaring even to simply raise the weapon over his own shoulder. He huffed as his people charged from behind. Veins writhed and pulsed all over his body. Muscles went taut with the monstrous strain needed to lift the weapon again.

With one final, bone-chilling roar, the cudgel smashed against the barrier and a layer of reality shattered and dissipated. There was no sound. Nonetheless, a ringing filled all our ears—and so began the bloodshed.

Chapter Eighty-Nine

EREFIEL

Museya embraces art in many forms. Dancers, poets, musicians, painters. But if one is lucky enough to be an Inspired, it does not mean they are lucky enough to be a Muse. To uphold the same level of skill and potential after years, to be able to maintain it in the face of an audience, to be able to maintain your voice even though the rules of art will threaten it: that is what makes one truly an Inspired. Even more so, if you decide to take your skills to the battlefield, to sing courage into the hearts of men or screech shrill madness into the souls of the enemy, know that a single second of broken concentration can mean the end of your men, or even your life.

—Introductory lecture for Inspired in Museya

T he clash of spears inevitably went in the favour of the akar, though many fell on their side as well. The tide pushed us in as I rushed forward on horseback.

Supporting our troops was a choir of four. They married their unique instruments to form a tapestry of emboldening power. The bard's lute imparted us with courage, the drums bestowed power, the flute gave us morale and the violin quelled our fear: they were the conductors of our battle.

The dancers were lost within the ebb and flow, but I could feel their rhythm. The way they shifted on their heels and performed, guiding the formation of my army. Pushing into the clashing enemy, tightening soldiers into robust forms who could not even tell that their cohesion hung upon the fragile focus of performers. I felt their dance in the way my men shuffled, in the way Zephyr moved left and right like a boat at sea.

Hidden spears under foliage sprung erect as the aurochs ran straight into them, their painful cries indicative of mortal wounds. Those that passed through were met by a shield wall that offered little resistance. The aurochs blew right past despite the brown ink brushed upon the shields. The stampede stripped one of our dancers from their spot, and I felt the formation buckle to the right.

As the beasts lost themselves among our troops, the archmages were already at work. Their magic dragged the panicking beasts underground, until their fearful cries were silenced beneath the dirt.

The akar forces were truly terrifying, but the tight neck of our position and our overbearing numbers funnelled their efforts and allowed us to hold the line.

"From above!" Called someone.

I barely noticed it from my visor, but there, streaking across the sky, were giant bats. Then came ruin. Round spheres were dropped from above, the contents bursting on impact. I only got a glimpse of the horror that ensued, but I knew that it would be burnt in my mind until my dying day.

My men shuddered, their skin beginning to split and sizzle. Pallid faces suddenly turning a sickly grey as eyes withered and shrunk in their sockets. Coloured spores glistened in the air. The spores seemed to die out and wither quickly themselves, but whoever stood within the area had sudden fungi sprout from their skin while their own bodies turned into withered husks.

I retreated to the next line, grabbing a young soldier, easily no older than sixteen, and pulled him up to me. Terror and confusion gripped his body; I barely managed to hold his terrified gaze.

Again, I felt the death of another dancer through the buckling formation of our troops, their magnetic pull was gone and our men spread haplessly within the untended chaos.

"Soldier! I need you to listen!" With whatever measure of lucidity the boy could muster, he nodded his head in stutters.

"Go and order the mages to provide us with cover from the airdrop!" I thought back to the Haar. The supply we had was enough only for a single barrier. There wasn't enough left for a second aerial one. "No matter what it takes, remove the bats!" The boy shook himself lucid and ran without another word.

Another round of bats swarmed from above and dropped their loads before arcing back. I saw riding atop the bats were akar with animal skulls as masks.

One of the payloads dropped right above me. I was closed in from all sides, unable to retreat. All I could do was turn away and brace for the impact but it never came. The shouts of combat continued about me.

I turned and saw one of the mages close by use Haar to grasp the falling bag of spores and fling it at the akar.

"Thank you!" I called out, unable to fully make out the features of the mage. He nodded and moved onto wherever else he was needed. From the rear, I was glad to find my own captains having an answer of their own. Archery units stepped forward and let loose a volley of arrows that arched through the sky and pierced the enclosing akar. One of the bats was shot dead and began to spiral. Another had their package destroyed and became victim to the spores along with their rider; they too hurtled down from above.

"Hold!" I roared. The sounds became more fervent, the muses playing their song and instilling us with strength. I doubted anyone could hear me. The chaos of battle had already unravelled the cross-stitched coherence of our troops.

The dancers that remained tried desperately to maintain formation, but the clustered troops and advancing akar made it nigh impossible.

Javelins, and arrows too, tried to strike down our musicians from their posts, but small bubbles of erected barriers kept them safe.

I returned to the fray; my sword was a quick gust of wind gaining momentum with every strike and slash deep enough to be fatal, but not too far as to break my building speed.

I rode on horseback. Zephyr rushing to and fro from the line wherever I was needed. My blade shrouded in a casing of wind and my shield by my side.

"No matter what happens! They cannot breach!" I roared, stained in the blood of the conquered. What few men could hear me and weren't occupied gave their affirming cries in turn.

Slowly, as I found myself within the rhythm of this exchange, I realized that the incoming force of akar was truly oppressive. It wasn't just a couple hundred. They came as an endless flood of forces.

Again, the next round of bats came from above and dropped their loads. Javelins and arrows breaking from canopies and arching into our forces like parasitic needles hungry for our blood.

Our archers fired up into the sky but the enemy had grown wise to our move. The bats flying ever higher and out of reach of our attack. Yet they continued to travel further into our forces and dropped their packages on our backlines—our rear recognized too late what was happening. The packages were delivered and the spores devoured everything within its reach.

Panic spread. I heard the momentary doubt cause the violinist to slip up and birth a costly screech from his instrument. Quickly, he shifted tone to focus their fear-abating song on our rear. Our frontline broke as a result. All it took was one or two fear stricken soldiers to flee and for the enemy to break through.

I tried my best to stem the flow, but more and more of our line steadily retreated.

Again, the bats came and soared high above from the reach of our lamed archers. What I didn't expect was the sudden spear of lightning which struck down from the heavens. A clear branching pillar of light that split the world into two dark halves. The clouds roiled and spun.

There was a deep and furious rumble from above. Roasted and smoking, one of the winged beasts dropped from the sky and so too did lightning bend and streak for the remaining aerial akar.

What few of the bats remained paused. Strikes of lightning wreaked havoc on the enemy's rear. The forest caught fire with a furious roar as the very sky itself became alight with a hungry glow. It was almost as if Thickwood itself was granted a voice to speak of its frenzy.

The battlefield was alight, and all the shadows were chased away. There was a great, pained moan as a blazing tree fell. Akar stepped forward from the forest like demons of flame rolling around in the filth and blood of their brethren. Embers like distant fiery stars danced in our vision.

"For Cleria!" I shouted, despite the encroaching enemy.

The akar had pushed in enough to spring our improvised defences. From the sides, where marked stones were inconspicuously laid, golems began to form into large and hulking bodies.

They attacked inwards through the flanks and provided a moment of respite for our own forces.

All it took was for the akar to take a single step back for me to see the fallen sons and fathers trampled underneath their tide.

Finally, our troops took their foothold and pushed back the enemy; the ensuing volley of archers, lightning strikes and artillery of mages showed their merit. The enemy tripped over their fallen allies.

"Push them back!" I cried over the masses. My men's morale boosted from the shifting tide. The muses picked up pace as well, their notes giving the shove we needed to push.

Shields held the enemy back while hidden spears poked out and killed one after another. Their bodies fell limp to the ground.

We could win. Suddenly, the body of a golem was sundered into boulders. The other golem was swarmed and taken down by a troop of akar that tore and ripped its granular limbs apart. My own men were flung into the air from the sides as blood splattered in great streaks of red: their leader was taking action. The reserved patience and silence of this individual unnerved me. Recognizing the pivotal shift, he must have lunged into battle to save their momentum.

I had to stop him.

I snapped my reins and charged, Zephyr huffing and puffing heavily as I strode forward with sword at the ready. Zephyr crashed into something, whinnying as I was flung forward into a huddle of stacked bodies. Grime and dirt, muddled with blood, clung to me. Zephyr gave panicked cries in the background. I turned in horror to find his stomach torn open; an impish and hunched akar was feasting on his innards.

"No!" I cried. Fury claimed me. I realised then the absolute chaos on the front lines. Chaos unravelled formations until it became a skirmish between lone soldiers. It was something else entirely to be above this tide of carnage, rather than to be drowning in its sea of blood.

Quickly, I noticed the overbearing club held above my head and I narrowly rolled away to the side. On my upturn, my blade found the akar's neck. I was now in the middle of the fray with no time to mourn Zephyr's death.

I stepped into the skirmish, my sword swinging and whipping on its own. Quickly, and as light as a feather, it cut through the enemies standing in my way until I came to stand before the impish akar feasting on Zephyr. The being was hideous. Blood smeared her mouth and all the way up her forearms. Her chest was bare, allowing breasts with no meat to sag. Zephyr was still alive, huffing and trying to raise his head in agony.

She did not move before my blade liberated her head from her shoulders.

I advanced. My blade was an unnoticeable scythe, silently slitting the throats of akar as if a whispered claim of Kaelu. Yet their leader was an indomitable force that flung my men side to side.

His movements were refined. I was at awe how deliberate his attacks were. Each strike had a beautiful savagery to it; dictating the flow of exchange. Even the way he wielded the Black Conduit spoke of a certain creativity. Two of my men charged from the side. His circular shield caught the brunt of one on his right, while the cudgel absorbed a blow from his left. He gyrated, sending the men stumbling through their momentum and bringing the weight of the cudgel down onto the right-attacker.

Two more soldiers charged from the front. The akar knocked aside the first blow with his cudgel and swung it with both hands into the attacker. The explosive force sent the soldier straight into his own men and knocked them to the ground.

As another slew came charging from the side the cudgel slammed into the ground to form a crater. The weapon was then dragged through the dirt and swung upwards, sending my men into the air.

The attacks stopped. The akar turned to face me, my own men stepping away. Blood splattered all about. Cries and roars intermingled with one another. We sized one another; him with his stripped down and bare body, just a round shield and his cudgel at hand, while I stood there with my own dented and grimy armour. Light from the burning forest reflected off what little polish my armour still had. I noticed the cudgel was giving off a slight ember-glow beneath its obsidian exterior. A glow which pulsed and ebbed until it was completely gone.

I went to remove my helmet, failing to notice the akar coming from my side. I would have easily fallen underneath the weight of his axe if it weren't for their leader barking an order to a halt. He snarled something. It was enough to make the other akar back away disgruntled but with a respecting bow.

I nodded. "Thank you." I had to shout and was unsure if the enemy could understand me.

"You fight with strength and honour. It is only right that I face you with the respect you deserve." I was impressed at the akar's mastery of the Bayrish language, despite the crude and guttural accent attached to it.

"Retreat, and we can stop with all this bloodshed."

"I could say the same thing," their leader said, though we both knew that neither was going to relent. "Tell me the name of the man I will kill."

"Erefiel Numyana."

The akar nodded. "I am Sun'Ra, son of Muktow. Warlord of all akar." And with that, he got into a low stance, his shield at the ready and cudgel in hand.

I had heard of the name before; Muktow. But at that moment, my mind was too muddled with war to ponder more on it. I leered at his umbral weapon and discerned its properties. It was the complete opposite of mine. While each unhindered swing of my sword bid it speed and lightness, his weapon of choice only gained weight and heft with each subsequent attack.

We stood there in the aurora of a burning forest, the cries of our men surrounding us as we heard the last bit of life slip through their lips. Sweat, blood and the scent of burning enveloped our world. The dancing fire formed beautiful contours about us.

I poised myself, shield and sword at the ready as the remaining fighters spread out, leaving a small island unto ourselves.

I pounced.

Chapter Ninety

EREFIEL

*Not all legendary artefacts stem from the hands of Blacksmith. There
are the fabled Seven weapons, made from primordial colour and with their
whereabouts unknown. Yet there are some even more divine and mysterious.
The Cragged Staff is such one weapon. It is made from twisted wood and
appears warped. It is said that trapped within is the first lightning strike
to have ever been created. Since it was never thrown, the surrounding of
the lightning calcified and became encased. One can only shudder at what
immense power would be unleashed if freed.*

—PRIMORDIAL WEAPONS — THE FLIGHT

I swung my blade up high before Sun'Ra's shield could react,
causing him to duck under my strike. Quickly, I pressed the
momentum. My blade redirected course and slashed the akar
on his right shoulder. I pushed my momentum.

Sun'Ra did not retreat at my advance. Instead, he brashly stepped
in. His cudgel swung at my side. My shield caught its weight and I
realised too late my error.

His next strike made my ears ring, though my own blade did not
lose its momentum. Sun'Ra's shield rose to bat my swing over his head.

The Black Conduit came again from the same side. I felt its meta-
physical weight rise and, instead of retreating, I allowed the path of

my blade to dictate my currents. I followed through with my attack, knowing full well if I were to draw back my swinging arm, it would lose half its gained speed. I had to dive deeper into this fluid stroke of blinding attacks; our weapons grazing a breath's length from one another as even the slightest error meant death.

In one swift and fluid motion, I went low. I spun in a complete circle and allowed myself to explode upwards; it granted my sword even more speed.

Sun'Ra had no choice but to step back, but I could tell he adapted quickly. As he stumbled, Sun'Ra swung his cudgel at the ground. The proceeding impact forming a small crater, adding weight to his weapon, and providing him with an extra bounce to distance himself.

There he stood, waiting. Taking his weapon before him and banging it against his shield to taunt me, but in truth, he was keeping his cudgel's weight right where he wanted it. The soft embers within the black weapon pulsed like a waiting heart.

I acted in kind, my sword dancing in my grip, spinning in complete circles until the surrounding wind attached itself to the blade's steel and concealed its length in a shroud.

Again, I charged forward, and Sun'Ra struck, but his swing was too early. Did he make a mistake?

No.

His cudgel turned the ground before him into upheaved dirt and dust, simultaneously creating cover for himself as well as robbing me of my footing.

Still, I had to persist. I attempted an overhead swing; the dust formed eddies on either side from where I cut downwards.

From my flank came the hidden strike. I was only able to lift my shield at the last moment.

I went back in time to when Nora's punch flung me through the air. The world spun about me.

I gasped, my vision unclear as I tried to orient myself. The rising flames of the forest were the growing curtains of this hellish performance, a spotlight to reveal our battle. I could see the ribbons of fire dancing like spectators until Sun'Ra's approach blocked out the starkness.

The akar stood there, cudgel tapping with immaculate control against his shield.

I rose to my feet, looking at my own shield that was now ruined, and the face of my father formed into a contorted dent. I realized then that the shield was a liability. It only made Sun'Ra's strikes heavier.

I allowed the shield to slip from my off-hand and clatter to the ground, its bottom point stabbing into the earth before toppling completely.

Sun'Ra's shield made things harder. Any attempt at hindering my momentum made me lose advantage, while his weapon became only more dangerous.

The shield wasn't enough.

Stabbing my sword into the ground, I began to steadily remove my armour. First, I removed the cape, usually a vibrant white, now a dirty and ragged thing that puddled to the ground. One gauntlet removed after another. My unclasped pauldrons slipped from my shoulders and plopped onto the wide-eyed gaze of a dead Clerian soldier. My cuirass unbuckled and brought over my head. My greaves and cuisses unfastened, so they would part from me. And finally, I doffed my hauberk that clinked like linked coins. What was left behind was a man in a sweat-drenched tunic, left barefooted and in brown pants.

"Your people carry more and more and more on their shoulder in the face of death, believing it keeps you safe. This look suits you better," Sun'Ra said, his cudgel tapping against his shield with remarkable restraint.

I said nothing in return, feeling my toes wiggle against the blood-stained soil and a breeze of wind tousled the feathers on my scalp. I stepped forward. Dancing embers brushed past and the scent of burnt flesh and wood filled my nostrils.

"Be ready," I said. I raised my weapon with both hands and prepared myself.

It must have seemed like a single step to Sun'Ra when I closed the gap in an instant. If it weren't for his wild instincts, his head would have already belonged to me. Sun'Ra barely managed to dodge my sword, and that was at a breath's length as he collapsed to the ground.

I was behind him, skidding to a stop and running back. My blade switched between the grip of my left and right hand like a dance partner tossed between two leads.

The roar of battle encased me, surrounded me on all sides. My bare feet now battered against soil, and I could feel the heartbeat of war as if it were my own.

I called upon the blood of my father to course through me unrestrained. I was truly a bird in flight. Somewhere in the back of my mind, I thought of Nora and when I first showed her my blade; I wished she were here to see me in action.

Without the encumbering joints, weight, and all else to hold me back, I could insert all my focus into offence and allow my blade to guide my course. I gave myself to the flow of battle; my thoughts going silent as the song of clashing steel and the dance of war were all that mattered.

Again and again, Sun'Ra swung his cudgel all about me, the flow of my body weaving and dodging only to move back in when he was stuck in his movements.

Though his left side was mostly untouched on account of the shield, his right was a display of dozens of cuts and blood pooled from him. Desperate and long swings to his rear collided with nothing. The rush and pull of air sounding like a hungry wail coming from the weapon—it desired collision. I vaulted above the giant's head and nicked him behind the knee.

Sun'Ra's reflexes were terrifying; there was an almost prophetic instinct to this man.

Eventually, with his weapon starved of momentum, I started to parry his swings. A slight angle of my blade gave him zero weight while simultaneously redirecting his attacks.

All my attacks were surgical and precise, only skin deep so as to never lose momentum.

Again I charged forward, closing in on the end as the akar began to fall from exhaustion alone.

Aiming at his right hip, my blade shrouded in wind swung true. Yet Sun'Ra did something that I could never have expected. He jumped towards my weapon. My blade struck deep, but that didn't matter.

Before I could pull out my weapon, his hand grasped the distorted wind before him and found purchase on its cutting edge. Like tattered, invisible rags, the wind unravelled. "I got you." Sun'Ra growled victoriously; only a light seam of blood trickling down his lip.

His forehead struck mine, the attack disoriented and filled my vision with dots.

Again there came another one, and the world seemed to slip past me.

The third brought me to my knees, as I no longer knew where I was. Blood melded with the colours of rising flames.

Everything was in a daze. I could smell the intermingled scent of blood and sweat all about me. There were distant war cries and death throes.

I felt a force break my sword arm. The lancing pain turned me lucid again as I cried out. I was violently brought back into reality. The scent of death and burning decay remained thick in the air. In the distance, I could sense a blinding light burning away the dark.

Sun'Ra took a pause. "Day is coming. It seems the Elder King wishes to witness your demise," he said, his own words heavy and laboured, yet no less stoic.

Was this it?

I fell to my rear, feeling what could have only been the black cudgel strike down and break my leg. This sent me back into the disorientating depths.

A wince escaped me. I crawled away with my one good arm. Soldiers all around me witnessed my desperate situation and tried to run to my aid, but were swatted away by rallying akar. My fall filled the invaders with renewed vigour until they even trampled over the bodies of their own dead brethren.

I was broken, sundered, the pride of the troops brought to prostrate himself before the enemy. Sun'Ra made sure to make it a spectacle, to show all how their pride had been brought low and sundered their morale.

Sun'Ra stepped patiently towards me. His cudgel now hammered once more against his shield. He looked close to death himself. Many incisions across his body left a trail of blood behind him. His feet left scarlet prints with each limp. The wound I had inflicted on his hip continued to bleed with the sword of Bereniel jutting out.

His cudgel picked up speed, faster and faster as the rhythm hammered until a hefty strike imbued it with power. A small shock wave spread from where the man stood as his shield split in two, both parts dropping to the ground, forgotten. The weapon's ember-glow trailed within like trapped ribbons.

I shuddered a private gasp, as if it were my soul readying itself to escape my body. I saw my life flash before my eyes. I thought of Nora, all the things I wished for her, of all the things she could be. I thought of Chroma, wishing that he'd become the man I believed he could be. I thought of Dalila, praying that she could find happiness in spite of everything.

Saru stood there in my mind's eye, waiting for me to return. Even in my final moment, I hoped that Saru would still find purpose without me.

Mother, her glacial presence suddenly seemed so soft and welcoming. I felt a cold drift over me and thought back to a time when I was but a child cradled in her arms. Was I just imagining it? A wistful fantasy in my final moments?

All about me, the chants of the akar grew, yet somehow they sounded so distant.

"Husa Bok Nala, Husa Bok Nala, Husa Bok Nala."

"Do you hear that, Erefiel Numyana? It means 'Our folk have risen.' We will bring low the Elders. Know that you have fought valiantly, son of White-Hawk." Sun'Ra leveraged a foot to turn me onto my back.

The act sent pain throughout my entire body.

It didn't matter, didn't matter at all what the hazy voice of Sun'Ra said in a distant realm. I imagined father with me, training me in the yard or telling me stories about this magical world. I recalled my bed time where he shared his battle against the dragons. The memory felt like it was within my grasp. War suddenly seemed so trivial; the concepts of honour and prestige so hollow and empty.

I thought of my father. Perhaps the most prolific zerub to have ever lived. Would he have been proud of me? I hoped so.

I blinked one last time, my hazy vision clearing as the world spread a greyish hue across its sky. For one final time, I took in the surrounding sight. There, standing upon a clearing to the east, I saw Nora break free with Chroma in tow.

I smiled. They made it back alive. Good. I was glad.

Sun'Ra's cudgel raised itself above his head. The akar roared victoriously, their very cry making my whole shattered body tremble.

I closed my eyes. It was time. I didn't even feel it when the mace came crashing down on me.

Chapter Ninety-One

DALILA

Some spirits in Minethria are said to be so engrossed in their final tasks in life that they are loath to abandon it. Still they roam Minethria, unwilling to let go. If you happen upon such a spirit, consider it best to avoid them.

—Guide to the foolish traveller, by Glassius Adams

Watching the endless gathering of troops depart towards Greyhill left behind a foreboding omen. There were rumours that spread among the people like a whisper brought from a distant land. War? Ruin? The threat of a siege? These were concepts that were entirely alien to citizens, so people spoke of it like a distant relative that nobody really felt comfortable to meet, but that everyone had an opinion on.

This gave my conviction further gravity as I saw the inherent need to visit my old home.

Though, truth be told, I was afraid and conflicted more than anything else. Would they welcome me with open arms? Would the wrinkles of time show themselves as tender lines or erosion? I wondered if mother would still be smiling so lovingly. I imagined father doing anything other than working his farm and failed—I just hoped that Fredrick was helping him out. Though I wondered suddenly if he ever did get married to the Horsestead girl. What was her name? I felt a pang of guilt when all that came to mind was '*rat-face*'; I was astutely aware of how much I had changed since then.

I thought of Ben. How he must have grown! Did he still play pretend wizard with Erefiel's feather? I grinned at the thought of being greeted by the *White Mage*. Then again, he must have grown up quite a bit since last I saw him. There was also Tom. I remembered him as just a helpless child. The old Tom I had known would be gone, replaced by a walking, talking boy. Was he as exuberant as Ben? Maybe as unlikable as Fredrick? Perhaps someone else altogether.

Did he know about me? Did father, mother, or the others ever tell him about his older sister? Or perhaps it was a past better left unspoken. This thought made my doubt resurface.

The sun was at its peak. The battle had not yet begun.

I sat within my coach with Ievarus opposite me. I couldn't help but feel growing excitement. The fear was still there: fear of rejection, fear of them wishing I had never returned. It was terrifying enough to make me grasp my own hands tightly until they turned bone-white.

There was also another conflicting emotion. I felt guilt. So many men had come together and now fought on the front lines, giving their lives for us. And here I was, leaving them to visit my family. I could use my magic. I could help all of them.

There was an unease in the air that told me the war was coming that very night. Yet the thought of never seeing my family again terrified me. If nothing else, I felt I was permitted this one selfish act.

As I sat inside the drawn coach, I thought of Erefiel and prayed for his safety. My mind also spared a moment for Nora. Her story was one of suffering and plight. I thought of Chroma; there was a goodness to that akar. I wished him no ill either. I never did get to thank him personally. I wondered if he even remembered who I was.

We trundled past Crowtown. The akar settlement just behind it was out of sight. Then there was Basksin somewhere in the distance.

I heard the whinnying of Horsestead's stable and knew we were getting close.

As we neared the Reed farm, there was a quiet and unsettling air all about it. My chest tightened, and a tension filled me. Was it because I was about to see my family? My subdued fear suddenly returned with greater intensity. Perhaps it was the miasmic cloud of terror which built above Greyhill, transported across the lands by a gust of seaward wind.

As the coach came to a halt, Ievarus and I stepped out, walking towards what used to be my home so long ago. Everything seemed smaller to me as we paced up the gravel road. I remembered the well as being old and dilapidated, yet with an ominous energy to it. I recalled seeing something hidden in its bowels, something which wanted to pull me under. Now, it just looked like a rather sorry thing. Even the size of the planted crops was bigger in memory; a great clustered field of reeds hiding predators in its embrace. Now, the reeds simply bent at our passing with the slightest breeze running through them. I began to realise how humbly small my youth was. In the distance, I watched with repressed shame at the goat barn where I spent my private nights etching another scar to my collection. That was the only part of my past that had grown with me.

Ievarus stepped forward and spoke, one of those rare moments they chose to. "This is your home?"

"Yes. I used to live here. My family still does."

"What is... family?" Ievarus asked in that drawn out way they did.

"Family is... family. I don't know how to explain it. I am bound by blood to mine. My brothers and I shared the same mother and father."

"The Elder King is my father."

I quickly realized how trite it would be to try and explain such things that we mortals simply took for granted. "A woman and a man, they come together and..." it felt almost wrong trying to explain sex to such a clueless being as Ievarus. "They commit in intercourse, think of it as a ritual. Then the mother gives birth. The bond you have with the Elder King is something else entirely."

"Birth? Like a surrogate?" Ievarus asked.

I wasn't quite sure as to what Ievarus meant, but I nodded. "I suppose so. Yes."

"Dalila. Am I a man? Or a woman?"

I paused and looked at Ievarus, who looked at me with a deep curiosity. "You have some features of a woman, but mostly those of a man. Elder beings have no gender, not unless you choose them yourself."

"Why not?"

"To be a man or woman is very much a mortal concept. A higher being such as yourself doesn't need such things. It is not for me to say if you are a man or a woman; that is for you to decide. Your predecessor, Kaelu, never did decide. And Vikma bore the body of a woman but decided to be a man."

"How will I know which one I am?"

I shrugged. "There are some things that even I don't know, Ievarus."

⋘ ⋙

As we neared my old home, the strangeness about this place became even more apparent. Something felt off. The sun had already begun its descent and I could see in the distance several pillars of smoke coming from Greyhill. I did a private prayer and spiralled my chest. I felt a nauseating cloud far, far away; a constant entity with such a presence that it took but an inkling of my awareness and held onto it. I assumed hundreds of men were dying at Greyhill. But from where I stood, their cries were but silent screams to my deaf ears.

I dismissed the thought when I reached the end of the steep path. The home was far bigger in my memories; it seemed almost impossible that we all lived in this small house.

The words were caught in my throat. It felt wrong to call upon mother and father, as if it were a right I had lost long ago.

One of the windows kept slamming over and over on account of a passing breeze; it was as if it were trying to break free from its hinges. Surprisingly, I was glad Ievarus was here, in case things worsened.

Father should be well at work, verbally lashing at my siblings to stop being lazy. So why was everything so silent? There was barely a sliver of sunlight left as the world warped into darkness. The barn door was still open. Someone needed to close the shutters.

Instead of calling for mother or father, I instead settled on my siblings. "Fredrick?" I called out cautiously.

"Ben? Tom?" The last name felt alien to me.

I walked to the swaying front door of my home. Just a small gap gave purview inside. "Dad?" I called out. "Mom?"

Hesitantly, I pushed open the door. What a horrible wail escaped me. My mother drifted slowly through the air alongside father. Their disembowelled organs floated as if through water. A red light pulsed from them like a faint heartbeat. Blood ran from the abyss of their emptied sockets and I felt as if mother's frozen expression of horror was trained on me. Immediately my mind went into denial and shock. I fell to the floor and shuddered. Then I wailed.

My tears came as a stream. My pain was unbearable. My sobs turned painful.

Mother's form was draped in a dress streaked in red, the hems of it rippled from a passing gust as if to make sure she wasn't just sleeping. Father drifted, his jaw open as if to scream.

"Fredrick?" I called out with my broken voice, praying for a response.

My wobbling legs came to stand as I worked my way to the barn. Inside, I found the drifting forms of Ben and another. I assumed this child was Tom. Barely seen six summers, his infantile lips were slightly parted with his last words still stuck to them. I could sense his final moments being bathed in confusion and terror. I made out dirty blonde hair underneath the dirt and blood which stuck to him. He was wearing suspenders, and I imagined him to have been healthy and kind. I watched him drift with a red glow of his own.

I turned to Ben; he had grown for sure, and I sensed that it had been more than just a physical growth. He was wearing a brown shirt and overalls. His hair had grown out. Ben looked as if he had been in the middle of a great growth spurt.

The goats were bleating, biting and prodding at my siblings' lifeless corpses.

On the floor, in a pool of their own blood, there drifted like a small boat of Erefiel's white feather, now stained red.

"Fredrick?!" I called out. The only one to not be among the dead.

I searched endlessly around the field, the barns and the rooms. Ievarus shadowed me all the while, watching the carnage with vapid disinterest and me with great curiosity. It sickened me for this tragedy of mine, for this play that mirrored The Futile Resistance of Mellezi to be of such interest to this spawn.

I turned to Ievarus. "Leave me alone!" I screamed shrilly. Sobs escaped me. Ievarus blinked emotionlessly and followed behind. The world was so unbearably quiet here. So lonely. I screamed for my family. The wails coming unbidden.

I only barely took notice of the fading light, the abstract shadows which stretched and stitched together like an extension of my own despair. Time and time again, I went to my house and gazed upon my parents' lifeless bodies drifting through the air. Again and again, I would hug the wall, carefully sliding along its contours while my eyes remained peeled. It was as if there was some magical barrier compelling me to not get close, not touch their desecrated forms.

I tore through the field over and over, the erect reed crops bobbing at my discordant passing. How many hours had I been searching, how many hours had it been since I mindlessly returned to the same locations and checked again and again with silent pleads, endless tears and a wordless Seed to witness my suffering? I never did find Fredrick but a set of footprints behind the house.

The sight immediately grabbed my attention, tears continued to flow unabated, and I had to wipe my cheeks to take a closer look. The set of footprints belonged to a man with an irregular gait. A little further down, I found a trail of blood leading into the forest alongside a white and bloodstained rag knotted to form a loop, almost as if it were a blindfold.

Realisation struck me like a knife through the chest, twisting and tugging at my insides. I wailed my contempt, my disparity, gave voice to my bottomless sense of betrayal. Brother Clemence deceived me. I did not know why, nor did I care. *Your suffering is beautiful.* His words rung in my ears. *When your friend died, how did you feel?* He was curious. *Tell me about your family.* How sickening his smile now was. My soul wrenched itself apart, thinking about how nurturing Brother Clemence acted, talking to me of kindness when Yasmin's blood still clung to his hands. But why? It didn't matter.

"Ievarus." My voice was a smouldering and deep thing. "Find Brother Clemence. Kill him."

Ievarus blinked apathetically. "I do not interfere with mortal affairs."

I looked up at Ievarus with a seething ire in my eyes. There was a brief moment of understanding in Ievarus. "I feel… rage."

I reached out to the Seed, fumbling at their chest with quivering arms, until finally I pulled out the coloured disk.

"You wish to learn about fear? Find him! Find that *creature* and make him see terror! Tear him apart! Disembowel him. Carve it into his flesh. Tear out his eyes and destroy him and you will see this turn into the colour of such beautiful fear like *nothing* else ever will be." I did not recognize this person. Did not know where this voice came from. But I relished in it. I let myself sink into its pernicious embrace.

I slammed the disc into Ievarus' chest, my words laced with such caustic venom that I feared it would burn my very skin. I was drunk on loss, drunk on rage, drunk on feelings of betrayal to such an extent that I knew these words were not my own.

Again, Ievarus repeated themselves. "I do not interfere in the affairs of mortals."

"Ievarus! So help me, if you do not do as I say, I will *vanish*. No longer will you know about aspects, no longer will I answer your questions. You will *never* find your purpose."

I knew deep inside that this wasn't me. This distasteful and horrid voice was something pitiful and grown out of grief.

Ievarus was gone in a blink, leaving behind a gust of wind where they had stood, and leaving me to my despondent sorrow. I fell again to my knees, huddled and weeping. My throat ached and turned hoarse as I looked into the uncaring depths of Dreamwood in front of me. In my hand, I held the bloodstained rag of Brother Clemence. Why did he do it? Did he wish to hurt me? To see me suffer? I did not understand.

For some peculiar reason, I brought the rag close to my chest as if bringing it into the fold of my mourning. I cried with such unfettered sorrow.

This was all I had for the time being: grief. Left with unending melancholy, I sank ever deeper into a pit of umbral tar.

I looked to the skies. It was already nightfall. Far in the distance, there was a glowing halo of flame that cried out against the night. I cried and wailed. From Mount Morniar, the rumble of a storm formed.

Chapter Ninety-Two
NORA

The Plague Knight is a walking distributor and liberator of disease. Whatever illness he accepts will be removed from the victim. Can you imagine? The pain he endures from all those illnesses? Never able to die? To suffer like that in eternal silence? And he will continue to do so, until he imparts his gifts through way of his coiled sword.

—BANNED SCRIPTUM OF THE EXILED SCHOLAR
MARCENDIUS DELEFRAM

Erefiel died before my eyes and turned my world red. My battle cry was fuelled with fire. My heart beat with such unmatched energy that I felt the scales upon my limbs rattle like a hundred hornet wings.

My feet turned into curved blades as I leapt into the fray.

The impact of the cudgel was embedded in my mind, the way the dust rose, the limp and caved in form of Erefiel on the ground. I let rage consume me.

Up in the air, my two arms turned into bladed whips linked by a thread of molten gold between each segment. My knee-guard knocked with crushing force into the temple of an akar as I pushed in from their flank.

I whirred and slashed without any thought in mind, my whips

thrashing with such virility as if sentient. The power of the prosthetics was indiscriminate. My whirlwind of blades continued to rend more and more of the enemy to shreds.

All around us, the dark of night was burnt away with the premature rising of the sun and the smouldering flames of the forest. The enemy fell to my onslaught. My left arm stretched out as far as it could, swinging through the crowds. Its momentum was robbed. Too many akar clogged its path as they all clambered onto my stretched arm in a game of tug. Again, my feet transformed. Heavy devices which punctured the earth and rooted me like an obsidian tree. I did not pull, instead, the whip receded back to me with such speed that any akar that still held on was drawn in too.

It felt like my shoulder was going to rip from its socket. I imbued even more power into my limbs. A melting warmth burnt in my chest as the fruit glowed even brighter. The liquid fire that flowed within me shone so bright that its currents were visible through my skin.

My right whip transformed back into an arm. The chittering of the scales was deafening as I gave a defying roar and punched with all the strength I had channelled. The akar I hooked received the full brunt of it as the ground ruptured. Bodies were flung into the air in a shower of viscera, blood and limbs.

I panted. My arms and legs transformed back into regular limbs. The excited chittering of my scales dampened as I readied myself for the horde that still remained.

I just bit a chunk out of the enemy's flank; an unexpected variable in this slaughter. Yet the element of surprise was only momentary. Exhaustion came over me, but I still stood my ground. The akar before me were pushed back from the small crater I left in the earth, its hole mounting with the remains of the dead.

"Nora!" I heard Chroma cry from behind.

"Come! I will deliver you all to your deaths!" I cried at the stunned dozen or so akar, feeling the taste of burnt wood cake my throat.

Chroma came to my side and scavenged a Clerian sword from the ground. He was obviously out of his depth as he struggled to make the weapon his own.

"Nora! Instruct me!" He cried.

"What?"

"Tell me what to do!"

"Guard my back!" I said instinctively. Chroma obliged.

All about us, the war raged on. The burning forest was losing its battle against the rising sun. Our collective gathering of akar, Chroma and myself were an island unto ourselves, separate from the disparaging clash of Cleria versus akar horde. The ones who eyed me collected themselves, their axes, spears, claws and bludgeoning clubs at the ready. They advanced.

There was an echoing cry from above. It sounded like thunder scraping against metal. My gaze craned to see the silhouette of a great manta ray stretched over the clouds. The akar came to a stop as their gazes, too, wandered to the sky. There was the sound again. Deafening. Majestic. Ear-piercingly shrill and as if distorted by water.

The manta ray dove, its fins flapping. It was the largest I had ever seen.

Plummeting from above was a streaking ball as white as snow. It was coming right at us.

"Move!" Chroma cried. He tried his best to lend me haste as we veered away. My prosthetics were exhausted and all I managed was to limp.

There was a shrill screech, different from the distorted echo from before. The crash sent Chroma and me forward as we landed flat on our stomachs. I coughed. A cloud of dust rose and slowly settled. I turned to see what cannonball had nearly flattened us.

It was no cannonball.

The being rose to their full height and gave another shrill screech that punctured ears. It was the size of two mighty bears and was a walking boulder in comparison to the akar. There were feathers instead of fur. It turned. The being was some mixture of bear with the head of an owl. Its face pressed into its head with a small beak and its beady eyes. It spread its arms to reveal the hefty weight of its paws with razor-sharp claws.

It did not wait for the akar. Immediately, the being leapt forward and swiped at the enemy. The charcoal-skinned warriors were torn open, revealing the scarlet contents packed within. If the force of the impact didn't kill them, then the rending claws did.

The akar redirected their attention towards this beast, which threatened their flank.

Chroma ducked his neck under my prosthetic to support my weight. My right leg practically dragged behind. I turned to the surreal display of power from this beast. But the akar stood their ground with frightening ferociousness. Their numbers swarmed about and cut its flesh. The beast roared shrilly, turning to punch down a crushing palm, before swinging in an arc to toss aside the building numbers.

Chroma urged me to move faster. Two akar came rushing from the side. My right arm took its shield form to block the incoming axe, while Chroma jumped out from cover to stab them through the throat. His scavenged sword was lodged tight. The second akar came swinging with their club. Thinking quick, Chroma took the dead akar's axe and, with surprising reflexes, deflected the strike and ended the second akar by embedding the axe into their skull.

We scampered through the side, and stopped every so often to deal with a stray akar or two.

I looked up to the manta ray again and noticed a towering form of armour plagued by rust. It leapt from the manta ray. The being was in free fall, its long limbs spread open. Its cape was a deep copper-rust that was in tatters, billowing frantically from the dragging wind. It held in one hand a spiralling and thin sword as it crashed right into the midst of the akar forces.

The sight was incredible.

It rose from its squatted position, revealing a pointed stinger upon its helmet which skewered an akar. The akar was lifted off the ground, helplessly pawing at the rusted stinger. Instantly, the akar was inflicted by some quick-acting malaise as boils and pustules formed all over their body. They went limp quickly and slid off the stinger. The towering force was almost sickly thin; it looked like a torturous contraption. I recognized the being as the Plague Knight. They had a pocked visor in the likeness of a many-eyed insect. Its stinger was like the pointed proboscis of a mosquito. Wordlessly, without even telegraphing its movements, the Plague Knight sundered and reaped through the field of invading akar.

The way it moved was almost insect-like. Fast. Unnatural. Long, gauntleted digits grabbing at akar with the precision and speed of a praying mantis, only to then fling the bodies into enemy lines. I watched as its rusted sword bestowed afflictions of horror onto the enemy and then kicked them into gathered groups. Disease spread that caused blood to seep from eyes and ears, big clumps of it to be vomited like a coagulated embryo containing the souls of these pitiful warriors.

The Plague Knight's rusted sword swung with such surgical accuracy that the diseases it spread had a life of their own. Others had their limbs blackened and fell, some swelled to such terrifying bloat that they scratched at their suffocated throats.

But it wasn't over. Another figure appeared in the sky. This one was majestic while the last was a crude instrument of pestilence.

White-Hawk dove, glistening cape billowing, his flawless armour reflecting the light of the Elder King's eye so that all would know of Mount Morniar's insurmountable power.

White-Hawk unsheathed his blade, its end pointed forward and his own kite-shield held to the side. At the last moment, he brought his armoured feet beneath him and pointed straight down with his glistening longsword. Like a divine spear, White-Hawk impaled through the chest of an akar and surfed upon his body. I only got glimpses through the battle's flow of how majestic this zerub was, yet still it left me speechless. The sight reminded me of Erefiel and the way he would dance and weave with such elegance. But the way White-Hawk moved was something else entirely. He fought on the ground the way a hawk soared in the sky. He cut through them in the blink of an eye and rushed back and forth on the tail of the wind. Not a single movement was wasted as shield battered away weapons with such choreographed grace before snipping away at the delicate life-threads that bound akars' spirit to their bodies.

As the numbers piled about White-Hawk and the Clerian forces gave wide berth, wind blew through the crags and filled the zerub's sword. The enveloped gust was sent forth like a slice of wind, cutting through opponents with repeated slashes.

The combined forces from Mount Morniar wreaked havoc through the battlefield. The inhuman and limber form of a bending Plague Knight bringing plagues onto the akar. The body of a monstrous beast rampaging through the backline and streaked in its own blood and that of its prey. The silent grace of White-Hawk culling the enemy vanguard without ever catching a single drop on himself.

"Stop," I instructed Chroma. We were almost back to our own troops.

"What is it?" Chroma asked. He noticed I was scouring the enemy lines for something.

"I need to find the bastard that killed Erefiel." I spat.

"Nora! We need to fall back."

"I won't let him get away."

"Nora!" I turned to find Chroma staring at me. Not with admonishment, but rather pleadingly. The look gave me pause. "Erefiel is dead, but we are still alive. There is no way to find the leader in all that turmoil." There was something else there. Sorrow.

I eventually relented. "I will make him pay."

Chroma nodded. "I will help you, but we need to get out of here."

Tucking his body under my left arm, Chroma dragged me back to our side.

"He's with me! Drop your weapons." I ordered. Discordant men from improvised formations pointed their spears at us. My visage gave them pause as they evoked my new moniker: *The Metal Dragon*. The men obeyed me, albeit reluctantly, their spears lowered to provide us safe passage.

There was the deep sound of a horn being blown. It must have been the sound to retreat. The akar gave a wide berth between the higher beings and Clerian forces.

So much death littered the field. The strewn limbs and bodies so carelessly piled in droves. These deaths were so senseless. Both sides had suffered incredibly. The sun's light revealed more and more of how truly monstrous this glut of despair was. The akar fell back, taking in the mounds of their fallen brethren.

The Plague Knight did not pursue. Their insect-like helmet only turning slightly; the seam between helmet and cuirass grinding, their tall and slender body entirely still.

They didn't speak, but it seemed that the rampaging beast with feathers of white understood the Plague Knight and gave pause. There was a haunting moment of stillness with the odd sight. The being turned towards us. I felt the human troops simultaneously gasp and lean back at the monster's gaze. It was deafeningly silent. A breeze howled through Greyhill's vale and wrapped itself about the stick-like body of rusted armour. The beast huffed, its coat painted in blood. Eventually, the beast collapsed on all fours again.

The flow of battle ebbed. Weapons held back from their swings as bodies of the living parted to reveal the dead.

One akar dared to attack the snowy beast despite the stillness and was chomped down in an instant. No one else was foolish enough to disturb the behemoth's gait. The creature ambled through the parting akar and back towards the front line. A nervous clatter of weapons and armour spread among our troops as we watched the beast prowl towards us.

The akar numbers had truly thinned. A fact that was obvious when nobody was running about with bloodlust. But it was even more so for our Clerian numbers. The enemy's slow retreat was like a receding wave. The lapping tide pulled back to reveal the souls drowned in ruin.

Erefiel's own grave was left upon a hollow crater, sectioned off from the rest of the littered bodies.

White-Hawk stepped forward without a morsel of despair to mar his grace. His mourning, though visible to all, was a private affair. White-Hawk held his son's body close to his chest. I could only imagine what deep sorrow such an old being must have felt. The concept of personal loss must have been alien to him.

The sound of clanking platemail boots rang with ominous power. The Plague Knight shifted with the threat of malaise.

I took in its sight. Its form was covered in rusted plate mail, almost as if old beyond compare. Its cape was a tattered ruin of auburn so deep it was practically black. Its pocked visor was of many holes along with its sickly stinger.

My ire flared as Erefiels' murderer stepped to the forefront. His body was covered in cuts as he stared at the Plague Knight with such fury. He hadn't escaped unharmed from his bout. A great gash was prominent at his side from where the sword of Bereniel still jutted. The remaining akar looked to their leader for some kind of command, an order, anything at all. There was such knotted conviction in him that for a moment, I thought he would commit all their resources to this final attack. I braced myself for the chance to kill him.

Suddenly, the akar seized at the sword of Bereniel and painfully pulled it out of his hip. With a gasp audible to all, the sword plopped out and was tossed to the floor, limp and impotent.

The leader grasped at his hip, his burning gaze not faltering. Two akar came swiftly to stem the bleeding with improvised bandages, but he pushed them away. The leader stumbled forward, refusing to fall.

"Is this who you serve?!" His voice bellowed across the open plain, his words retold from the sea of dead. "These abhorrent beasts? You worship oppressors, self-anointed gods living on top of their tower. Elder King. Hear me! Look at me writhe like a vile worm, but heed me nonetheless! You cannot rule forever! Cannot force my kind into servile submission, nor wish that we fall into destitute." The leader's ringing voice stunned all of us. The fluency with which he spoke was captivating. He turned and faced the floating sun. His cudgel, smeared in Erefiel's blood, raised to it. "Heed me, King Aemir. My name is Sun'Ra, son of Muktow. One day, the sun shall set on your realm, and you shall be thrown down from your mountain." Next, his gaze settled on us. "You know not what happens beyond the safety of your domain, of what horrors lurk in the dying realm of Minethria. You know naught of the malaise which chokes this land and chews on its roots." He panted. There was nothing else needed to be said.

The beast by our side snarled and growled a shrill sound of defiance. The Plague Knight simply watched, their spiralled sword sheened in rust, giving off a noisome aura.

The horn sounded a second time. It was the hollow drone of disappointment. Reluctantly, the akar turned towards the forest, leaving behind this sea of dead as a testament towards a depressing end.

Chapter Ninety-Three

Black Baynard Jerry, the infamous painter, was found at early hours in his apartment in Museya murdered. His profession by trade was painting and we had received several reports that he had swindled unknowing nobles in believing that his art was that of an Inspired. He was found with his eyes gouged out. It is believed that one of his clients had learnt the truth and decided to enact a most poetic punishment.

—MUSEYAN GUARD REPORT ABOUT THE MURDER
OF BLACK BAYNARD JERRY

Though the sun had begun its steady rise, the depths of Dreamwood seemed to lag behind in time, for the shadows clung darker within, reluctant to leave.

In this place limped a single man, his side wounded and bleeding out a trail of scarlet drops. His heavy breath misted within this twilight of warmth and absence. Again and again, his glowing, fiery, red eyes would look over his shoulder in fear, certain that death wouldn't be lagging too far behind. Thus, when eventually he reached a drop, he failed to notice and his foot gave way.

The man rolled down the slope, dust rising at his descent. He grunted and coughed, disoriented, as the world spun about him. The uneven growth of roots and foliage below him knocked and bruised his body until finally he came to a stop. A light fog of dirt shrouded the man as if to provide some futile extra seconds until he got to his feet.

It didn't take too long, as he rose with a wince, urgency lending him strength. His cane was discarded at some point during his run. Yet still the man continued his limp. His thoughts were scrambled as his side continued to ache and burn. Each time the man withdrew his hand from there, the blood didn't seem to relent.

The gust of wind trailed through the forest like a foreboding breath; it was the exhale of death.

There it came from behind him. Within the distant shadows the man could see a blanched wraith move with such eerie quiet that one would believe their feet never even touched the ground. So swift, so quick, the Silver Prince came like a fated premonition.

❧ ☙

Brother Clemence stumbled until his back found itself a tree and slid down its trunk.

Ievarus stared down at the man, whose typical holy robes of the Serving were grimy and caked in dirt. With the blindfold gone, one could see the fitted orbs within the man's sockets. They were like spherical balls of fire, the centre of which had a black silhouette as it radiated a wreath of flame like some sort of red sun in an eclipse. A single trail of blood had escaped the corner of Clemence's lips and trailed down his chin.

Ievarus simply watched the man with listless and curious eyes. Removing the disk, Ievarus' arm elongated until it would practically hang at their knee and held the disk in front of Brother Clemence; a soft yellow tinge revealed itself upon the domed surface.

Brother Clemence couldn't help but laugh. "We are nothing more than insects to you, aren't we?" he asked.

Ievarus knelt down and tilted their head to one side. "Dalila said you can teach me about fear. I need only to kill you."

Brother Clemence chuckled. "I didn't think that bitch had it in her," he said, spitting out a clump of blood as his breathing grew evermore forced. "Tell me something, Ievarus. You trailed her, followed her to learn about mortals, to learn about aspects. What did you *see* when she saw her family? Was there suffering? Pain? Fear? What kind of madness did I invoke?"

Ievarus blinked, the long stretched out arm receding back into its standard length. "I think I saw sadness. I believe I saw rage soon after. She was... distraught."

Brother Clemence nodded, satisfied. "Good. That is a good word. Distraught. Perhaps even, consternation?" His head knocked against the bark of the tree. His fiery, dark eyes stared out into the woods. "What I would have given to see her reaction. After everything I did to regain my sight... Tell me Ievarus, she is supposed to be compassion. Did you learn much about that?"

Ievarus paused for a moment, contemplating their response. "I have seen very little compassion from her. I sense only sadness."

"Ievarus. If you free me, I can teach you about all the emotions. I am an Inspired! Touched by the spirits to see the truth in blood, enough to even gift me new sight! I will certainly teach you about fear. Fear has been my accomplice since I started sacrificing my offerings. Fear was harboured even within me. Fear of remaining sightless, fear of what would happen if I did regain my vision! I have given compassion to those who deserve it, and rage comes through in my art! As for Will, my will is second to *none*." Brother Clemence recited with such unwavering confidence.

Ievarus came closer. "And what of hope?"

Brother Clemence scoffed. "Look into my eyes and what do you see? I *am* hope. I was lost, forlorned, when without my sight, made to serve those absurd monsters up in their realm. Yet my power came to me, nurtured by the sacrifice of the believers. Their emotions, their beliefs empowered me. Now I can see again, more than I ever could in the past. I can see things that some can only dream of. These eyes are not what I had before. They are improved constructions of my design, created through my devotion."

Ievarus blinked. "Why did you kill Dalila's family? Her friend?" Ievarus used these words without familiarity. The words were seemingly tasteless to them.

Brother Clemence chuckled meekly. "Faith, Ievarus. Faith. My sight could only be restored through faith. Truth be told, I did not think Dalila would come here so soon. She was supposed to be my final sacrifice, aged with such sweet sorrow." Brother Clemence drew out his words. "Those who represented the wanderers? There is power in that belief, in what they represent. But it was nothing compared to the kind of faith Yasmin had. Nothing compared to the isolated love of a family living out here with simple lives. And Dalila? With her family dead… just watch as that sorrow festers inside her." Brother Clemence shook his head. "She is no good to you anymore."

Ievarus said nothing and simply observed. Brother Clemence continued. "I was wrong about you. You can also be great; I can give you everything that you want, more than Dalila ever could. That is what you want… isn't it? To find your purpose?"

"You misunderstand. I have learnt a great many things from Dalila, from Nora, from all of my aspects. Dalila is compassionate despite her grief and sadness. Nora emits rage, but she stands as hope not for herself, but for all others. Chroma is rage, but if Will fights so desperately to conserve Chroma's rage, then it must be for a reason." As Ievarus spoke, their arms began to stretch out again with long and lithe fingers towards Brother Clemence.

The disk's yellow light brightened hungrily. "Very well! Then let me be your fear!"

"That is my intention."

As Ievarus began to take Brother Clemence apart bit by bit, their actions emotionless curiosity, they wondered if the screams were similar to Dalila's. It sounded wrathful, primitive, coming from a deep place that was capable of giving such breath to true agony. Ievarus was like a child plucking the wings from a dragonfly.

First, Ievarus removed the digits. The howling cry that swept across the forest. Did that sound like Dalila's cry? No. It wasn't quite right. As bones broke and limbs were pulled out until the stretched skin and ligaments tore themselves into two halves. There was truly agony. But it didn't sound like the desperation that Dalila gave from herself.

Next, Ievarus tried their own hair, wrapping strands of it and pulling it taut until the strands cut into Brother Clemence's skin. No. This was even further off.

Brother Clemence had become a novelty, an instrument of flesh and bones to be prodded until one got the desired sound. With absolute indifference, Ievarus played away at this new instrument without any remorse or pleasure.

"You are all monsters! Monsters! I was right!" Brother Clemence yelled, the pain breaking at his sanity as laughter bled into the cries.

Finally, when all else failed, Ievarus plucked away the fiery, glowing eyes of Brother Clemence. Blood tears streaked down vacated sockets and then the scream came. This one was like Dalila's; this one imparted the sound of true and utter loss as the disk enshrouded itself with a pure and bright yellow.

Epilogue

Some traditions of the Elders are beyond mortal understanding. It is said that once an Ascension is complete and the Haar is pushed back, that a zerub is sent out with a cube designed by the Puzzler. Where this box is taken, however, no one knows.

—A TREATISE ON ELDER POLITICS, BY BARTHOLOMEW CHESWICK

Within Mount Morniar, Ievarus was once more guided by the Maiden.

Finally, within the tall yet narrow halls of the winding tunnels within the mountain, the double doors awaited them.

Ievarus wore a ceremonial piece, the entire thing seemingly made of sparkling gossamer like the sparkle of diamonds in a ravine. The clothing flowed and billowed behind them as Ievarus walked forward and through the vast throne room of the Elder King.

There sat Ievarus' father at the end, their throne thick and tall, holding the king's wizened body.

Within the hall stood a small congregation of entities.

The long-limbed Sieli, with their willowy body of rough obsidian armour, along with their porcelain mask. The being had their curved toe boots pointing outward and the knees prominently bent. Long dragging arms hung in front as the eerie mask observed Ievarus. On the other side, close to the king, was Preceptor. They floated a few steps up on the dais and with a curious stare towards Ievarus.

Standing right beside the king was Sirmy, the headless Elder with a worming body that grew hands to hold further extremities. At this point, from its headless neck sprouted a single boneless arm, the hand holding eyes.

The only other members to fill the chamber were Aeolus, the Yungblood's sprout with ever shifting horns and a prehensile tail, and two Elder Guards standing at the entrance to guard the doors.

Ievarus's feet echoed upon the stone floor, not due to wearing any hefty footwear. Their feet were bare, but rather because of the construction of this place. Everything was made to be heard and nothing was to be hidden from the Elder King.

When Ievarus came to stand still, the Elder King's ethereal voice spoke out. *"Ye' blood of mine, thou beseeched me with a plea. When mine eyes changeth and the moon did rise, thou absconded from mine realm despite my wishes. And when thou'st did return, tis with a wish to liveth 'mongst mine own subjects as to bestow upon thee an idea."* The Elder King rose from his throne with his ever hanging sashes and draped robe made out of the night sky. He stepped forward, hanging necklaces imbued with power clattering together. His own curling horns and crown of yew prominent atop the Elder King's head and flowing mane of hair.

The King approached Ievarus with powerful staff in hand, towering above the Seed at three times their height. *"Telleth, Eleventh Seed, what has't thou learnt? For I am certain mine own blood wouldst not disappoint me."*

Ievarus looked up to their father, to this figure of absolute yet elusive power. From one eye gleamed the power of the sun, and nothing from the other; rightly so for the world of minethria behind the throne was bathed in silver night.

"The mortals are strange. They act in so many ways that contradict themselves. I found that people with compassion sought the pain of another. I found that those with the strongest wills still died. Ones who are given a second chance risk wasting it on fruitless vengeance whilst those who are shunned and despised continue to fight for those who shun and despise them. I know of hate the same way a demon may know of love: they understand the concept, but do not relate to it."

The Elder King nodded. *"Tis the way. We higher beings art beyond such whims. To burneth so fiercely be but a luxury of the short-lived. We court progress. Now telleth me thy reason."*

"Mortals intrigue me: their rules, their way of life. I wish for them to live on, to see how their story concludes. I have grown fond of watching their exchanges, to see how relationships unfold, what wars are won and what is lost. I wish to see the shape of their progress. Beings of such vibrancy deserve to find the end of their want." Ievarus lowered their gaze. Perhaps there was even a tug of sadness within. "My only regret would be that I would not be able to witness this."

The Elder King was silent for a moment, the sagging folds of his face contorting as the king considered Ievarus' words. *"And if their progress leadeth to ruin?"*

"I care not for the end, only for the path taken."

The Elder King turned back towards Preceptor; the tentacle-faced being said nothing, but surely a private conversation unfolded between them and the king.

"So be it, Ievarus. Thou art prepared for the Evil of this land."

AFTERWORD

If you've gotten this far, then I hope that you close the pages of this book feeling myriad of things. Not all of them good. So what's next? If you want to know how the Mistland continues, you can look forward to the second book: *Forgotten Seed*. Otherwise, I do also recommend sticking around and following me on social media! *Eleventh Cycle* will also be coming out as an audiobook thanks to Podium Audio.

I have one favour. If you truly did enjoy this book and want the sequel to come out as soon as possible, please make sure to review the book if you enjoyed it. Any post on social media also helps. The more people who buy the book, the more I can invest for the sequels including rad new art!

Feel free to reach out to me on any of these social media platforms:

Twitter: @ArdalanKian
Instagram: ardalan.writes
Reddit: KikiWrites
Website: www.kiannardalan.com
Email: kiannardalan@gmail.com

Enjoyed this book and want to know what else I wrote? Check out *The Fantastically Underwhelming Epic*!

ACKNOWLEDGEMENTS

This book was a behemoth in its own right, and would never have been possible with the people I am about to mention. Thank you to my girlfriend, Veronika. Without your encouragement and support, I don't know if I would have persisted. Special thanks to my parents for supporting me. For asking how it is going. For believing in me.

Thank you to Christopher Boucher. Your mentoring and belief meant the world to me and I will be eternally grateful that I now get to write for a living.

If you haven't checked out Bryce O'Connor's work, absolutely do. Not only is he one of the most recognized indie-pub names, he taught me how to traverse the landscape of indie publishing and helped me find my contacts. (I recommend starting with Shadows of Ivory if you enjoyed this book.)

Thank you to Mark Lawrence for your guidance. Your feedback was invaluable to me as a writer. Another big thanks to all the people on his discord. Including Shauna, Josh, Thiago, Saeed, John and many others!

In order to get disability right, I had the help of several sensitivity readers. A very special thanks goes out to Henry. Your feedback was paramount to ensuring that I respectfully dealt with the subject matter of disability in a fantasy setting.

Thank you to my editor, Aubrey. Your comments reassured me but also helped tighten up this book. I am also very fortunate for all the feedback and help I got over at Clubhouse. Thank you to Jennifer,

Everly, Vanessa, Rachel, and other Rachel, Jordan, Piotr, Collings, Yvonne, Ngozi, Ale, Wendy, Marlayna and many more.

This wouldn't have been possible without my beta readers. As always, thank you Scotty for being a number one fan and reading all the nonsense I throw at you. Thank you to Stephan for being such a supportive friend and giving me your candid feedback. Thanks to Patrick for reading the final product and putting my fears to rest!

Obviously, I have to acknowledge all the support and help from Varun. You asked to read my work and helped polish it even more. You really made this work possible.

Thank you to my audiobook publisher, Podium, for the privilege of working with them. Thank you to my artists! Especially Shawn T. King. You went above and beyond.

ABOUT THE AUTHOR

Kian N. Ardalan was born in Germany and raised in Dubai by persian parents. Yes. That's a lot of nationalities. From a young age, there wasn't very much he was good at. He barely got by in mathematics or other academic subjects, and he couldn't even write an essay to save his life. But when it was time to do some creative writing, people held their breaths.

Today, he lives in Vienna, Austria with his girlfriend and gets to dream up worlds for a living. He is living his dream life. He has several more works and stories lined up for the future and is currently working with ActorsEverywhere to deliver new and exciting stories. So if you are itching for more, make sure to follow him and his future career.